Kate Mosse is an international bestselling novelist, non-fiction writer, essayist and playwright. With sales of more than 8 million copies worldwide, her books have been translated into 37 languages and published in 40 countries. Her fiction includes the Languedoc trilogy (*Labyrinth*, *Sepulchre* and *Citadel*), the gothic novels *The Winter Ghosts* and *The Taxidermist's Daughter*, a short story collection (*The Mistletoe Bride*) and more recently a historical adventure series, *The Burning Chambers* and *The City of Tears*. Her non-fiction includes the highly acclaimed memoir *An Extra Pair of Hands* and she is working on a book and television series based on her global 'Woman in History' campaign. The Founder Director of the Women's Prize for Fiction, Kate is a Visiting Professor of Creative Writing and Contemporary Fiction at the University of Chichester and a Fellow of the Royal Society of Literature. An interviewer and presenter, she hosts the pre-show series at Chichester Festival Theatre, chairs Platform events for the National Theatre and is an Ambassador for Parkinson's UK. She was awarded an OBE in 2013 for services to literature and women.

SEPULCHRE

Kate Mosse

PHOENIX

First published in Great Britain in 2007 by Orion Books
This edition published in 2022 by Phoenix Books,
an imprint of The Orion Publishing Group Ltd
Carmelite House, 50 Victoria Embankment
London EC4Y 0DZ

An Hachette UK Company

1 3 5 7 9 10 8 6 4 2

A CIP catalogue record for this book is
available from the British Library.

ISBN (Mass Market Paperback) 978 1 4746 2591 3
ISBN (eBook) 978 1 4091 0834 4
ISBN (Audio) 978 0 7528 9892 6

Typeset by Input Data Services Ltd, Somerset

Printed in Great Britain by Clays Ltd, Elcograph S.p.A.

www.orionbooks.co.uk

Although *Sepulchre* is part of The Languedoc Trilogy, each of the three books – *Labyrinth, Sepulchre* and *Citadel* – was written to be read as a stand-alone novel. There are, however, a handful of characters, most notably Audric Baillard, who appear in two or all three stories at different times of their lives and each novel is a love letter to Carcassonne and its history.

Praise for Sepulchre

'Mosse's gifts for historical fiction are considerable . . . Mosse does what good popular historical novelists do best – make the past enticingly otherworldly, while also claiming it as our own'
Independent

'Ghosts, duels, ill-fated love and conspiracy . . . addictively readable'
Daily Mail

'A compulsive, fantastic, historical yarn. Mosse's skills lie in the precise nature of her storytelling'
Observer

'Her narrative lyricism, beautifully drawn female characters and deft journey from the past to the present day, are a cut above'
Scotland on Sunday

'A sure, deft momentum . . . the secrets begin to slip out thick and fast'
Daily Express

'The *Labyrinth* author is back with another brilliantly absorbing story . . . Richly evocative and full of compelling twists and turns'
Red

'The latest from the author of bestselling *Labyrinth*, this adventure will keep you engrossed'
Eve

To my wonderful mother, Barbara Mosse
(1931–2014),
for that first piano

And, as ever, my beloved Greg –
for all things present, past and yet to come

Paris

Lyon

Bordeaux

Carcassonne Marseille

CARCASSONNE

La Cité

Aude R

St
Hilaire

Limoux

Alet-les-Bains

Montazels

Espéraza

Couiza

Coustaussa

Arques

Quillan

Rennes-le-Château

Rennes-les-Bains

Domaine de la Cade

vers Sougraigne

vers

CONTENTS

SÉPULTURE

Si par une nuit lourde et sombre
Un bon chrétien, par charité
Derrière quelque vieux décombre
Enterre votre corps vanté,

A l'heure où les chastes étoiles
Ferment leurs yeux appesantis,
L'araignée y fera ses toiles,
Et la vipère ses petits;

Vous entendrez toute l'année
Sur votre tête condamnée
Les cris lamentables des loups

Et des sorcières faméliques,
Les ébats des vieillards lubriques
Et les complots des noirs filous.

If, one dark, oppressive night,
A Christian, moved by charity,
Should bury your lauded corpse
Behind some ancient ruin,

As the eyes of the chaste stars
Let fall their heavy lids,
The spider will spin its webs there
And the viper lay its eggs;

Season upon season
Your damned head will ring
With the baleful cries

Of wolves and rawboned witches,
The groans of decrepit lotharios
And conspirators' dark designs.

CHARLES BAUDELAIRE, 1857

L'âme d'autrui est une forêt obscure où il faut marcher avec précaution.
The soul of another is a dark forest in which one must tread carefully.

Letter, 1891
Claude Debussy

The true Tarot is symbolism; it speaks no other language and offers no other signs.

The Pictorial Key to the Tarot, 1910
Arthur Edward Waite

PRELUDE

March 1891

This story begins in a city of bones. In the alleyways of the dead. In the silent boulevards, promenades and impasses of the Cimetière de Montmartre in Paris, a place inhabited by tombs and stone angels and the loitering ghosts of those forgotten before they are even cold in their graves.

This story begins with the watchers at the gates, with the poor and the desperate of Paris who have come to profit from another's loss. The gawping beggars and sharp-eyed *chiffonniers*, the wreath makers and peddlers of *ex-voto* trinkets, the girls twisting paper flowers, the carriages waiting with black hoods and smeared glass.

This story begins with the pantomime of a burial. A small paid notice in *Le Figaro* advertised the place and the date and the hour, although few have come. It is a sparse crowd; dark veils and morning coats, polished boots and extravagant umbrellas to shelter from the unseasonable March rain.

Léonie stands beside the open grave with her brother and their mother, her striking face obscured behind black lace. From the priest's lips fall platitudes, words of absolution that leave all hearts cold and all emotion untouched. Ugly in his unstarched white necktie, his vulgar buckled shoes and greasy complexion, he knows nothing of the lies and threads of deceit that have led to this patch of ground in the 18th *arrondissement*, on the northern outskirts of Paris.

Léonie's cheeks are dry. Like the priest, she is ignorant of the events being played out on this wet afternoon. She believes she has come to attend a funeral, the marking of a life cut short. She has come to pay her last respects to her brother's lover – a woman she never met in life – to support her brother in his grief.

Her eyes are fixed upon the coffin being lowered into the damp earth where the worms and the spiders dwell. If she were to turn quickly now, catching Anatole unawares, she would see the expression upon her beloved brother's face and puzzle at it. It is not loss that swims in his eyes, but relief.

And because she does not turn, she does not notice the man in a grey top hat and frock coat, sheltering from the rain under the cypress trees in the furthest corner of the cemetery. He cuts a sharp figure, the sort of man to make *une belle Parisienne* touch her hair and raise her eyes a little beneath her veils. His broad, strong hands, tailored in calfskin gloves, rest perfectly upon the silver head of his mahogany walking stick. They are such hands as might circle a waist, might draw a lover to him, might caress a pale cheek.

He is watching, an expression of great intensity on his face. His pupils are black pinpricks in bright, blue eyes.

The heavy thud of earth on the coffin lid. The priest's dying words echo in the sombre air.

'*In nomine Patri, et Filii et Spiritus Sancti*. Amen. In the name of the Father, the Son and the Holy Ghost.'

He makes the sign of the cross, then walks away.

Amen. So be it.

Léonie lets fall her flower, picked freshly in the Parc Monceau this morning: a rose for remembrance. The bloom spirals down, down through the chill air, a flash of white slowly slipping from her black-gloved fingers.

Let the dead rest. Let the dead sleep.

The rain is falling more heavily. Beyond the high wrought-iron gates of the cemetery, the roofs, spires and domes of Paris are shrouded in a silver mist. It muffles the sounds of the rattling carriages in the boulevard de Clichy and the distant shrieks of the trains pulling out from the Gare Saint-Lazare.

The mourning party turns to depart the graveside. Léonie touches her brother's arm. He pats her hand, lowers his head. As they walk out of the cemetery, more than anything, Léonie hopes that this may be an end to it. That, after the last dismal months of persecution and tragedy, they might put it all behind them.

That they might step out from the shadows and begin to live again.

But now, many hundreds of miles to the south of Paris, something is stirring.

A reaction, a connection, a consequence. In the ancient beech woods above the fashionable spa town of Rennes-les-Bains, a breath of wind lifts the leaves. Music heard, but not heard.

Enfin.

The word is breathed on the wind. At last.

Compelled by the act of an innocent girl in a graveyard in Paris, something is moving within the stone sepulchre. Long forgotten in the tangled and overgrown alleyways of the Domaine de la Cade, something is waking. To the casual observer it would appear no more than a trick of the light in the fading afternoon, but for a fleeting instant, the plaster statues appear to breathe, to move, to sigh.

And the portraits on the cards that lie buried beneath the earth and stone, where the river runs dry, momentarily seem to be alive. Fleeting figures, impressions, shades – not yet more than that. A suggestion, an illusion, a promise. The refraction of light, the movement of air beneath the turn of the stone stair. The inescapable relationship between place and moment.

For, in truth, this story begins not with bones in a Parisian graveyard, but with a deck of cards.

The Devil's Picture Book.

PART I

Paris
September 1891

CHAPTER 1

Paris
Wednesday, 16th September 1891

Léonie Vernier stood on the steps of the Palais Garnier, clutching her chatelaine bag and tapping her foot impatiently.

Where is he?

Dusk cloaked the place de l'Opéra in a silky blue light.

Léonie frowned. It was quite maddening. For almost one hour she had waited for her brother at the agreed rendezvous, beneath the impassive bronze gaze of the statues that graced the roof of the opera house. She had endured impertinent looks. She had watched the *fiacres* come and go, private carriages with their hoods up, public conveyances open to the elements, four-wheelers, gigs, all disembarking their passengers. A sea of black silk top hats and fine evening gowns from the showrooms of Maison Léoty and Charles Worth. It was an elegant first-night audience, a sophisticated crowd come to see and be seen.

But no Anatole.

Once, Léonie thought she spied him. A gentleman of her brother's bearing and proportions, tall and broad, and with the same measured step. From a distance, she even imagined his shining brown eyes and fine moustache and raised her hand to wave. But then the man turned and she saw it was not he.

Léonie returned her gaze to the avenue de l'Opéra. It stretched diagonally all the way down to the Palais du Louvre, a remnant of fragile monarchy from when a nervous French king sought a safe and direct route to his evening's entertainment. The lanterns twinkled in the dusk, and squares of warm light spilled out through the lighted windows of the cafés and bars. The gas jets spat and spluttered.

Around her, the air was filled with the sounds of a city at dusk, as day gave way to night. *Entre chien et loup.* The clink of harness and wheels on the busy streets. The song of distant birds in the trees in the boulevard des Capucines. The raucous cries of hawkers and ostlers, the sweeter tones of the girls selling artificial flowers on the steps of the Opéra, the high-pitched shouts of the boys who, for a *sou*, would blacken and shine a gentleman's shoes.

Another omnibus passed between Léonie and the magnificent façade of the Palais Garnier on its way to the boulevard Haussmann, the conductor whistling on the upper deck as he punched tickets. An intoxicated soldier with a Tonquin medal pinned to his breast stumbled back and forth, singing an old army song. Léonie even saw a clown with a whitened face under his black domino felt cap, his costume covered with gold spangles.

How could he leave me waiting?

The bells began to ring out for evensong, the plangent tones echoing across the cobbles. From Saint-Gervais or another church nearby?

Léonie could delay no longer. If she wished to hear Monsieur Wagner's *Lohengrin,* then she must take her courage in both hands and go in alone.

Could she?

Although without an escort, by good fortune she was in possession of her own ticket.

But dare she?

She considered. It was the Parisian premiere. Why should she be deprived of such an experience because of Anatole's poor timekeeping?

Inside the opera house, the magnificent chandeliers glittered. It was all light and elegance, an occasion not to be missed.

Léonie made her decision. She ran up the steps, through the glass doors, and joined the crowd.

The warning bell was ringing. Two minutes until curtain up.

In a flash of petticoat and silk stockings, Léonie dashed across the marble expanse of the Grand Foyer, attracting approbation and admiration in equal measure. At seventeen, she was on the verge of becoming a great beauty, no longer a child, yet retaining a glimmer of the girl she had been. She was fortunate to have the fashionable good features and nostalgic colouring held in high regard by Monsieur Moreau and his Pre-Raphaelite friends.

But her looks were misleading. Léonie was determined rather than obedient, bold rather than modest, a girl of contemporary passions, not a demure medieval damsel. Indeed, Anatole teased that while she appeared the very portrait of Rossetti's *La Damoiselle élue*, she was in point of fact her mirror image. Of the four elements, Léonie was fire, not water; earth, not air.

Now, her alabaster cheeks were flushed. Thick ringlets of copper hair had come loose from their combs and tumbled down over bare shoulders. Her green eyes, framed by long auburn lashes, flashed with anger.

He gave his word that he would not be late.

Clutching her evening bag in one hand, as if it was a shield, the skirts of her green silk satin gown in the other, Léonie hurtled across the gleaming floor, paying no heed to the disapproving stares of matrons and widows. The faux pearls and silver beads on the fringe of her dress clipped against the steps as she rushed through the rose marble columns, the gilded statues and the friezes, towards the sweeping Grand Escalier. Confined in her corset, her breath came ragged and her heart pumped like a metronome set too fast.

Ahead, she could see the flunkeys moving to secure the doors into the Grande Salle. With a final spurt of energy, Léonie propelled herself forward to the entrance.

'*Voilà*,' she said, thrusting her ticket at the usher. '*Mon frère va arriver . . .*'

He stepped aside and permitted her to pass.

After the echoing caverns of the Grand Foyer, the auditorium was particularly quiet. Filled with hushed murmurings, words of salutation, enquiries after health and family, all half swallowed by the thick carpets and row upon row of red velvet seats.

The familiar flights of woodwind and brass, scales and arpeggios and fragments of the opera, increasingly loud, issued up from the orchestra pit like trails of autumn smoke.

Léonie composed herself and smoothed her gown. A new purchase, delivered from La Samaritaine this afternoon, it was still stiff from lack of wear. She pulled her long green gloves up above her elbows, so that no more than a sliver of bare skin could be seen, then walked down through the stalls towards the stage.

Their seats were in the front row, two of the best in the house, courtesy of Anatole's composer friend and their neighbour, Achille Debussy. To left and right, as she passed, were lines of black top hats and feathered headdresses and fluttering sequined fans. Choleric faces of red and purple, heavily powdered dowagers with set white hair. She returned every look with a cordial smile, a slight tilt of the head.

There is a strange intensity in the atmosphere.

Léonie's gaze sharpened. The further she went into the Grande Salle, the clearer it became that something was amiss. There was a watchfulness in the faces, something simmering only just beneath the surface.

She felt a prickling at the base of her neck. The audience was on its guard. She saw it in the darting glances and mistrustful expressions on every other face.

Don't be absurd.

Léonie had a faint memory of a newspaper article read aloud at the supper table by Anatole about protests against the presentation in Paris of works of Prussian artists. But this was the Palais Garnier, not some secluded alleyway in Clichy or Montmartre.

What could happen at the Opéra?

Léonie picked her way through the forest of knees and gowns along the row and with a sense of relief sat down in her seat. She took a moment to compose herself and then glanced at her neighbours. To her left were a heavily jewelled matron and her elderly husband, his watery eyes all but obscured beneath bushy white brows. To her right, with Anatole's empty seat making a barrier between them like a country ditch, sat four scowling and bearded men of middle years with sour expressions, each set of hands resting upon undistinguished boxwood walking sticks. There was something rather unnerving about the way they sat in silence, facing forward, an expression of intense concentration upon their faces.

It passed through Léonie's mind how singular it was that they should all be wearing leather gloves, and how uncomfortably hot they must be. Then one turned his head and stared at her. Léonie blushed and, fixing her eyes front, admired instead the magnificent *trompe l'oeil* curtains, which hung in folds of crimson and gold from the top of the proscenium arch to the wooden surface of the stage.

Maybe he is not late. What if some ill has befallen him?

Léonie shook her head at this new and unwelcome thought.

She pulled her fan from her bag and flicked it open with a snap. However much she might wish to make excuses for her brother, it was more likely to be a matter of poor timekeeping.

As so often these days.

Indeed, since the dismal events in the Cimetière de Montmartre, Anatole had been even less reliable than usual. Léonie frowned at how, yet again, the memory slipped back into her mind. The day haunted her. She relived it endlessly.

In March, she had hoped it was all over and done with, but his behaviour was still erratic. Often, he disappeared for days on end, returning at odd hours of the night, avoiding many of his friends and acquaintances and throwing himself instead into his work.

But tonight he promised he would not be late.

The *chef d'orchestre* walked onto the rostrum, scattering Léonie's thoughts. A round of applause filled the auditorium, like a volley of gunfire, sudden and intense. Léonie clapped with vigour and enthusiasm, all the stronger for her anxious state. The quartet of gentlemen beside her did not move. Their hands remained motionless, perched on their cheap, ugly walking sticks. She threw them a look, thinking them discourteous and boorish and wondering why they would even bother to come if they were determined not to appreciate the music. And she wished, although it irritated her to acknowledge such nerves, that she was not sitting so very close to them.

The conductor bowed deeply, then turned to face the stage.

The applause faded. Silence fell over the Grande Salle. He tapped his baton upon his wooden stand. The blue jets of gaslight in the auditorium spluttered and flickered, then dimmed. The atmosphere became charged with promise. Every eye was upon the *chef d'orchestre*. The players straightened their backs, lifted their bows, raised instruments to their lips.

The *chef* raised his baton. Léonie caught her breath as the opening chords of Monsieur Wagner's *Lohengrin* filled the palatial spaces of the Palais Garnier.

The seat beside her remained empty.

CHAPTER 2

The whistling and catcalling began almost immediately in the higher tiers. At first, the majority of the audience paid no heed to the disturbance. But then it became more obtrusive, louder. Voices were heard in the circle and from the stalls also.

Léonie could not quite make out what the protesters were saying.

She kept her eyes fixed resolutely on the orchestra pit and attempted to ignore each new hiss or whisper. But as the Overture continued, an increasing restlessness stirred through the auditorium from top to bottom, sly and insidious. Unable to hold her tongue any longer, Léonie leaned over to her neighbour.

'Who are these people?' she whispered.

The dowager frowned at the interruption but answered all the same.

'They call themselves the *abonnés*,' she replied, behind her fan. 'They oppose the performance of any but French composers. Musical patriots, they would claim. In principle, I have some sympathy, but this is not the way to go about things.'

Léonie nodded her thanks and sat back in her seat, reassured by the woman's matter-of-fact manner, though the disturbance seemed only to be growing.

The closing bars of the Overture had barely faded when the protest commenced in earnest. As the curtain rose on a scene of a chorus of tenth-century Teutonic Knights standing on the banks of an ancient river in Antwerp, a louder commotion began in the upper dress circle. A group of eight or nine men leapt to their feet in a cacophony of whistling and booing and slow hand-clapping. A wave of disapproval washed along the rows of the stalls, the upper tiers, countered by other outbursts of objection. Then taunting from the protesters, a chant that at first Léonie could not properly distinguish. A crescendo of noise, and it became unmistakable.

'*Boche! Boche!*'

The protest had reached the ears of the singers. Léonie saw darting glances pass between the chorus and principals, alarm writ large on every face.

'*Boche! Boche! Boche!*'

While not wishing the performance to be disrupted, Léonie could not deny it was exciting. She was witnessing the sort of event that in usual circumstances she only heard about in the pages of Anatole's *Le Figaro*.

For, in truth, Léonie was thoroughly bored by the restrictions of her daily existence, the ennui of accompanying Maman to dull afternoon soirées at the drab town houses of distant relations and former comrades of her father. Having to make painful small talk with her mother's current friend, an old military man who treated Léonie as if she was still in short skirts.

What a story I shall have to tell Anatole.

But the mood of the protest was changing.

The cast, pale and uncertain beneath their heavy stage make-up, continued to sing. Indeed, they did not falter until the first missile was thrown onto the stage. A bottle, narrowly missing the bass taking the role of King Heinrich.

For an instant, it seemed as if the orchestra must have stopped playing, so deep and suspended was the silence. The audience appeared to be holding its collective breath as the glass spun, as if in slow motion, catching the harsh limelight. Then it hit the canvas scenery with a thump, fell and rolled back into the pit.

The real world rushed back. Pandemonium broke loose, on stage and off. There was an upsurge of noise. Then a second missile soared over the heads of the stupefied audience, bursting on contact with the stage. A woman in the front row screamed and covered her mouth as a foul stench filtered out over the stalls.

'*Boche! Boche! Boche!*'

The smile faded from Léonie's face. She felt sick to her stomach. This was ugly, frightening, not an adventure at all.

The quartet to her left suddenly leapt to their feet as one and began to clap, perfectly in time, slowly at first, baying like animals. Their faces were cruel as they chanted their anti-Prussian leitmotif, now taken up in every corner of the auditorium.

'In God's name, sit down, man!'

A heavily bearded and bespectacled gentleman, with the sallow complexion of one who spent his time with inkwell and wax and papers, tapped one of the protesters on the back with his programme.

'This is neither the time nor the place. Be seated!'

'No, indeed,' agreed his companion. 'Sit down!'

The protester turned and delivered a glancing blow across the man's knuckles with his stick. Léonie gasped. Taken by surprise, the man howled and dropped his programme. His companion leapt to his feet as beads of blood sprang up along the line of the wound. He attempted to grab hold of the protester's weapon, seeing now that there was a metal pin deliberately lodged in the head, but rough hands pushed him back, and he fell.

The conductor attempted to keep the orchestra to time, but the players were throwing fearful glances all around and the tempo grew ragged and uneven, at once too fast and too slow. Backstage, a decision had been taken. Stagehands in their blacks, their sleeves rolled to the elbows, swarmed from the wings and began to usher the singers out of the direct line of fire. The musicians began to pack up their instruments.

The management attempted to drop the curtain. The weights clanged as they flew up too fast. The heavy material tumbled through the air, then caught on a piece of scenery and stuck.

The shouting intensified.

The exodus began from the private boxes. In a flurry of feathers and gold and silk, the bourgeoisie made hurried exits. The rows behind Léonie were also emptying into the aisles. From every part of the Grande Salle, she heard seats snapping shut. At the exits, the rattle of the brass rings on their rails as the heavy velvet curtains were pulled roughly open.

But the protesters had not yet achieved their goal of stopping the performance. More missiles were hurled at the stage. Bottles, stones and bricks, rotting fruit. The orchestra evacuated the pit, snatching up precious music and bows and instrument cases, shoving through the obstacles of chairs and wooden stands to exit under the stage.

At last, through the half-gap in the curtain, the theatre manager appeared on stage to appeal for calm. He was sweating and dabbed at his face with a grey handkerchief.

'Mesdames, messieurs, s'il vous plaît. S'il vous plaît!'

He was a substantial man, but neither his voice nor his manner commanded authority. Léonie saw how wild his eyes were, as he flapped his arms and attempted to impose some sort of order upon the mounting chaos.

It was too little, too late.

Another missile was thrown, this time not a bottle nor some acquired object, but a piece of wood with nails embedded in it. The manager was struck above the eye. He staggered back, clutching his face with his hand. Blood seeped through his fingers from the wound, and he fell sideways, crumpling like a child's rag doll to the surface of the stage.

At this last sight, Léonie's courage finally deserted her.

I must get out.

Terrified now, she threw desperate glances around the auditorium, but she was trapped, hemmed in by the mob behind her and to the side, and by the violence in front. Léonie clutched at the backs of the seats, supposing she might escape by scaling the rows, but when she tried to move, she discovered the beaded hem of her dress had caught in the metal bolts beneath her seat. With increasingly desperate fingers, she bent down and tried to pull, to tear herself free.

Now, a new cry of protest filtered through the auditorium.

'À bas! À bas!'

She looked up.

What now? The cry was taken up from every corner of the auditorium.

'À bas. À l'attaque!'

Like crusaders besieging a castle, the protesters surged forward, waving sticks and cudgels. Here and there, the glint of a blade. With a shudder, Léonie realised the protesters meant to storm the stage and that she was directly in their path.

Hysteria swept through the auditorium. Lawyers and newspapermen, painters and scholars, bankers and civil servants, courtesans and wives, all stampeding towards the doors in their desperation to escape.

Sauvez qui peut. Every man for himself.

The nationalists moved on the stage. With military precision, they marched forward from every section of the auditorium, vaulting seats and rails, swarming over the orchestra pit and up onto the boards. Léonie pulled at her dress, harder, harder, until, with a ripping of material, she freed herself.

'*Boche! Alsace française! Lorraine française!*'

The protesters were tearing down the backcloth, kicking over the scenery. Painted trees and water and rocks and stones, the imaginary soldiers of the tenth century destroyed by a very real nineteenth-century mob. The stage became littered with splintered wood, torn canvas and dust as the world of *Lohengrin* fell in the battle.

At last, resistance was mustered. A cohort of idealistic young men and veterans of past campaigns came together in the stalls and pursued the nationalists to the stage. The pass door separating the auditorium from the back of house was breached. They charged into the wings and joined forces with the opera-house stage crew, who were advancing upon the anti-Prussian nationalists between the flats and the scenery dock.

Léonie watched, appalled yet transfixed by the spectacle. A handsome man, not much more than a boy, in a borrowed evening suit too big for him and with a long, waxed moustache, launched himself on the ringleader of the protesters. Hurling his arms around the man's throat, he attempted to pull him down, but found himself on the ground instead. He shrieked in pain as a steel-capped boot drove into his stomach.

'*Vive la France! À bas.*'

Bloodlust had taken hold. Léonie could see eyes wide with excitement, with frenzy, as the violence escalated.

'*S'il vous plaît,*' she cried in desperation, but no one could hear and there was still no way through for her.

Léonie shrank back as another stagehand was thrown from the stage. His body somersaulted over the abandoned orchestra pit and was caught on the brass rail. His arm and shoulder hung loose, twisted. His eyes remained open.

You must move back. Get back.

Not more than five feet from where she stood, frozen to the spot, a man was crawling on hands and knees, his waistcoat and jacket trailing open. He left a smear of bloody handprints upon the wooden boards of the stage.

Léonie tried to call out a warning, but shock stole her voice. Down the weapon came. Made contact. The man slipped, falling heavily on his side. He looked up at his attacker, saw the knife and threw up his hand to protect himself as the blade came down. He howled as the knife was withdrawn and plunged again, deep into his chest.

The man's body jerked and twitched like a puppet in the kiosk on the Champs-Élysées, his arms and legs flailing, then was still.

Léonie realised she was crying. Then fear rushed back fiercer than ever.

'*S'il vous plaît*,' she shouted, 'let me pass.'

She attempted to push through with her shoulders, but she was too small, too light. A mass of people stood between her and the exit, and the central aisle was now blockaded with crimson cushions. Beneath the stage, the gas jets had sent sparks showering down onto the sheets of music left abandoned and lying on the ground. A splutter of orange, a hiss of yellow, then a billowing as the wooden underside of the stage began to glow.

'*Au feu! Au feu!*'

At this, a new level of panic swept through the auditorium. The memory of the inferno that had torn through the Opéra-Comique four years ago, killing more than eighty, took hold.

'Let me through!' Léonie shouted. 'I beg you.'

No one heeded her. The floor beneath her feet was carpeted with abandoned programmes and feather headdresses, lorgnettes and opera glasses.

Léonie could see nothing but elbows and the bare backs of heads, yet she kept moving forward, inch by painful inch, succeeding in putting a little distance between herself and the worst of the fighting, from the smouldering fire.

Then, at her side, she felt an elderly lady stumble and begin to fall.

Afraid she might be trampled, Léonie shot out her hand and caught hold of the woman's elbow. Beneath the starched fabric, she found herself gripping a spindly arm.

'I wished only to hear the music,' the woman was weeping. 'German, French, it matters nothing to me. That we should see such sights in our times. That it should come again.'

Léonie stumbled forward, taking the entire weight of the old lady, staggering towards the exit. The burden seemed to become greater with every step. The woman was slipping into unconsciousness.

'Not much further,' Léonie cried. 'Please try, please' – anything to keep the old woman upon her feet. 'We are nearly at the doors. Nearly safe.'

At last, she glimpsed the familiar livery of a flunkey.

'*Mais aidez-moi, bon Dieu!*' she shouted. '*Par ici. Vite!*'

The usher obeyed at once. Without a word, he relieved Léonie of her charge, sweeping the old lady up into his arms and carrying her out into the Grand Foyer.

Léonie's legs buckled, exhausted, but she forced herself on. Only a few steps more.

Suddenly a hand grabbed her wrist.

'No,' she cried. 'No!'

She would not let herself be trapped inside with the fire and the mob and the barricades. Léonie struck out blindly but connected only with air.

23

CHAPTER 3

'Léonie, *c'est moi*. Léonie!'
A man's voice, familiar and reassuring. And the smell of sandalwood hair oil and Turkish tobacco.

Anatole? Here?

And now strong hands were circling her waist and lifting her up out of the crowd.

Léonie opened her eyes. 'Anatole!' she cried, throwing her arms around his neck. 'Where have you been? How could you!' Her embrace turned to attack, as she pummelled his chest with furious fists. 'I waited and waited, yet you did not come. How could you leave me to—'

'I know,' he replied. 'And you have every right to rebuke me, but not now.' Her anger left her as quickly as it had come. She let her head fall forward onto her big brother's chest.

'I saw—'

'I know, *petite*,' he said softly, running his hand over her dishevelled hair, 'but the soldiers are outside already. We must leave or risk being caught up in the fighting.'

'Such hatred in their faces, Anatole. They destroyed everything. Did you see?' Léonie felt panic building inside her. 'With their bare hands, they—'

'You can tell me later,' he said sharply, 'but now we must get away from here. *Vas-y.*'

Léonie came back to her senses. She took a deep breath, wanting to be brave.

'Good girl,' he said, seeing the determination return to her eyes. 'Quick now!'

Anatole used his height and strength to forge a path through the mass of bodies fleeing the auditorium.

They emerged through the velvet curtains into the chaos. Hand in hand, they ran along the balconies, then down the Grand Escalier. Slipping, but never quite losing their footing, they reached the glazed doors and were out into the place de l'Opéra.

Instantly, behind them, came the sound of glass breaking.

'Léonie, this way!'

If she had thought the scenes inside the Grande Salle impossible, on the streets outside it was worse. The nationalist protesters, the *abonnés*, had taken possession of the steps of the Palais Garnier too. Armed with sticks and bottles and knives, they stood in lines three deep, waiting and chanting. Below, in the place de l'Opéra itself, rows of soldiers in short red jackets and gold helmets knelt with rifles trained on the protesters, hoping for the command to fire.

'There are so many of them,' she wailed.

Anatole pulled her through the crowds in front of the baroque façade of the Palais Garnier. He reached the corner, and then turned right into rue Scribe, out of the direct line of fire. They were carried along for almost a block by the mass of people, their fingers laced tight so as not to be separated from one another, borne like flotsam on a fast-flowing river.

But for a moment, Léonie felt herself safe. She was with Anatole.

Then the sound of a single shot from a rifle. The tide of people halted briefly, then, as if in one single movement, pushed once more. Léonie could feel her slippers coming unfastened from her feet and was aware of men's boots snapping at her ankles. She struggled to keep her balance.

A volley of bullets erupted behind them. The only fixed point was Anatole's hand.

'Don't let go,' she cried.

Behind them, an explosion ripped through the air. The pavement shuddered. Léonie, half twisting around, saw the dirty mushroom of smoke, grey against the city sky, rising up from the direction of the place de l'Opéra. A second blast reverberated up through the pavement. The air around them seemed first to solidify, then fold in on itself.

'*Des canons! Ils tirent!*'

'*Non, non, c'est des pétards.*'

Léonie grasped Anatole's hand more tightly. They surged forward, no sense of where they would end up, no sense of time, driven only by an animal instinct that told them not to stop, not until the noise and the blood and the dust were far behind.

Léonie felt her limbs tire as fatigue took hold, but she kept running, running, until she could go no further. Little by little, the crowd thinned, until at last they found themselves in a quiet street, far removed from the fighting and the explosions and the barrels of the guns. Her legs were weak and her skin flushed and damp with the night.

Coming to a halt, Léonie reached out with a hand to steady herself. Her heart was thudding feverishly. The blood was hammering in her ears, heavy and loud.

Anatole stopped too, leaning back against the wall. Léonie sagged against him and felt his arms go protectively around her shoulders. She gulped at the night air, trying to regain her breath, then pulled off her stained gloves, discoloured by soot, and let them drop to the pavement.

Anatole smoothed his fingers through the thick black hair that had fallen down over his high forehead and sharp cheekbones. He too was breathing hard, despite the hours he spent training in the fencing halls.

Extraordinarily, he seemed to be smiling.

For a while, neither spoke. The only sound was the rise and fall of their breath, clouds of white in the cool September evening. At last, Léonie drew herself up.

'Why were you late?' she demanded, fear making her petulant.

Anatole stared at her in disbelief; then he started to laugh, softly at first, then more loudly, struggling to speak.

'You would scold me, *petite*, even at such a moment?'

Léonie fixed him with a look but quickly felt the corners of her own mouth starting to twitch. A giggle burst out of her, then another, until she too was shaking with laughter and the tears were rolling down her grimy cheeks.

Anatole removed his evening jacket and draped it across her bare shoulders.

'You are really the most extraordinary creature,' he said. 'Quite extraordinary!'

Léonie contrasted her dishevelled state with his elegance. She glanced down at her tattered green gown. The hem hung loose like a train behind her, and the remaining glass beads were chipped and hanging by a thread. Despite their headlong flight through the streets of Paris, Anatole looked all but immaculate. His shirtsleeves were white and crisp, the tips of his collar still starched and upright, his blue dress waistcoat unmarked.

He stepped back and looked up to read the sign on the wall.

'Rue de Caumartin,' he said. 'Excellent. Supper? You are hungry, I suppose?'

'Ravenous.'

'I know a café not far from here. Downstairs is popular with the performers, and their admirers, from the cabaret La Grande-Pinte, but there are respectable private rooms on the first floor. Does that sound acceptable?'

Léonie beamed with delight. 'Perfectly so.'

He smiled. 'That's settled then. And for once, I shall keep you out late, well past a reasonable bedtime.' He grinned. 'I dare not deliver you home to Maman in such a state. She would never forgive me.'

CHAPTER 4

Marguerite Vernier disembarked from the *fiacre* at the corner of the rue Cambon and the rue Sainte-Honoré, accompanied by General Georges Du Pont.

While her escort settled the fare, she pulled her stole around her against the chill of the evening and smiled with satisfaction. Voisin's was the best restaurant in town, the famous windows curtained, as ever, with the finest Brittany lace. It was a measure of Du Pont's growing regard for her that he had brought her here.

Arm in arm, they walked inside. They were greeted by discreet conversation. Marguerite felt Georges puff out his chest and raise his head a little higher, aware that every man in the room was jealous of him. She squeezed his arm and felt him return the gesture, a reminder of how they had passed the last two hours. He turned a proprietorial look upon her. Marguerite granted him a gentle smile, then parted her lips slightly, enjoying the way he coloured from beneath his collar to the tips of his ears. It was her mouth – her generous smile and her full lips – that elevated her beauty. It carried both promise and invitation.

His hand went to his neck and he pulled at his stiff white collar, loosening his black tie. Dignified and entirely proper, his evening jacket was skilfully cut to disguise the fact that, at sixty, he was no longer quite the physical specimen he had been in his army heyday. In his buttonhole were threads of coloured ribbon signifying the medals he had gained at

Sedan and Metz. Rather than a waistcoat, which might have accentuated his prominent stomach, he wore instead a dark crimson cummerbund. Grey-haired and with a full and bushy cropped moustache, Georges was a diplomat now, formal and sober, and wished the world to know it.

To please him, Marguerite had dressed modestly in a purple silk moiré dinner dress with silver trim and beads. The arms were full, drawing attention all the more to the tapered waist and full skirts. The neck was high, allowing no more than the slightest hint of skin, although on Marguerite this made the outfit all the more provocative. Her dark hair was twisted artfully in a chignon, with a single spray of purple feathers, showing to best advantage her slim, white neck.

Every bored matron and upholstered wife in the restaurant stared with dislike and envy, the more so because Marguerite was in her middle forties rather than in the first flush of youth. The combination of her beauty and figure, matched with the lack of a ring on her finger, offended their sense of fairness and propriety. Was it right that such a liaison should be flaunted in such a place as Voisin's?

The proprietor, grey-headed and as distinguished-looking as his clientele, swept forward to greet Georges. General Du Pont was a customer of long standing, who ordered the best champagne and tipped generously. But he had been a less than frequent visitor of late. Clearly, the owner feared they had lost his custom to the Café Paillard or the Café Anglais.

'Monsieur, it is a great pleasure to welcome you once more. We surmised that perhaps you had received a posting abroad.'

Georges looked thoroughly embarrassed. So strait-laced, Marguerite thought, although she did not dislike him for it. He had better manners, and was simpler in his needs, than many men she had known.

'The fault is entirely mine,' she said. 'I have been keeping him to myself.'

The proprietor laughed. He clicked his fingers. While the cloakroom attendant relieved Marguerite of her stole and Georges of his walking stick, the men exchanged courtesies, talking of the weather and the current situation in Algeria. There were rumours of an anti-Prussian demonstration.

Marguerite allowed her thoughts to drift away. She cast her eyes over the famous show table of the finest fruit. It was too late for strawberries, of course, and, in any case, Georges preferred to retire early, so it was unlikely he would wish to remain for dessert.

Marguerite expertly stifled a sigh while the men concluded their business. Despite the fact that every table around them was occupied, there was a sense of peace and quiet comfort. Her son would dismiss the place as dull and old-fashioned, but she, who too often had been on the outside of such establishments looking in, found it delightful and an indication of the measure of security she had found with Du Pont's patronage.

The conversation over, the proprietor raised his hand. The maître d' stepped forward and led them through the candlelit room to a superior table in an alcove, not overlooked by any other diners and a long way from the swinging doors of the kitchen. Marguerite noticed the man was perspiring, his top lip glistening beneath his cropped moustache, and wondered what it really was that Georges did at the embassy that meant that his good opinion was so very important.

'Monsieur, Madame, an aperitif to start?' asked the wine waiter.

Georges looked across at Marguerite. 'Champagne?'

'That would be perfectly delightful, yes.'

'A bottle of Cristal,' he said, leaning back in his chair as if to spare Marguerite the vulgar knowledge of hearing that he had ordered the best in the house.

As soon as the maître d' had gone, Marguerite moved her feet to touch Du Pont's beneath the table and again had the pleasure of seeing him start, then shift on his chair.

'Marguerite, really,' he said, although his protest carried no conviction.

She slipped her foot from her slipper and rested it lightly against him. She could feel the seam of his dress trousers through her gossamer-thin stocking.

'They have the best cellar of red wines in Paris,' he said gruffly, as if he needed to clear his throat. 'Burgundies, Bordeaux, all arranged in their proper precedence – the wines from the great vineyards first and the rest in their correct order down to the merest bourgeois tipple.'

Marguerite disliked red wine, which gave her terrible headaches, and preferred champagne, but she was resigned to drinking whatever Georges put in front of her.

'You are very clever, Georges.' She paused, then looked around. 'And to find us a table. It is so busy for a Wednesday evening.'

'It's just a matter of knowing to whom to talk,' he said, although she could see he was pleased with the flattery. 'You have not dined here before?'

Marguerite shook her head. Meticulous, detailed, pedantic, Georges gathered facts and liked to parade his knowledge. She, of course, like every other Parisian, knew the history of Voisin's, but was prepared to pretend she did not. During the painful months of the Commune, the restaurant had witnessed some of the most violent of the altercations between the Communards and the government forces. Where now *fiacres* and two-wheelers waited to ferry customers from one side of Paris to the other, twenty years ago had stood the barricades: iron bedsteads, upturned wooden carts, pallets and munitions boxes. She, with her husband – her wonderful, heroic Leo – had stood on those barricades, for a brief and glorious moment united as equal partners against the ruling class.

'After Louis-Napoleon's shameful failure at the Battle of Sedan,' wheezed Georges, 'the Prussians marched upon Paris.'

'Yes,' she murmured, wondering not for the first time how young he thought she was that he should give her a history lesson of events she had witnessed at first hand.

'As the siege and bombardment deepened, of course there were food shortages. It was the only way to teach those Communards a lesson. It meant, however, that many of the better restaurants could not open. Not enough food, you see. Sparrows, cats, dogs – not a creature to be seen on the streets of Paris that was not fair game. Even the animals from the zoo were slaughtered for meat.'

Marguerite smiled encouragement.

'So what do you think Voisin's offered on their menu that night?'

'I cannot imagine,' she said, wide-eyed with perfectly judged innocence. 'Indeed, I hardly dare to. Snake, perhaps?'

'No,' he said, with a satisfied bark of laughter. 'Guess again.'

'Oh, I cannot say, Georges. Crocodile?'

'Elephant,' he said triumphantly. 'A dish concocted from the trunks of elephants. I ask you. Wonderful, really. Quite wonderful. Shows marvellous spirit, don't you think?'

'Oh yes,' Marguerite agreed, and she laughed too, although her memory of the summer of 1871 was somewhat different. Weeks of starvation, trying to fight, to support her wild, idealistic, passionate husband, at the same time as finding enough food for their beloved Anatole. Coarse brown bread and chestnuts and berries stolen at night from the fruit bushes in the Jardin des Tuileries.

When the Commune fell, Leo escaped, and remained at large, hidden by friends for nearly two years. In the end, he too was captured and only narrowly escaped the firing squad. More than a week passed, during which Marguerite tried every police station and court in Paris, before she discovered he had been tried and sentenced. His name was published on a list posted on the wall of a municipal building: deportation to the French Pacific Colony of New Caledonia.

The amnesty for the Communards came too late for him. He died in the galleys crossing the ocean, without even knowing he now had a daughter too.

'Marguerite?' Du Pont said testily.

Realising she had been silent for too long, Marguerite rearranged her face.

'I was just thinking how extraordinary that must have been,' she said quickly, 'but it says so much, does it not, for the skill and ingenuity of the chef at Voisin's that he was able to make such a dish? It is quite wonderful to sit here, where history was made.' She paused, and then added, 'And with you.'

Georges smiled complacently. 'Strength of character will out in the end,' he said. 'There's always a way to turn a bad situation to one's advantage, not that it's something today's generation has any knowledge about.'

'Excuse me for intruding upon your dinner.'

Du Pont got to his feet, courteous despite the irritation clouding his eyes. Marguerite turned to see a tall, patrician gentleman with thick dark hair and a high forehead. He looked down at her with sharp, pinpoint pupils, black in eyes of startling blue.

'Monsieur?' said Georges sharply.

The look of the man sent a memory scuttling across Marguerite's mind, although she was certain she did not know him. Perhaps about the same sort of age as she, he was dressed in the usual evening uniform of black jacket and trousers, but immaculately so, flattering the strong and impressive physique that lay beneath. Broad shoulders; a man accustomed to getting his own way. Marguerite glanced at the gold signet ring on his left hand, looking for clues as to his identity. He was holding a silk top hat, together with his white evening gloves and a white cashmere scarf, suggesting he had either just arrived or was on the point of making his departure.

Marguerite felt herself blush at the way his eyes seemed to strip her bare, her skin grow hot.

'Forgive me,' she said, throwing an anxious glance to Du Pont, 'but do I—'

'Sir,' he said, nodding at Du Pont by way of apology. 'If I may?'

Mollified, Du Pont gave a slight bow of the head.

'I am an acquaintance of your son's, Madame Vernier,' he said, pulling a calling card from his waistcoat book. 'Victor Constant, Comte de Tourmaline.'

Marguerite hesitated, and then took the card.

'Most discourteous of me to interrupt, I know, but I am anxious to be in contact with Vernier over a matter of some importance. I have been in the country, only arriving in town this evening, and was hoping to find your son at home. However . . .' He gave a shrug.

Marguerite had known many men. She always knew the best way to be, to speak, to flatter, to charm on a moment's acquaintance. But this man? She could not read him.

She looked down at the card in her hand. Anatole did not confide much of his business to her, but Marguerite was certain she had never heard him mention so distinguished a name, either as a friend or as a client.

'Do you know where I might find him, Madame Vernier?'

Marguerite felt a frisson of attraction, then fear. Both were pleasurable. Both alarmed her. His eyes narrowed as if he could read her mind.

'I am afraid, Monsieur, I do not,' she replied, struggling to keep her voice steady. 'Perhaps if you were to leave your card for him at his offices . . .'

Constant inclined his head. 'Indeed, I will. And they are to be found . . .'

'In the rue Montorgueil. I cannot remember the precise number.'

Constant continued to look hard at her. 'Very well,' he said in the end. 'Again, my apologies for intruding. If you might be so kind, Madame Vernier, as to tell your son that I am looking for him, I would be most grateful.'

Without warning, he reached down, took her hand from where it lay in her lap and raised it to his mouth. Marguerite felt his breath and the tickle of his moustache through her glove, and felt betrayed by the way her body responded to his touch.

'*À bientôt*, Madame Vernier. *Mon Général.*'

Then he gave a half-bow and left. The waiter came and refreshed their glasses. Du Pont exploded.

'Of all the insolent, impertinent scoundrels,' he growled, leaning back in his chair. 'Quite disgraceful. Who does the blackguard think he is, insulting you in such a manner?'

'Insulting me? Did he, Georges?'

'Fellow couldn't keep his eyes off you.'

'Really, Georges, I did not notice. He did not interest me,' she said, not wishing for a scene. 'Please do not concern yourself on my account.'

'Do you know the fellow?' Du Pont said, suddenly suspicious.

'I said I did not,' she replied calmly.

'Fellow knew my name,' he persisted.

'Perhaps he recognised you from the newspapers, Georges,' she said. 'You underestimate how many people know you. You forget how familiar a figure you are.'

Marguerite saw him relax his guard at the careful flattery. Intending to finish the matter, she took Constant's expensive card by the corner and held it to the flame of the candle set in the centre of the table. It took a moment to catch, then burned brightly and furiously.

'What in the name of God do you think you're doing?'

Marguerite kept her eyes on the flame, watching until it guttered and died away.

'There,' she said, brushing the grey ash from the tips of her gloves into the ashtray. 'Forgotten. And if the Count is someone with whom my son wishes to do business, then the proper place for such matters is between the hours of ten and five at his offices.'

Georges nodded in approval. With relief, she saw the suspicion melt from his eyes.

'Do you really not know where that boy of yours is tonight?'

'Of course I do,' she said, smiling as if letting him in on a joke, 'but it always pays to be circumspect. I do dislike gossiping women.'

It suited Marguerite for Georges to think of her as discreet and reliable.

He nodded again. 'Quite right, quite right.'

'As it happens, Anatole has taken Léonie to the opera. The premiere of the latest work by Wagner.'

'Damned Prussian propaganda,' Georges grumbled. 'Shouldn't be allowed.'

'And I believe he was intending to take her to supper afterwards.'

'To one of those ghastly bohemian places like Le Café de la Place Blanche, I shouldn't wonder. Crammed to the gills with artists and what have you.' He drummed his fingers on the table. 'What's that other place on the boulevard Rochechouart? They should shut it down.'

'Le Chat Noir,' Marguerite said.

37

'Layabouts, the lot of them,' pronounced Georges, warming to this new theme. 'Daubing dots on a scrap of canvas and calling it art: what kind of occupation is that for a man? That thoroughly insolent fellow, Debussy, who lives in your building? Chaps like that. Should be horsewhipped.'

'Achille is a composer, darling,' she chided mildly.

'Always scowling. Banging away on that piano day and night – I'm surprised his father doesn't take a stick to him. Might beat some sense into him.'

Marguerite hid a smile. Since Achille was a contemporary of Anatole's, she thought it was a little late for such disciplinary measures. In any case, Madame Debussy had been much too free with her hands when the children were young and it had clearly done not the slightest bit of good.

'This champagne is really quite delicious, Georges,' she said, moving the conversation on. She stretched across the table and took his fingers, then turned his hand over and pressed her nails into the soft flesh of his palm. 'You are most thoughtful,' she said, watching the wince of pain turn to pleasure in his eyes. 'Now, Georges. Will you order for me? We have been sitting here for such a time that I find I have quite an appetite.'

CHAPTER 5

Léonie and Anatole were shown to a private room on the first floor of Le Bar Romain, overlooking the street.

Léonie returned Anatole's evening jacket to him, then went to wash her face and hands, and repair her hair, in the small adjoining closet. She stared at her reflection in the looking glass, tilting it towards her. Her skin glowed from their night-time chase through the streets of Paris and her eyes glittered brightly from the light of the candles. Now the danger had passed, in her mind, Léonie was painting the scene in bright, bold colours, like a story. Already she had forgotten the hate on the men's faces, how terrified she had been.

Anatole ordered two glasses of Madeira, followed by red wine to accompany a simple supper of lamb chops and white creamed potatoes.

'Pear soufflé to follow, if you are still hungry,' he said, dismissing the *garçon*.

As they ate, Léonie related what had happened up until the moment Anatole had found her.

'They are a curious lot, *les abonnés*,' said Anatole. 'Only French music should be performed on French soil, that's the aim. Back in 1860, they pelted *Tannhäuser* from the stage.' He shrugged. 'It's a commonly held belief that they do not care about the music in the slightest.'

'Then why?'

'Chauvinism, pure and simple.' Anatole pushed back his chair from the table, stretched out his long, slim legs and took his cigarette case from the pocket of his waistcoat. 'I do not believe Paris will ever again welcome Wagner. Not now.'

Léonie thought a moment. 'Why did Achille make you a gift of the opera tickets? Is he not a fervent admirer of Monsieur Wagner?'

'Was,' he said, banging a cigarette on the silver lid to tighten the tobacco, 'but is no longer.' He leaned into his jacket pocket, pulled out a box of wax Vestas and struck a match. '"A beautiful sunset mistaken for a wonderful dawn", that is Achille's latest pronouncement on Wagner.' He tapped his head with a mocking half-smile. 'Forgive me, *Claude*-Achille as we are now supposed to address him.'

Debussy, a brilliant, if mercurial, pianist and composer, lived with his siblings and parents in the same apartment block as the Verniers on the rue de Berlin. He was both the *enfant terrible* of the Conservatoire and, reluctantly, their greatest hope. However, in their small circle of friends, Debussy's complex love life attracted more notoriety than his growing professional reputation. The current lady in favour was twenty-four-year-old Gabrielle Dupont.

'It is serious this time,' Anatole confided. 'Gaby understands his music must come first and that is, of course, most attractive to him. She is tolerant of the way he disappears each Tuesday to the salons of Maître Mallarmé. It raises his spirits in the face of the continuing drizzle of complaint from the Académie, who simply do not understand his genius. They are all too old, too stupid.'

Léonie raised her eyebrows. 'It is my belief that Achille brings most of his misfortunes down upon his own head. He is quick to fall out with those who might support him. He's too sharp-tongued, too ready to cause offence. Indeed, he goes quite out of his way to be churlish, rude and difficult.'

Anatole smoked and did not disagree.

'And friendship aside,' she continued, stirring a third spoonful of sugar into her coffee, 'I confess I have some sympathy with his critics. For me, his compositions are a little vague and unstructured and . . . well, disquieting. Meandering. Too often, I feel that I am waiting for the tune to reveal itself. As if one is listening underwater.'

Anatole smiled. 'Ah, but that is precisely the point. Debussy says that one must drown the sense of key. He is seeking to illuminate, through his music, the connections between the material and the spiritual worlds, the seen and the unseen, and such a thing cannot be presented in the traditional ways.'

Léonie pulled a face. 'That sounds like one of those clever things people say that mean precisely nothing!'

Anatole ignored the interruption. 'He believes that evocation and suggestion and nuance are more powerful, more truthful, more illuminating than statement and description. That the value and power of distant memories surpass that of conscious, explicit thought.'

Léonie admired her brother's loyalty to his friend but suspected he was only repeating verbatim words he'd heard previously issue from Achille's lips. For all Anatole's passionate advocacy of his friend's work, she knew very well that his tastes ran more to Offenbach and the orchestra of the Folies Bergère than to anything Debussy or Dukas or any of their Conservatoire friends might produce.

'Since we're trading confidences,' he added, 'I admit that I did return last week to the rue de la Chaussée d'Antin to purchase a copy of Achille's *Cinq poèmes*.'

Léonie's eyes flashed with frustration. 'Anatole, you gave Maman your word.'

He shrugged. 'I know, but I could not help myself. The price was so reasonable and it is sure to be a good investment, seeing as how Bailly printed only a hundred and fifty copies.'

'We must be more careful with our money. Maman relies on you to be prudent. We cannot afford to run up any more debts.' She paused, then added, 'Indeed, how much do we owe?'

Their eyes locked.

'Really, Léonie. Our household finances are not something for you to concern yourself with.'

'But—'

'But nothing,' he said firmly.

Sulking, she turned her back on him. 'You treat me like a child!'

'You are still a child,' he laughed. 'When you marry, you can drive your husband to distraction with queries about your own household budget, but until that time . . . However, I give you my word that, from now on, I will not spend a *sou* without your permission.'

'Now you're making fun of me.'

'Indeed, not even a *centime*,' he teased.

Hating them to be at odds, she surrendered. 'I shall hold you to it, mind,' she sighed.

Anatole drew a cross on his chest with his finger. 'On my honour.'

They smiled at one another, and then the teasing look fell from his face. He reached across the table and covered her small white hand with his own.

'To speak seriously for an instant, *petite*,' he said, 'I will find it hard to forgive myself for the fact that, because I was late, I left you facing tonight's ordeal alone. Can you forgive me?'

Léonie nodded. 'It is already forgotten.'

'Your generosity is more than I deserve. And you behaved with great courage. Most girls would have lost their heads. I am proud of you.' He sat back in his chair and lit another cigarette. 'Although you may find that the evening comes back to you. Shock has a habit of taking hold after the event.'

'I am not so timid,' she said firmly, pleased at having won his good opinion. She felt completely alive; taller, bolder, more precisely herself.

The clock on the mantelshelf chimed the hour.

'But at the same time, Anatole, I have never known you to miss the curtain before.'

Anatole took a mouthful of cognac. 'Always a first time.'

'What did keep you? Why were you delayed?'

Straight away, she knew he wasn't going to tell her the truth. He placed the broad-bellied glass on the table, then pulled at the waxed ends of his moustache.

'Anatole?'

'I was committed to meeting a customer from out of town. He was due at six but arrived rather later and remained longer than I had anticipated.'

'And yet you had your dress clothes with you? Or did you return home before joining me at the Palais Garnier?'

He didn't meet her eye. 'I had taken the precaution of bringing my evening clothes with me to the office.'

Quickly, he crossed the room and pulled the bell, stopping the conversation in its tracks. Before Léonie could quiz him further, the servants appeared to clear the table, making any further dialogue between them impossible.

'Time to get you home,' he said, putting his hand on her elbow and helping her to her feet. 'I will settle up once I have seen you into a carriage.'

Moments later, they were standing outside on the pavement.

'You are not returning with me?'

Anatole helped her up into the cab and fastened the catch. 'I think I'll pay a visit *chez* Frascati. Perhaps play a couple of hands of cards.'

Léonie felt a flutter of concern. 'What shall I tell Maman?'

'She will already have retired.'

'But what if she has not?'

He kissed her hand. 'In which case, tell her not to wait up.' Anatole reached up to press a note into the driver's hand. 'Rue de Berlin,' he said, then stepped back and banged on the side of the carriage. 'Sleep well, *petite*. I shall see you at breakfast.'

The whip cracked. The lamps banged against the side of the gig as the horses jerked forward in a clinking of harness and iron shoes on the cobbles. Léonie pushed down the glass and leaned out of the window. Anatole stood in a pool of smoggy yellow light beneath the hissing gas lamps, a trail of white smoke twisting up from his cigarette.

Why would he not tell me the real reason he was late?

She kept looking, reluctant to let him out of her sight, as the cab rattled up the rue de Caumartin past the Hotel Saint-Petersbourg, past Anatole's alma mater, the Lycée Fontanes, heading for the junction with rue Saint-Lazare.

Léonie's last glimpse, before the carriage turned the corner, was of Anatole flicking the burning end of his cigarette into the gutter. Then he turned on his heel and walked back into Le Bar Romain.

CHAPTER 6

The building in the rue de Berlin was quiet. Léonie let herself into the apartment with a latchkey. An oil lamp had been left burning to light her way. Léonie dropped the key into the china bowl that stood beside the silver post salver, empty of letters or calling cards. Pushing her mother's stole off the cushion, she sank down on a hall chair, slipped off her stained slippers and silk stockings and thought. If there was no shame attached to Anatole's actions, why hadn't he told her the truth?

Léonie glanced along the passageway and saw that her mother's door was closed. For once, she was disappointed. Though she tried not to, she too often found Marguerite's company irritating. Her topics of conversation were so limited and predictable. But tonight she would have been grateful for a little late-night company.

She took up the lamp and walked into the drawing room. A large and generous room, it occupied the entire front of the house, overlooking the rue de Berlin itself. The three sets of windows were closed, but the curtains of yellow chintz that hung ceiling to floor had been left open.

Léonie looked down on the deserted street and thought of her beloved brother, somewhere in the city, and hoped he was safe.

At last, thoughts of what could have been started to creep up on her. The high spirits that had supported her through the long evening drained away, leaving her frightened and fearful. She felt as if every limb, every muscle, every sense was overtaken by the memory of what she had witnessed.

Blood and cracked bones and hate.

Léonie closed her eyes, but still each separate incident flooded back, distinct, as if caught in the click of the shutter of a box camera. The stench as the home-made bombs of excrement and rotting food burst. The frozen eyes of the man as the knife plunged into his chest; that single paralysing moment between life and death.

There was a green woollen shawl hanging over the back of the *chaise longue*. She wrapped it around her shoulders, turned down the gas lamp and curled up in her favourite armchair, her legs tucked beneath her.

Suddenly, from the floor below, the sound of music began to filter up through the floorboards. Léonie smiled. Achille at his piano again. She looked to the clock on the mantelshelf.

Past midnight.

Léonie welcomed the knowledge that she was not the only one awake in the rue de Berlin. There was something soothing about his presence. She burrowed deeper into the folds of the chair, recognising the piece. *La Damoiselle élue*, a composition Anatole often claimed Debussy had written with Léonie in mind. She knew the assertion to be untrue. Achille had told her that the libretto was a prose setting of a poem by Rossetti, which in its turn had been inspired by Monsieur Poe's 'The Raven'. But false or not, she held the piece close to her heart, and its ethereal chords precisely suited her mood.

Without warning, another memory swooped down upon her. The morning of the funeral. Then, as now, Achille hammering endlessly on the piano, black notes and white seeping up through the floorboards until Léonie thought she would be driven mad with his playing. The single palm leaf floating in the glass bowl. The sickly aroma of ritual and death that insinuated itself into every corner of the apartment, the burning of incense and candles to mask the cloying sweetness of the corpse in the closed casket.

You are confusing what was with what is.

Back in the spring, Anatole had disappeared from the apartment most mornings before light had given shape back to the world. Most evenings, he returned home long after the household had retired. Once, he had been absent for a week without explanation. When Léonie finally mustered the courage to ask him where he had been, he told her only not to concern herself. She supposed he spent his nights at the *rouge et noir* tables. She knew, too, from the gossip of the servants, that he was being subjected to vociferous and anonymous denunciations in the columns of the newspapers. Léonie had tried to take refuge in her books, but even the words of Madame Oliphant had not helped.

The physical toll upon Anatole was obvious. His cheeks had grown hollow and his skin transparent. His brown eyes were dulled, permanently bloodshot, his lips parched. Léonie would do anything to prevent such a deterioration again.

Only when the leaves were returning to the trees in the boulevard Malesherbes, and when the paths of the Parc Monceau were filled once more with pink and white and lilac blooms, did the attacks upon his good name cease. From then, his spirits improved and his health recovered. The older brother she knew and loved was restored to her. Since then, there had been no more disappearances, no more evasions, no more half-truths.

Until this evening.

Léonie realised her cheeks were wet. She wiped away the tears with cold fingers, then wrapped the shawl more tightly around her.

This is September, not March.

But Léonie remained sick at heart. She knew he had lied to her. So she kept vigil at the window, allowing Achille's music below to lull her into a half-sleep, while all the time listening for the sound of Anatole's latchkey in the door.

CHAPTER 7

Leaving the lady sleeping, Anatole crept from the tiny rented room. Careful not to disturb the other lodgers in the boarding house, he walked slowly down the narrow and dusty wooden stairs in stockinged feet. A gas jet burned on each landing, as he descended one flight, then another and another.

It was not quite dawn, yet Paris was waking. In the distance, Anatole could hear the sounds of delivery carts. Wooden traps over the cobbles delivering milk and freshly baked bread to the cafés and bars of the Faubourg Montmartre.

He stopped to put on his shoes, then set off. The rue Feydeau was deserted and there was no sound except the clip of his heels on the pavement. Deep in thought, Anatole walked quickly to the junction with the rue Saint-Marc. He saw no one, heard no one.

His thoughts were rattling around in his head. Would their plan succeed? Could he get out of Paris unobserved and without raising suspicion? For all the fighting talk of the past hours, Anatole entertained doubts. He knew that his conduct over the coming hours, days, would determine their success or failure. Already Léonie was suspicious and since her support would be critical to the success of the endeavour, he cursed the sequence of events that had de- layed his arrival at the opera house, then the extraordinary ill fortune that the *abonnés* should have chosen that very night to stage their most bloody and violent protest to date.

He took a deep breath, feeling the crisp September dawn seeping into his lungs, mixed with the steam and smoke and soot of the city. The guilt he had felt at having failed Léonie had been forgotten while he held his lover in his arms. Now it returned, like a sharp pain in his chest.

He determined he would make it up to her.

The hand of time was on his back, pushing him homewards. He walked faster, wrapped in thought – delight at the night just past, the memory of his lover imprinted upon his mind and body, the fragrance of skin on his fingers, the texture of her hair. He was weary with the endless secrecy and obfuscation. As soon as they were away from Paris, there would be no more need for intrigue, to invent imaginary visits to the *rouge et noir* tables or opium dens or houses of ill repute to cover his true whereabouts.

That he had been under attack from the newspapers and unable to defend his own reputation was a state of affairs that sat uneasily with him. He suspected Constant to have had a hand in it. The blackening of his name affected the situation of both his mother and his sister. All he could hope was that when the matter was out in the open, there would be time enough to repair his standing.

As he turned the corner, a gust of autumn wind blew at his heels. He pulled his jacket tight around him and regretted the lack of a neck scarf. He crossed the rue Saint-Marc, thinking of the days, the weeks, to come, not the present within which he walked.

At first, he did not hear the sound of footsteps behind him. Two sets of feet, walking fast, getting closer. Then his mind sharpened. He glanced down at his evening clothes, realising he looked an easy target. Unarmed, unaccompanied and possibly with winnings from a night at the tables in his pockets.

Anatole walked faster. The footsteps, too, quickened.

Certain now that he was being marked, he darted right into the passage des Panoramas, thinking that if he could cut through to the boulevard Montmartre, where the cafés would be opening their doors and there was likely to be early-morning traffic, milk deliveries, carts, he would be safe.

The few remaining gas lamps burned with a cold blue light as he passed along the narrow row of glass-fronted shops selling stamps and *ex-voto* trinkets, the furniture maker displaying an ancient cabinet with dilapidated gilding, the various antiques dealers and sellers of *objets d'art*.

The men followed.

Anatole felt a spike of fear. His hand went to his pocket, looking for something with which to defend himself, but found nothing that would serve as a weapon.

He walked faster, resisting the impulse to start running. Better to keep his head up. Pretend all was well. Trust that he would make it through to the other side where there were witnesses before they had the chance to strike.

But behind him now, the sound of running. A flash of movement reflected in Stern's window, a refracting of the light, and Anatole spun round. He took a hit above his left eye but managed to land a punch. The man grunted, but Anatole felt his arms pinned from behind, leaving him exposed. The first blow, to his stomach, knocked the wind out of him, then a volley of blows smashed into his face that sent his head cracking from side to side.

The second assailant was also wearing a neck scarf across his face, but his head was uncovered and his hard scalp covered in angry red blisters. Anatole managed to send his foot smashing back into the man's shin, then grabbed at the open collar of his shirt and sent him staggering against the sharp-edged pillars in the doorway.

Anatole launched himself forward, using the weight of his body to try to get past, but the first man caught him with a glancing jab. Swinging out as he fell, Anatole hit the man in the ribs, but then he felt a blow on the back of his neck, sending him staggering. A vicious kick had him sprawling forward on the ground. He threw his hands over his head and pulled his knees up to his chin in a futile attempt to protect himself. As one blow, then another followed to his ribs, his kidneys, his arms, he realised for the first time that the beating might not stop.

'Hey!'

At the end of the passageway, through his bloodied eyes, Anatole thought he saw a light.

'Hey! You! What's going on?'

For a moment, time stood still. Then Anatole felt the breath of one of the assailants in his ear.

'*Une leçon.*'

Then the sensation of hands crawling over his battered body, fingers pushing into the pocket of his waistcoat, a sharp tug, and his father's fob watch being torn from its clip.

Finally Anatole found his voice.

'Over here! Here!'

With a final kick to his ribs, the two attackers left, running in the opposite direction from the inconstant light of the nightwatchman's lamp.

'Over here!' Anatole cried again.

He heard the shuffling feet coming towards him, then the clink of glass and metal on the ground and the old nightwatchman was peering down at him.

'Monsieur, *qu'est-ce qui s'est passé ici?*'

Anatole pulled himself up into a sitting position. 'I'm all right,' he said, trying to catch his breath. He put his hand up to his eye and his fingers came away red.

'You've taken quite a beating.'

52

'It's nothing,' he insisted. 'A cut.'

'Monsieur, you were robbed?'

Anatole reached up for the nightwatchman to help him to his feet. Pain shot across his back and down his legs. He examined his hands, turning them over. His knuckles were cracked and bleeding. He could feel a gash on his ankle where the skin was open, rubbing against the material of his trousers.

Anatole took a moment more to compose himself, then straightened his clothes.

'Did they take much, sir?'

He patted himself down and was surprised to find his pocket book and cigarette case still there.

'They appear to have taken only my watch,' he said. His words seemed to be coming from a long way away as the reality slipped into his head and took root. It had not been a random robbery. Indeed, not a robbery at all, but a lesson, as the man had said.

Pushing the thought from his mind, Anatole pulled out a note and slipped it into the old man's tobacco-stained fingers. 'In gratitude for your assistance, my friend.'

The watchman looked down. A smile broke out. 'Most generous, Monsieur.'

'But no need to mention this to anyone, there's a good chap. Now, if you could find me a cab?'

The old man touched his hat. 'Whatever you say, sir.'

CHAPTER 8

Léonie woke with a jolt. For a moment, she couldn't recall why she was wrapped in a woollen blanket in the drawing room, curled up in a chair. Then she looked down at her torn evening dress and remembered. The riot at the Palais Garnier. The late supper with Anatole. Achille playing lullabies through the night. She glanced at the Sèvres clock on the mantelshelf.

A quarter past five.

Chilled to the bone, and a little nauseous, she slipped into the hall and made her way along the passageway, noticing that Anatole's door was also now closed. The observation was comforting.

Her bedroom was at the end. Pleasant and airy, it was the smallest of the private rooms. Léonie stepped out of her bedraggled evening dress, letting it fall to the ground, and untied her petticoats. With clumsy fingers, she unlaced her corset and undid the hooks until she could wriggle out, then threw it over the chair. She splashed a little of last evening's water, now ice cold, on her face, then slipped on her nightdress and crawled into bed.

She was woken some hours later by the sounds of the servants.

Realising she was hungry, Léonie rose quickly, drew her own curtains and pinned back the shutters. Daylight had brought the unremarkable world back to life. She marvelled, after the excitements of last evening, at how Paris outside her window looked entirely unchanged. As she brushed her hair, she examined her reflection in the looking glass for signs of the night upon her face. Disappointingly, there were none.

The aroma of freshly brewed coffee rushed to meet her as she entered the drawing room, then came to a standstill. She was pleased to see both her mother and Anatole were already seated at the table. Most often, Léonie ate breakfast alone.

Even at this early hour, Marguerite's dark hair was twisted artfully into her habitual chignon, and she had a dusting of powder on her cheeks and neck. She sat with her back to the window, but in the unforgiving light of morning, the faintest of lines of age around her eyes and her mouth were discernible. Léonie noticed she was wearing a new negligée – pink silk with a yellow bow – and sighed. Presumably another gift from the pompous Du Pont.

The more generous he is, the longer we shall have to put up with him.

Feeling a stab of guilt at her uncharitable thoughts, Léonie walked to the table and kissed her mother on the cheek with more enthusiasm than usual.

'*Bon matin*, Maman,' she said, then turned to greet her brother.

Her eyes flashed wide at the sight of him. His left eye swollen shut, one hand wrapped in a white bandage, and a ring of green and purple bruising around his jaw.

'Anatole, what on earth—'

He leapt in. 'I have been telling Maman how we were caught up in the protests at the Palais Garnier last evening,' he said sharply, fixing her with a look. 'And how I was unlucky enough to take a few blows.'

Léonie looked at him in astonishment.

'It has even made the front page of *Le Figaro*,' Marguerite said, tapping the newspaper with her immaculate nails. 'When I think of what might have happened! You could have been killed, Anatole. Thank goodness he was there to look after you, Léonie. Several dead, it claims here.'

'Don't fuss, Maman, I've already been checked by the doctor,' he said. 'It looks worse than it is.'

Léonie opened her mouth to speak, then caught a warning glance from Anatole.

'More than a hundred arrests,' Marguerite continued. 'Several dead! And explosions! At the Palais Garnier, I ask you. Paris has become intolerable. The city is quite lawless. Really, I cannot bear it.'

'There is nothing whatsoever for you to bear,' Léonie couldn't help saying. 'You were not there. I am fine. And Anatole—' She broke off and fixed him with a long stare. 'Anatole has told you he is fine. You are only distressing yourself.'

Marguerite gave a wan smile. 'You have no idea what a mother suffers.'

'Nor do I wish to,' Léonie muttered under her breath, taking a piece of bread and spreading it liberally with butter and apricot preserve.

For a while, breakfast continued in silence. Léonie continued to throw enquiring glances at Anatole, which he ignored.

The maid came in with the post on a tray.

'Anything for me?' said Anatole, gesturing with his butter knife.

'Nothing, *chéri*. No.'

Marguerite picked up a heavy cream envelope with a look of puzzlement on her face. She examined the postmark. 'If you will excuse me,' she said, rising from the table and leaving the room before either of her children could protest.

The moment she was gone, Léonie turned on her brother.

'What on earth happened to you?' she hissed. 'Tell me. Before Maman returns.'

Anatole put down his coffee cup. 'I regret to say that I found myself in a disagreement with the croupier *chez* Frascati. He was trying to swindle me, I knew it, and I made the mistake of taking it up with the manager.'

'And?'

'And,' he sighed, 'the long and the short of it is that I was escorted from the premises. I had not gone more than five hundred yards when I was set upon by a pair of ruffians.'

'Sent from the club?'

'I assume so, yes.'

She stared, certain that there was more to the situation than Anatole was admitting. 'Do you owe money there?'

'A little, but . . .' He shrugged and discomfort flickered across his face. 'Coming on the heels of all that has gone before this year, it has made me consider it might be wise to make myself scarce for a week or so,' he added. 'Get out of Paris, just till the fuss has died down.'

Léonie's face fell. The thought of Anatole going away, even for a few days, did not bear thinking about. To be alone in the apartment, with her mother and the tedious Du Pont. She poured herself a second cup of coffee.

'But I could not bear it if you left. Besides, where would you go?'

Anatole put his elbows on the table and dropped his voice. 'I have an idea, *petite*, but I will need your assistance.' He touched her arm. 'Will you help me?'

'Of course, anything, but I—'

At that moment, their mother reappeared in the doorway. Anatole pulled back, touching his finger to his lips. Marguerite was holding both the envelope and the letter in her hand. Léonie was quite concerned at how pale she looked.

'Is everything all right, Maman? Anatole and I both were concerned that you had . . . perhaps received bad news.'

Marguerite said nothing, just stared intently at the letter.

'Who is it from?' Léonie asked in the end, when her mother still showed no signs of responding. Indeed, she gave the impression that she had almost forgotten they were there at all.

'Maman?' said Anatole. 'May I fetch you something? Do you feel unwell?'

'Thank you, *chéri*, but no.' Marguerite was frowning. 'The letter comes from the Domaine de la Cade,' she said quietly. 'From your Tante Isolde. The widow of my half-brother, Jules.'

'The uncle who died in January?' Léonie said.

Marguerite winced. 'Passed away, *disparu*; "died" is so vulgar,' she corrected, although Léonie could hear her heart was not in the rebuke.

'Why is she writing to you so long after the event?'

'Oh, she has written on a couple of previous occasions,' Marguerite replied. 'Once on their marriage, then again to inform me of Jules's death and the details of his funeral.' She paused. 'It is to my regret that ill health prevented me from making the journey and at such a time of the year.'

Léonie knew perfectly well that her mother would never have returned to the house in which she had grown up outside Rennes-les-Bains, regardless of the season or circumstance. Marguerite and her half-brother were estranged.

Léonie knew the bare bones of the story from Anatole. Marguerite's father, Guy Lascombe, had married young and in haste. When his first wife died giving birth to Jules some six months later, Lascombe immediately gave his son into the care of a governess, then a series of tutors, and returned to Paris. He paid for his son's education and the upkeep of the family estate, and when Jules came of age, he settled a fair annual allowance on him, but otherwise paid him no more attention than before.

Only at the end of his life had Grandpère Lascombe married again, although he had continued to live much the same dissolute life. He dispatched his gentle second wife and tiny daughter to live at the Domaine de la Cade with Jules, visiting only when the mood took him. From the pained expression that came over Marguerite's face on the rare occasion the subject of her childhood came up, Léonie understood that her mother had been less than happy.

Grandpère Lascombe and his wife had been killed one night when their carriage overturned. When the will was read, it transpired that Guy had left his entire estate to Jules, with not a *sou* for his daughter. Marguerite fled instantly north to Paris, where, in the February of 1865, she had met and married Leo Vernier, a radical idealist. Since Jules was a supporter of the *ancien régime*, there had been no contact between the half-siblings from that point onwards.

Léonie bit back her impatience. 'Well, then why is she writing to you again?'

Marguerite looked down at the letter, as if she could still not quite believe the contents of it.

'It is an invitation for you, Léonie, to pay a visit. For some four weeks, indeed.'

'What!' Léonie all but snatched the letter from her mother's fingers. 'How can that be?'

'*Chérie*, please. You will make my head ache.'

Léonie paid no attention. 'Does Tante Isolde give an explanation for why she is issuing such an invitation now?'

Anatole lit a cigarette. 'Perhaps she wishes to make amends for her late husband's lack of familial duty.'

'It is possible,' Marguerite said thoughtfully, 'although there is nothing in the letter to suggest that is the intention.'

He laughed. 'It is hardly the manner of thing one would commit to paper.'

Léonie folded her arms. 'Well, it is quite absurd to imagine that I should accept an invitation to sojourn with an aunt to whom I have never been introduced, and for so prolonged a period. Indeed,' she added crossly, 'I can think of nothing worse than being buried in the country with some elderly widow talking about the old days.'

'Oh no, Isolde is quite young,' said Marguerite. 'She was many years Jules's junior – little more than thirty years of age, I believe.'

For a moment, silence fell over the breakfast table, then Marguerite looked at her son. 'Anatole, what would you advise?'

'I do not wish to go,' said Léonie, looking to her brother for support but getting none.

Anatole smiled. 'Come now, Léonie, a visit to the mountains? It sounds just the thing. You were telling me only last week how bored you had become of life in town and that you stood in need of a rest.'

'I did, yes, but—'

'A change of scenery might restore your spirits. Besides, the weather in Paris is intolerable. Blustery and wet one day, and temperatures that would not shame the Algerian deserts the next.'

'I own that is true, but—'

'You were telling me how much you wished for an adventure. Yet when an opportunity presents itself, you are too timid to take it.'

'But Tante Isolde might be thoroughly disagreeable. And how would I occupy my time in the country? There will be nothing for me to do. No one to talk to, no books, no society.'

'Oh, there is a marvellous library,' her mother said vaguely. 'All the books you could ever hope to read.'

Léonie didn't know what to make of things. 'But, Maman, you never talk about the Domaine de la Cade with anything other than dislike.'

'It was a long time ago,' Marguerite said quietly. 'Perhaps things are different.'

Léonie tried an alternative approach.

'But the journey will take days and days. I cannot possibly travel so far. Not without a chaperone.'

Marguerite let her gaze settle on her daughter. 'No, no . . . of course not. But, as it happens, last evening General Du Pont suggested he and I might visit the Marne Valley for a few weeks. If I were able to accept his invitation . . .' She broke off and turned to her son. 'Might I prevail upon you, Anatole, to accompany Léonie to the Midi?'

'I am certain I could be spared for a few days.'

'But I don't want to go,' Léonie objected.

Her brother talked over her. 'In point of fact, I was just saying how I was considering a few days out of town. This way, the two things could be combined to everybody's satisfaction. And,' he added, fixing his sister with a conspiratorial smile, 'if you are anxious about being so far from home, *petite*, and alone in an unfamiliar environment, I am sure Tante Isolde could be prevailed upon to extend her invitation to me also.'

At last, Léonie caught up with Anatole's reasoning. 'Oh,' she said, her distress at the thought that she was being sent away instantly evaporating. 'A library, did you say?'

'Yes, indeed. Could you manage to be away for a week or two, Anatole?' Marguerite repeated.

'*Pour ma petite sœur*, anything.' He smiled at Léonie. 'If you wish to accept the invitation, then I am at your service.'

Léonie felt the first prickling of excitement. To be at liberty to walk in the open countryside, and to breathe unpolluted air. To be free to read what she wished and when she wished without fear of criticism or rebuke. Marguerite was always telling her that reading would spoil her eyes, or that gentlemen did not look favourably on girls who spent their lives with their noses stuck in a book.

And I would have Anatole to myself.

Léonie weighed the matter a little longer, not wishing it to be obvious that she and Anatole were in league together. The fact that her mother had not cared for the Domaine de la Cade did not mean that she would not. She looked sideways at Anatole's battered, handsome face. She had thought the whole business behind them. Last evening had brought it home to her that it was not.

'Very well,' she said, feeling a rush of blood to her head. 'If Anatole will accompany me and stay until I am comfortably settled.' She turned to her mother. 'Maman, please would you write to thank Tante Isolde and say that I – *we* – will be delighted to accept her generous invitation.'

'I shall send a wire and confirm the dates she has suggested.'

Anatole grinned. He raised his coffee cup. '*À l'avenir,*' he said.

Léonie returned the toast. 'To the future,' she laughed. 'And to the Domaine de la Cade.'

PART II

Paris
October 2007

PART II

Paris
October 2007

CHAPTER 9

PARIS
FRIDAY, 26TH OCTOBER 2007

Meredith Martin stared at her reflection in the window as the train hurtled towards the Eurostar terminal in Paris. Black hair unwashed, her pale face stripped of colour, she wasn't looking her best.

She glanced at her watch.

Eight forty-five. Nearly there, thank God.

The compartment was pretty empty. A couple of French businesswomen in grey pantsuits. Two students asleep on their backpacks. The soft tapping of computer keys, low calls made on cell phones, the rustle of the late-edition newspapers. Across the aisle, a quartet of lawyers in striped shirts and chinos with razor-sharp creases, talking loudly about a fraud case. Their table was covered in glass bottles and plastic cups.

Meredith's eyes drifted to the glossy hotel brochure on the plastic table, even though she'd read it cover to cover already.

L'HÔTEL DOMAINE DE LA CADE

RENNES-LES-BAINS

11190

Set in delightful wooded parkland above the picturesque town of Rennes-les-Bains in the beautiful Langue-doc, the Hôtel Domaine de la Cade is the epitome of nineteenth-century grandeur and elegance, but with all the comfort and leisure facilities expected by the discriminating twenty-first-century visitor. The hotel is situated on the location of the original maison de maître, *which was partially destroyed by fire in 1897. Run as a hotel since the 1950s, it reopened after a major refurbishment under new management in 2004 and is now recognised as one of the premier hotels in south-west France.*

For full tariff and detailed facilities, see opposite.

The same information was repeated in French.

It sounded wonderful. Come Monday, she'd be there. It was her treat to herself – a recommendation from one of her colleagues at work, who'd 'done' Europe the previous summer. It would be a couple of days of five-star luxury after all the budget flights and cheap motels. She pushed the brochure back into her plastic travel file and put the whole thing in her purse.

Meredith stretched her arms above her head, then rolled her neck. She couldn't remember when she'd last been so tired. She had checked out of her hotel in London at noon, taken in an afternoon concert at the Wigmore Hall – seriously dull – before grabbing a sandwich at Waterloo Station and boarding the train, hot and exhausted.

After all that, they'd been late leaving. When they finally got going, she spent most of the first part of the journey in a daze, watching the green English countryside zoom by, rather than typing up her notes. Then the train plunged beneath the Channel and was swallowed up by the tunnel. The atmosphere became oppressive, but at least it killed the cell-phone chatter. Thirty minutes later, they emerged the other side to the flat, brown landscape of northern France.

Chalet-style farmhouses, the flash of small towns and long, straight farm tracks leading nowhere. One or two larger towns, the slag heaps grassed over by time. Then Charles de Gaulle Airport and the suburbs, *la banlieue*, the drab and depressing rent-controlled high-rises that stood mute on the outskirts of the French capital.

Meredith leant back in her seat and let her thoughts wander. She was partway through a four-week work trip to France and the UK, writing a biography of the nineteenth-century French composer Achille-Claude Debussy and the women in his life. After a couple of years of researching and planning – but getting nowhere – she'd caught a break. Six months ago, a small start-up academic press made a modest offer for the book. The advance wasn't great, but, given that she didn't have a reputation in the field of music criticism, it was pretty good. Enough to make her dream of coming to Europe a reality. She was determined to write not just another Debussy biography, but *the* book that would put him and his life into context for the twenty-first century.

Her second piece of luck had been getting a part-time teaching post at a private college outside Raleigh Durham, starting the spring semester. It had the advantage of being close to where her adoptive parents now lived – which saved on laundry, phone bills and groceries – and not far from her alma mater, the University of North Carolina.

After ten years of paying her way through college, Meredith had racked up a lot of debt. But with the money she made from teaching piano, combined with the advance from the publishing company and now the promise of a regular salary, she summoned up the courage to go ahead and book the tickets to Europe.

The typescript was due with her publisher at the end of April. Right now, she was on track – ahead of schedule, in fact. She had spent ten days in England. Now she had nearly two weeks in France – Paris mostly, but she'd also scheduled a quick trip down to a small town in the south-west, Rennes-les-Bains.

The official reason for the detour was that she needed to check out a lead about Debussy's first wife, Lilly, having been sent there to convalesce after an operation, before heading back to Paris. If it had only been a matter of tracking down the first Mrs Debussy, she wouldn't have gone to so much trouble. But she had another motive for going to Rennes-les-Bains – a personal one.

Meredith reached into the inside pocket of her purse and pulled out a manila envelope with DO NOT BEND printed on it in red. She slid out a couple of old sepia photographs, the corners dog-eared and bent, and a printed sheet of piano music. She looked at the now-familiar faces, as she'd done so many times, before turning her attention to the piece of music. Handwritten on yellow manuscript paper, it was a simple melody in common time, key of A minor, the title and the date hand-printed in old-fashioned italic script at the top: *Sepulchre 1891*.

She knew it off by heart – every bar, every note. The music and the three photos she carried with it were the only things Meredith had inherited from her birth mother. An heirloom, a talisman.

She was well aware the trip might turn up nothing of interest. It was a long time ago; the stories were faded. On the other hand, Meredith figured she couldn't be worse off than she was right now, knowing virtually nothing about her family's past. For the price of the air ticket, it seemed worth it.

Meredith realised the train was slowing. The rail tracks had multiplied and the lights of the Gare du Nord were coming into view. The atmosphere in the carriage shifted again. A return to the real world, a sense of purpose at the end of a shared journey nearly over. Ties straightened, coats reclaimed.

With her sharp cheekbones, clear brown eyes and petite figure, Meredith looked more like a senior in high school than a twenty-eight-year-old academic. At home, she still carried her ID if she wanted to be sure of getting served in a bar. She reached up to the luggage rack for her jacket and tote bag, revealing a tanned, flat stomach between her green top and Banana Republic denims, aware that the four men across the aisle were staring.

Meredith put the jacket on.

'Have a good trip, guys,' she said, then headed for the door.

A wall of sound hit her the second she stepped down to the platform. People shouting, rushing, waving. Everybody in a hurry. Announcements were blaring out over the loud-speakers. Information about the next departure, introduced by a kind of fanfare on a glockenspiel. It was too much, too loud, after the hushed silence of the train.

Meredith smiled, breathing in the sights, smells, character of Paris. Already she felt like a different person.

Hoisting her bags high on each shoulder, she followed the signs across the station concourse and got in line for a taxi. The guy in front of her was shouting and waving, a Gi-tanes wedged deep between his fingers. Blue-white tendrils of vanilla-scented smoke twisted up into the night air.

She gave the address to the driver, a hotel in the 4th *arrondissement*, on the rue du Temple in the Marais district. It was a good location for the regular tourist stuff if she had time – the Centre Pompidou and Musée Picasso were nearby – but mostly for the Conservatoire, and the various concert halls, archives and private addresses she needed to visit for research.

Meredith was thrown back in her seat as the taxi accelerated sharply into the wild Parisian traffic. She put her arm protectively around her purse and hugged it tightly to her, watching as the cafés, boulevards, scooters and street lamps zoomed past.

Meredith felt she knew Debussy's muses, mistresses, lovers, wives – Marie Vasnier, Gaby Dupont, Thérèse Roger, his first wife Lilly Texier, his second, Emma Bardac, his beloved daughter Chouchou. Their faces, their stories, their features were right there, at the front of her mind – the dates, the references, the music. She had a first draft of the biography and was pretty satisfied with how the text was shaping up. What she needed now was to bring them to life on the page – a little more colour, a little nineteenth-century atmosphere.

From time to time, she worried that Debussy's life was more real to her than her own. Then she dismissed the thought. It was good to be focused. If she wanted to hit her deadline, she needed to keep at it for just a while longer.

The cab screamed to a halt.

'Hôtel Axial-Beaubourg. *Voilà.*'

The place was more like a boutique hotel in New York than what she had expected to find in Paris. It was all straight lines and glass; stylish, minimalist. Art magazines, copies of *Vogue* and *Paris Match* were stacked up in brushed chrome racks on the walls. Huge lampshades hung from the ceiling. It was all trying a bit too hard.

At the far end of the small lobby was the bar, with a line of men and women drinking. Lots of toned flesh and good tailoring. The rattle of ice and the chink of glasses.

Meredith approached the desk. The clerk was friendly and efficient, and Meredith was pleased her rusty French was understood. She hadn't spoken the language in a while.

Got to be a good sign.

Turning down the offer of help with her bags, she made a note of the Wi-Fi password, then took the narrow elevator to the third floor and walked along a dark passageway until she found the number she was looking for.

The room was small, but clean and stylish. Meredith ran her hand over the sheets. Good-quality bed linen, comfortable. Lots of space in the closet. She dropped her tote on the bed, took out her laptop and plugged it in to charge.

Then she went to the window, pulled back the net curtain and opened the shutters. The sound of traffic surged into the room. Down below, a glamorous young crowd was enjoying the surprisingly mild October evening. Meredith leaned out. She could see in all four directions. A department store on the corner opposite, its shutters closed. Cafés and bars, a patisserie and a deli were all open, and music filtered out onto the sidewalks. Orange street lamps, neon; everything floodlit or silhouetted.

With her elbows resting on the wrought-iron balustrade, Meredith just watched awhile, wishing she had enough energy to go down and join in. Then she rubbed her arms, realising her skin was covered in goosebumps.

She unpacked and took a quick shower, then, wrapped in a towelling robe, poured herself a glass of red wine from the minibar and sat down to check her mail.

There was nothing much – a couple of emails from friends asking how things were going, one from her mother, Mary, checking she was OK. Meredith sighed. Nothing from her publisher. The first part of the advance had been due at the end of September, but it hadn't come through. It was now the end of October and she was getting jumpy. She'd sent a couple of reminders and been reassured that everything was in hand. Her financial situation wasn't too bad – she had her credit cards and she could always borrow a little from Mary, if absolutely necessary, to tide her over – but she'd be relieved to know the money was on its way.

Meredith logged off. She drained the last of the wine, brushed her teeth and then climbed into bed with a book for company.

She lasted about five minutes.

The sounds of Paris faded. Meredith drifted asleep, the light still on, her battered copy of the stories of Edgar Allan Poe abandoned on the pillow beside her.

CHAPTER 10

When Meredith woke next morning, light was streaming through the window.

She leapt out of bed. She ran a brush through her hair, tied it back in a ponytail and pulled on blue jeans, a green sweater and her jacket. She checked she'd got all she needed in her purse – wallet, map, notebook, sunglasses, camera – then, feeling good about the day ahead, was out of the door.

It was a perfect fall day, bright and sunny and fresh. Meredith headed for the brasserie opposite for breakfast. Rows of round tables with faux-marble tops were set out on the sidewalk to catch the best of the morning sun. Inside, two middle-aged waiters in black and white were moving with astonishing speed through the crowded restaurant.

Meredith got the last free table outside, next to two thin and immaculately dressed women sipping *café noisette* from tiny white cups. She ordered the *petit-déjeuner complet* – juice, baguette with butter and jelly, pastries and *café au lait* – then pulled out her notebook, a replica of Hemingway's famous Moleskine jotters. She planned to spend the day visiting the private locations important to Debussy, as opposed to the big public spaces and concert halls. She'd take a few photos, see how far she got.

Debussy had been born in St-Germain-en-Laye on 22nd August 1862, in what was now commuter belt. But he was a Parisian through and through and spent pretty much all his fifty-five years in the capital, from his childhood home to the house at 80 avenue du Bois de Boulogne, where he'd died on 25th March 1918, four days after the German long-range bombardment of Paris had begun. The last stop on her itinerary, maybe when she came back at the end of the week, would be the Cimetière de Passy in the 16th *arrondissement* where he was buried.

Meredith took a deep breath. She already felt at home in Paris. Everything had been so frantic leading up to her departure, she could hardly believe she was actually here. She sat still, enjoying the scene and being right at the heart of things. Then she found her map and spread it out on the table.

The first address on her list was the rue de Berlin, where Debussy had lived with his parents and siblings from the early 1860s until he was twenty-nine years old. It was just around the block from the apartment of the Symbolist poet Stéphane Mallarmé, where Debussy had attended the famous Tuesday-afternoon salons. After the First World War, like many French streets with German names, it had been renamed and was now the rue de Liège.

Meredith followed the line with her finger to the rue de Londres, where Debussy had taken a furnished apartment with his lover Gaby Dupont in January 1892. Next came an apartment in the tiny rue Gustave Doré in the 17th, then just around the corner from the rue Cardinet, where they lived until Gaby walked out on him on New Year's Day 1899. Debussy remained at the same address for the next five years with his first wife, Lilly, before that relationship, too, broke down.

In terms of planning, Paris was pretty manageable. Everything was within walking distance, helped by the fact that Debussy had spent his life within a relatively small area: a star-like quartet of streets around the place d'Europe on the boundary of the 8th and 9th *arrondissements*, over-looking the Gare Saint-Lazare.

Meredith ringed each of the locations on the map with a black marker pen, looked at the pattern a moment, then decided she'd start at the furthest point and work her way back in the direction of the hotel.

She finished her coffee, brushed the buttery flakes of croissant from her sweater and licked her fingers one by one, resisting the temptation to order anything else. Despite her athletic appearance, Meredith loved food. Pastries, bread, cookies – all the stuff that nobody was supposed to eat any more. She left a ten-euro note to cover the check, then set off.

It took her just short of fifteen minutes to reach the place de la Concorde. From there, she turned north, then along the boulevard Malesherbes and avenue Velasquez towards the Parc Monceau. After the roar of traffic on the main thoroughfare, the imposing dead-end street seemed eerily silent. Plane trees with variegated bark, mottled like the back of an old man's hand, lined the sidewalk. Many of the trunks were tagged with graffiti.

As Meredith walked through black wrought-iron gates into the wide green space, she found it easy to imagine Lilly or Gaby, or even Debussy himself, hand in hand with his daughter, strolling along the generous pathways. Long white summer dresses swirling in the dust or ladies sitting beneath wide-brimmed hats on one of the green metal benches set along the edges of the lawns. Through the trees, she glimpsed a folly in the style of a Greek temple. A little further away, there was a stone pyramid icehouse, fenced off from the public, and marble statues of the Muses. Across the park, tawny ponies roped in a line carried excited children up and down the gravel.

Meredith took plenty of photographs. Apart from the clothes and the cell phones, the Parc Monceau seemed hardly changed from the photos she'd seen of a hundred years ago. Everything was so vivid, so clear.

Having spent half an hour wandering in contented circles, she found herself at the subway station on the north side. The sign MONCEAU LIGNE NO. 2 above the entrance, with its elaborate Art Nouveau design, looked like it might have been there since Debussy's day. She took a couple more shots, then walked into the 17th *arrondissement*. The neighbourhood seemed drab after the *fin-de-siècle* elegance of the park. The stores looked cheap, the buildings unremarkable.

She found the rue Cardinet easily and identified the block where Lilly and Debussy had lived. She felt a prick of disappointment. From the outside, it was plain, nondescript, dull. There was no character to it. In letters, Debussy talked of the modest apartment with affection, describing the watercolours on the walls, the oil paintings.

For a moment, she thought of ringing the bell and seeing if she could persuade anyone to let her in to look around. It was here, after all, that Debussy had written the work that had transformed his life: his only opera, *Pelléas et Mélisande*. It was here that Lilly Debussy had shot herself, days before their fifth wedding anniversary, when she realised Debussy was leaving her for good to set up home with the mother of one of his piano pupils, Emma Bardac. Lilly survived, but the surgeons never got the bullet out. Meredith thought the fact that she had lived the rest of her life with a physical reminder of Debussy lodged inside her was, somehow, the most poignant part of the whole awful story.

She raised her hand to the silver intercom, then checked herself. Meredith believed in the spirit of place. She bought into the idea that, in certain circumstances, a kind of echo of the past might remain. But here in the city, too much time had passed. Even if the bricks and mortar were the same, in a hundred years of bustling human life there'd be too many ghosts. Too many footsteps, too many shadows.

Instead, she went in search of the Square Claude Debussy. When she found it, it was, if anything, a bigger let-down. Ugly, brutalist six-storey buildings. And there was no one about. The whole place had an air of abandonment. Thinking of the elegant statues in the Parc Monceau celebrating writers, painters, architects, Meredith felt a spurt of anger that Paris had honoured one of its most famous sons so shabbily.

Meredith continued on to the rue de Londres, where Gaby and Debussy had rented their first apartment in January 1892, wanting to feel something, some nostalgia, some sense of place, but getting nothing. She checked the numbers, coming to a halt where Debussy's home should have been. It looked like the building had been swallowed up by the Gare Saint-Lazare. There wasn't anything here to link the old days with the new. There wasn't even anything worth photographing. Just an absence.

Meredith looked around and saw a small restaurant on the opposite side of the street, Le Petit Chablisien. It wasn't that long since breakfast, but she'd been walking for a while and she was hungry and disappointed. More than that, she felt she could do with a glass of wine.

She crossed the street. The menu was chalked up on a blackboard on an easel on the sidewalk. The large glass windows were modestly covered by lace half-curtains so she couldn't see inside. When she pushed down the old-fashioned handle, a shrill bell jangled and she was met instantly by an elderly waiter with a crisp white linen apron tied around his waist.

'*Pour manger?*'

Meredith nodded and was shown to a table for one in the corner. Paper tablecloths, clunky silver knives and forks, a bottle of water waiting on the table. She ordered the *plat du jour* and a glass of Fitou.

While she was eating, Meredith looked at the black-and-white photographs on the walls. Images of the *quartier* in days gone by, the staff of the restaurant standing proudly outside, the waiters with black moustaches and white collars and the patron and his matronly wife in the centre in their starched Sunday best. Best of all, though, was a photograph she recognised. Meredith smiled. Above the door to the kitchen, beside a portrait of a woman with a younger man and a girl with a mass of tumbling hair piled on her head, was a copy of one of the most famous photographs of Debussy, taken at the Villa Medici in Rome in 1885. Only twenty-two years old, he glowered out of the picture with his distinctive dark expression. His black curly hair was short over his forehead, and with the beginnings of a moustache, his face was immediately recognisable. Meredith hoped to use the image as the illustration on the back jacket of her book.

'He lived in this very street,' she said to the waiter, while she paid the bill. She gestured at the photo. 'Claude Debussy. Right here.'

The waiter shrugged, uninterested, until he saw the size of the tip. Then he smiled.

CHAPTER 11

By the time she got back to the hotel at six, Meredith had visited everywhere Debussy had ever lived in Paris. She showered and changed into a pair of white jeans and a pale blue sweater. She loaded the photos from her digital camera to her laptop, checked her mail – still no money – had a light supper in the brasserie opposite, then rounded off the evening with a cocktail at the hotel bar.

Back in her room, she felt the need to hear a familiar voice. She called home.

'Hi, Mary. It's me.'

'Meredith!'

The catch in her mother's voice brought tears to Meredith's eyes. She felt a long way from home.

'How are things?' she asked.

They talked for a while. Meredith filled Mary in on everything she'd done since they'd last spoken, and all the places she'd visited already since arriving in Paris, although she was painfully aware of the dollars mounting up every minute they chatted.

She heard the pause long distance. 'And how's the other project?' Mary asked.

'I'm not thinking about that right now. Too much to do here in Paris. I'll get onto it when I reach Rennes-les-Bains after the weekend.'

'There's nothing to worry about,' Mary said, the words coming out in a rush, making it obvious how much it was on her mind. She'd always been supportive of Meredith's need to find out about her past, though Meredith knew Mary feared what might come to light. She felt the same. What if it came out that the illness, the misery that had overshadowed her birth mother's entire life, was there in her family stretching way back? What if she started to show the same signs?

'I'm not worried,' she said, a little snappy, then felt immediately guilty. 'I'm excited more than anything. I'll let you know how I get on. Promise.'

They talked a few minutes more, then said goodbye.

'Love you.'

'Love you too,' came the answer from thousands of miles away.

On Sunday morning, Meredith headed for the Opéra de Paris at the Palais Garnier. In Debussy's time, the exuberant, over-the-top baroque building was the place to see and be seen. The site of the notorious anti-Wagner riots in September 1891, it was also the backdrop for Gaston Leroux's novel *The Phantom of the Opera*.

It took Meredith fifteen minutes to walk to the theatre, weaving in and out of the tourists looking for the Louvre, then all the way up the avenue de l'Opéra. The building itself was pure nineteenth century, but the traffic was strictly twenty-first – cars, scooters, trucks, buses and bikes coming at her from all angles. Taking her life in her hands, she dodged the lanes until she made it to the island on which the Palais Garnier stood.

It blew her away – the imposing façade, the grand balustrades, the rose marble columns, the gilded statues, the ornate gold-and-white roof and green copper dome glinting in the October sunshine. Meredith tried to picture the marshy wasteland on which the theatre had been constructed. Tried to imagine carriages, and women in long, sweeping dresses and men in top hats, instead of trucks and cars hitting their horns. But it was all too noisy, too strident to let echoes of the past slip through.

She was relieved to find that because there was a charity concert later, the theatre was open even though it was Sunday. The second she stepped inside, the silence of the historic staircases and balconies wrapped her in its arms. The Grand Foyer was just as she'd imagined from the pictures, an expanse of marble stretching before her like the nave of a monumental cathedral. Ahead of her, the Grand Escalier soared up beneath the burnished dome.

Was she allowed in here? Her sneakers squeaked on the floor. The doors into the auditorium were propped open, so she went inside. She wanted to see for herself the famous six-tonne chandelier and the Chagall ceiling.

Down at the front, a quartet was practising. Meredith slipped into the back row. For a moment, she felt the ghost of her former self – the performer she might have been – slide in and sit beside her. The feeling was so strong, she almost turned to look.

As strands of repeated notes soared out of the orchestra pit and into the empty aisles, Meredith thought of the countless times she had waited in the wings with her violin and bow in her hand. That sharp feeling of anticipation in the pit of her stomach, half adrenaline, half fear, before stepping out before the audience. Tuning up, the tiniest adjustments to the strings and bow, the shower of powdery rosin catching on the black polyester of her full-length orchestra skirt.

Mary had bought Meredith her first violin when she was eight, just after she had come to live with them for good. No more going back to her 'real' mother at weekends. The case had been waiting for her on the bed in the bedroom that was to be hers, a welcome gift for a little girl bewildered by life. A child who had already seen too much.

She had seized the chance offered with both hands. Music was her escape. She had an aptitude for it, was a quick learner and a hard worker. At the age of nine, she played in a city schools prom at the Milwaukee Ballet Company Studio at Walker's Point. Pretty soon, she was started on piano too. Before long, music dominated her life.

Her dreams of being a professional musician lasted all the way until her last year of high school. Her tutors encouraged her to apply to one of the conservatoires and told her she had a good chance of being accepted. So did Mary.

But at the last minute, Meredith flunked it. Talked herself into believing she wasn't good enough. That she didn't have what it took to make it. She applied to UNC instead to major in English, wrapped her violin in its red silk cloth and put it away in the blue velveteen-lined case. Loosened her expensive bows, clipped them in place in the lid. Put the block of golden rosin into its special compartment. Stood the case at the back of her closet and left it behind when she left Milwaukee and went off to college.

At UNC, Meredith studied hard and graduated *magna cum laude*. She still played piano in the holidays and gave lessons to the children of Bill and Mary's friends, but that was all. The violin remained at the back of the closet. Never, during that time, did she think she'd done the wrong thing.

But in the last couple of years, as she discovered the tiniest connections with her birth family, she'd started to question her decision. Now, sitting in the auditorium of the Palais Garnier at the age of twenty-eight, regret for what might have been tightened like a fist around her heart.

The music stopped.

Down in the orchestra pit, someone laughed.

The present came rushing back. Meredith quietly stood up and left. She'd come to the Opéra in search of Debussy. All she'd succeeded in doing was raising her own ghosts.

*

Outside, the sun was now hot.

Trying to shake herself out of her melancholic mood, Meredith doubled back along the side of the building and headed up the rue Scribe, intending to cut up to the boulevard Haussmann and from there to the Paris Conservatoire in the 8th.

All of Paris seemed to be out enjoying the golden day, and Meredith had to dodge in and out of the crowds to get through. There was a carnival atmosphere. A busker singing on the street corner; students handing out flyers for discount meals or designer-clothing sales; a juggler with a diabolo, flinging it impossibly high into the air and catching it in one smooth gesture; a guy selling watches and beads out of a suitcase.

Her cell rang. Meredith stopped and dug around in her purse. A woman following right behind drove her stroller into her ankles.

'*Excusez-moi, Madame.*'

Meredith raised her hand in apology. '*Non, non. C'est moi. Désolée.*'

By the time she found the phone, it had stopped ringing. She stepped out of the way and accessed her list of missed calls. It was a French number, one she vaguely recognised. She was about to press redial when someone pushed a flyer into her hand.

'*C'est vous, n'est-ce pas?*'

Meredith jerked her head up. 'Excuse me?'

A young woman was staring at her. Wearing a vest and combats, with her strawberry-blonde braids held off her face by a bandanna, she looked like one of the many New Age travellers and hippies on the streets of Paris.

The girl smiled. 'I said, she looks like you,' she said, this time in English. She tapped the leaflet in Meredith's hand. 'The picture on the front.'

Meredith looked down at the flyer. Advertising Tarot readings, palmistry and psychic insights, the front was dominated by an image of a woman with a crown on her head. In her right hand, she held a sword. In her left, a set of scales. Around the hem of her long skirt was a series of musical notes.

'In fact,' the girl added, 'she could be you.'

At the top of the smudged picture, Meredith could just make out the number eleven in Roman numerals. At the bottom, the words 'La Justice'. She peered closer. It was true. The woman did look kind of like her.

'I can't really see it,' she said, then coloured up at the lie. 'Anyhow, I'm leaving town tomorrow, so . . .'

'Keep it anyway,' the girl insisted. 'We're open seven days a week and we're only just round the corner. Five minutes' walk.'

'Thanks, but it's not my kind of thing,' Meredith said.

'My mother is very good.'

'Mother?'

'She does the Tarot readings.' The girl smiled. 'Interprets the cards. You should come.'

Meredith opened her mouth, and then shut it again. Easier to take it and throw it in the trash later. With a tight smile, she pushed the flyer into the inside pocket of her denim jacket.

'There's no such thing as coincidence, you know,' the girl added. 'Everything happens for a reason.'

Meredith nodded, unwilling to prolong the one-sided conversation, then moved away. At the corner, she stopped. The girl was still standing in the same place, watching her.

CHAPTER 12

Meredith forgot all about the flyer tucked inside her jacket pocket. She returned the call she'd missed – just the French travel agent confirming her hotel reservation – and rang the airline to check her departure time the following day.

She got back to the hotel at five, feeling tired and with sore feet from pounding the streets all afternoon. She uploaded the images onto the hard drive of her laptop, then started the process of transcribing the notes she'd made in the last three days. She grabbed a sandwich from the brasserie opposite at nine-thirty and ate in her room as she carried on working.

That night, Meredith lay in the comfortable semi-dark of the room, her hands above her head and her toes buried deep in the sheets, thinking not about Debussy, but rather about her own family history. Remembering the weekend when she had finally got up the courage to ask Mary to tell her everything she knew about Meredith's birth family.

The Pfister Hotel, Milwaukee, December 2000. The Pfister was where they went for every major family celebration – birthdays, weddings, special occasions – usually just for dinner, but this time Mary had booked them in for the whole weekend, a belated treat for Meredith's birthday and Thanksgiving, and to do a little early Christmas holiday shopping.

Enjoying the elegant, understated nineteenth-century

ambience, the colours and *fin-de-siècle* style, Meredith had gone down alone to the lobby café to wait for Bill and Mary. She'd settled herself in the corner of a deep sofa and ordered her first legal glass of wine in a bar: Sonoma-Cutrer Chardonnay – $7.50 a pop, but worth it. Buttery, holding the scent of the cask in its yellow tones.

How odd, of all things, to remember that.

Outside, snow had been falling. Steady flakes, persistent, in a white sky, covering the world with silence. At the counter, an old lady, in a red coat and a woollen hat pulled low over her brow. She'd shouted at the bartender, 'Speak to me! Why don't you speak to me?' Like the woman in Eliot's *The Waste Land*. Like Meredith, her fellow guests had pretended not to notice.

Meredith had just split from her boyfriend, so was happy to be off campus for the weekend. A visiting math professor on a sabbatical to UNC. She had fallen into the affair. Him sitting on the edge of the piano stool while she played, a hand dropped casually on her shoulder in the darkened library stacks late at night. It was never destined to go anywhere – they wanted different things – and Meredith wasn't heartbroken.

Meredith couldn't remember now why it was that weekend in particular she'd asked all the questions about her birth mother's life and early death she'd always wanted to, but she and Mary had talked most of the snowbound weekend. About the circumstances of her adoption, her mother's suicide, the painful memories under her skin like splinters of glass.

Meredith knew the basics. Her birth mother, Jeanette, had fallen pregnant in Senior High, not even realising it until it was too late to do anything about it. For the first few years, Jeanette's mother, Louisa, had tried to be supportive, but her swift death from cancer robbed Meredith of a reliable and stable influence in her life and things quickly deteriorated. When things got really bad, it was Mary – a distant cousin of Jeanette's – who stepped in when it became clear that, for her own safety, the eight-year-old Meredith could not go back. When Jeanette killed herself two years later, Mary and her husband Bill formally adopted the now ten-year-old Meredith. Although she kept her surname, and continued to call Mary by her first name, as she always had, Meredith at last felt free to think of Mary as her mother.

It was that weekend in the Pfister Hotel that Mary had given Meredith the photographs and the piece of piano music. The first was a shot of a young man in soldier's uniform, standing in a village square. Black curly hair and a direct gaze. There was no name, but the date, 1914, the photographer and the place, Rennes-les-Bains, were printed on the back. The second was of a little girl in old-fashioned clothes. There was no name, no date, no place. The third was of a woman Meredith knew was her grandmother, Louisa Martin, taken some years later – late 1930s or early 1940s, judging by her clothes – seated at a grand piano. Mary explained that Louisa had been a concert pianist of some reputation. The piece of music in the envelope had been her signature piece. She played it for every encore.

As she had looked at the photograph for the first time, Meredith had wondered whether, if she'd known about Louisa earlier, she would not have turned her back on a music career. She didn't know. She couldn't remember Jeanette playing the piano or singing. Only the shouting, the crying, and what came after.

Music had come into Meredith's life when she was eight years old, or so she'd thought. So, to later discover that there'd been something there all along, lying undiscovered beneath the surface, changed the story. That cold weekend in December 2000, Meredith's world shifted. The photos, the music became an anchor, connecting her to a past she knew she would go in search of one day.

Seven years on, she was finally doing it. Tomorrow she'd be in Rennes-les-Bains in person, a place that she'd imagined so many times. She was excited, but she was also nervous. She just hoped there was something there for her to find.

She glanced at the time. Twelve thirty-three. She smiled. *Not tomorrow, today.*

When Meredith woke the next morning, her night-time nerves had evaporated. Whatever she achieved, a few days in the mountains was just what she needed.

Her flight to Toulouse wasn't until mid-afternoon. She had brunch in the sun at her regular brasserie, before setting out to do some of the tourist sites.

She wound her way in and out of the shadows of the familiar colonnades on the rue de Rivoli, dodging swarms of students with backpacks and parties of tourists on the *Da Vinci Code* trail. She considered the Pyramide du Louvre, but the length of the entrance line put her off.

She found a seat in the Tuileries Gardens, wishing she'd worn something lighter. She loved Paris, but today the humid air seemed thick with pollution, gas fumes from the traffic and cigarette smoke from the café terraces. She thought about paying a visit to Shakespeare & Co., the legendary bookstore on the Left Bank, which was almost a shrine for Americans visiting Paris, but she couldn't summon the energy. Truth was, she wanted to do the tourist stuff, but without having to mix with any other tourists.

For want of anything better to do, Meredith decided to return to Debussy's childhood home in the former rue de Berlin. No longer needing the map to find her way through the network of streets, she walked fast, taking a different route this time. After five minutes, she stopped to get her bearings and saw she'd ended up in the rue de la Chaussée d'Antin.

In Debussy's day, the notorious Cabaret Grande-Pinte had stood at the top of the street, near the place de la Trinité. A little further down was the famous seventeenth-century Hôtel-Dieu. And at the bottom, pretty much where she was standing, was Edmond Bailly's notorious esoteric bookstore. There, in the glory days of the turn of the century, poets and occultists and composers had met to talk through new ideas, of mysticism and alternative worlds. In Bailly's bookshop, the prickly young Debussy would never have had to explain himself.

Meredith checked the street numbers. Here, as elsewhere, new buildings had replaced old, new streets had expanded, old addresses had been eaten up by the remorseless march of time. No. 2 rue de la Chaussée d'Antin was now a featureless modern concrete building. There was no bookstore. There wasn't even a plaque on the wall.

Then Meredith noticed a narrow door set right back in the masonry, hardly visible from the street at all. On it was a colourful hand-painted sign.

SORTILÈGE. TAROT READINGS.

Beneath, in smaller letters: 'French and English spoken'.

Her hand flew to the pocket of her denim jacket. Pulling out the flyer the girl had given her yesterday, Meredith peered at the picture. Though it was blurred and badly photocopied, there was no denying the resemblance.

She looks like me.

Meredith glanced back to the sign. Now the door stood open. As if someone had slipped out when she wasn't looking and undone the latch. She peered inside. There was a small lobby with purple walls, decorated with silver stars and moons and astrological symbols. Mobiles of crystals or glass, she wasn't certain which, were spiralling down from the ceiling, catching the light.

Meredith pulled herself up. Astrology, crystals, fortune-telling – she didn't buy the idea that the future was somehow already there, all written out. She didn't even check her horoscope in the paper, although Mary did every morning, while drinking her first cup of coffee of the day.

It's stupid. Superstition.

Yet at the same time, something was keeping her from walking away. Was it the coincidence of the picture? The happenstance of the address?

Now Meredith noticed a narrow flight of stairs leading up from the lobby, the treads painted alternately red and green. At the top, she could see a second door just visible through a covering of yellow wooden beads. Sky blue.

So much colour.

She'd read somewhere that certain people saw music in their heads in colour. Synaesthesia, was that it?

Meredith stepped inside. It was cool. Air trickled from a rattling old fan above the door; particles of dust were dancing in the sluggish October air. If she really wanted some *fin-de-siècle* atmosphere, then what better than to have the same kind of experience that might have been on offer, right here, a hundred years ago? Debussy was interested in such things, after all. It would be a kind of research.

For a moment, everything hung in the balance. It seemed as if the building itself was holding its breath. Waiting, watching. Holding the flyer in her hand, like some kind of talisman, Meredith set her foot on the bottom step and went up.

Many hundreds of miles to the south, in the beech woods above Rennes-les-Bains, a sudden breath of wind lifted the copper leaves on the branches of the ancient trees. The sound of a long-dead sigh, like fingers moving lightly over a keyboard.

Enfin.

The shifting of light upon the turn of a different stair.

CHAPTER 13

DOMAINE DE LA CADE

'*Oui, Abbé, et merci à vous pour votre gentillesse. A tout à l'heure.*'

Julian Lawrence held the phone in his hand a moment, and then replaced the receiver. Tanned and in good shape, he looked younger than his fifty years. He pulled a packet of cigarettes from his pocket, flipped open his Zippo and lit a Gauloises. The smoke wreathed up into the still air.

The arrangements for this evening's service were in place. Now, provided his nephew didn't make a scene, everything should go smoothly. He sympathised with the boy for his loss, but it was awkward that Hal had been asking questions around the town about his father's accident. Stirring things up. Hal had even approached the coroner's office to query the cause of death on the certificate. Since the officer in charge of the case in the police commissariat in Couiza was a friend of Julian's – and the only witness to the incident itself was the local drunk – the matter had been gently dealt with. Hal's questions had been seen as the understandable reaction of a grieving son rather than comments of substance.

All the same, Julian would be glad when the boy had gone. There was nothing to unearth, but Hal was digging and, sooner or later, in a small town like Rennes-les-Bains, the gossip would start. No smoke without fire. Julian was banking on the fact that, once the funeral was over, Hal would leave the Domaine de la Cade and head back to England.

Julian and his brother Seymour, Hal's father, had jointly acquired the place four years before. Seymour, the elder by ten years and bored after retiring from the City, was obsessed with profit forecasts and spreadsheets and how to grow the business.

Julian's preoccupation was different.

From the first time he'd travelled through the region in 1997, he had been intrigued by rumours about Rennes-les-Bains in general, and the Domaine de la Cade in particular. The whole area was riddled with mystery and legends: allegations of buried treasure, conspiracies, cock-and-bull stories of secret societies – anything and everything, from the Templars and the Cathars back to the Romans and the Celts. Though the one story that had caught Julian's imagination was more contemporary. Written accounts, dating back to the end of the last century, of a deconsecrated sepulchre set within the grounds, a deck of Tarot cards believed to have been painted as some kind of treasure map and the fire that had destroyed part of the original house.

The region around Couiza and Rennes-le-Château in the fifth century AD had been at the heart of the Visigoth empire. This was common knowledge. Historians and archaeologists had long speculated that the legendary treasure plundered by the Visigoths in the sack of Rome had been brought to the south-west of France. There, the evidence ran out. But the more Julian discovered, the more convinced he'd become that the greatest part of the Visigoth treasure was still there for the finding. And that the cards – the originals, not printed copies – were the key.

Julian became obsessed. He applied for licences to excavate, sinking all his money and resources into the search. His success was limited, turning up little more than a few Visigoth grave goods: swords, buckles, drinking cups – nothing special. When his permit to dig expired, he continued illegally. Like a gambler, he was hooked, convinced that it was only a matter of time.

When the hotel had come up for sale four years ago, Julian had persuaded Seymour to make an offer. Ironically, despite the huge differences between them, it had turned out to be a good move. The partnership had worked well until the final few months, when Seymour had become more involved in the day-to-day running of the business. And he had asked to see the books.

The sun on the lawn was strong, flooding the room through the high windows of the old study in the Domaine de la Cade. Julian glanced up at the painting on the wall above his desk. It was an old Tarot symbol, similar to a figure of eight lying on its side. The infinity symbol.

'Are you ready?'

Julian turned to see his nephew, in a black suit and tie, standing in the doorway. In his late twenties, with his broad shoulders and clear skin, Hal looked like the sportsman he had been in his university days. A rugby and tennis blue.

Julian ground the stub of his cigarette into the glass ashtray, then drained his whisky. He was impatient for the funeral to be over and for things to get back to normal. He'd had more than enough of Hal drifting around the place.

'I'll be right with you,' he said. 'Two minutes.'

CHAPTER 14

PARIS

Meredith reached the top of the stairs, drew back the beaded curtain and opened the bright blue door.

The entrance was tiny. To her left was a bright chart of the signs of the zodiac, a swirl of colour and pattern and symbols, most of which Meredith didn't recognise. On the wall to her right hung an old-fashioned mirror with an ornate gilt frame. She instinctively checked her reflection, then tapped on the second door straight ahead.

'Hello? Anybody here?'

There was no answer.

Meredith waited a moment, then knocked again, a little louder this time.

Still nothing. She tried the handle. The door opened.

'Hi?' she said, stepping inside. 'Anyone home? Hello?'

The room was small, but full of life. The walls were painted in more bright colours, like a day-care centre – yellow, red, green, with patterns of lines, stripes, triangles and zigzags in purple, blue, silver. A single window, right opposite the door, was covered by a curtain of transparent lilac gauze. Through it, Meredith could see the pale stone walls of the nineteenth-century building behind, its balustrade cheered up by boxes of geraniums and tumbling pansies.

The only pieces of furniture in the room were a small square wooden table right in the centre, the legs visible beneath a black-and-white linen cloth covered with circles and more astrological symbols, and two straight-backed wooden chairs either side.

Meredith heard a door slam someplace else in the building, then footsteps. She flushed, embarrassed to be standing there, uninvited, and was about to go when a woman appeared from behind a bamboo screen on the far side of the room.

She was dressed in a fitted shirt and khaki pants, with expensively cut shoulder-length brown hair flecked with grey and an easy smile – not at all how Meredith imagined a Tarot reader to look. No hoop earrings, no headscarf.

'I did knock,' Meredith said awkwardly. 'No one answered, so I came right on in. I hope that was OK.'

The woman smiled. 'That's fine.'

'You're English?'

She smiled. 'Guilty as charged. I hope you haven't been waiting long.'

Meredith shook her head. 'A couple of minutes.'

The woman held out her hand. 'I'm Laura.'

They shook. 'Meredith.'

Laura pulled out a chair and gestured. 'Take a seat.'

Meredith hesitated.

'It's natural to feel nervous,' said Laura. 'Most people do their first time.'

Meredith pulled the flyer from her pocket and put it down on the table.

'It's not that, it's just . . . a girl gave me this in the street yesterday. Since I was passing . . .' She tailed off again.

Laura took the flyer, then recognition passed across her face. 'La Justice. My daughter mentioned you.'

Meredith frowned. 'She did?'

'She said you were the spitting image.' She paused, as if expecting Meredith to say something. When she didn't,

Laura sat down at the table. 'Do you live in Paris?' she asked, gesturing to the chair opposite her.

Without quite intending to, Meredith found herself sitting down. 'Just visiting.'

Laura nodded. 'Am I right in thinking this is the first time you've had a reading?'

'Yes,' Meredith replied, still perching on the edge of the seat. 'It's for research. I don't want to waste your time.'

'Assuming you've read the flyer, you know that a half-hour session is thirty euros; fifty for a full hour?'

'A half-hour will do fine,' said Meredith.

Her mouth was suddenly dry. Laura was looking at her, *really* looking at her, like she was trying to read every line, every nuance, every shadow of her face.

'Right you are, although I have no one after you, so if you change your mind we can always carry on. Is there some particular issue you'd like to explore, or is it just a general interest?'

'Like I said, it's research. I'm working on a biography. In this street, actually right here, there was a famous bookstore that comes up a lot. The coincidence, I suppose you could say, rather appealed to me.' She smiled, trying to relax herself. 'Although your – your daughter, was it?' – Laura nodded – 'said there was no such thing as coincidence.'

Laura smiled. 'I understand. You're hoping to find some sort of echo of the past.'

'That's it,' Meredith said, with a sigh of relief.

'The next decision is the deck you would like to use.'

Meredith pulled an apologetic face. 'I'm sorry, I really don't know anything about it. I'm happy for you to choose for me.'

Laura gestured to a row of different decks of cards, all face down, set along the side of the table. 'I appreciate it's confusing to start with, but it's better if you choose. Just see if you like the feel of any of them in particular, OK?'

Meredith shrugged. 'Sure.'

Laura picked up the deck closest to her and fanned the cards across the table. They had royal-blue backs with long-tailed golden stars on them.

'They're beautiful,' Meredith said.

'Yes. This is the Universal Waite Tarot, a very popular deck.'

The next pack had a simple white-and-red repeat pattern on the back.

'This one is, in many ways, the classic deck,' Laura said. 'It's called the Marseille Tarot. It dates from the sixteenth century. It's a deck I occasionally use, although it's a little plain for contemporary tastes. Most querents prefer modern packs.'

Meredith raised her eyebrows. 'Querents?'

'Sorry,' Laura grinned. 'The querent is the person having the reading, the person asking the questions.'

Meredith looked along the line and then pointed to a deck that was a little smaller than the rest. The cards had beautiful deep-green backs with filigree lines of gold and silver.

'What's this one?'

Laura smiled. 'That's the Bousquet Tarot.'

'Bousquet?' Meredith repeated. She was sure she'd run up against that name someplace. 'Is that the name of the artist?'

Laura shook her head. 'No, the name of the original publisher of the deck. No one knows the artist or who commissioned the cards. Pretty much all we know is that it originates from south-west France towards the very end of the 1890s.'

Meredith felt a prickling on the back of her neck.

'Where, precisely, in the south-west?'

'I can't recall exactly. Somewhere in the Carcassonne area, I think.'

'I know of it,' Meredith replied.

She realised Laura was looking at her with sharpened interest. 'Is there something . . .?'

'No, it's nothing,' Meredith said quickly. 'I thought the name was familiar, that's all.' She smiled. 'I'm sorry, I really know nothing about this. Can I ask a couple of questions before we go any further?'

Laura laughed. 'Of course.'

'OK, very basic to start. How many cards are there?'

'With a couple of minor contemporary exceptions, there are seventy-eight cards in a standard Tarot pack, divided into the major and the minor arcana – *arcana* is the Latin word for "secrets". The major arcana, twenty-two cards in all, are numbered one to twenty-one – the Fool being unnumbered – and are unique to the Tarot deck. Each has an allegorical picture and a set of clear narrative meanings.'

Meredith glanced at the picture of La Justice on the flyer.

'Like this, for example.'

'Absolutely. The remaining fifty-six cards, the minor arcana – pip cards, as they're sometimes known – are divided into four suits and resemble ordinary playing cards, except that they have an extra court card. So in a standard Tarot deck we have King, Queen, Knight, then the additional card – the Page – before ten. Different decks give the suits different names: pentacles or coins, cups, wands or batons, and swords. Broadly speaking, they correspond to the suits of standard playing cards of diamonds, hearts, clubs and spades.'

'Right.'

'Most experts agree that the earliest Tarot cards date from northern Italy in the middle of the fifteenth century. The modern Tarot revival, however, began in the early years of the last century, when an English occultist, Arthur Edward Waite, produced a new deck. His key innovation was to give an individual and symbolic scene to each of the seventy-eight cards. Before that, the pip cards had only numbers.'

'What about the Bousquet deck?'

'The court cards in each of the four suits are illustrated. The style of painting suggests they date from the late sixteenth century. Certainly pre-Waite. But the major arcana are different; they have characteristics that suggest they were added, or at least modified, later. The designs and the clothes of the characters on certain of the cards are contemporaneous with *fin-de-siècle* styles.'

'How come?'

'The general consensus is that the publisher – Bousquet – didn't have a full set of cards to work from, so either had the major arcana painted or else copied them in the style and character of the extant cards.'

'Copied them from what?'

Laura shrugged. 'From fragments of surviving cards, or possibly from illustrations of the original deck in a book.'

Meredith looked back down at the green-backed cards. 'Someone did a good job.'

Laura made a fan of the suit of pentacles, facing Meredith on the table, starting from the ace at the beginning to the King at the end.

Laura tapped one of the cards. 'Here's another unique modification in the Bousquet Tarot. As well as the names of the court cards having been changed – Maître and Maîtresse, for example, instead of King and Queen – there are personal touches in some of the major arcana too. This one, for example, card II, is usually called the High Priestess. Here, she has the title La Prêtresse. The same figure appears here in card VI as one of the lovers – Les Amoureux. Also, if you look on card XV, Le Diable, it is the same woman again chained at the demon's feet.'

'And that's unusual?'

'Many packs link cards VI and XV, but not usually II as well.'

'So someone', said Meredith slowly, thinking aloud, 'either independently or on instruction, went to a lot of trouble to personalise these cards.'

Laura nodded. 'In fact, I've sometimes wondered if the major arcana of this deck might actually be based on real people. The expressions on some of the faces seem so vivid.'

Meredith glanced down at the image of La Justice on the front of the flyer.

Her face is my face.

She looked across the table at Laura, suddenly wanting to say something about the personal quest that had brought her to France. To tell her that in a matter of hours she was heading for Rennes-les-Bains. But Laura started speaking again and the moment was lost.

'The Bousquet Tarot also respects traditional associations. For example, swords is the suit of air, representing intelligence and intellect; wands is the suit of fire, energy and conflict; cups is the suit associated with water and the emotions. Finally, pentacles' – she tapped the card of the King sitting on his throne surrounded by what looked like gold coins – 'is the suit of earth, of physical reality, of treasure.'

Meredith scanned the images, concentrating hard as if committing each to memory, then nodded to let Laura know she was done.

Laura cleared the table, leaving only the major arcana, which she dealt into three rows of seven cards facing Meredith, lowest number to highest. Le Mat, card o, the unnumbered Fool, she placed alone at the top.

'I like to see the major arcana in terms of a journey,' Laura said. 'They are the imponderables, the big issues of life that cannot be changed or fought against. Laid out like this, it's clear how these three rows represent the three different levels of development – the conscious, the unconscious and the higher consciousness.'

This is where the facts run out.

'At the start of each row is a powerful image: Le Pagad, the Magician, at the beginning of the first row. La Force at the beginning of the second. Finally, at the head of the bottom row, we have card XV, Le Diable.'

Something stirred in Meredith's mind as she looked at the image of the twisted demon. She glanced at the faces of the man and woman chained at the devil's feet with a spark of recognition, but then it faded.

'The advantage of laying the major arcana out like this is that it not only shows the journey of the Fool – Le Mat – from ignorance to enlightenment, but it also makes explicit the vertical connections between the cards,' Laura continued. 'So, you can see how Strength is the octave of the Magician, and the Devil is the octave of Strength.'

'Like two sides of the same person.'

Laura nodded. 'Tarot is all about the patterns, about the relationships between one card and another.'

Meredith was only half listening. Something Laura had just said had caught her attention.

Octaves. That was it.

'Do you usually explain these principles in terms of music?' she asked.

'Sometimes,' Laura replied. 'It depends on the querent. There are lots of ways to explain how Tarot can be interpreted; music is just one of them. Why do you ask?'

Meredith shrugged it off. 'Because it's my area of work. I guess I was just wondering if you had somehow picked up on that.'

Laura gave a slight smile. 'Does that idea bother you?'

'No,' she said, though actually she didn't like the way it was making her feel. Her heart was telling her she might learn something about herself, about who she really was. At the same time, her head was telling her it was all nonsense.

Meredith pointed to La Justice. 'There are musical notes around the hem of her skirt.'

Laura smiled. 'Like my daughter said, there's no such thing as coincidence.'

Meredith laughed, although she didn't think it was funny.

'All systems of divination, like music itself, work through patterns,' Laura continued. 'If you're interested, there was an American cartomancer, Paul Foster Case, who came up with a whole theory linking particulars of the major arcana to individual notes of the musical scale.'

'Maybe I'll check that out,' Meredith said.

Laura gathered up the cards and tidied the deck. She held Meredith's gaze, and for one clear, sharp moment, Meredith was certain she was looking right into her soul; seeing all the anxiety, the doubt – the hope too – reflected in her eyes.

'Shall we make a start?' Laura asked.

Meredith's heart lurched.

'Sure,' she said. 'Why not?'

CHAPTER 15

'Shall we stick with the Bousquet deck?' Laura said. 'You clearly feel some connection with it.'

Meredith didn't really trust herself to speak. She nodded. 'OK.'

Laura removed everything else from the table.

'As we discussed, I'll do a general reading,' she said. 'It's my own spread based on a version of the Celtic Cross, a ten-card reading using the whole pack. It will offer an excellent overview of where you are now, what has happened in your recent past and what the future might hold.'

And although Meredith was trying to remain sceptical, she found she desperately wanted to hear what Laura had to say.

'Modern Tarot readers seek to empower people,' Laura explained, 'to give them the tools, the courage if you like, to change themselves and their lives. A reading is more likely to be of value if the querent confronts their hidden motivations or unconscious patterns of behaviour.'

Meredith nodded.

'The downside with this is that there is an almost infinite variety of interpretations. Some people will tell you, for example, that a majority of major arcana cards in a reading indicates that the situation is outside your control, whereas a majority of minor arcana suggests your fate is in your own hands. All I can advise before we start is that I see a reading as a guide to what *might* happen, not what *will* happen.'

'OK.'

Laura put the deck of cards down on the table between them. 'Shuffle them well, Meredith. Don't hurry. And while you're doing it, think of what it is you most want to discover, what brought you here today. Some people find it helps to shut their eyes.'

A light breeze was coming in through the open window, a relief after the earlier humidity. Meredith reached out, picked up the cards and began to shuffle. Slowly, the present started to recede from her conscious mind as she lost herself in the repetitive motion.

Fragments of memory, images and faces, floated into her mind, then melted away. Her beautiful, vulnerable, damaged mother. Her grandmother, Louisa, sitting at the piano. The serious-looking young man in military uniform.

All the family she had never known.

For a moment, Meredith felt she was floating, weightless. The table, the two chairs, the colours, herself – all seen from a different perspective.

'OK. When you're ready, open your eyes.' Laura's voice was very distant now, heard but not heard, like the sound of music after the note has ended.

Meredith blinked as the room rushed back to meet her, blurred at first, then somehow brighter than before.

'Now put the deck down on the table and cut it in three, using your left hand.'

Meredith did so.

'Put the cards back together, the middle pile first, then the top, then the bottom.' She felt Laura waiting until she was done. 'OK, the first card you're going to draw is what we call the significator. This is the card that will represent you, the querent, the person you are now. The sex of the figure on the card isn't important because each carries within it archetypal masculine or feminine qualities.'

Meredith slid out a card from the middle of the deck and laid it face up in front of her.

'La Fille d'Epées,' said Laura. 'The Daughter of Swords. Swords is the suit of air, remember, of intellect. In the Bousquet deck, the Daughter of Swords is a powerful figure, a thinker, someone strong. At the same time, she is someone perhaps not fully connected to others. This could be because of her youth – the card often indicates a young person – or because of decisions taken. Sometimes it can indicate someone at the beginning of a journey.'

Meredith looked down at the image on the card. A slender and petite woman, wearing a knee-length red dress, with straight black hair to her shoulders. She looked like a dancer. She held the sword with both hands, neither threatening, nor as if she herself was under threat, but as if she was protecting something. Behind her, a jagged mountain peak was set against a fierce blue sky dotted with white clouds.

'It is an active card,' Laura said, 'a positive card. One of the few unequivocally positive sword cards.'

Meredith nodded. She could see that.

'Draw again,' said Laura. 'Put this next card beneath La Fille d'Epées to your left. This second card denotes your situation as it is now. The environment in which you are working or living, the influences acting on you.'

Meredith placed it in position.

'The Ten of Cups,' Laura said. 'Cups is the suit of water, of emotion. This is also a positive card. Ten is the number of completion. It marks the end of one cycle and the beginning of another. It suggests you are standing upon a threshold, that you are ready to move on and to make changes from a current position, which is already one of fulfilment, of success.'

'What kind of threshold?'

'It could be work, could be in your personal life, or both. Things will become clearer to you the further on in the reading we get. Draw again.'

Meredith took a third card from the deck.

'Place this below and to the right of the significator,' Laura instructed. 'This indicates any possible obstacles in your way. Things, circumstances, people even, that might prevent you from moving on or making changes or achieving your goal.'

Meredith turned the card over and placed it on the table.

'Le Pagad,' said Laura. 'Card I, the Magician. *Pagad* is an archaic word used in the Bousquet Tarot and not in many other decks.'

Meredith looked hard at the image. 'Does it represent a person?'

'Usually, yes.'

'Someone to be trusted?'

'It depends. As the name suggests, the Magician may be on your side, but he – or she – may not. Often, he is someone who acts as a powerful catalyst for transformation, although always with this card there is a hint of trickery, of balancing judgement with intuition. The Magician has control over all the elements – water, air, fire and earth – and the four suit symbols: cups, swords, wands and pentacles. Its appearance indicates perhaps someone who could use their skills, with language or knowledge, for your benefit. Equally, the person might use the same gifts to obstruct you in some way.'

Meredith looked at the face on the card. Piercing blue eyes.

'Is there someone in your life you feel might have this role?'

She shook her head. 'Not that I can think of.'

'It could be someone from the past who still has some sort of influence over how you see yourself. Someone who, despite his or her absence, is a negative influence. Or someone you've yet to meet. Equally, someone you do know, whose role in your life has not yet become central.'

Meredith looked down at the card again, attracted by the image and the contradictions contained within it, willing it to mean something. Nothing struck her. No one came to her.

She drew another. This time her reaction was quite different. She felt a rush of emotion, of warmth. The image was of a young girl standing beside a lion. Above her head was the infinity symbol, like a crown. She was wearing a formal, old-fashioned green-and-white dress with mutton sleeves. Her auburn hair tumbled in loose curls all the way down her back to a narrow waist. Exactly the way, Meredith realised, she'd always pictured Debussy's *La Damoiselle élue*, the chosen maiden, half Rossetti, half Moreau.

Remembering what Laura had said, Meredith had no doubt that this illustration might have been based on a real person. She read the name on the card: La Force. Number VIII. The eyes were so green, so vivid.

And the longer she looked, the surer she became that she'd seen this image in a photograph or a painting or a book. Of course, it wasn't possible. But still, the idea took root.

Meredith looked across the table at Laura.

'Tell me about this one,' she said.

CHAPTER 16

'Card VIII, Strength, is associated with the star sign Leo,' said Laura. 'The fourth card in the reading is taken to indicate one single, overriding issue – very often unconscious, unacknowledged by the querent – that has influenced the decision to seek a reading. A powerful motivator. Something guiding the querent.'

Meredith immediately protested. 'But that's not—'

Laura raised her hand. 'Yes, I know you told me it was chance – my daughter pressing a leaflet into your hands, you being in the area today and having time to come up – but at the same time, Meredith, might there also be something more to it? The fact that you are sitting here?' She paused. 'You could have walked by. Not chosen to come in.'

'Maybe. I don't know.' She considered. 'I guess.'

'Is there a particular situation or person you might associate with this card?'

'Not that I can think of, although . . .'

'Yes?'

'The girl. Her face. There's something familiar about her, although I can't pin it down.'

Meredith could see Laura was frowning.

'What?'

Laura dropped her eyes to the four cards laid on the table. 'Readings based on the Celtic Cross spread mostly have a straightforward sequential pattern.' Meredith could hear the hesitation in her voice. 'Even though it's early in the reading, usually by this time it's clear to me which events belong to the past, the present and the future.' She paused. 'But here, for some reason, the timeline is confused. The sequence seems to be jumping backwards and forwards, as if there is some blurring of events. Things slipping between past and present.'

Meredith leaned forward. 'What are you saying? That you can't interpret the cards as I'm drawing them?'

'No, not quite that.' She hesitated again. 'To be honest, Meredith, I'm not entirely sure what I'm saying.' She shrugged. 'Things will fall into place if we keep going.'

Meredith didn't know how to react. She wanted Laura to be more explicit but couldn't think of the questions to ask to get the answers she needed.

'Draw again,' Laura said. 'The fifth card, signifying the recent past.'

Meredith drew the Eight of Pentacles reversed, and pulled a face at Laura's suggestion that the card could indicate that hard work and skill might not reap the benefits they should.

The sixth card, associated with the near future, was the Eight of Wands reversed. Meredith felt the short hairs on the back of her neck stand on end. She glanced up at Laura.

'This is a card of motion, of clear action,' Laura said. 'It suggests hard work and projects coming to fruition. Things about to take off. In some ways, it is the most optimistic of the eights.' She broke off and looked across at Meredith. 'I assume all these references to work mean something to you?'

Meredith nodded. 'I'm in the process of writing a book,' she said, 'so yes, it all makes sense.' She paused. 'But . . . does the meaning change if the card is upside down? Like here?'

'Reversed it indicates delay,' said Laura. 'A disruption of energy as a project remains suspended.'

Like abandoning Paris for Rennes-les-Bains, for example, Meredith thought. Like putting the personal rather than the professional centre stage.

'That, unfortunately,' she said with a wry smile, 'also makes sense. Would you see this as a warning not to get diverted or caught up in other stuff?'

'Probably,' agreed Laura, 'although delay is not necessarily bad. It could be that it is the right thing for you to do at this particular time.'

Meredith felt Laura waiting, watching, until she had finished with that card, before inviting her to draw again.

'This represents the environment in which current or future events are to be – or are already being – played out. Place this above card six.'

Meredith drew the seventh card and laid it down.

The image showed a tall grey tower under a lowering sky. A single fork of lightning seemed to cut the picture in two. Meredith shivered, feeling an immediate antipathy to the card. And although she was still trying to tell herself it was all nonsense, she wished she had not drawn it.

'La Tour,' she read. 'Not a great card?'

'No card is either good or bad,' Laura replied automatically, although her expression gave a different message. 'It depends on where it comes in a reading and its relationship to the cards around it.' She paused. 'Having said that, the Tower is traditionally interpreted as indicating dramatic change. It can suggest destruction.' She glanced up at Meredith, then back to the card. 'Read positively, it's a card of liberation – when the edifice of our illusions, limitations, boundaries comes crashing down, leaving us free to start afresh. A flash of inspiration, if you like. It's not necessarily negative.'

'Sure, I get that,' Meredith said, a little impatient. 'But I don't think that's how you're interpreting it, right?'

Laura met her gaze. 'Conflict is how I see it.'

'Between?' Meredith threw back.

'That's something only you can know. It could be what you've alluded to before – conflict between personal demands and professional ones. Equally, it could be a discrepancy between people's expectations of you and what you can give.'

Meredith said nothing, trying to squash the thought pushing into her conscious mind from where she'd buried it. The fear that, on this quest of hers, she might find something about her background that would turn her whole life on its head.

'Is there something particular that you think this card might be referring to?' asked Laura softly.

'I ...' Meredith started to speak, then stopped again. 'No,' she replied, more firmly than she felt. 'Like you say, it could be so many things.'

She hesitated, almost unwilling to go on, but then drew again.

The next card, representing the self, was the Eight of Cups, followed by the Eight of Swords. Another octave.

She heard Laura catch her breath.

'All the eights – what are the odds?' Meredith said, trying to make light of it.

Laura didn't immediately answer. 'It's unusual, certainly,' she said eventually.

Meredith studied the spread. It wasn't just the octaves linking the cards of the major arcana, or the repetition of the number eight. It was also the notes on the dress of La Justice and the green eyes of the girl in La Force.

'The probability of any card being turned is of course the same for each,' Laura said, although Meredith could see she was now saying what she thought she ought to, not what she was actually thinking.

'But have you ever had this happen before?' Meredith said, unwilling to let her off the hook. 'Seriously? All of one number coming up like this?' She cast her eye over the table. 'And La Tour, card XVI too. That's a multiple of eight.'

Reluctantly, Laura shook her head. 'Not that I can recall.'

Meredith tapped the card with her finger. 'What does the Eight of Swords signify?'

'Interference. An indication of something – or someone – holding you back.'

'Like Le Pagad?'

'Maybe, although …' Laura stopped, clearly choosing her words with care. 'There are parallel stories here. On the one hand, there is the clear evidence of the imminent culmination of a major project, either work or in your personal life, or possibly both.' She looked up. 'Yes?'

Meredith frowned. 'Go on.'

'Running alongside that, there are hints of a journey or a change of circumstances.'

'OK, let's say that fits, but—'

Laura interrupted. 'I sense there's something else. It's not altogether clear, but I feel there *is* something. This final card … something you are about to discover, or uncover.'

Meredith caught her breath. All the way through, she'd been telling herself how it was just a bit of harmless fun. How it didn't mean anything. So why was her heart turning somersaults?

'Remember, Meredith,' said Laura urgently, 'the art of divination by the drawing and interpretation of cards is not about saying this *will* happen or will *not* happen. It's about investigating possibilities, discovering unconscious motivations and desires that might, or might not, result in any given pattern of behaviour.'

Just harmless fun.

But something about Laura's intensity, the fierce concentration on her face, was making it deathly serious.

'A Tarot reading should increase free will, not diminish it,' Laura said, 'for the simple reason that a reading tells us more about ourselves and the issues facing us. You're free to make your own decisions, better decisions. Decide which path to take.'

Meredith nodded. 'I understand.'

Suddenly, all she wanted to do was get this over with.

'So long as you remember that.'

Meredith heard the very real warning in Laura's voice and knew, without a shadow of a doubt, that Laura was alarmed by the fall of the cards.

'This final card, card ten, will complete the reading. It goes at the top, on the right-hand side.'

For a moment, Meredith's hand seemed to hover over the Tarot deck. She could almost see the invisible lines connecting her skin to the green and gold and silver of the backs of the cards.

Then she took the card and turned it over. She heard Laura catch her breath.

Somehow, Meredith kept her voice level. 'Justice,' she said. 'That makes sense. Your daughter said I looked like her.'

Laura did not meet her eye. 'The stone associated with La Justice is opal,' she said. Meredith thought she sounded as if she was reading the information from the pages of a book. 'The colours associated with this card are sapphire, topaz. There is also an astrological sign linked to this card. Libra.'

Meredith gave a hollow laugh.

'I'm Libra,' she said. 'My birthday's October eighth.'

Still Laura didn't react, as if she wasn't surprised by this piece of information either.

'La Justice in the Bousquet Tarot is a powerful card,' she continued.

'And it means?'

'Usually, when it comes up in a reading, it is an instruction to keep a balanced view.'

Meredith smiled. 'But it's reversed,' she said, amazed at how calm she sounded. 'That changes things, doesn't it?'

Laura didn't answer.

'Doesn't it?' Meredith pressed.

'Reversed, the card warns of some injustice. Perhaps prejudice and bias, or a miscarriage of justice in legal terms. It also carries with it a sense of anger at being judged or judged wrongly.'

'And do you think this card represents me?'

'I think it does,' she said eventually. 'Not only because it's come up last in the reading.' She hesitated. 'And not only because there is obviously a physical resemblance.' She stopped again.

Meredith looked at her. 'Laura?'

'OK. I believe it represents you, but at the same time, I don't think it's indicating an injustice done to you. I'm inclined to think that it's more that you might find yourself called upon to right some wrong. You as an agent of justice.' She looked up.

Meredith cast her eyes over the ten cards lying upon the table: the Magician and the Devil, both with ice-blue eyes, the former the double octave of the latter. All the eights, the number of recognition, of achievement. She reached forward and took out first the fourth card from the spread and then the last. Strength and Justice.

Somehow, they seemed to belong together.

'For a moment,' she said quietly, talking as much to herself as to Laura, 'I thought I understood. As if, somewhere beneath the surface, it all made sense.'

'And now?'

Meredith hesitated. 'Now it's just pictures. Just patterns and colours.'

The words hung between them. Then, without warning, Laura's hands darted forward and she gathered up the cards.

'You should take them,' she said. 'Work things out for yourself.'

Meredith was sure she must have misheard. 'Excuse me?'

But Laura was holding out the cards. 'This deck belongs with you.'

'I couldn't possibly ...'

But now Laura was reaching under the table. She brought out a large square of black silk and folded the cards up within it. 'There,' she said, pushing them across the table. 'Another Tarot tradition. Many people believe you should never buy a deck of cards for yourself. That you should always wait for the right deck to be given to you as a gift.'

Meredith shook her head. 'Laura, I can't possibly accept them. Besides, I wouldn't know what to do with them.'

She stood up and put on her jacket.

Laura stood too. 'I believe you need them.'

Their eyes met once more.

'But I don't want them.'

If I accept them, there'll be no way back.

'The deck belongs with you.' Laura paused. 'And I think, deep down, you know it.'

Meredith felt the room pressing in on her. The colourful walls, the patterned cloth on the table, the stars and sickle moons and suns, pulsating, growing larger, smaller, shifting shape. And there was something else – a rhythm sounding in her head, almost like music. Or the wind in the trees.

Enfin. At last.

Meredith heard the word as clearly as if she'd spoken herself. It was so sharp, so loud, that she turned around, thinking that perhaps a person had come in behind her. There was no one there.

Things shifting between past and present.

She wanted nothing to do with the cards, but in the face of Laura's determination, she felt she'd never get out of the room if she didn't accept them.

She took them. Then, without another word, she turned and ran down the stairs.

CHAPTER 17

Meredith wandered the Parisian streets, holding the cards in her hands and feeling like, at any moment, they might blow up and somehow take her with them.

It was only when she heard the bells of the church of Saint-Gervais striking one o'clock that she realised she was on track to miss her flight to Toulouse.

Meredith pulled herself together. She flagged down a taxi and, yelling at the driver that there'd be a good tip if he could get her there quickly, they screeched out into the traffic.

They made it to rue du Temple in ten minutes flat. Meredith threw herself out of the cab and, leaving it on the meter, charged into the hotel lobby to pick up the bags she'd left with the concierge, confirmed she'd be back in Paris at the end of the week for a couple more nights, then jumped back into the taxi and headed across town to Orly Airport.

Her efficient, organised self had kicked in, but she was only going through the physical motions while her brain was elsewhere. Half-remembered phrases, ideas grasped, subtleties missed. All the things Laura had said.

How it made me feel.

Meredith made it with just fifteen minutes to spare. It was only when she was going through security that she realised that in her hurry to get out of the tiny room, she'd forgotten to pay Laura for the session. A wave of embarrassment washed over her. Working out that she'd been there for at least an hour – maybe closer to two – she made a mental note to mail the money and extra besides as soon as she got to Rennes-les-Bains.

As the plane took off, Meredith pulled her notebook from her bag and started to scribble down everything she could remember. A journey. The Magician and the Devil, both with blue eyes, neither to be entirely trusted. Herself as an agent of justice. All the eights.

As they swept through the blue skies of northern France, over the Massif Central, chasing the sun down to the south, Meredith listened to Debussy's *Suite bergamasque* on her headphones and wrote until her arm ached, filling page after small, lined page with neat notes and sketches. Laura's words replayed over and over in her head, like they were on some kind of loop, fighting with the music.

Things slipping between past and present.

And all the time, like an unwanted guest, the presence of the cards lurking in her bag in the luggage bins above her head.

The Devil's Picture Book.

PART III

Rennes-les-Bains
September 1891

CHAPTER 18

Having accepted Isolde Lascombe's invitation to La Domaine de la Cade, Anatole set things in motion for their immediate departure.

As soon as breakfast was finished, he sent a wire giving their time of arrival and purchased train tickets for the following day, leaving Marguerite to take Léonie shopping for items she might need during her month in the country. They went first to La Maison Léoty for new undergarments, then to La Samaritaine, where her mother bought her a new tea dress and walking suit appropriate for autumn in the country. It was unusual for them to spend so much time together – Léonie had always known that Anatole was her mother's favourite and had trained herself not to mind – but the idea of the adventure to come in the country made her less impatient than usual. Marguerite was warm but distant, and Léonie realised she had something on her mind. She suspected it was Du Pont's credit against which Marguerite made their purchases and resigned herself to the fact that they might return to Paris in November and find themselves with a new father.

Léonie was excited, but also curiously out of sorts, a state of affairs she put down to the events of the previous evening. She had no chance to speak to Anatole to find out what had really happened to him, nor to discuss with him the coincidence of timing that had led to the invitation arriving just when he most needed it.

After lunch, making the most of the mild and pleasant afternoon, Marguerite and Léonie went walking in Parc Monceau, a favourite haunt of the ambassadors' children from the embassies nearby. A group of boys were playing *un, deux, trois, loup* with great exuberance, shouting and yelling encouragement to one another. Girls in ribbons and white petticoats, watched over by nannies and dark-skinned bodyguards, were engaged in a game of hopscotch. *La marelle* had been one of Léonie's favourite childhood games, and she and Marguerite stopped to watch the girls throw the pebble into the square and jump. From the look on her mother's face, Léonie knew she, too, was remembering the past. She took advantage to ask a question.

'Why is it that you were not happy at the Domaine de la Cade?'

Marguerite shrugged, as she always did, unwilling to be drawn. 'It was not an environment in which I felt comfortable, *chérie*, that is all.'

'But why? Was it the company? The place itself? There must be a reason,' Léonie pressed.

Marguerite finally looked at her. 'My half-brother was a strange, solitary man,' she said. 'He did not wish for the company of a much younger sibling, let alone to be partly responsible for his father's second wife. We felt like unwelcome guests.'

Léonie thought a moment. 'Do you think I will enjoy myself there?'

'Oh yes, I am certain of it,' Marguerite said quickly. 'The estate is quite beautiful, and I imagine that in thirty years there will have been many improvements. And, of course, the library.' She smiled, but Léonie could see her heart wasn't in it.

'And the rest of the house?'

Marguerite did not answer.

'Maman?'

'It was a long time ago,' she said firmly. 'Everything will have changed.'

The morning of their departure, Friday, 18th September, dawned damp and blustery.

Léonie woke early, with a fluttering of nerves. Now the day had arrived, she was nostalgic for the world she was leaving behind. The sounds of the city, the rows of sparrows sitting upon the rooftops of the buildings opposite, the familiar faces of neighbours and tradesmen – all seemed invested with a poignant charm. Everything brought tears to her eyes.

Something of the same seemed to have affected Anatole also, for he was ill at ease. His mouth was pinched and his eyes wary, as he stood watchful at the drawing-room windows, casting nervous glances up and down the street until the maid announced that the carriage had arrived.

'Inform the driver we will be down immediately,' he said.

'You are travelling in those clothes?' Léonie teased, looking at his grey morning suit and frock coat. 'You look as if you are going to your offices.'

'That is the idea,' he said grimly, walking across the drawing room towards her. 'Once we are away from Paris, I will change into something less formal.'

Léonie blushed, feeling stupid not to have remembered why he had to leave Paris for a while. 'Of course.'

He picked up his top hat. 'Hurry, *petite*. We do not wish to miss our train.'

In the street below, their luggage was loaded into the *fiacre*.

'Gare Saint-Lazare,' Anatole shouted, to make his voice heard over the cracking of the wind.

Marguerite's eyes were rimmed red, which surprised Léonie and made her tearful in turn. Too often, she felt her mother barely noticed her at all, so she embraced her more affectionately than usual and promised to write.

The *fiacre* pulled away. At the last moment, as the gig rounded the corner into the rue d'Amsterdam, Léonie pushed down the window and called back to where Marguerite stood, alone, on the pavement. She felt an unexpected sense of loss.

'*Au revoir*, Maman.'

When she sat back in the seat, Anatole took her hand.

'I am certain she will get along fine without us,' he reassured her. 'Du Pont will look after her. He's a solid chap.'

Léonie dabbed at her eyes until the desire to weep had passed.

'Does the Express not depart from the Gare Montparnasse rather than Saint-Lazare?' she asked.

'If anyone comes calling,' he said in a conspiratorial whisper, 'I wish them to believe in the fiction that we are heading for the western suburbs. Yes?'

She nodded. 'I see. A bluff.'

Anatole grinned and tapped the side of his nose.

On their arrival at the Gare Saint-Lazare, he had their luggage moved to a second cab. He made a great play of chatting with the driver, but Léonie noticed he was sweating, even though it was cold. His cheeks were flushed and his temples slicked with beads of perspiration.

'Are you unwell?'

Anatole found a smile. 'Don't worry, *petite*. This . . . subterfuge, it is a strain on my nerves. I shall be fine once we are away from Paris.'

'What would you have done,' Léonie continued, 'had the invitation not arrived when it did?'

He shrugged. 'Made alternative arrangements.'

Léonie waited for him to say more, but he remained silent.

'Does Maman know about your ... commitments *chez* Frascati?' she asked in the end.

Anatole avoided the question. 'If anyone should come asking, she is well primed to perpetrate the fiction that we have gone to Saint-Germain-en-Laye. Debussy's people are from there, so ...' He put both hands on her shoulders and turned her to face him. 'Now, *petite*, are you satisfied?'

Léonie tilted her chin. 'I am.'

'And no more questions?' he teased.

She gave an apologetic grin. 'I will try.'

On their arrival at the Gare Montparnasse, Anatole all but threw the fare at the driver and shot into the station as if he had a pack of hunting dogs at his heels. Léonie played along with the pantomime, understanding that whereas he had wanted them to be noticed at Saint-Lazare, here he wished to be inconspicuous.

Inside the station, he looked at the departures board, then put his hand to the pocket of his waistcoat before appearing to think better of it.

'Have you mislaid your watch?'

Anatole pulled a face. 'It was taken during the assault,' he said. 'But no matter.'

They walked along the platform to find their seats. Léonie read the names of the towns at which the train was scheduled to stop on their way down to Marseille. Tomorrow, they were due to take the coast train from Marseille to Carcassonne. Then, on Sunday morning, they would depart Carcassonne for Couiza-Montazels, the closest railway station to Rennes-les-Bains. From there, according to their aunt's instructions, it was only a short carriage ride to the Domaine de la Cade, in the foothills of the Corbières.

Anatole purchased a newspaper and buried himself behind it, while Léonie watched the people go by. Top hats and morning suits, ladies in wide, sweeping skirts. A beggar with a thin face and dirty fingers lifted up the window of their first-class carriage until the guard chased him off.

There was a final shrill, sharp blast from the whistle, then a bellow from the engine as it spat out its first jet of steam. Sparks flew. Then the grind of metal against metal, another belch from the black funnel and, slowly, the wheels started to turn.

Enfin.

The train began to pick up speed as it pulled away from the platform. Léonie sat forward in her seat watching Paris disappear in folds of white smoke.

CHAPTER 19

Léonie had enjoyed their long journey through France. Anatole had quickly recovered his good spirits and kept her amused with stories, playing hands of cards, discussing how they would spend their time in the mountains.

At a little after six o'clock on Friday evening, they had disembarked in Marseille. The following day, they continued along the coast to Carcassonne and passed an uncomfortable night in a hotel with no hot water and surly staff. Léonie had woken with a headache. But as soon as they were on their way into the mountains, her mood improved as the living, breathing landscape of the Midi began to work its charm.

The track followed the line of the curving river south, through the silver valley of the Aude towards the Pyrenees. At first, the rails ran alongside the road. The land was flat and unoccupied. But soon she saw rows of vines and the occasional field of sunflowers still in bloom, bright and yellow, their heads bowed to the east.

She glimpsed a small village – no more than a handful of houses – perched on a picturesque distant hill. Then another, the red-tiled roofs clustered around the dominating spire of the church. Near at hand, on the outskirts of the railway towns, were pink hibiscus, bougainvillea, poignant syringas, lavender bushes and wild poppies. In the distance, gold and polished copper silhouettes, the only hint that autumn was waiting in the wings.

All along the line, peasants were working in the fields, their starched blue smocks stiff and shining as if varnished. The women wore wide, flat straw hats to keep off the blistering sun. The men bore expressions of resignation upon their leathery faces, turned away from the relentless wind, working so late a harvest.

The train halted for a quarter of an hour at a town called Limoux. After that, the countryside became steeper, rockier, as the plains gave way to the *garrigue* of the Hautes Corbières. They rattled precariously on, perched on thin tracks above the river, until, rounding a curve, the blue-white Pyrenees suddenly appeared in the distance, shimmering in a heat haze.

Léonie caught her breath. The mountains seemed to rise up out of the very land, connecting earth to heaven. Magnificent, unchanging. In the face of such natural splendour, the man-made constructions of Paris seemed as nothing. The controversies about Monsieur Eiffel's celebrated metal tower, Baron Haussmann's grand boulevards, even Monsieur Garnier's opera house, paled into insignificance. This was a landscape built on an altogether different scale – earth, air, fire and water were laid out in plain view, like keys on a piano.

Léonie pushed down the glass and felt the air of the Midi upon her cheeks. Wooded hills, green and brown and crimson, rose abruptly in the shadow of grey granite cliffs. Lulled by the swaying motion of the train and the singing of the wheels upon the metal tracks, she found her eyelids flickering shut.

She was jolted awake by a squeal of brakes.

For an instant, she forgot where she was. Then she glanced down at the guidebook on her lap, and across to

Anatole, and remembered. Not Paris, but in a rattling railway carriage in the Midi.

She realised the train was slowing.

Léonie peered out of the window. It was hard to make out the lettering on the painted wooden board on the platform. Then she heard the stationmaster, in a heavy southern accent, announce: 'Couiza-Montazels. *Dix minutes d'arrêt.*'

She tapped her brother on the knee. 'Anatole, *nous sommes là. Lève-toi.*'

Already she could hear doors opening and falling back against the painted green side of the train with a heavy slap.

'Anatole' – anxious that they might miss their stop – 'we have arrived at Couiza.'

She leaned out and raised her arm. Even this late in the season, there was a line of porters leaning on high-backed wooden trolleys. Most had their caps set back on their heads and waistcoats open, shirtsleeves rolled up to the elbow.

'*Porteur, s'il vous plaît.*'

Without warning, the door was pulled open. 'Allow me, Mademoiselle.'

A man was standing on the platform looking up into the carriage.

'No, really, we can manage . . .' she began to say, but he cast his eyes over the compartment, taking in Anatole's sleeping figure and the luggage still upon the rack, then without invitation stepped up into the carriage. 'Anatole, wake up.'

'I insist.'

Léonie took an instant dislike to him. His high collar, double-breasted waistcoat and top hat marked him a gentleman, and yet there was something not quite *comme il faut* about him. His gaze was impertinent.

'Thank you, but there is no need,' she said, recoiling from the smell of plum brandy on his breath. 'I am more than . . .'

But he was already lifting the first of their valises and boxes down from the wooden rack. Léonie noticed him glance at the initials inscribed in the leather as he placed Anatole's portmanteau on the dirty floor.

Léonie winced as the man dropped Anatole's personal trunk with a thud on the platform. Then he reached back inside for her lacquered workbox.

'Please take care,' she said. 'It is precious.'

The man ran his eyes over her, then over the two gold initials on the top: L.V.

'But of course. Do not concern yourself.'

Thoroughly frustrated by her brother's languor, she shook him roughly by the arm.

'Anatole, *voilà Couiza*. Wake up!'

At last, and to her relief, he showed signs of stirring. He stared lazily around him, as if bewildered to find himself in a railway carriage. Then he caught sight of her anxious face and smiled.

'Must have dozed off,' he said, smoothing his long white fingers over his black, oiled hair. '*Desolé.*'

He stood up and, in an instant, the compartment seemed very much smaller. He glanced at himself in the looking glass below the luggage rack, adjusted his waistcoat and shot his cuffs, then swept up his hat, gloves and cane in one easy motion.

'Shall we?' he said casually, offering Léonie his hand.

Only then did he seem to notice that their belongings had been set down from the carriage. He looked at their companion.

'My thanks, Monsieur. We are most grateful.'

'Not at all. I was in the adjacent carriage, Monsieur . . .'

'Vernier. Anatole Vernier. And this is my sister, Léonie.'

'Raymond Denarnaud, at your service.' He tipped his hat. 'Are you putting up in Couiza? If so, I would be delighted to—'

The whistle blew once more.

'*En voiture!* Passengers for Quillan and Espéraza, *en voiture!*'

'We should step away,' said Léonie.

'Not in Couiza itself,' Anatole replied to the man, almost shouting to make himself heard over the roar of the furnace. 'But close by. Rennes-les-Bains.'

Denarnaud beamed. 'My home town.'

'Excellent. We are staying at the Domaine de la Cade. Do you know it?'

Léonie stared at Anatole in astonishment. Having pressed upon her the need for discretion, here he was, only two days out of Paris, announcing their business to a complete stranger without a second thought.

'Domaine de la Cade,' Denarnaud replied carefully. 'Yes, I know of it.'

The engine let out an explosion of steam and clatter. Léonie stepped nervously back and Denarnaud climbed aboard.

'Again, I must thank you for your courtesy,' Anatole repeated.

Denarnaud leaned out. The two men exchanged cards, then shook hands as the steam swamped the platform.

Anatole stood back from the edge. 'Seemed a nice enough fellow.'

Léonie's eyes flashed. 'You insisted we should keep our plans private, and yet—'

Anatole cut in. 'Never hurts to be courteous.'

The station clock on the tower began to strike the hour.

'It seems that we are still, after all, in France,' said Anatole, then he saw the expression on her face. 'Is something the matter?'

Léonie didn't want to be at odds with him. 'I am hot and tired. It was dull having no one to talk to for so long. And you left me quite at the mercies of that disagreeable man.'

'Oh, Denarnaud wasn't so bad,' he objected, squeezing her hand. 'But I ask your forgiveness anyway for the heinous crime of falling asleep!'

Léonie pulled a face.

'Come, *petite*. Let's be friends. You will feel more yourself when we have had something to eat and drink.'

CHAPTER 20

The full force of the sun hit them the instant they were out of the shadow of the station building. Brown clouds of grit and dust blew into their faces, agitated by the swirling wind that seemed to come from all directions at once. Léonie fumbled with the clasp of her parasol.

As Anatole made arrangements with the porter for their luggage, she took in their surroundings. She had never travelled this far south before. Indeed, her visits beyond the outskirts of Paris had been only as far as Chartres or childhood picnics on the banks of the Marne. This was a different France. Léonie recognised some road signs and advertising posters for aperitifs, for wax polish and cough linctus, but it was not a world she knew.

The concourse gave directly onto a small and busy street lined with spreading lime trees. Dark women with broad, weather-beaten faces, waggoners and railway workers, unkempt children with bare legs and dirty feet – Léonie had the sensation she had stepped into a scene from Offenbach's *Tales of Hoffmann*, where the old ways held sway and time all but stood still.

'Apparently there's a passable restaurant on the avenue de Limoux,' said Anatole, reappearing at her side with a copy of a local newspaper, *La Dépêche de Toulouse*, tucked under his arm. 'There's also a telegraph office, a telephone and a poste restante, so we're not completely cut off from civilisation.' He pulled a box of wax Vestas from his pocket, took a cigarette from his case, tapped it on the lid and then struck a match. 'But I fear there's no such luxury as a carriage, at least not this late in the year and on a Sunday.'

The Grand Café Guilhem was on the far side of the bridge. A handful of tables were set outside in the shade of a large awning that ran the length of the restaurant.

'Hardly the Café Paillard,' said Léonie, 'but it will do.'

Anatole smiled fondly. 'I doubt if there will be private rooms, but the public terrace looks acceptable. Yes?'

They were shown to a pleasantly situated table. Anatole ordered for them both and fell into easy conversation with the *patron*.

The waiter arrived promptly with a tray of drinks – a jug of water, a large glass of cold beer for Anatole and a *pichet* of the local *vin de table*. It was followed shortly afterwards by a luncheon of bread, hard-boiled eggs, a galantine of cured meats, a couple of centimes' worth of local cheese and a slice of chicken pie carved and embedded in aspic – plain but satisfying.

'Not at all bad,' said Anatole. 'In fact, surprisingly good.'

Léonie excused herself between courses. When she returned some ten minutes later, it was to find that Anatole had fallen into conversation with their fellow diners on an adjacent table. An older gentleman, dressed in the formal attire of a banker or lawyer, with a high black top hat, and a dark suit, starched collar and necktie despite the heat. And opposite him, a younger man with straw-coloured hair and a bushy moustache. She had rarely known her brother be so companionable.

'Dr Gabignaud, Maître Fromilhague,' he said, 'may I present my sister, Léonie.'

Both men half rose to their feet and lifted their hats.

'Gabignaud was telling me of his work in Rennes-les-Bains,' Anatole explained, as Léonie sat back down at the table. 'You were saying you have been apprenticed to Dr Courrent for three years?'

Gabignaud nodded. 'Indeed. Our baths in Rennes-les-Bains are not only the oldest in the region, but we also are lucky enough to have several different types of water, so can treat a wider range of symptoms and pathologies than any other equivalent thermal establishment. The group of thermal waters includes the *source du Bain Fort*, at fifty-two degrees, the—'

'They don't need every detail, Gabignaud,' growled Fromilhague.

The doctor reddened. 'Yes, quite. Well. I have been fortunate enough to be invited to visit similar establishments elsewhere,' he continued. 'I have had the honour to spend some weeks studying under Dr Privat in Lamalou-les-Bains.'

'I am not familiar with Lamalou.'

'You amaze me, Mademoiselle Vernier. It's a charming spa town, also Roman in origin, just to the north of Béziers.' He dropped his voice. 'Although it is rather a sombre place, of course. In medical circles, it is best known for its treatment of ataxics.'

Maître Fromilhague brought his hand down with a bang on the table, making the coffee cups and Léonie jump. 'Gabignaud, you are forgetting yourself!'

The young doctor turned scarlet. 'Forgive me, Mademoiselle Vernier. I did not intend to cause any offence.'

Puzzled, Léonie fixed Maître Fromilhague with a cold look. 'Rest assured, Dr Gabignaud, *I* have taken none.'

She glanced at Anatole, who was attempting not to laugh.

'Nevertheless, Gabignaud, it might not be an appropriate conversation for mixed company.'

'Of course, of course,' gabbled the doctor. 'My interest as a medical man often leads me to forget that such matters are not—'

'You are visiting Rennes-les-Bains for the spa?' asked Fromilhague with ponderous courtesy.

Anatole shook his head. 'We are to stay with our aunt at her estate just outside of the town. At the Domaine de la Cade.'

Léonie saw alarm in the doctor's eyes, quickly veiled. Her interest sharpened.

'Your aunt?' Gabignaud queried.

'To be precise, our late uncle's wife,' Anatole replied, clearly also noticing the hesitation in Gabignaud's manner. 'Jules Lascombe was our mother's half-brother. We have not yet had the pleasure of making our aunt's acquaintance.'

'Is there something the matter, Dr Gabignaud?' enquired Léonie.

'No, no. Not in the slightest. Forgive me, I . . . I was not aware Lascombe was fortunate enough to have such close relations. He lived a quiet life and did not mention . . . To be frank, Mademoiselle Vernier, we were all taken by surprise when he took the decision to marry, and so late in life. Lascombe seemed a confirmed bachelor. And to take a wife to such a house, with such an ill reputation, well . . .'

Léonie leant forward. Perhaps, now, they were going to come to the heart of things. 'An ill reputation?'

But Anatole had moved to a different question. 'You knew Lascombe, Gabignaud?'

'Not well, but we were acquainted. They summered here, I believe, in the first years of their marriage. Madame Lascombe, preferring life in town, was often away from the Domaine for some months at a time.'

'You were not Lascombe's personal physician?'

Gabignaud shook his head. 'I did not have that honour, no. He had his own man in Toulouse. He had been in poor health for many years, although his decline was more sudden than expected, brought on by the fearsome cold at the beginning of the year. When it was clear that he would not recover, your aunt returned to the Domaine de la Cade at the beginning of January. Lascombe died days afterwards. Of course, there were rumours that he died as a result of—'

'Gabignaud!' interrupted Fromilhague. 'Hold your tongue!'

The young doctor again flushed.

Fromilhague signalled his continuing displeasure by summoning the waiter, then insisting on relating precisely what they had eaten to confirm the bill, making further conversation between the two tables impossible.

Anatole left a generous tip. Fromilhague threw a note onto the table and stood up. 'Mademoiselle Vernier, Vernier,' he said, raising his hat. 'Gabignaud. We have matters to attend to.'

The doctor followed without a word.

'Why may Lamalou not be spoken of?' Léonie demanded as soon as they were out of earshot. 'And why does Dr Gabignaud permit Maître Fromilhague to bully him so?'

Anatole grinned. 'Lamalou is notorious as the place where the latest medical advancements in the treatment of syphilis – ataxia – are being pioneered,' he replied. 'As for his manner, I would imagine Gabignaud needs the Maître's sponsorship. In such a small town, it is the difference between a successful and a failing practice.' He gave a brief laugh. 'Lamalou-les-Bains! I ask you!'

Léonie frowned. 'But why was Dr Gabignaud so odd when I told him we were to be staying at the Domaine de la Cade? And what did he mean by the house having an ill reputation?'

'Gabignaud talks too much and Fromilhague disapproves of gossip. That's all there is to it.'

'It was more than that.'

'Everything isn't like in those books you so love,' he teased. 'In real life, most things are as they seem.'

Léonie shook her head. 'No. Maître Fromilhague was determined not to permit him to speak.'

Anatole laughed. 'Fromilhague has the choleric complexion of a man who is frequently aggravated. He merely dislikes Gabignaud prattling on like a woman!'

Léonie poked out her tongue at this slight to her sex. 'Beast!'

Anatole wiped his moustache, then stood up. '*Alors, on y va.* We have some time to spare. Let us acquaint ourselves with the modest delights of Couiza.'

CHAPTER 21

PARIS

Hundreds of miles to the north, Paris was becalmed. After the bustle of a busy morning of commerce, the afternoon air was choked with dust and the smells of rotten fruit and vegetables. The ostlers, the traders of the 8th *arrondissement* had gone. The beggars had moved on, leaving behind the detritus, the dregs of another day.

The apartment of the Vernier family in the rue de Berlin was silent in the blue light of the fading afternoon. The furniture was shrouded in white dust sheets, the long windows of the drawing room were closed, the curtains of yellow chintz had been drawn. The floral wallpaper was faded where the daily passage of the sun had stripped the colour away. Particles of dust hung suspended above the few sticks of furniture left uncovered.

On the table, forgotten roses in a glass bowl hung their heads, almost without scent. There was another smell, barely discernible, a sour smell that did not belong. A hint of the souk, Turkish tobacco, and a strange aroma this far from the sea, carried in upon the grey clothes of the man who stood silently in front of the fireplace, obscuring the porcelain face of the Sèvres clock on the mantel.

He was strong and powerfully built, with broad shoulders and a high forehead. Dark clipped eyebrows sat above sharp blue eyes with pupils as black as coal.

Marguerite Vernier was sitting upright on one of the mahogany dining chairs. Her rose-coloured negligée, tied at the neck with a yellow silk bow, lay draped across perfect white shoulders. The material fell, exquisitely, over the cushioned seat and the fabric arms of the chair, as if for an artist's still life. It was only the alarm in her eyes that told a different story. That, and the fact that her arms were pulled awkwardly behind her, bound tightly by picture wire.

A second man, his shaved scalp covered in an angry rash, stood on guard behind the chair, waiting for his master's instructions.

'Where is he?' his master said in a cold voice.

Marguerite looked at him. She remembered the flush of attraction that had come over her in his presence before and hated him for it.

'You were at the restaurant,' she said. 'At Voisin's.'

He ignored her. 'Where is Vernier?'

'I do not know,' said Marguerite again. 'I give you my word. He keeps his own hours. Often, he is gone for days without a word.'

'Your son, yes. But your daughter does not come and go as she pleases, unchaperoned. She keeps regular hours. And yet she, too, is absent.'

'She is with friends.'

'Is Vernier with her?'

'I . . .'

His eyes swept over the sheets and empty cupboards.

'How long is the apartment to be empty?' he said.

'Some four weeks. Indeed, I am expecting General Du Pont at any moment,' she said, struggling to keep her voice level.

The words were lost in her scream, as the manservant grabbed her by the hair and jerked back her head.

'No!'

The tip of the knife pressed against her skin.

'If you leave now,' she said, struggling to keep her voice steady, 'I will say nothing, I give you my word. Leave me, go.'

The man stroked the side of her face with the back of his gloved hand.

'Marguerite, no one will come. The piano downstairs is silent. The neighbours upstairs are in the country for the weekend. And as for your maid and cook, I watched them leave. They, too, believe that you have already departed with Du Pont.'

Fear flashed in her eyes as Victor Constant pulled up a chair, so close that Marguerite could feel his breath upon her face.

'My friend will soon—'

'I regret to say your esteemed General is already in receipt of a note postponing your liaison until half past eight this evening.' He glanced at the clock on the mantelshelf. 'Some five hours and more away. So, you see, we have no need to hurry. And what he discovers when he does arrive is entirely up to you. Alive, dead. It matters little to me.'

The point of his knife was now pressing beneath her eye.

'I fear that you would fare ill in the world without your looks.'

'What is it you want? Money? Does Anatole owe you money? I can settle his debts.'

Constant gave a hollow laugh. 'If only it were that simple. Besides, your financial situation is, shall we say, perilous. And generous as I am certain your lover can be, I do not think General Du Pont would pay to keep your son from the bankruptcy courts.' He pressed the tip of the blade a little harder against her pale skin. 'It is not a question of money. Vernier has taken something that belongs to me.'

Marguerite heard the change in his voice and began to struggle. She tried to pull her arms free but succeeded only in causing her bonds to tighten. The wire cut sharply into the skin of her bare wrists. Blood began to drip, bead by red bead, onto the blue carpet.

'I beg you,' she bargained. 'Let me speak with my son. I'm sure it is no more than a misunderstanding. I will persuade him to give back to you whatever it was he took, I give you my word.'

'Ah, but it is too late for that,' he said softly, running his fingers down her cheek and to her throat. 'I wonder if you even presented my card to your son, *chère* Marguerite?' Constant increased the pressure and Marguerite began to choke, struggling to stretch away from his grasp. The look in his eyes terrified her quite as much as the suffocating violence.

Then, without warning, he released her.

Marguerite fell back against the chair, gulping for air. Her eyes were sore and her throat was marked red.

'Start with Vernier's room,' he instructed his man. 'Look for his journal.' He made a shape with his hands. 'About so large.'

The servant withdrew.

'Now, again,' he said, as if in the midst of a perfectly normal conversation. 'Where is your son?'

Marguerite met his eye, her heart thudding with dread, but she had endured ill treatment at the hands of others in her past and survived. She could do so again.

'Truly, I do not know,' she said.

This time, he struck her. Hard, and with his fist, sending her head snapping back. Marguerite gasped as blood welled in her mouth. She dropped her chin and spat into her lap. Then she flinched as she felt the tug of silk at her neck and the rasp of his leather gloves untying the yellow bow.

With his other hand, she felt him pushing up the folds of material above her knees, above her thighs, higher.

'Please, no,' she whispered.

'It is barely shy of three,' he said, tucking a curl of hair behind her ear, in a parody of tenderness. 'We have more than enough time for me to persuade you to talk. And think of Léonie, Marguerite. Such a pretty girl. A little high-spirited for my tastes, but I am sure I could learn to make an exception.'

He pushed the silk from her shoulders.

Marguerite became calm, vanishing into herself as she had been forced to do many times before. She cleared her mind, wiping out the image of him. Even now, her strongest emotion was shame at the way her heart had lurched when she had first opened the door and allowed him into the apartment.

Sex and violence, the old alliance. She had seen it countless times. On the barricades in the Commune, in the backstreets, hidden beneath the respectable veneer of the society salons through which latterly she had moved. So many men driven by hate, not desire. Marguerite had made good use of it. She had exploited her looks, her charms, so that her daughter would never have to live the life she had.

'Where is Vernier?'

He untied her and dragged her from the chair to the floor.

'Where is Vernier?'

'I do not—'

He struck her again. 'Where is your son?'

As Marguerite slipped from consciousness, her only thought was how to protect her children. How not to betray them to this man. She must give him something.

'Rouen,' she lied through her bloodied lips. 'They have gone to Rouen.'

CHAPTER 22

RENNES-LES-BAINS

By a quarter past four, having taken in the modest sights of Couiza, Léonie and Anatole were standing on the concourse in front of the station, waiting while the cabman loaded the luggage into the *courrier publique*.

The horses, both greys, wore white embroidered fringes over their ears and eyes to keep the insects away. Unlike the conveyances Léonie had noticed in Carcassonne, with black leather seats, the *courrier* was an altogether more rustic form of transport. Indeed, it resembled a farmhouse cart, with two wooden bench seats running up each side facing inwards, painted red. There were no cushions and it was open to the sides, with a piece of dark canvas, stretched over a thin metal frame, for shade.

The other passengers included an elderly husband and his much younger wife, from Toulouse. Two elderly bird-like sisters twittered to one another in low voices beneath their hats.

Léonie was pleased to see that their lunch companion from the Grand Café Guilhem, Dr Gabignaud, was to take the same carriage. Frustratingly, Maître Fromilhague kept Gabignaud close to him. Every few minutes, he drew out his watch from his waistcoat pocket by the chain and tapped the glass face, as if suspicious it had stopped working, before putting it away again.

'Clearly a man with pressing matters to attend to,' Anatole whispered. 'He'll be driving the carriage himself soon if we don't look out!'

As soon as everyone was settled, the driver climbed up to his cab. He perched himself on top of the sundry collection of suitcases and valises, his legs spread wide, and looked up at the clock on the front of the railway station building. Not until it struck the half-hour did he flick his whip and they were away.

Within moments, they were on the open road, heading west out of Couiza. The route ran along the river valley between high hills on either side. The bitter winter and wet spring that punished most of France for so much of the year had, here, created an Eden. Lush pastures, green and fertile, rather than sun-scorched earth, thickly wooded hillsides of fir and holm oak, hazel and Mediterranean chestnut and beech. High on a hill to their left, Léonie glimpsed the outline of a ruined castle. An old wooden sign at the side of the road announced it to be the village of Coustaussa.

Gabignaud, seated next to Anatole, was pointing out landmarks. Léonie caught only fragments of their conversation over the crescendo of the wheels on the road and the rattling harness of the horses.

'And that?' Anatole said.

Léonie followed her brother's pointing finger. High on a rocky outcrop to the right, well above the road, she could just discern a tiny hillside village, shimmering in the fierce afternoon heat, no more than a collection of dwellings clinging to the precipitous side of the mountain.

'Rennes-le-Château,' replied Gabignaud. 'You would not believe it to look at it now, but it once was the ancient Visigoth capital of the region, Rhedae.'

'What caused its decline?'

'Charlemagne, the Crusade against the Albigensians, bandits from Spain, plague, the relentless and unforgiving march of history. Now it's just another forgotten mountain village. Rather in the shadow of Rennes-les-Bains.' He paused. 'Having said that, the curé works hard for his parishioners. An interesting man.'

Anatole leaned closer to hear. 'Why so?'

'He is erudite, clearly ambitious and forceful. It is a matter of much local speculation as to why he should choose to stay so close to home and bury himself away in such a poor parish.'

'Perhaps he believes this is where he can be most effective?'

'Certainly the village loves him. He's done a lot of good.'

'In practical matters or of merely a spiritual nature?'

'Both. As an example, the church of Sainte Marie-Madeleine was no more than a ruin when he arrived. In the summer of 1886, the *mairie* voted him two thousand five hundred francs to begin restoration work.'

Anatole raised his eyebrows. 'A sizeable sum!'

He nodded. 'I only know what I hear indirectly. It is said that many items of archaeological interest have come to light, which of course greatly interested your uncle.'

'Such as?'

'An historical altarpiece, I gather. Also a pair of Visigoth pillars and an ancient tombstone – the Dalle des Chevaliers – possibly also from the Visigoth era. Being so interested in that period, your uncle was much engaged in the early stages of the renovations in Rennes-le-Château.'

'You, too, seem to be something of an historian,' ventured Léonie.

Gabignaud flushed with pleasure. 'A hobby, Mademoiselle Vernier, nothing more.'

Anatole took out his cigarette case. The doctor accepted. Shielding the flame with his arched hand, Anatole struck a match for both of them. 'And what is the name of this exemplary priest?' he asked, blowing out the question with the smoke.

'Saunière. Bérenger Saunière.'

They had reached a straight section of road and the horses picked up speed. The noise grew in volume until further discussion was all but impossible. Léonie did not altogether mind. Her thoughts were racing, for somewhere in the morass of Gabignaud's conversation, she had the sense that she had learned something of significance.

But what?

After a short while, they left the main road to follow the river valley of the Salz. Léonie leaned out as far as she dared, delighted by the beauty of the landscape, the extraordinary vista of sky and rock and woods. Here the ancient forest came almost down to the road's edge and she felt they were entering a secret place, like explorers in one of Monsieur Rider Haggard's entertainments venturing into lost African kingdoms.

Now the road began to curve elegantly, following the cut of the river. It was beautiful, an arcadia. Everything was fertile and lush – olive green, sea green, scrub the colour of absinthe. The silver underside of leaves, lifted by the breeze, shimmered in the sun between the darker tones of fir and oak. Above the treeline, the startling outline of crests and peaks, the ancient silhouettes of menhirs, dolmens and natural sculptures. The antique history of the region was laid out plain to see, like pages in a book.

And like a game of *cache-cache*, the water sang its continuous presence, chasing through the entangled branches of the willows that hung low over the river, a guide drawing them ever closer to their destination.

CHAPTER 23

Ahead, on the bend in the road, Léonie had her first glimpse of Rennes-les-Bains. She could see a white three-storey building with a sign announcing itself to be the Hôtel de la Reine. Beside it was a cluster of rather forbidding buildings that she presumed made up the establishment of the thermal spa.

The *courrier* crossed a low bridge and slowed to walking pace as they swung into the main street. To the right, it was bounded by the great grey wall of the mountain itself. To the left, there was a collection of homes, boarding houses and hotels. Heavy metal-framed gas lamps were set into the walls.

Her first impressions were not as she had expected. The town had an air of elegance and prosperity. Generous, scrubbed stone steps and thresholds abutted the roadway, which, although left as nature intended, was clean and passable. The street was lined with bay and laurel trees in wide planters, which seemed to bring the woods down into the town. She saw a rotund gentleman in a buttoned frock coat, two ladies with parasols and three nurses, each pushing a *chaise roulante*.

The driver pulled up the horses. '*La place du Pérou. S'il vous plaît. Terminus.*'

The small square was bordered by buildings on three sides and shaded by lime trees. The golden sunlight filtered down through the leaves, casting chequerboard patterns on the ground. There was a water trough for the horses and the respectable town houses were adorned with window boxes filled with the last of the tumbling summer flowers. At a small café with striped awnings, a collection of well-dressed, well-gloved ladies and their escorts were taking refreshment. In the corner was the approach to a modest church.

'All very picturesque,' muttered Anatole.

The driver jumped down from his cab and began to unload the luggage.

'*S'il vous plaît, Mesdames et Messieurs. La place du Pérou. Terminus.*'

One by one, the travellers disembarked. There were awkward farewells. Maître Fromilhague raised his hat and then disappeared. Gabignaud shook Anatole's hand and presented his card, saying how much he hoped there would be an opportunity to meet again during their stay, perhaps for a game of cards or at one of the musical soirées that took place in Limoux or Quillan. Then, tipping his hat to Léonie, he hurried away across the square.

Anatole put his arm around Léonie's shoulders.

'This does not look as unpromising as I had feared,' he said.

'It is charming. Quite charming.'

A young girl in the grey-and-white uniform of a parlour-maid appeared, out of breath, at one corner of the square. She was plump and pretty, with deep black eyes. Strands of thick dark hair were escaping from beneath a white cap.

'Ah! Perhaps our reception committee?' said Anatole.

Behind her, also out of breath, came a young man with a broad, pleasant face. He wore an open-necked shirt with a red scarf.

'*Et voilà*,' Anatole grinned, 'unless I am much mistaken, the explanation for the girl's lack of punctuality.'

The maid attempted to tidy her hair, then ran towards them.

'Sénher Vernier? Madomaisèla. Madama sent me to fetch you to the Domaine de la Cade. She asked me to present her apologies, but there is a difficulty with the gig. It's being repaired, but Madama suggests that it might be quicker on foot ...' The maid glanced doubtfully down at Léonie's calfskin boots. 'If you don't mind ...'

Anatole looked the girl up and down. 'And you are?'

'Marieta, Sénher.'

'Very good. And how long might we have to wait for the gig to be repaired, Marieta?'

'I couldn't say. There is a broken wheel.'

'Well, how far is it to Domaine de la Cade?'

'*Pas luènh.*' Not far.

Anatole peered over her shoulder at the breathless boy. 'And the luggage will be brought on later?'

'*Oc,* Sénher,' she said. 'Pascal will bring it.'

Anatole turned to Léonie. 'In which case, with the lack of any promising alternative, I vote we do as our aunt suggests – and walk.'

'What?' The word burst from Léonie's lips before she could help herself. 'But you hate to walk!' She touched her fingers to her own ribs, to remind him of his injuries. 'Besides, might it not be too much for you?'

He shrugged. 'I admit, it's a bore, but what can one do? I would rather press on than kick our heels here.'

Taking Anatole's words as assent, Marieta gave a quick curtsey, then turned and set off.

Léonie stared after her, open-mouthed. Anatole threw back his head and laughed.

'Welcome to the country,' he said, taking Léonie's hand. 'Come, *petite*. Otherwise, we will be left behind!'

Marieta led them down a shadowed passageway between the houses. They emerged into bright sunlight on an old arched stone bridge. Far below, the water flowed over flat rocks. Léonie caught her breath, made dizzy by the sensation of light and space and height, but there was no time to enjoy the view.

The maid was making for a narrow, unmade path that ran steeply up into the trees of the wooded hillside. Léonie and Anatole followed in silent single file, each saving their breath for the climb.

Higher and steeper they went, along a dappled track of stones and fallen leaves, venturing ever deeper into thick forest. Before long, the path opened out into a wider country track.

Léonie turned and looked back in the direction they had come. Now she could see, steeply below them but close still, the red and grey sloping roofs of Rennes-les-Bains. She could even identify the hotels and the central square where they had disembarked from the carriage. The water shimmered and teased, a ribbon of green and silver, even red with the reflection of autumn leaves, running as smooth as silk.

After a slight dip in the track, they reached a plateau.

Ahead stood the stone pillars and gates of a country estate. Wrought-iron railings disappeared as far as the eye could see, shielded by fir and yew. The property seemed both forbidding and aloof. Léonie shivered. For a moment, her spirit of adventure abandoned her. She recalled her mother's reluctance to discuss the Domaine and her childhood spent within it. And then the words of Dr Gabignaud at luncheon echoing in her ears.

Such an ill reputation.

'*Cade?*' Anatole queried.

'It is a local name for juniper, Sénher,' the maid replied.

Léonie glanced at her brother, then stepped forward with determination and put both hands upon the railings, peering through the iron bars at the gardens beyond.

Everything was shrouded in a dark, filtered green, chinks of sun reflected through an ancient canopy of leaves. Elderberry trees, shrubs, formal hedges and once-elegant borders were unkempt and lacking colour.

A large stone birdbath stood dry in the centre of a wide gravelled path that led straight from the gates into the grounds. To Léonie's left, there was a round ornamental pond, a rusty metal frame stretched over it. It, too, was dry. To the right was a row of juniper bushes, growing wild and untended. A little further back were the remains of an orangery, the glass missing and the frame twisted.

If she had come upon this place by accident, Léonie would have thought it abandoned. She glanced to her right and saw there was a sign of grey slate hanging upon the fence, the words partly obscured by deep scratches scored in the stone. Like claw marks.

DOMAINE DE LA CADE.

The house did not look as if it would welcome visitors.

CHAPTER 24

'There is another approach to the house, I presume?' asked Anatole.

'*Oc*, Sénher,' replied Marieta. 'The main entrance is on the north side of the estate. The late master had a track built, up from the Sougraigne road. But it is a good hour's walk, all the way round the town of Rennes-les-Bains, then back up the hillside. Much longer than the old forest path.'

'And did your mistress instruct you to bring us this way, Marieta?'

The girl blushed. 'She did not say *not* to bring you through the woods,' she said defensively.

They stood patiently while Marieta hunted in the pocket of her apron to retrieve a large brass key. There was a heavy clunk as the gate opened. Once they were through, she locked it behind them. It juddered and creaked, then clattered back into position.

Léonie had butterflies in her stomach, a mixture of nerves and excitement. She felt herself the heroine of her own story as she followed Anatole along narrow green pathways, clearly little used, past a box hedge with an arch cut into it. Marieta went straight on until they emerged onto a generous driveway. This was gravelled and well kept, no hints of moss or wild grass, and was flanked by an avenue of *châtaigniers* with fruit hanging from their branches.

At last, Léonie caught her first glimpse of the house itself.

'Oh,' she gasped in admiration.

The house was magnificent. Imposing, yet well proportioned, it was perfectly situated both to catch the best of the sun and to benefit from the views to the south and west afforded by its position looking out over the valley. There were three storeys, a gently sloping roof and rows of shuttered windows set within elegant whitewashed walls. Each of the windows on the first floor gave onto stone balconies with curved iron balustrades. The entire edifice was covered with flaming red and green ivy, gleaming as if the leaves themselves had been polished.

As they drew closer, Léonie saw that a wall ran unbroken along the ledge of the entire top storey of the house, behind which were visible eight round attic windows.

Perhaps Maman once looked down from one of those very windows?

A wide, sweeping semicircular stone staircase led to a substantial double front door, painted raven black, with a brass knocker and trim. It sheltered beneath a curved stone portico, bordered by two substantial planters holding ornamental cherry trees.

Léonie followed the maid and Anatole into a large elegant entrance hall. The floor was a chequerboard of black and red tiles and the walls were covered in a delicate cream paper decorated with yellow and green flowers, giving an impression of light and space. In the centre was a mahogany table with a wide glass bowl of white roses, the highly polished wood contributing to an atmosphere of intimacy and warmth.

To the left of a grand staircase was a miniature grand piano, with a whisper of dust upon the closed lid.

'Madama will receive you on the afternoon terrace,' Marieta said.

She took them through a set of glazed glass doors, which gave onto a south-facing terrace, shaded by vines and honeysuckle. It ran the width of the house and was situated to overlook the formal lawns and planted beds. A distant avenue of horse chestnut trees and evergreen firs marked the furthest boundary; a gazebo of glass and wood painted white glinted in the sun. In the foreground was the smooth surface of an ornamental lake.

'This way, Madomaisèla, Sénher.'

In a patch of shade, created by a generous yellow awning, a table was laid for three. White linen tablecloth, white china, silver spoons and a centrepiece of meadow flowers, Parma violets, pink and white geraniums, purple Pyrenean lilies.

'I will tell the mistress you are here,' Marieta said, and disappeared back into the shadows of the house.

Léonie leant back against the stone balustrade. Her cheeks were flushed. She unbuttoned her gloves at the wrist and untied her hat, using it as a fan.

'She has led us around full circle,' she said.

'I beg your pardon?'

Léonie pointed at the high box hedge at the distant reaches of the lawn. 'If we had come through the arch, we could have walked across the park. But the girl has led us through the grounds in a circle so as to approach from the front.'

Anatole removed his straw hat and gloves and placed them on the wall.

'Well, it is a splendid building, and the prospect was excellent.'

'And no carriage, no housekeeper to greet us,' Léonie continued. 'It is all most peculiar.'

'These gardens are exquisite.'

'Here, yes, but at the rear, the entire property appears quite derelict. Abandoned. The orangery, the overgrown beds, the—'

He laughed. 'Derelict, Léonie, you exaggerate! I admit it is more in the state that nature intended, but more than that . . .'

Her eyes glinted. 'It is completely overgrown,' she argued. 'No wonder the Domaine is viewed with suspicion locally.'

'Whatever are you talking about?'

'That impertinent man, Monsieur Denarnaud, at the railway station – did you see the expression upon his face when you said where we were headed? And poor Dr Gabignaud. The manner in which that disagreeable Maître Fromilhague chastised him and forbade him to speak. It's all most mysterious.'

'It is not,' Anatole said with exasperation. 'Do you imagine we have stumbled accidentally into one of those ghastly little stories of Monsieur Poe you have such a taste for?' He pulled a grotesque face. '"We have put her living in the tomb",' he quoted in a trembling voice. '"I tell you that she now stands without the door!" I can be Roderick Usher to your Madeline.'

'And the lock on the gate was rusty,' she said doggedly. 'No one had passed that way for some time. I tell you, Anatole, it is most peculiar.'

From behind them came a woman's voice, soft and clear and calm.

'I am sorry to hear you find it so, but you are most welcome all the same.'

Léonie heard Anatole catch his breath.

Mortified to have been overheard, she spun round, her face aflame. The woman standing in the doorway suited her voice precisely. Elegant and assured, she was slender and tall. Her thick blonde hair was piled high on her head, not a strand out of place. Most striking of all were her eyes, a pale grey, the colour of moonstone.

Léonie's hand flew to her own ungovernable curls, wayward in comparison.

'Tante, I . . .'

Isolde was stepping forwards. 'You must be Léonie,' she said, extending long, slim fingers. 'And Anatole?'

With a half-bow, Anatole took Isolde's hand and raised it to his lips.

'Tante,' he said with a smile, looking up at her from beneath his dark lashes. 'It is a great pleasure.'

'The pleasure is mine. And, please, Isolde. Tante is so formal and makes me feel quite old.'

'Your girl brought us through the rear gates,' Anatole said. 'It is that, and the heat, that have disturbed my sister.' He took in the house and grounds with a sweep of his arm. 'But if this is our reward, then the tribulations of our journey are already a distant memory.'

Isolde inclined her head at the compliment, then turned to Léonie.

'I did ask Marieta to explain the unfortunate situation with the carriage, but she is easily flustered,' she said lightly. 'I am sorry that your first impressions have not been favourable. But no matter. You are here now.'

Léonie found her tongue at last. 'Tante Isolde, please forgive my discourtesy. It was inexcusable.'

Isolde smiled. 'There is nothing to forgive. Now, do sit. Tea first – *à l'anglaise* – then Marieta will show you to your rooms.'

They took their seats. Immediately, a silver teapot and a jug of fresh lemonade were brought to the table, followed by plates of both savoury and sweet dishes. Isolde leaned forward and poured the tea – a delicate pale liquid that smelled of sandalwood and the Orient.

'What a wonderful scent,' said Anatole, breathing in the aroma. 'What is it?'

'It is my own blend of lapsang souchong and *verveine*. I find it so much more refreshing than those heavy English teas that are currently so popular.'

Isolde offered Léonie a white china dish filled with large slices of bright yellow lemon.

'Your mother's wire, accepting my invitation on your behalf, Léonie, was perfectly charming. I do hope I shall have the opportunity to meet her too. Perhaps she might visit in the spring?'

Léonie thought of her mother's dislike of the Domaine and how she had never regarded it as home, but she remembered her manners and lied prettily.

'Maman would be delighted. She suffered a period of illness at the beginning of this past year, brought on by the inclement weather, otherwise she would of course have come to pay her last respects to Oncle Jules.'

Isolde smiled, then turned to Anatole. 'I read in the newspapers that temperatures fell well below zero in Paris. Can that be true?'

Anatole's eyes glittered bright. 'It seemed the world had turned to ice. The Seine itself froze and so many were dying at night on the streets that the authorities were obliged to open shelters in gymnasiums, shooting galleries, schools and public baths; they even set up a dormitory in the Palais des Arts Libéraux in the Champs-de-Mars, in the shadow of Monsieur Eiffel's magnificent tower.'

'The fencing halls too?'

Anatole looked puzzled. 'Fencing halls?'

'Forgive me,' Isolde said, 'the mark above your eye. I thought, perhaps, you were a swordsman.'

Léonie jumped in. 'Anatole was assaulted four nights ago, on the night of the Palais Garnier riots.'

'Léonie, please,' he protested.

'Were you hurt?' Isolde said quickly.

'A few cuts and bruises; it was nothing,' he said, throwing a fierce look at Léonie.

'Did word of the riots not reach here?' asked Léonie. 'The newspapers in Paris carried nothing but news of the arrests of the *abonnés*.'

Isolde kept her eyes fixed upon Anatole.

'Were you robbed?'

'My watch – my father's timepiece – was taken. They were interrupted before they could take anything else.'

'A street robbery then?' Isolde repeated, as if wishing to convince herself of it.

'That's right. Nothing more. It was bad luck.'

For a moment, an awkward silence fell over the table.

Then, remembering her duties, Isolde turned to Léonie. 'Your mother spent some time here at the Domaine de la Cade in her childhood, did she not?'

Léonie nodded.

'It must have been rather lonely for her growing up here alone,' Isolde suggested. 'No other children for company.'

Léonie smiled with relief that she did not have to pretend an affection for the Domaine de la Cade her mother did not feel and spoke without thinking.

'Do you intend to make this your home or return to Toulouse?'

Isolde allowed confusion to cloud her grey eyes. 'Toulouse? I am afraid I don't . . .'

'Léonie,' said Anatole sharply.

She blushed but met her brother's eye. 'I was under the impression from something Maman said that Tante Isolde came from Toulouse.'

'Really, Anatole, I am not in the least offended,' Isolde said. 'But, in point of fact, I grew up in Paris.'

Léonie leaned closer, pointedly ignoring her brother. She was intrigued to know how her aunt and uncle had first made one another's acquaintance. From what little she knew of Oncle Jules, it seemed an unlikely marriage.

'I was wondering—' she began, but Anatole leapt in.

'Do you have much contact with Rennes-les-Bains?'

Isolde shook her head. 'My late husband was not interested in entertaining, and since his death, I regret to say I have neglected my responsibilities as a hostess.'

'I am sure people are sympathetic to your situation,' Anatole said.

'Many of our neighbours were most kind during the final weeks of my husband's life. Prior to that, his health had not been good for some time. After his death, there were so many matters to take care of, away from the Domaine de la Cade, and I was here less than perhaps I should have been. But . . .' She broke off and drew Léonie into the conversation with another of her calm, steady smiles. 'If it would be pleasing for you, I had thought to use the excuse of your visit to hold a dinner party for one or two local guests this coming Saturday evening. Would you like that? Nothing on a grand scale, but it will be an opportunity to introduce you.'

'That would be delightful,' Léonie replied.

After that, the afternoon rolled pleasantly on. Isolde was an excellent hostess – conscientious, careful and charming – and Léonie enjoyed herself hugely. Slices of thick-crusted white bread, spread with goat's cheese and sprinkled with chopped garlic, thin fingers of toast topped with anchovy paste and black pepper, a platter of cured mountain ham with purple half-moons of ripe fig. A rhubarb tart, the pastry sugared and golden, sat beside a blue china bowl filled to the brim with a compote of mulberries and black-heart cherries, and a jug of cream, a long-handled silver spoon lying beside it.

'And what are these?' Léonie asked, pointing to a dish of purple bonbons coated with a white frosting. 'They look delicious.'

'Pearls of the Pyrenees, drops of schoenanthus scent crystallised in pieces of sugar.'

'How fortunate, they are some of my favourite sweets,' Anatole said.

'I'm so glad. And these' – Isolde gestured to another dish – 'are home-made chocolate creams. Jules's cook is really quite excellent. She has served the family for almost forty years.'

There was a wistfulness to her tone that made Léonie wonder if perhaps Isolde felt, as their mother had done, something of an unwelcome guest rather than the rightful chatelaine of the Domaine de la Cade.

'You work in newspapers?' Isolde was asking Anatole.

Anatole shook his head. 'Not for some time. The life of a journalist did not suit me: domestic disputes, the Algerian conflict, the latest election crisis at the Académie des Beaux-Arts; I found it dispiriting to be forced to consider matters that did not interest me in the slightest. Now, although I write the odd review for *La Revue blanche* and *La Revue contemporaine*, mostly I pursue my literary endeavours in a less commercial arena.'

'Anatole is on the editorial board of a magazine for collectors, antique editions and suchlike,' Léonie said.

Isolde smiled and turned her attention back to Léonie. 'I must say again how delighted I was you felt able to accept my invitation. I feared a month in the country might seem rather dull after the excitements of Paris.'

'One can be just as easily bored in Paris,' Léonie replied. 'Too often, I am obliged to spend my time at tedious soirées listening to widows and old maids complaining of how things were so much better under the Emperor. I prefer to read!'

'Léonie is *une lectrice assidue*,' Anatole smiled. 'Always has her nose in a book. Although her reading matter is often rather – how shall I put it? – sensationalist! Not to my taste at all. Ghost stories and Gothic horrors ... Our mother said there was a splendid library here.'

'Indeed there is. My late husband was an avid historian and was interested in other, less usual ...' Isolde broke off, as if searching for the appropriate word. 'More select matters of study, shall we say.' She hesitated again. Léonie looked at her with interest, but Isolde said nothing more about what these matters might be. 'There are many first editions and rare volumes,' she continued, 'which I am certain will be of interest to you, Anatole, as well as a good selection of novels and back editions of *Le Petit journal* that might appeal to you, Léonie. Please, treat the collection as if it were your own.'

It was now just short of seven o'clock. In the shade of the tall chestnut trees, the sun had all but gone from the terrace, and the shadows were stretching across the far edges of the lawn. Isolde rang a small silver bell that sat beside her on the table.

Marieta appeared immediately.

'Has Pascal returned with the luggage?'

'Some time ago, Madama.'

'Good. Léonie, I have put you in the Yellow Room. Anatole, you have the Anjou Suite, at the front of the house. It faces north, but it is a pleasant room.'

'I'm certain it will be most comfortable,' he said.

'Since we have eaten so well at tea, and I thought you might both wish to retire early tonight after the rigours of the journey from Paris, I have not arranged for us to dine formally this evening. Please feel at liberty to ring for anything you need. It has become my custom to have a nightcap in the drawing room at nine o'clock. If you would care to join me, I would be delighted.'

'Thank you.'

'Yes, thank you,' Léonie added.

They all three rose to their feet.

'I thought I might take a stroll around the gardens before dusk. Smoke a cigarette?' said Anatole.

Léonie saw some reaction flare in Isolde's still, grey eyes.

'If it is not too much of an imposition, may I suggest you save your exploration of the Domaine until the morning. It will be dark soon. I would not wish to have to send out a search party for you on your very first evening.'

For a moment, nobody spoke. Then, to Léonie's astonishment, rather than object to this restriction on his freedom, Anatole smiled. He took Isolde's hand and raised it to his lips.

'Of course, Tante, whatever you wish,' said Anatole. 'I am your servant.'

CHAPTER 25

Having taken leave of her brother and her aunt, Léonie followed Marieta up the staircase and along the first-floor passageway that ran the length of the house. The maid paused to indicate to her the location of the water closet and, adjacent to it, a spacious bathroom, in the centre of which stood a huge copper bath, before continuing to her bedroom.

'The Yellow Room, Madomaisèla,' said Marieta, standing back to allow Léonie to enter. 'Hot water is on the washstand. Is there anything else you need?'

'Everything looks wonderful.'

The maid bobbed and withdrew.

Léonie looked around with pleasure at the room that was to be her home for the next four weeks. It was a well-appointed chamber, both handsome and comfortable, overlooking the lawns to the south of the property. The window was open, and from below she could hear the quiet chink of crockery and china as the servants cleared the table.

The walls were covered in a delicate paper of pink and purple flowers, matching the curtains and linen, which gave an impression of light despite the deep hues of the mahogany furniture. The bed – quite the largest Léonie had ever seen – sat like an Egyptian barge in the centre of the room, its ornate head- and footboards polished and gleaming. Beside it sat a claw-footed armoire, on which stood a candle in a brass holder, a glass and a jug of water covered with an embroidered white napkin to keep away the flies. Her workbox had also been placed there, together with her book of cartridge papers and painting accoutrements. Her travelling easel was propped up against the armoire on the floor.

Léonie crossed the room to a tall wardrobe. The surround was carved in the same elaborate Egyptian style and there were two long mirrors set into the doors, which reflected the room behind her. She opened the right-hand door, setting the hangers rattling on the rail, to see her petticoats, afternoon dresses, evening gowns and jackets arranged in neat rows. Everything had been unpacked.

The fireplace was on the wall facing the door, and above it, a mirror with a mahogany frame. In the centre of the mantelpiece was a gilt and porcelain Sèvres clock, much like the one in the drawing room at home.

Léonie removed her dress, cotton lisle stockings, combinations and corset, draping garments across the carpet and armchair. In her chemise and undergarments, she poured the steaming water from the jug into the basin. When she had finished washing, she pulled her blue cashmere dressing gown from where it had been hung on a heavy brass hook on the back of the door, then sat down at the dressing table in front of the middle of the three long casement windows.

Pin by metal pin, she undid her unruly hair, letting it fall loose to her waist, then tilted the looking glass towards her and began to brush in wide, long strokes until it lay unravelled like a skein of silk down her back.

Out of the corner of her eye, a movement in the gardens below snagged her attention.

'Anatole,' she muttered, fearing that perhaps her brother had decided to ignore Isolde's request that he remain inside after all. His character in the country – so obliging and engaging – was rather different from his hot-headedness in Paris.

Léonie replaced her hairbrush on the dressing table and slipped round to stand before the centre window. The last vestiges of day had all but bade farewell to the sky. As her eyes became accustomed to the dusk, she noticed another movement, this time at the far boundary of the lawns by the high box hedge, beyond the ornamental lake.

Now she could clearly see a figure. He was bare-headed and had a furtive walk, every few steps turning and glancing behind him, as if he thought he was being followed.

A trick of the light?

The figure disappeared into the shadows. Léonie fancied she heard a church bell toll in the valley below, a thin and mournful single note, but when she strained to listen, the only sounds she could distinguish were those of the countryside at dusk. The whispering of the wind in the trees and the mixed twilight chorus of birdsong. Then the piercing shriek of an owl preparing for a night's hunting.

The figure had almost certainly been one of the gardeners, the worse for drink, or a boy on a dare taking an illicit short cut across the lawns, but she felt uncomfortable at having watched. A rap on the door made her jump.

'*C'est moi*,' Anatole called back. 'Are you decent? May I come in?'

'*Attend, j'arrive.*'

'Whatever is wrong?' he said, when she opened the door. 'You sounded quite alarmed.'

'You were not out walking on the lawns?' she asked. 'No more than a few minutes past?'

Anatole shook his head. 'I did remain on the terrace for a few moments after you had withdrawn, but for no longer than the time it took to smoke a cigarette. Why?'

'I . . .' Léonie began, then reconsidered. 'Never mind. It doesn't matter.'

He tipped her clothes to the floor and took possession of the armchair.

Probably just one of the stable boys.

Anatole fished his cigarette case and his box of wax Vestas from his pocket and put them on the table.

'Not in here,' pleaded Léonie. 'Your tobacco is noxious stuff.'

He shrugged, then reached into his other pocket and pulled out a small blue pamphlet.

'Here. I have brought you something to help pass the time.'

He strolled across the room, handed the monograph to her and then sat back in the chair.

'*Voilà*,' he said. '*Diables et esprits maléfiques et phantômes de la montagne.*'

Léonie wasn't listening. Wondering if whatever she had seen was still out there.

'Are you certain you are all right? You really are awfully pale.'

Anatole's voice drew her back. Léonie looked down at the volume in her hand, as if wondering how it had got to be there, and felt embarrassed.

'I am fine. Whatever manner of book is it?'

'Haven't a clue. Looks quite dreadful, but it seems your sort of thing! Found it gathering dust in the library. The author is someone Isolde intends to invite to supper on Saturday night, a Monsieur Audric Baillard. There are passages about the Domaine de la Cade. It appears there are all sorts of stories about devils, evil spirits and ghosts associated with this region, particularly this estate, stretching back to the religious wars of the seventeenth century.' He smiled across at her.

Léonie grinned. 'And what spurred you to this act of generosity?'

'Can a brother not, out of the goodness of his heart, undertake an act of random kindness for his sister?'

'Certain brothers, indeed, yes. But you?'

He held up his hands in surrender. 'Very well, I confess I thought it might keep you out of mischief.'

Anatole ducked as Léonie threw a pillow at him.

'Missed,' he laughed. 'Very poor shot.' He swept up his cigarette case and matches from the table, sprang to his feet and within a matter of strides was at the door. 'Let me know how you get on with Monsieur Baillard. I think we should accept Isolde's invitation to join her for drinks later in the drawing room. Yes?'

'Do you not think it odd that there is to be no dinner this evening?'

He raised his eyebrows. 'Do you have an appetite?'

'Well, no. I do not, but even—'

Anatole put his finger to his lips. 'Well then, stop looking to find fault with everything.'

'I'm not,' Léonie protested, though she realised he was right. 'It's just all so, so ... different.'

He opened the door. 'Enjoy the book, *petite*. I shall expect a full report later.'

Léonie listened to his whistling and the firm tread of his boots getting fainter as he made his way along the passage to his own room. Then, the closing of another door. Peace descended upon the house once more.

Léonie fetched the pillow from where it had fallen and climbed up onto the bed. She drew up her knees, settled herself comfortably and opened the book.

The clock on the mantelpiece chimed the half-hour.

CHAPTER 26

Paris

The fashionable streets and boulevards were smothered in a thick brown twilight. The *quartiers perdus*, the down-at-heel neighbourhoods, the alleyways and labyrinthine network of apartments and slums, also gasped for breath in the polluted dusk.

The air grew cold.

Buildings and people, trams and landaus, seemed to loom out of the shadows, appearing and then disappearing like phantoms. The awnings of the cafés on the rue d'Amsterdam were flapping in the blustering wind, plunging like tethered horses trying to break free. On the Grands Boulevards, the branches of the trees shook.

Leaves skimmed and danced along the pavements of the 9th *arrondissement* and the green paths of the Parc Monceau. The new telegraph wires of the Post Office began to vibrate and sing, and the tram rails to whistle.

At seven-thirty, the fog gave way to rain. It fell, as cold and grey as iron filings, slowly at first, then heavier and faster. Servants closed the shutters of apartments and houses with a clatter. In the 8th *arrondissement*, those still outside sought refuge from the impending tempest, ordered beer and absinthe and quarrelled over the few remaining tables inside at the Café Wéber on the rue Royale.

The beggars and *chiffonniers* with no homes to go to sought shelter beneath the bridges and railway arches.

In the rue de Berlin, Marguerite Vernier lay on the *chaise longue* in her apartment. One arm was folded beneath her head, the other was draped over the side of the divan, her fingers trailing the carpet like a dreamy girl in a summertime boat. Only the tinge of blue on her lips, the purple bruising like a collar around her jaw, the ugly bracelet of congealed blood on her abused wrist betrayed the fact that she was not sleeping. The knife, the blade stained red by its task, lay beside her hand as if it had dropped from her dying fingers.

Victor Constant was insensible to her presence. She had ceased to exist for him the instant he had realised he had obtained as much as he would from her.

Save the ticking of the clock on the mantelpiece, all was silent.

Save the pool of light cast by the single candle, all was darkness.

Constant lit a Turkish cigarette, then took a seat at the dining table to examine the journal his manservant had found in Vernier's nightstand.

'Get me a brandy.'

With his other knife, a Nontron blade with a yellow handle, Constant cut the string, then unfolded the waxed brown paper and lifted out a royal-blue pocket notebook. The journal was a record of Vernier's day-to-day personal activities for the year: the salons he had frequented; a list of debts, recorded neatly in two columns and scored through when the obligation had been met; mention of a brief flirtation with the occultists in the cold early months of the year, as a buyer of books rather than an acolyte; purchases made, such as an umbrella, and a limited edition of *Cinq poèmes* from Edmond Bailly's bookshop in the rue de la Chaussée d'Antin.

Constant was not interested in the tedious domestic details. He was looking for details of the affair between Vernier and the only woman he had ever loved. He still could not bring himself even to think her name, let alone speak it. On 31st October of last year, she had told him their relationship must end. Before, indeed, their liaison was worthy of the word. He had taken her reluctance for modesty and had not pressed her. His shock had yielded instantly to uncontrolled rage, and he had all but killed her. Indeed, he might have done so had not her cries been overheard by neighbours in the adjoining building.

He had not intended to hurt her. He loved her, worshipped her, adored her. But she had driven him to it. After their misunderstanding, as Constant thought of it, she disappeared from Paris. Throughout November and December, Constant thought of her endlessly. It was simple. He loved her, and in return, she had betrayed him. His body and mind would throw out relentless reminders of their time together – her scent, her grace, how grateful she had been for his love. Then, the humiliation of how she had abandoned him would come flooding back, together with an anger fiercer and more savage than before.

To obliterate the memory of her, Constant took refuge in the usual pastimes open to a gentleman of urbane habits and deep pockets. Gambling dens, nightclubs, laudanum to counteract the increasingly heavy doses of mercury he was obliged to take to alleviate the symptoms of his worsening condition. There was a succession of *midinettes* – whores who looked in passing like her – their soft flesh paying the price for her disloyalty. He was strikingly good-looking. He could be generous. He knew how to charm and coax, and the girls were willing enough, until the moment they realised how depraved were his appetites.

Nothing gave him respite. Nothing eased his anguish at her treachery. She belonged to him.

For three months, Constant survived without her. At the end of January, however, everything changed. As the ice on the Seine began to melt, a rumour reached his ears that not only was she back in Paris, and a widow now, but that there was a lover. That she had given to another man what she had withheld from him.

It was a simple matter to discover his rival's name, though the knowledge made him mad. The fact that Vernier and she were lovers was the first thought that came to him each dawn as the sun rose. It was the last thought that was left to him as the moon arrived to greet the night.

As January yielded to February, Constant started his campaign of persecution and retribution. He began with Vernier, intending to destroy his good name. His tactic was simple. Gossip dripped into the ear of the less reputable newspaper columnists, drop by drop. Forged letters passed palm to greasy palm. Rumours fed into the labyrinthine networks of clandestine groups of initiates and acolytes and mesmerists that swarmed beneath the respectable façade of Paris, each obligingly suspicious and in constant fear of betrayal. The rotting titbits of news, twilight whisperings, the anonymous publication of slanders.

Lies all, but plausible lies.

But even his crusade against Vernier, well executed as it was, gave Constant no respite. Nightmares still stalked his dreams and even his days were filled with images of the lovers entwined in one another's arms. The relentless progress of his illness, too, stole sleep from him. When Constant shut his eyes, he was assaulted by nightmarish images of himself, scourged and nailed to a cross.

In March came a resolution of sorts. She died. Her death came as something of a release. Constant watched from the sidelines as her casket was lowered into the wet ground of the Cimetière de Montmartre, feeling as if a burden had been taken from his shoulders. After that, with great satisfaction, he had watched Vernier's life crumble under the weight of his grief.

Spring gave way to the heat of July and August. For a while, Constant had been at peace. September arrived. Then a chance comment overheard, a glimpse of blonde hair beneath a blue hat on the boulevard Haussmann, whisperings in Montmartre of a coffin buried six months previously without a tenant. Constant sent two men to question Vernier on the night of the riot at the Palais Garnier, but they were interrupted before they could learn anything of value.

He flicked through the pages of the journal once more until he reached the date of 16th September last. The page was empty. Vernier had made no record of the riot at the Opéra, no reference to the attack upon him in the passage des Panoramas. The last entry in the journal was dated two days previously. Constant turned the page and read it. Large, confident letters – a solitary word.

'*Fin.*'

He felt cold rage flood through him. The three letters seemed to dance on the page before his eyes, mocking him. After everything he had endured, to discover that he was the victim of a hoax pulled at the cords of his bitterness. How lunatic it seemed with hindsight to ever have thought that dishonouring Vernier would be sufficient. Constant knew, now, what he had to do.

He would hunt them down and kill them. He understood, now, that it was the only thing that would bring him peace.

The servant placed the tumbler of brandy at his elbow. 'General Du Pont may soon be here . . .' he murmured, then withdrew to the window.

Conscious of the time passing, Constant picked up the sheet of greased brown paper in which the notebook had been wrapped. The presence in the apartment of the journal puzzled him. Why would Vernier have left the journal behind if he were not intending to return? Because he had left in such haste? Or perhaps because he did not propose to be absent from Paris for long.

Constant downed the brandy in one and hurled the glass into the grate. It shattered into a thousand glittering pieces. The servant flinched. For a moment, the air seemed to vibrate.

Constant stood and replaced the dining chair precisely beneath the table. He walked to the mantelpiece and opened the glass face of the clock. He pushed the hands forward until they showed half past eight. Then he struck the heavy back of the clock against the edge of the marble surround until the mechanism stopped working. Crouching down, he placed the clock face down among the glinting shards of glass.

'Open the champagne and fetch two glasses.'

The man did as instructed. Constant went to the couch. He took a fistful of hair in his hand and lifted Marguerite Vernier's head into his arms. A sweet metallic smell hung about her. The pale cushions around her were dyed crimson and a pool of blood stained her chest, like the overblown bloom of a hothouse flower.

Constant tipped a little champagne into Marguerite's mouth. He pressed the rim of a glass against her split lips until the faintest smear of lipstick was visible, then filled it halfway with champagne and placed it on the table beside her. He poured a little into the second glass too, and then laid the bottle on its side on the floor. Slowly the liquid began to empty, a ribbon of bubbles streaming onto the carpet.

'Our reptilian comrades of the Fourth Estate are aware that there might be something for them tonight?'

'Yes, Monsieur.' For an instant, the servant's mask slipped. 'The lady . . . Is she dead?'

Constant did not answer.

The servant crossed himself. Constant walked to the sideboard and picked up a framed photograph. Marguerite was seated in the centre of the picture, with her children standing behind her. He read the name of the studio and the date. October 1890. The daughter's hair was worn loose. A child still.

The servant coughed. 'Are we to travel to Rouen, Monsieur?'

'Rouen?'

He twisted his fingers nervously, recognising the look in his master's eyes.

'Forgive me, Monsieur, but did not Madame Vernier say her son and daughter had travelled to Rouen?'

'Ah. Yes, she showed more courage . . . initiative . . . than I expected. But Rouen? I doubt that was their destination. Perhaps she really did not know.'

He thrust the photograph at his man.

'Get out and ask after the girl. Someone will talk. Somebody always does. People will remember her.' He gave a cold smile. 'She will lead us to Vernier and his whore.'

CHAPTER 27

DOMAINE DE LA CADE

Léonie screamed. She threw herself upright, her heart thudding against her ribs. The candle had blown itself out and the room was cloaked in darkness.

For a moment, she thought she was back in the drawing room at the rue de Berlin. Then she looked down and saw Monsieur Baillard's monograph lying on the pillow beside her, and realised.

Un cauchemar.

Of demons and spirits, of phantoms and clawed creatures and the ancient ruins where the spider spins her web. The hollow eyes of ghosts.

Léonie sat back against the wooden headboard, waiting for her pulse to stop racing. Images of a stone sepulchre beneath a grey sky, withered garlands draped over a worn escutcheon. A coat of arms, of a family long corrupt and dishonoured.

She waited for her pulse to stop racing, but, if anything, the hammering inside her head was getting louder.

'Madomaisèla? Madama has sent me to ask if there is anything you need?'

With relief, Léonie recognised that it was Marieta knocking at the door.

'Viens.' Come in.

There was a rattling at the door, then, 'Forgive me, but it is locked.'

Léonie did not remember turning the key. Swiftly, she slipped her chilled feet into her silk *savates* and ran to open the door.

Marieta gave a quick bob. 'Madama Lascombe and Sénher Vernier have sent me to ask if you are intending to join them.'

'What is the time?'

'Nearly half past nine.'

Léonie rubbed the nightmare from her eyes. 'Of course. I lost track of the time. If you could tell them I will be down presently?'

She put on a plain evening dress, nothing elaborate. She arranged her hair with combs and pins, dabbed a little eau de cologne behind her ears and on her wrists, and then descended to the drawing room.

Both Anatole and Isolde stood up as she entered. Isolde was dressed simply in a high-necked turquoise dress with half-sleeves decorated with French jet glass beads.

'I am sorry to have kept you waiting,' Léonie apologised, kissing first her aunt and then her brother.

'We were about to give up on you,' Anatole said. 'What would you like? We are drinking champagne – no, my apologies, Isolde, not champagne. Would you like the same? Or something else?'

Léonie frowned. 'Not champagne?'

Isolde smiled. 'He is teasing you. It is a *blanquette de Limoux*, not champagne, but a local wine much like it. It is sweeter and lighter, more thirst-quenching. I confess, I have quite a taste for it now.'

'Thank you,' Léonie said, accepting a glass. 'I began to read Monsieur Baillard's pamphlet. The next I knew, it was past nine o'clock.'

Anatole laughed. 'Is it so very dull that it sent you to sleep?'

Léonie shook her head. 'Quite the opposite. It was fascinating. It appears the Domaine de la Cade – or, rather, the site that the house and grounds currently occupy – has long been at the heart of a great many superstitions and local legends. Ghosts, devils, spirits walking at night. Most common are stories concerning a black wild creature, half devil, half beast, stalking the countryside when times are bad, snatching children and livestock.'

Anatole and Isolde caught one another's eye.

'According to Monsieur Baillard,' Léonie continued, 'that is why so many of the local landmarks have names that hint at this supernatural past. He relates one tale concerning a lake in the Tabe mountain, the étang du Diable, which is said to communicate with Hell itself. If one throws stones into it, clouds of sulphurous gas apparently rise up out of the water, bringing ferocious storms. And another story, going back to the summer of 1840, which was particularly dry. Desperate for the rains, a miller from the village of Montségur climbed up to the Tabe mountain and threw a live cat into the lake. The animal thrashed and struggled like a demon, so vexing the Devil that he made it rain upon the mountains for the two months following.'

Anatole stretched back, draping his arm along the back of the settee. In the grate, a good fire crackled and spat.

'What superstitious nonsense!' he said affectionately. 'I almost regret putting such a book into your hands.'

Léonie pulled a face. 'You may mock, but there is always some measure of truth in these stories.'

'Well spoken, Léonie,' said Isolde. 'My late husband was much interested in the legends associated with the Domaine de la Cade. His particular passion was the Visigoth period of history, but he and Monsieur Baillard sometimes talked late into the night about all manner of subjects. The curé from our sister village of Rennes-le-Château also sometimes joined them.'

An image of the three men huddled together over books flashed into Léonie's mind, and she wondered if Isolde had resented being excluded.

'Abbé Saunière.' Anatole nodded. 'Gabignaud mentioned him on the journey from Couiza this afternoon.'

'Having said that,' Isolde continued, 'it would be fair to say that Jules was always cautious in Monsieur Baillard's company.'

'Cautious? How so?'

Isolde waved her slim white hand. 'Oh, perhaps *cautious* is the wrong word. Reverential, almost. I am not entirely certain what I mean. He had great respect for Monsieur Baillard's age and knowledge but was also somewhat in awe of his learning.'

Anatole replenished the glasses, then rang the bell for another bottle.

'You say Baillard is a local man?'

Isolde nodded. 'He has furnished lodgings in Rennes-les-Bains, although his main residence is elsewhere. Somewhere in the Sabarthès, I believe. He is an extraordinary man, but a very private one. He is circumspect about his past experiences and his interests are wide-ranging. In addition to local folklore and customs, he is also an expert on the Albigensian Heresy.' She gave a light laugh. 'Indeed, Jules remarked once that one might almost believe Monsieur Baillard had been a witness at some of those medieval battles, so vivid were his descriptions.'

They all smiled.

'It is not the best time of year, but perhaps you would like to visit some of the ruined frontier castles?' Isolde said to Léonie. 'Weather permitting.'

'I would like that very much.'

'And I shall place you next to Monsieur Baillard at dinner on Saturday, so you may question him all you wish about devils and superstitions and the myths of the mountains.'

Léonie nodded, remembering Monsieur Baillard's tales. Anatole, too, fell silent. A different mood had entered the room, slipping in among the easy conversation when no one was watching. For a while, the only sounds were the ticking of the golden hands of the long-case clock and the spitting of the flames in the hearth.

Léonie found her eyes drawn to the windows. They were shuttered against the evening, yet she was strongly aware of the darkness beyond. It seemed to have a living, breathing presence. It was only the wind whistling around the corners of the building, but it seemed to her as if the night itself was murmuring, conjuring up the ancient spirits of the woods.

She glanced at her aunt.

Does she feel it too?

Isolde's expression was impassive. It was impossible for Léonie to tell what she might be thinking. Her eyes did not flicker with the grief of her husband's absence. And there was no suggestion of anxiety or nervousness at what might lie beyond the stone walls of the house.

Léonie looked down at the *blanquette* in her glass, then drained the last of it.

The clock chimed the half-hour.

Isolde announced her intention to write the invitations for Saturday's supper party and withdrew to the study. Anatole took the squat green bottle of Bénédictine from the tray and declared he would remain a while longer and smoke a cigar.

Léonie kissed her brother goodnight and left the drawing room. She walked across the hall, a little unsteady on her feet, with memories of the day in her mind. Of those things that had given her pleasure, and those that had intrigued. How lucky it was that Tante Isolde had chosen what Anatole said were his favourite bonbons, Pearls of the Pyrenees, though she didn't remember him ever saying so before. How comfortable, for the most part, the three of them had been in one another's company.

Her hand was already upon the banister rail when she observed that the piano lid stood temptingly open. The black and white keys were bright in the candlelight, as if they had recently been polished. The rich surround seemed to glow.

Léonie was not an accomplished pianist, but she was unable to resist the invitation of the untouched keyboard. She played a scale, an arpeggio, then a chord. The piano had a sweet voice, soft and precise, as if it was kept tuned and cared for. She let her fingers go where they wished, sounding out a mournful and antique pattern of notes in a minor key – A, E, C and D. A single strand of melody echoed briefly in the silence of the hall, then faded. Sorrowful, evocative, pleasing to the ear.

Léonie ran the backs of her fingers up the climbing octaves with a final flourish, then continued up the stairs to bed.

As the hours passed, the house fell, room by room, into silence. One by one, the candles were extinguished. Beyond the grey walls, the grounds, the lawns, the lake, the beech wood lay quietly beneath a white moon. All was still.

And yet.

PART IV

Rennes-les-Bains
October 2007

CHAPTER 28

Meredith's plane touched down at Toulouse–Blagnac Airport ten minutes ahead of schedule. By four-thirty, she'd picked up her rental car and was negotiating her way out of the parking lot.

The evening rush hour on the beltway was like *Grand Theft Auto* without the weapons. Meredith gripped the wheel tightly, nervous about the traffic coming at her from all sides.

But once she hit the autoroute, things calmed down. She started to feel confident enough to turn on the radio. She found a station, Classique, on pre-set and turned the volume up high. The usual. Bach, Mozart, Puccini, even a little Debussy.

By six o'clock, feeling a mixture of anticipation and excitement, she was driving into the town she'd thought about for so long.

Her first impressions of Rennes-les-Bains were encouraging. It was much smaller than she'd expected and the main street – although 'main' was pushing it some – was narrow, barely wide enough for two cars to pass, but there was something charming about it. Even the fact that it was completely deserted didn't really bother her.

She drove by an ugly stone building, then pretty gardens set down from the road with a metal sign over the entrance,

JARDIN DE PAUL COURRENT, and a sign on the wall, LE PONT DE FER. Suddenly her foot hit the floor. The car slid to a halt, just in time to avoid slamming into the back of a blue Peugeot stopped in the road ahead.

It was the last in a short line of cars. Meredith killed the radio, pressed the button to open her window and leaned out to get a better look. Ahead was a small group of workmen standing beside a yellow road sign: ROUTE BARRÉE.

The driver of the Peugeot got out and walked towards the men, shouting. Meredith waited, then, when another couple of drivers got out of their cars too, she did the same, just as the Peugeot guy turned and strode back towards his car. In his forties or fifties, a little grey around the temples, a little extra weight, but carrying it well. Attractive, with the bearing and demeanour of someone used to getting his own way. What caught Meredith's eye was how he was dressed. Very formal, in black jacket, black pants and tie, polished shoes.

She darted a glance at his licence plate. It ended with eleven, the local tag.

'*Qu'est-ce qui se passe?*' she asked, as he drew level.

'Tree's down,' he replied in English, paying her little attention.

'Well, did they say how long it would be?'

'At least half an hour,' he replied, getting into his car. 'Could mean anything up to three hours, Midi time. To-morrow even.'

He was clearly impatient to be gone. Meredith stepped forward and put a hand on the door. 'Is there another way round?'

This time, he at least looked at her. Steely blue eyes, very direct.

'Back to Couiza, over the hills via Rennes-le-Château,' he said. 'Take you forty minutes at this time of night. I'd wait. Confusing in the dusk.' He glanced at her hand, then back to her face. 'Now, if you'll excuse me?'

Meredith coloured. 'Thank you for your help,' she said, taking a step back. She watched as he reversed up onto the sidewalk, got out, then strode off down the main street. 'Not a guy to fall out with,' she muttered to herself, not sure why she felt so cross.

Some of the other drivers were doing awkward three-point turns in the tight street and heading back in the direction they'd come. Meredith hesitated. However abrupt the guy had been, she figured his advice was probably good. No sense getting lost in the hills.

She decided to explore the town on foot. She backed her rental car onto the sidewalk and parked beside his blue Peugeot. Meredith wasn't sure if Rennes-les-Bains was actually where her ancestors had come from, or if it was just an accident of timing that the photograph of the soldier from 1914 had been taken here. But it was one of the only leads she had.

She locked the car, then walked to the main entrance of the Station Thermale et Climatique. There was a hand-printed notice on the door saying it was now closed for the winter: 1st October through 30th April 2008. Meredith stared at the sign. She'd just assumed it would be open year-round and hadn't thought to call ahead.

Hands in her pockets, she stood outside awhile. The windows were dark, the building apparently empty. Even though she admitted that the search for traces of Lilly Debussy was, in part at any rate, an excuse to get herself down here, she'd had high hopes of the spa. Old records, photographs dating back to the turn of the last century when Rennes-les-Bains was one of the most fashionable resorts in the area.

Now, looking at the shuttered doors of the Station Thermale, even if there was evidence inside of Lilly being sent here to convalesce in the summer of 1900 – or else of her young man in military uniform – she wasn't going to find out.

Meredith turned away and walked back to the street. A footpath ran down the right of the spa buildings, the allée des Bains de la Reine. She followed it down to the river-bank, pulling her jacket tight around her against the sharp wind that had come up, past a large swimming pool drained of water. An air of neglect hung about the deserted terrace. The chipped blue tiles, the peeling pink-washed deck, the broken white plastic recliners. Hard to believe the pool was used at all.

She moved on. The riverbank also felt abandoned, empty of human life. Like tailgate parties in high school, the morning after the night before, when the fields were muddy and skidded with tyre tracks. The path was lined with metal benches, crooked and dispirited-looking; there was a rickety metal pergola in the shape of a crown with a wooden bench set beneath. It looked as if it hadn't been used for years.

Through force of habit, she dug into her bag and pulled out her camera. She adjusted the setting to deal with the poor light before taking a couple of shots, not convinced they'd come out. She tried to picture Lilly sitting on one of the benches, in a white shirt and black skirt, her face sheltered beneath a wide-brimmed hat, dreaming of Debussy and Paris. She tried to imagine her sepia soldier strolling along the riverbank, maybe with a girl on his arm, but couldn't. Everything was derelict, abandoned. The world had moved on.

Feeling somehow sad, nostalgic for an imagined past she'd never known, Meredith walked slowly along the bank. She followed the curved course of the river to a flat concrete bridge that crossed the water. She hesitated before walking over. The opposite bank was wilder, clearly less frequented. It was dumb to wander around a strange town alone, especially with a laptop and camera in her purse.

But Meredith felt something tugging at her. A spirit of exploration, she guessed, or adventure. She wanted to get under the skin of the town. The real place, that had been here for hundreds of years, not just the main street with its modern cafés and cars. And if it turned out she did have some sort of personal connection with the town, she didn't want to feel she'd wasted her brief amount of time here.

There was a different atmosphere on the far side of the river. Right away, Meredith had the sense of a more enduring landscape, one less influenced by people and fashions. The rough-hewn, jutting hillside seemed to rise straight out of the ground in front of her. The variegated greens and browns and coppers of the bushes and trees taking on the rich hues of dusk. It should have been a landscape that appealed, but something felt wrong about it. Two-dimensional, somehow, as if the true character of the place was concealed beneath a painted exterior.

Meredith followed the path until she could go no further. She found herself standing at the mouth of a black tunnel that led away beneath the road into the mountainside.

Some kind of storm drain?

Resting her hand on the cold brick wall of the surround, Meredith peered inside, feeling the moist air trapped beneath the stone arch whisper across her skin. The water was flowing faster here, funnelled into the narrow channel. White flecks splashed up against the brick walls as the river ran over jagged rocks.

There was a narrow ledge, just wide enough for her to stand on.

Not a smart idea to go in.

Yet she found herself taking a step into the gloom. Straight away, the smell of wet air, spray, moss and lichen hit her. The ledge was slippery as she edged in further, a little further, further still, until the twilight was just a shimmer and she could no longer see the riverbank.

Bending her head so as not to knock it on the curved wall, Meredith stopped and looked down into the water. Small black fish darting, trailing tendrils of green weed flattened by the force of the current.

Lulled by the white noise and the motion of the water, Meredith crouched down. Her eyes lost focus. It was peaceful beneath the bridge, hidden, a secret place. Here, she could more easily summon the past.

She was aware the silence seemed to have deepened. The air was empty and cold, as if all the life had been sucked out of it. She felt her heart catch and her senses sharpen. Every nerve in her body was alert. For a fleeting second, she thought she saw the outline of a face looking up at her.

It can't be. Just my own reflection.

She looked again into the choppy mirror of the water. This time, there was no doubt. A face was staring up at her from beneath the surface of the river. It was not a reflection, although Meredith had the sense of her own features hidden behind the image, but a girl with long flowing hair swaying and shifting in the current, a modern-day Ophelia. Then the eyes beneath the water seemed, slowly, to open and hold Meredith's own in their clear and direct gaze. Eyes like green glass, containing within them all the shifting colours of the water.

Meredith cried out, but now there was nothing there. No reflection, no ghostly face in the water, just the distorted shapes of the rocks and driftwood stirred up by the moving current.

Desperate to get out of the tunnel now, Meredith inched along the ledge until she was in the open air, then thumped down on a dry patch of grass.

Was it starting?

Meredith's greatest fear was that the illness that had afflicted her birth mother would one day show up in her. Ghosts, voices, haunted by things no one else could hear or see.

I'm not her.

She took deep breaths, in and out, in and out, until she felt calmer. Meredith was still shaken, but more, she was mad at herself for getting so spooked. She used the same techniques she'd taught herself way back, calling on good memories to push out the bad. Now, rather than the painful memory of Jeanette crying, she heard instead Mary's voice in her head. If Mary was here right now, she'd be cross with Meredith for wandering off on her own, for poking her nose into places she had no business to be, just like always.

A wave of homesickness washed over her. For the first time since she'd flown to Europe two weeks ago, Meredith wished she was curled up safe and sound with a book in her favourite armchair. Home, rather than wandering alone on what might turn out to be a wild goose chase, in a forgotten corner of France.

Rather than go back the way she'd come, Meredith stayed on the walkway that ran along the backs of the houses at river level. The street lights had come on and she could just make out an old woman in a flowered bathing suit and swim hat lying face up in the water, within a ring of stones, her towel folded neatly nearby. Meredith shivered, before noticing that steam was rising from the surface. Alongside the woman, an old man, his lean brown body wrinkled, was drying himself down.

Meredith admired their spirit. She tried to picture the glory days of the *fin de siècle* when Rennes-les-Bains was a thriving resort. The bathing huts on wheels, ladies and gentlemen in old-fashioned swimsuits stepping down into the hot therapeutic waters, their servants and nurses standing behind them on this same riverbank.

She failed. Like a theatre after the curtain has fallen and the house manager has turned off the lights, Rennes-les-Bains seemed too desolate for such flights of imagination.

A narrow staircase handrail led up to a pedestrian bridge of blue painted metal. She remembered the sign from earlier: LE PONT DE FER. It was right where she'd left the rental car.

Meredith climbed up. Back to civilisation.

CHAPTER 29

Her rental car was just as she'd left it, behind the blue Peugeot, but the road was still shut. A couple of other cars had joined them on the sidewalk.

To pass the time, Meredith walked past the Jardin Paul Courrent, then right up a very steep road that seemed to run straight into the hillside itself. It led to a car park. She read the tourist information board, a rustic wooden sign advertising walks to local landmarks: L'Homme Mort, La Cabanasse, La Source de la Madeleine, and a cross-country route to a neighbouring village, Rennes-le-Château.

It wasn't raining, but the air was damp and everything seemed muffled and subdued. Meredith peered up alleyways that seemed to lead nowhere, glanced into the brightly lit windows of houses, then doubled back to the main street. Straight ahead was the *mairie*, with the *tricolore* fluttering blue, white and red in the evening air. She turned left and found herself in the place des Deux Rennes.

There was a charming pizzeria on the right with wooden tables outside. Only a couple of the tables were occupied, both with groups of English people. On one, the men were talking football and Steve Reich, while the women were sharing a bottle of wine and discussing the latest Ian Rankin. On the second table was a crowd of students, eating pizza and drinking beer. One of the boys was wearing a blue studded leather jacket. Another was talking about Cuba to a darker-haired friend. The last member of the group, a girl with streaks of pink in her hair, was making the shape of a square with her hands as if framing the scene for a photograph. Meredith smiled as she walked by, reminded of her own students. The girl noticed and smiled back.

In the far corner of the square, Meredith noticed a *cloche-mur* with a single bell above the rooftops of the buildings and realised she'd found the church.

She walked down a cobbled approach that led to l'église de Saint-Celse et Saint-Nazaire. A single overhead lamp was burning in the unassuming porch, open to the elements to north and south. There were two trestle tables too, incongruous-looking and empty.

The sign on the parish noticeboard next to the door stated that the church was open from ten every morning through dusk, except for feast days, weddings and funerals. But when she tried the handle, it was locked, even though lights were on inside.

She looked at her watch. Almost seven o'clock. Maybe she'd just missed it.

Meredith turned around. On the opposite wall was a board of names, a roll call of the men of Rennes-les-Bains who'd given their lives in the First World War.

À SES GLORIEUX MORTS.

Was death ever glorious? Meredith wondered, thinking of her sepia soldier. Of her birth mother walking into Lake Michigan with her pockets weighted down with stones. Was the sacrifice worth it?

She stepped forward and read down the alphabetical list of names right to the end, knowing that it was pointless to expect Martin to be there. From what little background Mary had been able to pass on, Meredith knew that Martin was Louisa's mother's surname, not her father's. In fact, on her birth certificate it said FATHER UNKNOWN. But Meredith did know her ancestors had emigrated from France to

America in the years after the First World War, and after the research she'd done, she was pretty certain the soldier in the photograph was Louisa's father.

She just needed a name.

Something caught her eye. BOUSQUET was there on the memorial. Like the Tarot cards sitting in her bag in the trunk. Maybe the same family? Something else to check out. She moved on. At the bottom of the plaque, an unusual name: SAINT-LOUP.

Next to the board were a stone plaque in memory of Henri Boudet, curé of the parish from 1872 to 1915, and a black metal cross. Meredith thought about it. If her unknown soldier had come from here, Henri Boudet might have known him. It was a small town after all, and the dates were about right.

She copied it all down: first rule of research – and the second and third – write everything down. You never knew until later what might turn out to be relevant.

Beneath the cross were inscribed the Emperor Constantine's famous words: IN HOC SIGNO VINCES. Meredith had come across the phrase plenty of times before, although this time it set some other thought racing through her head. 'By this sign shall you conquer,' she murmured, trying to figure out what was bugging her, but nothing came.

She walked through the porch, past the main door into the church, and out into the graveyard itself. Straight ahead there was another war memorial, the same names, with one or two additions and discrepancies of spelling, as if to mark their sacrifice only once would be too little.

Generations of men, fathers, brothers, sons, all those lives.

Meredith walked slowly in the sombre twilight down the gravelled path that ran alongside the church. Tombs, graves, stone angels and crosses loomed up at her as she passed. Every now and again, she paused to read an inscription. Certain names repeated over, generation after generation of local families, remembered in granite and marble – Fromilhague and Saunière, Denarnaud and Gabignaud.

At the furthest boundary of the cemetery, overlooking the river gorge, Meredith found herself standing before an ornate mausoleum with the words FAMILLE LASCOMBE-BOUSQUET carved above the metal grille.

She crouched down and, in the last vestiges of daylight, read of the marriages and births that had united the Lascombe and Bousquet families in life and now in death. Guy Lascombe and his wife had been killed in October 1864. The last of the Lascombe line had been Jules, who died in January 1891. The final surviving member of the Bousquet branch of the family, Madeleine Bousquet, had passed on in 1955.

Meredith straightened up, aware of the familiar prickling feeling on the back of her neck. It wasn't just the Tarot deck Laura had pressed on her and the coincidence of the Bousquet name, but something else. Something about the date, something she'd seen but not paid enough attention to at the time.

Then she got it. The year 1891 kept coming up, more than its fair share. She noticed that date in particular because of its personal significance. It was the date printed on the piece of music. *Sepulchre 1891*. She could see the title and the number in her mind's eye as clearly as if she was holding it in her hand.

But there was something more. She ran back over everything in her mind from the second she'd walked into the churchyard, until she figured it out. Not only the year but the same date.

With a burst of adrenaline, Meredith hurried back through the tombs, weaving in and out, checking the inscriptions, and found she was right. Her memory wasn't playing tricks on her. She pulled out her notebook and started to scribble, recording the same date of death for different people, three, four times over.

All had died 31st October in 1891 or 1897.

Behind her, the bell began to toll.

Meredith turned round and looked at the lights inside the church, then glanced up and saw that there were now stars dotted across the sky. She could hear voices too, a low murmuring. She heard the church door open, a rush of louder voices before it shut again with a clatter.

She retraced her steps back into the porch. The wooden trestle tables were now in use. One was covered in gifts – flowers in cellophane, bouquets, houseplants in terracotta pots. The second was laid with a thick red felt cloth with a large book of condolence set on it.

Meredith couldn't resist taking a look. Beneath that day's date was a name and dates of birth and death: SEYMOUR FREDERICK LAWRENCE: 15 SEPTEMBRE 1938–24 SEPTEMBRE 2007.

She realised the funeral was about to begin. Not wanting to get caught up, she walked quickly back into the place de Deux Rennes. The square was busy now. Thronging around, quiet but not silent, were people of all ages. Men in blazers, women in pressed pastels, kids in suits and smart dresses. What Mary would call Sunday best.

Standing in the shadow of the pizzeria, not wanting to look like she was rubber-necking, Meredith watched as the mourners disappeared into the presbytery next to the church for a few minutes, then emerged and went into the porch to sign the book of condolence. It seemed the whole town had turned out.

'Do you know what's going on?' she asked the waitress.

'*Funérailles, Madame. Un bien-aimé.*'

A thin woman with short dark hair was leaning against the wall. She was standing perfectly still, but her eyes were darting around all over. When she lifted her hand to light her cigarette, the sleeves of her shirt slipped down and Meredith noticed scars around both wrists.

As if sensing someone was looking, the woman turned her head and looked right at her.

'*Un bien-aimé?*' Meredith said, casting round for something to say.

'Someone popular. Well respected,' the woman replied in English.

Of course. Pretty obvious.

'Thanks.' Meredith gave an embarrassed smile. 'I wasn't thinking.'

The woman kept staring a moment longer, then turned her head away. The bell began to toll more insistently, a thin and reedy sound. The crowd stood back as four men came out of the presbytery carrying a closed casket. Behind them, a young guy dressed in black, late twenties maybe, with a mop of black hair. His face was white, his jaw rigid, as if struggling to keep control.

Beside him was an older man, also dressed in black. Meredith recognised the driver of the blue Peugeot. She felt a shot of guilt at her reaction earlier.

No wonder he was so abrupt.

Meredith watched as the coffin made its short journey from the presbytery to the church. The tourists at the café opposite got to their feet as the mourners filed past. The students stopped talking and stood in silence with their hands clasped in front of them as the slowly moving mass of people disappeared down the passageway.

The door of the church fell shut with a clatter. The bell stopped ringing, leaving only an echo in the evening air. Quickly, everything in the square returned to normal. Then Meredith noticed a car driving up the main street and realised, to her relief, that the road must be open again. She wanted to get to the hotel.

As she stepped out of the lee of the building and took in the whole vista, rather than just one detail of it, suddenly she saw it. The photograph of the young soldier, her ancestor, had been taken here, the precise spot framed by the buildings leading to the Pont Vieux, between a line of *platanes* and the wooded hillside glimpsed through the gap in the houses.

Meredith dug into her purse, pulled out the envelope and held up the image.

An exact match.

The café signs and the bed and breakfast on the east side of the square were new, but otherwise it was the same view. Right here, in 1914, a young man had stood and smiled at the camera before going off to fight. Her great-great-grandfather, she was certain of it.

With renewed enthusiasm for the task she'd set herself, Meredith walked back to her car. She'd been here little more than an hour and already she'd found something out.

CHAPTER 30

Meredith started her car. As she drove past the place de Deux Rennes, she glanced at the spot where the photograph had been taken, as if she might see the outline of her long-dead ancestor standing smiling at her from between the trees.

Pretty soon, she had cleared the outskirts of the town and was out onto the unlit road beyond. The trees took on strange, shifting shapes. The occasional building, a house or a shed for animals loomed at her out of the dark. She locked her door with her elbow and heard the reassuring click of the mechanism. The silence of the country seemed absolute. Beside her was a mass of forest. Above, an expanse of sky lit only with a few stars. There was no sign of life, not even a fox or a cat.

Meredith found the road to Sougraigne marked on the brochure and turned left. She rubbed her eyes, aware that she was too beat to be driving. The bushes and telegraph poles at the verge seemed to be swaying, vibrating. A couple of times, she thought there was someone walking along the side of the road, backlit by her headlamps, but when she got level, she discovered it was only a sign or a roadside shrine.

She tried to keep focused, but she could feel her tired thoughts wandering. It had been a long day – the Tarot reading, the cab ride across Paris, the drive down here, the rollercoaster of emotions – her energy had run out. All she could think about now was a long, hot shower, then a glass of wine and dinner. Then a long, long sleep.

Jesus!

Meredith slammed on the brakes. There was someone standing right in the middle of the road. A woman in a long red cloak, the hood pulled up over her head. Meredith jerked the steering wheel, knowing there was no way to avoid the collision. As if in slow motion, she felt the tyres lose the road. She threw up her hands to brace herself for the impact. The last thing she saw was a pair of wide green eyes staring right at her.

No!

The car skidded. The rear wheels swung round, sliding across the road, rocking to a stop inches away from a ditch. There was a roaring noise coming from somewhere, hammering her senses. It was a moment before she realised it was only the sound of her own blood in her ears.

Meredith opened her eyes.

For a few seconds, she sat gripping the wheel, as if afraid to let go. Then, with a rush of cold dread, she realised she had to force herself to get out. She might have hit someone. Killed someone.

She fumbled with the lock and stepped out of the car on shaking legs. Dreading what she was going to find, she walked carefully round to the front, bracing herself to see a body caught under the wheels.

There was nothing. Not knowing what to think, Meredith cast her disbelieving eyes all around, back in the direction she had come, ahead to where the light from the headlights disappeared into a pinpoint of black.

Nothing. The forest was silent. No sign of life.

'Hello?' she called. 'Is anybody there? Are you OK? Hello?'

Nothing but her own voice echoing back at her.

Bewildered, she examined the front of the car. There were no marks at all. She walked round the vehicle, running her hand over the bodywork, but it was clean.

Meredith got back in the car. She was certain she'd seen someone. She hadn't imagined it. Had she? She glanced in the mirror but saw only her own ghostly reflection looking back at her. Then, out of the shadows, the desperate face of her birth mother.

I am not going crazy.

She rubbed her eyes, gave herself a couple of minutes more, then started the car. Spooked by what had happened – what *hadn't* happened – she took it steady, leaving the window open to clear her head.

Meredith was relieved when she saw the sign for the hotel. She turned off the road onto a winding single track, which climbed steeply up the hillside. After a couple of minutes more, she arrived at two stone pillars and a pair of ornate black wrought-iron gates. On the wall was a grey slate sign: HÔTEL DOMAINE DE LA CADE.

Triggered by a motion sensor, the gates slowly opened to let her through. There was something eerie about the silence, and Meredith shivered. The woods seemed almost to be alive, living and breathing, watching. Malevolent, somehow. She'd be glad to get inside.

The tyres crunched as she drove slowly up a long drive lined with sweet chestnut trees, like sentinels on duty. The lawns stretched out on either side into blackness. Finally she rounded a slight curve in the drive and, at last, got sight of the hotel.

Even after everything that had happened tonight, the unexpected beauty of the place blew her away. The hotel was an elegant three-storey building, with whitewashed walls covered with flaming red and green ivy. Balustrades on the first floor and a row of round windows at the very top – the old servants' quarters. A house perfectly in proportion; amazing when she considered that part of the original *maison de maître* had been destroyed by fire. It all looked totally authentic.

Meredith found a parking space at the front of the hotel and carried her bags up the curved stone steps. She was glad to have arrived in one piece, although she couldn't quite shake the queasy feeling in the pit of her stomach from her near miss on the road. And the scene at the river.

Just tired, she told herself.

She felt better the second she stepped inside the spacious and elegant lobby. There was a black-and-red chequerboard tiled floor and a delicate cream paper of yellow and green flowers on the walls. Everywhere, mirrors and glass reflected the light from the chandeliers, gilt frames and glass wall sconces.

Straight ahead was a sweeping central staircase, the handrails glinting in the diffused light of the glass chandelier, with the front desk to the right – a large wooden clawfooted table rather than a counter. The walls were covered in period photographs. Men in military uniform – Napoleonic rather than First World War at first glance – ladies in puffed sleeves and wide skirts, family portraits, scenes of Rennes-les-Bains in days gone by. Meredith smiled. Plenty to check out over the next few days.

She stepped up to the desk.

'*Bienvenue, Madame.*'

'Hi.'

'Welcome to the Domaine de la Cade. You have a reservation?'

'Yes, it's Martin. M-A-R-T-I-N.'

'It is your first time with us?'

'It is.'

Meredith filled in the form and gave her credit card details, the third she'd used that day. She was handed a map of the hotel and grounds, another of the surrounding area, and an old-fashioned brass key with a red tassel and a disc with the name of her room on it: LA CHAMBRE JAUNE.

She suddenly felt a prickling on the back of her neck again, as if a person had come up behind her and was standing a little too close. She glanced over her shoulder, but there was no one there.

'The Yellow Room is on the first floor, Madame Martin.'

'Excuse me?' Meredith turned back to the clerk.

'Your room is on the first floor. The elevator is opposite the concierge,' the woman continued, indicating a discreet sign. 'Or, if you wish, take the stairs up and go to the right. Last orders for dinner are at nine-thirty. You wish for me to reserve a table?'

Meredith glanced at her watch. Seven forty-five. 'That'd be great. Eight-thirty?'

'Very good, Madame. The terrace bar – the entrance is through the library – is open until midnight.'

'Great. Thank you.'

'Do you need help with your luggage?'

'No, I'm good, thanks.'

With a backward glance at the empty lobby, Meredith took the stairs to the impressive first-floor landing. At the top, she looked down and noticed there was a boudoir grand tucked into the shadows beneath the staircase. Nice instrument, by the look of it, although it seemed a weird place to put a piano. The lid was closed.

As she walked along the passage, she grinned at the fact that all the rooms had names rather than numbers. The Anjou Suite, the Blue Room, Blanche de Castille, Henri IV.

Her room was right at the end. With the shimmer of anticipation she always got when going to a hotel for the first time, she fumbled with the heavy key, pushed the door open with the toe of her sneaker and then flicked the switch.

She gave a wide smile.

There was a huge mahogany bed in the centre of the room. The dresser, closet and two nightstands all matched in the same deep-red wood. She opened the doors of the closet and found that the minibar, TV and remote were all hidden inside. On a small wooden book-holder placed on top of the bureau, a selection of old books. Meredith ran her eyes along the spines – the usual thrillers and classics, a guide to some kind of hat museum in Espéraza, a couple of books on local history.

She crossed the room to the window and opened the shutters, breathing in the heady smell of earth and night air. The dark lawns stretched away for what seemed like miles. She could just make out an ornamental lake, then a tall hedge separating the formal part of the garden from the woods beyond.

Meredith unpacked – properly this time, rather than leaving everything in the bag as she had in Paris – then tried out the fancy Molton Brown soaps and shampoo in the bathroom.

Thirty minutes later, feeling more like herself, she was wrapped in a huge white bathrobe and sitting down at her laptop. Discovering she couldn't get internet access, she reached over and dialled reception to request the password.

She was struck by the coincidence as she typed it in – CONSTANTINE. She sent her daily email to Mary, letting her know she'd arrived safely. Next, she looked into her checking account and saw with relief that the money from the publisher had at last come through.

Finally.

She was about to log off when she thought she might as well see if there was anything about the fire at the Domaine de la Cade in October 1897. There wasn't much more than she'd learned already from the hotel brochure.

Next, she typed LASCOMBE into the search engine.

This did yield a little new information about Jules Lascombe. He appeared to have been some sort of amateur historian, an expert on the Visigoth era and local folklore and superstitions. He'd even had a few books – pamphlets – privately published by a local printing company, Bousquet.

Meredith's eyes narrowed. She clicked on a link and information flashed up on the screen. A well-known local family, as well as being the owners of the largest department store in Rennes-les-Bains and a substantial printing business, the Bousquets were also first cousins of Jules Lascombe and had inherited the Domaine de la Cade on his death.

Meredith scrolled down the page until she found what she was looking for. She clicked, then started to read:

The Bousquet Tarot is a rare deck, not used much outside France. The earliest examples of this deck were printed by the Bousquet publishing company, located outside Rennes-les-Bains in south-west France, in the late 1890s.

Said to be based on a far older deck, dating back to the seventeenth century, aspects unique to this deck include the substitution of Maître, Maîtresse, Fils and Fille for the four court cards in each suit and the period clothing and iconography. The artist of the major arcana cards, which are contemporaneous with the first printed deck, is unknown.

Beside her on the desk, the phone rang. Meredith jumped, the sound raucous in the silence of the room. Without taking her eyes from the screen, Meredith grabbed the receiver.

'Yes? Yes, this is she.'

It was the restaurant asking if she still required her table. Meredith glanced at the clock on her laptop and was amazed to find it was eight-forty.

'Actually, I think I'll get something sent up instead,' she said, but was swiftly informed that room service stopped at six.

Meredith was torn. She didn't want to stop, not now she was getting somewhere – although whether it mattered or what it meant was another issue. But she was ravenous.

'I'll be right down,' she said.

CHAPTER 31

'What's wrong with you?' Julian Lawrence said.

'Apart from having just buried my father?' Hal shot back. 'Apart from that, you mean?'

He slammed the door of the Peugeot shut, too hard, then started to walk towards the steps, yanking off his tie and shoving it into his jacket pocket as he went.

'Keep your voice down,' his uncle hissed. 'We don't want another scene. There's been enough of that this evening.' He followed his nephew across the staff car park towards the back entrance of the hotel. 'What the devil were you playing at? And in front of the whole town.'

From a distance, they looked like a father and son going to some sort of formal dinner. Smart, dressed in black jacket and suit, polished shoes. Only the expressions on their faces indicated the dislike the two men felt for one another.

'That's it, isn't it?' Hal said. 'All you care about. Reputation. What people might think.' He tapped his head. 'Has the fact that it was your brother – my father – in that box even penetrated your consciousness? I doubt it!'

Julian reached out and put his hand on his nephew's shoulder.

'Look, Hal,' in a softer voice. 'I understand you're upset. Everybody understands. It's only natural. But throwing around wild accusations isn't helping. If anything, it's making it worse. It's starting to make people think there is some substance to the allegations.'

Hal tried to shake himself free. His uncle's grip tightened.

'The town – the commissariat, the *mairie* – everyone's sympathetic to your loss. And your father was well liked. But if you keep on—'

Hal glared at him. 'Are you threatening me?' He jerked his shoulder, shrugging his uncle's hand away.

The shutters came down over Julian Lawrence's eyes. Gone was the look of compassion, familial concern. In its place, irritation, and something else. Contempt.

'For Christ's sake, pull yourself together. You're twenty-eight years old, not some spoiled public schoolboy!' He walked into the hotel. 'We'll talk in the morning,' he said over his shoulder.

Hal strode past him. 'There's nothing more to say. Nothing you can say or do is going to make me change my mind.'

He veered to the right and headed for the bar. His uncle waited a moment, watching him until the glass door had swung shut between them. Then he walked round to the front desk.

'Evening, Eloise. Everything fine?'

'Very quiet tonight.' She smiled up at him with sympathy. 'Funerals are always so difficult, no?'

He rolled his eyes. 'You have no idea,' he said. He put his hands on the desk between them. 'Any messages?'

'Only one,' she said, handing him a white envelope. 'But everything went all right in the church, *oui*?'

He nodded grimly. 'As well as could be expected in the circumstances.'

He glanced at the handwriting on the envelope. A slow smile broke across his face. It was the information he'd been waiting for about a Visigoth burial chamber discovered in Quillan, which Julian hoped might have some relevance to his excavations at the Domaine de la Cade. The Quillan site was sealed; no inventory had yet been released.

'What time did this come, Eloise?'

'At eight o'clock, Monsieur Lawrence. Delivered by hand.'

He drummed his fingers on the counter in a tattoo. 'Excellent. Thank you, Eloise. Have a good evening now. I'll be in my office if anyone needs me.'

CHAPTER 32

By nine forty-five, Meredith had finished dinner. Although she was wiped out, there was no point turning in just yet. She had too much on her mind.

She looked out through the front door to the darkness beyond.

Maybe a walk? The paths were brightly lit but deserted and quiet. She pulled her red cardigan around her slim frame and dismissed the idea.

Not after what happened earlier.

Meredith pushed the thought away. There was a murmur of noise slipping down the passageway leading to the terrace bar.

Walking past display cases filled with china and porcelain, she pushed open the glass door and walked in. The room looked more like a library than a bar. The walls were covered floor to ceiling with books in glass-fronted cabinets. In the corner, there was a set of sliding wooden steps, for reaching the higher shelves.

Leather armchairs were grouped at low round tables, like a gentlemen's country club. The atmosphere was comfortable and relaxed. Two couples, a family group and several men on their own.

There wasn't a free table, so Meredith took a stool at the counter. She put her key and the brochure down and picked up the bar list.

The bartender smiled. '*Cocktails d'un coté, vins de l'autre.*'

Meredith turned the card over and read the wines by the glass on the reverse, then put the menu down.

'*Quelque chose de la région?*' she suggested. '*Qu'est-ce que vous recommandez?*'

'*Blanc, rouge, rosé?*'

'*Blanc.*'

'Try the Domaine Begude Chardonnay,' said another voice. An English voice.

Meredith turned to see a guy sitting a couple of stools further down the bar. A smart, well-cut jacket was draped over the two seats between them and his smart shirt, pants and shoes seemed at odds with his defeated air. A mop of thick black hair hung over his face.

'Local vineyard. Cépie, just north of Limoux. Good stuff.'

He turned his head and looked at her, as if checking she was listening to him, then went back to staring into the bottom of his glass of red wine.

Such blue eyes.

Meredith realised she recognised him. It was the younger guy she'd seen earlier in the place des Deux Rennes, walking behind the casket in the funeral cortège. Somehow, the fact that she knew that about him made her feel awkward. Like she'd been snooping, even though she hadn't meant to.

She looked at him. 'OK.' Then back to the bartender. '*S'il vous plaît.*' She glanced back at the guy along the bar. 'Thanks for the recommendation.'

'Don't mention it,' he said.

Meredith shifted on her stool, not sure if they were going to have a conversation or not. He made the decision for her, turning round and offering his hand across the expanse of black leather and wood.

'I'm Hal, by the way,' he said.

'Meredith. Meredith Martin.'

The barman put a paper mat in front of her, then a glass filled with a rich, deep-yellow wine. Acutely aware of Hal watching her, Meredith took a sip. Light, lemony, clean, it was reminiscent of the white wines Mary and Bill served on special occasions or when she came home on weekends.

'It's great. Good call.'

The barman glanced at Hal. '*Encore un verre, Monsieur?*'

He nodded. 'Thanks, Xavier.' He twisted round so he was half facing her. 'So, Meredith Martin. You're American.'

The moment the words were out of his mouth, he dropped his elbows to the bar and pushed his fingers through his unruly hair. Meredith wondered if he might be a little drunk.

'Sorry, what a ridiculous thing to say.'

'It's OK.' She smiled. 'And yes, I am.'

'Just arrived?'

'A couple of hours ago.' She took another sip of wine and felt the alcohol hit her stomach. 'What about you?'

'My father ...' He stopped, a despairing expression on his face. 'My uncle owns the place,' he finished.

Meredith figured it was Hal's father's funeral she'd witnessed, and felt even worse for him. She waited until she felt his eyes come back to her.

'Sorry,' he said. 'Not a great day.' He drained his glass, then reached out for the refill the barman had placed in front of him. 'Are you here for business or pleasure?'

Meredith felt like she was stuck in some kind of surreal play. She knew why he was so distracted but couldn't admit it. And Hal, trying to make small talk with a total stranger, missing all his cues. The pauses between comments were all way too long, his train of thought disjointed.

'Both,' she replied. 'I'm a writer.'

'A journalist?' he said quickly.

'No. I'm working on a book. A biography of the composer Claude Debussy.'

Meredith saw the spark go out of his eyes and the same hooded look come down again. Not the reaction she was looking for.

'It's a beautiful place,' she said quickly, taking in the bar. 'Has your uncle been here long?'

Hal sighed. 'He and my father bought it together in 2003. Spent a fortune doing it up.'

Meredith couldn't think of what to say next. He wasn't exactly making it easy.

'Dad only came out here full-time back in May. He wanted to get more involved in the day-to-day running of the . . . He . . .' He stopped. Meredith heard the catch in his voice. 'He died in a car crash four weeks ago.' He swallowed hard. 'It was his funeral today.'

In her relief that the information was out in the open, Meredith reached over and took Hal's hand before she even realised she'd done it.

'I'm sorry.'

Meredith saw some of the tension leave his shoulders. They just sat there awhile, hand in silent hand, then she gently slid her fingers away under the cover of picking up her glass.

'Four weeks? That's quite a time before . . .'

He looked at her. 'It wasn't straightforward. Post-mortem took a while. The body was only released last week.'

Meredith nodded, wondering what the issue had been. Hal sat in silence.

'Do you live here?' she asked, trying to get the conversation going again.

Hal shook his head. 'London. Investment banker, although just handed in my notice.' He hesitated. 'I'd had enough anyway. Even before this. I was working fourteen-hour days, seven days a week. Great money, but no time to spend it.'

'Do you have other family out here? I mean, relatives in this part of France?'

'No. English through and through.'

Meredith paused a moment. 'What are your plans now?'

He shrugged.

'Will you stay in London?'

'Don't know,' he said. 'Doubt it.'

Meredith took another mouthful of wine.

'Debussy,' Hal said, as if he had only just registered what she'd said. 'I'm embarrassed to admit I don't know the first thing about him.'

Meredith smiled, relieved he was at least making an effort.

'No reason why you should,' she said.

'What's his connection with this part of France?'

Meredith laughed. 'Tenuous,' she said. 'In August 1900, Debussy wrote a letter to a friend saying he was sending his wife Lilly to the Pyrenees to convalesce after an operation. Reading between the lines, a termination. So far, no one's proved the story one way or the other – and if Lilly did go, it sure wasn't for long because she was back in Paris in October.'

Hal pulled a face. 'It's possible. It's hard to imagine it now, but I believe Rennes-les-Bains was a very popular resort at that time.'

'It was,' Meredith agreed. 'Particularly with Parisians.'

'It seems a lot of effort to go to,' he said. 'Coming all this way on the off-chance Lilly Debussy was here. Is it that important in the overall scheme of things?'

'If I'm honest, no, not really,' she replied, surprised at how defensive she felt. As if her real motive for coming to Rennes-les-Bains was painfully transparent. 'But it would be a great piece of original research, something no one else has got. That can make all the difference to making one book stand out from the others.' She paused. 'And it's an interesting period of Debussy's life too. Lilly Texier was only twenty-four when she met him, working as a mannequin. They married a year later in 1899. He dedicated a lot of his works to friends, lovers, colleagues, and it's undeniable that Lilly's name doesn't figure on many scores, songs or piano pieces.' Meredith was aware she was gabbling, but she was caught up in her own story now and couldn't stop. 'The way I see it, Lilly was right there during the crucial years leading up to the first performance of Debussy's only opera, *Pelléas et Mélisande*, in 1902. That was when his fortunes, his reputation, his status changed for good. Lilly was by his side when he made it. I figure that's got to count for something.'

She stopped to draw breath and saw, for the first time since they'd started talking, that Hal was smiling.

'Sorry,' she grinned. 'I didn't mean to get so carried away. It's a terrible habit, assuming everyone will be as interested as I am.'

'I think it's great there's something you're so passionate about,' he said quietly. Caught by the shifting tone of his voice, Meredith looked across at him and saw that his blue eyes were fixed firmly on her. To her embarrassment, she felt herself blush.

'I like the research process better than the actual writing,' she said. 'All the mental excavation. All the obsessing over scores and old articles and letters, trying to bring to life a moment, a snapshot, from the past. It's all about reconstruction, about context, about getting under the skin of a different time and place, but with the benefit of hindsight.'

'Detective work.'

'In a way.'

'When are you hoping to finish?'

'I'm due to be done April next year. I've got way too much material as it is. All the academic papers published in the *Cahiers Debussy* and the *Œuvres complètes de Claude Debussy*, notes on every biography ever published. Added to which, Debussy himself was a prolific letter writer. He wrote for a daily newspaper, *Gil Blas*, as well as producing a handful of reviews for *La Revue blanche*. You name it, I've read it.'

Embarrassment hit her when she realised she was doing it again. She glanced over at him, intending to apologise, but something caught her. His boyish expression reminded her of someone, though she couldn't remember who.

A wave of tiredness washed over her. She looked at Hal, lost in his own thoughts, so slipped from her stool.

Hal's head snapped up. 'You're not going?'

Meredith smiled. 'It's been a long day.'

'Of course.' He got down from his stool too. 'Look, I know this probably sounds outrageous – I don't know – but if you're around tomorrow, maybe we could go out. Or meet for a drink?'

Meredith blinked. On the one hand, she liked Hal. He was charming, and clearly needed company. On the other, she needed to focus on finding out what she could about her birth family. She didn't want to get distracted.

'Of course, if you're busy . . .' he started to say.

It was the undercurrent of disappointment in his voice that made her mind up. Besides, apart from the time spent with Laura during the reading – and that hardly counted – she'd not had a face-to-face conversation with anyone longer than a couple of sentences in weeks.

'Sure, why not,' she heard herself say.

Hal smiled, properly this time, transforming his face. 'Great.'

'But I was intending to head out pretty early to do some research.'

'I could come along for the ride,' he suggested. 'Might be able to help out a little. I'm not an expert, but I've been coming here on and off for the last few years. I know the area quite well.'

'It might be pretty boring.'

Hal shrugged. 'I can do boring. Do you have a list of places you want to visit?'

'I thought I'd play it by ear. I had hoped to get something from the old spa buildings in Rennes-les-Bains, but they're all closed up for the winter. I thought maybe if I went to the *mairie* there might be a person who could help.'

Hal's face clouded over. 'They're useless,' he said. 'Like beating your head against a brick wall.'

'Sorry,' she said quickly. 'I didn't mean to remind you of . . .'

Hal raised his hands. 'No, I'm sorry. It's me.' He sighed, then smiled at her again. 'I have a suggestion. Given the period of time you're interested in for Lilly Debussy, you might find something useful in the museum in Rennes-le-Château. I've only been there once, but I remember it gave a pretty good account of what life might have been like round here at that time.'

Meredith felt a spike of excitement. 'That sounds great.'

'Shall we meet in reception at ten?'

Meredith hesitated, then decided she was being too cautious.

'OK,' she said. 'Ten is good.'

He pushed his hands deep into his pockets. 'Night, then.'

Meredith nodded. 'See you tomorrow.'

CHAPTER 33

Back in her room, Meredith was too wound up to sleep. She ran the conversation between them over in her mind, trying to work out if she was reading too much into things. He was clearly lonely, and no wonder if he'd recently lost his father.

She stared at her reflection in the mirror as she brushed her teeth, feeling sorry for him. Hal seemed so vulnerable. She spat the toothpaste into the basin. He probably wasn't interested in her at all. He probably just needed a little company.

She climbed into bed and turned off the light, plunging the room into an inky darkness. But as she started to drift off, the face Meredith had seen in the water, the weird experience on the road, came rushing into her mind. Worse, the tortured face of her birth mother, begging the voices to leave her in peace.

Meredith's eyes snapped open.

She was here to find out who she was, about her family, to escape the shadow of her mother, not bring her back, more real than ever. Meredith pushed her childhood memories away, replacing them with the Tarot images she'd been carrying around in her head all day. Le Mat and La Justice. The Devil with blue eyes, the Lovers chained, hopeless, at his feet.

She replayed Laura's words in her mind, let her thoughts wander from card to card, slipping down into sleep. Her eyes grew heavy. Now, Meredith was thinking of Lilly Debussy, with a bullet lodged for eternity in her chest. Of Debussy scowling and smoking at the piano as he played. Of Mary sitting on the porch in Chapel Hill, her chair rocking back and forwards as she read. Of the soldier framed by the *platanes* in the place de Deux Rennes.

The hotel fell silent. Night wrapped its black arms around the house. The grounds of the Domaine de la Cade lay sleeping beneath a pale moon.

The hours passed. Midnight, two o'clock, four.

Suddenly, Meredith jolted awake, her eyes wide open in the dark. Every nerve in her body was vibrating, alert. Every muscle, every sinew, pulled as tight as a violin string.

Someone was singing.

No, not singing. Playing the piano. And close.

She sat up. The room was cold. The same penetrating chill she'd felt under the bridge. The darkness was different too, less dense, more fragmented. Meredith felt almost as if she could see the particles of light and dark and shadow breaking down in front of her. There was a breeze coming in from somewhere, even though she could swear all the windows were shut – a light breeze brushing over her shoulders and neck, skimming without touching, pressing, whispering.

There's someone in the room.

She told herself it was impossible. She'd have heard something. Yet she was gripped with an overwhelming certainty that someone was standing at the foot of the bed, watching. Two eyes burning in the darkness. Trails of sweat slid cold between her shoulder blades and into the hollow between her breasts.

Adrenaline kicked in.

Now. Do it.

She counted to three, then rolled over and flicked on the light.

The darkness was scattered. All the regular everyday objects rushed back to greet her. Nothing out of place. Closet, table, window, mantelpiece, bureau – all just as they should be. The cheval mirror, standing by the door to the bathroom, reflecting the light.

No one.

Meredith slumped back against the mahogany head-board. Relief washed over her. On the nightstand, the clock blinked the time in red. Four forty-five. Not eyes at all, just the flashing LED of the radio alarm reflected in the mirror.

Just a regular nightmare.

She should have expected it after the stuff that had happened yesterday.

Meredith kicked back the covers to cool herself down and lay still awhile, hands folded on her chest like a figure on a tomb. Then she got out of bed. She needed to move around, do something physical. She grabbed a bottle of mineral water from the minibar, then walked over to the window and looked down over the silent gardens, still in the moonlight. The weather had broken and the terrace below glistened with rain. There was a veil of white mist floating in the air above the line of the trees.

Meredith pressed her warm hand against the cold glass, as if she could push the bad thoughts away. Not for the first time, doubt at what she was getting herself into slipped in. What if there was nothing to find? All the time, the idea of coming to Rennes-les-Bains, armed with only a handful of old photographs and a piece of piano music, had kept her going. But now she was here, and could see what a small place it was, she felt less certain. The whole idea of tracing her birth family back here, without even having proper names to search for, seemed ridiculous.

Meredith had no idea how long she stood there, just thinking, working things through at the window. Only when she realised that her toes were numb with cold did she turn to look at the clock. She gave a sigh of relief. It was past five o'clock in the morning. She'd killed enough time. Chased away the ghosts, the demons of the night. The face in the water, the figure on the road, the intimidating images on the cards.

This time when she lay down to sleep, the room was peaceful. No eyes staring at her, no shimmering presence in the darkness, just the blinking electric numbers of the alarm clock. She closed her eyes.

Her soldier melted into Debussy, became Hal.

PART V

Domaine de la Cade
September 1891

CHAPTER 34

Léonie yawned and opened her eyes. She stretched her arms above her head, then propped herself up on her generous white pillows. Despite the surfeit of *blanquette de Limoux* drunk last evening – or perhaps as a consequence of it – she had slept well.

The Yellow Room was pretty in the morning light. For a while, she lay in bed listening to the rare sounds that broke the deep silence of the countryside. The dawn songs of the birds, the wind in the trees. It was more pleasant by far than waking at home to a grey Parisian daybreak, the sounds of screeching metal from the Gare Saint-Lazare.

At eight o'clock, Marieta brought the breakfast tray. She placed it upon the table by the window, then drew the curtains, flooding the room with the first refracted rays of sunlight. Through the imperfect glass of the old casements, Léonie could see that the sky was bright and blue, flecked with trailing wisps of purple and white cloud.

'Thank you, Marieta,' she said. 'I can manage.'

'Very good, Madomaisèla.'

Léonie threw off the covers and swung her feet down to the carpet, finding her slippers and her dressing gown. She splashed a little of last night's water on her face, then sat down at the table in front of the window, feeling sophisticated to be breakfasting alone in her bedchamber.

The only time she did so at home was when Du Pont was visiting Maman.

She lifted the lid on the pot of steaming coffee, releasing the delicious aroma of freshly roasted beans, like a genie from a lamp. Beside the silver pot stood a jug of frothy warm milk, a bowl of white sugar cubes and a pair of silver tongs. She lifted the pressed linen napkin to discover a plate of warm white bread, a dish of creamy whipped butter and three different jams in individual china dishes.

As she ate, she gazed out across the gardens. A white mist hung suspended over the valley between the hills, skimming the tops of the trees. The lawns lay peaceful and calm under the September sun, no evidence of the wind that had threatened the previous evening.

Léonie dressed in a plain woollen skirt and high-necked blouse, then picked up the book Anatole had brought for her last evening. She had a fancy to see the library for herself, investigate the dusty stacks and polished spines. If she were challenged – although she saw no reason why she should be, given that Isolde had asked them to treat the house as their own – she would have the excuse that she was returning Monsieur Baillard's pamphlet.

She opened the door and stepped out into the passage. The rest of the household appeared to be sleeping. Everything was still. No rattle of coffee cups, no whistling from Anatole's bedroom as he made his morning toilette, no sign of life at all. Downstairs, the hall also was deserted, although behind the pass door that led to the servants' quarters, she could hear the sound of voices and the distant clattering of pots in the kitchen.

The library occupied the south-west corner of the house and was accessed by means of a small passageway, tucked in between the drawing room and the door to the study. Indeed, it was amazing that Anatole had stumbled upon it at all. There had been so little time to explore yesterday afternoon.

The corridor was bright and airy and wide enough to accommodate several glass cases mounted upon the walls. The first displayed Marseille and Rouen china; the second a small, ancient *cuirasse*, two sabres, a foil that resembled Anatole's favourite fencing weapon and a musket; the third case, smaller than the others, contained a selection of military medals and ribbons, laid out on blue velvet. There was nothing to indicate to whom they had been awarded or for what. Léonie presumed they belonged to their Oncle Jules.

She lifted the handle of the library door and slipped inside. Instantly, she felt the room's peace and tranquillity – the smell of beeswax, honey and ink, dusty velvet and blotters. It was more generous in size than she had expected and had a dual aspect, with windows looking out to the south and the west. The curtains, fashioned from heavy gold-and-blue brocade, fell in folds from ceiling to floor.

The sound of her clipped heels was swallowed up by the thick oval rug that filled the centre of the room and upon which stood a pedestal table, large enough to accommodate even the most substantial volume. There was an inkwell and pen, beside a leather writing pad with a fresh blotter.

Léonie decided to start her exploration at the corner furthest from the door. She ran her eyes along each shelf in turn, reading the names on the spines, letting her fingers trail over the leather bindings, pausing from time to time when a particular volume caught her interest.

She came upon a beautiful missal with an ornate double clasp, printed in Tours, with rich green-and-gold endpapers and delicate, tissue-thin paper protecting the engravings. She read, upon the flyleaf, her late uncle's name – Jules Lascombe – inscribed with the date of his confirmation.

In the next stack, she discovered a first edition of Maistre's *Voyage autour de ma chambre*. It was battered and dog-eared, unlike Anatole's pristine copy at home. In another alcove, she found a collection of both religious and fervently anti-religious texts, grouped together as if to cancel one another out.

In the section devoted to contemporary French literature, there was a complete set of Zola's *Rougon-Macquart* novels, as well as Flaubert, Maupassant and Huysmans – indeed, many of the intellectually improving texts Anatole tried in vain to press upon her, even a first edition of Stendhal's *Le Rouge et le noir*. There were a few works in translation, but nothing entirely to her taste except for Baudelaire's translations of Monsieur Poe. Nothing by Madame Radcliffe or Monsieur Le Fanu.

In the furthest corner of the library, Léonie found herself in an alcove dedicated to books on local history, where, she presumed, Anatole had come upon Monsieur Baillard's monograph. She found her spirits quickening as she stepped from the warmth and space of the main area into the confined, sombre stacks. The alcove harboured a damp mugginess that caught at the back of her throat.

She cast her eyes along the serried rows of spines and covers until she reached the letter 'B'. There was no obviously vacant space. Puzzled, she squeezed the slim volume in where she believed it should go. Her task completed, she turned back towards the door.

Only then did she notice the three or four glass display cases high up on the wall to the right of the door, presumably to house the more valuable volumes. A set of wooden sliding steps was attached to a brass rail. Léonie took hold of the contraption with both hands and pulled as hard as she could. The steps creaked and complained but quickly surrendered. She slid them along the rail to the middle point, then, positioning the feet securely, folded them out and began to climb. Her taffeta petticoats rustled and caught between her legs.

She stopped on the second-to-top step. Bracing herself with her knees, she peered into the case. It was dark within, but by cupping her hands over the glass to shield her eyes from the light from the two tall windows, she could see just enough to enable her to read the titles upon the spines.

The first was *Dogme et rituel de la haute magie* by Éliphas Lévi. Next to it was a volume entitled *Traité méthodique de science occulte*. On the shelf above, several writings by Papus, Court de Gébelin, Etteilla and MacGregor Mathers. She had never read such authors, but knew they were occultist writers and considered subversive. Their names appeared regularly in the columns of newspapers and periodicals.

Léonie felt a frisson of excitement. Although she'd never been there herself, she knew Monsieur Bailly's bookshop on the rue de la Chaussée d'Antin was filled with such titles and that Anatole had sometimes bought books for his collection there.

Her attention was caught by a large, plain volume bound in black leather, less gaudy and ostentatious than the rest, displayed facing outwards. Her uncle's name was written upon the cover in gold embossed letters beneath the title: *Les Tarots*.

CHAPTER 35

PARIS

By the time a smoggy and hesitant dawn broke over the offices of the Commissariat of Police of the 8th *arrondissement* in the rue de Lisbonne, tempers were already frayed.

The body of a woman identified as Madame Marguerite Vernier had been discovered shortly after eight-thirty on the evening of Sunday, 20th September. Given that the deceased woman was associated with a war hero, General Du Pont, Prefect Laboughe had been summoned back from his country residence to take command.

In high ill-humour, he strode through the outer office and dropped a pile of early editions onto Inspector Thouron's desk.

Carmen Murder! War Hero Detained! Lovers' Quarrel Leads to Knife Death!

'What is the meaning of this?' Laboughe thundered.

Thouron stood and murmured a respectful greeting, then removed the other papers from the single vacant chair in the cramped and fuggy room, feeling Laboughe's simmering eyes on him. When it was done, the Prefect took off his silk top hat and sat down. The wooden back of the chair creaked under his impressive weight but did not give way.

'Well, Thouron?' he demanded. 'How did they get so many inside details? One of your men got a loose tongue?'

Inspector Thouron bore all the marks of a man who had seen daybreak without experiencing the luxury of his own bed. He had smudged dark shadows, like half-moons, beneath his eyes. His moustache drooped and there was stubble on his chin.

'I don't believe so, sir,' he said. 'The reporters were already there before we arrived on the night in question.'

Laboughe stared at him from beneath white, bushy eyebrows. 'Tipped off?'

'It appears so.'

'By whom?'

'No one will say. One of my *gendarmes* overheard a conversation between two of the vultures suggesting that at least two of the newspaper offices received a communication at approximately nine o'clock on Sunday evening intimating that it would be an expedient measure to dispatch a reporter to the rue de Berlin.'

Prefect Laboughe clenched his blue-veined hands on the ivory head of his cane. 'General Du Pont? Does he deny he and Marguerite Vernier were lovers?'

'He does not, although he has requested assurances that we will be discreet in the matter.'

'Which you gave?'

'I did, sir. The General most vigorously denies killing her. Claims that a note was passed to him as he came out of a lunchtime concert, postponing their assignation on the afternoon in question from five o'clock until later in the evening. They were due to travel to the Marne Valley this morning for a few days in the country. The servants were all dismissed for the duration. The apartment was certainly prepared for an absence.'

'Does Du Pont still have the note in his possession?'

Thouron sighed. 'Out of respect for the lady's reputation, or so he says, he claims he tore up the missive and threw it away outside the concert hall.' Thouron dropped his elbows to the desk as he ran tired fingers through his hair. 'I set a man onto it straight away, but the cleaners in that *arrondissement* had been surprisingly assiduous.'

'Evidence of relations of an intimate nature prior to her death?'

Thouron nodded.

'What does the fellow say to that?'

'Shaken by the information but held his composure. Not him, or so he says. Sticks to his story that he arrived to find her dead and a crowd of reporters milling around in the street outside.'

'Was his arrival witnessed?'

'At half past eight it was. The issue is whether or not he was there earlier in the evening. We have only his word that he was not.'

Laboughe shook his head. 'General Du Pont,' he muttered. 'Well connected ... Always awkward.' He peered at Thouron. 'How did he get in?'

'He has a latchkey.'

'Other members of the household?'

Thouron burrowed into one of the teetering stacks of paper upon his desk, nearly upsetting an inkwell. He found the manila folder he wanted and extracted a single sheet of paper.

'Apart from the servants, there's one son living there, Anatole Vernier, unmarried, aged twenty-six, an erstwhile journalist and *littérateur*, now on the board of some periodical dedicated to the subject of rare books, *beaux livres*, that manner of thing.' He glanced down at his notes. 'And one daughter, Léonie, seventeen, also unmarried and living at home.'

'Have they been informed of their mother's murder?'

Thouron sighed. 'Unfortunately, they have not. We have not been able to locate them.'

'Whyever not?'

'It is believed they have gone to the country. My men have questioned the neighbours, but they know little.'

Prefect Laboughe frowned, causing his white eyebrows to meet in the middle of his forehead. 'Vernier ... Why is that name familiar?'

'Could be one of a number of reasons, sir. The father, Leo Vernier, was a Communard. Arrested and brought to trial, sentenced to deportation. Died in the galleys.'

Laboughe shook his head. 'More recently than that.'

'During the course of this year, Vernier *fils* has appeared in the newspapers on more than one occasion. Allegations of gambling, opium dens, whoring, but all unproven. A suggestion of immorality, if you like, rather than evidence of it.'

'Some manner of smear campaign?'

'There is a strong smell of that, yes, sir.'

'Anonymous, I presume?'

Thouron nodded. '*La Croix* seems particularly to have had Vernier in its sights. They published, for example, an allegation that he had been involved in a duel on the Champs de Mars, admittedly as a second rather than as a principal, but even so ... The newspaper printed times, dates, names. Vernier was able to prove he was elsewhere. He claimed to be ignorant as to who might be behind the slanders.'

Laboughe caught his tone. 'You do not believe him?'

The inspector looked sceptical. 'Anonymous attacks are rarely that to those involved. Then on the twelfth of February last, he was implicated in a scandal involving the theft of a rare manuscript from the Bibliothèque de l'Arsenal.'

Laboughe slapped his knee. 'That's it. That is why the name's familiar.'

'Through his business activities, Vernier was a regular and trusted visitor. In February, after an anonymous tip-off, it was discovered that an extremely precious occultist text had gone missing.' Thouron glanced down at his notes once more. 'A work by a Robert Fludd.'

'Never heard of him.'

'Nothing was traced to Vernier and the matter revealed the rather inadequate security arrangements of the Bibliothèque, so the whole business was hushed up.'

'Is Vernier one of those esoterists?'

'It appears not, except in the course of his work as a collector.'

'Was he questioned?'

Thouron nodded. 'Again, it was a simple matter to prove he could not have been involved. And again, when he was asked if there were persons who might have some malicious intent towards him, he said not. We had no choice but to let the matter drop.'

Laboughe was silent for a moment as he absorbed the information.

'What about Vernier's sources of income?'

'Irregular,' replied Thouron, 'although by no means insignificant. He has some twelve thousand francs a year, from a variety of sources.' He glanced down. 'His position on the advisory board of the periodical, which pays him a retainer of some six thousand francs. Offices are in the rue Montorgueil. He supplements this with writing articles for other specialist magazines and journals and, no doubt, winnings at the *rouge et noir* tables and at cards.'

'Any expectations?'

Thouron shook his head. 'As a convicted Communard, his father's assets were confiscated. Vernier *père* was an only child and his parents are long dead.'

'And Marguerite Vernier?'

'We are investigating. Neighbours knew of no close relatives, but we will see.'

'Does Du Pont make a contribution to the household expenses of the rue de Berlin?'

Thouron shrugged. 'He claims not, although I doubt he is being entirely candid on that matter.'

Laboughe shifted position, causing the chair to creak and complain. Thouron waited patiently while his superior considered the facts.

'You said Vernier was unmarried,' he said finally. 'He has a mistress?'

'He was involved with a woman. She died in March. Medical records suggest that some two weeks previously she had undergone an operation at a clinic, the Maison Dubois.'

Laboughe pulled an expression of distaste. 'A termination?'

'Possibly, sir. The medical records have been mislaid. Stolen, the staff claim. The clinic did confirm, however, that the expenses were paid by Vernier.'

'March, you say,' Laboughe said. 'So unlikely to be connected with Marguerite Vernier's murder?'

'I think it more likely, if indeed Vernier has been the victim of some whispering campaign, that those two things might well be connected.'

Laboughe snorted. 'Come, Thouron. Slandering a man is hardly the act of a person of honour. But from that to murder?'

'Quite, Monsieur le Préfet, and in usual circumstances I would agree. But there is something else that makes me wonder if there has been an escalation of ill will.'

Realising his inspector was still not finished, Laboughe pulled a black meerschaum pipe from his pocket, knocked it upon the corner of the desk to loosen the tobacco, then struck a match and drew until the flame took. A muggy, sour smell filled the cramped office.

'Vernier himself was the victim of an assault in the passage des Panoramas in the early hours of the seventeenth of September, Thursday last,' Thouron continued. 'Reported by a neighbour, who saw two men running away.'

'Morning after the Palais Garnier riot?'

'That's it, sir. When questioned, the nightwatchman of the passage admitted he had known of the attack – witnessed it, in point of fact – but confessed that Vernier had paid him handsomely to say nothing of it.'

'Did you pursue the matter?'

'Since Vernier had chosen not to report the incident, there was little we could do. I only mention it to support the suggestion that perhaps it was an indication of an escalation in hostilities.'

'But in that case, why is it Marguerite Vernier lying dead on a slab rather than Vernier himself? It makes no sense.' Prefect Laboughe sat back in his chair, drawing on his pipe. 'Do you believe Du Pont is guilty of the murder, Inspector, yes or no?'

'I am keeping an open mind, sir, until we have gathered more information.'

Laboughe waved his hand impatiently. 'Yes, yes, but your instinct?'

'I don't think he is our man. There are too many things that do not seem to fit.' Thouron took a deep breath. 'The tip-off, for one. If, indeed, it was a lovers' quarrel that got out of hand, who was it that made contact with the papers? Du Pont himself? I hardly think so. The servants had all been dismissed. It can only have been a third party.'

Laboughe nodded. 'Go on.'

'There were two champagne glasses, but also one whisky tumbler smashed in the grate. Also, the timing of both the son and daughter being out of town and the apartment closed up for the duration.' He sighed. 'I don't know, sir. Something staged about the whole thing.'

'You think Du Pont was set up to take the fall?'

'I think it is something we should consider, sir. If it was him, why would he only postpone the assignation? Surely he would take care to be nowhere in the vicinity?'

Laboughe sighed. 'I can't deny that it would be a relief not to have to pursue an army hero through the courts.' He caught Thouron's eye. 'Not that it should influence your decision, Inspector. If you believe him guilty . . .'

'I, too, would be distressed to prosecute a hero of the *patrie*!'

Laboughe glanced down at the shrill newspaper headlines. 'On the other hand, Thouron, we must not forget that a woman lies dead.'

'No, sir.'

'Our priority must be to locate Vernier and inform him of his mother's murder. If he was unwilling to talk to the police before, perhaps this tragedy will loosen his tongue.' He shifted position. The chair creaked under his weight. 'But no indication of where he is?'

Thouron shook his head. 'We know he left Paris three days ago, in the company of his sister. A cabman – one of the regulars who work the rue d'Amsterdam – reports picking up a fare in the rue de Berlin, a man and a girl matching the description of the Verniers, and taking them to the Gare Saint-Lazare on Friday, shortly after nine o'clock in the morning.'

'Any sightings of them once they were inside Saint-Lazare?'

'None, sir. Trains from Saint-Lazare service the western suburbs as well, of course, as do the boat trains for Caen. Nothing. My men are onto it.'

Laboughe was gazing at his pipe. 'And you have the word out with the railway authorities, I presume?'

'Notices have been posted throughout the Île-de-France and we are checking the passenger lists for Channel sailings.'

The Prefect drew himself heavily to his feet, wheezing at the effort of it. He put his pipe in the pocket of his coat, then picked up his top hat and gloves.

Thouron also stood.

'Pay another visit to Du Pont,' Laboughe said. 'He is the most obvious candidate in this unfortunate business, although I am inclined to think that your reading of the situation is correct.'

Laboughe moved slowly across the room, his cane tapping on the floor, until he reached the door.

'And Inspector?'

'Préfet?'

'Keep me informed. Any developments in this case, I want to hear the facts from you, not from the pages of *Le Petit journal*. I am not interested in tittle-tattle, Thouron. Leave such things to the *journalistes* and writers of fictions. Do I make myself clear?'

'Perfectly, sir.'

CHAPTER 36

There was a tiny brass key in the lock of the cabinet. It was stiff and did not want to give, but Léonie rattled at it until eventually it turned. She pulled open the door and lifted out the intriguing volume.

Perching on the polished top step, Léonie opened *Les Tarots*, folding back the hard covers, releasing the scent of dust and old paper and antiquity. Inside was a slim pamphlet, hardly a book at all. No more than eight pages, jagged, as if they had been cut by a knife. The heavy cream paper spoke of an older age – not an antique, but not a recent publication either. The words within were handwritten, in a clear italic hand.

On the first page was repeated her uncle's name, Jules Lascombe, and the title, *Les Tarots*, this time with a secondary heading underneath it: *Au delà du voile et l'art musicale de tirer les cartes.* Beneath that was an illustration, much like a figure of eight, lying flat upon its side. At the bottom of the page was a date, presumably when her uncle had written the monograph: 1870.

After my mother fled the Domaine de la Cade and before Isolde arrived.

The frontispiece was protected by a sheet of waxed tissue paper. Léonie lifted it, then gasped. The illustration was a black-and-white engraving of a devil, staring malevolently up from the page with a lewd and bold stare. His body was hunched, with vulgar twisted shoulders, long arms and claws in place of hands. His head was too large, distorted, suggesting somehow a travesty of the human form.

As Léonie looked closer, she saw that set within the creature's brow were horns, so small as to be almost indistinct. There was an unpleasant suggestion of fur rather than skin. Most disagreeable of all were the two clearly human figures, a man and a woman, chained to the base of the tomb on which the devil was standing.

At the bottom of the engraving was a number in Roman numerals: XV.

Léonie looked to the foot of the page. No artist was credited, no information given as to the provenance or origin of the piece. Just a single word, a name, inscribed in careful block capitals beneath: ASMODEUS.

Not wishing to linger longer, she turned to the next page. She was confronted with line after line of introductory explanation of the subject of the book, tightly spaced. She skimmed the text, certain words catching her eye as she read. The promise of devils and Tarot cards and music set her pulse racing with a delightful frisson of horror. Deciding to make herself more comfortable, she descended her wooden tower, jumping down the last few steps, then carried the volume to the table in the centre of the library and plunged deep into the heart of the story.

Upon the scrubbed flagstones within the sepulchre was the square, painted in black by my very hand earlier that day and which, now, seemed to give a faint glowing light.

At each of the four corners of the square, like compass points, the musical note corresponding therewith. C to the north, A to the west, D to the south and E to the east. Within the square were placed the cards, into which life was to be breathed and through the power of which I would walk in another dimension.

I lit the one lamp on the wall, which cast a pallid white light.

Instantly, it seemed as if the sepulchre was filled with a mist, choking the wholesome air from the atmosphere. The wind, too, asserted its presence, for to what else could I ascribe the notes that were now murmuring inside the stone chamber, like the sound of a distant pianoforte?

Through the twilight atmosphere, the cards, or so it seemed to me, came to life. The figures, released from their prisons of pigment and paint, took form and shape and walked once more upon the earth.

There was a rushing of air and the sensation that I was not alone. Now I was certain that the sepulchre was full of beings. Spirits – I cannot say they were human. All natural rules were vanquished. The entities were all around. My self and my other selves, both past and yet to come, were equally present. They brushed my shoulders and my neck, skimmed my forehead, surrounded me without ever touching, yet always pressing closer and closer. It seemed to me they flew and swept through the air, so that I was aware always of their fleeting presence. Yet they seemed to have weight and mass. Especially in the air above my head, there seemed ceaseless movement, accompanied by a cacophony of whispering and sighing and weeping that caused me to bow my neck as if under a burden.

It became clear to me that they wished to deny me access, although I knew not why. I only knew that I must regain the square or I would be in mortal danger. I took a step towards it, whereupon instantly there descended upon me a great wind, pushing me back, shrieking and howling, a fearsome melody, if I may call it that, which seemed to be both inside my head and without. The vibrations made me fear the very walls and roof of the sepulchre building would collapse.

I gathered my strength and then launched myself towards the centre of the square, as a drowning man reaches in desperation for the shore. Instantly, a single creature, a devil distinct, yet as invisible as its hellish companions, threw itself upon me. I felt supernatural claws upon my neck and talons on my back, its fishlike breath upon my skin, and yet not a mark was laid upon me.

I drew my arms over my head to protect myself. Perspiration flowed from my brow. My heart began to lose its rhythm and I became aware of a growing incapacity. Breathless, shaking, with every muscle strained to the utmost, I summoned the last vestiges of courage and forced myself forward once more. The music was growing louder. I dug my nails deep into the cracks in the flagstones upon the floor and, by some miracle, succeeded in dragging myself into the square marked out.

Instantly, a terrible silence oppressed the room with the force of a mighty scream, so violent, and bringing with it the stench of Hell and the depths of the sea. I thought my head would split open with the very pressure of it. Babbling wildly, I continued to recite the names upon the cards: Fool, Tower, Strength, Justice, Judgement. Was I calling the spirits of the cards, now made manifest to aid me, or was it they who attempted to prevent me gaining the square? My voice seemed not to be of my making but to issue from somewhere outside of me, low at first, but gradually increasing in volume and intensity, growing in power and filling the sepulchre.

Then, when I believed I could withstand it no longer, something withdrew from within me, from my presence, from beneath my very skin with a scraping noise, like the claws of a wild animal along the surface of my bones.

There was a rushing of air. The pressure on my failing heart was relieved.

I fell prostrate to the ground, all but unconscious, I was yet aware that the notes – those same four notes – were fading and the whisperings and sighings of the spirits growing weaker till at last I could hear nothing.

I opened my eyes. The cards were returned to their sleeping state once more. On the walls of the apse, the paintings now were inert. Then a sense of emptiness and peace suddenly came over the sepulchre, and I knew that all was finished. Darkness closed over me. I know not for how long I remained unconscious.

I have notated the music to the best of my ability. The marks on the palms of my hands, stigmata, have not faded.

Léonie hadn't realised she was holding her breath, but now she exhaled before turning the page. There was no more.

She sat staring at the pamphlet and the extraordinary tale it contained. The occult interplay of music and place had brought the images upon the cards to life and, if she had understood, summoned those who had passed over to the other side. *Au delà du voile* – beyond the veil – as the title inscribed upon the wrapper declared.

And written by my uncle.

As much as anything, it was astounding to Léonie that there could be an author of such quality within her family and yet it had never been mentioned. She wondered if Anatole knew. As a collector of rare books, surely he must have known?

And yet . . .

Léonie paused. In the introduction, her uncle claimed it to be true testimony. So what did he mean when he wrote of the power to 'walk in another dimension'? What did he mean when he said 'my other selves, both past and yet to come'? And had the spirits, once summoned, withdrawn whence they had come?

The hairs on the back of her neck stood on end. Léonie found herself glancing over her shoulder, feeling as if there was someone standing behind her. She peered into the shadows of the alcoves either side of the fireplace and the dusty corners behind the tables and curtains. Were there spirits still within the estate? She thought of the figure she had seen crossing the lawns the previous evening.

A premonition? Or something other?

Léonie shook her head, amused that she was allowing her imagination to be the master of her. Anatole would tease her for it. She returned her attention to the book. If she took her uncle at his word, and believed the story as fact, not a fiction, then did the sepulchre stand within the Domaine de la Cade itself? She was inclined to think it might, not least because the musical notes required to summon the spirits – c, d, e, a – corresponded to the letters of the name of the estate: Cade.

And does it still exist?

Léonie dropped her chin into her hand. It should be a simple matter to ascertain if there was some manner of structure such as her uncle described within the grounds. It would be in keeping for a country estate of this size to have its own chapel or mausoleum within the park. Her mother had never spoken of such a thing, but then she had said little about the estate. Tante Isolde, also, had not mentioned it, but the matter had not come up during the course of the conversation last evening and, as she herself had admitted, her knowledge of the history of her late husband's family estate was limited.

If the sepulchre still stands, I shall find it.

A noise in the passageway outside caught Léonie's attention.

Immediately, she hid the volume in her lap. She did not wish to be found reading such a book. Not out of embarrassment, but because it was her private adventure and she did not wish to share it with anyone, except perhaps Anatole. She wondered where he was.

The footsteps became fainter. She stood up, wondering if she could take *Les Tarots* with her. She did not think her aunt would object to the loan, given that she had invited her and Anatole to treat the house as their own. And although the book had been locked within a case, Léonie was certain that was as protection against the ravages of dust and time and sunlight, rather than from a sense of it being forbidden. Why else should the key have been so obligingly left in the lock?

CHAPTER 37

PARIS

Victor Constant folded the newspaper and placed it on the seat beside him.

Carmen Murder – Police Seek Son!

His eyes narrowed with contempt. 'The Carmen Murder'. It offended him, after all the help he had given them, that the gentlemen of the press were so predictable. No two women could be less alike than Marguerite Vernier and Bizet's impetuous, flawed heroine, but the opera had seeped into French public consciousness to a distressing degree. All it took for the comparison to be made was a soldier and a knife, and the story was written.

In the space of hours, Du Pont had gone from prime suspect to innocent victim and forced the press to cast their nets a little wider. Now – thanks in no small part to Constant's own endeavours – the reporters had Anatole Vernier in their sights. He was not yet quite a suspect, but the fact that his whereabouts were unknown was seen as suspicious. It was said the police were unable to locate either Vernier or his sister to inform them of the tragedy. Would an innocent man be so hard to find?

Indeed, the more Inspector Thouron denied that Vernier himself was a suspect, the more virulent the rumours grew. Vernier's absence from Paris became, *de facto*, a presence in the apartment on the night of the murder.

It served Constant well that journalists were lazy. Present them with a tale, neatly wrapped like a parcel, and they would offer it, with little modification, to their readers. The suggestion that they might independently verify the information they had been given or satisfy themselves as to the veracity of the facts they had been fed did not occur.

Despite his hatred for Vernier, Constant was forced to admit he had been clever. Even with his deep pockets and web of informants, Constant had not at first been able to discover where Vernier and his sister had gone.

He threw an uninterested glance out of the window as the Marseille Express rattled south through the Parisian suburbs. Constant rarely ventured beyond the *banlieue*. He disliked the views, the indiscriminate light of the sun or dull grey skies that bleached everything under their broad gaze. He preferred to conduct his business in the twilight of artificially lit streets, in the semi-darkness of concealed rooms lighted in the old-fashioned way with tallow and wax. He despised open spaces. His milieu was the perfumed corridors of theatres filled by girls with feathers and fans, private rooms in private clubs.

All the same, in the end, Constant had unravelled the maze of confusion Vernier had woven around their departure. The neighbours, encouraged by a *sou* or two, claimed to know nothing definite, but had sufficient fragments of information. Certainly enough for Constant to piece together the Verniers' flight from Paris. The patron of Le Petit Chablisien, a restaurant close to the Vernier apartment in rue de Berlin, had admitted to overhearing a discussion about the medieval city of Carcassonne.

With a purse full of coins, Constant's manservant had tracked down the cabman who had transported the Verniers to Saint-Lazare on the Friday morning, then the second *fiacre* that had taken them thence to the Gare Montparnasse, something the *gendarmes* of the 8th *arrondissement* had thus far failed to discover.

It was enough to convince Constant it was worth the cost of the train ticket south. If the Verniers were staying in Carcassonne, that would be easier. With the whore, or without her. He did not know what name she lived under now, only that the name by which he had known her was carved upon the tombstone in the Cimetière de Montmartre. A dead end.

Constant would arrive at Marseille later that day. Tomorrow he would take the coast train from Marseille to Carcassonne and there would install himself. Sooner or later, people would talk. They always did. Whispers, rumours. The Vernier girl was striking. Among the black-haired, coal-eyed, dark-skinned people of the Midi, such white skin and auburn hair would be remembered.

It might take time, but he would find them.

Constant took Vernier's timepiece from his pocket in his gloved hands. A gold casing with a platinum monogram, it was a distinguished and distinctive watch. It gave him pleasure simply to possess it, to have taken something of Vernier's.

Tit for tat.

His expression hardened as he pictured her smiling at Vernier, as once she had smiled for him. An image flashed into his mind, of her uncovered before his rival's gaze. And he could not bear it.

To distract himself, Constant reached inside the leather travelling valise for something to help pass the journey. He pulled out *Niels Klim's Underground Travels* and Swedenborg's *Heaven and Hell*, but found neither to his taste. He chose again. This time he took out an essay, 'Chiromancy' by Robert Fludd.

Another souvenir. It suited his mood perfectly.

CHAPTER 38

Léonie had barely departed the library when she was accosted by the maid, Marieta, in the hall. She hid the book behind her back.

'Madomaisèla, your brother has sent me to inform you that he is planning a visit to Rennes-les-Bains this morning and would be pleased if you would accompany him.'

Léonie was excited at the thought of exploring the Domaine in search of the sepulchre, but that could wait. A trip to town with Anatole could not.

'Please give my brother my compliments. Tell him I shall be delighted.'

'The carriage is ordered for ten-thirty.'

Taking the stairs two by two, Léonie bounded up to her chamber and cast her eyes around for some secret place to conceal *Les Tarots*, not wishing to provoke interest on the part of the servants by leaving such a volume in plain view. Her eyes fell upon her workbox. She opened the mother-of-pearl lid and concealed the book deep within the reels of cotton and thread, the jumble of fabric scraps.

There was no sign of Anatole when Léonie descended to the hall.

She wandered out to the terrace at the back of the property and stood with her hands upon the balustrade, looking out over the lawns. Broad slatted shafts of sunlight, filtered through a veil of cloud, made it difficult to see clearly in the abrupt contrast between light and shade. Léonie took a deep breath, drawing in the fresh, clean, unpolluted air. It was so unlike Paris, with its stink of soot and hot iron and the perpetual mantle of smog.

The gardener and his boy were working on the beds below, strapping the smaller bushes and trees to wooden stakes. A barrow stood filled with raked red autumn leaves the colour of wine. The older man wore a short brown jacket and a cap, with a red handkerchief tied at his neck. The boy, no more than eleven or twelve, was bare-headed.

Léonie descended the steps. The gardener snatched his cap from his head as she approached.

'Good morning.'

'*Bonjorn*, Madomaisèla,' he mumbled.

'A beautiful day.'

'Storm's coming.'

Léonie looked doubtfully up at the perfectly blue sky, flecked with floating islands of cloud. 'It seems so still.'

'Biding its time.'

He leaned towards her, revealing a mouth of blackened, crooked teeth like a row of old gravestones.

'The devil's work, the storm. All the old signs. Music over the lake last evening.'

His breath was peaty and sour and Léonie instinctively pulled back, affected by the old man's sincerity.

'Whatever do you mean?'

The gardener crossed himself. 'Hereabouts the devil walks. Each time he comes out of the lac de Barrenc, he brings with him violent storms chasing one another across the country. The late master sent men to fill in the lake, but the devil came and told them plain that if they continued their work, Rennes-les-Bains would be drowned.'

Léonie tried to laugh. 'These are just folk tales.'

He shook his head. 'A bargain was struck – not for me to say why or how, but the fact of the matter was, the workmen withdrew. Lake was let be. But now, *mas ara*, the natural order again is overturned. All the signs are there. The devil will come to claim his due.'

'Natural order?' she heard herself repeat. 'I don't understand what you mean.'

'Twenty-one years ago,' he muttered. 'Late master raised the devil. Music comes when the ghosts are walking out of the tomb. Not for me to say the why and how of it. The priest came.'

'The priest? Which priest?'

'Léonie!'

With a mixture of guilt and relief, she spun round at the sound of her brother's voice. Anatole was waving at her from the terrace.

'The gig is here!' he shouted.

'Keep your soul close, Madomaisèla,' said the gardener. 'When storms come, the spirits are released to walk.'

She worked the dates out in her head. Twenty-one years ago, he had said, which would make it 1870. She shivered. In her mind's eye, she saw the same date, the year of publication, printed upon the front page of *Les Tarots*.

The spirits are released to walk.

She didn't believe it – of course she didn't. At the same time, the gardener's words chimed precisely with what she had read that morning. Léonie opened her mouth to ask another question, but the old man had already returned to his digging. She hesitated, then hitched up her skirts and ran lightly up the steps to where her brother stood waiting.

It was intriguing, yes. Disquieting also. But she would not permit anything to spoil her time with Anatole.

'Good morning,' he said, leaning forward to plant a kiss on her flushed cheek, and looking her up and down. 'Perhaps a little more modesty is called for?'

Léonie glanced down at her stockings, clearly visible and flecked with touches of mud from the path. She grinned as she smoothed down her skirts with her hands.

'There,' she said. 'Quite respectable!'

Anatole shook his head, half amused. 'Have you been sewing already?' he asked, noticing a piece of red cotton thread stuck to her sleeve. 'How very industrious!'

Léonie picked off the strand. 'I was searching for something in my workbox, that's all,' she replied, not even blushing at the unrehearsed lie.

They climbed into the carriage, the driver cracked the whip and the gig jerked forward and down the drive.

'Tante Isolde did not wish to accompany us?' she asked, raising her voice to be heard over the rattling of the harness and hooves.

'She had estate matters requiring her attention.'

'But the supper party is settled for Saturday evening?'

Anatole patted his jacket pocket. 'It is. And I have promised we will play messenger and deliver the invitations.'

The night winds had shaken loose twigs and leaves from the smooth silver trunks of the beech trees, but the track down from the Domaine de la Cade was clear of debris and they covered the terrain quickly. The horses were blinkered and held steady, even though the lamps bumped and knocked against the side of the carriage in the holders as they made the descent.

'Did you hear the thunder last night?' said Léonie. 'It was so strange. Dry rumblings, then sudden outbursts, all the time the wind howling.'

He nodded. 'It is apparently quite commonplace to have thunderstorms with no rain, especially in the summer, when there might be a string of such storms, one after the other.'

'It sounded as if the thunder was trapped in the valley between the hills. As if it was angry.'

Anatole smiled. 'That might have been the *blanquette*!'

Léonie stuck out her tongue. 'I am suffering no ill effects whatsoever,' she said. She paused. 'The gardener was telling me how the storms are said to come when the ghosts are walking. Or is it the other way round? I am not certain.'

Anatole raised his eyebrows. 'Indeed?'

Léonie twisted round to address the driver on his bench.

'Do you know of a place called the lac de Barrenc?' she said.

'*Oc,* Madomaisèla.'

'Is it far from here?'

'*Pas luènh.*' Not far. 'Tourists visit, though I would not venture there.' He pointed with his whip at a dense parcel of woodland and a clearing with three or four stone megaliths sticking out of the ground as if dropped there by some giant hand. 'Up there is the Devil's Armchair. And, not above a morning's walk, the étang du Diable and the Horned Mountain.'

Léonie turned back to face Anatole with an expression of triumph on her face.

'You see,' she said. 'Everywhere evidence of devils and phantoms.'

Anatole laughed. 'Superstition, *petite,* certainly. Hardly evidence.'

The gig set them down in the place du Pérou.

Anatole found a boy willing to deliver the invitations to Isolde's guests for a *sou,* then they set off. They began by promenading along the Gran'Rue in the direction of the thermal establishment. They halted awhile at a small pavement café, where Léonie drank a cup of strong, sweet coffee and Anatole a glass of absinthe. Ladies and gentlemen in frock coats and walking suits passed. A nurse pushing a perambulator. Girls, their flowing hair decorated with silk ribbons of red and blue, and a boy in knee-length britches with a hoop and stick.

They paid a visit to the largest shop in the town, the Magasins Bousquet, where Anatole passed to Léonie Isolde's list for provisions to be delivered to the Domaine de la Cade on Saturday, then continued their exploration of the town.

Many of the buildings on the *rive gauche* were more substantial than they appeared from the road; indeed, several were many storeys taller and deeper and built down into the gorge of the river.

Léonie had excellent views of the terraces of the thermal spa. Narrow stone steps led down directly to the water's edge, where stood a collection of individual bathing huts. It was a testament to progress, to science; a modern-day shrine for contemporary pilgrims.

A solitary nurse, her winged white hat perched on her head like a giant sea bird, was pushing a patient in a *chaise roulante*. By the water's edge, a wrought-iron pergola in the shape of a crown provided shade from the sun. Outside a small travelling kiosk, a woman with a pale headscarf and broad, suntanned arms was selling cups of apple cider for a couple of *centimes*.

Anatole stood in line and purchased two cups. It was too sweet for his palate. Léonie, however, declared it delicious and drank first hers, then the dregs of his, spitting out the stray pips into her handkerchief.

The *rive droite* – the far bank – had a different character. There were fewer buildings and those that did cling to the hillside were domestic dwellings, small and modest. Here lived the artisans, the servants, the shopkeepers whose livelihoods depended upon the ailments of the urban middle classes from Toulouse, from Perpignan, from Bordeaux. Léonie could see patients sitting in the steaming, iron-rich water of the *bains forts*. A line of nurses and servants waited patiently on the bank, towels draped across their arms, for their charges to emerge.

They lunched in a pretty brasserie on the south side of the square.

'Is this acceptable?' he asked, pointing at the sole available table with his walking stick. 'Or would you prefer to eat inside, out of the wind?'

'Outside,' she said. 'It is quite perfect.'

Anatole smiled. 'I wonder if this is the wind they call the Cers,' he mused, sitting down opposite her. 'I believe this is a north-westerly, which comes down from the mountains, according to Isolde, as opposed to the Marin, which comes from the Mediterranean.' He shook out his napkin. 'Or is that the Mistral?'

Léonie shrugged.

'I visited the library this morning,' she said, once they had ordered and their food had arrived. 'A most interesting selection of books, I thought. I am astonished we had the pleasure of your company at all last night.'

'Whatever do you mean?'

Léonie stared at him. 'Only that there are more than enough books to keep one occupied for some time and, indeed, that I was impressed you managed to locate Monsieur Baillard's volume among so many. Why? What did you think I meant?'

'Nothing,' replied Anatole, twisting the ends of his moustache.

Sensing some evasion, Léonie put down her fork. 'Although now you come to mention it, I do confess I am at a loss that you did not remark upon the collection when you came to my chamber last evening before dinner.'

'Remark upon . . .?'

'Why, the collection of *beaux livres*, for a start.' She fixed her eyes on his face to watch his reaction. 'And the occultist books also. Some of them looked to be rare editions.'

Anatole did not immediately answer. 'Well, you have accused me, on more than one occasion, of being somewhat tiresome on the matter of antiquarian books,' he said finally. 'I did not wish to bore you.'

Léonie laughed. 'Oh, for goodness' sake, Anatole, whatever is the matter with you? I know, from what you yourself have told me, that a good many of these books are considered quite disreputable. Even in Paris. It's not what one would expect in a place like this. And for you to not even mention it, well, it is . . .'

Anatole sat drawing on his cigarette.

'Well?' she demanded, crossing her arms.

'Well what?'

'Well, to start with, *why* are you determined to show no interest? And why should our uncle have such a wide collection of books of such a character? It is strange that Tante Isolde did not say.'

'In point of fact, she did,' he said sharply. 'You seem determined to be critical of Isolde. Evidently you do not care for her.'

Léonie flushed, unsure as to how they were suddenly at odds with one another. 'You are mistaken. I think Tante Isolde quite charming.' She raised her voice slightly. 'It is not our aunt, but more the character of the place that is disquieting, especially when taken together with the presence of such occultist books in the library.'

Anatole sighed. 'I did not notice them. You are making something over nothing. The most *obvious* explanation, to use your words, is that Oncle Jules had catholic – or, rather, liberal – tastes. Or, perhaps, that he inherited many of the books with the house.'

'Some of them are very recent,' she said doggedly.

She knew she was being provoking, and she didn't want them to be bad friends, but she couldn't help herself.

'And you are the expert on such publications,' he said sceptically.

'That is precisely my point. You are! Hence my surprise that you did not see fit to mention the collection at all.'

'I cannot account for why you are so determined to find some mystery in this – indeed, in everything here.'

Léonie leaned forward. 'I tell you, Anatole, there is something strange about the Domaine, whether or not you will admit it.' She paused. 'Indeed, I even find myself wondering if you did go into the library at all.'

'That is enough,' he said, his voice thick with warning. 'I don't know what the devil has got into you today.'

'You accuse me of wishing to inject some sort of mystery into the house. I admit that might be so. But, by the same token, you appear determined to do the opposite.'

Anatole rolled his eyes in exasperation. 'Isolde has made us both most welcome. Her position is an uncomfortable one, and if there is any awkwardness, surely this can be put down to the fact that she herself is a stranger here, living among long-established servants who probably resent an outsider coming in as mistress of the house. From what I gather, Lascombe was often absent and I suppose the staff had the run of the place. Such comments are not worthy of you.'

Realising she had gone too far, Léonie relented. 'I only wanted—'

Anatole tossed his napkin upon the table. 'All I intended was to find you some interesting volume to keep you company last evening,' he said, 'not wishing you to be homesick in an unfamiliar house. Isolde has shown you nothing but kindness and yet you seem determined to find fault in everything.'

'That's not what I intended—' she began, but it was too late.

'Nothing I say seems to stop this childish mischief-making, so there is nothing to profit from continuing the conversation further.' He left a note on the table, then took up his hat and cane. 'Come along. The gig is waiting.'

'Anatole,' she pleaded, but he was already striding across the square. Léonie, torn between regret and resentment, had no choice but to follow. More than anything, she wished she had held her tongue.

But as they drove out of Rennes-les-Bains, she began to feel aggrieved. Anatole had determined to take insult when none was intended. And hard on the heels of such excuses was another, more insidious consideration.

He defends our aunt over me.

CHAPTER 39

The journey back to the Domaine de la Cade was an uncomfortable one.

Léonie tried to make conversation, but Anatole paid no attention. As soon as they arrived, he leapt down from the carriage and vanished into the house without a backward glance, leaving her alone to contemplate a dull and solitary afternoon stretching out before her.

Upset with both herself and her brother, she repaired to her chamber and flung herself face down upon the bed. She kicked off her shoes, letting them drop with a satisfying thump to the floor, leaving her feet to dangle over the edge as if she was floating on a raft.

The clock on the mantelshelf chimed two.

Léonie picked at the stray threads on the embroidered cover, teasing out the strands of gold until she had made a pile worthy of Rumpelstiltskin on the bed beside her. She threw a frustrated glance at the clock.

Two minutes past two. Time was barely moving.

She slid off the bed and walked over to the window, lifting the corner of the curtain with her hand. The lawns were flooded with light, rich and golden.

Everywhere, Léonie could see evidence of the damage wrought by the mischievous wind. Yet at the same time, the gardens looked serene. Perhaps she would take a walk. Explore the grounds a little.

Her eyes alighted upon her workbox, and she burrowed through the materials and sequins to where the black book lay.

Of course.

It was the ideal opportunity to search for the sepulchre. Perhaps she would even find the Tarot cards. She took out the book. This time, Léonie read every word.

An hour later, dressed in her new worsted jacket and sturdy walking boots, and with her hat perched on her head, Léonie sneaked out onto the terrace.

There was nobody in the gardens, but she walked fast nonetheless, not wishing to have to explain herself. She passed the cluster of rhododendron and juniper bushes almost at a run, keeping up the pace until she was out of plain view of the house. Only once she was through the opening in the high box hedge did she slow and catch her breath. She removed her scratchy hat, enjoying the feel of the wholesome air on her bare head, and pushed her gloves deep into her pockets. She felt exhilarated to be so completely alone and unobserved, the mistress of herself.

At the edge of the woods, she stopped, feeling the first prickings of caution. There was a palpable sense of quiet, the scent of bracken and fallen leaves. She glanced back over her shoulder, in the direction that she had come, then into the sombre light of the wood. The house was all but out of sight.

What if I cannot find my way back?

Léonie looked up at the sky. Provided she was not too long, provided the weather held, she could simply head home to the west, in the direction of the setting sun. Besides, these were private woods, managed and tended, set within an estate. It was hardly like venturing into the unknown.

Having talked herself into continuing, feeling much like a heroine in an adventure serial, Léonie set out along an overgrown path. Soon, she found herself standing at the crossroads of two paths. To the left, there was an air of neglect and stillness. The box trees and laurel seemed to drip with condensation. The downy oak and sharp needles of the *pins maritimes* seemed to bow under the unwelcome weight of time with a blighted and exhausted aspect. The right-hand path was positively mundane in comparison.

If there was a long-forgotten sepulchre within the grounds, then surely it would be deep within the woods, away from the house itself.

Léonie took the path to the left, into the shadows. The track had an unfrequented air. There were no fresh wheel ruts made by the gardener's barrow, no indication that the leaves had been raked, no sense that anyone had recently passed this way.

Léonie realised she was walking uphill. The path was growing rougher and less clear. Stones, uneven earth and fallen branches tumbled from the overgrown thicket on either side. She felt enclosed, as if the landscape was pushing in upon her, shrinking. On one side, above the path, was a steep embankment, covered with dense green undergrowth, boughs of hawthorn and an intense tangle of yew, knitted together in the half-light. Léonie felt a fluttering of nerves in her chest. Even the animals seemed to have forsaken these woods. No birds sang. No rabbits or foxes or mice moved in the undergrowth to their burrows.

Soon, the ground beside the path fell away sharply to the right. Several times, Léonie dislodged a stone with her foot and heard it tumble into the chasm below. Her misgivings grew. It required no great leap of imagination to summon the spirits that both the gardener and Monsieur Baillard, in his book, claimed haunted these glades.

She emerged onto a platform in the hillside, open on one side to reveal the panorama of the distant mountains. There was a small stone bridge over a culvert, where a strip of brown earth intersected the path beneath it at right angles, a low channel worn away by the fierce rushing of meltwaters in spring. It was dry now.

Far away, through the opening, glimpsed over the heads of the smaller trees, the entire world seemed spread out before her like a picture. The clouds scudding across the seemingly endless sky; a late-summer-afternoon heat haze or mist floating in the troughs and curves of the hills.

Léonie took a deep breath. She felt magnificently distant from all of civilisation, from the river and the grey and red roofs of the houses below in Rennes-les-Bains, from the thin outline of the *cloche-mur* and the silhouette of the Hôtel de la Reine. The thin tolling of the church bell carried on the wind.

Three o'clock already.

Léonie listened until the faint echo had died away. Her spirit of adventure faded with the sound. The words of the gardener came back to her.

Keep your soul close.

She wished she had asked him – asked somebody – for directions. Always wishing to do things for herself, she hated to ask for help. She had brought paper and a pencil but had failed to bring with her either the book itself or a map of the estate, if such a thing existed.

Léonie raised her chin and walked on with determination, fighting the fear that she was going in the wrong direction entirely. Instinct had led her this way in the first place. It crossed her mind that no one knew where she had gone. If she should fall or lose her way, nobody would know where to find her. It occurred to her, too, that she should have left some sort of trail. Fragments of paper or, like Hansel and Gretel in their woods, white pebbles to mark the way home.

Now she found herself in a wooded glade, ringed by a circle of wild juniper bushes covered with late-ripening berries, as if birds never penetrated this deep into the forest.

Shadows, distorted shades, slipped in and out of her vision. Within the green mantle of the wood, the light was thickening, stripping away the reassuring and familiar world and replacing it with something unknowable, something more ancient. Winding through the trees, the briars, the copse, an afternoon mist had set in, stealing up without a word of warning. There was an impenetrable stillness as the sodden air muffled all sound.

Then, ahead of her through the trees, she glimpsed the outline of something. A small stone chapel, no bigger than would accommodate six or eight worshippers, its roof steeply pitched and a small stone cross upon the arched entrance.

Léonie caught her breath.

The sepulchre was surrounded by a host of gnarled yew trees, their roots twisted and misshapen like an old man's hands, overshadowing the path. There were no impressions in the mud. The brambles and briars were all overgrown.

Feeling pride and anticipation in equal measure, Léonie stepped forward. Leaves rustled and twigs snapped beneath her boots. Another step. Closer, now, until she stood before the door. She tilted her head and looked up. Above the wooden arch, symmetrical and perfectly pointed, were two lines of verse painted in antique black lettering.

AÏCI LO TEMS S'EN
VA RES L'ETERNITAT.

Léonie read the words twice aloud, rolling the strange sounds over in her mouth. She pulled her pencil from her pocket and scribbled them down on a scrap of paper.

There was a noise behind her. A wild animal? A mountain cat? Then a different sound, as if a rope was being drawn across the deck of a ship. A snake? The dark eyes of the forest seemed to be pressing in upon her. The words in the book now came back to her with a dreadful clarity. Premonitions, hauntings, a place where the veil between worlds was drawn back.

Léonie felt suddenly reluctant to enter the sepulchre. But the alternative, remaining alone, unprotected, in the clearing, seemed far worse. With the blood pounding inside her head, she grasped the heavy metal ring upon the door and pushed.

At first, nothing happened. She pushed again. This time, there was the sound of metal grinding out of place and then a sharp click as the catch gave. She put her narrow shoulder against the timber and, with the weight of her whole body, gave a sharp shove.

The door juddered slowly open.

CHAPTER 40

Léonie stepped inside the sepulchre. Chill air rushed to meet her, together with the unmistakable scent of dust and antiquity and the memory of centuries-old incense. There was something else too. She wrinkled her nose. A lingering smell of fish, the salted hull of a wrecked boat.

She clenched her hands at her sides to stop them from shaking.

This is the place.

Immediately to the right of the main door on the west wall was the confessional, about six feet tall by eight wide and no more than two feet deep. It was made of dark wood and plain, nothing like the elaborate or ornate carved versions in the cathedrals and churches of Paris. The grille was shut. A single drab curtain hung in front of one of the seats. On the other side of the compartment, the curtain was missing.

To the left of the door was the *bénitier*, the stoup for holy water. Léonie stared. The basin was of red-and-white marble, but it was supported upon the back of a grinning, diabolic figure. Blistered red skin, clawed hands and feet, malevolent eyes of piercing blue.

The statue was the twin of the engraving from the frontispiece of *Les Tarots*.

Despite the burden upon his back, the defiance remained. Carefully, as if afraid he might come to life, Léonie edged closer. Beneath, printed upon a small white card, yellowed by age, was the confirmation: ASMODÉE, MAÇON AU TEMPLE DE SALOMON, DÉMON DU COUROUX.

'Asmodeus, builder of the Temple of Solomon, the demon of wrath,' she read aloud.

Standing on her cold tiptoes, Léonie peered inside. The *bénitier* was dry. But there were letters carved into the marble. She traced them with her fingers.

'*Par ce signe tu le vaincras*,' she murmured out loud. 'By this sign shall you conquer him.'

She frowned. To whom did 'him' refer? The devil Asmodeus himself? Straight away, another thought: which had come first, the illustration in the book or the *bénitier*? Which was the copy, which the original?

All she knew was that the date in the book was 1870.

Bending down, her worsted skirts making swirling patterns in the dust on the flagstoned floor, Léonie examined the base of the statue to see if there was any date or mark upon it. There was nothing to indicate either its age or its provenance.

She made a note to ask her aunt. It was possible her late husband might have told her something about it.

Léonie stood up and turned to face the nave. There were three rows of simple wooden pews on the south side of the sepulchre, facing front, like a classroom in elementary school but no wider than could accommodate two worshippers apiece. No decoration, no carvings at the end of the row and no cushions on which to kneel, just a single thin wooden footrest running the length of each.

The walls of the sepulchre were whitewashed and peeling. Plain arched windows – no coloured glass – let in the light but stripped the space of warmth. The Stations of the Cross were small illustrations set into the frame of wooden crosses – hardly paintings at all, more medallions, and all unremarkable, at least to Léonie's untrained eye.

She began to walk slowly up the nave, like a reluctant bride, becoming more anxious the further she travelled from the door. Once, thinking there was someone behind her, she turned.

Again, no one.

To her left, the narrow nave was flanked by statues of plaster saints, all half-sized, like malevolent children. Their eyes seemed to follow her as she passed by. She halted from time to time to read the names painted in black on wooden signs beneath each: Saint-Antoine, the Egyptian Hermit; Sainte-Germaine, her apron full of Pyrenean mountain flowers; the lame Saint-Roch with his staff. Saints of local significance, she presumed.

The last statue, closest to the altar, was of a petite woman wearing a knee-length red dress, with straight black hair hanging to her shoulders. With both hands she held a sword, not threatening, nor as if she was under attack, but rather as if she herself was the protector.

Beneath it was a printed card with the words: LA FILLE D'ÉPÉES.

Léonie wrinkled her brow. The Daughter of Swords. Perhaps it was intended to be a representation of Sainte-Jeanne d'Arc?

There was another noise. She glanced up at the high windows. Just the branches of the sweet chestnut trees tapping like nails upon the glass. Just the sombre call of the birds.

At the end of the nave, Léonie stopped, then crouched down and examined the floor, seeking evidence of the black square the author had described, and for the four letters – C, A, D, E – she believed her uncle had marked upon the ground. She could not see anything, not even the faintest memory, but she did uncover an inscription scratched into the stone flagstones.

'Fujhi, poudes; escapa, non,' she read. She copied this down too.

Léonie straightened up and stepped forward to the altar. It matched precisely, to her memory, the description in *Les Tarots*: a bare table, none of the artefacts of religion – no candles, no silver cross, no missal, no antiphoner. It was set in an octagonal apse, the ceiling above a bright cerulean blue, like the opulent roof of the Palais Garnier. Each of the eight panels was lined with a patterned wallpaper, with a detail of blue discs or coins, batons or wands.

Within each was a single painted image.

Léonie suddenly realised what she was looking at. Eight individual tableaux taken from the Tarot, as if each figure had stepped out of its card and up onto the wall. Printed beneath each one was a title: LE MAT; LE PAGAD; LA PRÊTRESSE; LES AMOUREUX; LA FORCE; LA JUSTICE; LE DIABLE; LE TOUR. Black antique ink on yellowed card.

It is the same hand as the book.

What better evidence that her uncle's testimony was based on true events? She moved closer. The question was – why these eight, of the seventy-eight cards her uncle's book had detailed? With excitement fluttering in her chest, she started to copy out the names, but she was running out of space on the tiny scrap of paper. She cast her eyes around the sepulchre, looking for something else on which to write.

Peeking out from beneath the stone feet of the altar, she noticed the corner of a sheet of paper. She pulled it out. It was a leaf of piano music, handwritten on heavy yellow parchment. Treble and bass clef, common time, with no flats or sharps. The memory of the subtitle on the front cover of her uncle's book came into her mind.

She flattened out the music and attempted to sing the opening bars but could not catch the melody even though it was very plain. There were but a limited number of notes, which at first glance reminded her of nothing so much as the sort of four-finger exercises she had been obliged to struggle through in her childhood piano lessons.

Then a slow smile came to her lips. Now she could see the pattern – c-a-d-e. The same notes repeating in sequence. Beautiful. As the book had claimed, music to summon the spirits.

Now another thought, following on the heels of the last. *If the music remains in the sepulchre, why not also the cards?*

Léonie hesitated, then scribbled the date and the word 'Sepulchre' across the top, as evidence of where she had found the music, then slipped it into her pocket and began a methodical search of the stone chapel. She pushed her fingers into dusty corners and crevices, looking for concealed spaces, but found nothing. There were no pieces of furniture or furnishings behind which a deck of cards could be hidden.

But if not here, then where?

She moved around behind the altar. Now her eyes were accustomed to the gloom, she fancied she could see the outline of a small door concealed within the eight panels of the apse. She reached out, looking for some disturbance in the surface, and found a slight depression, perhaps the markings of an old opening that once had done service. She pushed hard with her hand, but nothing happened. It was quite firmly fixed. If there had been a door here, it was no longer in use.

Léonie stood back, hands on her hips. She was reluctant to accept that the cards were not here, but she had exhausted every possible hiding place. She could think of nothing else for it but to go back to the book once more and seek answers there. Now she had seen the place, surely she would be able to read the hidden meanings in the text?

If indeed there are any.

Léonie again glanced up at the windows. Shafts of tree-filtered light had slipped away, leaving the glass dark. Now, as before, she felt the eyes of the plaster statues were turned upon her, watching. And as she became aware of their presence, the atmosphere within the tomb seemed to tip, to shift.

There was a rushing of air. She could discern music, inside her head, coming from somewhere within her. Heard, but not heard. Then a presence, behind her, surrounding her, skimming past without ever touching, yet pressing closer, a ceaseless movement, accompanied by a silent cacophony of whispering and sighing and weeping.

Her pulse started to race.

It is but my imagination.

She heard a different noise. She tried to dismiss it, as she had dismissed all other sounds. But it came again. A scratching, a shuffling. The clip of nails or claws upon the flagstones, coming from behind the altar.

Now Léonie felt as if she was a trespasser. She had disturbed the silence of the sepulchre and of the listeners, the watchers who inhabited its dusty stone corridors. She was not welcome. She had looked upon the painted images on the walls and stared into the eyes of the plaster saints that kept vigil. She turned, held in the malicious blue eyes of Asmodeus. The descriptions of the demons of the book came back to her with full force. She recalled her uncle's terror as he wrote of how the black wings, the presences, bore down upon him. Tore into him.

The marks on the palms of my hands, like stigmata, have not faded.

Léonie looked down and saw, or imagined she saw, red marks spreading across her cold, upturned hands. Scars in the form of a figure eight on its side upon her pale skin.

Her courage finally abandoned her.

She picked up her skirts and bolted for the door. The malignant gaze of Asmodeus seemed to mock her as she passed, his eyes following her down the short nave. In terror, she threw the full weight of her body at the door, succeeding only in closing it more firmly. Frantic, she remembered it opened inwards. She grabbed at the handle and pulled.

Now Léonie was certain there were footsteps behind her. The devils of the place had been released to protect the sanctuary of the sepulchre. A sob escaped from her throat as she stumbled out into the darkening woods.

The door fell heavily shut behind her, rattling on its ancient hinges. She was no longer afraid of what might be lying in wait in the twilight of the trees.

Léonie plunged back through the autumn air, dropping her hat, stumbling and half falling, retracing her steps all the way through the dusk-draped woods to the safety of the lawns and the gardens. And some of the words she'd heard were ringing in her ears.

Fujhi, poudes; escapa, non.

CHAPTER 41

Léonie arrived back at the house to find Anatole pacing the hall. Not only had her absence been noted, it had also caused great consternation. Isolde threw her arms around her, and then quickly withdrew, as if embarrassed by her display of affection. Anatole hugged her, clearly torn between wanting to chastise her and the relief he felt that no ill had befallen her. Nothing was said about the earlier quarrel that had driven her out alone into the grounds.

'Where have you been? We have been worried sick.'

'Walking in the gardens.'

'Walking! It is almost dark!'

'I lost track of the time.'

Anatole continued to fire question after question at her. Had she seen anyone? Had she strayed beyond the boundaries of the Domaine? Had she noticed or heard anything out of the ordinary? Under such a sustained verbal interrogation, the fear that had taken hold of her in the sepulchre loosened its grip. His reaction seemed entirely out of all proportion. Léonie rallied and started to defend herself, his determination to make so much of the incident encouraging her to do the opposite.

'I am not a child,' she threw back at him. 'I am perfectly capable of looking after myself.'

'No, you are not!' he shouted. 'You are only seventeen.'

'You talk as if you feared I had been kidnapped!'

'Don't be absurd,' he snapped, although Léonie intercepted a glance passed between him and Isolde.

'What?' she said slowly. 'Has something happened to make you worried? What is it that you are not telling me?'

Anatole opened his mouth, then closed it again, leaving Isolde to step in.

'I am sorry if our concern seems excessive to you. Of course you are perfectly at liberty to walk wherever you please. It is just that there have been reports of wild animals coming right down into the valley at dusk. Sightings of mountain cats, wolves perhaps, not far from Rennes-les-Bains.'

Léonie was on the point of challenging the explanation when the memory of the sound of claws in the sepulchre came sharply back to her. Even so close to the event, she could not say what had turned the adventure into something altogether else, and so abruptly. Only that in the moment she began to run, she had believed herself in danger of her life. From what, she did not know.

'See, you have made yourself quite ill,' Anatole said. 'You're as white as a sheet.'

'Anatole, enough,' Isolde said quietly, lightly touching him on the arm.

He turned away, his hands on his hips.

'Really, I am quite all right,' Léonie said.

'There are also warnings of more bad weather coming in from the mountains,' Isolde added. 'We were fearful you would be caught out in the storm.'

All three looked to the windows. Brooding clouds could now be seen scudding across the tops of the mountain. A white mist, like the smoke from a bonfire, hung suspended between the hills in the distance.

'Come,' said Isolde, taking Léonie's arm. 'I will have the maid draw you a hot bath, then we will have supper and a fire in the drawing room. And, perhaps, a game of cards? Bezique, *vingt-et-un*, whatever you wish.'

Léonie remembered. She looked down at the palms of her hands, white with the cold. There was nothing there.

It was only some time later, when the bell for supper had rung, that Léonie paused to contemplate her reflection. Her eyes, although bright, were feverish. She could see plainly the memory of the fear etched upon her skin and wondered if it would be evident to Isolde or Anatole.

All the same, Léonie retrieved *Les Tarots* from her workbox. With cautious fingers, she turned the pages until she came to the passage she wanted.

There was a rushing of air and the sensation that I was not alone. Now I was certain that the sepulchre was full of beings. Spirits – I cannot say they were human. All natural rules were vanquished. The entities were all around. My self and my other selves, both past and yet to come . . . It seemed to me they flew and swept through the air, so that I was aware always of their fleeting presence . . . Especially in the air above my head, there seemed ceaseless movement, accompanied by a cacophony of whispering and sighing and weeping.

Léonie closed the book.

It so precisely matched her experience. The question was, had the words lodged themselves somewhere deep in her mind and thus directed her emotions and reactions? Or had she independently experienced something of what her uncle had seen?

And can Isolde really know nothing of this?

That both her mother and Isolde felt something disturbing in the character of the place, Léonie had no doubt. In their different manners, they had hinted at a sense of disquiet, although admittedly neither was explicit. Léonie, too, had felt it on that first afternoon when she and Anatole arrived at the Domaine de la Cade.

Still turning the matter over in her mind, she returned the book to its hiding place, slipping the sheet of piano music within the covers, then hastened downstairs to join the others. Now her fear had retreated, she was intrigued, determined to discover more. She had many questions she wished to ask of Isolde. Perhaps, she would write to Maman, too, to enquire as to whether there were any specific incidents in her childhood that had caused her alarm. For without knowing what she was so certain about, Léonie was sure that it was the place itself that held captive the terrors, the woods, the lake, the ancient trees.

As she closed the bedroom door behind her, Léonie realised she could not mention her expedition for fear she would be forbidden to return to the sepulchre. For the time being at least, her adventure must remain secret.

Night slowly fell over the Domaine de la Cade, bringing with it a sense of anticipation.

Supper passed agreeably, with occasional rumbles of disconsolate thunder in the distance. Anatole seemed in better spirits and the matter of Léonie's adventure into the grounds was not mentioned. Instead, they talked of Rennes-les-Bains and adjoining towns, of the preparations for Saturday's supper party and the guests, of how much there was to do and the enjoyment they would have doing it.

After they had eaten, they withdrew to the drawing room and their moods changed. The darkness without the walls seemed almost to be alive. It was, at last, a relief when the storm struck. The very sky itself began to growl and shudder. Forked lightning ripped silver through the black clouds. Thunder ricocheted off rock and branch, echoing between the valleys.

Then the wind, stilled momentarily as if gathering up its strength, hit the house in full force, bringing with it the first of the rain that had threatened all evening. Gusts of hail lashed against the windows, until it seemed to those cowering within the house that an avalanche of water was cascading over the face of the building, like waves breaking upon the shore.

From time to time, Léonie thought that she could hear music. The notes that lay inscribed on the sheet hidden in her bedroom, taken up and sounded by the wind. As, indeed, the old gardener had warned.

For the most part, Anatole, Isolde and Léonie attempted to pay no heed to the tempest beyond the walls. A good fire crackled and spat in the grate. All the lamps were lit and the servants had brought extra candles. They had been made as comfortable as possible.

In the hall, a door came unlatched, blown open by the wind, and was quickly secured. Léonie could hear the servants moving around the house, checking that all the windows were shuttered. Because there was a danger that the thin glass of the windows in the oldest casements would shatter, all the curtains had been drawn. In the upstairs corridors, they heard footsteps and the chink of pails and buckets set at intervals to catch the drips – the leaks that Isolde told them allowed rain through the loose tiles on the roof.

Confined to the drawing room, the three of them sat, strolled, paced, talked. They drank a little wine. At ten o'clock, Léonie suggested a game of bezique. She and Isolde settled themselves at the card table. Anatole stood, his arm resting upon the mantelshelf, smoking a cigarette and holding a glass of brandy.

They spoke little. Léonie noticed how very pale Isolde had become, as if there was some further threat, some warning within the storm. Her fingers plucked at the fabric of her skirts, at the corners of the playing cards, at the green baize.

A crack of thunder struck directly overhead. Isolde's eyes flared wide. In an instant, Anatole was at her side. For a moment, Léonie felt rather the odd one out, as if they had forgotten she was there.

'According to Monsieur Baillard,' she said, 'local legend holds that the storms are sent by the devil when the world is out of kilter. When the natural order of things is disturbed. The gardener said much the same this morning. He said that music was heard over the lake last evening, which—'

'That's enough!' Anatole said sharply. 'All these sorts of tales, demons and diabolic happenings, those curses and maledictions, they are merely stories to scare children.'

Isolde threw another glance at the window. 'How much longer can this last? I do not think I can bear it.'

Anatole fleetingly let his hand drop onto her shoulder, then withdrew it, but not so quickly that Léonie did not observe the gesture and feel jealous of it.

'The storm will blow itself out soon,' Anatole said again. 'It's just the wind.'

'It's not the wind. I feel something . . . something terrible is going to happen,' Isolde whispered. 'I feel as if he is coming. Getting closer to us.'

'He?' Léonie echoed. 'Who? Who is coming?'

Neither of them paid her any attention.

Another gust of wind rattled the shutters. The sky cracked. 'I am certain that this dignified old house has seen much worse than this,' Anatole said, trying to inject a lightness into his voice. 'Indeed, I wager it will still be standing many years after we are all dead and buried. There's nothing to fear.'

Isolde tried to smile, but it was clear that Anatole's words had not comforted her. For a fraction of an instant, Léonie thought she saw the grimacing face of the demon

Asmodeus looking out at her from the leaping flames of the fire. She felt herself recoil.

The wind did not relent. Nor did her unquiet imagination give her any rest.

CHAPTER 42

When Léonie woke the following morning, she was surprised to find herself on the *chaise longue* in the drawing room of the Domaine de la Cade, rather than in her bedroom. Someone had put a blanket over her.

Shafts of golden early-morning light were slipping in through the cracks in the curtains. The fire was dead in the grate. The playing cards and empty glasses sat on the table, abandoned.

After all the hammering of rain and wind, everything was now quiet. The old house no longer creaked and groaned. The storm had passed on.

Last night's terrors – thoughts of ghosts and devils – seemed quite absurd in the benign morning light. Soon, hunger drove Léonie from the sanctuary of the sofa. She tiptoed to the door and out into the hall. She went through the pass door separating the front of the house from the servants' quarters, feeling the cold tiles through the thin soles of her *savates*, and found herself in a long flagstoned corridor. At the end, behind a second door, she could hear voices and the clattering of cooking utensils, someone whistling.

Léonie entered the kitchen. It was smaller than she had imagined, a pleasant square room with waxed walls and black beams from which hung a variety of pans and cooking implements. On the blackened top of the stove, set within a chimney large enough to accommodate a stone bench on either side, was a bubbling pot.

The cook was holding a long-handled wooden paddle in her hand as she turned towards the unexpected visitor. There was a scrape of chair legs on the flagstones as the other servants, eating breakfast at a scarred wooden table in the middle of the kitchen, rose to their feet.

'Please, don't get up,' said Léonie quickly, awkward at her intrusion. 'I wonder if I might have some coffee. Some bread, too, perhaps.'

The cook nodded. 'I will prepare a tray, Madomaisèla. In the morning room?'

'Yes, thank you. Has anybody else come down?' she asked.

'No, Madomaisèla. You are the first.'

The tone was courteous, but the dismissal clear.

'Has there been any damage from the storm?'

'Nothing that can't be put right,' the cook said.

'No flooding?' she asked, worried that perhaps Saturday's dinner party, although some days off, would be postponed if the road up from the village was impassable.

'Nothing serious reported from Rennes-les-Bains. One of the girls heard tell there's been a landslide at Alet-les-Bains. The mail coach is held over at Limoux.' The cook wiped her hands on her apron. 'Now, if there's nothing else, Madomaisèla, perhaps you will excuse me. I have a great deal to do.'

Léonie had no choice but to withdraw. 'Of course.'

As she left the kitchen, the clock in the hall struck seven. She looked through the windows to see a pink sky behind white clouds. Outside, work had begun sweeping up the leaves and gathering the wood and branches that had blown loose from the trees.

The next few days passed quietly.

Léonie had the run of the house and grounds. She breakfasted in her rooms and was free to spend the morning howsoever she chose. She had hoped to spend time with

Anatole – he was always so busy in Paris – but, if anything, she saw less of him. Often, she did not see him until the evening. In the afternoons, she and Isolde walked in the grounds, weather permitting, or explored the house. Her aunt was unfailingly attentive, gentle, with an amusing wit. They played Rubinstein duets on the piano, clumsily and with more enjoyment than skill, and amused themselves with parlour games in the evenings. Léonie read and paint-ed a landscape of the house from the small promontory overlooking the lake.

Her uncle's book and the sheet of music she had taken from the sepulchre were much on her mind, but she did not return to them. She wanted to share her discovery with Anatole, though at the same time she feared his censure. So in her perambulations of the estate, Léonie deliberately did not allow her feet to take her in the direction of the over-grown path in the woods that led to the deserted Visigoth chapel.

The day of the dinner party dawned bright and clear.

By the time Léonie had finished breakfast, the first of the delivery carts from Rennes-les-Bains was rattling up the drive of the Domaine de la Cade. The boy jumped down and unloaded two large blocks of ice. Not long after, another arrived with the *viande*, cheeses and fresh milk and cream.

In every room of the house, or so it seemed to Léonie, servants polished and primed and folded linen and set out ashtrays or glasses under the eye of the old housekeeper.

At nine o'clock, Isolde appeared from her room and took Léonie with her into the gardens. Armed with a pair of secateurs and thick rubber overshoes as protection against the damp paths, they cut flowers for the table displays while the first dew was still on them.

By the time they returned to the house at eleven o'clock, they had filled four flat trug baskets with blooms. They found steaming coffee waiting for them in the morning room and Anatole, in excellent spirits, smiling up at them from behind the newspaper.

At midday, Léonie finished the last of the *placement* cards, the names printed and designed to Isolde's specifications. She extracted a promise from her aunt that, when the table was ready, she could lay out the cards herself.

By one, there was nothing left to do. After a light lunch, Isolde announced her intention to retire to her chamber to rest for a few hours. Anatole withdrew to attend to some correspondence. Léonie was left with no alternative but to do the same.

In her room, she glanced to her workbox where *Les Tarots* lay hidden, but even though some days had passed since her expedition to the sepulchre, she was reluctant to disturb her own peace of mind by getting caught up again in the mysteries of the book. Her eyes instead darted to where her colours, brushes, easel and book of cartridge papers sat on the floor. She stood up, feeling a wave of affection for her mother. This would be the ideal opportunity to make good use of her time and paint something as a souvenir. A gift to present to her on their return to town at the end of October. Perhaps it would help eclipse her unhappy childhood memories of the Domaine de la Cade.

Léonie rang for Marieta and asked her to fetch a bowl of water for her brushes and a sheet of thick cotton to cover the table. Then she took out her palette and tubes of paint and began to squeeze out beads of crimson, ochre, tourmaline blue, yellow and moss green, with ebony black for edging. From her book of cartridge paper, she took a single heavy cream sheet.

She sat for a while, waiting for inspiration to strike. Without having any clear idea of what she might choose to attempt, she began to sketch the outline of a figure in thin, black strokes. As her brush glided over the paper, her mind was concentrated on the excitements of the evening ahead. The painting began to find its shape without her. She wondered how she would find the society of Rennes-les-Bains. Everyone invited had accepted Isolde's hospitality. Léonie saw herself admired and complimented, picturing herself first in her blue gown, then the red, then her green dress from La Samaritaine. She imagined various pairs of evening gloves, favouring the particular trim of one pair or the length of another. She imagined her hair held in check by mother-of-pearl combs or silver hairpins that would best flatter her colouring. She toyed with a variety of necklaces and earrings and bracelets to complete the look.

As the shadows lengthened on the lawns below, as she passed the time in pleasurable thought, stroke by stroke the colours thickened upon the sheet of cartridge paper and the image came to life.

Only when Marieta had returned to clear away and quitted the room did Léonie take stock of what she had painted. What she saw astonished her. Without in the least intending to do so, she had painted a figure from one of the Tarot tableaux on the wall of the sepulchre: La Force. The only difference was that she had given the girl long copper hair and a morning dress that looked quite the copy of a gown she had hanging in her own closet in the rue de Berlin. She had painted herself into the picture.

Caught between pride at the quality of her handiwork and her intriguing choice of subject matter, Léonie held the self-portrait up to the light. As a rule, all her figures looked rather similar and bore little relationship to the subject she had been attempting. But on this occasion, there was more than a passing resemblance.

Strength?

Was that how she saw herself? Léonie would not have said so, but, aware that the afternoon was drawing to a close, she left it on the table to dry and put it out of her mind.

Marieta knocked upon her door at seven o'clock.

'Madomaisèla, Madama Isolde has sent me to help you dress. Are you decided upon what you will wear?'

Léonie nodded, as if she hadn't spent most of the afternoon thinking about it. 'The green gown with the square neck. And the *sous-jupe* with the broderie anglaise trim.'

'Very good, Madomaisèla.'

Marieta carried the garments over outstretched arms and laid them carefully upon the bed. With deft fingers, she helped Léonie into her corset over her chemise and undergarments, lacing it tight at the back and fastening the hooks and eyes at the front, then climbed onto the chair and lowered first the petticoat, then the dress itself over Léonie's head. The green silk was cool against her skin as it fell in shimmering folds like water touched by sunlight.

Marieta dealt with the fastenings, then sat back on her heels to arrange the hemline, while Léonie adjusted the sleeves.

'You look a picture, Madomaisèla,' Marieta said, and the two girls smiled at one another. 'How would you like me to dress your hair?'

Léonie pulled forward her small brown leather jewellery case. 'I have tortoiseshell combs with inlaid abalone pearls, which match the earrings and pendant I intend to wear.'

Marieta worked quickly, but carefully. She fixed the clasp of the platinum leaf-and-pearl necklace around Léonie's neck, then stood back to admire her handiwork.

Léonie smiled, pleased with what she saw in the cheval glass. The gown hung well, neither too plain nor too extravagant for a private dinner. Like the heroine in a novel, she thought.

From downstairs, the raucous clamour of the bell. Then the sound of the front door being opened as the first guests arrived.

'Which gloves would you like, the green or the white?'

'The green with the beading around the cuff,' said Léonie. 'There is a fan of much the same colour in one of the hat boxes at the top of the closet.'

When she was ready, Léonie swept up her chatelaine bag from the top of the chest of drawers, then slipped her stockinged feet into green silk slippers.

'There,' Marieta said, pleased with her handiwork.

A volley of noise hit Léonie when she emerged from her room. She peeped over the balcony to the hall below. The servants were dressed in smart hired livery for the evening, which added to the sense of occasion. She fixed a dazzling smile on her face, smoothed her dress and then, feeling a mixture of excited and a little nervous, went down to the join the party.

At the entrance to the drawing room, Pascal announced her in a strong and clear voice, and then rather spoiled the effect by giving her a wink of encouragement as she walked through.

Isolde was standing before the fireplace talking to an ill-complexioned young woman. With her eyes, she called Léonie over to join them.

'Mademoiselle Denarnaud, may I present my niece, Léonie Vernier, the daughter of my late husband's sister.'

'*Enchantée*, Mademoiselle,' said Léonie prettily.

It transpired that Mademoiselle Denarnaud was an unmarried sister of the gentleman who had helped them with their luggage at Couiza on the day of their arrival. Denarnaud himself raised his hand and waved when he saw Léonie looking across the room at him. A rather more distant cousin, she learned, worked as the housekeeper to the curé of Rennes-le-Château. Léonie remembered how Isolde had mentioned at supper two nights ago that the Abbé Saunière himself was one of eleven siblings.

Her attempts at conversation were met with a cold stare. Although perhaps no older than Isolde, Mademoiselle Denarnaud was wearing a matronly heavy brocade gown more suited to a woman of twice her years. The contrast between her and their hostess could not have been greater. Isolde's golden taffeta and ivory silk gown, fine enough to Léonie's eye to have come from the latest collection by Charles Worth, was shot through with crystal and metallic thread. At her neck, she wore a high choker in the same fabric, with a pearl brooch set in the middle.

With relief, Léonie spotted Anatole standing by the windows, smoking and talking to Dr Gabignaud. She excused herself and slipped across the room to join the gentlemen. Anatole's face lit up when he saw her.

'Léonie!' He slipped an arm around her waist and hugged her tightly. 'May I say, you look quite charming.' He took a step back to let the doctor into the conversation. 'Gabignaud, you remember my sister?'

'Indeed I do.' The doctor gave a crisp bow. 'Mademoiselle Vernier. And may I add my compliments to those of your brother.'

Léonie blushed. 'It is quite a gathering,' she said.

Anatole identified the other guests for her. 'You remember Maître Fromilhague? And Denarnaud and his sister, who keeps house for him.'

Léonie nodded. 'Tante Isolde introduced me.'

'And that is Bérenger Saunière, the parish priest of Rennes-le-Château and friend of our late uncle.'

He pointed to a tall, muscular man, with a high forehead and strong features that were rather at odds with his long black robes.

'Seems a charming fellow,' Anatole continued, 'although not a man given to trivialities.' He nodded to the doctor. 'He was rather more interested in Gabignaud's medical investigations than the mundane pleasantries I had to offer.'

Gabignaud smiled, acknowledging the truth of it. 'Saunière is an extremely informed man, in all manner of things. He has an appetite for knowledge. Always asking questions.'

Léonie looked at the priest a moment longer, then her gaze moved on.

'And the lady with him?'

'Madame Bousquet, a distant relative of our late uncle.' Anatole dropped his voice. 'Had not Lascombe taken it upon himself to marry, she would have inherited the Domaine de la Cade.'

'Yet she has accepted the invitation to dine?'

He nodded. 'The bond between Madame Bousquet and Isolde is hardly that of sisters, but it is civilised. They receive one another. Indeed, Isolde admires her.'

Only now did Léonie notice a tall, very thin man standing a little behind their small group. She half turned to observe him. He was dressed most unusually, in a white suit, rather than the customary black evening wear, and sported a yellow handkerchief in the breast pocket of his jacket. His waistcoat, too, was yellow.

His face was lined and his skin almost transparent with antiquity, and yet it seemed to Léonie that no great sense of age hung about him. There was, though, she thought, an underlying sadness. As if he was a man who had suffered and seen much.

Anatole turned to see who or what had so caught her attention. He leaned closer to whisper in her ear. 'Ah, that is Rennes-les-Bains's most celebrated visitor, Audric Baillard, author of that strange little pamphlet that engaged you so.' He smiled. 'Quite the eccentric, apparently. Gabignaud's been telling me that he always dresses in that singular manner, regardless of the occasion. Always in a pale suit, always with a yellow cravat.'

Léonie turned to the doctor. 'Why is that?' she asked, *sotto voce*.

Gabignaud smiled and shrugged. 'I believe in memory of friends once lost, Mademoiselle Vernier. Fallen comrades – I'm not entirely certain.'

'You can ask him yourself, *petite*, at dinner,' said Anatole.

The conversation prospered until the sound of the gong being struck called the party in to dinner.

Pascal, splendid in borrowed red-and-gold livery, threw open the doors as the guests approached. There was an immediate murmur of appreciation. Even Léonie, who had seen the dining room in various stages of preparation during the course of the morning, was dazzled by the transformation. The glass chandelier was alight with three tiers of white wax candles. The long oval table was dressed with armfuls of fresh lilies, lit by three silver candelabra. On the sideboard were serving tureens, their lids domed and gleaming like armour. Light from the candles sent shadows dancing along the walls across the painted faces of past generations of the Lascombe family that hung upon the walls.

Once everyone had taken their seats, the servants poured generous measures of *blanquette de Limoux* into coupes as wide as coffee bowls. Fromilhague concentrated his attentions on his hostess, all but ignoring Denarnaud's sister. It was discourteous, although Léonie could not entirely blame him for it. In their brief conversation, she had thought her most dull.

After a few formal exchanges with Madame Bousquet, Léonie could hear Anatole was already launched into animated conversation with Maître Fromilhague about literature. Fromilhague was a man of strong opinions, dismissing Monsieur Zola's latest novel, *L'Argent*, as dreary and immoral. In vain did Anatole try to suggest that a man's life and his work might be treated separately.

'Immorality in life debases the art,' was Fromilhague's stubborn response.

Soon, most of the table were engaged in the debate.

'You are quiet, Madomaisèla Léonie,' came a voice at her ear. 'Does literature not interest you?'

She turned to Audric Baillard. 'I adore to read. But in company such as this, it is difficult to make one's opinions heard.'

He smiled. 'Ah, yes.'

'And I confess,' she continued, 'I find much contemporary literature utterly wearisome. Page after page of ideas, exquisite turns of phrase and clever ideas, but where nothing ever happens!'

A smile flickered in his eyes. 'It is stories that capture your imagination?'

Léonie smiled. 'My brother, Anatole, always tells me I have rather low tastes, and I suppose he is right. The most thrilling novel I have read is *The Castle of Otranto*, but I am also a fan of Amelia B. Edwards' ghost stories and anything by Monsieur Poe.'

Baillard nodded. 'He was gifted. A troubled man, but so adept at capturing the dark side of our human nature, don't you think?'

Léonie felt pleased. She had endured too many tedious soirées in Paris being all but ignored by the majority of guests, who seemed to believe that she was too young to have any opinions worth hearing.

'I do,' she agreed eagerly. 'My favourite of Monsieur Poe's stories, although I confess it gives me nightmares each time I read it, is "The Tell-Tale Heart". A murderer driven mad by the sounds of the beating heart of the man he has slaughtered and concealed beneath the floorboards. Quite brilliant!'

'Guilt is a powerful emotion,' he said quietly.

Léonie looked at him closely for a moment, waiting for him to expound, but he said nothing more.

'May I be impertinent and ask you a question, Monsieur Baillard?'

'Of course.'

'You are dressed, well . . .' She broke off, not wishing to cause offence.

Baillard smiled. 'Unconventionally? Not in the usual uniform?'

'Uniform?'

'Of a gentleman these days at dinner,' he said, his eyes twinkling.

Léonie gave a sigh. 'Well, yes. Although it was not that so much as that my brother said you were known to always wear yellow. In memory of fallen comrades, he said.'

Audric Baillard's face seemed to cloud over.

'That is so,' he said quietly.

'Did you fight at Sedan?' she asked, then hesitated. 'Or . . . my papa fought for the Commune. I never knew him. He was deported and . . .'

For a moment, Baillard's hand covered hers. She felt his skin, paper thin, through the material of her gloves, and the lightness of his touch. Léonie did not know what overcame her at that moment, only that an anguish she had never realised she felt had been put into words.

'Is it always right to fight for what you believe in, Monsieur Baillard?' she said. 'I have often wondered. Even if the cost to those around you is so great?'

'Always,' he said quietly. 'And to remember those who fall.'

For an instant, the noise of the room receded. All the voices, the laughter, the chink of glasses and silver cutlery. Léonie looked directly at him and felt her gaze, her thoughts, absorbed by the wisdom and experience flickering in his pale, dignified eyes.

Then he smiled. His eyes crinkled and the intimacy was broken.

'The Good Christians, the Cathar believers, were forced to wear a yellow cross pinned to their clothing to mark them out.' His fingers patted the sunflower-yellow handkerchief in his pocket. 'I wear this in remembrance.'

Léonie tilted her head. 'You feel deeply for them, Monsieur Baillard,' she said, smiling.

'Those who have gone before us are not necessarily gone, Madomaisèla Vernier.' He tapped his chest. 'They live here.' He smiled. 'You did not know your father, you say, and yet he lives in you. Yes?'

Léonie felt tears spring to her eyes. She nodded, unable to trust herself to speak. And, perhaps for the first time, she thought about how it must have been for her mother to live the whole of her life without the man she loved.

'Yes,' she said.

CHAPTER 43

Course after course was brought to the table. Fresh trout, pink and melting from the bone like butter, followed by dainty lamb cutlets served on a bed of late asparagus. The men were poured a strong Corbières, a hearty local red wine from Jules Lascombe's excellent cellar. For the ladies, a semi-sweet white wine from Tarascon, rich and dark, the colour of singed onion skins.

The air grew hot with conversation and opinion, arguments of faith and politics, of north and south, of country versus town. Léonie glanced across at her brother. Anatole was in his element. His brown eyes sparkling, she could see how he was charming both Madame Bousquet and Isolde herself. At the same time, she could not fail to notice there were shadows beneath his eyes. And that, in the dancing light of the candles, the scar on his eyebrow looked particularly vivid.

Léonie took a little time to recover from the strong emotions her conversation with Audric Baillard had aroused in her. Little by little, self-consciousness and embarrassment at having revealed herself so openly – and so unexpectedly – began to give way to curiosity that she should have done so. Having recovered her composure, she became impatient for an opportunity to rekindle their conversation. But Monsieur Baillard was now deeply engaged in debate with the curé, Bérenger Saunière. To her other side, Dr Gabignaud seemed determined to fill every moment with talking. Only with the arrival of dessert did the opportunity present itself.

'Tante Isolde says you are an expert in many matters, Monsieur Baillard. Not only the Albigensians, but Visigoth history, also Egyptian hieroglyphs. On my first evening here, I read your monograph, *Diables et esprits maléfiques et phantômes de la montagne*. There is a copy here in the library.'

He smiled, and Léonie hoped that he, too, was pleased to return to their conversation.

'I made a gift of it to Jules Lascombe myself.'

'It must have taken a long time to gather so many stories together in one volume,' she continued.

'Not so long,' he said lightly. 'It is but a matter of listening to the landscape, to the people who inhabit this land. The stories often recorded as myth or legend, spirits and demons and creatures, are as much woven into the character of the region as the rocks and mountains and lakes.'

'Of course,' she said. 'But do you not also think there are mysteries that cannot be explained?'

'*Oc*, Madomaisèla, *ieu tanben*. I believe that too.'

Léonie's eyes widened. 'You speak Occitan?'

'It is my mother tongue.'

'You are not French?'

He gave a sharp smile. 'No, indeed not.'

'Tante Isolde wishes the servants to speak French within the house, but they lapse into Occitan so frequently that she has given up reprimanding them.'

'Occitan is the language of these lands. Aude, Ariège, Corbières, Razès – and beyond, into Spain and Piedmont. The language of poetry, of stories and folklore.'

'So you come from this region then, Monsieur Baillard?'

'*Pas luènh*,' he replied, passing lightly over her enquiry.

'But are such stories true, Monsieur Baillard?' she asked. 'Of evil spirits and phantoms and demons. Are they true?'

'*Vertat?*' he repeated, holding her gaze with his pale eyes for a moment longer. 'True? Who is to say, Madomaisèla? There are those who believe that the veil that separates one dimension from the other is so transparent, so lucent, as to be almost invisible. Others would say that only the laws of science dictate what we may and may not believe.' He paused. 'For my part, I can only tell you that attitudes change over time. What one century holds as fact, another will see as heresy.'

'Monsieur Baillard,' Léonie said quickly, 'when I was reading your book, I found myself wondering if the legends followed the natural landscape. Were the fauteuil du Diable or the étang du Diable named for stories that were told in these parts, or did the stories grow up as a way of giving character to the place?'

He nodded and smiled. 'That is a perceptive question.'

Baillard spoke softly and yet Léonie felt all other sound retreat in the face of his clear, timeless voice. 'What we call civilisation is merely man's way of trying to impose his values upon the natural world. Books, music, painting – all these constructed things that have so occupied our fellow guests this evening – are but attempts to capture the soul of what we see around us. A way of making sense of, ordering, our human experiences into something manageable, containable.'

Léonie stared at him for a moment. 'But ghosts, Monsieur Baillard, and devils,' she said slowly. 'Do you believe in ghosts?'

'*Benleu*,' he said, in his soft and steady voice. Perhaps.

He turned his head to the windows, as if looking for someone beyond, then back to Léonie.

'This much I will say. Twice before, the devil that haunts this place has been summoned. Twice, he has been defeated.' He glanced to his right. 'Most recently, with the help of our friend here.' He paused. 'I should not wish to live through such times again, unless there was no choice.'

Léonie followed his gaze. 'Abbé Saunière?'

Baillard gave no indication he had heard her. 'These mountains, these valleys, these stones – and the spirit that gave life to them – existed long before people came and tried to capture the essence of ancient things with language. It is our fears that are reflected in those names to which you refer.'

Léonie considered what he had said. 'But I am not sure you have answered my question, Monsieur Baillard.'

He placed his hands upon the table. Léonie could see blue veins and the brown marks of age written upon his white skin. 'There is a spirit that lives in all things. Here we sit in a house several hundred years old. It is established – one might say antique – by modern human standards. But it stands within a place that is many thousands and thousands of years old. Our influence upon the universe is nothing more than a whisper. Its essential character, its qualities of light and dark, were set millennia before man attempted to make his mark upon the landscape. The ghosts of those who have gone before are all around us, absorbed into the pattern, the music of the world, if you like.'

Léonie suddenly felt the room was spinning, swaying, shifting. The candles, the voices, the rush of servants moving to and fro, everything was blurred around the edges. She took another sip of wine to steady her nerves.

'Music,' she said, although her voice sounded as if it came from a long way off. 'Can you tell me about the music, Monsieur Baillard?'

She saw the expression on his face, and for a moment thought he had somehow understood the unspoken question behind her words.

Why, when I sleep, when I enter the woods, do I hear music in the wind?

'Music is an art form that involves organised sounds and silence, Madomaisèla Léonie. We consider it now an entertainment, a diversion, but it is so much more than that. Think instead of knowledge expressed in terms of pitch – that is to say, melody and harmony; in terms of rhythm – that is tempo and metre; and in terms of the quality of sound, timbre, dynamics and texture. Put simply, music is a personal response to vibration.'

She nodded. 'I have read that it may, in certain situations, provide a link between this world and the next. That a person might pass from one dimension to another. Do you think there could be some veracity in such claims, Monsieur Baillard?'

He met her gaze. 'There is no pattern the human mind can devise that does not exist already within the bounds of nature,' he said. 'Everything we do, see, write, notate, all are an echo of the deep seams of the univèrse. Music is the invisible world made visible through sound.'

Léonie felt her heart contract. Now they were approaching the core of it. All along, now she knew, she had been moving towards this one moment when she would tell of how she had found the sepulchre concealed in the woods, led there by the promise of arcane secrets laid out within the book. Such a man as Audric Baillard would understand. He would tell her what she wished to know.

Léonie took a deep breath.

'Are you acquainted with the game of Tarot, Monsieur Baillard?'

The expression on his face did not alter, but his attention sharpened.

Indeed, almost as if he was expecting such a question.

'Tell me, Madomaisèla,' he said at last, 'is your enquiry related to matters we have been discussing previously? Or separate from it?'

'Both.' Léonie felt her cheeks grow hot. 'Although I ask because … because I came upon a book in the library. It was written in a most old-fashioned manner, the words

themselves are obscure, and yet there was something ...'
She paused. 'I am not certain that I divined the true
meaning.'

'Go on.'

'This text, which purported to be a real testimony and
was ...' She stumbled, not certain if she should reveal the
authorship of the text. Monsieur Baillard completed
the thought for her.

'Written by your late uncle,' he said, smiling at her startled expression. 'I am aware of the book.'

'You have read it?'

He nodded.

Léonie breathed a sigh of relief. 'The author – that is,
my uncle – talked of music woven into the fabric of the
corporeal world. Certain notes that could, or so he claimed,
summon the spirits. And the Tarot cards, also, were associated with both the music and the place itself, pictures that
came to life only during the course of this communication
between worlds.' She paused. 'A tomb within these grounds
was mentioned, and claim of an event that had once taken
place here.' She raised her head. 'Have you heard stories of
such happenings, Monsieur Baillard?'

'I have.'

She had intended to conceal the fact of her expedition
from him, but under his wise, searching eyes, she found she
could not dissemble.

'I ... I found it,' she said. 'It lies higher up, in the woods
to the east.'

Léonie turned her flushed face towards the open
windows. She longed, now, to be out of doors, away from
the candles, the conversation, the stale air in the over-
heated room. Then she shivered, as if a shadow had fallen
behind her.

'I know it too,' he said. He stopped, waited, then added,
'And I believe there is a question you wish to ask of me?'

Léonie turned her head back to face him. 'There was an inscription written upon the arch above the door of the sepulchre.'

She recited it as best she could, the unfamiliar words clumsy in her mouth.

'Aïci lo tems s'en, va res l'eternitat.'

He smiled. 'You have a good memory, Madomaisèla.'

'What does it mean?'

'It is something of a corruption, but in essence it means: "Here, in this place, time moves away towards eternity."'

For a moment, their eyes met. Hers sparkling with *blanquette*, his steady and calm and wise. Then he smiled. 'You remind me very much, Madomaisèla Léonie, of a girl I once knew.'

'What happened to her?' Léonie asked, momentarily diverted.

'Oh, it is another story,' he said lightly. 'One that is not yet ready for the telling.'

Léonie saw him withdraw, wrapping his memories around himself. His skin seemed transparent, the lines on his thin face deeper, as if etched in stone.

'You were telling of how you found the sepulchre,' he said. 'Did you enter?'

Léonie took her mind back to that afternoon. 'I did.'

'So you read the inscription upon the floor: "*Fujhi, poudes; escapa, non.*" And now you find the words haunt you?'

'Yes! But how could you know? I do not even know their meaning, only that they repeat endlessly in my head.'

He paused, then said: 'Tell me, what do you think you found there? Within the sepulchre?'

'The place where spirits walk,' she heard herself say, and knew it to be true.

Baillard was silent for what seemed an age. 'You asked me before if I believed in ghosts,' he said eventually. 'There are many types of ghosts. Those who cannot rest because they have done wrong, who must seek forgiveness or atonement. Also those to whom wrong has been done and who are condemned to walk until they can find an agent of justice to speak their cause.' He looked at her. 'Did you look for the cards, Madomaisèla Léonie?'

'Yes, but I did not find them.'

She stopped, feeling suddenly sick. Her stomach was churning, lurching, as if she was on board a boat on a rough sea. 'All I found was a sheet of music for the piano.'

Her voice sounded muffled, as if she was speaking from under water.

'Did you take it from the sepulchre?'

Léonie pictured herself thrusting the music, with the words written upon it, into the deep pocket of her worsted jacket, as she ran down the nave of the sepulchre and out into the twilight of the forest. Then, later, slipping it between the pages of *Les Tarots*.

'Perhaps I should not have, but I did.'

'Listen to me. You are steadfast and you are courageous. *Forca e vertu* – good qualities both when used wisely. You know how to love, and well.' He glanced across the table to where Anatole sat, then his gaze flickered to Isolde, before returning to Léonie. 'I fear there are great trials ahead for you. Your love will be tested. You will be called upon to act. The living will be in need of your services, not the dead. Do not return to the sepulchre until – *if* – it becomes absolutely necessary for you to do so.'

'But I—'

'My advice is that you return *Les Tarots* to the library. Forget all that you read within it. It is, in so many ways, an enchanting book, a seductive book, but for now, you should put the whole matter from your mind.'

'Monsieur Baillard, I—'

'You said perhaps you feared you had misunderstood the words in the book.' He paused. 'You did not, Léonie. You understood very well.'

The unadorned use of her name pulled her up. 'So it is true? That the cards can summon the spirits of the dead?'

He did not reply directly. 'With the correct patterning of sound and image and place, such things might happen.'

Her head was spinning. She wanted to ask a thousand questions, but she could not find the words.

'Léonie,' he said, drawing her back to him. 'Save your strength for the living. For your brother. For his wife and child. It is they who will need you.'

His wife and child?

Her confidence in Monsieur Baillard momentarily faltered. 'No, you are mistaken. Anatole has no—'

At that moment, Isolde's voice rang out from the end of the table.

'Ladies, shall we?'

Immediately, the room was filled with the scrape and slide of the chairs on the polished wooden floor as the guests rose from the table.

Léonie got unsteadily to her feet. The folds of her green dress fell like water to the floor.

'I do not understand, Monsieur Baillard. I thought I did, but now I find I was mistaken.' She halted, realising how intoxicated she was. The effort of remaining upright was quite overwhelming. She put out a hand to steady herself on the back of his chair.

'And you will heed my advice?'

'I shall do my best,' she said, giving a crooked smile. Her thoughts were going round in circles. She could no longer remember which words had been spoken out loud and which only uttered within her muddled head.

'*Ben, ben.* Good. I am reassured to hear it. Although . . .' He paused again, as if he was undecided whether to speak

300

further. 'If the time does come when you need the agency of the cards, Madomaisèla, then know this. You may call upon me. And I will help you.'

She nodded, the room spinning wildly.

'Monsieur Baillard,' she said, 'you did not tell me what the second inscription meant. Upon the floor.'

'*Fujhi, poudes; escapa, non?*'

'Those words, yes.'

His eyes clouded. 'Flee, you may; escape, you cannot.'

PART VI

Rennes-le-Château
October 2007

CHAPTER 44

Meredith woke the next morning with a thudding head after broken sleep. The combination of wine, the whispering of the wind in the trees and her wild dreams had made her restless.

She didn't want to think about the night. Ghosts, visions. What it might mean. She was here to work, yes, but also to relax and enjoy being in such a beautiful part of France.

Meredith stood under the shower until the water ran cold, took a couple of Tylenol, dressed in comfortable blue jeans and a red sweater, then went down to breakfast. A supersize plate of scrambled eggs, bacon and baguette, washed down with several cups of strong, sweet French coffee, and she felt human again.

She checked her purse – phone, camera, notebook, pen, sunglasses and a map of the local area – then, a little nervous, went down to the lobby to meet Hal. There was a line at the desk. A Spanish couple complaining about having too few towels in their room, a French businessman challenging the additional charges on his bill and, by the concierge's station, a mountain of luggage waiting to be taken out to the coach of an English tour group en route to Andorra. The clerk looked strung out already.

There was no sign of Hal. Meredith was prepared for the fact that he might not show. In the cold light of day, without the courage that comes with alcohol, he might be regretting the impulse that had led him to ask a stranger out. At the same time, she kind of hoped he would come. She would enjoy having company.

While she waited, she looked at the photographs and paintings hanging on the wall around the lobby. They were the standard oil paintings to be found in every countryside hotel. Rural views, misty towers, shepherds, mountains – nothing remarkable. The photographs were more interesting, clearly all chosen to reinforce the *fin-de-siècle* ambience. Framed portraits in sepia tones, brown and grey. Women with serious expressions, tight-nipped waists and big skirts, hair swept up. Men with moustaches and beards, in formal poses, straight-backed and staring into the lens.

Meredith ran her eyes over the walls, taking in the general impression rather than the specifics of each shot, until she came to one portrait tucked in right by the curve of the staircase, just above the piano she'd noticed last night. She recognised the square in Rennes-les-Bains. In the centre of the photograph, on an ornate metal chair, sat a man with a black moustache, his dark hair swept back from his forehead and his top hat and cane balanced across his knees. Behind him, to his left, was an ethereal-looking woman in a well-cut dark jacket, high-collared shirt and long skirt. Her black half-veil was lifted off her face, revealing light hair pinned back in an artful chignon. Her gloved hand rested lightly upon his shoulder. To the other side was a younger girl – her curly hair arranged beneath a felt hat – dressed in a cropped jacket with shining buttons and velvet trim, looking straight into the lens.

I've seen her before.

Meredith peered closer. There was something about the girl's direct, bold gaze that drew her in, sending an echo slipping through her mind. A shadow of another photograph like it? A painting? The cards, maybe? She dragged the heavy piano stool to one side and leaned in, racking her brains, but the memory refused to come.

Meredith looked back to the man. There was a clear family resemblance. Brother and sister maybe? They had the same long lashes, the same unswerving focus, the same tilt of the head. The other woman seemed less definite, somehow. For all her physical proximity to the others, she seemed insubstantial. There, but not there. As if, at any moment, she might slip from sight altogether. Like Debussy's Mélisande, Meredith thought, she carried a suggestion of belonging to another time and place.

Meredith reached forward and lifted the photograph away from the wall, looking for any identifying marks. The creased brown waxed paper was coming unstuck from the frame, but the words printed on the back in block capitals were clear.

RENNES-LES-BAINS, OCTOBRE 1891, and then the studio credit, EDITIONS BOUSQUET.

Beneath that, three names.

MADEMOISELLE LÉONIE VERNIER, MONSIEUR ANATOLE VERNIER, MADAME ISOLDE LASCOMBE.

Meredith felt the hairs on the back of her neck stand on end, remembering the tomb at the far edge of the cemetery in Rennes-les-Bains: FAMILLE LASCOMBE-BOUSQUET. Now, on a photograph hanging on the wall, the two names joined once more.

She was certain the two younger figures were the Verniers – brother and sister, surely, rather than husband and wife, given the physical similarities between them? The older woman had the air of someone who had lived a less sheltered existence. Then, Meredith realised where she'd seen the Verniers before. A snapshot of a moment in Paris, settling the check in Le Petit Chablisien in the street in which Debussy had once lived. The composer looking down from the frame, saturnine and discontented. And beside him, his neighbours on the restaurant wall, a photograph of this same man, this same striking girl, although with a different and older woman.

Meredith kicked herself for not paying more attention at the time. For a moment, she even thought about calling the restaurant and asking if they had any information about the family portrait. Then the thought of having such a conversation in French, on the telephone, made her dismiss the idea.

As she stared at the photograph, in her mind's eye, the other portrait seemed to shimmer behind it, shadows of the girl and the boy, the people they had been once and were now. For a second, she knew – *thought* she knew – how, if not yet why, the stories she had been following might be interlinked.

She hung the frame back on the wall, thinking she could borrow it later. As she pushed the heavy piano stool back to its original position, she noticed the lid of the instrument was now open. The ivory keys were a little yellow, the edges chipped like old teeth. Late nineteenth century, she reckoned. A Blüthner boudoir grand.

She pressed middle c. The note echoed clear and loud into the private space. She looked round, guilty, but no one was paying any attention. Still standing, as if sitting down would commit herself to something, Meredith played the scale of a minor. Just a couple of low octaves in the left hand. Then the arpeggio with her right. The touch of the keys on her fingertips felt like she had come home.

The stool was a deep mahogany with ornate carved legs and a red velvet cushion. To Meredith, snooping around in other people's music collections was as interesting as running one's fingers along a friend's bookshelves. The brass hinges creaked as she opened the lid, releasing the distinctive scent of wood, old music and pencil lead.

Inside was a neat pile of books and loose sheet music. Meredith went through the stack, smiling as she came across sheet music for Debussy's *Clair de lune* and *La Cathédrale engloutie*, in their distinctive pale-yellow Durand covers. The regular collections of Beethoven and Mozart sonatas, as well as Bach's *The Well-Tempered Clavier*, volumes one and two. Even a couple of show tunes from Offenbach's *La Vie parisienne* and *Gigi*.

'Go ahead,' said a voice at her shoulder. 'I'm happy to wait.'

'Hal!'

She let the lid of the stool fall shut with a snap, then turned to see him smiling at her. He looked better this morning. The lines of worry, of misery, had gone from the corners of his eyes and he wasn't so pale.

'You sound surprised,' he said. 'Did you think I was going to stand you up?'

'Not at all . . .' She grinned. 'Well, yes, maybe. It crossed my mind.'

He spread his arms out. 'As you can see, present and correct and ready to go.'

They stood, a little awkward, then Hal leaned over the piano stool and kissed her on the cheek.

'I'm sorry I was late.' He gestured at the piano. 'Are you sure you don't want—'

'Maybe later.'

They walked together across the tiled floor of the lobby, Meredith aware of the small distance between them and the smell of his soap and aftershave.

'Do you know where you want to start looking for her?'

'Her?' she said quickly.

'Lilly Debussy,' he frowned. 'I'm sorry, isn't that what you said you were hoping to do this morning? A little research?'

'Sure, yes. Absolutely.'

Meredith experienced a rush of embarrassment. She didn't want to explain her personal reason for being in Rennes-les-Bains – her real reason, she guessed – it felt too soon. She hardly knew the man.

'Absolutely,' she repeated. 'On the trail of the first Mrs Debussy. If Lilly ever was here, I'm going to find out how, why and when.'

Hal smiled. 'Shall we take my car? I'm happy to drive you wherever you want to go.'

Meredith thought about it. It would leave her freer to take notes and look around properly, check out the map.

'That would be great, thank you.'

As they walked out the door and down the steps, Meredith thought she could feel the eyes of the girl in the photograph on her back.

CHAPTER 45

The drive and the grounds looked very different in daylight.

October sun flooded the gardens, burnishing everything with intense colour. Meredith caught the smell of burning bonfires and the perfume of sun on wet leaves through the half-opened car window. A little further away, a more dappled light fell on the deep-green bushes and high box hedge. Everything was outlined as if in gold and silver.

'I'm taking the back way, cross-country to Rennes-le-Château. Much quicker than heading into Couiza and out again,' Hal said.

The road doubled back and twisted up on itself as it climbed through the wooded hills. A final hairpin bend, and then they were out of the woods and into wide expanses of meadows and pasture.

Meredith felt her spirits soar at the views unfolding before her.

'It's wonderful. So amazingly beautiful.'

'I remembered something I think will really interest you,' Hal said. She heard the smile in his voice. 'When I told my uncle I was going to be out this morning – and why – he reminded me that there are allegations of a connection between Debussy and Rennes-le-Château. He was unusually helpful, in fact.'

'Really?'

'I'm assuming you know the basic stories about the place?'

She shook her head. 'Don't think so . . .'

'It's the village that sparked all the *Holy Blood and the Holy Grail* stuff? *Da Vinci Code*? *The Templar Legacy*? Ringing any bells? Bloodline of Christ?'

Meredith pulled a face. 'Sorry. I'm more a non-fiction girl – biography, history, theory, that kind of stuff. Facts.'

Hal laughed. 'OK, quick précis. The story is that Mary Magdalene was in fact married to Jesus and had children by him. After the Crucifixion, she fled, some say to France. Marseille, lots of places along the Mediterranean coast, all lay claim to being where she came ashore. Fast-forward nine hundred years, to 1891, when it's alleged the priest of Rennes-le-Château, Bérenger Saunière, came across parchments demonstrating this bloodline of Christ, going all the way from the present day to the first century AD.'

Meredith caught her breath. That same year again. 'Eighteen ninety-one?'

Hal nodded. 'That's when Saunière began a massive renovation project that was to last for many years – starting with the church, but in the end, gardens, graveyard, house – everything.' He stopped. Meredith felt him glance at her.

'Sorry, it's fascinating. Go on.'

'The bloodline parchments were supposed to have been hidden inside a Visigoth pillar, way back when. Most locals think the whole thing was a hoax from start to finish. Anyway, the church hierarchy accused him of simony – that is, selling masses for money. His parishioners were more charitable. They thought he had discovered some cache of Visigoth treasure and didn't begrudge him, since he spent so much of it on the church and his parishioners.'

'When did Saunière die?' she asked, remembering the dates on Henri Boudet's memorial in the church in Rennes-les-Bains.

Hal glanced at her. 'Nineteen seventeen,' he said, 'leaving everything to his housekeeper, Marie Denarnaud. It wasn't until the late 1970s that all the religious conspiracy theories began to surface.'

'This is all so useful, Hal, thank you.'

'My pleasure.'

She scribbled that information down too. The name Denarnaud had appeared on several tombs in the graveyard.

'What does your uncle think about all the stories?'

Hal frowned. 'That it's good for business,' he said.

Since there was clearly no love lost between him and his uncle, Meredith wondered why Hal was sticking around now the funeral was over. One look at his face suggested he wouldn't welcome the question and she didn't want to spoil things. She was enjoying his company and hoped he felt the same.

'So, Debussy?' she prompted.

Hal pulled his thoughts together. 'There was supposed to have been a secret society formed to act as guardians of the bloodline parchments, the things Saunière may or may not have found in the Visigoth pillar. This organisation was alleged to have had some very famous leaders – figureheads if you like. Newton, for one, Leonardo da Vinci for another. And Debussy.'

Meredith burst out laughing.

'I know, I know,' Hal said, starting to grin. 'But I'm just giving you the story as my uncle told it.'

'Debussy lived for his music. And he was not a clubbable person. Very private, very loyal to a small group of friends. The thought of him running some secret society . . . well, it's just crazy!' She wiped the corner of her eye with her sleeve. 'What's the evidence to support this bizarre theory?'

Hal shrugged. 'Saunière did entertain many important Parisians and guests at Rennes-le-Château around the turn of the last century – something else that fuelled the conspiracy theories – heads of state, singers. Someone called Emma Calvé? Ring any bells?'

Meredith thought. 'French soprano, around at the right sort of time, but I'm pretty certain she never sang a major role for Debussy.' She wrote down the name. 'I'll check it out.'

'So it could fit?'

'Any theory can be made to fit if you try hard enough. Doesn't make it true.'

'Says the scholar.'

Meredith could hear the gentle teasing in his voice and decided she liked it. 'Says the person who's spent half her life in a library. Real life is never so neat. It's messy. Stuff overlaps, facts contradict each other. You find one piece of evidence, think it's all going on. You've nailed it. Next thing you know, you come across something else that turns it all on its head.'

For a while, they drove on in companionable silence. Apart from the clear antipathy he felt for his uncle, Hal was easy company. Meredith noticed the landscape this side of the hill was different, not so green. Grey rocks, like teeth, seemed to push out of the rust-coloured earth as if a series of violent earthquakes had forced up the hidden heart of the world. Slashes of red soil, like wounds in the land.

'It makes you realise,' she said, 'how little the essential landscape has changed. Take the cars and the buildings out of the equation, and you're left with mountains, gorges, valleys that have been here tens of thousands of years.'

She was intensely aware of the gentle rise and fall of his breathing in the confined space.

'I couldn't see it last night,' she rushed on, to hide her embarrassment. 'It all seemed too small, too insignificant to have been the centre of anything. But now ...' Meredith broke off. 'Up here, the sheer scale of things is different. It makes it more plausible that Saunière might have found something of value.' She paused. 'I'm not saying he did or he didn't, only that it gives substance to the theory.'

Hal nodded. 'Rhedae – the old name for Rennes-le-Château – was at the heart of the Visigoth empire in the south. Fifth, sixth and early seventh centuries.' He glanced at her, then back to the road. 'But from your professional standpoint, doesn't it seem a long time – too long – for something to lie undiscovered? If there was anything genuine to find – Visigoth or even earlier; Roman, I guess – surely it would have come to light before 1891?'

'Not necessarily,' Meredith replied. 'Think of the Dead Sea Scrolls. It's surprising how some things turn up, while others stay hidden for thousands of years. According to the guidebook, there are the remains of a Visigoth watch-tower nearby in the village of Fa and Visigoth crosses in the cemetery at the village of Cassaignes, both discovered pretty recently.'

Hal raised his eyebrows. 'They were Christians? I'm not sure I knew that.'

Meredith nodded. 'Another interesting thing is that it was Visigoth practice to bury their kings and noblemen with their treasure in hidden graves, rather than in graveyards round a church building. Swords, buckle clasps, jewellery, fibulae, drinking cups, crosses, you name it. Of course, this brought with it the same problems as the Ancient Egyptians.'

'How to deter grave robbers.'

'Exactly. So the Visigoths developed a way of constructing secret chambers below riverbeds. The technique was to dam the river and temporarily divert its course while the site was excavated and the burial chamber prepared. Once the king or warrior and his treasure were safely stowed, the chamber would be sealed and camouflaged with mud, sand, gravel, whatever, then the dam demolished. The water rushes back and the king and his treasure are hidden for eternity.'

Meredith turned to look at Hal, realising he had withdrawn into himself again. Something she'd said had triggered thoughts about something else.

'Are you all right?'

He looked as if he was about to speak, then at the last moment he stopped himself.

'We're nearly there.'

She couldn't figure him out. Even bearing in mind what he had been through, yesterday in particular, he seemed to switch from open and relaxed one moment, to a guy with the world on his shoulders the next.

Meredith looked straight ahead, not wanting to put him under pressure. If he wanted to confide in her, he would. No sense pushing it.

CHAPTER 46

Meredith peered through the windshield as Hal edged the car up the last bend in the road, and suddenly they had arrived.

Set high on the vertiginous hillside above them was a collection of houses and other buildings. There was a painted board welcoming them to Rennes-le-Château.

Son site, ses mystères.

White and purple flowers peeped out from the steep hedgerow at the side of the road, and big blooms, like giant, overblown hyacinths.

'There are poppies everywhere in the spring,' Hal said. 'It's really something.'

'It must be beautiful.'

They parked in a dusty lot with panoramic views over the entire southern expanse of the Haute Vallée and the mountains beyond.

Immediately behind them, there was a circular stone water tower. A square sundial painted on the south-facing curve marked the summer and winter solstices. At the top, there was an inscription. Meredith shielded her eyes to read it.

AÏCI LO TEMS S'EN
VA RES L'ETERNITAT.

At the edge of the parking lot was a map mounted on a viewing board. Hal jumped up onto the low wall and began to point things out: the mountain peaks of Bugarach, Soularac and Bézu, the towns of Quillan to the south, Espéraza to the south-west, Arques and Rennes-les-Bains to the east.

Meredith breathed out deeply. The endless sky, the outline of the peaks behind, the distinctive profile of the fir trees, the mountain flowers at the side of the road, the tower in the distance. It was reminiscent, she realised, of the background she remembered on La Fille d'Épées. The Tarot cards could easily have been painted with this landscape in mind.

'It says here,' Hal said, 'that on a clear day in the summer you can see twenty-two villages from this one point.'

He smiled, then jumped down and pointed to a gravel path.

'If I remember rightly, the church and museum are down that way.'

'What's that?' asked Meredith, pointing at a squat, crenellated tower built overlooking the valley.

'The Tour Magdala,' he replied. 'Saunière built the belvedere – the stone walkway that runs along the south side of his gardens – with this incredible view, at the very end of the renovation programme, 1898, 1899. The tower was to house his library.'

'The original collection's not in there, surely?'

'I doubt it,' he said. 'I suspect they've done what my dad did at the Domaine de la Cade – put a few replacement volumes in the cases, for atmosphere. He called, really pleased with himself, after he'd managed to buy a whole load of second-hand books from a *vide grenier* in Quillan.'

Meredith frowned.

'A second-hand sale,' he explained.

'Right.' She smiled. 'So, does that mean your father was pretty involved in the day-to-day running of the place?'

Hal sighed. 'Dad was the money – came over from the UK from time to time. It was my uncle's project. He found the place, persuaded my father to put up the cash, supervised the renovation, made all the decisions.' He paused. 'Until this year, that is. Dad retired and changed. For the better, really. Relaxed, enjoyed himself. He came over quite a few times in January and February, then moved over for good in May.'

'How did your uncle feel about that?'

Hal stuck his hands into his pockets and looked at the ground. 'I'm not sure.'

'Had your father always intended to retire to France?'

'I really don't know,' he said. Meredith heard the confusion in his voice and felt a rush of sympathy.

'You want to piece together the last few months of your father's life,' she said gently, understanding all too well.

Hal raised his head. 'That's it. We weren't exactly close. My mother died when I was eight and I was packed off to boarding school. Even when I was home in the holidays, Dad was always working. I can't say we really knew each other.' He paused. 'But we'd been starting to see a little more of each other in the past couple of years. I feel I owe it to him.'

Sensing Hal needed to go at his own pace, Meredith didn't press him on what he meant.

'So what kind of business was he in? Before he retired?'

'Investment banking. With a singular lack of imagination, I followed him into the same firm after I graduated from university.'

'Another reason you quit your job?' she asked. 'Do you inherit your father's share of the Domaine de la Cade?'

'An excuse, rather than a reason.' He paused. 'My uncle wants to buy me out. Not that he's said as much. But I keep thinking that maybe Dad would want me to get involved. Take over where he left off.'

'Did you ever talk to your father about it?'

'No. There didn't seem any point.'

They had been walking slowly while they were talking and were now standing outside an elegant villa giving directly onto the narrow street. Opposite was a pretty, formal garden with a generous stone pond and a café. The wooden shutters were down.

'I first came here with Dad,' Hal said, 'sixteen, seventeen years ago. Way before he and my uncle had ever thought of going into business together.'

Meredith smiled to herself, now understanding why Hal knew so much about Rennes-le-Château. The place was special to him because of the bond it gave him with his father.

'It's all been completely done up now, but then it was pretty derelict. The church was open for a couple of hours a day, watched over by a terrifying *gardienne* dressed all in black, who scared the living daylights out of me. The Villa Béthania here,' he pointed up at the impressive house, 'Saunière built for guests rather than for himself. When I came with Dad, it was open to the public, but in a totally haphazard way. You'd wander into one of the rooms and see a waxwork figure of Saunière sitting up in bed.'

Meredith laughed. 'Sounds awful.'

'All the papers and documents were lying about in unlocked display cases, in damp, unheated rooms beneath the belvedere.'

'An archivist's nightmare.'

He gestured through the railings. 'Now, as you can see, the place is a major tourist attraction. The cemetery itself, where Saunière is buried next to his housekeeper, was closed to the public in December 2004, when *The Da Vinci Code* took off and the number of visitors coming to Rennes-le-Château went through the roof. It's down here.'

They walked on in silence until they reached the high, solid metal gates protecting the graveyard.

Meredith tilted her head back to read the inscription set in a porcelain pendant above the locked gates.

'*Memento homo quia pulvis es et in pulverem reverteris.*'

'Which means?' Hal asked.

'Dust to dust,' she said. A shiver went down her spine. There was something about the place that made her uncomfortable. A brooding quality in the air, a watchfulness despite the deserted streets. She dug out her notepad and copied down the Latin.

'Do you write everything down?'

'Sure do. Occupational hazard.'

Meredith was glad to leave the graveyard behind them. She followed Hal past a stone Calvary, then doubled back up another tiny path to a small statue dedicated to Notre Dame de Lourdes behind wrought-iron railings.

The words PÉNITENCE, PÉNITENCE and MISSION 1891 were carved on the base of the ornate stone pillar.

Meredith stared. There was no getting away from it. That same date kept coming up.

'This is apparently the actual Visigoth pillar inside which the parchments were found,' Hal said.

'Is it hollow?'

'I suppose it must be.'

'If it is the original, it's crazy that they would leave it sitting here,' Meredith said. 'If this place is such a magnet for conspiracy theorists and treasure hunters, you'd think the authorities would worry someone would take it.'

Meredith looked attentively at the benign eyes and silent lips of the statue standing on top of the pillar. As she gazed at the stone features, imperceptibly at first, then deeper and more insistent, she saw scratch marks begin to appear on the gentle face. Ridges and furrows, like someone was gouging at the surface with a chisel.

Not trusting the evidence of her own eyes, she stepped forward and touched the stone.

'Meredith?' said Hal.

The surface was smooth. Quickly, she withdrew her fingers as if she'd been burnt. Nothing. She turned her palms over, as if expecting to see some mark there.

'Is something wrong?' he asked.

Only that I'm starting to see things.

'Just a trick of the light,' she said. 'That sun is bright.'

Hal looked concerned, which Meredith realised she didn't mind at all.

'Anyhow, what happened to the parchments after Saunière found them?'

'He was supposed to have taken them to Paris to have them verified.'

She frowned. 'That makes no sense. Why would he go to Paris? The logical thing for a Catholic priest would be to head straight to the Vatican.'

He laughed. 'I can see you don't read much fiction!'

'Although playing devil's advocate for a moment,' she continued, 'the counter-explanation would be, presumably, that he didn't trust the Church not to destroy the documents.'

Hal nodded. 'That's the most popular theory. Dad made the point that if a parish priest in a far corner of France really had stumbled upon some amazing secret – such as a marriage document or proof of descendants going back to the first century AD – then it would have been simpler for the Church to get rid of him rather than go to all the trouble of paying him off.'

'Good point.'

Hal paused. 'Although, he had an entirely different theory.'

Meredith turned to face him. 'Which was?'

'That the whole Rennes-le-Château saga was just a cover-up, a deliberate attempt to draw attention away from events going on at the same time in Rennes-les-Bains.'

Meredith felt a lurch in her stomach. 'Covering up what?'

'Saunière was known to be a friend of the family who owned the Domaine de la Cade. There was a run of unexplained deaths in the region – some kind of wolf, mountain cat most likely – but rumours built up about there being some sort of devil marauding across the countryside.'

Claw marks.

'Although the cause of the fire that destroyed much of the original house in 1897 was never proved, there's strong evidence that it was started deliberately. Maybe to rid the area of this devil they believed was being harboured in the grounds of the Domaine de la Cade. There was also something about a deck of Tarot cards associated with the Domaine. Saunière was supposed to have been involved in that too.'

The Bousquet Tarot.

'All I do know is that my uncle and Dad fell out over it,' Hal said.

Meredith forced herself to keep her voice steady. 'What happened?'

'At the end of April, just before my dad made the decision to come out here for good, I was staying with him in his London flat. I came into the room to catch the tail-end of the conversation. Argument, really. I didn't hear much of it: something about the interior of Saunière's church being a copy of an earlier tomb.'

'Did you ask your father what he meant?'

'He didn't want to talk about it. All he would say was that he'd learned there was a Visigoth mausoleum within the grounds of the Domaine de la Cade, a sepulchre, which was destroyed at the same time as the house caught fire. All that is left is a few old stones, ruins.'

For a second, Meredith was tempted to confide in Hal. Tell him all about the Tarot reading in Paris, about her nightmare last night, about the cards sitting, right now, at the bottom of her closet. About the additional reason she had come to Rennes-les-Bains at all, but something still held her back. Hal was fighting his own demons right now; he didn't need her adding to them. Then she remembered again the four-week delay between the accident and the funeral.

'What precisely happened to your father, Hal?' she asked, then worried she'd gone too far, too fast. 'I'm sorry, it was presumptuous of me to . . .'

Hal traced a pattern on the ground with his foot. 'No, it's fine. His car ran off the road, on the bend coming into Rennes-les-Bains. Went over into the river.' He spoke in a monotone. 'Police couldn't understand it. It was a clear night. It wasn't raining or anything. The worst thing was . . .'

He broke off.

'You don't have to tell me if it's too difficult,' she said softly, resting her hand in the small of his back.

'It happened in the early hours of the morning, so the car wasn't discovered until some hours later. He had been trying to get out, so the door was half open. It seemed the animals had got to him first. His body and face were badly scratched.'

'I'm so sorry.'

Meredith glanced back towards the statue on the path, fighting not to link in her mind a tragic accident in 2007 with the older superstitions that seemed to haunt the region. But the connections were hard to ignore.

All systems of divination, like music itself, work through patterns.

'The thing is, I could accept the situation if it was an accident. But they said he'd been drinking, Meredith. And that's the one thing I know he'd never do.' He dropped his voice. 'If I knew for sure what had happened, one way or the other, it would be all right. Not all right, but I mean I could deal with it. But it's the not knowing. Why was he there at all, on that stretch of road, at that time? I just want to know.'

Meredith thought of her birth mother's tear-stained face and the blood under her nails. She thought of the sepia photographs and the piece of music and the hollowness inside that had driven her to this corner of France.

'I can't deal with not knowing,' he repeated. 'Do you understand?'

It seemed the most natural thing to do to wrap her arms around him. He responded, putting his arms around her and folding her into him. Meredith fitted perfectly beneath his broad shoulders. She could smell his aftershave and soap, the soft wool of his sweater tickling her nose. Could feel the heat of him, his anger, his rage, then the despair behind both.

'Yes,' she said quietly. 'I understand.'

CHAPTER 47

DOMAINE DE LA CADE

Julian Lawrence waited until the chambermaids had finished the first floor before leaving his study. His nephew's trip to Rennes-le-Château and back would take two hours at least. He had plenty of time.

When Hal told him he was going out, and with a girl, Julian's first reaction had been relief. They had even talked for a couple of minutes without Hal storming out. Maybe it meant the boy was going to accept what had happened and get on with life? Let his doubts go.

As things stood, there were loose ends. Julian had hinted that he'd be willing to buy his nephew out of his inherited share of the Domaine de la Cade but had not pushed it. He had expected to have to wait until after the funeral, but he was getting impatient.

Then Hal had let drop that the girl in question was a writer and Julian had started to wonder. Given Hal's behaviour over the past four weeks, he wouldn't put it past the boy to try to get a journalist interested in the story of his father's accident, just for the hell of it.

Julian had checked the register and discovered she was an American, Meredith Martin, booked in until Friday. He'd no idea if she knew Hal or if his nephew was simply taking advantage of finding someone who might listen to his sob story. Either way, he couldn't risk Hal using the girl to stir up more trouble. He wasn't prepared to let his plans be damaged by rumour and innuendo.

Julian went up the back stairs and along the corridor. With the master key, he let himself into Meredith Martin's room. He took a couple of Polaroids, to make certain he could return the room to the exact state in which he'd found it – a basic precaution – then started to search, beginning with the bedside table. He went quickly through the drawers but found nothing of interest other than two plane tickets: one for Toulouse to Paris Orly on Friday afternoon, the other her return flight to the States on 11th November.

He moved to the bureau. Her laptop was plugged in. He opened the lid and booted it up. It was easy. There was no password protection on her operating system and she had been using the hotel's wireless system.

Ten minutes later, Julian had read through her emails – tedious, domestic stuff, nothing relevant – tracked her online trail through recent sites she'd visited and looked at a few of the stored files. None of it suggested she was a journalist out for a story. Local history, mainly. There were notes about research in England, then very basic stuff – addresses, dates, times – about Paris.

Next, Julian went into her picture files, going through them in date order. The first few were taken in London. There was a folder of shots from Paris – streets scenes, landmarks, even one of a sign showing the opening hours of the Parc Monceau.

The final folder was marked Rennes-les-Bains. He opened it and began to peruse the images. These worried him more. There were several photographs of the riverbank at the entrance to the town to the north, specifically a couple of the road bridge and the tunnel at exactly the place where his brother Seymour's car had left the road.

There were other photographs of the graveyard at the rear of the church. One, taken from the covered porch looking back to the place des Deux Rennes, enabled him to identify exactly when they had been taken. Julian laced his fingers behind his head. He could just make out, in the bottom right-hand corner of the picture, part of the tablecloth on which the book of condolence had sat.

His brow furrowed. Why had Meredith Martin been in Rennes-les-Bains last night taking photographs of the funeral and the town?

He exited the programme and shut the computer down, leaving everything just as he'd found it, then moved to the wardrobe. He took a couple more Polaroids, then worked methodically through every pocket, the piles of T-shirts and shoes, finding nothing of interest. He had no compunction about going through the woman's personal belongings. If she was doing nothing wrong, then she'd have nothing to worry about.

At the bottom of the wardrobe, beneath a pair of boots and a pair of high-heeled shoes, was a soft black travel bag. Squatting down, Julian undid the zip and looked inside the main compartment. It was empty apart from a pair of socks and a bead bracelet, caught in the stiff lining. He pushed his fingers into every corner but found nothing, then went through the outside pockets. Two large compartments at either end, both empty, then along either side three small-er compartments. He turned the bag upside down and shook it. It seemed heavy. He turned the bag over again and pulled at the cardboard base. With a tearing sound of Velcro, the lining came up to reveal another compart-ment. He reached in and drew out a square package of black silk. With his thumb and forefinger, he unfolded the four corners.

Julian froze. The face of Justice was staring up at him.

For a split second, he thought he was seeing things, then he realised it was just another reproduction set. He fanned them out to make sure, cutting the deck twice.

Printed, laminated, not the original Bousquet Tarot. Stupid that, even for a second, he'd thought it could possibly be.

'Who are you?' he muttered.

He flicked through the cards in case there was something unique, something different about this deck. There wasn't. It appeared the same as the one he had downstairs in his safe. No additional words, no variation in the images.

Julian thought. This discovery turned everything on its head, especially coming on the heels of the information coming out of the Visigoth burial site at Quillan. With the grave goods, a slate had been found confirming the existence of other sites in the vicinity of the Domaine de la Cade.

But the immediate question was: why did Meredith Martin have a reproduction set of the Bousquet deck? It couldn't be coincidence. Presumably, at the very least, she knew about the original deck of cards and their association with the Domaine de la Cade?

What else? Maybe Seymour had said more to his son than Julian had realised? And if Hal had brought her down here, rather than just taking advantage of meeting her here, maybe it wasn't to investigate the circumstances of the crash, but to do with the cards?

He needed a drink, not least from the shock of believing, if only for a moment, that he was holding the original cards in his hands.

Julian wrapped the replica deck back up in the black silk, returned the package to the bag and replaced it at the bottom of the wardrobe. He glanced round the room one last time. Everything looked as it had before. If anything was misplaced, Ms Martin would put it down to the chambermaids. He let himself out into the corridor and walked briskly back towards the service stairs.

CHAPTER 48

Hal was the first to break away.
'I'm sorry.'

Meredith also stepped back. The strength of their attraction to one another, now the emotion of the moment had passed, left them both a little awkward.

'There's no need to be sorry,' she said, pushing her hands into her pockets. Like her, she could see he wasn't sure quite what had just happened.

'Anyway,' Hal said, turning to the wooden gates at right angles to the path and trying the lock. 'Unbelievable, but it seems it's closed. I'm sorry. I should have called ahead.'

They looked at one another. Then they both burst out laughing.

'The spa in Rennes-les-Bains was closed too,' she said. 'Until April thirtieth.'

A lock of unruly hair had fallen forward. Meredith's fingers ached to push it back from his face, but she kept her hands in her pockets.

'But at least the church is open,' he said.

Meredith stood beside him, very aware of his physical presence now. He seemed to fill the entire path.

Hal pointed up at the triangular porch above the door.

'That inscription – TERRIBILIS EST LOCUS ISTE – is another reason all the conspiracy theories surrounding

Rennes-le-Château took hold,' he said, clearing his throat. 'The phrase actually translates as "this place is awe-inspiring" – *terribilis* in an Old Testament sense, rather than "terrible" in a modern sense – but you can imagine how it's been interpreted.'

Meredith did look, but it was the other, partially legible inscription on the apex that she was concentrating on. IN HOC SIGNO VINCES. Constantine again, the Christian emperor of Byzantium. The same inscription as on Henri Boudet's memorial in Rennes-les-Bains. She pictured Laura's spread of cards on the table. The Emperor was one of the major arcana, near the Magician and La Prêtresse, at the beginning of the deck. And the internet password . . .

'Who came up with the password for the hotel network?' she asked.

If Hal was surprised at the non sequitur, he didn't miss a beat.

'My uncle,' he said. 'Dad wasn't into computers.' Then he reached out and took her hand. 'Shall we?'

The first thing that struck Meredith as they walked into the church was how very small it was, like it had been built on a three-quarter scale. The perspectives seemed all wrong.

On the wall to the right were handwritten notices: some French, some awkward English. Piped choral music, some kind of mediocre plainsong, filtered in over thin silver speakers suspended in the corners.

'They've sanitised the place,' Hal said in a low voice. 'To counteract all the rumours of mysterious treasure and secret societies, they've tried to inject a Catholic message into everything. Like this, for example.' He tapped one of the signs. 'Look. "*Dans cette église, le trésor c'est vous.*" In this church, the treasure is you.'

But Meredith was staring at the stoup for holy water on the immediate left of the door. The *bénitier* was balanced on the shoulders of a three-foot-high statue of a devil. The malevolent red face, the twisted body, the unnerving, piercing blue eyes. She'd seen the demon before. At least, an image of him. Lying on the table in Paris as Laura spread out the major arcana at the beginning of the reading.

Le Diable. Card XV of the Bousquet Tarot.

'That's Asmodeus,' said Hal. 'The traditional guardian of treasure, keeper of secrets and builder of the Temple of Solomon.'

Meredith touched the grimacing demon, which felt cold and chalky beneath her fingers. She looked at his hands, clawed and twisted, and couldn't help glancing back through the open door to where the statue of Notre Dame of Lourdes stood immobile upon the pillar.

She gave a small shake of her head and raised her eyes to the frieze above. A tableau of four angels, each making one part of the sign of the cross, and Constantine's words yet again, although this time in French. The colours were faded and chipped, as if the angels were fighting a losing battle.

On the base, two basilisks framed a red inset containing the letters BS.

'The initials could stand for Bérenger Saunière,' said Hal. 'Or for Boudet and Saunière, or for La Blanque and La Salz, two local rivers that meet at a pool nearby known as *le bénitier*.'

'The two priests knew each other well?' she asked.

'By all accounts, yes. Boudet was a mentor to the younger Saunière. In the early days of Boudet's ministry, when he spent some months in the parish of Durban nearby, he also became friendly with a third priest, Antoine Gélis, who subsequently took over the parish at Coustaussa.'

'I drove by there yesterday,' Meredith said. 'It looked ruined.'

'The castle is. The village is inhabited, though it's tiny. No more than a handful of houses. Gélis died in somewhat strange circumstances. Murdered on Hallowe'en 1897.'

'The thirty-first again,' she muttered. 'They never found out who was responsible?'

'Don't think so, no.' Hal stopped in front of another plaster statue. 'Saint Anthony, the Hermit,' he said. 'Famous Egyptian saint of the third, fourth century.'

This information drove any thoughts of Gélis out of Meredith's mind.

The Hermit. Another card from the major arcana.

The evidence to prove that the Bousquet Tarot had been painted in the area was overwhelming. This tiny church dedicated to Mary Magdalene was testament to that. The only thing Meredith wasn't clear about was how the Domaine de la Cade fitted in.

And how, if at all, this connects with my own family.

Meredith forced herself to concentrate on the matter in hand. No sense muddling everything up together. What if Hal's father was right in his suggestion that everything in Rennes-le-Château had been constructed precisely to draw attention away from its sister village down in the valley? There was a logic to it, but Meredith needed to know more before jumping to any conclusions.

'Shall I leave you to look around on your own?' Hal asked.

Meredith shook her head. 'No, I'm done.'

They didn't talk much as they walked back up to the car. It was a comfortable silence, but Meredith was very aware of the sound of their feet on the gravel, crunching like tightly packed snow.

'Three corpses were found buried in the grounds of the Villa Béthania in the 1950s,' Hal said. 'All were male, aged between thirty and forty, and they had all been shot, although one of the bodies at least had been very badly mauled by wild animals. The official verdict was that they'd been killed during the war – the Nazis occupied some of this part of France, and the Resistance was pretty active down here. But local belief is that the bodies were older, end of the nineteenth century, that they were connected with the fire at the Domaine de la Cade and, possibly, also the murder of the priest in Coustaussa.'

Meredith looked at Hal over the roof of the car. 'Was the fire started deliberately? I read it was.'

Hal shrugged. 'Local history is sketchy on the point, but the general consensus is that it was.'

'But if these three men were involved – in either the fire or the murder – who do people think killed them?'

At that moment, Hal's cell phone rang. He flipped the lid and glanced at the number. His eyes sharpened.

'I need to take this,' he said, covering the speaker. 'Sorry.'

Inwardly, Meredith groaned with frustration. 'Of course, go ahead,' she said.

She climbed into the car and watched as Hal wandered over to a fir tree near the Tour Magdala to talk.

No such thing as coincidence. Everything happens for a reason.

She leant back against the headrest and ran through everything that had happened, the sequence of events from the moment she'd stepped off the train at the Gare du Nord. No, after that. From the moment she set foot on the colourful painted steps that led up to Laura's rooms.

Meredith pulled her notebook out of her purse and glanced over her notes, looking for answers. The real question was: which was the story she was chasing down here, which the echo? She was in Rennes-les-Bains searching for her own family history. Did the cards fit in with that in any way? Or was it a completely different, unrelated story? Of academic interest, but nothing to do with her? Did she even have a connection with the Domaine de la Cade? The Verniers?

What had Laura said? Meredith flipped back through her notes until she found it.

'The timeline is confused. The sequence seems to be jumping backwards and forwards, as if there is some blurring of events. Things slipping between past and present.'

She glanced through the window at Hal, who was now walking back towards the car, holding his cell clenched in his hand. The other was dug deep in his pocket.

Where does he fit into all this?

'Is everything all right?' she said, as he opened the door.

He got in. 'I'm so sorry, Meredith. I was going to suggest we went for lunch, but something's come up that I need to sort out first.'

'Something good?' she asked.

'The police commissariat handling the case in Couiza have finally agreed to let me have sight of the file into my father's accident. I've been asking for this for weeks, so it's a step forward.'

'That's great, Hal,' she said, hoping he wasn't getting his hopes up for no reason.

'So I can either drop you back at the hotel,' he continued, 'or you could come with me and we'll find somewhere to eat later. Only problem with that is I'm not sure how long I'll be. They don't always move fast down here.'

For a moment, Meredith was tempted to tag along to give him moral support, but she figured it was something he needed to do on his own.

'Sounds like you might be a while,' she said. 'If you don't mind dropping me back at the hotel on your way, that would be fine.'

She was gratified to see Hal's expression falter, just for a moment.

'Then what about later?' he said, as he negotiated the narrow street out of Rennes-le-Château. 'We could meet for a drink. Dinner, even? If you've not got plans.'

'I'd like that.' She smiled.

CHAPTER 49

Julian Lawrence was standing at his study window at the Domaine de la Cade as his nephew turned the car and drove back down the long drive. He switched his attention to the woman who'd just got out and who was now waving goodbye.

He nodded his approval. Good figure, athletic but petite, straight dark hair to her shoulders. It wouldn't be such a trial to spend a little time in her company.

Then she turned around and Julian recognised her, although he couldn't place her. He dug into his memory until it came to him. The pushy bitch from the traffic hold-up in Rennes-les-Bains last night. The American accent.

Another flash of concern. If Ms Martin was here working with Hal, and had mentioned she'd seen him driving into the town, his nephew might legitimately question where he'd been. Might realise the excuse Julian had given for being late for the funeral didn't make sense.

He drained his glass, then pulled his jacket from the back of the door and walked out to intercept her in the lobby.

On the journey back from Rennes-le-Château, Meredith started to feel excited. Before, Laura's gift had felt like a burden. Now, the Tarot cards seemed full of intriguing possibilities.

She waited until Hal's car had disappeared from view, then turned and headed up the steps to the main door of the hotel. The same contradictory feelings she'd experienced when sitting with Laura were back, big time. Hope versus scepticism, the prickling anticipation versus the fear that she was putting two and two together and coming up with five.

'Ms Martin?'

Meredith turned in the direction of the voice to see Hal's uncle striding towards her across the lobby. She tensed, hoping that after their bad-tempered exchange in Rennes-les-Bains last night he wouldn't recognise her. But today he was smiling.

'Ms Martin?' he said, holding out his hand. 'Julian Lawrence. I just wanted to welcome you to the Domaine de la Cade,' he said.

'Thank you.'

They shook hands.

'Also,' he stopped, giving a slight shrug, 'I wanted to apologise if I was rather abrupt yesterday, in the town. If I'd known you were a friend of my nephew's, I would of course have introduced myself then.'

Meredith blushed. 'I didn't think you'd remember me, Mr Lawrence. I'm afraid I was pretty rude myself.'

'Not in the slightest. As I'm sure Hal told you, it was a rather difficult day for us all yesterday. It's no excuse, I know, but . . .'

He left the apology hanging.

Meredith noticed how he had the same habit as Hal of staring right at a person with an unwavering gaze that seemed to blot out everything else. And, although some thirty years older, he had that same kind of charisma as Hal. A way of filling the space. She wondered if Hal's father had been the same.

'Of course,' she said. 'I'm sorry for your loss, Mr Lawrence.'

'Julian, please. And thank you. It was a shock.' He paused. 'Speaking of my nephew, Ms Martin, I don't suppose you know where he's disappeared off to? I was under the impression you were going to Rennes-le-Château this morning, but that he would be here this afternoon.'

'We did go, but a call just came through from the police station, so he dropped me off before going on to deal with things. Couiza, I think he said.'

She sensed a sharpening of interest, even though Julian's expression didn't change. Immediately, Meredith regretted saying so much.

'What sort of things?' he asked.

'He didn't really say,' she said in a rush.

'Pity, I had hoped for a word with him.' He shrugged. 'But it's nothing that can't wait.' He smiled again, but this time it failed to reach his eyes. 'I trust you're enjoying your stay with us? You have everything you need?'

'Everything's great.' She glanced at the stairs.

'Forgive me,' he said. 'I'm holding you up.'

'I've got some stuff I need to . . .'

Julian nodded. 'Ah, yes. Hal mentioned you were a writer. Are you here working on an assignment?'

'Just a little research,' she replied.

'Is that so?' He offered his hand. 'In which case, I won't delay you further.'

Not wishing to be rude, Meredith took it. This time, the touch of his skin made her uncomfortable. Too personal, somehow.

'If you see my nephew before I catch up with him,' he said, squeezing her fingers a little, 'do let him know I'm looking for him, won't you?'

Meredith nodded. 'I will.'

Then he turned and walked back across the lobby without a backward glance. Clear message. He was confident, sure of himself, in control.

Meredith let a long whistle escape from between her lips, wondering exactly what had just happened. She stood staring into the empty space where Julian had been. A normal, casual enquiry, or something more?

Don't overthink everything.

She glanced around. The desk clerk was dealing with a query and facing the opposite direction. From the noise coming from the restaurant, Meredith figured most guests were already in the dining room having lunch. Perfect for what she had in mind.

She walked quickly across the red-and-black tiles, ducked round beside the piano, then reached up and took the photograph of Anatole and Léonie Vernier and Isolde Lascombe from the wall. She slipped it beneath her jacket, then doubled back and ran up the stairs, taking them two at a time.

Only when she was back in her room, with the door safely shut behind her, did her breathing return to normal. She paused a moment and looked around the room.

There was something about the atmosphere that seemed different. An alien smell, very subtle, but there all the same. She wrapped her arms around herself, remembering her nightmare. Then she shook her head. *Don't do this.* The maids had been in to make up the bed. Besides, she thought, it wasn't at all like what she'd felt in the night.

Dreamed, she corrected herself.

Just a dream.

Then, there was a definite sense of someone being in the room with her. A presence, a chill in the air. Now, it was just . . .

Meredith shrugged. Polish or a cleaning product, that was all. It wasn't so strong. Not really. Although she couldn't help wrinkling her nose. Like the smell of the sea washing stagnant on the shore.

CHAPTER 50

Meredith retrieved the Tarot deck, unfolding the four corners of black silk as if the cards inside were made of glass.

The unsettling image of the Tower was on the top, the trees more vivid here in the clouded afternoon than they had seemed in Paris. Then she paused. Hadn't the Justice card been at the top of the pile when Laura pressed the cards upon her? Obviously not.

She cleared a space on the bureau and put the cards down, then pulled out her notebook from her purse, wishing she'd taken the time last night to transpose her scribbled notes about the reading from page to screen.

Meredith thought for a moment, trying to figure out whether, if she laid out the ten cards that had come up yesterday, in the peace and quiet of her own thoughts, she might see something more in them. She decided against it. She was less interested in the reading *per se* than in the historical data she was gathering about the Bousquet Tarot and how the cards fitted in to the story of the Domaine de la Cade, the Verniers and the Lascombe family.

Meredith searched the deck until she had found all twenty-two of the major arcana. Putting the other cards to one side, she then laid them out in three rows, one above the other, placing the Fool at the top on his own, just like Laura had done. The cards felt different to the touch. Yesterday they'd made her nervous. As if she was committing herself to something even by handling them. Today they seemed – and she knew it sounded stupid – kind of well meaning.

She slid the stolen framed photograph from under her jacket, propped it on the bureau in front of her and studied the three black-and-white figures, frozen in time. Then she dropped her eyes to the colourful images.

For a moment, her attention rested on Le Pagad, with his blue eyes and thick black hair, gathering all the symbols of the Tarot to him. An attractive image, but a man to be trusted?

Then that same tingling feeling on the back of her neck as a new idea took hold. Was it possible? She put the Magician to one side. She picked up The Fool, Le Mat, and held it against the framed photograph, then nodded with satisfaction. There was no doubt the man was 'Monsieur Vernier' brought to life. Though less formal, in a pale suit and boater, it was the same debonair expression, the slim figure, the black moustache.

Next, card II, La Prêtresse. The ethereal, pale, distant features of 'Madame Lascombe', although in an evening gown, cut low at the neck, rather than the formal day clothes of the photograph.

Finally, card VIII, La Force: 'Mademoiselle Léonie Vernier'.

Meredith felt herself smiling. She felt the greatest connection with this card, almost as if she knew the girl. In a way, she guessed, it was because Léonie resembled her mental image of Lilly Debussy. Léonie was younger, but there was that same wide-eyed innocence, the same thick auburn hair, although loose on the card and tumbling down over her shoulders, rather than tied up in a formal style. Most of all, that same way of gazing directly into the lens.

A glint of understanding rippled beneath the surface of her mind but was gone before Meredith could grasp it.

She turned her attention to the other cards of the major arcana that had come up in the course of the day: the Devil, the Tower, the Hermit, the Emperor. She studied each in turn, but increasingly with the sense that they were taking her further away from where she wanted to be, not closer.

Meredith sat back in her chair, put her hands behind her head and closed her eyes.

What am I not seeing?

She let her thoughts wander back to the reading. Allowed Laura's words to flow over her, in no particular order, letting the patterns emerge.

Octaves. All the eights.

Eight was the number of completion, of successful outcomes. There was also an explicit message about interference, obstacles and conflict. Both Strength and Justice, in older packs, carried the number eight. Both La Justice and Le Pagad had the infinity symbol, like a sideways figure of eight.

Music linked everything together. Her family background, the Bousquet Tarot, the Verniers, the reading in Paris, the sheet of piano music. She reached for her notebook, going back through the pages until she found the name she was looking for, the American cartomancer who'd linked the Tarot with music. She switched on her laptop, tapping her fingers impatiently as it sought a connection. Finally, the search box flashed up on the screen. Meredith typed PAUL FOSTER CASE. Moments later, a list of sites appeared.

She went straight to the Wikipedia entry, which was thorough and straightforward. An American, Paul Foster Case became interested in cards in the early 1900s while he was working the steamboats playing piano and organ in vaudeville. Thirty years later in Los Angeles, he set up an organisation to promote his own Tarot system, the Builders of the Adytum, known as BOTA. One of the distinguishing features of BOTA was that Case went public with his philosophy, in sharp contrast to most esoteric systems of the time, which relied on absolute secrecy and the idea of an elite. It was also interactive. Unlike any other decks, the BOTA cards were black and white, the idea being that each individual could colour them in, put their own mark upon them. This, as much as anything, helped bring Tarot into the US mainstream.

Another of Case's innovations was the association of musical notes with certain of the major arcana. All of them, with the exception of card XX, the Sun, and IX, the Hermit – as if those two images alone stood outside the common run of things – were linked with a specific note.

Meredith looked at the illustration of a keyboard, with arrows showing which card went with which.

The Tower, Judgement and the Emperor were all assigned to the note C; the Devil was linked with A; D connected with the Lovers and Strength; the Magician and the unnumbered Fool were E.

C–A–D–E. Domaine de la Cade.

C–A–D–E. All white notes, all associated with particular cards of the major arcana that had come up already.

And more than that, Meredith saw another connection that had been staring her in the face all along. She reached for her inherited sheet of piano music: *Sepulchre 1891*. She knew the piece backwards – the forty-five bars, the change of tempo in the middle section – in style and character suggesting nineteenth-century gardens and girls in white dresses. Echoes of Debussy and Satie and Dukas.

And built around the notes of A, C, D and E.

For a moment, Meredith forgot what she was doing, picturing her fingers flying over the keyboard. Nothing but the music existed. A, C, D and E. The final split arpeggio, the last chord fading away.

She sat back in her chair. Everything fitted together, sure. *But what, if anything, does it mean?*

In a moment, Meredith was back in Milwaukee, Miss Bridge's advanced music class in senior high, repeating the same mantra over and over. A smile came to her lips. 'An octave is made up of twelve plus one chromatic tones.' She could all but hear her teacher's voice in her head. 'The semitone and the whole tone are the building blocks of the diatonic scale. There are eight tones in the diatonic scale, five in the pentatonic. The first, third and fifth tones in the diatonic scale are the building blocks of root chords, the formula for perfection, for beauty.'

Meredith let her memories come. Music and math, seeking the connections, not the coincidences. She typed FIBONACCI into the search box. Watched as new words appeared in front of her. In 1202, Leonardo of Pisa, known as Fibonacci, developed a mathematical theory where numbers formed a sequence. After two starting values, each number was the sum of the two preceding numbers.

0, 1, 1, 2, 3, 5, 8, 13, 21, 34, 55, 89, 144, 233, 377.

The relationship between pairs of consecutive numbers was said to approach the golden proportion, the golden mean.

In music, the Fibonacci principle was sometimes used to determine tunings. Fibonacci numbers also appeared in natural settings, such as branching in trees, the curve of waves, the arrangement of a pine cone. In sunflowers, for example, there were always eighty-nine seeds. Meredith smiled.

I remember.

Debussy had flirted with the Fibonacci sequence in his great orchestral tone poem *La Mer*. It was one of the wonderful contradictions of Debussy that, although he was seen as a composer primarily concerned with mood and colour, some of his most popular works were in fact constructed around mathematical models. Or, rather, could be divided into sections that reflected the golden ratio, frequently by using the numbers of the standard Fibonacci sequence. So in *La Mer* the first movement was fifty-five bars long – a Fibonacci number – and it broke down into five sections of 21, 8, 8, 5 and 13 bars, all also Fibonacci numbers.

Meredith forced herself to slow down, to order her thoughts.

She went back to the Paul Foster Case entry. Three of the four notes linked to the name of the Domaine – c, a and e – were Fibonacci numbers: the Fool was zero, the Magician was I and Strength was VIII.

Only d, card VI, the Lovers, wasn't a Fibonacci number.

Meredith ran a hand through her hair. Did that mean she'd got it wrong? Or that it was the exception that reinforced the rule?

She looked at the card again and, this time, saw that the two figures resembled Madame Lascombe and Anatole Vernier. If that was the case, then the Lovers did fit the sequence if treated as individuals rather than as a pair: Le Mat was zero, the Priestess was card II. And zero and two were both Fibonacci numbers, even if six was not.

Meredith frowned. All well and good, but even if those connections were valid, how could there be a link between the Bousquet Tarot, the Domaine de la Cade and Paul Foster Case? The dates didn't work.

Case set up BOTA in the 1930s in America. The Bousquet deck dated back to the 1890s, the minor arcana cards possibly even earlier. There was no way it could have been based on Case's system.

What if I turn it on its head?

Meredith thought harder. What if Case had heard of the association of Tarot with music and then refined it for his own system? What if he'd heard of the Bousquet Tarot? Or maybe the Domaine de la Cade itself? Could the ideas have passed not from America to France, but the other way round?

She pulled the battered envelope from her purse and extracted the picture of the young man in soldier's uniform. How had she been so blind? She had seen how the figure of Le Mat was Anatole Vernier, but hadn't taken seriously the obvious resemblance between Vernier and her soldier. The family resemblance to Léonie too.

She glanced back to the portrait. These dates were right. The boy in the soldier's uniform could be a younger brother, a cousin. Even a son.

And through him, down the generations, to me.

Meredith felt as if a great weight was being lifted from her chest. The burden of not knowing, like Hal had said earlier, crumbling and folding in on itself as she edged closer to the truth. But instantly, the cautious voice in her head kicked in, warning her against seeing what she wanted to see rather than what was there.

Verify it. The facts are out there. Test it.

Her determined fingers flying over the keys, Meredith hammered the word VERNIER into the search box but found nothing of use.

Try again. There's got to be something.

She added Bousquet and Rennes-les-Bains. This time, she got a few sites selling Tarot cards, and a couple of paragraphs about the Bousquet deck, but nothing more than she'd already found out.

Meredith sat back in her chair. The obvious way forward was to register with family search websites in this part of France and see if she could pick her way back to the past that way, although it would take a while. But maybe Mary could help out from the other end.

She fired off an email to Mary, asking her to check the Milwaukee local history websites and electoral rolls for the name Vernier, aware that if the soldier was Léonie's son, rather than Anatole's, she still might not have the right name. As an afterthought, she added the name Lascombe as well, then signed off with a long line of kisses.

The phone beside the bed rang.

For a moment, she just stared at it. Then, she grabbed the receiver. 'Hello?'

'Meredith? It's Hal.'

She could hear straight off that things weren't good. 'Are you OK?'

'I was just letting you know I was back.'

'How did it go?

A pause, then, 'I'll tell you when I see you. I'll wait in the bar. I don't want to drag you away from your work.'

Meredith glanced at the time and was amazed to see it was a quarter after six already. She looked at the chaotic mess of cards, tagged internet sites and photographs lying on the bureau, evidence of her afternoon's work. Her head felt ready to explode. She had found out plenty but still felt she was in the dark.

She didn't want to stop, but she knew she could no longer think straight. All those high-school nights when Bill would come into her room and tell her it was time to take a break. Tell her that everything would be clearer after a good night's sleep. He was always so steady, so matter-of-fact.

'Actually, now is a good time to stop.'

'Really? You're sure I'm not interrupting anything?'

The relief in his voice made Meredith smile. 'I'm sure,' she said. 'I'll finish up and be down in ten.'

Meredith changed into a fresh white shirt and her favourite black skirt, put a little powder on her cheeks and a couple of strokes of mascara, then twisted her hair up into a knot.

She was putting on her boots, ready to go down, when her laptop bleeped. The email from Mary was only two lines long, but the message contained a name, dates, an address and the promise to email again as soon as she had more to tell.

A smile broke out across Meredith's face.

Nailed it.

She picked up the photograph, no longer an unknown soldier. There was still way more to pin down, but she was on her way. She tucked the picture into the frame of the photograph, where it belonged. The family reunited. Her family.

Still standing, she leaned over and clicked reply.

'You're totally amazing,' she typed. 'All further info gratefully received! Love you.'

Meredith pressed send. Then, still smiling, she went down to find Hal.

PART VII

Carcassonne
September–October 1891

CHAPTER 51

SUNDAY, 27TH SEPTEMBER 1891

The morning after the dinner party, Léonie, Anatole and Isolde rose late. The evening had been a great success, everyone agreed. The generous rooms and passageways of the Domaine de la Cade, so long silent, had been brought back to life. The servants whistled in the corridors. Pascal grinned as he went about his business. Marieta skipped lightly across the hall with a smile on her face.

Only Léonie was out of sorts. She had a headache brought on by the unaccustomed quantity of wine she had consumed and the after-effects of Monsieur Baillard's confidences.

She spent much of the morning lying upon the *chaise longue* with a cold compress on her head. She thought of her mother and half wished she was here to look after her, although, in truth, Marguerite had never been at her best in the sickroom. She determined to finish her letter to her mother, which remained unfinished in her bedroom. When Léonie did feel recovered enough to eat a little toasted bread and beef consommé for luncheon, she found herself subject to the sort of malaise that inevitably follows the passing of a big event. The dinner party having loomed in her mind for so long, she felt there was no longer anything to look forward to.

Meanwhile, she saw Isolde move from room to room in her customary calm and unhurried manner, but as if a burden had been lifted from her shoulders. The look upon her face suggested that now, perhaps for the first time, she felt as if she were the chatelaine of the Domaine. That she owned the house rather than that the house owned her. Anatole, too, whistled as he walked from hall to library, from drawing room to the terrace, looking like a man who had the world at his feet.

Later that afternoon, Léonie accepted Isolde's invitation to walk in the gardens. She needed to clear her head and, feeling slightly better, was glad of the opportunity to stretch her legs. The air was still and warm, the afternoon sun gentle upon her cheeks. Quickly, she felt her spirits restored.

They chatted pleasantly on the usual topics as Isolde led Léonie down in the direction of the lake. Music, books, the latest fashions.

'So, now,' said Isolde. 'How shall we occupy your time while you are here? Anatole tells me you are interested in local history and archaeology? There are several excellent trips. To the ruined castle at Coustaussa, for example?'

'I would like that.'

'And, of course, reading. Anatole always says you have a hunger for books as other women have for jewellery and clothes.'

Léonie pulled a face. 'He thinks I read too much, but only because he does not read sufficiently! He knows all about books as objects but is not interested in the stories that lie between the pages.'

Isolde laughed. 'Which, of course, may be why he was obliged to resit his examinations for his baccalaureate!'

Léonie shot a look at Isolde. 'He told you this?'

'Of course not, no,' she said quickly. 'What man brags of his failures?'

'Then—'

'Despite the lack of intimacy between my late husband and your mother, Jules liked to be kept informed of the events in his nephew's education and upbringing.'

Léonie glanced at her aunt with interest. Her mother had been quite clear that the communication between her and her half-brother had been minimal. She was on the point of pressing Isolde further, but her aunt was speaking again and the moment was lost.

'Have I mentioned I have recently taken out a subscription with the Société Musicale de la Lyre in Carcassonne, although so far I have been unable to attend any concerts? I am aware that it might become rather dull for you, cooped up here in the country, so far from any entertainments.'

'I am perfectly content,' Léonie said.

Isolde smiled her appreciation. 'I am obliged to make a trip to Carcassonne some time in the next few weeks, so I thought we might make an outing of it. Spend a few days in the city. How would that be?'

Léonie's eyes widened with delight. 'That would be wonderful, Aunt. When?'

'I am waiting for a letter from my late husband's lawyers. A point of query. As soon as I receive word, we will make the arrangements to travel.'

'Anatole too?'

'Of course,' Isolde replied, smiling. 'He tells me you would like to see something of the restored medieval Cité. It looks quite unchanged, they say, from the thirteenth century. It is really quite remarkable what they have achieved. Until some fifty years ago, it was a ruin. Thanks to the work of Monsieur Viollet-le-Duc, and those who carry on his work, the slums have almost all been cleared. Nowadays, it is safe for tourists to visit.'

They had reached the end of the path. They struck out towards the lake, then on in the direction of the small, shaded promontory that afforded a wonderful view of the water.

'So now that we are better acquainted, would you mind if I asked you a question of a rather personal nature?' Isolde asked.

'Well, no,' Léonie said cautiously, 'although I suppose it would depend on the nature of the question.'

Isolde laughed. 'I wondered, only, if you had an admirer?'

Léonie blushed. 'I . . .'

'Forgive me, have I presumed too much on our friendship?'

'No,' Léonie said quickly, not wishing to appear gauche or naive, although, in truth, all her notions of romantic love had been acquired from novels and opera. 'Not in the slightest. It is just that you . . . you took me by surprise.'

Isolde turned to her. 'Well, then? Is there someone?'

Léonie experienced a momentary flash of regret that there was not. She had dreamed, but of characters she had met between the pages of books or of heroes glimpsed upon the stage singing of love and honour. Never, yet, had her unspoken fantasies attached themselves to a living, breathing person.

'I have no interest in such things,' she said firmly. 'Indeed, in my opinion, marriage is a form of servitude.'

Isolde hid a smile. 'You are young. All girls dream of love.'

'Not I. I have seen Maman—'

She broke off, not wishing to be disloyal, but remembering the scenes, the tears, the days when there was no money to put food on the table, the procession of men coming and going.

Isolde's serene expression was sombre. 'Marguerite's situation has been a difficult one. She has done what she can to make things comfortable for you and Anatole. You should try not to judge her harshly.'

'I do not judge her,' she said, stung by the rebuke. 'I . . . I just do not wish such a life for myself.'

'Love – true love – is a precious thing, Léonie,' Isolde continued. 'It is painful, uncomfortable, makes fools of us all, but it is what breathes meaning and colour and purpose into our lives. Love is the one thing that lifts our common experience to the extraordinary.'

Léonie stared at her feet. 'It is not only Maman who has made me turn my face away from love,' she added. 'I have witnessed how sorely Anatole has suffered. I dare say this affects the way I see things.'

Isolde turned. Léonie felt the full force of her grey eyes upon her and found she could not meet her gaze.

'There was a girl he loved very much,' she continued. 'She died. This past March. I do not know precisely the manner of her death, only that the circumstances were distressing.' She swallowed hard. 'For months afterwards, Maman and I feared for him. His spirit was broken and his nerves shot to pieces, so much so that he took refuge in all manner of ill . . . ill practices. He would spend whole nights away and—'

Isolde squeezed Léonie's arm against her. 'A gentleman's constitution can cope with forms of relaxation that to us seem insidious. You should not take such things as an indication of a deeper malaise.'

'You did not see him,' she cried. 'He was a man lost to himself.'

To me.

'Your affection for your brother is a credit to you, Léonie,' Isolde said, 'but perhaps the time has come to worry less about him. Whatever was the situation, he appears to be in good spirits now. Would you not agree?'

Reluctantly, Léonie nodded. 'I admit he is much improved on the spring.'

'There. So this is the time to think more of your own needs and less of his. You accepted my invitation because you, yourself, stood in need of a rest. Is that not so?'

'I suppose so.'

'So now you are here, you should think of yourself. Anatole is in safe hands.'

Léonie thought of their headlong exit from Paris, her promise that she would help him, the sense of threat that came and went, the scar upon his eyebrow as a reminder of the danger he faced, and then, in a moment, felt a burden was being lifted from her shoulders.

'He is in safe hands,' Isolde repeated firmly. 'As are you.'

They were now on the far side of the lake. It was peaceful and green, quite isolated and yet in full view of the house. The only sounds were the crack of twigs underfoot, the occasional flurry of a rabbit in the undergrowth behind. High above the treeline, the caw of distant crows.

Isolde led Léonie to a curved stone bench set on the rise of ground. It was the shape of a crescent moon, its edges softened by time. She sat down and patted the seat to invite Léonie to join her.

'In the days immediately after my husband's death,' she said, 'I came often to this spot. I find it a most restful place.'

Isolde unpinned her wide-brimmed hat and placed it on the seat beside her. Léonie did the same, removing her gloves too. She glanced at her aunt. She sat, as ever, perfectly straight, her hands resting gently in her lap and her boots peeking out neatly from the bottom of her pale blue cotton skirt.

'Was it not rather ... rather solitary? Being here alone?' Léonie said.

'Sometimes. We were married only a matter of years. Jules was a man of fixed habits and customs and, well, for much of that time we were not in residence here. At least, I was not.'

'But you are happy here now?'

'I have grown accustomed to it,' she said quietly.

All of Léonie's previous curiosity about her aunt, which had faded somewhat into the background during the excitements of the preparation for the dinner party, flooded back. A hundred questions leapt into her mind. Not least of them why, if Isolde did not feel entirely comfortable at the Domaine de la Cade, she chose to remain here.

'Do you miss Oncle Jules so very much?'

Above them, the leaves swayed in the wind, whispering, murmuring, eavesdropping. Isolde sighed.

'He was a considerate man,' she replied carefully. 'And a kind and generous husband.'

Léonie's eyes narrowed. 'But your words about love—'

'One cannot always marry the person one loves,' Isolde replied. 'Circumstance, opportunity, need – all these things play a part.'

Léonie thought of her mother – how her love for their father had never dimmed and the compromises she was forced to make – and felt a rare moment of sympathy. She wished Anatole was here so she could show him how she understood. Her distance from their mother always distressed him.

'I wondered how it was that you made the acquaintance of Oncle Jules?' Léonie asked. 'From Maman, I was under the impression that my uncle rarely left the Domaine de la Cade, so—'

'It is true that Jules disliked travelling far from home. He had everything he wished for here. He kept himself well occupied with his books and took his responsibilities for the estate seriously. However, it was his custom to pay a visit once a year to Paris, as he had done when his father was still alive.'

'And it was during one of those visits that you were introduced?'

'It was,' she said.

Léonie's attention was caught, not by Isolde's words, but by her actions. Her aunt's hand had stolen to her neck, which, today, was covered by a delicate high lace collar despite the mildness of the weather. Léonie realised how habitual a gesture it was.

'So you do not miss him so much?' Léonie pressed.

Isolde gave one of her slow, enigmatic smiles.

There was no doubt in Léonie's mind, now, that the man about whom Isolde had talked with such longing, such tenderness, was not her husband.

Léonie was trying to summon the courage to pursue the conversation further, but at the same time she did not wish to be impertinent. For all the confidences Isolde appeared to have shared, she had explained little of the history of her courtship and marriage. More, Léonie had the suspicion several times during the course of the conversation that Isolde was on the point of raising some other issue, unsaid between them, although what this could be, she did not know.

'Shall we return to the house?' said Isolde. 'Anatole will be wondering where we are.'

She stood up. Léonie gathered her hat and gloves and did likewise. 'So do you think you will continue to live here, Tante Isolde?' she asked, as they made their way down from the promontory and headed back towards the path.

Isolde waited a moment before answering. 'We will see,' she said. 'For all its undoubted beauty, this is a disquieting place.'

CHAPTER 52

The porter opened the door to the first-class carriage and Victor Constant stepped down to the station platform at Carcassonne.

Un, deux, trois, loup. Like a game of grandmother's footsteps. Coming to get you, ready or not.

The wind was ferocious. According to the porter, the region was forecast to suffer the worst series of autumn storms for many years. Another, predicted to be even more devastating than those preceding it, was expected to hit Carcassonne perhaps as early as next week.

Constant looked around. Above the railway sidings, the trees were plunging like unbroken horses. The sky was as grey as steel. Menacing black clouds scudded across the tops of the buildings.

'This is just the overture,' he said, then smiled at his own joke.

He glanced along the platform to where his manservant had disembarked with the luggage. In silence, they made their way out through the concourse and Constant waited while his man procured a cab. He watched with little interest as the bargemen on the canal du Midi lashed their *péniches* to double moorings, or even to the bases of the lime trees that lined the bank. Water slapped against the brick embankments. In the kiosk selling newspapers, the headline of the *Dépêche de Toulouse*, the local journal, was about a storm that would strike that very evening, with worse to come.

Constant secured lodgings in a narrow side street in the nineteenth-century Bastide Saint-Louis. Then, leaving his man to begin the tedious process of visiting every boarding house, every hotel, every house with private rooms, to show the portrait of Marguerite, Anatole and Léonie Vernier purloined from the apartment in the rue de Berlin, he set out immediately on foot for the old town, the medieval citadel that stood on the opposite bank of the River Aude.

Despite his loathing of Vernier, Constant could not but admire how well he had kicked over the traces. At the same time, he hoped that Vernier's apparent success in disappearing might lead him to be arrogant, foolish. Constant had paid the concierge in the rue de Berlin handsomely to intercept any communication addressed to the apartment from Carcassonne, relying on the fact that Vernier's need to remain undiscovered would mean that he did not yet know of his mother's death. The thought of how the net in Paris was tightening, even while he remained ignorant, gave him pleasure.

Constant crossed to the far side via the Pont Vieux. Far below, the Aude swirled black against the sodden banks, and sped over flat rocks and choked river weeds. The water was very high. He adjusted his gloves, attempting to alleviate the discomfort of the soft blistering between the second and third fingers of his left hand.

Carcassonne had changed a great deal since last Constant had set foot in the Cité. Despite the inclement weather, entertainers and men with sandwich boards now handed out tourist brochures on every street corner. He skimmed the tawdry pamphlet, his unforgiving eyes passing over the advertisements for Marseille soaps and La

Micheline, a local liqueur; for bicycles and boarding houses. The text itself was a mixture of civic self-aggrandisement and history rewritten.

Constant hated Carcassonne and had good cause to do so. Thirty years ago, his uncle had taken him to the slums of La Cité. He had walked among the ruins, seen the filthy *citadins* who lived within its crumbling walls. Later that same day, full of plum brandy and opium, in a damask-draped room above a bar in the place d'Armes, he had had his first experience of a working girl, courtesy of his uncle.

That same uncle was now sequestered in Lamalou-les-Bains, infected by one *connasse* or another, syphilitic and mad. Constant did not visit. He had no desire to see how the disease might work, over time, upon him.

That woman was the first Constant had killed. It was unintentional and the incident had shocked him. Not because he had taken a life, but because it had been so easy to do so. The hand on the throat, the thrill of seeing the fear in the girl's eyes when she realised that the violence of their coupling was but a precursor to a possession more absolute.

Had it not been for his uncle's deep pockets and connections in the *mairie*, Constant would have had nothing but the galleys or the guillotine to look forward to. As it was, they had left swiftly and without ceremony.

The experience had taught him much, not least that money could rewrite history, amend the ending to any story. There was no such thing as a 'fact' when gold was involved. Constant had learned well. He had spent a lifetime binding to him friends and enemies alike, through a combination of obligation, debt and, when that failed, fear. It was only some years later that he understood that all lessons came at a cost. The girl had her revenge after all. She had given him the sickness that was painfully leaching the life from his uncle and would from him.

As he descended the bridge, he thought again of Marguerite Vernier's death. A flush of heat shot through him. She had, for a passing moment at least, obliterated the memory of the humiliation he had suffered at the hands of her son. The fact remained that, even after so many had passed beneath his hands, the experience was the more pleasurable when the woman was beautiful. It made the game worth the candle.

Stimulated more than he wished by the memory of those hours in the rue de Berlin with Marguerite, Constant loosened his collar at the neck. He could all but smell the intoxicating mix of blood and fear, the distinctive scent of such liaisons. He clenched his fists, remembering the delicious feel of her resistance, the pull and stretch of her unwilling skin.

Constant stepped down onto the rough cobbles of the rue Trivalle and cast a supercilious eye over the vista before him. The hundreds, thousands of francs spent on the restoration of the thirteenth-century citadel did not seem to have affected the lives of the people of the *quartier* Trivalle. It was as impoverished and run-down as it had been thirty years ago.

He crossed the place Saint-Gimer in front of Monsieur Viollet-le-Duc's ugly new church. A pack of dogs and children were snapping at his heels, calling out for coins, offering their services as guides or messengers. He paid them no heed, until one boy ventured too close. Constant struck him a blow on his leg with the metal head of his cane, and the gaggle of urchins backed away.

He arrived at a narrow cul-de-sac on the left, little more than an alleyway, which led up to the base of the ramparts of the Cité. He picked his way up the filthy, slippery alleyway. Debris covered the streets. Paper wrappings, animal excrement, rotting vegetables too decayed for even the mange-bitten dogs to eat. He was aware of unseen dark eyes watching him from behind slatted shutters.

He stopped before a tiny house in the shadows of the walls and rapped on the door with his walking stick. To find Vernier and his whore, Constant had need of the services of the man who lived within. He could be patient. He was willing to wait for as long as it might take once he had proved to his own satisfaction that the Verniers were in the area.

A wooden hatch shot back.

Two bloodshot eyes widened first in shock, then in fear. The hatch was slammed shut. Then, after the sliding of a bolt and the painful turning of the key in the lock, the door was opened.

Constant stepped inside.

CHAPTER 53

The blustery and changeable September gave way to a mild and gentle October.

It was only two weeks since Léonie had left Paris, but already she found it hard to remember the pattern of days at home. She missed less about her former life than she had expected. Not the views, not the streets, the shops. Her absence from her mother had softened her heart and she was surprised to not yet have received a letter, though Anatole reminded her that since Marguerite was still in Du Pont's company, she might have few opportunities to write.

Both Isolde and Anatole appeared to have undergone something of a permanent transformation since the night of the dinner. Isolde's eyes were no longer clouded with anxiety, and although she tired easily and often kept to her room in the mornings, her complexion was radiant and Léonie marvelled at it. She could only assume it was relief that after the success of the gathering, and the genuine warmth of the letters of thanks, Rennes-les-Bains was prepared to welcome Jules Lascombe's widow into their society and Isolde was grateful for it.

During these tranquil weeks, Léonie spent as much of her time as possible out of doors, exploring every inch of the estate, although she avoided the abandoned path that led to the sepulchre. The combination of sun and early-autumn rain had painted the world in vivid colours. Birdsong, the bark of a solitary dog carried up from the valley, the rustle of the undergrowth as a rabbit ran for cover, the heels of her boots dislodging pebbles and twigs underfoot, the growing chorus of cicadas vibrating in the trees; the Domaine de la Cade was spectacular. As time put a distance between the shadows she had perceived on her first evening and the chill of the sepulchre, Léonie felt herself absolutely at home. That her mother, as a child, had felt something disquieting about the grounds and house, she now could not comprehend. Or so Léonie told herself. It was a place of such tranquillity.

Her days fell into an easy routine. Most mornings, she painted a little. She had intended to embark on a series of landscapes. Instead, she found herself embarking on a sequence, from her fading memory, of the remaining seven Tarot tableaux from the sepulchre. Rather than a gift for her mother, she now had the idea that the paintings might be a souvenir for Anatole of their sojourn. And although in Paris the charms of nature had hitherto left her unmoved, here Léonie found she had an affinity with the trees and views she saw from her window. She found herself painting the landscape of the Domaine de la Cade into each illustration.

Some of the tableaux came more readily to mind and more easily to her brush than others. The image of Le Mat took on the character of Anatole, the expression on his face, his figure, his colouring, his summer suit and hat. La Prêtresse possessed an elegance, a charm that Léonie associated with Isolde.

She did not attempt Le Diable.

Her afternoon walks with Isolde became a fixture. Léonie could see how their friendship pleased Anatole, and although she still had less time on her own with him than she had hoped, she no longer minded so much as she grew closer to their aunt. Isolde continued to be discreet and circumspect about the circumstances of her marriage, but little by little, Léonie managed to acquire enough fragments of information to piece together a satisfying history.

Isolde had grown up in the Parisian suburbs in the care of an elderly relative, a cold and bitter woman to whom she was little more than an unpaid companion. Liberated by her aunt's death, and left with few means with which to support herself, she had been fortunate enough to find her way into the city, at the age of twenty-one, in the employ of a financier and his wife. An acquaintance of Isolde's aunt, the lady had lost her sight some years earlier and required day-to-day assistance. Isolde's duties were light. She took dictation of letters and other correspondences, read aloud from the newspapers and the latest novels and accompanied her employer to concerts and the opera. From the softness of Isolde's tone as she talked of those few years, Léonie understood that she had been fond of the financier and his wife. Through them she also acquired a good working knowledge of culture and society and *couture*. Isolde was not explicit about the reasons for her dismissal, but Léonie inferred that inappropriate behaviour on the part of the financier's son had played its part.

On the matter of her marriage, Isolde was more guarded. It was clear, however, that need and opportunity had played a significant part in her acceptance of Jules Lascombe's proposal.

Léonie also learned more about the series of incidents in the area that had caused disquiet in Rennes-les-Bains, to which Monsieur Baillard had alluded, and which had become associated with the Domaine de la Cade. Isolde was not clear on the specifics. There had also been allegations in the 1870s of depraved and inappropriate ceremonies within the deconsecrated chapel in the woods of the estate.

Léonie found it difficult to conceal her innermost feelings and dearly wanted to admit that she had found the sepulchre.

She remembered Monsieur Baillard's comments about how Abbé Saunière had been called upon to attempt to quiet the spirits of the place and wished to know more, but it was a story told second-hand by Isolde and heard some time after the event, so she could not, or would not, tell her.

In another conversation, Isolde told her niece how Jules Lascombe was considered by the town to be something of a recluse. Alone since the death of his stepmother and departure of his half-sister, he was content in his solitude. As Isolde explained it, he had no wish for company of any description, least of all a wife. However, Rennes-les-Bains had increasingly come to mistrust his bachelor status and Lascombe found himself the focus of suspicion. Why had his sister fled the estate several years previously – if, indeed, she ever actually left?

As Isolde explained it, the drizzle of gossip and innuendo grew stronger until Lascombe was obliged to act. It was in the summer of 1885 that the new parish priest of Rennes-le-Château, Bérenger Saunière, suggested to Lascombe that the presence of a woman at the Domaine de la Cade might go some way to reassuring the neighbourhood.

A mutual friend introduced Isolde to Lascombe in Paris. Lascombe made it clear that it would be acceptable – indeed, agreeable – to him for his young wife to remain for most of the year in town at his expense, provided she was available in Rennes-les-Bains when he required it. The question flitted into Léonie's mind – although she was not bold enough to ask – whether or not the marriage had ever been consummated.

It was a pragmatic and unromantic story. And although it answered many of the questions Léonie had about the nature of her aunt and uncle's marriage, it did not explain whom Isolde had been speaking of when she had talked so tenderly on that first walk they had taken together. On that occasion, she had hinted at a grand passion straight from the pages of a novel. She had given tantalising glimpses of experiences about which Léonie could only dream.

During these peaceful early weeks of October, the storms forecast failed to materialise. The sun shone brightly. There was a temperate, but moderate, breeze – nothing to disrupt the tranquillity of their days. It was a pleasant time, with little to disturb the surface of the domestic and self-contained life they were constructing for themselves at the Domaine de la Cade.

The only shadow on the horizon was the continuing lack of word from their mother. Marguerite was a lackadaisical correspondent, but to have received no communication whatsoever was strange. Anatole tried to reassure Léonie that the most likely explanation was that a letter had been mislaid on the mail coach that had overturned outside Limoux on the night of the storm. The postmaster had told him that an entire consignment of letters, packages and telegrams had been lost, hurled by the force of the accident into the River Salz and carried downstream in the floods.

At Léonie's persistent prompting, Anatole agreed he would write to the apartment on the rue de Berlin. It was possible that, by now, Du Pont had been obliged to return to Paris and that Marguerite therefore might be there to receive the letter.

As Léonie watched Anatole seal the envelope and give it to the boy to be taken to the post office in Rennes-les-Bains, a feeling of dread overwhelmed her. She all but reached out a hand to stop him but checked herself. She was being foolish. She could not think that Anatole's creditors were still pursuing him.

At the end of the second week of October, Léonie made so bold as to suggest to Isolde that perhaps they might pay Monsieur Baillard a visit. Or, indeed, invite him to the Domaine de la Cade. She was disappointed when Isolde said she had heard it reported that Monsieur Baillard had quit his lodgings in Rennes-les-Bains and was not expected to return before the feast day of Saint Martin in November.

'Wherever has he gone?'

Isolde shook her head. 'No one knows. Into the mountains, it is believed, but no one knows for certain.'

Léonie still wished to go to the town. Although Isolde and Anatole were reluctant, they capitulated, and a visit was arranged for the following day.

They passed an agreeable morning in Rennes-les-Bains.

They ran into Charles Denarnaud and took coffee with him on the terrace of the Hôtel de la Reine. Despite his *bonhomie* and cordiality, Léonie still could not bring herself to like him, and from Isolde's manner and reserve, she realised her aunt felt similarly.

'I do not trust him,' Léonie whispered. 'There is something false in his manner.'

Isolde did not say anything in response but raised her eyebrows in such a manner as to confirm she shared Léonie's misgivings. Léonie was relieved when Anatole stood up to take his leave.

'So you'll join me for a morning of shooting, Vernier?' said Denarnaud, shaking Anatole's hand. 'Plenty of *sanglier* at this time of year. Woodcock and pigeon also.'

Anatole's eyes glinted brightly at the prospect. 'I would be delighted, Denarnaud, although I warn you I have more enthusiasm than skill. And, I am embarrassed to inform you, I am ill prepared. I have no gun.'

Denarnaud slapped him on the back. 'I'll provide the weapons and ammunition, if you stand the cost of the breakfast.'

Anatole smiled. 'A deal,' he said, and, despite her antipathy to the man, Léonie was cheered by the look of pleasure the promise of the hunt had brought to her brother's face.

'Ladies,' said Denarnaud, raising his hat. 'Vernier. Monday next? I'll send what you need up to the house ahead of time, if that is agreeable to you, Madame Lascombe.'

Isolde nodded. 'Of course.'

As they promenaded, Léonie could not help but notice that Isolde attracted a certain amount of interest. There was no hostility or suspicion in the scrutiny, but there was a watchfulness. Isolde was dressed in sombre clothes and wore her half-veil lowered in the street. It shocked Léonie that, even nine months after the event, she was still expected to dress as Jules Lascombe's widow. Periods of mourning in Paris were brief. Here, there was clearly a requirement for a longer observation.

The highlight of their visit was the presence of a travelling photographer in the place du Pérou. His face was hidden beneath a thick black cloth, and the box contraption was balanced on the spindly wooden legs of a tripod with metal feet. He came from a studio in Toulouse. On a mission to record the life of the villages and towns of the Haute Vallée for posterity, he had already visited Rennes-le-Château, Couiza and Coustaussa. After Rennes-les-Bains, he was to progress to Espéraza and Quillan.

'May we? It will be a souvenir of our time here.' Léonie pulled at Anatole's sleeve. 'Please? A gift for Maman.'

To her astonishment, tears sprang into her eyes. Léonie found herself sentimental at the thought of her mother's delight at receiving the present. Surely, by now, she must be missing their company?

Perhaps observing her high emotions, Anatole capitulated. He sat in the middle upon an old metal chair, its legs uneven and wobbling upon the cobbles, holding his cane across his knees and with his hat in his lap. Isolde, elegant in her dark jacket and skirt, stood behind him to his left with her slim black fingers in silk on his shoulder. Léonie, pretty in her russet walking jacket with brass buttons and velvet trim, stood at his right, looking directly into the camera.

'There,' Léonie said, when it was over. 'Now we shall always remember Friday, the sixteenth of October. A permanent record.'

Before they departed Rennes-les-Bains, Anatole made his regular pilgrimage to the poste restante, while Léonie, wishing to be convinced that Audric Baillard truly was not in residence, made her way to his modest lodgings. She had slipped the sheet of music taken from the sepulchre into her pocket and she was determined to show it to him. She wished, too, to confide how she had begun to make a record on paper of the paintings on the wall of the apse. And to ask him more of the rumours surrounding the Domaine de la Cade.

Isolde waited as Léonie knocked upon the blue wooden door, as if she could draw Monsieur Baillard out by force of will. The window boards were all closed and the flowers in the boxes on the outer sills were covered in felt, in anticipation of the autumn frosts that might soon come. An air of hibernation hung about the building, as if it was not expecting anyone to return for some time.

She knocked again.

As she gazed at the shuttered house, the strength of Monsieur Baillard's warning not to return to the sepulchre or seek the cards came back to her more strongly than ever. Although she had only spent one evening in his company, she had complete confidence in him. Some weeks had passed since the dinner party. Now, as she stood silently waiting at a door that did not open, she realised how much she wished him to know that she had remained obedient to his wishes.

Almost completely so.

She had not retraced her steps through the woods, she had not tried to learn more. It was true she had not yet returned her uncle's book to the library, but she had not

371

studied it. Indeed, she had barely even opened it since that first visit.

Now, although it frustrated her that Monsieur Baillard truly was absent, it nonetheless strengthened her resolve to abide by his advice. The thought flashed through her mind that it would not be safe to do otherwise.

Léonie turned away and took Isolde's arm.

When they arrived back at the Domaine de la Cade some half an hour later, Léonie ran to the corner beneath the stairs and placed the sheet of music in the piano stool, beneath a moth-eaten copy of Bach's *Well-Tempered Clavier*. Now, it seemed significant to her that in all that time she had possessed it, she had not ever actually tried to play it.

That night, when Léonie blew out the light in her bed-chamber, for the first time she regretted that she had not returned *Les Tarots* to the library. She was sensitive to the presence of her uncle's book in her chamber, albeit hidden beneath her spools of cotton, thread and ribbon. Thoughts of devils slipped into her mind, of children stolen from their beds, of markings upon the ground and stones that seemed to tell of some evil unchained. In the middle of the long night, she jolted awake with the image of the eight Tarot tableaux pressing down upon her. She lit a candle and set the ghosts to flight. She would not allow them to draw her back.

For Léonie now understood absolutely the nature of Audric Baillard's warning. The spirits of the place had come close to claiming her. She should not give them such an opportunity again.

CHAPTER 54

The clement weather held until the following Tuesday. A gunmetal-grey sky sat low on the horizon. A damp and obscuring mist wrapped the Domaine in chill fingers and the surface of the lake was choppy.

Léonie was glad that Anatole had had his day's hunting with Charles Denarnaud before the rain set in. He had set off with a brown leather *etui à fusil* slung across his shoulder holding his borrowed guns, the buckles gleaming in the sun. Late in the afternoon, he returned home with a brace of wood pigeon and eyes flushed with the thrill of the shoot.

As she glanced out of the window, she thought how much less pleasurable an experience it would have been today.

After breakfast, Léonie took herself into the morning room and was curled up on the *chaise longue* with the collected stories of Madame Oliphant when the post was delivered from the village. She heard the front door open, a murmuring of greetings, then the clipped footsteps of the maid on the tiled floor crossing the hall to the study.

For Isolde, it was approaching a particularly busy time of year on the estate. Saint Martin's Day, 11th November, was three weeks away. It was the day of annual accounting and, on certain estates, evictions. Isolde explained to Léonie that it was the day the tenants' rents were settled for the coming year, and as chatelaine, she was determined to fulfil her role.

It was more a question of listening to the estate manager and acting on his advice than making decisions *per se*, but the matter had kept her cloistered away in her study the past two mornings.

Léonie carried on reading. But a few minutes later, she heard raised voices, then the unaccustomed sound of the study bell jangling. Puzzled, Léonie put down her book and, in stockinged feet, ran across the room and opened the door a fraction. She was in time to see Anatole bounding down the stairs and disappearing into the study.

'Anatole?' she called after him. 'Is there news from Paris?'

But evidently he did not hear as he slammed the door firmly shut behind him. Léonie waited a moment longer, peering inquisitively around the door frame, hoping to glimpse her brother, but soon she grew weary of watching and returned to her settee. Five minutes passed, then ten. Léonie continued to read, even though her attention was elsewhere.

At eleven o'clock, Marieta brought a tray of coffee into the morning room and set it out on the table. There were, as usual, three cups.

'My aunt and brother will be joining me?'

'I have not been given orders to the contrary, Madomaisèla.'

At that moment, Anatole and Isolde appeared together in the doorway. It slipped into Léonie's mind how comfortable they looked together.

'Good morning, *petite*,' Anatole said warmly.

Léonie stood up. 'I wondered if you had received news from Paris.'

His expression faltered a moment. 'I'm sorry, no. Nothing from Maman.'

'Then ... whatever has happened?' she asked, realising that Isolde, too, was in a state of some excitement.

She crossed the room and squeezed Léonie's hand. 'This morning I received the letter I have been waiting for from Carcassonne.'

Anatole had taken a position in front of the fire, his hands behind his back. 'I believe Isolde may have promised a concert ...'

'So we are going!' Léonie kissed her aunt. 'That is perfectly wonderful!'

Anatole laughed. 'We had hoped you would be pleased. It is not the best time of year for such a journey, of course, but we are at the mercy of circumstances.'

'When?' Léonie asked, looking from one to the other.

'We will depart this Thursday morning. Isolde has wired to inform the lawyers she will be there at two o'clock.' He paused, exchanged another glance with Isolde. Léonie caught it.

There is something more he wishes to tell me.

'In point of fact, there was one other matter we wished to raise with you. Isolde has most generously suggested that we might extend our stay here. Perhaps even until the New Year. What would you say to that?'

Léonie stared, astonished, not immediately knowing what she thought of such a suggestion. Would the pleasures of the country pall if they remained longer?

'What about your work? Can the magazine spare you for so long? Do you not need to oversee your interests from closer at hand?'

'Oh, I dare say the magazine can manage a little longer without me,' he said lightly. He accepted a cup of coffee from Isolde.

'But, Maman?' Léonie said, assailed suddenly by an image of her beautiful mother sitting alone in the drawing room of the rue de Berlin.

'If Du Pont can spare her, we had thought, perhaps, to invite her to join us here.'

Léonie could hardly believe what she was hearing.

He cannot believe she will ever leave Paris. Or return here.

'I cannot see General Du Pont being agreeable to that,' she said.

'Or perhaps you are too bored with my company to wish to remain here longer?' Anatole said, crossing the room and draping his arm around her shoulders. 'Does the thought of further weeks spent confined here with your brother distress you so?'

The moment stretched, then Léonie giggled. 'You are a fool, Anatole! Of course I would be delighted to stay longer. I cannot think of anything I would like more, although—'

'Although?' Anatole said quickly.

The smile slipped from her lips. 'I should be glad to hear from Maman.'

Anatole lit a cigarette. 'As would I,' he said quietly. 'I am certain it is only that she is having so agreeable a time that she has not yet found the opportunity to write. And, of course, allowing time for my letter to be forwarded to the Marne.'

Léonie frowned. 'I thought you believed they must have returned to Paris?'

'I suggested only that they *might* have done so,' he said mildly. Then his expression lightened again. 'But the thought of a trip to Carcassonne pleases you?'

'Indeed, yes.'

He nodded. 'Good. On Thursday, we will take the morning train from Couiza. The *courrier publique* leaves from the place du Pérou at five o'clock.'

'How long will we be staying?'

'Two days, maybe three.'

Léonie's face fell in disappointment. 'But that is hardly any time at all.'

376

'Quite long enough,' he smiled.

This time, Léonie could not fail to notice the intimate glance that passed between him and Isolde, and wondered at it. She resolved to ask him about Isolde as soon as they had a few moments to themselves.

CHAPTER 55

The lovers lay beneath the sheets, their faces lit only by the flickering light of a single candle.

'I think she suspects,' Isolde said.

'Léonie, for all her undoubted qualities, is very much concerned with her own feelings.'

'That is unjust. She is curious.'

'Young,' Anatole grinned.

'We should tell her.'

'Soon. Let us keep our secret a little longer.'

Isolde sighed and placed her hand upon his chest. 'You should return to your rooms. It is late.'

Anatole folded his arms behind his head. 'Quite. Everyone is in bed.'

Isolde smiled. 'I did not believe I could experience such happiness,' she said quietly. 'That we would ever be together here.' Then the smile fell from her face. Her hand went, automatically, to the hollow of her throat. 'I fear it will not last.'

Anatole bent over and kissed the damaged skin. Even now he felt her desire to pull away from the touch of his lips. The scar was a constant reminder of her brief and violent affair with Victor Constant.

It was only some months into their romance, after the death of her husband, that Isolde had permitted Anatole to see her uncovered and without her customary high collar, scarf or choker concealing the ugly red scar on her neck. It was some weeks later still before he succeeded in persuading her to tell him the story of how she had come by the injury.

He had thought – mistakenly – that speaking of the past might help her gain mastery over her memories. It had not done so. Moreover, it had disturbed his peace of mind. Even now, some nine months after their first meeting and when the litany of the physical punishments Isolde had suffered at Constant's hands was familiar to him, Anatole still found himself flinching as he remembered her calm and expressionless recitation of how, in an attack of jealousy, Constant had used fire tongs to hold his signet ring to the coals, then pressed the hot metal to her throat until she passed out from the pain. He had branded her. So vivid was her description that Anatole could all but smell the sickly-sweet scent of her burning flesh.

Isolde's liaison with Constant had lasted only a matter of weeks. Broken fingers had healed, the bruises had faded; only that one scar remained as a physical souvenir of the damage Constant had inflicted upon her during the course of those thirty days. But the psychological damage remained.

'It will last,' Anatole said firmly.

He let his hand move lower, smoothing over the beloved, familiar bone and form, until it came to rest upon the soft white skin at the top of her thighs.

'Everything is in place. We have the licence. Tomorrow we will meet with Lascombe's lawyers in Carcassonne. Once we know where you stand with regard to this place, we can make our final arrangements.'

He reached over to the nightstand, the muscles in his back stretched visible beneath his bare skin. He retrieved his case and matches, lit two cigarettes, then handed one to Isolde.

'There will be those who refuse to receive us,' she said. 'Madame Bousquet, Maître Fromilhague.'

'I dare say,' he shrugged. 'But do you care so greatly for their good opinion?'

Isolde did not answer the question. 'Madame Bousquet has reason to be aggrieved. If Jules had not taken it upon himself to marry, she would have inherited the estate. She might even challenge the will.'

Anatole shook his head. 'Instinct tells me that if she had intended to do so, she would have done it when Lascombe died and the will was published. Let's see what the codicil says before we concern ourselves with imagined objections.' He inhaled another mouthful of smoke. 'I do concede that Maître Fromilhague might deplore the haste of our marriage. He might object, even though there is no blood tie between us, but what business is it of his?' He shrugged. 'He will come round, given time. When all is said and done, Fromilhague is a pragmatist. He will not wish to sever links with the estate.'

Isolde nodded, although Anatole suspected it was because she wished to believe him rather than because he had convinced her.

'Are you still of the opinion we should live here? Not hide ourselves in the anonymity of Paris?' she asked.

Anatole remembered how distressed Isolde became whenever she returned to town. How every smell, every sound, every sight seemed to cause her pain and remind her of her brief liaison with Constant. He could not live like that and he doubted she could either.

'Yes, if we can do so, then I think we should make our home here.' He broke off, then gently placed his hand upon her lightly swelling stomach. 'Especially if your suspicions are correct.' He looked at her, flushed with pride. 'I still cannot believe I am to be a father.'

'It is early days yet,' she said gently. 'Very early. Although for all that, I do not think I am mistaken.'

She placed her hand upon his and for a moment they were silent.

'You do not fear that we will be punished for our wickedness in March?' she whispered.

Anatole frowned, not understanding her meaning.

'The clinic. Pretending that I was obliged to ... interrupt a pregnancy.'

'Not in the slightest,' he said firmly.

She fell silent once more. 'Do you promise me that your decision not to return to the capital is nothing to do with Victor. Paris is your home, Anatole. Are you sure you wish to relinquish it for good?'

Anatole extinguished his cigarette. 'We have discussed this too many times, but if it reassures you for me to say it again, I give you my word that it is my considered opinion that the Domaine de la Cade is the most appropriate domicile for us.' He made the mark of a cross on his bare chest. 'It is nothing to do with Constant. Nothing to do with Paris. Here, we can live simply, quietly, establish ourselves.'

'And Léonie too?'

'I hope she will make her home with us, yes.'

Anatole could feel Isolde's entire body become quite still, tense, as if ready for flight.

'Why do you allow him still to have such a hold over you?'

She caught her breath and immediately Anatole regretted speaking his mind. Isolde was well aware how it frustrated him that Constant was so often in her thoughts. In the early days, he had made the mistake of telling her how inadequate her continuing fear of Constant made him feel. As if he was not man enough to banish the spectres of her past.

As a consequence, he knew, not that her memories of the suffering she had endured troubled her any less, but that she kept her fears to herself. Now he understood how the remembrance of mistreatment took longer to heal than the physical evidence. But what he still struggled to comprehend was why she felt so ashamed. On more than one occasion, she had attempted to explain how humiliated his abuse of her made her feel. How she felt disgraced by her emotions, polluted, that she had been so deceived as to believe she could fall in love with such a man.

In his darkest hours, Anatole feared that Isolde believed she had forfeited the right to any future happiness because of that one fleeting error of judgement. And it saddened him that, despite his reassurances and the extraordinary measures they had taken to escape Constant's attentions – going so far as the pantomime in the Cimetière de Montmartre – she still did not feel safe.

'If Constant was looking for us, we would know of it by now. He made little attempt to conceal his malevolent intentions in the early months of the year.' He paused. 'Did he ever know your real name?'

'No. He knew I had a husband in the country who, within the usual bounds of respectability, was tolerant of my need for a measure of independence, provided I was discreet. It was not something we discussed. When I told him I was leaving, I cited the need to be with my husband.'

She shivered, and Anatole knew she was thinking of the night he had nearly killed her.

'Constant never knew Lascombe,' he said, pressing his point. 'That is right, is it not?'

'He did not.'

'Nor know of any address, any connection, other than the apartment in the rue Feydeau?'

'No.' She paused. 'At least, never from my lips.'

'Well then,' Anatole said, as if he had proved his case. 'It has been six months since the burial, has it not? And nothing has happened to disturb our tranquillity.'

'Except the attack upon you in the passage des Panoramas.'

'I've told you. That was nothing whatsoever to do with Constant,' he said immediately.

'But they took only your father's timepiece,' she protested. 'What thief leaves a notebook full of francs?'

'I was in the wrong place, at the wrong time,' he said. 'That's all.' He stroked her cheek with the back of his hand. 'Since we arrived at the Domaine de la Cade, I have kept my ears and eyes open, Isolde. I have heard nothing, seen nothing untoward. Nothing that could cause us a moment's disquiet. No questions have been asked in the village. No strangers have been reported around the estate.'

Isolde was still frowning. 'Does it concern you that there has still been no word from Marguerite?'

He pushed his fingers through his hair. 'I admit, it does. I was reluctant to write, after all the efforts to obscure our whereabouts. I can only assume it is because she is engaged with Du Pont.'

Isolde smiled. 'His only crime is to love your mother.'

'Then why does he not marry her?' he said, more sharply than he had intended.

'You know why,' she said gently. 'She is the widow of a Communard. He is not the sort of man to flout convention.'

Anatole sighed. 'The simple truth is that Du Pont occupies her time and, God help me, despite my antipathy to the man, I worry less about Maman knowing she is in his company in the Marne than if she were alone in Paris.'

Isolde took her *peignoir* from the chair beside the bed and draped it over her shoulders.

Concern flickered in his eyes. 'Are you cold?'

'A little.'

'Is there anything I can fetch you?'

Isolde put her hand upon his arm. 'I am fine.'

'But in your condition, you should—'

She smiled. 'I am not ill, Anatole. My condition, as you put it, is perfectly natural. Please, do not worry so.'

The smile slid from her lips. 'But, on the question of your family, I am still of the view that we should confide the real reason for our visit to Carcassonne to Léonie. Tell her what we intend.'

Anatole lit another cigarette. 'And I am still of the opinion that it is better she does not know until after the event.'

White wisps of smoke floated up into the room, like writing in the air.

'Can you really believe that Léonie will forgive you for keeping her so in the dark?' Isolde paused. 'Forgive us.'

'You are fond of her, are you not?' he said. 'I am glad of it.'

Isolde nodded. 'It is why I would like to bring her into our confidence.'

Anatole drew deeply on his cigarette. 'She will understand that we considered it too great a burden to place upon her.'

'I hold the opposite opinion. Léonie would do anything for you, accept anything you trust her with. However ...' She gave a slight shrug of her shoulders. 'If she feels slighted, then I fear that her pique might lead her to behave in ways that she – and we too – might very much regret.' She took his hand. 'She is not a child, Anatole.'

'She is only seventeen,' he protested.

'She is already jealous of the attention you pay to me and starting to wonder at it.'

'Nonsense.'

'How do you think she will feel when she discovers we – you – have deceived her?'

'It is not a question of deceit,' he said. 'It is a question of discretion. The fewer people who are aware of what we intend, the better.'

He placed his hand upon Isolde's belly, making it clear he considered the subject closed.

'Soon, my love, it will all be over.'

He cupped her head with the other hand and drew her to him, kissing her lips. Then, slowly, he slipped the *peignoir* from her shoulders. Isolde closed her eyes.

'Soon,' he murmured, 'everything will be out in the open. We can start a new chapter of our lives.'

CHAPTER 56

At half past four in the morning, the gig pulled away down the long drive of the Domaine de la Cade with Anatole, Léonie and Isolde inside. Marieta sat up front with Pascal driving, a single blanket draped over their knees.

The carriage was closed, but the cracked leather hood was inadequate protection against the hour. Léonie was swaddled in her long black cloak, drawn up over her head, squashed warmly between her brother and her aunt. She could smell the must and mothballs of the fur throws, used for the first time this autumn.

For Léonie, the blue light of the early hour and the cold only added to the adventure. The romance of setting out before dawn, the prospect of two days in Carcassonne to explore and go to a concert and eat in restaurants – she could not wait.

The lamps clinked and knocked against the cab as they made their way down to the Sougraigne road, two points of light in the darkness. Isolde admitted she had slept badly and consequently felt a little nauseous. She said little. Anatole, too, was silent.

Léonie was wide awake. She had the scent of the damp earth in her nose and the fragrant mingling scents of cyclamen and box, the mulberry bushes and sweet chestnut trees. It was too early, yet, for the sound of lark or pigeon, but she heard the hoot of owls returning from a night's hunting.

Despite their early start, the blustery weather conditions resulted in the train arriving more than an hour late into Carcassonne.

Léonie and Isolde waited while Anatole hailed a cab. Within moments, they were flying across the Pont Marengo to a hotel in the northern *quartier* of the Bastide Saint-Louis, recommended by Dr Gabignaud.

Situated in the rue du Port, on the corner of a quiet side street close to the église Saint-Vincent, it was modest, yet comfortable. A semicircle of three stone steps led up from the pavement to the entrance, a black-painted door framed in chiselled stone. Ornamental trees stood along the outer wall in terracotta pots, and window boxes upon the sills cast their green-and-white shadows against freshly painted shutters. On the side wall, the words HôTEL ET RESTAURANT were painted in high block capital letters.

Anatole took care of the formalities and oversaw the bags being carried to the rooms. They took a first-floor suite for Isolde, Léonie and the maid, with a single room for himself across the corridor.

After a light lunch in the brasserie of the hotel, they agreed to rendezvous at the hotel at half past five, in time for an early supper before the concert. Isolde's appointment with her late husband's lawyers was fixed for two o'clock and Anatole had offered to accompany her. As they departed, he exacted a promise from Léonie that she would go nowhere without Marieta and that she would not venture unchaperoned across the river beyond the boundaries of the Bastide.

It was raining again. Léonie occupied herself talking to another guest: an elderly widow, Madame Sanchez, who had been visiting Carcassonne for many years. She explained how the lower town – the Basse Ville, she termed it – was constructed on a grid system, much like the modern American cities. Madame Sanchez ringed the hotel and central square on the *plan de la ville* provided by the proprietor. She also warned how many of the street names were out of date.

'Saints have yielded to generals,' she said, shaking her head. 'So now we listen to the band in the Square Gambetta rather than the Square Sainte-Cécile. All I can tell you is that the music sounds exactly the same!'

Noticing the rain was easing off and impatient to begin her explorations, Léonie hastily excused herself, reassuring Madame Sanchez that she would manage perfectly well.

With Marieta struggling to keep up, she headed for the main square, la place aux Herbes, led by the shouts of the hawkers and market traders, the rattling of cartwheels and harness filtering up the narrow street. There was a delicious smell of roasting chestnuts and freshly baked bread. Punch flavoured with sugar and cinnamon was being ladled from steaming metal containers hanging from the back of a wooden handcart.

The place aux Herbes was an unassuming but well-proportioned square, lined on all four sides by six-storey buildings and with small roads and passageways leading in from each corner. The centre was dominated by an ornate eighteenth-century fountain dedicated to Neptune.

The branches of the spreading *platanes* were losing their leaves. Everywhere were umbrellas and brightly coloured parasols, sheltering from the wind and the rain that came and went; willow *paniers* containing fresh vegetables, fruit, garden herbs and the autumn flowers. From wicker *corbeilles,* black-draped women with weather-beaten faces sold bread and *chèvres*.

To Léonie's delight, almost the entire façade of one side of the square was occupied by a department store. Its name in bold letters was attached by twisted threads of wire to the wrought-iron balcony railings – PARIS CARCASSONNE. Although it was only just past two-thirty, the trays of bargain goods – *solde d'articles, réclame absolûment sacrifiés* – were being laid out on tables at the front of the store. Hanging from the awnings on metal display hooks were hunting guns, *prêt-à-porter* dresses, baskets, all manner of household objects, frying skillets, even stoves and ovens.

I could purchase some item of hunting equipment for Anatole.

The thought flashed in and then out of her mind. She had only a little money and no possibility of acquiring credit. Instead, she strolled around the *marché*. She picked up vegetables, rubbed herbs between her fingers, breathed in the scent of tall-stemmed flowers, in a manner she would never have done in Paris.

When she had seen all the place aux Herbes had to offer, she decided to venture into the side streets. She walked west and found herself in Carriere Mage, the street where Isolde's lawyers were situated. At the top end were mostly offices and *ateliers de couturières*. She paused awhile outside the workshops of Tissus Cathala. Through the glass door, she could see displays of cloth of every colour, as well as all manner of sewing materials. On the wooden shutters either side of the entrance, paper drawings of *les modes masculines et féminines* were tacked up with pins, from gentlemen's morning suits to ladies' tea dresses and capes.

Léonie occupied herself by examining the sewing patterns, regularly glancing up the street towards the lawyers' offices, thinking perhaps to see Isolde and Anatole emerge. But as the minutes passed and there was no sign of them, the lure of the shops further down the street drew her instead.

With Marieta trailing behind, she walked in the direction of the river. She stopped to look through the plate-glass windows of the several establishments trading in antiquaries. There was a *librairie*, its windows filled with dark wooden bookcases and leather spines. At number 75, an *épicerie fine*, there was the enticing smell of bitter ground and roasted coffee. For a moment, she stood on the pavement looking in through the three tall windows. Inside, shelves of glass and wood displayed examples of beans, paraphernalia, pots for the stove and for the fire. The letters above the door read ÉLIE HUC. Inside, strings of dried sausage hung on hooks to one side of the store.

Léonie decided she would make a purchase for Isolde, a gift to thank her for arranging this trip to Carcassonne. She stepped inside the Aladdin's cave, leaving Marieta to twist her anxious hands on the pavement, returning some ten minutes later holding a white paper packet containing the finest Arabian coffee beans and a tall glass jar of crystallised fruit.

She was becoming bored with Marieta trailing after her. *Dare I?*

Léonie felt a spark of excitement at the mischievous idea that had slipped into her mind. Anatole would scold her. But there was no need for him to find out if she was quick and if Marieta held her tongue. Léonie glanced up and down the street. There were some unaccompanied women of her class out taking the air and no one seemed to pay the slightest attention. Anatole fussed too much.

In such an environment, I do not need a guard dog.

'I wonder if you might take these back to the hotel for me,' she said, passing the packages to Marieta. 'I fear it might rain again and everything will be spoiled.' She glanced up at the sky. 'I will wait for you here.'

Marieta looked instantly concerned. 'But Sénher Vernier said to stay with you.'

'It will take no more than ten minutes,' she said. 'You will be there and back without him ever knowing.' She patted the white package. 'The coffee is a gift for my aunt. You could bring an umbrella back with you. My brother would not thank you were I to catch a cold.'

Marieta hesitated, looking down at the packages.

'Hurry,' said Léonie. 'I will wait for you here.'

With a doubtful glance behind her, the girl scurried away back up Carriere Mage, repeatedly looking over her shoulder to reassure herself that her young mistress had not vanished.

Léonie was delighted by her harmless subterfuge. She did not intend to go against Anatole's instructions and leave the Bastide, but she felt she could, with clear conscience, walk as far as the river and catch her first glimpse of the medieval citadel from the right bank of the Aude. She was curious to see the Cité about which Isolde had spoken and for which Monsieur Baillard had told her he had such affection.

She removed the map from her pocket and studied it.

It cannot be so far.

If Marieta did, by bad luck, arrive back before she did, Léonie would say she had taken it upon herself to seek out the lawyers' offices in order to be able to walk back with Isolde and Anatole.

Pleased with her plan, she crossed the rue Pelisserie, her head held high. She felt adventurous and liked the sensation. Léonie exited the tight grid of bustling streets and entered the tree-lined calm of the Square Gambetta. A plaque commemorated the work of the Carcassonnais architect Léopold Petit, who had designed and supervised the gardens. There was a lake in the centre of the park, with single jets of water shooting to the heavens from beneath the surface, creating a white haze all round. A bandstand in the Japanese style was surrounded by white chairs. The ramshackle arrangement of the seating, the debris of ice-cream biscuits and waxed paper and the wet ends of cigars suggested that the concert had finished some time ago. The ground was littered with discarded flyers for a concert, muddy footprints upon the white paper. Léonie bent down and picked one up.

From the green and pleasant spaces of Gambetta, she turned right along a rather dull cobblestoned street that ran down the side of the hospital and promised to lead to a panoramic viewpoint at the foot of the Pont Vieux.

Saint Vincent de Paul surveyed the scene from the Hôpital des Malades at the approach to the bridge. His benign stone gaze and open arms seemed to gather in the chapel alongside, with its high arched stone doorway and rose window above.

The whole spoke of beneficence, money, affluence.

Léonie looked straight ahead and had her first uninterrupted sight of La Cité, the citadel set high on a hill on the opposite bank of the river. She caught her breath. It was both more magnificent and more human in scale than she had pictured. She had seen the popular postcards of the Cité that carried the famous words of Gustave Nadaud: '*Il ne faut pas mourir sans avoir vu Carcassonne*' – one must not die without having seen Carcassonne – but had thought it no more than an advertising slogan. Now she was here, it seemed a true reflection of fact.

Léonie could see the water was very high. Indeed, in places it was lapping over the bank and up on the grass, washing against the stone foundations of the hospital buildings. She had no intention of disobeying Anatole further, and yet she found herself stepping up onto the gentle slope of the bridge, which spanned the river in a series of stone arches.

A few steps further and I will turn back.

The far bank was mostly wooded. Through the treetops and branches, Léonie could see watermills, the flat roofs of the distilleries and the textile workshops with their *filatures mécaniques*. It was surprisingly rural, she thought; remnants of another, older world.

Léonie looked up to see a battered stone Jesus hanging upon a cross in the central *bec* of the bridge, a niche in the low wall where travellers could sit awhile or remove themselves from the path of carriages or draymen's carts.

She took another step, and so, without ever actually deciding to do so, crossed from the safety of the Bastide to the romance of the Cité.

CHAPTER 57

Anatole and Isolde stood before the altar.

An hour past, all the papers had been signed. The conditions of Jules Lascombe's will, after the delays of the summer, had finally been verified.

Lascombe had left his estate to his widow for her lifetime. In an unexpected twist of fortune, he had willed that in the event of her remarrying, the property should pass to the son of his half-sister, Marguerite Vernier, *née* Lascombe.

When the lawyer had read the terms out loud in his dry and scratchy voice, it had taken a moment for Anatole to realise that it was to him that the document referred. It was all he could do not to laugh out loud. The Domaine de la Cade, one way or another, in time would belong to them.

Now, half an hour later, as they stood in the small Jesuit chapel and the priest spoke the closing words of the brief ceremony that joined them together as man and wife, Anatole reached out and took Isolde's hands.

'Madame Vernier, *enfin*,' he whispered.

The witnesses, chosen at random on the street, smiled at their open signs of affection, although they considered it a pity it was such a modest affair.

Anatole and Isolde stepped out into the street to the peal of bells. They heard the thunder. Wishing to spend the first hour of their married life alone – and reassured that Léonie and Marieta were comfortably in the hotel awaiting their return – they ran down the street and ducked into the first suitable establishment they came to.

Anatole ordered a bottle of Cristal, the most expensive champagne on the menu. They exchanged gifts. Anatole gave Isolde a silver locket with a miniature of her on one side, him on the other. She presented him with a fine gold-plated timepiece with his initials engraved on the top to replace the one stolen in the attack in the passage des Panoramas.

'Madame Vernier,' Anatole said, raising his wife's hand to his lips. 'How I have longed to be able to say that.'

For the next hour, as the first spots of rain struck the wide plate-glass windows, they drank and talked, delighting in one another's company. Remembering how they first met in Paris, at a private concert given by a friend. Anatole claimed he could remember nothing of the compositions performed that night, only the way Isolde's hair shone beneath the light of the candles and how they discovered they were united in their admiration for Debussy. They relived their stolen moments as they endeavoured to keep their love affair secret – meeting, as if by chance, in the Jardin de Tuileries, or beside the *Venus de Milo* in the statue galleries at the Louvre, or leaving mass at the Sainte-Chapelle on a Sunday morning. Books, music, the light and shade of paintings they liked and shops they frequented. Finding all the points of similarity, marvelling at the points of difference. Of Constant and violence and subterfuge, they said nothing. For this afternoon, nothing mattered but the two of them.

'We should go,' Isolde said, glancing at the clock, but she, too, was reluctant to break the spell. 'Léonie will be wondering where we are.'

Anatole raised his hand and ordered a second bottle of champagne.

'This is our honeymoon,' he said, realising he had tears in his eyes. 'Forgive me. I am not usually so sentimental.'

'My love,' Isolde whispered.

Outside, the rain continued to fall.

CHAPTER 58

Léonie felt a moment of disquiet as she descended the bridge. She could no longer pretend that she was not disobeying Anatole's express instructions. She pushed the thought from her mind, then looked back over her shoulder to observe that black storm clouds were massing over the Bastide.

At this instant, she told herself, it would be wiser to remain on the far side of the river away from the worst of the weather. Indeed, it would be inadvisable to return to the Basse Ville quite yet. Besides, an adventuress, a lady explorer, would not give up the chase simply because her brother told her to.

The *quartier* Trivalle was more unnerving, far poorer, even than a scene in a novel by Monsieur Zola. She dropped a coin into the bowl of a beggar and picked her way cautiously up the cobblestoned road, which was lined with plain buildings. The shutters were all peeling and in a state of disrepair. The street smelled of overcrowding and neglect. But wasn't this the same in Paris, the elegant streets and the forgotten alleyways existing cheek by jowl?

The road was sloping upwards. The buildings fell away and the Cité itself came into view. To her left, at the top of a crumbling set of stone steps, she glimpsed a heavy wooden door set deep within ancient grey walls. The sign, battered and worn, announced that this was the Capuchin convent.

Had once been.

Neither Léonie nor Anatole had been brought up in the repressive shadow of the Church. Her mother was too free a spirit and her father's Republican sympathies meant that, as Anatole had once explained it to her, Leo Vernier considered clerics as much of an enemy to the establishment of a true Republic as the aristocracy. Nevertheless, Léonie's romantic imagination caused her to regret the intransigence of politics and progress that demanded all beauty should be sacrificed for principle. The architecture spoke to her, even if the words that echoed within the convent did not.

At the top of the rue Trivalle, she turned to the right. Straight ahead, she could see the high and narrow sand-coloured towers of the Porte Narbonnaise, the primary entrance into the Cité. Her heart rejoiced at the sight of the double ring of walls, punctuated by towers, some with red-tiled roofs, some with grey slates, all in silhouette against the glowering sky. As she drew closer, she saw the tops of grey tombstones with soaring angels and monumental crosses behind the high walls of a cemetery.

Beyond, all was pasture and grasslands.

Léonie paused a moment to catch her breath. The approach into the citadel was by means of a cobblestoned bridge over a grassy moat, flat and wide. At the head of the bridge was a small, rectangular toll office. A man wearing a battered top hat and old-fashioned whiskers stood, hands in his pockets, looking out and claiming payment from the drivers of goods carts, merchants carrying barrels of ale for the Cité.

Perched on the wide and low stone wall of the bridge was a man, in the company of two soldiers. He was wearing an old blue Napoleonic cape and smoking a long-stemmed pipe as black as his teeth. All three men were laughing. For a moment, Léonie fancied his eyes widened a fraction as he caught sight of her. He held her in his gaze a little too long, his stare slightly impertinent, then looked away. Unnerved by his attention, she walked quickly past.

As she stepped out onto the bridge, the direct force of the north-westerly wind struck her. She was obliged to put one hand on her hat to hold it in place and with the other keep her swirling skirts free from tangling around her legs. She fought her way forward, eyes screwed tight against the dust and grit thrown up into her face.

But the instant she passed into the Cité, she was sheltered from the wind. She paused a moment, then made her way through into the open space between the inner and outer fortifications. She could see the outline of the remains of the humble shanty houses that had recently been demolished. At upper-storey height, hanging in mid-air, was a hearthstone, black with soot, left behind when the lodgings had been torn down.

Wishing she had had the foresight to put her guidebook in her pocket before departing the hotel, rather than the map of the Bastide only, Léonie asked for directions and was informed that the castle was straight ahead. As she walked on, she felt another flutter of misgiving. After the distant grandeur of the exterior and the windswept spaces of the *hautes lices* – the space between the inner and outer walls – the interior was darker and more sombre than she had expected. And it was dirty. Mud covered the slippery cobbles. Debris and detritus of all kinds littered the gutters.

Léonie picked her way up the narrow street, following a hand-painted wooden sign for the Château Comtal, where the garrison was quartered. This, too, disappointed. From previous reading, she knew it had once been the home of the Trencavel dynasty, lords of the Cité many hundreds of years ago. Léonie had imagined a grand castle, such as those that stood on the banks of the Loire. She had pictured courtyards and great halls, filled with ladies in sweeping dresses, and *chevaliers* riding out to battle.

The Château Comtal looked like what it now was: a plain military building; efficient, workaday, drab. The Tour de Vade, in the shadow of the walls, was a powder depot. A single sentinel stood guard, picking his teeth. The place wore a mantle of neglect; a building tolerated but not cherished.

Léonie attempted to see some romance in the plain bridge and the functional narrow gateway into the château itself but could find none. As she strolled up and down the passageways, the thought came into her mind that attempts to rejuvenate the Cité as a tourist landmark were likely to fail. The newly repaired walls, the machine-cut stone and tiles only emphasised how ruined were the authentic surroundings.

A few fellow travellers – ladies with their hands warm in fur muffs, gentlemen with walking sticks and top hats – bade her good afternoon, but the wind was even stronger on the western side and Léonie was obliged to hold her handkerchief across her mouth and nose.

She found herself standing beside an old stone cross looking out over terraced market gardens, with vegetable plots, vines, chicken coops and rabbit hutches. Below, a cluster of small, cramped houses.

From this vantage point, she could see the river was a restless, swirling black mass of water, speeding through the mills, setting the blades spinning. Rain was already falling over the Bastide – she could only just pick out the tall, thin bell tower of the église Saint-Vincent, hard by their hotel – and she felt a spike of anxiety. She could easily find herself trapped by rising water levels on this side of the river. The story she had concocted in her mind to tell Anatole of how she had become disorientated and lost in the narrow streets of the Bastide would be of no matter if she was caught by flooding.

A movement above her head made her glance up. A flock of autumn crows, black against the grey sky, flew up over the turrets and battlements, struggling against the wind.

Léonie started to hurry, but she had left it too late. The first spot of rain landed upon her cheek. Then another and another, faster, heavier, colder. Then a rattle of sleet and a single, abrupt crack of thunder.

The storm, so long threatened, had arrived.

CHAPTER 59

Léonie cast around urgently for shelter, but there was nothing. Caught halfway down the steep and cobbled path that linked the citadel to the *quartier* Barbacane below, there were no trees, no buildings, no dwellings.

She stumbled on down the *calada*, holding her skirts above her ankles to prevent them being soaked by the water already cascading over the cobbles. The wind boxed her ears and blew the rain beneath the rim of her hat, causing her coat to flap and catch around her legs.

She did not see the two men watching her beside the stone cross at the top of the ramp. One was well dressed, clearly a person of some means and status. The other was short and dark, wrapped in a thick Napoleonic cloak. They exchanged a few words. There was a glint of coins passing from one gloved hand to the dirty palms of the old soldier, then the two men parted company. The soldier vanished into the Cité.

The gentleman followed Léonie down.

By the time Léonie reached the place Saint-Gimer, she was drenched.

Her only option was to take shelter in the church itself. She hurried up the charmless modern steps, through the metal gate standing partly open in the black railings, and stepped inside.

She shivered. Candles were lit on the altar and in the side chapels, but it was colder inside than out. She stamped her feet to shake off the rain, then, realising she could be stranded within the church for some time, decided that not catching a chill was of more importance than her appearance. She removed both her gloves and her sodden hat.

As her eyes became accustomed to the gloom, Léonie realised others had been drawn to the church to shelter from the storm. It was a strange congregation. In the nave and side chapels, people milled quietly about. A gentleman in a top hat and greatcoat with a lady on his arm sat bolt upright in one of the pews as if they had an unpleasant smell beneath their noses. Local residents of the *quartier*, many without boots or shoes and inadequately dressed, squatted on the flagstones. There was even a donkey, and a woman clutching two chickens, one under each arm.

'An extraordinary sight,' said a voice at her ear. 'But then one must remember that sanctuary welcomes all those who seek it.'

Startled to be addressed, Léonie spun around to see a gentleman standing at her elbow. His grey top hat and frock coat marked his class, as did the silver head and tip of his cane and his kid leather gloves. The traditional elegance of his attire made his blue eyes all the more startling. For an instant, Léonie thought she might have seen him before.

There was something else about him, something about his direct gaze that caused an unexpected tumult in Léonie's chest. Her heart began to beat a little harder.

She looked down.

'Forgive me, I did not mean to offend you,' he said. 'In normal circumstances, I would not, of course, address a lady without introduction.' He smiled. 'But these are somewhat unusual circumstances, no?'

His courtesy reassured her.

'They are rather.'

'So here we are, fellow travellers seeking refuge from the storm.' He tipped his hat to reveal a high forehead and glossy hair, precisely cut to the top of his high collar. 'So, can we be friends for the duration? I do not offend you to make such a request?'

Léonie shook her head, imagining how Anatole might think otherwise. 'Not in the slightest. Besides, we might find ourselves here, after all, for quite some time.'

She regretted that to her ears her voice sounded strained, too thin to be pleasing. But the stranger was smiling still and did not seem to notice.

He looked around. 'But bearing in mind the proprieties, perhaps if I might make so bold as to introduce myself to you, then we will no longer be strangers. And your guardians need not worry.'

'Oh, I am ...' Léonie stopped. It might not be prudent to reveal that she was alone. 'I should be delighted to accept your introduction.'

With a half-bow, he pulled a calling card from his pocket. 'Victor Constant, Mademoiselle.'

Léonie accepted the elegant embossed card with a frisson of excitement, which she attempted to mask by studying the name upon the card. She tried to think of something amusing to say. She wished, too, she had not previously removed her gloves.

'And may I be so impertinent as to ask your name?'

A laugh slipped out from between her lips. 'Of course. How stupid of me. I regret that I do not ... I have neglected to bring any visiting cards,' she lied, without questioning why. 'I am Léonie Vernier.'

Constant took her bare hand and raised it to his lips. '*Enchanté*.'

Léonie felt a jolt as his lips grazed her skin. She heard herself gasp, then felt the red rush into her cheeks, self-conscious at so obvious a reaction, and pulled her fingers away.

Gallantly, he affected not to notice. Léonie liked him for it.

'Why did you assume I am under the care of a guardian?' she said, when she could trust herself to speak. 'I might be accompanied by my husband.'

'Indeed you might,' he said, 'but for one thing, I cannot believe that any husband would be so lacking in chivalry as to leave so beautiful a young wife alone and in such company.'

They both cast their eyes around the bedraggled collection of people.

'My husband might have gone simply to summon assistance.'

'No man would be such a fool,' he said, and glanced down at her bare hand, devoid of any marriage band.

'Well, I admit you are quite perspicacious, Monsieur Constant. You are indeed correct in your assumption.'

'What husband would wish to be parted from such a wife, even for an instant?'

She tilted her head. 'You, of course, would not treat your wife in such a manner,' she said, the bold words slipping out before she could check herself.

'Alas, I am not married,' he said with a slow smile. 'I meant merely that if I were lucky enough to enjoy such a precious possession, I would take greater care.'

To cover the surge of emotion she was experiencing, Léonie laughed, causing several of the temporary citizens of Saint-Gimer to turn and stare.

Constant placed his finger to his lips. 'Our levity, clearly, is not appreciated.'

He had lowered his voice yet further, so she was obliged to draw nearer. Indeed, they were so close as to be almost touching. Léonie could feel the heat of him beside her. She remembered Isolde's words about love as they had sat on the promontory overlooking the lake. This was nothing of the sort, of course, and yet for the first time, Léonie understood what such feelings might be like.

'Shall I tell you a secret?' he asked.

'By all means.'

'I believe I know what drew you to this place, Mademoiselle Vernier.'

Léonie raised her eyebrows. 'Indeed?'

'You have the air of a young lady upon a solitary adventure. You entered the church alone, drenched from the downpour, which suggests you have no servant with you, for certainly they would have been equipped with an umbrella. And your eyes, quite like emeralds, dazzle with the excitement of the moment.'

A burst of loud and angry words came from a Spanish family close by, drawing Constant's attention. Léonie was glad of the reprieve. She felt quite unlike herself and realised that, in the intensity of the moment, she might say things she would subsequently wish she had not. But his compliment pleased her.

Your eyes dazzle quite like emeralds.

'There are many Spanish textile workers in this *quartier*,' Constant said. 'Until the renovations of the medieval fortress were commenced in 1847, the Cité was the centre of the local cloth industry.'

'You are well informed, Monsieur Constant,' she said, trying to keep concentration. 'Are you involved with the restoration? You are an architect, perhaps?'

'You flatter me, Mademoiselle Vernier, but no. I have merely an amateur interest.'

Léonie found that she could not think of a single amusing thing to say. She wished him to think her witty, intelligent, charming, but her words had left her.

'There has been a church dedicated to Saint-Gimer close by this site since the end of the eleventh century,' he continued. 'This particular building was consecrated in 1859, after it had become clear that such was the state of disrepair of the original that it would be advisable to build a new church, rather than attempt a restoration.'

'I see,' she said.

How dull I sound. How stupid.

'The church was begun under the auspices of Monsieur Viollet-le-Duc, although the construction was quickly handed over to a local architect to complete his designs.'

He placed his hands upon her shoulders and turned her round so she was facing up the nave. Léonie caught her breath as a shot of heat surged through her.

'The altar, the pulpit, the chapels and the screens are all Viollet-le-Duc's work,' he said. 'Quite typical. A blend of styles, north and south. They transferred many of the objects from the original building to here. And although it is rather modern for my tastes, it is nonetheless a place of some character. Do you not agree, Mademoiselle Vernier?'

Léonie felt his hands slip from her shoulders, brushing against the small of her back as they did so. She could only nod, not trusting herself to speak.

A woman sitting in the side aisle on the floor, in the golden shadow of a reliquary casket set into the wall, began to sing a lullaby to still the restless baby in her arms.

Grateful for the diversion, Léonie turned to look.

> *Aquèla Trivala*
> *Ah qu'un polit quartier*
> *Es plen de gitanòs.*

The words floated across the church to the nave where Léonie and Victor were standing.

'There is a great charm in simple things,' he said.

'That is the language of Occitan,' she said, wishing to impress. 'The maids at home speak it when they believe no one is listening.'

She felt his attention sharpen.

'At home?' he said. 'Forgive me, from your clothes and your bearing I assumed you were but travelling in this region. I had taken you for *une vraie Parisienne*.'

Léonie smiled at this second compliment. 'Again, Monsieur Constant, your perspicacity does you credit. My brother and I are indeed only guests in the Languedoc. We live in the eighth *arrondissement*, not far from the Gare Saint-Lazare. Do you know the *quartier*?'

'Only from the paintings of Monsieur Monet, I regret.'

'The place d'Europe is visible from our drawing-room windows,' she said. 'If you knew the area, you could place our lodgings precisely.'

He gave a regretful shrug. 'In which case, if it is not too impertinent a question, Mademoiselle Vernier, what brings you to the Languedoc? It is late in the season to be travelling.'

'We are staying with a relative for a month. An aunt.'

He pulled a face. 'My commiserations,' he said.

It was a moment before Léonie realised he was teasing her.

'Oh,' she laughed, 'Isolde is not at all that kind of aunt. All mothballs and eau de cologne. She is beautiful and young, also from Paris in the first instance.'

She saw something flash in his eyes – satisfaction, delight even – and was pleased to have amused him.

Constant placed his hand on his heart and gave a half-bow.

'I stand corrected,' he said.

'I forgive you for it.'

'And this beautiful and charming Isolde, previously of Paris, she is now resident in Carcassonne?'

Léonie shook her head. 'No. We are in town for a few days. My aunt has business to attend to, concerning her late husband's estate. We are to go to a concert this evening.'

He nodded. 'Carcassonne is a charming city. Much improved in the past ten years. There are now many excellent restaurants and shops, hotels too.' He paused. 'Or have you taken lodgings, perhaps?'

Léonie laughed. 'We are only here for a matter of days, Monsieur Constant. The Hôtel Saint-Vincent is more than adequate for our needs!'

The door to the church opened, with a gust of cold air, as more travellers came in from the rain. Léonie shivered as her wet skirts clung to her cold legs.

'The storm distresses you?' he asked.

'No, not in the slightest,' she said, although pleased at his concern. 'My aunt's estate is high in the mountains. In the past two weeks, we have experienced thunder and lightning considerably more severe than this.'

'So you are some distance outside Carcassonne?'

'We are situated south of Limoux, in the Haute Vallée. Not far from the spa town of Rennes-les-Bains.' She smiled up at him. 'Do you know it?'

'I regret I do not,' he said. 'Although, I admit, the region suddenly holds considerable interest for me, Mademoiselle Vernier. Perhaps I will be moved to pay a visit in the not too distant future, if that would not be too presumptuous.'

'It is rather isolated, but the countryside is magnificent.'

'Is there much society in Rennes-les-Bains?'

She laughed. 'No, but we are quite happy with the quiet life. My brother leads a busy existence in town. We are here to rest.'

The Spanish family, still arguing, got to their feet. Léonie turned round and saw that the main doors were now standing open.

'The rain appears to be stopping,' said Constant. 'A pity.'

The last word was spoken so quietly that Léonie threw a sideways glance at him. It seemed too clear a declaration of interest after so short an acquaintance. But his face was quite innocent and she was left wondering if she had mistaken his meaning. She looked back to the doors and saw that the sun had come out, flooding the wet steps with a blinding light.

The gentleman in the top hat helped his companion to her feet. They stepped carefully out of their pew into the nave and walked out. One by one, everyone else started to follow. Léonie was surprised to realise how large the congregation had become. She had barely noticed them.

Monsieur Constant held out his arm. 'Shall we?' he said.

His voice sent a shiver down her spine. Léonie hesitated for only a moment. Then, as if in slow motion, she saw herself reaching out her ungloved hand and resting it upon his grey sleeve.

'You are most kind,' she said.

Together, Léonie Vernier and Victor Constant left the church and processed into the place Saint-Gimer.

CHAPTER 60

Despite her dishevelled appearance, Léonie felt herself the most fortunate person in Carcassonne. Having often imagined a moment such as this and read such scenes in more novels than she could care to mention, it was nonetheless extraordinary that it felt so natural to be walking arm in arm with a man.

Victor Constant continued to be the perfect gentleman, attentive but not inappropriately so. He asked her permission to smoke and, when Léonie granted it, did her the honour of offering her one of his Turkish cigarettes, thick and brown unlike those Anatole favoured. She declined but was flattered to be treated as an adult.

The conversation between them continued along predictable lines – the weather, the delights of Carcassonne, the splendour of the Pyrenees – until they reached the far side of the Pont Vieux.

'This is, I regret, where I must leave you,' he said.

Disappointment washed through her, but Léonie succeeded in keeping her expression composed.

'You have been most kind, Monsieur Constant, most solicitous. I, too, must return. My brother will be wondering what has become of me.'

For a moment, they stood awkwardly together. It was one thing to make one another's acquaintance in so unorthodox a manner. It was quite another to take the association a step further.

Although she liked to think herself not bounded by convention, Léonie nonetheless waited for him to speak first. But she smiled at him, hoping to make it clear she would not rebuff him should he issue some kind of invitation.

'Mademoiselle Vernier,' he said. Léonie heard a tremor in his voice and liked him the more for it.

'Yes, Monsieur Constant?'

'I hope you will forgive me if this seems too bold a comment, but I was wondering if you had yet had the pleasure of visiting Square Gambetta,' he said, gesturing to the right. 'No more than two or three minutes from here.'

'I walked there this morning,' she said.

'Should you happen to enjoy music, there is an excellent concert every Friday morning at eleven o'clock.' He turned the full force of his blue eyes upon her. 'Certainly, I shall attend tomorrow.'

Léonie smiled, admiring the finesse with which he had invited her to meet him without transgressing the bounds of social proprieties.

'My aunt had intended for me to enjoy a range of musical activities while we are in Carcassonne,' she said.

'In which case, perhaps I may be fortunate and find that our paths cross again tomorrow, Mademoiselle,' he said, raising his hat. 'And to have the pleasure of meeting your aunt and brother.' She caught her breath, wishing for nothing more at that moment than that Monsieur Constant would circle her waist with his hands and kiss her.

'*À la prochaine*,' he said.

His words broke the spell. Léonie blushed, as if he could read her innermost thoughts.

'Yes, indeed,' she stammered. 'Until tomorrow.'

She turned and walked away up the rue du Pont Vieux before she shamed herself by revealing the extent of the hopes playing within her.

*

Constant watched her go, seeing from her posture and the way she held her head high that she was more than aware of his eyes upon her retreating back.

Like mother, like daughter.

In truth, it was almost too easy. The schoolgirl blushes, her widening eyes, the coyness. He could have enticed her away there and then had he so wished. That did not suit his purposes. It was infinitely more satisfying to play with her emotions. Ruin her, certainly, but by making her fall in love with him. That knowledge would torment Vernier more than the idea of her being taken by force.

And she *would* fall in love with him. She was impressionable and young and naïve – ripe for the taking.

Constant clicked his fingers and the man in the blue cloak appeared instantly at his side.

'Monsieur.'

Constant penned a curt note and gave instructions for it to be delivered to the Hôtel Saint-Vincent. The thought of Vernier's face when he read the letter was too much to resist. He wanted to see him suffer – both of them: Vernier and his whore. He wanted them to spend the next few days looking over their shoulders, waiting for the blow to fall. Knowing that, despite their subterfuge, he had hunted them down.

He thrust a purse of money into the man's hands. 'Follow them,' he said. 'Send word to me in the usual manner to let me know precisely where they go. Do you think you can deliver the note before the girl arrives back at the hotel?'

The man looked offended. 'It is my town,' he muttered, then turned on his heel and vanished into a narrow *allée* running along the back of the Hôpital des Malades.

Constant put the girl out of his mind and considered his next move. During the course of the tedious flirtation in the church, she had told him everything he needed to know. Not just where they were staying in Carcassonne, but, more importantly, where Vernier and his whore had gone to ground.

He was acquainted with Rennes-les-Bains and its therapeutic treatments. The location suited his purposes well. He could not move against them in Carcassonne. The city was too crowded and a confrontation here would attract too much attention. But an isolated estate in the country? He had some connections in the town – one man in particular: a person of few scruples and a cruel temperament to whom he had once been of service. Constant did not foresee any difficulties in persuading him that the time had come for the debt to be repaid.

Constant took a *fiacre* back into the heart of the Bastide, then threaded his way through the network of streets behind the Café des Négociants on the boulevard Barbès. There the most exclusive of private clubs was to be found. Champagne, perhaps a girl. There was mostly only dark meat this far south, not the pale skin and pale hair he preferred. But today he was prepared to make an exception. He was in the mood to celebrate.

CHAPTER 61

Léonie rushed through the Square Gambetta, its pathways and borders glinting with pools of rainwater reflecting the pale rays of the sun, all but oblivious to the rush of the world about her. The pavements were crowded, the streets swirled with black water and debris carried from the top of the town by the force of the storm, but she barely noticed.

The consequences of her afternoon's excursion were only now hitting her. Thoughts of how Anatole would chastise her filled her head.

Although I do not regret it.

She would be reprimanded for her disobedience, she had no doubt, but she could not say that she wished she had never gone.

She looked up at the street sign and found she was not in the rue Carriere Mage as she had supposed. Indeed, she was lost. The *plan de la ville* was soaking wet and disintegrated in her hands. The ink had run and the street names were now all but illegible. Léonie looked around, hoping for a landmark she might recognise, but all the shops were boarded up against the ill weather and the narrow streets in the Bastide now looked the same.

She mistook her way several times, so it was the best part of another hour before she managed to locate the hotel. As she charged up the steps of the main entrance, she heard the bells of the cathedral strike six.

She burst into the lobby, hoping at the very least to be able to regain the privacy of her room and change into dry clothes before facing her brother. But Anatole was standing in the reception hall, pacing up and down, a cigarette wedged deep between his fingers. When he saw her, he stormed across the floor and grabbed her by the shoulders.

'Where in the blazes have you been? I have been going out of my mind.'

Léonie stood fixed to the spot.

'Well?' he demanded.

'I got caught out in the storm.'

'Do not play with me, Léonie. I expressly forbade you to go out alone. You dismissed Marieta under some absurd pretext, and then disappeared. Where in God's name have you been? Tell me, damn it!'

Léonie's eyes widened. He had never sworn at her before.

'Anything could have happened to you! A girl alone in an unfamiliar place. Anything!'

Léonie glanced at the *patron*, who was listening with undisguised interest. Anatole noticed, too, and marched her into the corner of the lobby.

'Did you disobey me and go beyond the Bastide? Well? Did you?'

'No,' she lied, too frightened to tell the truth. 'I walked in the Square Gambetta and admired the architecture. I admit I did send Marieta back to fetch an umbrella and deposit our packages – and I should not have done that, I know – but when the rain started, I thought you would rather I sheltered than remain outdoors. Did she tell you we went to the Carriere Mage to find you?'

Anatole's expression darkened yet further.

'She did not inform me of that, no,' he said curtly. 'And did you see us?'

'No, I—'

Anatole renewed his tirade. 'Even so, the rain stopped more than an hour ago. We agreed that we would meet here at half past five. Or did you put that out of your mind?'

'I remember, but—'

'One cannot fail to be aware of the time in this city. One cannot take a single step without being assailed by bells. Do not lie to me, Léonie. Do not pretend you did not know how late it was, for I shall not believe it.'

'I was not going to,' she said in a small voice.

'Where did you take shelter?' he demanded.

'In a church,' she replied quickly.

'Which church? Where?'

'I do not know,' she said. 'Near the river.'

Anatole grabbed her arm. 'Are you telling me the truth, Léonie? Did you cross the river to the Cité?'

'The church was not in the Cité,' she cried, distressed at the tears that had sprung to her eyes. 'Anatole, you're hurting me.'

'And nobody approached you? Nobody tried to harm you?'

'You can see they did not,' she said, trying to pull her arm free.

He stared at her, his eyes blazing with a fury she had rarely provoked in him before. Then he let her go, all but pushing her away from him.

Léonie's cold fingers stole to the pocket in which she had put Monsieur Constant's calling card.

If he should find this now . . .

He took a step back. 'I am disappointed in you,' he said. The coldness and lack of affection in his voice chilled Léonie to the core. 'Always I expect better of you, then you go and behave in this manner.'

Her temper flared and she was on the point of exclaiming that she had done nothing more than go for a walk unaccompanied, but she bit her tongue.

Léonie dropped her head. 'I am sorry,' she said.

417

He turned away. 'Go to your room and pack.'

Her fighting spirit rushed back.

'Pack? Why must I pack?'

'Don't question me, Léonie, just do as you are told.'

If they left this evening, she would not be able to meet Victor Constant tomorrow in the Square Gambetta. Léonie had not determined she would go, yet she did not want the decision taken out of her hands.

What will he think if I do not attend the concert?

Léonie rushed to Anatole and seized his hand. 'Please, I have said I am sorry. Reprimand me if you like, but not in such a manner. I don't want to leave Carcassonne.'

He shook her off. 'Our plans have changed. There are warnings of further storms and flooding. This is nothing to do with you, but thanks to your disobedience, I have been obliged to send Isolde ahead to the station with Marieta.'

'But the concert,' Léonie cried. 'I want to stay! Please! You promised.'

'Go – and – pack!'

'What has happened?' she demanded, her voice rising to match his. 'Is it something to do with Isolde's meeting with the lawyers that we suddenly have to leave?'

To Léonie's relief, his expression softened. 'There will be other concerts,' he said. He tried to put his arm around her, but she pushed him away.

With tears stinging her eyes and not caring in the least who saw her, Léonie ran up the stairs and along the passageway into her room and threw herself face down on the bed in a storm of weeping.

I will not go. I will not.

But she knew there was nothing she could do. She had little money of her own. Whatever the true reason for their abrupt departure, she had no choice. He was determined to punish her for her wilfulness and had chosen the surest way to do it.

Her fit of sobbing over, Léonie went to the wardrobe to pick out something dry to wear and found it empty of all but her travelling cloak. She burst through the communicating door into the common part of the suite to find it deserted, and realised Marieta had packed everything.

Thoroughly miserable, her sodden clothes scratchy and uncomfortable, she gathered the few private items the maid had left on the dressing table, then snatched up her cloak and stormed into the corridor, where she encountered Anatole.

'Marieta has left nothing whatsoever for me to wear,' she protested, her eyes flashing with fury. 'My clothes are wet and I am cold.'

'Good,' he said, walking into his room opposite and slamming the door.

Léonie stamped back into her own room.

She would show him. She had been careful to behave properly and with decorum, but Anatole was forcing her to take more drastic measures. She would send word to Monsieur Constant explaining why she could not honour their arrangement in person. At least then he would not think ill of her. Perhaps he might even write to express his sadness at their friendship being cut short.

Her complexion flushed with defiance, Léonie rushed to the bureau. Quickly, before she lost her nerve, she scribbled a few lines of regret, suggesting that letters sent care of the poste restante in Rennes-les-Bains would find her in the event he might wish to put her mind at rest by confirming receipt of this note. She did not feel she could so far forget herself as to give the address of the Domaine de la Cade itself.

Anatole would be furious if he knew she was writing to a man of a mere afternoon's acquaintance, but Léonie did not care. It served him right. If he insisted on treating her like a child, then she would behave like one. If he would not allow her to make her own decisions, then she would henceforth take no account of his wishes.

She sealed the envelope and addressed it. After a moment's pause, she took a glass bottle of perfume from her bag and sprinkled a few drops over the letter, as the heroines of her favourite novels would have done. Then she held it to her lips, as if she could imprint a little of herself upon the white paper.

There. It is done.

Now all she had to do was find a way to leave it with the *patron* of the hotel without Anatole's knowledge, to be delivered at the appointed hour tomorrow morning to Monsieur Constant in the Square Gambetta.

Then, she could only wait and see what came of it.

In his bedroom opposite, Anatole sat with his head in his hands. Screwed in his fist he held a letter that had been delivered by hand to the hotel some half an hour before Léonie had reappeared.

It was barely a letter. Just five words that struck iron into his soul.

'*CE N'EST PAS LA FIN.*' It is not the end.

There was no signature, no return address, but Anatole feared he understood the meaning well enough. Was it possible it was a response to the single word he had written on the final page of the journal he had left in Paris? If so, how had Constant had sight of it?

'*FIN.*'

He raised his head in desperation. His cheeks were hollow and white with the shock. Somehow, Constant knew. He knew both that the burial in the Cimetière de Montmartre had been a hoax and that Isolde was alive, even that she was here, with him, in the Midi.

Anatole ran his fingers through his hair. How? How had Constant learned they were in Carcassonne? Nobody but he, Léonie, Isolde and the household servants knew that they were in the town, let alone at this hotel in particular.

The lawyer knew. And the priest.

But not that they were staying at this very hotel.

Anatole forced himself to concentrate. This was not the time to concern himself with how Constant had found them – there would be time enough for such morbid analysis later – but rather to decide what they should do now.

His shoulders slumped as the memory of Isolde's broken expression came back into his mind. He would have given anything to have kept it from her, but she had come upon him moments after the letter had arrived and he had been unable to hide the truth.

The joy of the afternoon had evaporated. The promise of a new life together, neither hiding nor fearful, had slipped from their grasp.

He had intended to tell Léonie their happy news this evening. After her outrageous performance this afternoon, he decided against it. His decision not to involve her in the wedding was vindicated, though even as he tried to persuade himself, he realised that if she had been with them, she would never have been wandering unaccompanied around Carcassonne.

Anatole strode to the window, parted the wooden slats of the blinds and looked out. There was no one in the street, except for one drunken fellow, wrapped in an old soldier's cloak, knees drawn up and slumped against the wall opposite.

He let the blind snap shut.

He had no way of knowing if Constant himself was actually present in Carcassonne. Or, if not, how close at hand he might be. Their only choice was to return immediately to Rennes-les-Bains.

He had to hold onto the slim hope that if Constant had known of the Domaine de la Cade, he would have sent the letter there instead.

CHAPTER 62

Léonie waited for Anatole in the lobby. She had given him what little money she had remaining, but her heart was thudding with fear that the *patron* would give her away.

Anatole descended the stairs without a word to her. He went to the desk, spoke briefly with the *patron*, then strode past her and out into the street where the *fiacre* was standing in readiness to convey them to the railway station.

'My thanks, Monsieur,' she said.

'*Je vous en prie*, Mademoiselle Vernier,' he said, winking at her. He patted his breast pocket. 'I will see the letter delivered as you wish.'

Léonie nodded her farewell, then hurried down the steps to catch up with Anatole.

'Get in,' he ordered as she climbed into the carriage, as if he was speaking to a lazy servant, then leant forward and slipped a silver coin to the driver. 'Fast as you can.'

He did not address another word to her during the short ride to the railway station. Indeed, he did not even look at her.

They made the train with only moments to spare, rushing along the slippery platform to the first-class carriages at the front. The guard held the door for them and ushered them on. Isolde and Marieta were settled in the corner.

'Tante Isolde,' Léonie cried, forgetting her ill humour at the sight of her. There was not a drop of colour in her cheeks and her grey eyes were rimmed red.

Marieta stood up. 'I thought it better to stay with Madama,' she said. 'Rather than withdraw to my carriage.'

'Quite right,' Anatole said, not taking his eyes off Isolde. 'I'll settle it with the guard.'

He sat down on the banquette beside Isolde and took her limp hand.

Léonie, too, drew closer. 'Whatever is the matter?'

'I fear I have caught a chill,' Isolde said. 'I am so very sorry that, for my sake, you should miss the concert. I know how much you were looking forward to it.'

'Léonie accepts that your health comes first,' Anatole said, not allowing her the chance to answer for herself. 'And that we cannot risk being stranded this far from home, despite her inconsiderate perambulations this afternoon.'

The unfairness of his rebuke stung her, but Léonie held her tongue. Whatever the real reason for their hasty departure from Carcassonne, there was no doubt Isolde needed to be in the comfort of her own home.

Indeed, if Anatole had said as much, I would have made no complaint.

Resentment pricked at her. She persuaded herself that Anatole had provoked the quarrel and that she, in fact, had done nothing. She looked pointedly out of the window.

The whistle blew. Steam exhaled into the blustery air and the train juddered forward.

On the opposite platform, a matter of minutes later, Inspector Thouron and two Parisian officers disembarked from the train from Marseille. They were some two hours late, having been held up by a landslide brought on by heavy rain on the track outside Béziers.

Thouron was greeted by Inspector Bouchou of the Carcassonne *gendarmerie*. The two men shook hands. Then, holding their flapping coats tightly about them and clasping their hats firmly on their heads, they battled their way down the squally concourse into the fierce headwind.

'Good of you to meet me, Bouchou,' said Thouron, tired after his long and uncomfortable journey.

Bouchou was a corpulent, red-faced man, close to the age of retirement, with the dark colouring and stocky physique Thouron associated with the Midi. But, on first acquaintance, he seemed an amiable enough fellow, and Thouron's concerns that as northerners – worse still, Parisians – he and his men might be treated with suspicion seemed ill-founded.

'Delighted to be of assistance,' Bouchou shouted to make himself heard over the wind. 'Although I confess I'm puzzled as to why someone of your standing should make such a journey in person. It is only a matter of finding Vernier to inform him of the murder of his mother, *è?*' He turned a shrewd eye on Thouron. 'Or is there more to it?'

The inspector sighed. 'Let's get out of this wind and I'll tell you.'

Ten minutes later, they were established in a small café hard by the Cour de Justice Présidial where they could talk without fear of being overheard. Most of the clientele were either fellow officers from the *gendarmerie* or personnel from the prison.

Bouchou ordered two glasses of a local liqueur, La Micheline, then pulled up his chair to listen. Thouron found it a fraction too sweet for his taste but drank gratefully all the same as he explained the bare bones of the case.

Marguerite Vernier, widow of a Communard and more recently the mistress of a prominent and highly decorated war hero, had been found murdered in the family apartment on the evening of Sunday, 20th September. Since then, a month had passed and yet they had still been unable to trace either her son or her daughter, as next of kin, to inform them of their loss.

Indeed, although there was no reason to consider Vernier a suspect, at the same time a number of points of interest had come to light. Not least the growing evidence that he and his sister had deliberately covered their traces. It had taken Thouron's men some time to discover that Monsieur and Mademoiselle Vernier had travelled south from the Gare Montparnasse, rather than west or north from the Gare Saint-Lazare as previously believed.

'In truth,' Thouron admitted, 'if one of my men had not been on his toes, we would have got no further than that.'

'Go on,' said Bouchou, his eyes sharp with interest.

'After four weeks, you understand,' explained Thouron, 'I could no longer justify a full-time watch on the apartment.'

Bouchou shrugged. '*Bien sûr.*'

'However, in the way of these things, one of my officers – sharp boy, Gaston Leblanc – has become friendly with a maid in the Debussy household, the family which resides in the apartment below the Verniers in the rue de Berlin. She told Leblanc that she had seen the concierge accepting money from a man and, in return, handing over some sort of envelope.'

Bouchou dropped his elbows to the table. 'The concierge admitted it?'

Thouron nodded. 'At first, he denied it. These people always do. But under threat of arrest, eventually he admitted that he had been paid – and handsomely – to pass over any correspondence addressed to the Vernier apartment.'

'By whom?'

Thouron shrugged. 'He claimed not to know. The transactions were always done with a servant.'

'And you believed him?'

'On balance,' he said, draining his glass, 'I did. The long and the short of it was that the concierge claimed, although he could not be certain, that the handwriting resembled that of Anatole Vernier. And that the postmark was Aude.'

'*Et voilà*, so you are here.'

Thouron pulled a face. 'It is not much, I know, but it is the only lead we have.'

Bouchou raised his hand to order another round of drinks. 'And the matter is sensitive because of Madame Vernier's romantic liaison.'

Thouron nodded. 'General Du Pont is a man of some reputation and influence. He is not suspected of the crime, but—'

'And you are certain of that?' Bouchou interrupted. 'It is not just that your préfet does not wish to find himself embroiled in some scandal?'

For the first time, Thouron allowed a smile to flicker across his lips. It transformed his face, making him seem younger than his forty years.

'I do not deny that my superiors would have been rather ... disquieted, shall we say, should there have been a case against Du Pont,' he replied carefully. 'But, fortunately for all concerned, there are too many mitigating factors against the General being responsible. He is, however, anxious not to have this shadow hanging over him. Understandably, he believes that until the killer is caught and brought to justice, there will be rumours, the possibility of a stain on his character.'

Bouchou listened in attentive silence as Thouron went through his reasoning for believing Du Pont innocent – the anonymous tip-off; the fact that the medical examiner's estimated time of death was some hours earlier than when the body was found, at which point Du Pont was attending a concert and in plain view; the issue of who had been bribing the concierge.

'A rival lover?' he suggested.

'I wondered about that, yes,' Thouron admitted. 'There were two champagne glasses, but also a whisky glass broken in the grate. Also, although there was some evidence that Vernier's room had been searched, the servants are adamant that the only thing taken was a framed family portrait that resided on the sideboard.'

Thouron produced a similar photograph from his pocket, from the same sitting at the Parisian studio. Bouchou looked at it without comment.

'I appreciate', continued Thouron, 'that even if the Verniers were in the Aude, they might not be so now. It is a large area, and if they are here in Carcassonne, or in a private house in the country, then it might be very difficult to gain information about their whereabouts.'

'Do you have copies?'

Thouron nodded.

'I will put out an alert in the hotels and boarding houses in Carcassonne in the first instance, then perhaps the major tourist towns to the south. They would stand out less in an urban environment than in the country.' He looked down at the photograph. 'The girl is striking, is she not?' He slipped the image into his waistcoat pocket. 'Leave it with me, Thouron. I'll see what we can do.'

The inspector gave a deep sigh. 'I am most grateful, Bouchou. This case drags on.'

The storm hit the Haute Vallée at a little after eight o'clock in the evening, just as the train carrying Léonie, Anatole and Isolde south approached the station at Limoux.

Thunder, then a jagged fork of lightning slashed the purple sky. Isolde cried out and Anatole took her hand.

'It will be all right, I promise you.'

And, finally, Léonie could no longer pretend that Anatole's attentions to their aunt were a matter of courtesy. All the passing looks, the moments she had come upon them talking together, their evident growing affection. She wanted to catch his eye, but her brother's entire attention was focused on Isolde. Léonie thought he had forgotten she was even there.

Another crack of thunder split the air, making her jump, followed by a second burst of lightning as the storm rolled ever closer across the plains. The *pins maritimes*, the *platanes*, the beech trees swayed in the gusting crescendo of the wind. Even the vines, regimented in neat rows, shook with the ferocity of the tempest.

Feeling alone and unloved, but also with the pleasing memory of her adventure in the church, Léonie rubbed at the steamy glass and watched, half horrified and half exhilarated, as the elements raged about them. The tempest outside of the window seemed to match her mood. Several times, they were obliged to stop while the rails were cleared of fallen branches and even small trees loosened from the steep slopes of the gorges by the pummelling rain.

At every station, more and more people seemed to board the train. Hats were pulled low over brows, collars turned up to provide protection against the rain that was driving into the thin glass of the windows. The period of delay at each station became more and more interminable, with people standing in the carriages.

Some hours later, they arrived in Couiza. The weather was less ferocious in the valleys, but still there was no cab for hire and the *courrier publique* had long departed. Anatole was obliged to knock up one of the shopkeepers to send his boy by mule up the valley to fetch Pascal to bring the gig to collect them.

While they waited, they took shelter in a miserable restaurant building adjoining the *gare*. It was too late for dinner, but on seeing Isolde's incapacity and Anatole's undisguised anguish, the owner's wife took pity on their bedraggled party and provided cups of steaming oxtail soup and a bottle of strong Tarascon wine.

Two men joined them, also seeking refuge from the storm, bringing with them news that the River Aude was close to bursting its banks in Carcassonne. There were already pockets of flooding in the *quartiers* Trivalle and Barbacane.

Léonie paled, picturing the black water lapping at the steps of the église de Saint-Gimer. How easily she could have been trapped. The streets through which she had walked were now, if the accounts were to be believed, submerged. Then another thought shot into her mind. Was Victor Constant safe?

The torment of imagining him in danger played on her nerves all the way back to the Domaine de la Cade, making her oblivious to the rigours of the journey and the struggle of the weary horses along the slippery and perilous roads leading home.

The instant they arrived, Anatole charged into the house, shouting instructions. Marieta was sent to mix a powder to help her mistress sleep, another maid to fetch the bedwarmer and frame, to take the chill from Isolde's sheets, a third to stoke the fire already burning in the grate. Then, without caring what the servants might think, Anatole lifted Isolde into his arms and carried her up the stairs.

Léonie watched them go, her suspicions that he loved Isolde confirmed beyond doubt. By the time Léonie had rallied her thoughts, everyone had disappeared, leaving her to fend for herself. She did not understand why he had not told her he had fallen in love with Isolde. Why she had not. All those afternoons they had walked together in the gardens and she had not said a word.

Hurt and cold to her bones, Léonie followed them up to the first floor. She undressed and climbed into her bed. No fire burned in her grate; the room was unwelcoming and cheerless. No one came to check upon her, to make sure that she was all right after the long and difficult journey. Léonie felt she had been pushed to one side, forgotten.

She slept badly. All night long, Léonie was aware of Anatole pacing the corridors. Later, she heard the clip of his boots on the tiles of the hall below, like a soldier on the night watch, and the sound of the front door opening.

Then silence.

At last, Léonie fell into a restless half-sleep, dreaming of Victor Constant.

PART VIII

Hôtel de la Cade
October 2007

CHAPTER 63

Meredith saw Hal before he saw her. Sprawled in one of three low armchairs set around a small table, he was wearing much the same clothes he'd had on earlier, blue jeans and a white T-shirt, but had changed his sweater. As she watched, he lifted his hand and pushed his unruly hair off his face.

Meredith smiled at the gesture, which already seemed familiar.

He stood up as she drew close.

'Hi,' she said. 'Tough afternoon?'

'I admit I've had better,' he said, waving to the waiter. 'What can I get you?'

'The wine you recommended last night was pretty good.'

Hal ordered. '*Une bouteille du Domaine Begude, s'il vous plaît, Xavier. Et trois verres.*'

'Three glasses?' Meredith queried. 'Is someone joining us?'

Hal frowned. 'I bumped into my uncle coming in. He seemed to think you wouldn't mind and invited himself. Said you had a good conversation earlier.'

Meredith could see Hal was upset by the idea that she'd made friends with his uncle.

'Hardly a conversation,' she said. 'He asked me if I knew where you had gone after you dropped me back here. I said I wasn't sure. That was the extent of it.'

Hal looked at her, then nodded. 'He's good at getting what he wants.'

'Five minutes at most,' she said, driving the point home. 'Anyhow, more to the point, what happened this afternoon?'

Hal glanced at the door. 'I tell you what, why don't I reserve us a table for dinner? I don't want to start, then have to break off in a few minutes when my uncle gets here. How does that sound?'

Meredith grinned. 'Dinner sounds great. I skipped lunch. I'm ravenous.'

Looking pleased, Hal stood up. 'Be back in a moment.'

Meredith watched him walk across the room to the door, liking the way he turned as if to check she was still there, then he disappeared into the corridor.

Meredith smiled, feeling surprisingly light-headed at this gentle flirtation, and shook her head at such schoolgirl silliness.

Xavier brought the wine in an ice bucket on a stand and poured her a large, tulip-shaped glass. Trying not to drink too fast, Meredith cast her eyes around at the floor-to-ceiling shelves of books, wondering if Hal knew which – if any of them – were part of the original library and had survived the fire. It had occurred to her that there might be some kind of link involving the Lascombe family and the Verniers, especially given the connection with printing through the Bousquet family.

Sipping her wine, she looked out of the window. On the furthest edges of the lawns, she could see the shapes of the trees, swaying, moving in the darkness. For a moment, she felt as if someone had passed just in front of the window and was looking in at her. Then she became aware that someone had come up behind her. She smiled, expecting to see Hal, but found herself instead looking up at his uncle.

'Ms Martin,' he said, lightly putting his hand on her shoulder. 'Please, don't get up.'

Julian sat in the leather armchair to Meredith's right, poured himself some wine and sat back before she had the chance to tell him he was in Hal's chair.

'*Santé*,' he said, raising his glass. 'My nephew's done another vanishing act?'

'He's gone to get us a reservation for dinner,' she replied.

Polite, to the point, but nothing more.

Julian Lawrence smiled as if she had said something witty. He was dressed in a pale linen suit and blue shirt, open at the neck. Meredith found her eyes drawn to his left hand resting on the arm of the chair. It betrayed his age: late fifties, rather than the mid-forties she would have given him. He wore no ring.

Feeling the silence pressing on her, Meredith looked back up to his face. He was staring right at her.

Julian put his glass back on the table. 'What do you know about Tarot cards, Ms Martin?'

His question took her totally by surprise. Wondering how the hell he'd struck upon that subject, she thought of the photograph she'd stolen from the lobby and the deck of cards in her room. He couldn't know about any of it, but she felt herself colouring all the same. Worse, she could see he was enjoying her discomfort.

'Jane Seymour in the movie *Live and Let Die*,' she said, trying to make a joke of it. 'That's about it.'

'Ah, the beautiful Solitaire,' he said, raising his eyebrows. 'Personally, I find myself attracted by the history of the Tarot, although I do not for a moment believe that fortune-telling is any sort of way to plan one's life.'

His voice was similar to Hal's, she realised. They had the same habit of rolling their words as if every one was special.

The difference was that Julian always sounded faintly mocking. Sarcastic. She glanced at the door, but it remained resolutely shut.

'Are you aware of the principles behind the interpretation of Tarot cards, Ms Martin?'

'It's not something I know much about,' she said, wishing he'd get off the subject.

'Really? My nephew gave me the impression that it was an interest of yours. He said Tarot cards had come up when you were walking around Rennes-le-Château this morning. Perhaps I misunderstood.'

Meredith racked her brains. Tarot had never been far from her mind, sure, but she didn't remember discussing it with Hal. Julian was still staring right at her, a hint of challenge in his unwavering scrutiny.

In the end, she found herself responding to cover the awkward silence. 'I believe the idea is that although it seems as if the cards are laid at random, in fact the process of shuffling is merely a way of allowing invisible connections to be made visible.'

'Well put. Have you ever had your cards read, Ms Martin?'

A strangled laugh escaped out of her. 'Why do you ask?'

He topped up his glass. 'Just interested.'

Meredith glared at him, at a loss as to why the conversation was making her so uncomfortable. Then she felt a hand on her shoulder and flinched.

'Sorry,' Hal said quickly. 'I didn't mean to make you jump.'

Hal nodded at his uncle, then sat down in the vacant seat opposite Meredith. He took the bottle from the ice bucket and poured himself some wine.

'We were just talking about Tarot cards,' Julian said.

'Really?' said Hal. 'What were you saying?'

Meredith looked into his eyes and read the message in them. Her heart sank. She did not want to get caught up in a discussion about Tarot, but she could see that Hal saw it as a good way of keeping his uncle off the subject of his visit to the police commissariat.

'I was just asking Ms Martin if she had ever been to a Tarot reading,' Julian said. 'She was about to answer.'

She looked at him, then at Hal, and realised that unless she could think of an alternative topic of conversation in the next couple of seconds, she was going to have to answer.

'Actually, I did have a reading,' she said, trying to make it sound as dull as possible. 'In Paris, a couple of days ago. First – and last – time.'

'And was it a pleasurable experience?'

'It was interesting, certainly. What about you, Mr Lawrence? Have you ever had your cards read?'

'Julian, please,' he said. Meredith caught a look of amusement flicker across his face, mixed with something else. 'Not my kind of thing, although I am interested in some of the symbolism associated with Tarot cards.'

Meredith felt her nerves tighten. This wasn't small talk. He was after something specific. She took another mouthful of wine and fixed a bland expression on her face. 'Is that right?'

'The symbolism of numbers, for example,' he continued.

'Like I said, it's not something I know much about.'

Julian reached into his pocket. Meredith tensed. It would be too appalling if he produced a deck of Tarot cards. He held her gaze a moment, as if he knew exactly what was going through her mind, then pulled a packet of Gauloises and a Zippo from his pocket.

'Cigarette?' he asked, offering her the packet. 'Although it will have to be outside, I'm afraid.'

Furious, now, that he was somehow making a fool of her, and in front of Hal, she shook her head. 'I don't smoke.'

'Very wise.' Julian placed the packet, the lighter on top, on the table between them. 'The number symbolism in the church at Rennes-le-Château, for example, is quite fascinating.'

Meredith glanced over at Hal, willing him to say something, but he was resolutely refusing to join in.

'I didn't notice.'

'The number twenty-two, in particular, comes up surprisingly often.'

'In what form?' she replied, drawn into the conversation despite her antipathy towards Julian himself.

'The baptismal font in the entrance, the statue of the devil Asmodeus. You must have seen it?'

Meredith nodded.

'Asmodeus was supposed to be one of the guardians of the Temple of Solomon. The Temple was destroyed in 598 BCE. If you add each digit to the next – five plus nine plus eight – you get twenty-two. You know, I presume, that there are twenty-two cards in the major arcana?'

'Everyone knows that.'

Julian shrugged. 'Well then.'

'I presume there are other occurrences of the number?'

'The twenty-second of July is the feast day of St Mary Magdalene, to whom the church is dedicated. There is a statue of her between paintings thirteen and fourteen of the Stations of the Cross; she is also depicted in two of the three stained-glass windows behind the altar. Another link is with Jacques de Molay, the last leader of the Templars – there are supposed to be Templar links at Bézu, across the valley. He was the twenty-second Grand Master of the Poor Knights of the Temple, to give the outfit its full name. Then the French transliteration of Christ's cry from the cross: "*Elie, Elie, lamah sabactani*" – my God, my God, why hast thou forsaken me? – has twenty-two letters. It's also the opening verse of Psalm 22.'

Meredith was interested, in a kind of abstract way, but she still couldn't figure out why he was telling her. Just to see her reaction? To find out how much she did know about Tarot?

'Finally, the priest of Rennes-le-Château, Bérenger Saunière, died on the twenty-second of January 1917. An odd story attached to his death. Allegedly, his body was placed on a throne on the belvedere of his estate; the villagers filed past and each plucked a tassel from the hem of his robe. Much like the image of the King of Pentacles in the Waite Tarot, in fact.' He shrugged. 'Or, if you add two plus two, plus the year of his death, you end up with—'

'Yes,' she said, her patience starting to run out. 'What time is our reservation, Hal?'

'Seven-fifteen. Ten minutes.'

Julian ignored her interruption. 'Of course, playing devil's advocate, one could just as easily take any number and find a whole string of things that suggested there was some special significance.'

He picked up the wine and leaned forward to top Meredith up. She covered her glass with her hand. Hal shook his head. Julian shrugged, then emptied the remains of the bottle into his own glass.

'It's not as if any of us have to drive,' he said casually.

Hal rolled his eyes.

'I don't know if my nephew mentioned it, but there is a theory that the design of the church at Rennes-le-Château is in fact based on a building that once stood within our grounds here.'

Meredith forced her attention back to Julian.

'Is that right?'

'There's a significant amount of Tarot imagery within the church,' he continued. 'The Emperor, the Hermit, the Hierophant – who is, as I'm sure you remember, the symbol of the established church in Tarot iconography.'

439

'I really—'

He carried on talking. 'Some would say the Magician is suggested, in the form, perhaps, of Christ, and of course four of the paintings of the Stations of the Cross have towers in them, not to mention the Tour Magdala on the belvedere.'

'But that looks nothing like it,' she said, before she could stop herself.

'Like what, Ms Martin?' Julian said. She could hear excitement in his voice, as if he thought he'd caught her out.

'Jerusalem,' she said, the first random thing that came into her mind.

He raised his eyebrows. 'Or perhaps like Tarot cards you've seen?'

A silence fell over the table. Hal was frowning. Meredith couldn't figure out if he was embarrassed or had picked up the tension between her and his uncle and misunderstood it.

Julian placed his glass on the table, pushed back his chair and stood up.

'I'll leave you two young people to it,' he said, smiling at them as if they'd just passed the most pleasant half-hour in one another's company. 'Ms Martin. I hope you enjoy the rest of your stay with us.' He put his hand on his nephew's shoulder and Meredith could see how Hal hated it. 'Can you pop your head into my study when you've finished your supper? There are a couple of things I need to discuss with you.'

'Tonight?'

Julian tightened his grip. 'Tonight,' he said.

They sat in silence until Julian had gone.

'I'm sorry,' Hal said. 'I don't know what to say.'

'I don't know how you …' Meredith began, then she stopped. Rule number one: never criticise anyone else's family.

'Put up with it?' Hal said. 'Answer: I can't. As soon as I've sorted things, I'm out of here.'

'And are you any closer to that?'

He gave a long sigh, then stood up. 'I'll tell you at dinner.'

CHAPTER 64

Julian broke the seal on a new bottle of whisky, poured a generous measure, then sat down at his desk with his Tarot pack in front of him.

He'd studied the reproduction Bousquet deck over many years, always looking for something – a hidden key or a code he might have missed. The search for the original cards had occupied him ever since he first came to the Aude valley and heard the rumours about the undiscovered caches of treasure buried beneath the mountains, the rocks, even the rivers.

Having acquired the Domaine de la Cade, Julian had quickly come to the conclusion, like many before him, that all the stories surrounding Rennes-le-Château were a hoax and the renegade nineteenth-century priest at the heart of the rumours – Saunière – was prospecting for more than spiritual treasures.

Then Julian started to pick up stories about how a deck of cards revealed the location not of a single tomb, but allegedly the entire treasury of the Visigoth Empire. Perhaps even the contents of the Temple of Solomon, looted by the Romans in the first century AD, then in turn plundered when Rome itself fell in the fifth century to the Visigoths. Priceless, exceptional, worth a great deal on the open market and even more to private collectors. And he needed the money.

The cards were rumoured to be hidden within the estate itself. Julian had sunk every penny into trying to find

them through systematic searching and excavation, starting with the area around the ruins of the Visigoth sepulchre
and working out from there. It was difficult terrain and
the effort was extremely labour-intensive – and therefore
expensive.

Still nothing.

When he'd exhausted his credit at the bank, he'd begun
borrowing from the hotel. It was useful that the hotel was –
at least in part – a cash business. It was also a tough market
in which to make money, but if he succeeded in finding the
cards, then what he'd spent would fade into insignificance.
The overheads were high. The place was still finding its feet
when the bank called in its loans. But he kept taking money
out all the same – gambling that, soon, he'd find what he
was looking for and everything would be all right.

Julian drained his glass in one.

It was his brother's fault. Seymour could have been patient. Should have trusted him. Not interfered. Julian would
have repaid the money; it was all a matter of timing. The
question was what, if anything, Seymour had told his son.

Julian flipped the lid of his Zippo with a snap, lit a cigarette and inhaled deeply. He had spoken with the police
commissariat in Couiza just after Hal had left the station,
who had suggested that it would be better if the boy stopped
asking questions. Julian had promised to have a word and
invited the commissaire for a drink the following week.

He reached for the bottle, pouring himself another
two fingers. He cast his mind back to the conversation in
the bar. He had been deliberately clumsy, hardly subtle
in his technique, but it had seemed the easiest way to flush
the American out. She had been reluctant to talk about the
Tarot. The girl was sharp. Attractive, too.

'What? What does she know?'

He realised the sound he could hear was the sound of
his fingers drumming on the desk. Julian looked down

at his hand, as if it didn't belong to him, then forced it to be still.

In a drawer of his locked desk, the deeds of the transfer of ownership lay ready to sign and return to the *notaire* in Espéraza. The boy wasn't stupid. He didn't want to stay at the Domaine de la Cade. He and Hal couldn't work together, any more than he and Seymour had been able to. Julian had been leaving a decent interval before talking any further to Hal about his plans.

'It wasn't my fault,' he said, his voice now a little slurred.

He should talk to her again, the American girl. She must know something about the original Bousquet deck, why else was she here? Her presence was nothing to do with Seymour's accident or his pathetic nephew or the hotel finances, he could see that now. He'd made a mistake thinking that. She was here for the same reason he was. He hadn't done all the dirty work to see some American bitch come in and take the cards from him.

He gazed out at the darkened woods. Night had fallen. Julian reached out and turned on the lamp, then cried out.

His brother was standing right behind him. Seymour, as waxy and lifeless as Julian had seen him in the morgue, the skin on his face scarred from the crash, lined, his eyes bloodshot.

He leapt out of his chair, sending it toppling to the ground. The whisky glass went flying across the polished wood of the desk.

Julian spun round.

'You can't be . . .'

The room was empty.

He stared, uncomprehending, his eyes darting around the room into the shadows, back to the window, until he realised. It was his own pallid reflection, stark in the darkened glass. His own eyes, not his brother's.

Julian took a deep breath.

His brother was dead. He had spiked his drink and driven the car to the bridge outside Rennes-les-Bains; struggled to manoeuvre Seymour into the driver's seat; released the handbrake. He had seen the car fall.

'You made me do it,' he muttered. He hadn't wanted to, but Seymour wouldn't listen. All the way through their lives, Seymour had never listened. He'd always made him feel small.

Julian exhaled a long, exhausted breath, then bent down and righted the chair. For a moment, he stood with his hands gripping the back, his head bowed. Hating what he had become.

Then he pulled himself together. He reached for another cigarette and looked back out to the black woods beyond.

The original cards were still out there, he knew it.

'Next time,' he murmured. He was so close, he could feel it. Then he'd make amends. To Hal, to his brother's memory. To himself.

CHAPTER 65

'OK,' Meredith said. 'Tell me what happened.'

Hal put his elbows on the table. 'Bottom line, they don't see any grounds for opening things up. They are satisfied with the verdict.' He shook his head. 'Accidental death. That Dad was drunk, lost control of the car, went over the bridge into the Salz. Three times over the limit, that's what the tox report claims.'

They were sitting in one of the window alcoves. The restaurant was quiet, so they could talk without being overheard. Across the white linen tablecloth, in the light of the candle flickering on the table, Meredith had to fight the urge to reach across and take his hand.

'There was a witness, apparently,' he continued. 'An English woman, Dr Shelagh O'Donnell, who lives locally.'

'That's helpful, isn't it? Did she see the accident?'

Hal shook his head. 'That's the problem. According to the file, she heard brakes, the sound of tyres. She didn't actually see anything.'

'Did she report it?'

'Not straight away. According to the commissaire, lots of people take the road too fast on the bend coming into Rennes-les-Bains. It was only the following morning, when she saw the ambulance and the police recovering the car from the river, that she put two and two together.' He paused. 'I thought I might talk to her. See if there's anything that's come back to her.'

446

'Wouldn't she have told the police already?'

'I didn't get the impression they thought her a reliable witness.'

'In what way?'

'They didn't say it in so many words, but they implied that she's an alcoholic. Also, since there were no tyre marks on the road, it's unlikely she could have heard anything. According to the police, that is.'

'So they think she's making it up?' Meredith said.

He shrugged. 'They wouldn't give me her address, but I managed to copy down her number from the file. In fact, I invited her up here tomorrow.'

'Is that a good idea?' said Meredith. 'If the police think you're interfering, won't that make them less, rather than more, likely to help?'

'They're already pissed off with me,' he said, 'but to tell you the truth, I don't care any more. I feel like I'm hitting my head against a brick wall. For weeks I've been trying to get the police to take my concerns seriously, but it's got me nowhere.' He raised his hand. 'Sorry, Meredith. This can't be much fun for you.'

'It's OK,' she said, thinking how similar Hal and his uncle were in some ways, though she knew how much Hal would hate such a comparison.

'I appreciate there's no reason for you to take what I say at face value, but I just don't believe the official version of events. I'm not saying my dad was perfect – to be honest, we didn't have much in common. He was distant and quiet, not the sort of man to make a fuss – but there's just no way he would drink and drive. Even in France. No way.'

'It's easy to misjudge that sort of thing, Hal,' she said carefully. 'Lots of people have one too many, play the odds.'

'Not Dad,' he said. 'He liked his wine, but he was fanatical about not getting behind the wheel if he'd been drinking. Not even one glass.' He met her gaze. 'The thing is, my mother was killed by a drunk driver. She was on her way to pick me up from school, at half past three in the afternoon. An idiot in a BMW, on his way back from the pub, tanked up on champagne and driving too fast.'

'Oh, Hal. That must have been devastating.'

'Yes,' he said simply.

'And when you were so young.'

This time, she did reach out. Briefly, she laid her hand across his and felt his fingers take hers. And now she understood why Hal couldn't bring himself to accept the verdict. But wishing things were different didn't make them so; she'd been there herself.

She sat back in her chair. 'So if the tox screen came back positive,' she said carefully, 'what other explanation could there be? What did the police say?'

'It was obvious they thought I was too upset to think straight.'

'OK. Let's come at it from another direction. Could the tests be wrong?'

'The police say no.'

'Did they search for anything else?'

'Like what?'

'Drugs?'

Hal shook his head. 'Didn't think there was any need.'

Meredith thought. 'Well, could he have been driving too fast? Just lost control on the bend?'

'Back to the lack of skid marks on the road and, in any case, that doesn't account for the alcohol in his bloodstream.'

A shiver went down her spine. Meredith looked at him. 'So what are you saying, Hal?'

'That either the tests are fake, or someone spiked his drink.'

Her face gave her away.

'You don't believe me,' he said.

'I'm not saying that, but think about it. Even supposing it was possible, who would do such a thing? Why would they?'

Hal didn't look away until Meredith realised.

'You think your uncle had something to do with it?'

He nodded.

'Are you serious?' she pressed. 'I mean, I know you don't see eye to eye, but even so, to accuse him of—'

'I know it sounds ridiculous, but who else stands to gain by my father's death?'

Meredith frowned. 'Did you make this accusation to the police?'

'Not in so many words, but I did request that the *gendarmerie nationale* were shown the file.'

'I'm sorry, I don't know what that means.'

'The *gendarmerie nationale* investigate crimes. At the moment, the crash is being treated as a traffic accident. But if I can find some sort of evidence linking it to Julian, then I could make them reconsider.'

Meredith didn't know what to think. She was desperately sorry for what had happened to him – to lose both his mother and now his father was awful – but she feared his judgement was clouded. She liked him, but she had to remind herself that she barely knew him. He needed someone to blame as a way of dealing with his loss.

'Meredith?'

She realised Hal was staring at her. 'Sorry,' she said. 'Just thinking.'

'Would you be able to be there when Dr O'Donnell comes tomorrow? I think she'd be more likely to open up with another woman there.'

She hesitated. She wanted to help, but what if she only made it worse?

'I'd really appreciate it.'

He looked so hopeful that Meredith gave in. 'OK,' she said in the end.

Hal smiled. 'Thank you.'

'But I'm not promising I'll be able to get anything out of her either.'

'I understand,' he said quietly, 'but you're helping. That means a lot.'

The waiter came over and the mood changed, became less intense. They both ordered steak and Hal chose a bottle of local red to go with it. For a moment, they sat looking a little awkwardly at one another, not sure how to pick up the conversation.

Hal broke the silence. 'So, Meredith Martin, you've heard all about my problems. Are you going to tell me now why you're really here?'

Meredith went still. 'Excuse me?'

'It's obviously not for the Debussy book, is it? Or, at least, not only for that.'

'Why do you say that?'

Hal flushed. 'Well, for a start, the stuff you were interested in today didn't seem to have much to do with Lilly Debussy. You seem more into the history of this place, Rennes-les-Bains, and the people here.' He grinned. 'Also, I noticed that the photograph hanging above the piano has disappeared. Someone's taken it.'

'You think I did?'

'You were looking at it this morning, so . . .' he said, pulling an apologetic smile.

For a moment, Meredith thought about brazening it out, then she grinned too.

'I'm intending to put it back.'

Hal laughed. 'I knew it!' Then his face grew serious. 'It's not something to do with my uncle, is it, your real reason for being here?'

Meredith simply stared at him. 'What do you mean?'

'Well, the way he behaved earlier, I wondered if you might be here checking up on him.'

He stumbled to a standstill.

Meredith held up her hand. 'Let me see if I've got this straight. You don't believe your father's accident was, in fact, an accident, because you think the results might have been tampered with or his drink was spiked and the car was forced from the road—'

'Yes, although—'

Meredith carried on talking. 'And so when I turn up, you jump to the conclusion that I'm somehow involved? Is that what you think, Hal? That I'm some kind of Nancy Drew? Is that why you invited me for dinner?'

'Of course not.'

'Well, it sounds like it.'

She took a large mouthful of wine, caught between disbelief at the turn the conversation had taken and disappointment.

Hal looked sheepish. 'I didn't mean to offend you,' he said quickly. 'But, well, it was something Dad said to me back in April that gave me the impression he was unhappy with the way Julian was running things out here and was going to do something. He might have . . .'

'. . . Hired someone,' she said.

'I'm sorry,' Hal said, now looking awkward.

'If that was the case,' she said, in a level voice, 'wouldn't your father have just come right out and told you?'

Hal shook his head. 'Dad wasn't like that. He hated gossip, rumour. He'd never say anything, even to me, until he was completely certain of his facts. Innocent until proven guilty.'

Meredith didn't know what to say. She didn't know what she felt.

'It might have been something trivial,' Hal continued, still trying to bridge the chasm that had opened up between them, 'but I got the impression it was serious. Something

451

to do with the Domaine de la Cade and its history, not just money.'

Meredith decided to put her own injured pride to one side. She had clearly read too much into the few hours they'd spent together.

'He didn't leave you anything? A file? Notes?'

'Believe me, I've looked everywhere. There's nothing.'

'When you started to think all this, Hal,' she said, 'why didn't you just ask me?'

'I thought there was more to your being here than the biography you're writing, but I only started to think you might be here because of my uncle after I'd come back from the police station.'

Meredith frowned. 'So it's not why you started talking to me in the bar last night?'

'No, of course not!' he said, looking genuinely appalled.

'Then why?'

Hal turned red. 'Christ, Meredith, you know why. It's obvious enough.'

And she realised she believed him.

'But you are right. Debussy is not the only reason I'm here,' she said.

CHAPTER 66

The rest of the meal was wonderful. Meredith told Hal a little about her family and, away from his grief and concern about his father's death, he was a wonderful dinner companion.

He insisted on paying for dinner, saying it was the least he could do, and as they walked out of the restaurant, Meredith felt Hal's fingers wrap around hers.

Hand in silent hand, they walked up the stairs. Meredith felt totally calm. She didn't have to think about whether this was what she wanted. It felt fine. They were attracted to one another, they were not otherwise attached, it seemed like the obvious end to the evening.

They reached the end of the first-floor passageway without bumping into any other guests. Meredith turned the key, loud in the hushed corridor, and pushed open the door to her room. Almost formal, they walked in still holding hands.

Slats of white light from a harvest moon shone in through the windows and patterned the floor and glinted on the reflective surface of the mirror, on the framed portrait of Anatole and Léonie Vernier and Isolde Lascombe propped on the desk.

Meredith reached out to put on the light.

'Don't,' Hal said quietly.

He cupped his hand behind her head and drew her to him. Meredith breathed in the smell of him, just like at Rennes-les-Bains outside the church – a mixture of wool and soap.

They kissed, their lips carrying the trace of red wine, softly at first, tentatively, the mark of friendship moving into something else, something more urgent. Meredith felt comfort give way to desire, a rush of blood to the head.

Hal gathered her into his arms in one movement and carried her to the bed. The key dropped from Meredith's hand, landing with a heavy thump on the thick pile carpet.

He placed her carefully down, then sat beside her, his feet still firmly planted on the floor, like a Hollywood matinée idol under fear of the censor.

'Are you . . .' he started. 'Are you sure you want—'

Meredith laid a single finger across his mouth. 'Ssshh.'

Slowly, she began to undo the buttons of her shirt, then guided his hand to her. She heard the rise and fall of his breathing in the dappled silver light of the room. Sitting cross-legged on the edge of the bed, Meredith leant forward to kiss him, her dark hair falling over her face, the difference in their heights eliminated now.

Hal struggled to remove his sweater as Meredith pushed her hands beneath the cotton of his T-shirt. They both laughed, a little shy.

Meredith didn't feel self-conscious as she undressed. It all felt like time out of time. As if for a few days she had stepped out of her regular life to a place where different rules applied.

She took a step towards Hal, their bare skin touching, top to toe, intimate and startling. She could feel how much he wanted her, but he let her lead the way.

She took his hand and pulled him back to the bed. They slipped between the sheets, the linen crisp and cool against their skin. For a moment, they lay side by side, arm to arm, like a knight and his lady on a stone tomb, then

Hal propped himself on one elbow and with his other hand started to stroke her head.

Meredith breathed deeply, relaxing under his touch.

Now his hand was moving lower, smoothing over her shoulders, the hollow of her throat, skimming her breasts, winding her fingers with his, his lips and his tongue whispering over the surface of her skin.

Meredith felt heat burn in her, along the lines of her veins. She raised herself towards him, her kisses hungry now. Just when the waiting was becoming intolerable, Hal shifted position and lowered himself into the space between her legs. Meredith looked up into his eyes and saw every possibility reflected, for an instant, in them. The best of her, and the worst.

'You're sure?'

Meredith smiled and reached down to guide him. Carefully, Hal eased himself inside her.

'It's OK,' she murmured.

For a moment, they lay still in one another's arms. Then Hal began to move, slowly at first, then a little more urgently. Meredith placed her hands firmly on his back, her body filled with the hammering of her own blood. She could feel the power of him, the strength in his arms and hands.

Hal was breathing harder, moving harder, as desire, need, drove him on. Meredith held him to her, tighter, rising to meet him, possessing him. He cried out her name, shuddered, and they both fell still.

The rushing in her head faded away. She felt the full weight of him come back, but she did not move. She stroked his thick black hair and held him in her arms.

'Tell me more about yourself,' he said a little later.

'I told you everything.'

Hal grabbed her fingers. 'I'm serious! You've told me where you grew up, what and where you studied, about Bill and Mary, about your publishing deal. But what lies behind all that. You didn't really tell me why you were here.'

Meredith caught her breath.

'Only if you want to,' he said quickly.

Meredith knitted her fingers through his. 'I do.'

She sat up in bed, pulling the sheet over her. It wasn't a part of herself she had shared with a lover before, for fear, perhaps, of putting them off. But she thought Hal would understand. Like her, he had lost his parents.

'My birth mother, Jeanette, was unable to take care of me,' she said. 'Mary is a distant cousin, a kind of aunt a couple of times removed. I'd spent time with them, on and off, when Jeanette was sick. When things finally got too bad, I went to live with them for good. They formally adopted me a couple of years later, when my birth mom died.'

The plain, carefully chosen words did not do justice to the years of late-night phone calls, the unannounced visits, the shouting in the street, the burden of responsibility the child Meredith had felt for her damaged and volatile mother. Nor did they hint at the guilt she carried with her still, that her first reaction on hearing her mother was dead had not been grief, but relief. She couldn't forgive herself for that.

'Sounds tough,' Hal said.

Meredith smiled at his British understatement. 'Mary is an amazing lady. It was she who got me started on the violin, then the piano. I owe everything to her and Bill.'

'So you really are writing a biography of Debussy?' he teased.

Meredith hit him on the arm. 'Have the money in my account to prove it!'

For a moment, they lay in companionable silence, still and touching.

'Until now,' Meredith continued, 'all I knew about Jeanette's family was that they might have come from this part of France, during – or just after – the First World War. I have a photograph of what I'm now pretty sure is my great-great-grandfather, in French army uniform, taken in the square in Rennes-les-Bains in 1914.'

'That's amazing.'

She nodded. 'The story is he ended up in Milwaukee, but, since I didn't have a name, I couldn't get much further. The city had a large European population from the early nineteenth century, so it was plausible enough.'

Meredith gave Hal a skeleton version of what she'd discovered since arriving at the Domaine de la Cade, about why she'd taken the portrait from the lobby and the piece of music she'd inherited from her grandmother. She also told him about the Bousquet Tarot cards and how she believed the images reflected real people.

'So you think your unknown soldier is a Vernier,' Hal said, when Meredith had finished.

She nodded. 'I think so. The physical resemblance is overwhelming. Colouring, features. He might be a younger brother or a cousin, I guess, but taking the dates and his age into consideration, I'm thinking he could be a direct descendant.' She stopped. 'Then, just before I came down to meet you, I got an email from Mary saying that there was the record of a Vernier in the graveyard at Mitchell Point in Milwaukee.'

'Do you think Anatole Vernier was his father?'

'That's the next step: to prove it one way or the other. He could be Léonie's son.'

'Then he wouldn't be a Vernier, would he?'

'He would if she wasn't married.'

Hal nodded. 'Fair enough.'

Meredith took his hand. 'So, here's the deal. Tomorrow, I help you talk to Dr O'Donnell, then in return you help me do a little research into the Verniers.'

'Deal,' he said, leaning across and kissing her. 'And, Meredith, I know you think I'm making something out of nothing, but I really appreciate it. She'll be here at ten.'

'As you said, she's more likely to talk with another woman there.'

Suddenly, Meredith was struggling to keep her eyes open. Slowly, she felt herself drifting away from Hal. The silver moon made her progress across the black Midi sky. Below in the valley, the bell tolled the passing of the hours.

CHAPTER 67

In her dream, Meredith was sitting at the piano at the foot of the stairs. The cool ivory of the keys and the melody were familiar beneath her fingers. She was playing Louisa's signature piece, better than she had ever played it before, sweet and yet haunting.

Then the piano vanished and she was walking along a narrow and empty corridor. There was a patch of light at the end and a set of stone stairs, dipped and worn away in the centre by the passage of feet and time. She turned to go but found herself always standing in the same place. It was somewhere within the Domaine de la Cade, she knew, but not a part of the house or grounds she recognised.

The light, a perfect square, was coming from a gas jet on the wall, which hissed at her as she passed. Facing her at the top of the steps was a dusty tapestry of a hunt. She stared a moment at the cruel expressions of the men, the smears of red blood on their spears. Except, as she looked with her dream eyes, she realised it was not a wild animal they were hunting. Not a bear, not a boar, not a wolf. Instead, a black creature, standing on two legs, with cloven feet, an expression of rage on its almost human features. A demon, his claws tipped red.

Asmodeus.

In the background, flames. The wood was burning.

Meredith moaned and shifted position as her dreaming hands, both weighed and weightless, pushed at an old wooden door. There was a carpet of silver dust on the ground, glinting in the moonlight or the halo from the gaslight.

The air was still. At the same time, the room didn't feel like a space left empty. Time jumped forward. Now Meredith could hear the piano again, except this time distorted. Like the sound of a fairground or a carousel, menacing and sinister.

Her breath came faster. She reached out and grasped the cold metal latch.

She pushed open the door. Stepped up over the stone step.

No birds flew up. There was no whispering of voices, hidden, behind the door. Now she was standing inside some kind of chapel. High ceilings, flagstone floors, an altar and stained-glass windows. Paintings covering the walls, immediately recognisable as the characters from the cards. A sepulchre. It was utterly silent. Nothing but the echo of her footsteps disturbed the hush. And yet, little by little, the air began to whisper. She could hear voices, noises in the darkness. At least, voices behind the silence. And singing.

Moving forward, she felt the air part. The very space itself seemed to be holding its breath.

Meredith kept walking until she arrived before the altar. She was now standing inside a square, marked in black upon the stone floor. Around it, letters inscribed upon the ground.

Help me.

Someone was there. In the darkness and the silence, something was moving. Meredith felt the space around her shrinking, fold in upon itself. She could see nothing, yet she knew she was there. A living, breathing presence. And she knew she had seen her before – beneath the bridge, on the road, at the foot of her bed. Air, water, fire and now earth. The four suits of the Tarot.

Hear me. Listen to me.

Meredith felt herself falling, down into a place of stillness and peace. She was not afraid. She was no longer herself, but instead standing outside, looking in. And, clear in the room, she heard her own sleeping voice speak calmly out.

'Léonie?'

At the foot of the bed, the figure gave a slight movement of her head. Long copper curls, colour without substance, unveiled as the hood fell from her hair. Skin translucent. Green eyes, although transparent. Form without substance. A long black dress beneath the cloak. Shape without form.

I am Léonie.

Meredith heard the words inside her head. A young girl's voice, a voice from an earlier time. Again, the atmosphere in the room seemed to shift.

I cannot sleep. Until I am found, I can never sleep. Hear the truth.

'The truth? About what?' Meredith whispered. The light was changing, loosening.

The story is in the cards.

There was a rushing of air, a fracturing of the light, a shimmering of something – someone – withdrawing. The atmosphere was different again now. There was a threat in the darkness, which Léonie had held at bay. But the gentle presence of the ghost had vanished, replaced by something destructive. A malevolence. It was now oppressively cold, pushing in upon Meredith. Like an early-morning mist at sea, the sharp tang of salt and fish and smoke. She was back in the sepulchre. She felt the need to run, although she did not know what from.

There was something behind her. A black figure or some kind of creature. Meredith could almost feel its breath on the back of her neck, puffs of white clouds in the frigid air. But the stone nave was shrinking. The wooden door was getting smaller and more distant.

Un, deux, trois, loup! Coming to get you, ready or not.

Something was snapping at her heels, gaining speed in the shadows, getting ready to leap. Meredith started to run, fear giving power to her shaking legs. Her sneakers were skidding, sliding, on the flagstone floor. Behind her, the breathing.

Nearly there.

She threw herself at the door, feeling her shoulder crashing into the frame, pain ricocheting down her arm. The creature was right behind her, the bristling of its fur, the stench of iron and blood, melting into her skin, the surface of her scalp and the soles of her feet. She fumbled at the latch, rattling, tugging, jerking it towards her, but it wouldn't open.

She started to bang on the door, trying not to look over her shoulder, trying not to be caught in the gaze of its hideous blue eyes. She could feel the silence deepen around her. Could feel its arms coming down around her neck, wet and cold and rough. The smell of the sea, dragging her down.

CHAPTER 68

'Meredith! Meredith. It's all right. You're safe, it's all right.'

She woke with a massive jolt that left her gasping for breath. Every muscle in her body was alert, every nerve screaming. The cotton sheets were knotted and her fingers were locked rigid. For a moment, she felt consumed with rage, as if the creature had forced its way down through the surface of her skin.

'Meredith, it's OK! I'm here.'

She was trying to prise herself free, disorientated, until gradually she realised that she felt warm skin, holding her tight to save her, not harm her.

'Hal.'

The tension fell from her shoulders.

'You were having a nightmare,' he said. 'You're all right.'

'She was here. She was here . . . then . . . it came and . . .'

'Ssshh, it's OK,' he said again.

Meredith reached up her hand and with her fingers traced the contours of his face.

'She came . . . and then. Behind her . . .'

'There's no one here but us. Just a nightmare. It's all over now.'

Meredith looked around the room, as if expecting at any moment someone to step out of the shadows. At the same time, she knew the dream had passed. She felt the warmth and the strength of him holding her closer, holding her safe.

She could feel the bones of her ribcage as they rose and fell, rose and fell.

'I saw her,' she murmured, although she was talking to herself now, not Hal.

'Who?' he whispered.

She didn't answer.

'It's all right,' he repeated gently. 'Go back to sleep.'

He began to stroke her head, smoothing her bangs back from her forehead like Mary used to do.

'She was here,' Meredith said again.

Gradually, beneath the repetitive and gentle motion of Hal's hand, the terror faded away. Her eyelids became heavy.

Four o'clock in the morning.

Clouds had covered the moon and it was completely dark. The lovers fell back to sleep in each other's arms, shrouded in the deep blue of early morning before the day comes.

PART IX

The Glade
October–November 1891

CHAPTER 69

FRIDAY, 23RD OCTOBER 1891

When Léonie woke the following morning, the first thought that came to her mind was of Victor Constant. If the ill weather was continuing in Carcassonne without respite, the *patron* of the hotel might be unable to deliver her letter to him. She was upset by the realisation that she had no way of being certain.

Her next thought was of Anatole.

Feeling out of sorts, she dressed quickly and let herself out into the early morning. Evidence of yesterday's storm was all around. Broken branches, leaves sent flying into spirals by the agitating wind. Everything was quite still now and the pink dawn sky was clear. But in the distance, over the Pyrenees, a grey bank of storm clouds threatened more bad weather to come.

As she walked back into the house, she couldn't decide if she wanted to see her brother or not. The memory of their quarrel and his coldness to her still stung. But when she walked into the breakfast room to find it empty, apart from Marieta, who was setting the coffee pot on the table, she was disappointed.

'Good morning. Has my brother come down?'

Marieta shook her head. 'You are the first.'

'And my aunt? Is she recovered after last evening?'

Marieta dropped her voice, as if confiding a great secret.

'Did you not hear, Madomaisèla? Madama was taken that bad in the night that Sénher Anatole was obliged to send to town for the doctor.'

Léonie was horrified. 'I had no idea. I should go to her.'

'Best to leave her. Madama has finally fallen asleep.'

Léonie hesitated, then sat down, feeling guilty that she hadn't thought of Isolde all night.

'Dr Gabignaud said she has caught a chill,' Marieta continued, 'which is threatening to develop into something worse. He gave her a powder to bring down the fever. He stayed with her – your brother too – all night.'

'Will she be all right?' Léonie asked in a quiet voice.

'You will have to ask Sénher Anatole. The doctor spoke with him in private.'

Léonie felt dreadful that she had slept through the night. She felt as if there was a ring of iron around her chest, stopping her breathing. She ate little, her mind running riot. First worrying about her aunt's health, then Monsieur Constant, then back to Isolde and her brother. She was no longer sure what she thought.

Finally, she heard the sound of footsteps crossing the hall. Tossing her napkin on the table, she leapt to her feet and ran to the door, coming face to face with Anatole in the hall.

He was pale and had hollow circles under his eyes.

'I have only just heard. Is the doctor returning this morning? Is—'

Despite his wretched appearance, Anatole smiled. He held up his hand, as if to deflect the volley of questions.

'*Calme-toi*,' he said, placing his arm around her shoulder. 'The worst is over.'

Léonie exhaled. 'I felt so hopeless. I didn't know what you would want me to do.'

'There's nothing to do now, *petite*. Isolde will be fine. Gabignaud was excellent. Gave her something to help her sleep. She is weak, but the fever has gone. It's nothing that a few days' bed rest will not cure.'

Léonie shocked herself by feeling tears come to her eyes – a mixture of guilt and relief that she and Anatole were friends again. Any previous thought of questioning him about his feelings for Isolde were pushed to one side.

'Come now,' he said affectionately, handing her his handkerchief. 'Everything will be fine.'

'Let's not ever argue any more,' Léonie said. 'I cannot bear it.'

'Nor I,' he said. 'Now, have you breakfasted?'

Léonie nodded.

'Well, I have not. Will you keep me company?'

Over the course of the weekend, Isolde kept to her bed on Gabignaud's orders but asked Léonie to sit with her in the afternoons. Her colour was coming back and she was distressed at causing everyone such a fright. She was particularly solicitous and careful of Léonie's feelings, suggesting what books Léonie might try next. Léonie enjoyed her company. She felt useful and at the heart of things. Anatole whistled as he walked around the house and busied himself with matters concerning the estate on Isolde's behalf. Once, he joined them in her chamber in the evenings and, if the servants found such familiarity surprising, they did not remark upon it in Léonie's hearing.

All the same, several times Léonie caught Anatole looking at her as if he was on the point of confiding something. For her part, she was no longer certain about what she had witnessed on the train back from Carcassonne – familial affection or something more – but she didn't want to damage the returning warmth between her and her brother, so she forced herself to be patient. If Anatole, or indeed Isolde, wished to confide in her, then they would.

The main topic of conversation in the servants' quarters was the damage the storm had wrought in Rennes-les-Bains and neighbouring Quillan. Communications were disrupted and in some areas suspended altogether. On Monday evening, news of the catastrophe that had struck Carcassonne reached the Domaine de la Cade. After three days of relentless rain, in the early hours of Sunday morning, the River Aude had finally burst its banks. Early reports had it that much of the *quartier* Trivalle and the *quartier* Barbacane were completely under water and the Pont Vieux, linking the medieval Cité to the Bastide, was submerged.

Léonie listened to the news with increasing anxiety. She feared for Monsieur Constant, her anguish all the worse for being unable to share it with anyone. She knew it was absurd to feel so strongly for a person in whose company she had spent little more than an hour, yet he had taken residence in her romantic mind and she could not shake her thoughts free of him. Earlier in October, she had worried about letters from their mother having gone astray; now she found herself wondering if there was a letter from Carcassonne for her lying unclaimed in the boxes at the poste restante in Rennes-les-Bains.

The question was, how could she make the trip down to town in person? She could hardly entrust so delicate a matter to one of the servants, not even the amiable Marieta. In novels, the heroine always found a way, but Léonie was at a loss. The thought that Constant might have written, and would now be thinking ill of her for her discourtesy in not replying, preyed on her mind in every idle moment.

CHAPTER 70

H er chance came three days later.

On Wednesday evening, Isolde was improved enough to join Anatole and Léonie for dinner in the dining room. Though she ate little – even the coffee, freshly brewed from the beans Léonie had purchased for her in Carcassonne, was not to her taste – she was attentive and charming, amusing Léonie with stories of the opera in Paris and the men who frequented the stage door of the ballet. Léonie could see how their friendship pleased Anatole, though he fussed endlessly.

'Is there anything you want? Whatever it is, I will endeavour to get it for you.'

Isolde smiled. 'Everything tastes so peculiar.'

'I can go down into Rennes-les-Bains tomorrow and purchase whatever you would like,' he continued.

Léonie suddenly saw the solution to her situation.

'I could go,' she said, trying to keep her voice light. 'Rather than tear you away, Anatole, it would be my pleasure to go down to the town. I am well acquainted with your tastes, Tante. If the gig could be spared in the morning, Pascal could drive me.' She paused. 'I could bring back a tin of crystallised ginger from the Magasins Bousquet.'

To Léonie's delight, Isolde smiled. 'Now I confess, that is something I could manage,' she admitted.

'Excellent,' Anatole said.

'And perhaps, also,' Léonie added, running through Isolde's favourite treats in her mind, 'I could visit the *pâtissier* and purchase a box of Jesuites?'

'They might be a little rich for me at present, but some of those black pepper biscuits might be quite the thing.'

Anatole was nodding. 'That is settled then.' He covered Léonie's hand with his. 'But I am more than happy to come with you, *petite*, if you wish it.'

'There is no need. It will be an adventure. I am certain there are plenty of things to occupy your time here.'

He glanced across at Isolde. 'Well, if you are certain, I would be most grateful.'

'Quite certain,' she said briskly. 'I will leave at ten o'clock, so as to be back in good time for luncheon. I shall compile a list.'

'You are kind to go to so much trouble,' Isolde said.

'It is my pleasure,' Léonie replied, truthfully.

She had done it. Provided she could slip away to the poste restante without Pascal's knowledge some time during the course of the morning, she would at least know if Monsieur Constant had thought of her at all. A letter, whatever its contents, would make that clear.

At a quarter past ten the following morning, Léonie stepped down from the gig in the place du Pérou. Dressed in her favourite crimson day dress, with matching jacket and hat, she promenaded along the Gran'Rue with her shopping list in hand, visiting every shop in turn. Pascal's arms became fuller. She paused for a *sirop de grenadine* at the street-side café adjoining the Maison Gravère, where she and Anatole had taken coffee on their first expedition, and felt quite at home.

Indeed, Léonie felt as if she belonged to the town and the town to her. And although one or two people with whom she had a passing acquaintance were a little cold to

472

her, or so it seemed – the wives looking away and the husbands barely lifting their hats as she passed – Léonie now believed that she felt more herself in the wooded landscape of mountains and lakes of the Aude than she had ever done in the city.

Now, the thought of the dirty streets and soot of the 8th *arrondissement*, not to mention the limitations placed upon her freedom, appalled her. Certainly, if Anatole could persuade their mother to join them for Christmas, then Léonie would be more than content to remain at the Domaine de la Cade until the New Year and beyond.

Her tasks were quickly accomplished. By eleven o'clock, all that remained was to slip away from Pascal for long enough to make her detour to the poste restante. She asked him to convey the packages back to the gig, which had been left in the care of one of his many nephews, declaring she intended to pay her respects to Monsieur Baillard.

Pascal's eyes narrowed. 'I was not aware he had returned to Rennes-les-Bains, Madomaisèla Léonie.'

Their eyes met. 'I do not know for certain that he has,' she admitted. 'But it is no trouble to walk there and back. I shall meet you in the place du Pérou presently.'

As she was speaking, Léonie realised how she could engineer an opportunity to read the letter in private.

'In point of fact, Pascal,' she added, 'I believe I shall walk all the way back to the Domaine de la Cade instead. You need not wait.'

Pascal shook his head. 'I am certain Sénher Anatole would not wish me to abandon you here to make the return journey on foot,' he said, his expression making it clear that he knew how Marieta had been reprimanded for letting Léonie slip from her charge in Carcassonne.

'Please, Pascal,' she said. 'I am confident of the path through the woods. Marieta brought us through the rear entrance to the Domaine de la Cade, as you know, so it is not unknown to me. It is such a fine day – possibly the last of this year's sun – I cannot believe my brother would not wish me to take advantage of the good air.'

Pascal stared at her a moment longer, weighing things up, then grinned. 'As you wish, Madomaisèla,' he said in his calm, steady voice, 'but I shall send Marieta to unlock the gates and walk to meet you halfway down.'

Léonie felt humbled, both by Pascal's good nature and also by his concern for her well-being. For the truth was that, despite her fighting talk, she was anxious at the thought of going alone through the woods.

'Thank you, Pascal,' she said softly. 'I promise I will be so quick that my aunt and brother will never know.'

Feeling a mixture of excitement and nerves, Léonie watched him go. As he turned the corner, she glimpsed a person in a blue cape darting into the passageway that led to the church, as if he did not wish to be seen. Léonie frowned, thinking perhaps she had seen him before, but she hurried on in case Pascal changed his mind and came back.

Léonie intended to walk to the poste restante via the road in which Monsieur Baillard's lodgings were to be found to make the story she had told true. To her delight, the blue shutters of his tiny house were pinned back. Isolde had been certain Monsieur Baillard had quit Rennes-les-Bains until the feast day of Saint Martin at least.

Léonie was desperate to know if she had a letter – she had thought of little else for days. But having enjoyed a period of anticipation, she was nervous that there might be no communication from Monsieur Constant.

And she had been regretting the absence of Monsieur Baillard now for some weeks. If she passed by without stopping and later discovered she had missed an opportunity to renew her acquaintance with him, she would never forgive herself. If there was a letter, it would still be there in ten minutes' time.

Léonie rapped upon the door.

For a moment, nothing happened. She leaned closer to the painted panels and could just pick out the sound of feet walking across a tiled floor.

She took a step back as the door was opened. A small dark-haired boy, with eyes the colour of blackberries, stood looking up at her.

'Is Monsieur Baillard at home?' she said. 'It is Léonie Vernier. The niece of Madame Lascombe. From the Domaine de la Cade.'

'He is expecting you?'

'I was passing, so took the liberty of paying an impromptu visit. If it is inconvenient . . .'

'*Que ès?*'

The boy turned. Léonie smiled with pleasure at the sound of Monsieur Baillard's voice. Emboldened, she called out.

'It is Léonie Vernier, Monsieur Baillard.'

Moments later, the distinctive figure in the white suit she remembered so clearly from the evening of the dinner party appeared at the end of a passageway.

'*Madomaisèla* Léonie,' he smiled. 'An unexpected pleasure.'

'I have been undertaking certain tasks for my aunt – she has been unwell – and Pascal has gone ahead. I had thought you were away, but when I saw the shutters pinned back, I . . .' She realised she was gabbling.

'I am delighted you did so,' Baillard said. 'Please, do come in.'

Léonie hesitated. Although he was a man of some reputation, an acquaintance of Tante Isolde and on visiting terms with the Domaine de la Cade, some might consider it inappropriate for a young girl to enter the house of a gentleman without a chaperone.

But then who is here to witness it?

'Thank you,' she said. 'I should be delighted.'

She stepped over the threshold.

CHAPTER 71

Léonie followed Monsieur Baillard down the passageway, which opened into a pleasant room at the rear of the tiny house. A single large window dominated the whole of one wall.

'Oh,' she exclaimed. 'The view is as perfect as a picture.'

He smiled. 'I am fortunate.'

He rang a small silver bell that sat on a low side table next to the wing armchair beside the wide stone fireplace. While he asked the boy to bring them a tray of drinks, Léonie discreetly cast her eyes around the room. It was a plain and simple chamber, with a selection of mismatched chairs, a boudoir table behind the sofa. Bookcases covered the length of the wall opposite the fireplace, every inch of them filled.

'Please, take a seat. Tell me your news, Madomaisèla Léonie. I trust all is well at the Domaine de la Cade. You said your aunt was indisposed. Nothing serious, I hope?'

Léonie removed her hat and gloves, then settled herself opposite him.

'She is much improved. We were caught out in the ill weather last week and my aunt became unwell. The doctor was called, but the worst is over and every day she grows stronger.'

'Her condition hangs in the balance,' he said, 'and it is early days. But all will be well.'

Léonie looked at him, puzzled at this non sequitur, but at that moment the boy returned carrying a brass tray with two ornate glass goblets and a silver jug on it.

'It comes from the Holy Land,' her host told her, noticing her admiration. 'A gift from an old friend, many years ago now.'

He handed her a glass filled with a thick red liquid.

'What is this, Monsieur Baillard?'

'A local cherry liqueur, *guignolet*. I am rather partial to it. It is particularly good when taken with these black pepper biscuits.' He nodded and the boy offered the plate to Léonie. 'They are a local speciality and can be purchased everywhere, but I judge those baked here at the Frères Marcel quite the best I have tasted.'

'I bought some myself,' Léonie replied.

She took a mouthful of *guignolet*, then immediately coughed. It was sweet, tasting intensely of wild cherries, but very strong indeed.

'You have returned earlier than we were expecting,' she said. 'My aunt led me to believe that you would be away until November.'

'My business was quicker to conclude than I had expected. There are stories coming up from the town. I felt here I might be of more use.'

'Where did you go, Monsieur?'

'To visit old friends,' he replied. 'Also, I have a house some way into the mountains. In a tiny village called Los Seres, not so far from the old fortress citadel of Montségur. I wished to ensure that it was ready, should I need to repair there in the foreseeable future.'

Léonie frowned. 'I was under the impression that you had taken lodgings here in town in order to avoid the rigours of winter in the mountains.'

His eyes sparkled. 'I have lived through many mountain winters, Madomaisèla,' he said softly. 'Some hard, others less so.' He fell silent a moment and seemed to drift into thought. 'But, tell me, what of you these past weeks? Have you had any further adventures, Madomaisèla Léonie, since last we met?'

She met his gaze. 'I have not returned to the sepulchre, Monsieur Baillard,' she said, 'if that is your meaning.'

He smiled. 'Indeed it was, and I am glad to hear it.'

'Although, I must confess, the subject of Tarot has continued to hold some interest for me.' She scrutinised his expression, but his time-worn face gave nothing away. 'I have begun a sequence of paintings also. Reproductions of the images from the walls.'

'Is that so?'

'They are studies, I suppose. Or rather copies.'

He leaned forward in his chair. 'And you have attempted all of them?'

'Well, no,' she answered, although thinking it a singular question. 'Just those they term the major arcana, and even then, not every character. I find that I am disinclined to attempt certain of the images. For example, Le Diable.'

'And La Tour?'

'Nor the Tower. How did—'

'When did you begin these paintings, Madomaisèla?'

'The afternoon of the supper party. I only wished to occupy myself, to fill the empty hours of waiting. Without the slightest conscious design, I found I had painted myself into the picture, Monsieur Baillard, so I felt moved to continue.'

'May I ask within which of them?'

'La Force.' She paused, recollecting the complication of emotions that had swept over her at that moment. 'The face was my face, though I had not set out to do that. Why do you think that should be?'

'The most obvious explanation would be that you see the characteristic of strength within yourself.'

Léonie waited, expecting more, until it became clear that again Monsieur Baillard had said all he intended on the matter.

'I find myself increasingly intrigued by my uncle and the experiences of which he writes in his monograph, *Les Tarots*,' Léonie continued. 'I do not wish to press you against your better judgement, Monsieur Baillard, but I have wondered if you knew my uncle at the time of the events detailed in the book?' She scanned his face, looking for signs of encouragement or else displeasure at the line of questioning, but his expression remained unreadable. 'I have realised the ... situation sits precisely within the period of time after my mother had left the Domaine de la Cade and yet before my aunt and uncle married.' She hesitated. 'I imagine, without intending to be disrespectful in any way, that he was by nature a solitary man. Not drawn much to the company of others?'

She stopped once again, giving Monsieur Baillard the opportunity to make some response. He remained perfectly still, his veined hands in his lap, seemingly content to listen.

'From comments Tante Isolde has made,' Léonie ploughed on, 'I gained the impression that you had been instrumental in effecting an introduction between my uncle and Abbé Saunière, when he was appointed to the parish at Rennes-le-Château. She also hinted, as did you, at some unpleasantness, rumours, incidents traced back to the sepulchre, which required the intervention of a priest.'

'Ah.' Audric Baillard pressed the tips of his fingers together.

She took a deep breath. 'I have ... Did the Abbé Saunière perform an exorcism on behalf of my uncle, is that it? Did such an ... an event take place within the sepulchre?'

This time, having asked the question, Léonie did not rush in. She allowed the silence to do the work of persuasion. For an endless time, or so it seemed, the only sound was the ticking of the clock.

CHAPTER 72

'To rid the place of evil,' she added eventually. 'Is that so? Once or twice, I have glimpsed it. But I realise now that my mother might have felt its presence, Monsieur, when she was a girl. She quitted the Domaine as soon as she was able.'

Still Baillard did not speak, then he sighed.

'In certain decks of Tarot cards,' he began, 'the card representing the Devil is modelled upon the head of Baphomet, the idol the Poor Knights of the Temple of Solomon were accused – falsely – of worshipping.'

Léonie nodded, although she had no idea what he meant.

He smiled. 'You observed, on your visit, the statue of Asmodeus in the sepulchre, *è*? Bearing the burden of the *bénitier*?'

'I did.'

'Asmodeus, also known as Ashmadia or Asmodai, is most likely derived from a form of Persian – the phrase *aeshma-daeva*, meaning demon of wrath.'

Léonie again nodded, even though her knowledge of the Old Testament was somewhat limited. Neither she nor Anatole had attended Sunday school or learned their catechism. Traditional in ways of society and manners, Marguerite was a vehement opponent of the Church. Léonie wondered whether the violence of her mother's feelings could be traced back to the atmosphere of the Domaine de la Cade. All being well, Marguerite would accept

Anatole's invitation to join them soon and Léonie would be able to ask her.

'The story tells of how King Solomon invokes Asmodeus to aid in the construction of the Temple – the great Temple. Asmodeus, a demon most particularly associated with lust, does appear, but his presence is disturbing. He predicts that Solomon's kingdom will one day be divided.

'Asmodeus, as I said previously, is a demon associated with carnal desires. He is most especially an enemy of newly-weds. In the apocryphal Book of Tobit, he torments a woman called Sarah, killing each of her seven husbands before the marriages can be consummated. On the eighth occasion, the angel Raphael instructs Sarah's latest suitor to place the heart and liver of a fish on red-hot cinders. The smoky, foul-smelling vapour repels Asmodeus and causes him to flee to Egypt, where Raphael binds him, his power broken.'

Léonie shivered, not at his words but at the memory of the disgusting stench that had assailed her senses in the sepulchre. An inexplicable scent of smoke and the sea.

'These parables seem rather archaic, do they not?' said her host. 'They are intended to convey some larger truth, but so often serve only to obscure. In the Book of Solomon, it is also said that Asmodeus detests being near water.'

Léonie sat up straighter. 'Hence, perhaps, the holy water stoup being set upon his shoulders? Could that be, Monsieur Baillard?'

'It could,' he agreed. 'Asmodeus appears in other works of religious commentary. In the Talmud, for example. Some years later, in the middle of the fifteenth century, Asmodai appears as the demon of lust in the *Malleus Maleficarum*. As a collector, it is a book perhaps your brother would know?'

'He might well, yes.'

'There are those who believe that different devils have particular potency at different times of the year.'

'And when is Asmodeus considered to be at his most powerful?'

'During the month of November.'

Léonie thought for a moment. 'But what does it mean, Monsieur Baillard, this marriage of superstition and supposition?'

He walked over to the window and placed his hands upon the sill with his back to her.

'Monsieur Baillard?'

He turned. For a moment, the sun coming in through the wide window seemed to cast a halo of light around him. Léonie had the impression that she was looking at an Old Testament prophet in an oil painting.

'It means that when village superstitions talk of a demon walking these valleys and wooded hillsides, we should take them seriously. There are certain places – the Domaine de la Cade is one – where older forces are at work.' He paused. 'Also, there are others who choose to raise such a creature, to commune with such spirits, failing to understand that evil cannot be mastered.'

She didn't want to believe what he was saying, yet her heart skipped a beat.

'Are you asking me to accept that my uncle, through the agency of the cards and the spirit of the place, called forth the devil Asmodeus and then found himself unable to master him? That my uncle was responsible, morally at least, for the killings in the valley? And he knew this?'

Audric Baillard held her gaze. 'He knew it.'

'And so that was why he was obliged to seek the services of Abbé Saunière, to banish the monster he had released?' She stopped. 'Did Tante Isolde know of this?'

'It was before her time here. She did not.'

Léonie didn't know what to think. She stood up and walked to the window. 'Such stories. Devils, demons. How can they be credited in the modern world?' She paused. 'I cannot believe it,' she said, but her voice was less certain.

'Blood will attract blood,' Baillard said quietly. 'There are some things that draw evil to them. A place, an object, a person may, by force of their ill will, draw to them ill circumstances, wrongdoings, sins.'

Léonie looked at her gentle host, then sat back down in her chair.

'Even supposing I could accept such things, what of the deck of cards, Monsieur Baillard? Unless I mistake your meaning, you are suggesting that they might be a force for good or for ill, depending on the circumstances of their use.'

'That is so. Consider how a sword is either an instrument for good or for bad. It is the hand that wields it that makes it so, not the steel.'

Léonie nodded. 'What is the provenance of the cards? Who painted them and for what purpose? When I first read my uncle's words, I understood him to be saying that the paintings upon the wall of the sepulchre might somehow step down and imprint themselves upon the cards.'

Audric Baillard smiled. 'If that were the case, Madomaisèla Léonie, there would be only eight cards, whereas there is a full deck.'

Her heart sank. 'Yes, I suppose so.'

'Although,' he continued, 'it does not mean that there is not some kernel of truth in what you say.'

'In which case, Monsieur Baillard, tell me, why those eight tableaux in particular?' Her eyes sparkled as a new idea came to her. 'Could it be that the images that remain imprinted upon the wall are those very same that my uncle drew to him? That in another such communication between worlds, it might be other tableaux visible upon the walls?' She paused. 'From paintings, perhaps?'

Audric Baillard allowed a faint smile to play across his lips. 'The lesser of the cards date from that unhappy time when, once more, men driven by faith to murder and oppress and extirpate heresy plunged the world into blood.'

'The Albigensians?' Léonie said.

He gave a resigned shake of his head. 'Ah, if only lessons were learned so quickly, Madomaisèla. But I fear they are not.'

In the gravitas of his voice, it seemed to Léonie that behind his words lay a wisdom that spanned centuries. And she, who had never taken the slightest interest in the events of the past, found herself wishing to understand how one consequence led to another.

'I speak of the conflicts of the sixteenth century between the Catholic house of Guise and what we might call, for the sake of clarity, the Huguenot house of Bourbon.' He raised his hands, and then let them drop. 'As always – perhaps it will be ever thus – the demands of faith quickly become inextricably bound to those of territory and control.'

'And the cards date from this period?' she urged.

'The original fifty-six of the cards, intended simply to help pass a long winter's evening, followed much in the tradition of the Italian game of *tarocchi*. A hundred years prior to the time of which I speak, the Italian court and nobility had given birth to a fashion for such entertainments. When the Republic was born, the court cards were replaced by Maître and Maîtresse, Fils and Fille, as you have seen.'

'La Fille d'Épées,' she said, remembering the painting upon the wall of the sepulchre. 'By when?'

'That is not so clear. It was at much the same time, on the eve, indeed, of the Revolution, that in France the harmless game of Tarot was transformed into something other. A system of divination, a way of linking the seen and known to the unseen and unknown.'

'So the deck of cards was already at the Domaine de la Cade?'

'The fifty-six cards were the possession of the house, if you like, rather than the individuals within it. The ancient spirit of the place worked upon the deck; the legends and rumours invested the cards with some further meaning and purpose. The cards were waiting, you see, for one who would complete the sequence.'

'My uncle . . .' she said.

Baillard nodded. 'Lascombe read the books published by the cartomancers in Paris and was seduced by them. To the deck of cards he had inherited, he added the twenty-two greater arcana – those speaking of the fundamental turns of life and what lies beyond – and fixed those he wished to summon upon the wall of the sepulchre.'

'My late uncle painted the twenty-two additional cards?'

'He did.' He paused. 'You believe absolutely, then, Madomaisèla Léonie, that through the agency of the Tarot cards – in the specific place and with the conditions that make such things possible – demons, ghosts might be summoned?'

Léonie thought of everything he had told her, all she had read, but, most of all, the overwhelming dread and terror she had felt in the sepulchre. The sense of something beyond the house in the darkness.

'It does not credit belief,' she said carefully, 'yet I find I cannot dismiss it.' She paused. 'I still do not understand, though, how the cards control the spirits.'

'Not control,' Baillard said swiftly. 'That was the mistake your uncle made. The cards may summon the spirits, yes, but never control them. All possibilities are contained within the images, but should they be released, they take on a life of their own.'

Léonie frowned. 'I don't understand.'

'The tableaux upon the wall are the imprints of the last cards summoned in that place. But if one were to alter,

486

through the touch of a brush, the features on one or other of the cards, they would take on other characteristics instead. The cards can tell different stories.'

'Would this be true of these cards wherever they were?' she asked immediately. 'Or only in the Domaine de la Cade, in the sepulchre?'

'It is the unique combination of image and sound and the spirit of the place. That one place,' he replied. 'At the same time, the place works upon the cards. So, for example, it might be that La Force, now, attaches itself specifically to you. Through your artistry.'

Léonie looked at him. 'But I have not seen the cards themselves. Indeed, I have not painted cards, only imitations on common paper.'

He gave a slow smile. 'Things do not always hold fast, Madomaisèla. And besides, you have painted more than yourself into the cards, have you not? You have painted your brother and your aunt into these pictures also.'

She blushed. 'They are just paintings intended as a memento of our time spent here.'

'Perhaps.' He inclined his head to one side. 'Through such pictures your stories will endure longer than you have tongue to tell them.'

'You are frightening me, Monsieur,' she said.

'That is not my intention.'

Léonie paused before asking the question that had been on her lips since the moment she had heard of the Tarot cards. 'Does the deck exist still?'

He fixed her with his wise eyes. 'The deck survives,' he said finally.

'Within the house?'

'The Abbé Saunière begged your uncle to destroy the cards, to burn them, so that no other man would be tempted to make use of them. The sepulchre too.' Baillard shook his head. 'But Jules Lascombe was a scholar. He could no more destroy something of such ancient origin than the abbé himself could denounce his God.'

'Are the cards hidden within the grounds, then? I am certain they are not in the sepulchre.'

'They are safe,' he said. 'Concealed where the river runs dry, in a place where once the ancient kings were buried.'

'But if that is the case, then—'

Audric Baillard raised his finger to his lips. 'I have told you all this as a way to curb your inquisitive nature, Madomaisèla Léonie, not to fan your curiosity. I understand how you have been drawn into this story, but I repeat my warning: no good will come of trying to find the cards, especially at such a time, when matters hang so delicately balanced.'

'At such a time? What do you mean, Monsieur Baillard? Because November approaches?'

But it was clear from the expression that had fallen over his face that he was prepared to say nothing further.

Through the open window came the sound of the bell of the tiny church of Saint-Celse and Saint-Nazaire tolling out the midday. An emaciated single note marking the passing of the morning.

The sound brought Léonie back into the present. She had quite forgotten her task. She leapt to her feet.

'Forgive me, Monsieur Baillard, I have taken up more than enough of your time.' She dragged her gloves on over her fingers. 'And in so doing have quite forgotten my own responsibilities this morning. The *bureau de poste* ... If I hurry, I might still ...'

Clutching her hat, Léonie ran across the room to the door.

'If I may, Monsieur, I will call again? *Au revoir.*'

'Of course, Madomaisèla. The pleasure will be mine.'

Léonie waved, then rushed down the passageway and out of the front door into the street, leaving Audric Baillard, a timeless figure, standing alone.

'*Si es atal es atal*,' he muttered, in the old language. Things will be as they will be. 'But with this child, I wish it were not so.'

CHAPTER 73

The wooden door of the post office was closed and barred. Léonie hammered on it with her fist.

'*S'il vous plaît?*' she called. It was only three minutes past midday. Surely, there must still be someone inside? '*Il y a quelqu'un? C'est vraiment important!*'

Nobody came. She knocked and called out again, until an ill-tempered woman with two thin grey plaits leaned out of the window opposite and shouted at her to stop banging.

Léonie realised how stupid she was being by drawing attention to herself in such a manner. If there was a letter waiting for her from Monsieur Constant, it was destined to remain there for the time being. She could hardly stay in Rennes-les-Bains until such time as the poste restante reopened later that afternoon.

Her emotions were contradictory. She was cross with herself for failing to fulfil the one task she had set herself. At the same time, she felt she had been granted a reprieve.

At least I do not know that Monsieur Constant has not written.

Léonie descended to the river walk, where the patients of the thermal spa were sitting in the steaming, iron-rich water of the *bains forts*. Behind them, a row of nurses in white uniforms, their wide sweeping hats perched upon their heads like giant seabirds, stood waiting patiently for their charges to emerge.

She crossed to the far bank and found the path along which Marieta had taken them easily enough. The woods had changed a great deal since they had last come this way. Some of the trees had lost their leaves, through either the natural approach of autumn or the ferocity of the storms that had battered the hillside.

Twigs, fallen branches, stones shaken loose from the banks on either side rattled and snapped under her feet. The ground was covered by fallen pine cones and shiny brown fruit from the horse chestnut trees. For a moment, she had a pang of homesickness, thinking of childhood autumns in Paris. Each October, when they were little, their mother had taken her and Anatole to the Parc Monceau to gather horse chestnuts.

Rennes-les-Bains had vanished from sight. Léonie walked faster, feeling she was now a long way from civilisation. A bird flew up, its wings beating heavily on the air, making her jump. She laughed nervously when she realised it was only a wood pigeon. In the distance, she heard the shots from hunting guns and wondered if Charles Denarnaud's hand was behind one of them.

Léonie pressed on and soon reached the estate. When the rear gates of the Domaine de la Cade came into view, she felt a rush of relief. She hurried forward, expecting at any moment to see the maid step out with the key.

'Marieta?'

Only the sound of her own voice echoed back. By the quality of the silence, Léonie knew there was no one there. She frowned. It was unlike Pascal not to keep his word. And although Marieta was easily flustered, she was reliable as a rule.

Léonie rattled the gates and found them locked. She did not wish to have to walk the entire perimeter to enter by the front gates. She was certain if she looked hard enough, she would find an opening wide enough for her to slip through. From there, it would be a simple matter to find her way back to familiar paths. If the worst came to the worst, she would simply follow the line of the boundary all the way around.

Léonie walked briskly, peering through the hedge growth, pulling at briars and avoiding the vicious tangle of blackberry bushes, and soon enough came across an interruption in the fencing. Removing her hat, she crouched down and squeezed through the narrow opening with a sense of relief.

The land here was steeper, the woods darker and more oppressive. It was not long before Léonie realised that she was on the far side of the beech woods.

There was a criss-cross of small tracks, rather than one clear path to follow. All the clearings and copses looked the same. Leonie told herself that so long as she kept walking forward, she would come upon the lawns and the house soon enough.

Suddenly, through a break in the trees, she saw the parcel of woodland within which stood the group of stone megaliths and realised with a sense of unease that all the diabolic place names around about were visible from the Domaine de la Cade. So, too, was the point at which the rivers La Blanque and La Salz met, a spot known locally as *le bénitier*.

Above her now was a steep wall of hillside, like a barrier set across her path. Directly over her head was a natural platform, almost like a bridge arching over the patch of ground on which she stood. She realised she was standing in a dry riverbed.

Something else Monsieur Baillard had told her came into her mind.

Concealed where the river runs dry, in a place where once the ancient kings were buried.

Feeling the first stirrings of excitement, Léonie looked around, searching for anything out of the ordinary. Her eye was drawn by a shallow depression in the ground and, beside it, a flat grey stone, just visible beneath the tangled roots of a wild juniper bush.

She crouched down, pulled at the knotted undergrowth and peered into the dank green space. Now she could see that there was a ring of stones, eight in all. She thrust her hands into the foliage, staining the tips of her gloves with green slime and mud, trying to see if anything was hidden beneath them.

The largest was quickly dislodged. Léonie sat back on her heels, resting it in her lap. There was something painted upon the surface in black tar or paint: a five-pointed star set within a circle.

Putting the stone to one side, Léonie used a piece of wood to dig around each of the others in turn and discovered a fragment of heavy material concealed in the mud.

She continued, her makeshift shovel scraping against stones and shards of tile until she was able to pull the material free from the earth. It covered a small hole. Léonie jabbed at it, trying to loosen what was buried beneath, until she hit something solid.

Now she was looking at a plain wooden casket with metal handles at each end. Fixing her filthy gloves on the clasps, she pulled. The ground was reluctant to yield, but Léonie wrenched and twisted until, finally, it gave up its treasure with a wet sucking sound.

Out of breath, Léonie dragged the box to an area of dry ground. Sacrificing her gloves to rub the surface clean, she opened the wooden lid. Inside the chest was another container, a metal strongbox of the kind in which Maman kept her most valuable possessions.

It was fitted with a tiny padlock, which hung open. Not wishing to damage anything, she slowly raised the lid, inching it up fraction by fraction. It creaked but gave easily enough.

The light was dim beneath the trees and whatever was inside the strongbox was dark. As her eyes adjusted, she thought she could make out a package wrapped in some dark fabric. She felt her nerves thudding in her chest. No doubt it was of the right size and proportion to be the deck of cards.

Carefully, Léonie folded back the corners of the fabric.

She was looking at the reverse side of a playing card, larger than those she was accustomed to. The back was painted a rich forest green, decorated with a swirling pattern of silver and gold filigree lines.

Léonie paused, gathering her courage. She counted to three in her head and turned over the top card.

A strange image of a dark man, attired in a long red tasselled robe and sitting upon a throne on a stone belvedere, looked up at her. The mountains in the distance seemed familiar. She read the inscription at the bottom: LE ROI DES PENTACLES.

She looked more closely, realising the figure of the King was familiar. Then it came to her. It was the image of the priest called upon to banish the demon from the sepulchre, who had begged her uncle to destroy the deck of cards. Bérenger Saunière.

'Madomaisèla. Madomaisèla Léonie?'

Léonie spun round in alarm, before realising it was Pascal. He was some way off, but she didn't want him to find her with the cards. Quickly, she wrapped them up once more, returned them to the inner box, then the box into the chest, which she slid back into the hole.

'Madomaisèla?' called Marieta.

Léonie kicked the earth back with the already muddy soles of her boots, dropping her spoiled gloves into the ground too and covering them over.

She had to trust in the fact that no one had discovered the deck previously and were therefore unlikely to now. She would return, under cover of darkness, and take the cards when it was discreet and safe to do so.

'Madomaisèla Léonie!'

She could hear the panic in the girl's voice.

Léonie climbed onto the platform and ran back down the woodland path towards the sound of the servants' voices. Finally, when she thought she had put enough distance between herself and the treasure, she stopped, caught her breath and then called out.

'I am here!' she cried. 'Marieta! Pascal! Over here.'

Within moments, their concerned faces burst through the opening in the trees.

'I mislaid my gloves.' The spontaneous lie rose easily to her lips. 'I was obliged to go back to search for them and lost my way.'

Pascal looked hard at her. 'And did you find them, Madomaisèla?'

'Sadly, no.'

'Your clothes,' Marieta said.

Léonie looked down at her muddy boots, her stained petticoats and skirts streaked with mud and lichen. 'I slipped on the damp ground, that is all.'

She could see Pascal doubted the explanation, but he said nothing. They walked back to the house in silence.

CHAPTER 74

Léonie was grateful to Pascal and Marieta for holding their tongues – she did not want a repeat of the scenes in Carcassonne the last time she had gone against Anatole's wishes. For the rest of that day, she kept Isolde company with stories of Rennes-les-Bains and her time with Monsieur Baillard, though she didn't share with her the substance of their conversation.

The skies clouded over at dusk and there was a flurry of rain down in the valley, but the Domaine de la Cade was little disturbed.

The following morning, Léonie slept late.

As she emerged onto the landing, she saw Marieta carrying the letter tray across the hall to the dining room. There was no reason to presume that Monsieur Constant could somehow have acquired her address and written to her directly, but such were the romantic imaginings Constant had awoken in her that she flew down the stairs with the sole intention of intercepting Marieta. How would she possibly explain a personal letter?

She was too late. The dining-room door closed. Léonie jumped from foot to foot until the maid came out again.

'I do not suppose you happened to observe if there were any letters from Carcassonne, Marieta?' she whispered.

The maid gave her an enquiring look. 'Not that I noticed, Madomaisèla.'

'You are certain?'

'There were the usual circulars, a letter from Paris for Sénher Anatole and a letter apiece for your brother and for Madama that came up from the town.'

Léonie gave a sigh of relief, tinged with disappointment.

'Invitations, I dare say,' Marieta added. 'Very fine-quality envelopes they were, and addressed in a most elegant hand. A distinguished family crest also. Pascal said they were hand-delivered. Strange fellow in an old cloak.'

Léonie grew still. 'What colour was the cloak?'

Marieta looked at her with surprise. 'I'm sure I don't know, Madomaisèla. Pascal did not say. Now, if you will excuse me . . .'

Léonie stood back. 'Yes, of course.'

She hesitated on the threshold, uncertain as to why she should feel anxious about being in her brother's company.

Anatole sat at the breakfast table, staring blindly at the letter.

His hand shook as he lit a third cigarette from the stub of his second. The air in the closed room was thick with smoke. There were three envelopes on the table. One – unopened – had a Paris postmark. The other two bore an embossed crest. A sheet of writing paper with the same aristocratic family emblem lay on the empty plate in front of him.

The truth was that Anatole had known that such a letter would, one day, find him. However much he had tried to reassure Isolde, ever since the attack in the passage des Panoramas back in September he had expected it. The taunting communication they had received in the hotel in Carcassonne a week past had merely confirmed that Constant knew of the hoax and – worse – had found them.

Although Anatole had attempted to make light of Isolde's fears, everything she had told him about Constant

497

had led him to dread what he might do. The pattern of Constant's illness and the nature of it, his neuroses and paranoias, his ungoverned temper, all spoke of a man who would do anything to be revenged upon the woman he believed had wronged him.

Anatole looked down again at the letter in his hand. It was a formal challenge by Victor Constant to a duel to be fought tomorrow, Saturday, 31st October, at dusk. Constant elected that they should fight with pistols. He would leave it to Vernier to propose some appropriate plot of land within the Domaine de la Cade – private land, so that their illegal combat would pass unobserved.

He concluded by informing Vernier that he was at the Hôtel de la Reine in Rennes-les-Bains, awaiting his confirmation that he was a man of honour and would accept the challenge.

Not for the first time, Anatole regretted the impulse that had stayed his hand at the Cimetière de Montmartre. He had felt Constant's presence in the graveyard. It had taken all of his strength not to turn round and shoot him there, in cold blood, and hang the consequences. When, this morning, he had opened the letter, his first thought had been to go to town and confront Constant. But he knew the man could not be appealed to. Words would not end the matter.

For some time, Anatole sat in the dining room. His cigarette burned down and he lit another, but he felt too consumed with lethargy to smoke it.

He would need a second for the duel – someone local, obviously. Perhaps he could ask Charles Denarnaud? He at least had the virtue of being a man of the world. He might be able to prevail on Gabignaud to attend in his capacity as a medical man and, although he was certain the young doctor would baulk at the request, he did not think he would refuse him. Anatole had been obliged to take Gabignaud into his confidence about the situation between him and Isolde, for the sake of Isolde's condition. He thought the doctor would agree, therefore, for her sake, if not for his own.

He tried to persuade himself of a satisfactory outcome. Constant wounded, forced to shake his hand, calling the feud to an end. But, somehow, he could not. Anatole was not convinced that Constant would abide by the rules of engagement.

He had no alternative but to accept the challenge. He was a man of honour, even if his actions this past year had been far from honourable. If he did not fight Constant, nothing would ever change. Isolde would live under an intolerable strain, always waiting for Constant to strike. So would they all. The man's appetite for persecution showed no signs of abating. If he refused to meet him, Anatole knew Constant's campaign against them – against everyone close to them – would intensify.

In the past days, Anatole had heard gossip from the servants' hall that there were stories about the Domaine de la Cade circulating in the town. Disturbing suggestions that the beast that had so terrorised the neighbourhood in Jules Lascombe's day had returned. Anatole had been inclined to dismiss the stories. Now he suspected Constant's hand behind the malicious rumours.

He screwed the paper tightly in his fist. He would not have his child grow up in the knowledge that his father was a coward. He had to accept the challenge. He had to shoot to win. To kill.

Anatole drummed his fingers on the table. He was not short of courage. The problem lay in the fact that he was far from being an assured shot. His skill lay with rapier and foil, not pistol. No doubt Constant was aware of that.

Anatole pushed that thought to one side. At this instant, the most pressing question was whether or not he should confide in his wife. But such news might bring on a relapse and threaten the health of the baby. No, he could not tell her.

He slipped the second letter, addressed to Isolde in Constant's hand, into the breast pocket of his jacket. He could not hope to conceal the situation indefinitely, but he could protect her peace of mind for a few hours more.

Less simple to resolve was whether or not he should confide in Léonie. Anatole had come to realise Isolde was right. His attitude to his sister was based more on the child she had once been than the young woman she had become. He still thought her impetuous and sometimes childish, unable or unwilling to hold her temper in check. Against that was her undoubted affection for Isolde and the solicitous way in which, since their return from Carcassonne, she had cared for her aunt.

Anatole had resolved to speak to Léonie over the course of last weekend. He had intended to tell her the truth, from the beginning of his love affair with Isolde to the situation in which they now found themselves. His wife's fragile health had delayed matters, but now the receipt of the challenge had brought the pressing need for the conversation to the fore.

Anatole twisted his cigarette case in his hand and decided to tell Léonie of their marriage this morning. Depending upon her reaction, he might or might not tell her he had been challenged to a duel.

Taking the letters with him, he strode across the dining room into the hall and rang the bell.

'Ah, Marieta. Will you ask Mademoiselle Léonie to join me in the library at midday? I would like to talk to her in private, so if she could keep the matter to herself? Please impress upon her the importance of that. Also, there is no need to mention the letters received this morning to Madame Isolde. I will appraise her of them myself.'

Marieta looked puzzled but did not question his orders. 'Where is Pascal at present?'

The maid blushed. 'In the kitchen, I believe, Sénher.'

'Tell him to meet me at the rear of the house in ten minutes,' he instructed.

Anatole returned to his room to change into outdoor clothes. He wrote a curt and formal reply to Constant, blotting the ink, then sealed the envelope to make it safe from prying eyes. Pascal could deliver the response. Now the only thought in his mind was how, for Isolde's sake and for that of their child, he could not afford to miss.

The letter from Paris remained unopened in his waist-coat pocket.

Léonie paced up and down her bedroom anxiously, wondering why Anatole had requested to see her at noon, and privately. Could he have discovered that she had again disobeyed his orders and returned alone from the town yesterday?

The sound of voices below her open window drew her attention. She leaned out to observe Anatole striding across the lawns with Pascal, who was carrying a long wooden box in both hands. It looked much like a pistol case. Léonie had never observed such equipment in the house, but she supposed her late uncle had possessed such weapons.

Perhaps they are going to hunt?

She frowned. Anatole was not dressed for hunting. Besides, neither he nor Pascal were carrying shotguns. Only pistols. For no reason she could explain, dread swooped down upon her. She snatched her hat and jacket, and pushed her feet into outdoor shoes, intending to follow him.

Then she checked her step.

Too often, Anatole accused her of acting without thinking. It went against her nature to sit idle and wait, but what good would it do to go after him? Whatever he was doing, he could not intend to be long, having fixed an appointment with her at noon. She glanced at the clock on the mantel. Two hours away.

She threw her hat upon the bed and kicked off her shoes, then looked around the chamber. She would do better to stay put and find some entertainment to pass the time.

Léonie looked at her painting equipment. She hesitated, then went to the bureau and began to unpack her brushes and papers. This was the ideal opportunity to continue her sequence of illustrations and it would keep her mind occupied. She had but three left to complete.

She fetched water, dipped her brush, then began to sketch with black ink the outlines of the sixth of the eight tableaux from the wall of the sepulchre.

Card XVI: La Tour.

CHAPTER 75

In the private drawing room on the first floor of the Hôtel de la Reine in Rennes-les-Bains, two men were seated in front of a fire. Two servants, one Parisian, the other Carcassonnais, stood behind at a respectful distance. From time to time, when they thought their master was not watching, they darted mistrustful glances at one another.

Charles Denarnaud, his face still flushed from the quantity of excellent brandy consumed last evening at dinner, drew deeply on his cigar, puffing until the sour, expensive leaves caught. There was an expression of complacency on his mottled face. He tilted his head back and blew a white ring of smoke up to the ceiling.

'Sure you won't join me, Constant?'

Victor Constant held up his hand, his diseased skin hidden beneath gloves. He felt unwell this morning. The anticipation of the hunt being almost at an end was playing on his nerves.

'You are confident Vernier will petition you?' he said.

Denarnaud heard the determination in his host's voice and sat up straight. 'I do not think I have mistaken the man,' he said. 'Vernier has few associates in Rennes-les-Bains, certainly no others with whom he is on such terms as to request such a service and in such a matter. I am certain he will make representation to me. The timings involved do not allow him the opportunity to send further afield.'

'Quite,' Constant said drily.

'My guess would be that he will approach Gabignaud, one of the resident doctors in the town, to be the medical man present.'

Constant turned to the servant standing closest to the door.

'The letters were delivered this morning?'

'Yes, Monsieur.'

'You did not make yourself known to the household?'

He shook his head. 'I passed them into the hands of a footman to be taken in with this morning's post.'

Constant thought a moment. 'And no one is aware you are the source of the stories circulating?'

He shook his head. 'I have simply dropped a word or two in the ears of those most likely to repeat them. Spite and superstition have done the rest. The storms are seen as evidence enough that all is not well.'

'Excellent.' Constant gestured with his hand. 'Return to the grounds of the Domaine and observe what Vernier does. Report at dusk.'

'Very good, Monsieur.'

Pulling his blue Napoleonic cloak from the back of the chair, he then slid out into the overcast street.

As soon as Constant heard the door close, he stood up.

'I wish the matter to be resolved quickly, Denarnaud, and with the minimum of attention. Is that clear?'

Taken aback by the abrupt end to the interview, Denarnaud also struggled to his feet.

'Of course. Everything is in hand.'

Constant clicked his fingers. His manservant stepped forward, holding out a drawstring bag. 'This is half of what you are promised. The remainder will follow once the business is concluded to my satisfaction. You understand me?'

Denarnaud's voracious hands closed round the purse.

'You will confirm that I am not in possession of any other weapon,' Constant said in a cold, hard voice. 'You are quite clear on this.'

'There will be a pair of duelling pistols, Monsieur, each with a single shot. Should you be carrying another instrument, I will fail to find it.' Denarnaud gave an ingratiating smile. 'Although I cannot believe such a man as you, Monsieur, would fail to hit your target on the first attempt.'

Constant looked contemptuous at the craven flattery.

'I never miss,' he said.

CHAPTER 76

'Damn and blast it to hell,' Anatole shouted, kicking the ground with the heel of his boot.

Pascal walked back to the makeshift shooting gallery he had set up in the clearing in the woods ringed by wild juniper bushes. He lined up the bottles again in a row, then returned to Anatole and reloaded the pistol for him.

Of the six shots, two had gone wide, one had hit the trunk of a beech tree and two the wooden fencing, dislodging three bottles through the vibration. Only one had hit its target, just nicking the base of the thick glass bottle.

'Try again, Sénher,' Pascal said quietly. 'Keep your eye steady.'

'That's what I'm doing,' Anatole muttered.

'Raise your eye to the target, then drop it again. Imagine the shot as it travels down the barrel.' Pascal stepped away. 'Steady, Sénher. Take your aim. Don't rush.'

Anatole raised his arm. This time, he imagined that, instead of a bottle that had once held ale, it was Victor Constant's face in front of him.

'Now,' said Pascal softly. 'Hold steady. Fire.'

Anatole hit it full square. The bottle shattered, exploding in a shower of glass like a cheap firework. The sound ricocheted off the trunks of the trees, sending birds flapping in alarm from their nests.

A tiny puff of smoke slipped from the end of the barrel. Anatole blew across the top, then turned with his eyes bright with satisfaction to face Pascal.

'An excellent shot,' the servant said, his broad, impassive face for once the mirror to his thoughts. 'And ... when is this engagement?'

The smile faded from Anatole's face. 'Tomorrow at dusk.'

Pascal walked across the glade and lined up the remaining bottles once again. 'Shall we see if you can hit a second time?'

'God willing, I shall only have to do it once,' Anatole said under his breath.

But he permitted Pascal to reload the pistol and keep him at it, until every last bottle had been struck and a smell of powder, gunshot and old ale hung in the air of the wooded clearing.

CHAPTER 77

At five minutes before midday, Léonie walked along the passageway and down the main staircase. Her heart was beating like a drum.

As she crossed the tiled hall, she noticed there were flecks of paint, green and black, on her nails. She had, during the course of her anxious morning, completed the illustration of La Tour, but she was not satisfied with it. However lightly she had flecked the leaves on the trees or tried to colour the sky, there was an unnerving and brooding presence that spoke through the strokes of her brush.

On the library threshold, she hesitated. Then she lifted her chin high, raised her hand, and knocked upon the door with more courage than she felt.

'Come.'

At the sound of Anatole's voice, Léonie opened the door and stepped inside.

'You wished to see me?' she said, feeling as if she had been summoned before the magistrates' bench rather than into the company of her beloved brother.

'I did,' he said, smiling at her. The expression on his face and the look in his brown eyes relieved her, although she realised that he, too, was nervous. 'Come in, Léonie. Sit down.'

'You are scaring me, Anatole,' she said quietly. 'You seem so grave.'

'There is no need to be scared,' he said, steering her to a chair, 'but it is a serious matter about which I wish to speak to you.'

He pulled out the chair for her to sit, then walked some distance off and turned to face her, hands behind his back. Now Léonie noticed he was holding something between his fingers. An envelope.

'Is it a letter from Maman? From Paris?'

A strange look came over Anatole's face.

'No. At least, yes, it is a letter, but it is one I have myself written. To you.'

Léonie frowned. 'To me? I don't understand.'

Anatole smoothed his hand over his hair. 'It is an awkward situation in which I find myself,' he said quietly. 'There are ... matters of which we must speak, but now that the moment is here, I find myself tongue-tied in your presence.'

Even more nervous now, Léonie laughed. 'I cannot see how that could be,' she said. 'You would not be embarrassed in front of me, surely?'

She had intended to tease him, but the sombre expression on Anatole's face stopped her in her tracks. She jumped from her chair and ran to him.

'Whatever is it?' she said. 'Is it Maman? Isolde?'

Anatole looked down at the letter in his hand. 'I have taken the liberty of committing the confession to paper.'

'Confession?'

'Contained within is information that I should – that *we* should – have shared with you some time ago. Isolde would have done so, but I believed I knew best.'

'Anatole!' she cried, shaking his arm. 'Tell me.'

'It is better you read it in private,' he said. 'There is a situation that has arisen, far more serious, which requires my immediate attention. And your help.'

He slipped his arm out of Léonie's small hand and pushed the letter at her.

'I hope you can forgive me,' he said, his voice breaking. 'I shall wait outside.'

Then, without further word, he strode across the room to the door, jerked it open and was gone.

Bewildered, and distressed by Anatole's anguish and uncertainty, Léonie looked down at the envelope. Her own name was printed in black ink in Anatole's elegant, romantic hand.

She stared at it, fearful of what might be inside, then ripped it open.

Vendredi, le 30 octobre

Ma chère petite soeur—

Always, you accused me of treating you like a child. Even when you were still in ribbons and short skirts and I struggling with my lessons. This time, the charge is fair. For tomorrow evening at dusk, I shall be in the clearing in the beech woods preparing to face the man who has made every attempt to ruin us.

If it does not fall out in my favour, then I do not wish you to be left without explanation to all those questions you would surely ask of me. Whatever the outcome of the duel, I wish you to know the truth of the matter.

I love Isolde with my heart and soul. It was she at whose graveside you stood in March, a desperate attempt for her – for us – to seek safety from the violent intentions of a man with whom she had a brief, ill-judged liaison. To dissemble her death and her burial seemed the only way for her to escape from the shadow under which she lived.

Léonie reached out and found the back of the chair. Carefully, she sat herself down upon it.

I admit that I expected you to uncover our deception. During those difficult spring months and the early summer, even while the attacks upon me in the newspapers continued, at every turn, I expected you to tear off the mask and denounce me, but I played my part too well. You, who are so true of heart and purpose, why would you doubt that my pinched lips and haggard eyes were the consequences of grief?

I must tell you that Isolde never wished to deceive you. From the moment we arrived at the Domaine de la Cade and she made your acquaintance, she had faith that your love for me — and she hoped in time that this same love would extend to her — would allow you to put moral considerations aside and support us in our deception. I disagreed.

I was a fool.

As I sit writing this, on what might be the eve of my last day upon this earth, I admit that my greatest fault was moral cowardice. One fault, among many.

But these have been glorious weeks here, with you and Isolde, in the peaceful paths and gardens of the Domaine de la Cade.

There is more. A final deception, for which I pray you can find it in your heart, if not to forgive, at least to understand. In Carcassonne, while you explored the innocent streets, Isolde and I were married. She is now Madame Vernier, your sister by the bonds of law as well as affection.

I am also to be a father.

But on that same happiest of days, we learned that he had discovered us. This is the true explanation for our abrupt departure. It is, too, the explanation for Isolde's decline and fragility. But it is clear that her health cannot withstand the assaults upon her nerves. The matter cannot remain unresolved.

Having discovered the deception of the funeral, some-how he has hunted us, first to Carcassonne, and now to Rennes-les-Bains. It is why I have accepted his challenge. It is the only way to settle the issue for good.

Tomorrow evening, I will face him. I seek your help, petite, as I should have sought it many months previously. I have great need of your service, to keep the particulars of the duel from my beloved Isolde. Should I not return, I commend the safety of my wife and child to you. The house is secure in possession.

Your affectionate and loving brother,
A—

Léonie's hands dropped into her lap. The tears she had struggled to keep at bay began to roll silently down her cheeks. She wept for the pity of it, for the deception and the misunderstandings that had kept them apart. She cried – for Isolde, for the fact that she and Anatole had deceived her, that she had ever deceived them – until all her emotion was spent.

Then her thoughts sharpened. The reason for Anatole's untimely expedition from the house this morning was now explained.

In a matter of a day, hours, he could be dead.

She ran to the window and threw the casement wide. After the brilliance of the early morning, an autumn fog was floating over the gardens, shrouding the world in a deceptive calm.

Tomorrow at dusk.

She looked at her reflection in the tall library window, thinking how strange it was that she could appear the same, yet be so utterly changed.

Léonie shivered. Tomorrow was Toussaint, the Eve of All Saints. A night of terrible beauty, when the veil between good and ill was at its slightest. It was a time when such events could take place. A time, already, of demons and evil deeds.

The duel must not be allowed to go ahead. It was down to her to prevent it. But even as the thought raced across her mind, Léonie knew it was no use. She would not deflect Anatole from his chosen course of action. For honour, for his wife, he was bound to accept.

She composed herself. She would be the sister, the ally, he needed her to be. Ready to face him, she went to the door and pulled it open.

Her brother was standing outside in a fug of cigarette smoke, the anguish of waiting carved clearly upon his face.

'Oh, my dear Anatole,' she said, throwing her arms around him.

His eyes filled with tears. 'Forgive me,' he whispered, allowing himself to be held. 'I am so very sorry. Can you forgive me, *petite*?'

CHAPTER 78

Léonie, Anatole and Isolde spent much of the rest of the afternoon in one another's company. Unaware of the shadow hanging over Anatole, Isolde was in good spirits, delighted that their marriage was no longer a secret.

'I wish I could have been there at the wedding,' Léonie said.

'I regret that you were not. When Marguerite comes to join us, we will hold a proper celebration then.'

Léonie put her arms around her, finding the pretence that all was well exhausting.

'And you know that you are to be an aunt? A summer baby.'

Léonie found a smile. 'It is the most wonderful news.'

When Isolde withdrew to change for dinner, Léonie and Anatole continued to talk. Her brother was as open as she had ever known him to be and answered almost any question she put to him.

'Did Maman know of the deception at Cimetière de Montmartre?' she asked, haunted by the idea that she might have been the only one present not party to the hoax.

'We told no one,' he assured her, 'although I believe she suspected there was more to the matter than met the eye.'

'And the clinic? Was there a child?'

'No. Another lie to shore up our deception.'

He would say little of his enemy, suffice that he had damaged Isolde greatly in the short time they had been acquainted. Anatole did admit that the man was a Parisian and that he had clearly been successful in unpicking the false trail laid for him and tracked them to the Midi. However, Anatole was at a loss as to how he had made the leap from Carcassonne to Rennes-les-Bains. He couldn't bring himself even to utter his name.

As Léonie listened to the story of the obsession, the lengths to which their enemy was prepared to go to ruin both Isolde and Anatole, she became ever more fearful of what might happen on the following day.

Léonie gave him her word that, should he fail in his task, she would find some immediate way of leaving the Domaine de la Cade under cover of night with Isolde.

'You do not believe he will abide by the rules of engagement, do you?' she said in a level voice.

'He is not a man of honour,' Anatole replied. 'Should things go ill tomorrow, I would not wish Isolde to be here when he comes to find her.'

'He sounds a devil.'

'And I, a fool,' said Anatole, 'for thinking it could end in any other way than this.'

Léonie found the evening difficult and felt uncomfortable keeping the truth from Isolde, especially having been the victim of one such concealment herself. But she accepted that, in her condition, Isolde should be spared the worry. God willing, all would be well and she would only hear of the duel after it was over.

As soon as Isolde retired for the night, Léonie and Anatole finalised the last of the next day's arrangements. She was to keep Isolde occupied so that, at the appointed hour, he and Pascal could slip away. Anatole had sent word to Charles Denarnaud inviting him to be his second – a request that had been accepted. Dr Gabignaud, though an unwilling participant, had agreed to provide medical assistance should it be required.

Though she nodded, Léonie had not the slightest intention of abiding by Anatole's wishes. She could not contemplate sitting idly in the drawing room, watching the hands of the clock, knowing that her brother was engaged in such combat. She didn't yet know how, but she was determined to find some way of passing off responsibility for Isolde between the hours of dusk and nightfall.

But Léonie gave no indication of her intended disobedience, in either word or deed. And Anatole was so absorbed in his fevered planning that he did not think to doubt her.

When he, too, retired for the night, Léonie remained behind for some time, thinking.

She would be strong. She would not permit her fears to master her. Anatole would wound or kill his enemy. She refused to entertain an alternative.

But even as the hours of night slipped by, she was aware that wishing would not make it so.

CHAPTER 79

The Eve of All Saints came in with a chill and pink dawn. Léonie had barely slept. After breakfast, when neither she nor Anatole could manage to eat much, he spent the morning closeted with Isolde.

As she sat in the library, she could hear them laughing, whispering, planning. Isolde's joy at her brother's company made Léonie's awareness of how easily such happiness might be snatched away the more painful.

When she joined them for coffee in the morning room, Anatole raised his head and the anguish in his eyes made her turn away, for fear her countenance would give him away.

Léonie felt her nerves were as tight as violin strings. The strain of pretence, the dissembling and lightness of conversation, exhausted her and she marvelled at how Anatole seemed able to hide his true feelings.

They passed the afternoon in playing cards and reading stories aloud, contriving to delay Isolde's afternoon rest as Léonie and Anatole had planned. It was not until four o'clock that Isolde declared her intention to withdraw to her chamber until supper. Anatole returned some quarter of an hour later with sorrow etched in lines upon his face.

'She is sleeping,' he said.

They both looked out at the apricot sky, the last vestiges of sun flecked bright behind the clouds. Léonie's strength finally deserted her. 'It is not too late.' She took his hand. 'For the sake of Isolde and your child, I beg you, Anatole, do not go through with this.'

He put his arms around her and drew her to him, enveloping her in the familiar scent of sandalwood and hair oil.

'I cannot default, *petite*,' he said softly. 'Or else it will never end. Besides, I would not have my son grow up believing his father a coward.'

'Or your daughter.'

Anatole smiled. 'Or daughter. Nor, indeed, my courageous and steadfast little sister.'

The sound of footsteps on the tiled floor made them both turn.

Pascal stopped at the bottom of the stairs, holding Anatole's greatcoat over his arm. The expression on his face betraying how little he wished to be part of the matter.

'It is time, Sénher,' he said.

Léonie raised her head. She had tried and failed to prevent him from going. Now, all she could do was to send him on his way with her confidence and support.

'I am proud of you,' she said.

Anatole caught his breath. 'Look after my Isolde,' he whispered. 'I have left a letter in my dressing room, should things …' He broke off. 'She must not want for anything. Neither she, nor the child. Keep them safe.'

Léonie watched in despair as Pascal helped him into his coat, then the two men walked briskly to the front door. On the threshold, Anatole turned. He raised his hands to his lips.

'I love you, *petite*.'

There was a rush of evening air, then the door shuddered to a close behind them and they were gone. Léonie listened to the muffled crunch of their boots upon the gravel until she could hear them no more.

Then her courage deserted her. She sank onto the bottom step, rested her head on her arms and sobbed. From the shadows beneath the stairs, Marieta crept out. The girl hesitated, then, deciding to forget herself, sat down on the step beside Léonie and put her arm around her shoulder.

'It will be all right, Madomaisèla,' she murmured. 'Pascal will not let any harm come to the master.'

Léonie clamped her hand over her mouth, so her weeping would not disturb Isolde, and was grateful for Marieta's kindness. She rubbed her eyes hard with the cuff of her sleeve.

'Is my . . .' She stopped, realising that she no longer knew quite how she should refer to Isolde. 'Is my aunt still sleeping?'

Marieta smoothed down her apron. The look on her face suggested that Pascal had confided the whole business to her.

'Do you wish me to go and see if Madama has woken?'

Léonie shook her head. 'No, let her be.'

'Can I fetch you something? A tisane, perhaps. A splash of brandy.'

Léonie stood up. 'No, I will be fine now. Thank you, Marieta.' She gave a weak smile. 'Besides, my brother will need refreshment when he returns. I would not have him wait.'

For a moment, the eyes of the two girls met.

'Very good, Madomaisèla. I shall make certain the kitchen is ready,' she said.

Léonie quickly took her hat and coat, which she had left ready beside the door, and was on the point of leaving when a wail from upstairs split the silence of the hall. Léonie looked up, then ran up the stairs two at a time. The sound seemed to be coming from her brother's chamber, but she had seen him depart the house not ten minutes previously in the company of Pascal. Was someone else there?

As she opened the door, Isolde all but fell into her arms. Léonie had never seen her aunt in such a state. Her hair was loose and her dress was open at the neck, revealing raw, red scarring at her throat.

'Isolde! Whatever is it? What has happened?'

Then she saw that Isolde was holding a letter in her hand and realised she had prematurely found the letter Anatole had left for her in his dressing room.

Quickly, she put her arm around Isolde's shoulder. 'Come back to your room,' she said.

'I could not sleep, so I went to find him and found this.' Isolde looked Léonie in the eye and saw her guilt reflected there. 'You knew,' she said.

Léonie hesitated but nodded. After everything that had happened, the evasions and half-truths and misunderstandings, it was time to be honest.

'The challenge was delivered by hand yesterday. Denarnaud and Gabignaud have accompanied him.'

Isolde became even whiter. 'So he is here. He has found us.'

'Anatole will not miss his mark,' Léonie said, with a conviction she did not feel.

Isolde suddenly became calm. 'I must dress. I have to go to him.'

'You cannot,' Léonie said desperately. 'Your condition, your recent illness, there is nothing he would hate more than for you to put yourself in harm's way.'

Isolde took no notice. 'Where is the contest to take place?'

'Your presence would distract him, Isolde, can't you see that?'

Isolde looked down at the hat and coat in Léonie's hands. 'Yet you, yourself, are intending to go?'

Léonie sighed. 'The contest is to take place at a clearing in the beech woods. I do not know precisely where. Truly.'

Isolde nodded. 'Where the wild juniper grows, there's a clearing where my late husband would sometimes go to practise.'

'It may be. He said nothing more.'

Isolde crossed the corridor to her own chamber.

'But even if we leave now and manage to find the precise location,' Léonie protested, 'Anatole left with Pascal some quarter of an hour ago.'

'If we go now, we may yet stop it.'

Isolde put on her grey walking jacket over her dress, laced her boots and then headed for the stairs, leaving Léonie no choice but to follow. As they ran through the hall, it seemed to Léonie that the world had taken on a harsher hue. Things once familiar and precious – the polished table and doors, the pianoforte and tapestried stool, within which Léonie had placed the music taken from the sepulchre – seemed to have turned their backs on them.

Léonie took down the heavy garden cloaks from the hooks inside the entrance for additional warmth, handed one to Isolde, wrapped the other around herself, then pulled open the door. She took the lighted lamp from the stand.

'At what precise time is the duel to take place?' Isolde asked.

'Dusk,' Léonie replied. 'Six o'clock.'

They looked up at the sky, a deep and darkening blue above them.

'If we are to be there in time,' Léonie said, 'we must hurry.'

CHAPTER 80

With Pascal holding a lantern aloft, the two men walked in silence to the end of the drive, where Denarnaud's carriage was waiting.

Anatole nodded at Gabignaud, whose expression revealed his distaste at the business. Charles Denarnaud clasped Anatole's hand.

'The principal and the doctor in the back,' Denarnaud announced, his voice clear. 'Your man and I will ride at the front.'

The hood was up. Gabignaud and Anatole climbed in. Pascal, looking uncomfortable in such company, and Denarnaud, balancing the long wooden pistol case on his lap, faced them.

'You know the place, Denarnaud?' Anatole asked. 'The glade in the beech wood to the east of the property?'

Denarnaud leaned out and gave the instructions. Anatole heard the driver flick his reins and the gig moved off, the harness and bridle rattling in the chill dusk air.

Denarnaud was the only one with an appetite for talk. Most of his stories involved duels with which he had been involved: close shaves all, but always ending well for his principal. Anatole understood he was trying to put him at ease but wished he would hold his tongue.

He sat bolt upright, looking out at the countryside, thinking that perhaps it was the last time he would see it. The avenue of trees lining the drive was covered in hoar frost. The heavy fall of the horses' hooves on the hard ground echoed around the park. The sky seemed to glint like a mirror, as a pale moon rose in white splendour.

'These are my own pistols,' Denarnaud explained. 'I loaded them myself. The case is sealed. You will draw lots to decide whether we use these or your opponent's.'

'Yes,' Anatole snapped, then added, 'My apologies, Denarnaud. My nerves are on edge. I am most grateful for your careful attention.'

'Always worth running through the etiquette,' Denarnaud said in a voice louder than the confined space of the carriage and the situation required. Anatole realised that Denarnaud too, for all his bluster, was nervous. 'We don't want any misunderstandings. For all I know, matters are conducted differently in Paris.'

'I do not think so.'

'You have been practising, Vernier?'

Anatole nodded. 'With the pistols from the house.'

'Are you confident with them? Is the sighting good?'

'I would have had more time,' he said abruptly, and turned away.

They turned and started to move across the rougher ground. Anatole tried to picture his cherished Isolde, sleeping with her hair fanned out on the pillow. He thought of Léonie's green, questioning eyes and the face of his child not yet born. Tried to fix their beloved features in his mind.

I am doing this for them.

But the world had shrunk to the rattling carriage, the wooden box upon Denarnaud's lap, the fast, nervous breathing of Gabignaud beside him.

Anatole felt the *fiacre* swing again to the left. Beneath the wheels, the ground became more rutted and uneven, until they emerged into a clearing. On the far side stood another carriage. Anatole recognised the crest of Victor Constant, Comte de Tourmaline, gold upon black, and struggled to breathe. Two bay horses, plumed and blinkered, were stamping their hooves. Beside them stood a knot of men.

Denarnaud passed the pistol case to Pascal, then alighted first, Gabignaud followed, then Pascal. Finally, Anatole stepped down. Even from this distance, with their opposite numbers all dressed alike in black, he could identify Constant. With a shudder of revulsion, he also recognised one of the two men who had set about him on the night of the riot at the Opéra. Beside him, a dissolute-looking old soldier in an archaic Napoleonic cloak. He, too, seemed familiar.

Anatole drew his breath. Even though Victor Constant had resided in his thoughts from the moment he had met and fallen in love with Isolde, the two men had not been in one another's company.

He was taken by surprise at the rage that rushed through him. A cool head was what was required, not an impetuous desire for revenge. But suddenly the wood seemed too small. The bare trunks of the beech trees appeared to be closing in upon him.

He stumbled on an exposed root, and nearly fell.

'Steady, Vernier,' murmured Gabignaud.

Anatole gathered his thoughts and watched as Denarnaud walked towards Constant's party, Pascal trailing behind him carrying the pistol box across his arms as if it was a child's coffin.

The seconds greeted one another formally, each bowing briefly, then they walked further up into the clearing. Anatole was aware of Constant's cold eyes upon him, piercing, across the frozen earth. He noted, too, that he looked unwell.

They moved to the centre of the clearing, not far from where Pascal had set up the makeshift shooting gallery the day before, then measured the paces from where each man would take aim. Pascal and Constant's man hammered two walking sticks into the ground to mark precisely the spot.

'How are you holding up?' Gabignaud murmured. 'Can I fetch any—'

'Nothing,' Anatole said quickly. 'I need nothing.'

Denarnaud returned. 'I regret we lost the toss for the pistols.' He slapped Anatole on the shoulder. 'It will make no difference, I am certain. It's the aim that counts, not the barrel.'

Anatole felt he was a man walking in his sleep. Everything around him seemed to be muffled, happening to someone else. He knew he should be concerned about the fact that he was to use his opponent's pistols, but he was numb.

The two groups moved closer to one another.

Denarnaud removed Anatole's greatcoat. Constant's second did the same for him. Anatole watched as Denarnaud ostentatiously patted down Constant's jacket pockets, his waistcoat pockets, to make sure he had no other weapons, no pocketbook, no papers that might act as a shield.

Denarnaud nodded. 'Nothing amiss.'

Anatole lifted his arms while Constant's man ran his hands over his body to check that he, too, had no concealed advantage. He felt his watch fob being taken from his pocket and unchained.

'A new watch, Monsieur? Monogrammed. Nice piece of workmanship.'

He recognised the voice. It was the same man who had stolen his father's timepiece from him. Anatole forced himself to look him in the eye but said nothing. He would not allow himself to be provoked.

The man glanced at his master, then shrugged and walked away.

Anatole felt Denarnaud take his elbow and lead him to one of the walking sticks. 'Vernier, this is your mark.'

I cannot miss.

He was handed a pistol. It was cold and heavy in his hand, a far finer weapon than those belonging to his late uncle. The barrel was long and polished, with Constant's gold monogrammed initials stamped into the handle.

Anatole felt as if he was looking down upon himself from a great height. He could see a man who much resembled him, the same jet-black hair, the same moustache, the pale face and nose tipped red from the cold. A man facing, for the last time, his enemy.

Now, as from a distance, came a voice. The business would soon be concluded.

'Are you ready, gentlemen?'

Anatole nodded. Constant nodded.

'One shot apiece.'

Anatole raised his arm. Constant did the same.

Then the same voice again. 'Fire.'

Anatole was aware of nothing – no sights, no sounds, no smells; he experienced a total absence of emotion. He believed himself to have done nothing, and yet the muscles in his arm contracted and his fingers squeezed, pressing the trigger, and there was a snap as the catch released. He saw the powder flare in the pan and the puff of smoke bloom on the air. Two reports echoed around the glade. The birds flew from the tops of the surrounding trees, their wings beating the air in their panic.

Anatole lost the air in his lungs. His legs went from under him. He was falling to his knees on the hard earth, thinking of Isolde and Léonie. Then a warmth spread over his chest, like the soothing ministrations of a hot bath.

'Is he struck?' Was it Gabignaud's voice?

Dark figures gathered around him, no longer identifiable, just a forest of black and grey-striped trouser legs, hands encased in thick fur gloves, heavy boots. Then he heard something. A wild shriek, his name carried in agony and despair.

Anatole slumped sideways onto the ground. He was imagining he could hear Isolde's voice calling to him. But, almost simultaneously, he realised that others could hear the shouting too. The crowd surrounding him parted and stood back, far enough for him to see her running towards him from the cover of the trees, with Léonie hard on her heels.

'No. Anatole, no!' Isolde was shouting. 'No!'

Something else caught his attention, just outside his line of vision. His eyes were darkening. He tried to sit, but a sharp pain in his side, like the stab of a knife, caused him to gasp. He reached out his hand but had no strength, and felt himself slumping back down to the ground.

Everything started to move in slow motion. Anatole realised what was going to happen. At first, his eyes could not accept it. Denarnaud had checked the rules of engagement were met. One shot and one shot only. And yet as he watched, Constant dropped the duelling pistol to the ground, reached into his jacket and pulled out a second weapon, so small that the barrel fitted between his second and third fingers. His arm continued its upward arc, then swung to the right and fired.

A second gun when there should have been only one.

Anatole shouted, at last finding his voice. But he was too late.

Her body came to a standstill, as if hanging momentarily in the air, then was thrown backwards by the force of the bullet. Her eyes widened in surprise, then shock, then pain as Anatole watched her fall. Like him, down to the ground.

Anatole felt a shout tear from his chest. All around him was chaos, yelling and shouting and pandemonium. And in the heart of it, he thought he heard the sound of someone laughing. His vision faded, black replacing white, stripping the colour from the world.

It was the last sound he heard before the darkness closed over him.

CHAPTER 81

A howl split the air. Léonie heard it but was at first unaware that the cry had issued from her own lips.

For a moment, she stood rooted to the spot, unable to accept the evidence of her own eyes. She fancied she looked at a stage set, the glade and each person captured in time with brush and paint or the shutter of a lens. Lifeless, motionless; a postcard image of their real, flesh-and-blood selves.

Then, with a kick, the world rushed back. Léonie cast her gaze into the darkness, the truth imprinting its bloody handprint.

Isolde, lying upon the damp earth, her grey dress stained red. Anatole, struggling to raise himself on one arm, his face creased with pain, before collapsing back to the ground. Gabignaud crouched at his side.

Most shocking, the face of their murderer. The man who Isolde so feared and Anatole so detested, revealed in plain sight.

Léonie turned cold, her courage ripped from her.

'No,' she whispered.

Guilt, sharp as glass, pierced her defences. Humiliation, then anger following on its heels, swept through her like a river bursting its banks. Here, but a couple of steps away from her, was the man about whom she had allowed herself to dream. Victor Constant.

Anatole's assassin. Isolde's persecutor.

Léonie raised her lamp higher until she could clearly see the crest on the side of the carriage standing some way off to the side, although she did not need confirmation that it was he.

Rage, violent and all-encompassing, swooped down over her. Insensible of her own safety, she charged out of the shadows of the trees and into the glade, running forward towards the knot of men standing around Anatole and Gabignaud.

The doctor seemed paralysed. Shock at what had transpired had stolen from him the ability to act. He lurched up, nearly losing his footing, looking wildly to Victor Constant and his men, then in bewilderment at Charles Denarnaud, who had checked the guns and pronounced that the conditions for the duel had been met.

Léonie reached Isolde first. She threw herself down on the ground beside her and lifted her cloak. The pale grey material on the left side of her dress was soaked crimson. Léonie pulled off her glove and, pushing Isolde's cuff higher up her arm, felt for a pulse. It was faint, but there. Some slight measure of life remained. Quickly, she ran her hands over Isolde's prostrate body and realised the bullet had hit her arm. Provided she did not lose too much blood, she would survive.

'Dr Gabignaud, *vite*,' she cried. '*Aidez-la*. Pascal!'

Her thoughts leapt to Anatole. The slightest frosting of white breath around his mouth and nose in the twilight gave her hope that he, too, was not mortally wounded.

She stood up and took a step towards her brother.

'I will thank you to stay where you are, Mademoiselle Vernier. You too, Gabignaud.'

Constant's voice stopped her in her tracks. Only now did Léonie register that he was still holding his weapon raised pointing at Pascal and the doctor, finger upon the trigger, ready to squeeze, and that it was not a duelling pistol, but a gun designed to be carried in the pocket or a purse.

And I led him to them.

Her legs were shaking and her heart hammering in her chest, but she held her nerve. She raised her chin and looked him straight in the eye.

'Monsieur Constant,' she said, his name like poison on her tongue.

'Mademoiselle Vernier,' he replied, not changing his aim. 'This is an unexpected pleasure. I had not thought Vernier would expose you to such ugliness.'

Her eyes darted to where Anatole lay on the ground, then back to Constant. He jerked his head and his man-servant stepped forward, followed by the filthy soldier whom Léonie now recognised as the same creature who had followed her as she walked into the medieval Cité of Carcassonne. With despair, she realised how complete had been Constant's planning.

The two men seized Gabignaud and pulled his arms behind his back, throwing his lamp to the ground. Léonie heard the glass smash as the flame was extinguished with a hiss in the wet leaves. Then, before she realised what was happening, the taller of the men drew a gun from beneath his coat, put it to Gabignaud's temple and pulled the trigger.

The force of the shot lifted Gabignaud from the ground. The back of his head exploded, showering his executioner with blood and bone. His body twitched, jerked, then lay still.

How little time it takes to kill a man.

The thought swooped in, then out of her mind. Léonie clamped her hand to her mouth, feeling the nausea rising in her throat, then doubled over and vomited.

Out of the corner of her eye, she saw Pascal taking a small step backwards, then another. She had never had to question his loyalty and steadfastness before, but was he going to leave them?

Then he caught her eye and glanced down to signal his intention.

Léonie understood. Straightening up, she turned to Charles Denarnaud. 'Monsieur,' she said loudly, creating a diversion, 'I am appalled to find you an ally of this man. You will be condemned when news of your duplicity is reported.'

He gave a complacent grimace. 'From whose mouth, Mademoiselle Vernier? There is none but us here.'

'Hold your tongue,' commanded Constant.

'Do you care nothing for your sister, for your family,' Léonie challenged, 'that you would disgrace them in such a manner?'

Denarnaud laughed. 'Money speaks louder.'

'Denarnaud, *ça suffit*!'

Léonie glanced at Constant, now noticing how his head seemed to tremble in permanent motion. Then, out of the corner of her eye, she saw Anatole's foot twitch on the ground.

Was he alive? Hope sparked inside her, driven out immediately by dread. If he was yet alive, he would remain so only as long as Constant thought him dead.

Night had fallen. Though the doctor's lamp was broken, the remaining lanterns cast uneven pools of yellow light on the ground.

Léonie forced herself to take a step towards the man she had thought she might love.

'Is it worth it, Monsieur? Damning yourself? And for what? Jealousy? Revenge? For it is certainly not for honour.' She took another pace, a little to the side this time, hoping to shield Pascal. 'Let me tend to my brother. To Isolde.'

She was now close enough to see the look of contempt on Constant's face. She could not believe she had ever thought his features distinguished, noble. Now, he repelled her.

531

'You are hardly in a position to issue orders, Mademoiselle Vernier.' He turned his head to where Isolde lay folded within her cloak. 'And the whore. A single shot was too good for her. I would wish that she had suffered as she has made me suffer.'

Léonie met his gaze without flinching. 'She is beyond your reach now,' she said, the lie coming without hesitation to her lips.

'You will forgive me, Mademoiselle Vernier, if I do not take your word for that. Besides, there is not a single tear on your cheek. You have strong nerves, but I do not believe you are so hard-hearted.'

He hesitated, now aiming at her, as if preparing to deliver the *coup de grâce*. Léonie felt her body tense, waiting for the shot she thought must surely now find her, and prayed Pascal was almost ready to act. It took great effort of will not to look in his direction.

'In point of fact,' Constant said, 'in character you remind me much of your mother.'

Everything stilled, as if the world was holding its breath. White clouds, cold on the evening air; the shivering of the wind in the bare branches of the trees; the rustling of the juniper bushes. At last, Léonie found her tongue.

'What do you mean?' she said. Each word seemed to drop like lead into the cold air.

She could sense his satisfaction. It rose from him like the stench from a tannery, acrid, pungent.

'You still do not know what has befallen your mother?'

Léonie didn't trust herself to speak.

'It has been quite the talk of Paris,' Constant said. 'I am told, one of the worst murders the pedestrian minds of the *gendarmes* of the eighth *arrondissement* have been obliged to deal with for some time.'

Léonie stepped back as if he had struck her. 'She is dead?'

She started to shake. She did not want to believe him, but she could hear the truth of what Constant claimed in the quality of his silence. She could not react. She could not let him under her skin. And all the time, Isolde and Anatole were growing weaker.

'I do not believe you,' she managed to articulate.

'Ah, but you do, Mademoiselle Vernier. I can see it in your face.' He let his arm drop, taking the gun off Léonie for an instant. She took another step backwards. Behind her, she felt Denarnaud moving closer, blocking her path. Constant stepped towards her, quickly covering the distance between them. Then, from the corner of her eye, she saw Pascal crouch, snatch up the spare pistols from the box they had brought from the house.

'*Attention!*' he shouted to her.

Léonie reacted without hesitation, throwing herself down to the ground as a shot whistled over her head.

Denarnaud fell, struck in the back.

Constant retaliated instantly, firing into the darkness but going wide of his target. Léonie could hear Pascal in the undergrowth and realised he had moved round behind Constant.

On Constant's command, the old soldier was advancing on where Léonie lay on the ground. The other man was running towards the edge of the glade, looking for Pascal, firing at random.

'*Il est ici!*' he shouted to his master.

Constant fired again. Again, the shot went wide.

Suddenly, the vibration of running feet echoed through the ground. Léonie raised her head in the direction of the noise and heard shouting.

'*Arèst!*'

She recognised Marieta's voice, calling through the darkness, others shouting too. She could make out the glow of several lanterns getting closer, larger, jolting in the darkness. Then the gardener's boy, Emile, burst into sight on the far side of the clearing, holding a flaming torch in one hand and a stick in the other.

Léonie saw Constant take stock. He fired, but the boy darted back behind the shelter of a beech tree. Constant raised his arm again, then turned the gun and sent two bullets slamming into Anatole's torso.

Léonie screamed, as the servants rushed forward. 'No!' she cried, crawling desperately on her hands and knees over the muddy ground to where her brother lay. 'No!'

Constant realised the numbers were against him. Throwing his coat behind him, he strode into the shadows to where his *fiacre* still stood in readiness to depart.

'No witnesses,' he said.

Without a word, his manservant turned and fired a bullet into the old soldier's head. For a moment, his face was fixed in an expression of bewilderment. Then he dropped to his knees and fell forward.

Pascal fired the second pistol. Léonie saw Constant stumble, his legs nearly buckling under him, but he kept walking. Through the mayhem and chaos, she heard the slamming of the carriage door, the rattling of the harness and the chink of the lamps as the conveyance vanished uphill into the woods.

Marieta was already tending to Isolde, Pascal crouching beside her. Léonie thought her heart had stopped; she could barely breathe with the horror of what had happened. Blocking out the images of bone and blood and torn skin, she struggled to her feet and stumbled across the last few yards to her brother.

'Anatole?' she whispered. Her arm tightened around his broad shoulders, shaking him, trying to wake him. 'Anatole, please.'

The stillness seemed to deepen.

Léonie grasped the thick material of Anatole's greatcoat and rolled him over. A sob slipped from her lips. So much blood, pooled on the ground where he had been lying; the holes in his body where the bullets had penetrated. She cradled his head in her arms and brushed his hair back from his face. His eyes were wide open, but the life was extinguished.

CHAPTER 82

With Pascal's help, Marieta carried the barely conscious Isolde to Denarnaud's carriage. Although the wound on her arm was not serious, she had lost a lot of blood. Léonie tried to speak to her, but Isolde made no answer. She seemed to know no one, recognise nothing. She was yet in the world but removed from it.

Léonie was cold, shivering, her hair and clothes infused with the stench of blood and gunshot and soil, but now she did not leave Anatole's side. The gardener's boy and the ostlers from the stables constructed a makeshift bier with their coats and carried Anatole's prostrate body on their shoulders back across the grounds, torches burning fiercely. Léonie followed behind, a solitary mourner at an unannounced funeral. For a moment, she imagined how distraught their mother would be at the loss of her beloved son. She would never recover. Then, with a swooping feeling, she remembered that Marguerite had been dead for weeks, without their knowing, and grief caught in her throat.

Other servants carried the body of Dr Gabignaud, covering his shattered head with a cloth. The dog cart would be sent to bring the bodies of Constant's messenger and the perfidious Denarnaud.

By the time Léonie regained the house, Pascal had dispatched a messenger to Rennes-le-Château to inform Bérenger Saunière of the catastrophe and to request his presence. Marieta had sent to Rennes-les-Bains for the services of the local woman who laid out the dead.

Léonie listened to all the arrangements but heard nothing. She was numb with shock. Anatole was dead. The light had gone out of her life, and it was her fault.

I led Constant here.

Madame Saint-Loup arrived with a small boy, carrying a large cotton bag twice his size. Realising that, for the time being, she would have to take responsibility for everything, Léonie tried to agree rates with the woman, but she was informed that costs had been met already by her neighbour, Monsieur Baillard. Even his kindness did not bring tears to her eyes. She knew that if she gave way to any emotion at all, she would collapse. And for the sake of Isolde, and the promise she had made to her brother to look after his wife and child, she had to remain strong.

The bodies were placed in the dining room. Léonie watched in disbelief as Madame Saint-Loup filled a china bowl with water from a glass bottle she had brought with her.

'Holy water, Madomaisèla,' she said in response to Léonie's unasked question. Into it she dipped a sprig of boxwood, then lit two scented candles, one for each, and began to recite her prayers for the dead. The boy bowed his head.

'*Peyre Sant*, Holy Father, take this thy servant . . .'

As the words washed over her – a mixture of old and new traditions – Léonie felt nothing. There was no moment of grace descending, no sense of peace in Anatole's passing, no light entering the soul and drawing together in a common circle. There was no consolation, no poetry to be found in the old woman's offerings, only a vast and echoing loss.

Madame Saint-Loup gestured to the boy to pass a pair of large-bladed scissors from her bag, then began to cut away Anatole's blood-sodden clothes.

'Madomaisèla?' she said, handing Léonie two envelopes from Anatole's pockets. The first bore the black crest of the letter from Constant. The second, with a Parisian postmark, was unopened. Both were edged in rust-red, as if a border had been painted across the thick weave of the paper.

Léonie opened the second letter. It was formal and official notification from the *gendarmerie* of the 8th *arrondissement* informing Anatole of their mother's murder, on the night of Sunday, 20th September. No criminal had yet been apprehended for the crime. The letter was signed by an Inspector Thouron and had been forwarded via a number of addresses before finally finding Anatole in Rennes-les-Bains. The letter concluded by requesting he should make contact at his earliest convenience.

Léonie let the letter fall from her hand. She had not doubted Constant, but reading the black-and-white official words brought it home to her that her mother, truly, was dead. And had been for more than a month. This fact – that her mother had been unmourned and unclaimed for so long – twisted at Leonie's conscience and, with Anatole gone, who was there left to mourn?

Madame Saint-Loup began to clean the body, wiping Anatole's face and hands with such tenderness that it pained Léonie to witness it. When she pulled out several linen sheets, each yellowing and criss-crossed with black looped stitching to sew Anatole into his shroud, she could no longer bear to watch.

'Send word when Abbé Saunière comes,' she said and left her brother.

As if her legs were weighted down by lead, Léonie slowly climbed the stairs and went to Isolde's chamber. Marieta was at her mistress's side. A new doctor, one Léonie did not recognise, was accompanied by a matronly nurse in a white starched apron. Resident staff from the thermal spa. She learned that they, too, had been engaged by Monsieur Baillard.

As Léonie entered the room, Dr Courrent was administering a sedative.

'How is she?' Léonie whispered to Marieta.

The maid gave a small shake of her head. 'She struggles to stay with us, Madomaisèla.'

Léonie stepped closer to the bed. Even to her untrained eyes, it was clear how Isolde, gripped by a fierce, consuming fever, hovered between life and death. Léonie sat down and took her hand. The nurse laid strips of cold linen cloth across her blazing forehead, which cooled her skin for no more than a moment.

Finally, the doctor's medicine took effect and Isolde's narrow frame now shook with cold, rather than fever, as one afflicted with Saint Vitus's dance.

Léonie's flashbacks to the violence she had witnessed were kept at bay by her fears for Isolde. The weight of loss threatened to overwhelm her. So many lost, and Isolde's life, and that of her unborn child, hanging in the balance.

The moon rose in the sky. The Eve of All Saints.

Shortly after the clock had struck eleven, there was a knock at the door and Pascal appeared.

'Madomaisèla Léonie,' he said in hushed tones. 'There are . . . men here to see you.'

'Abbé Saunière?'

'Police officers,' he said.

'I cannot see anyone. After all this, I cannot.'

Pascal briefly put his hand on her shoulder. 'There is no one else,' he said. 'Monsieur Baillard is with them.'

Léonie felt a rush of relief. She paused at the top of the staircase, trying to compose herself as she looked down at the collection of black top hats and greatcoats in the hall. Two wore the uniform of the Parisian *gendarme*, a third a shabby provincial version of it. In the forest of dark and sombre clothes, a pale suit on a lean figure.

'Monsieur Baillard,' she cried, running down the stairs and taking his hands in hers. 'I am so glad you are here.' She looked at him. 'Anatole . . .'

Her voice broke. She was unable to pronounce the words.

Baillard nodded. 'I know. I have come to pay my respects,' he said formally, then lowered his voice so that his companions could not overhear. 'And Madama Vernier? How goes it with her?'

Léonie shook her head. 'The state of her mind is of as much concern to the doctor at present as the consequences of her wound. Although it is important to ensure her blood does not become infected, the bullet only nicked the inside of her arm.' Léonie stopped abruptly, only now realising what Monsieur Baillard had said. 'How did you know they had married?'

Baillard put his finger to his lips. 'This is not a conversation to be had now and in such company.' He glanced at his companions, then raised his voice. 'By happenstance, Madomaisèla Léonie, these gentlemen and I found ourselves travelling the drive to the Domaine de la Cade. A coincidence of timing.'

The younger of the two smartly dressed officers removed his hat and stepped forward. He had black smudged rings under his eyes, as if he had not slept for days.

'Inspector Thouron,' he said, offering his hand. 'From Paris, the commissariat of the eighth *arrondissement*. My condolences for the loss of your brother, Mademoiselle Vernier. And I regret I am also the bearer of still more bad news. Worse, it is old news. For some weeks, I have been seeking your brother to inform him – indeed, you yourself also – that—'

Léonie withdrew the letter from her pocket. 'Do not distress yourself, Monsieur l'Inspecteur,' she said, struggling to control herself. 'I know of my mother's death. This arrived yesterday, albeit by a most circuitous route.'

Thouron looked at her. 'You and your late brother have been most difficult to locate,' he said.

Léonie was aware of a quickness and intelligence behind the dishevelled appearance and exhausted features.

'And in the light of the . . . tragedy of this evening, it leads me to wonder if perhaps the events of Paris a month ago and what happened here tonight are in some way connected?'

Léonie darted a glance at Monsieur Baillard, then at the older man standing beside Inspector Thouron. His hair was flecked with grey and he had the strong, dark features characteristic of the Midi.

'Forgive me,' Thouron said. 'This is Inspector Bouchou of the Carcassonne *gendarmerie*. Bouchou has been assisting me in locating you.'

Léonie looked from one to the other. 'I do not understand, Inspector Thouron. You sent a letter from Paris, yet have come in person also? And you are here tonight.'

The two men exchanged a look.

'May I suggest, gentlemen,' Audric Baillard said quietly, but in a tone of authority that invited no disagreement, 'that we continue this conversation in some more private setting?'

Léonie felt the touch of Baillard's fingers on her arm.

'There is a fire in the drawing room,' she said.

The small group crossed the chequerboard hall and Léonie pushed open the door.

The memory of Anatole held within the drawing room was so strong that she faltered. In her mind's eye, she saw him standing before the fire, his coat-tails held up to let the heat of the flames warm his back, his hair glistening. Or by the window, a cigarette wedged deep between his fingers, talking to Dr Gabignaud the night of the supper party. Or leaning over the green baize card table, watching while she and Isolde played *vingt-et-un*. He seemed to have written himself into the fabric of the room, although Léonie had never known it until this second.

She closed her eyes as despair swept over her. How could she possibly talk as if nothing had happened, behave as if nothing had happened?

It was left to Monsieur Baillard to invite the officers to take a seat and to steer her to a corner of the *chaise longue*, where she sat, as if half asleep. He remained standing behind her.

Thouron explained the sequence of events, as they had pieced them together, from the night of her mother's murder on 20th September, to the discovery of the body, and the small steps the investigation had taken to lead them to Carcassonne, and from there to Rennes-les-Bains.

Léonie heard the words as if they were being spoken from behind glass. They did not penetrate her mind. Even though it was her mother of whom Thouron spoke – and she had loved her mother – the loss of Anatole had set a wall of stone around her heart that allowed no other emotion to enter. There would be time enough to grieve for Marguerite. For the gentle and honourable doctor too. But for now, nothing but Anatole – and the promise she had made to him to protect his wife and child – had any purchase in her mind.

'So,' Thouron concluded, 'the concierge admitted he had been paid to pass on any correspondence. The maid in the Debussy household confirmed that she, too, had seen the man loitering around the rue de Berlin in the days leading up to and after the ... the incident.' Thouron paused. 'Indeed, had it not been for the letter your late brother

542

wrote to your mother, I cannot see how we would have found you yet.'

'Have you identified the man, Thouron?' enquired Baillard.

'By sight only. An unfortunate-looking individual. A raw and angry complexion, with little or no hair on a blistered scalp.'

'Oh.' The word slipped from her lips. Léonie felt three pairs of eyes look to her.

'Do you know him, Mademoiselle Vernier?'

An image of him holding the muzzle of his gun to Dr Gabignaud's temple and pulling the trigger.

She swallowed hard. 'He is Victor Constant's man. He was here tonight.'

Thouron exchanged another look with Bouchou. 'The Comte de Tourmaline?'

'I beg your pardon?'

'It is the same man, Constant, Tourmaline. He goes under either name depending on the circumstances or the company he is keeping.'

'He gave me his card,' she said in a hollow voice. 'Victor Constant.'

She felt the reassuring pressure of Audric Baillard's hand upon her shoulder. 'Is the Count of Tourmaline a suspect in this matter, Inspector Thouron?' he enquired.

The officer hesitated, then, clearly deciding that there was no benefit to concealment, he nodded. 'And he, too, we discovered, had travelled from Paris to the Midi, some days after the late Monsieur Vernier.'

Léonie did not hear. All she could think about was the way her heart had leapt when Victor Constant took her hand. How she had kept his card safe, deceiving Anatole. How, in her imagination, she had thought him a man she might care for.

She had led him to them. Because of her, Anatole lay dead.

'Léonie,' Baillard asked softly. 'Was Constant the man from whom Madama Vernier fled? With whom your brother duelled this evening?'

Léonie forced herself to reply. 'It was,' she managed to say.

Baillard walked across the room to the small, round drinks table and poured Léonie a glass of brandy.

'From your expressions, gentlemen,' he said, pressing the glass into her cold fingers, 'I think this man is known to you.'

Thouron nodded. 'Several times his name came up in the enquiry into Madame Vernier's murder, but never with evidence enough to associate him with the crime. He appears to have nursed a vendetta against Monsieur Vernier, a clever and sly campaign, until these last weeks, when he has become less careful.'

'There was an incident at a ... house of recreation in the *quartier* Barbès in Carcassonne,' Bouchou added, 'which left a girl badly disfigured.'

'We believe his increasingly erratic behaviour is, in part, due to the aggressive acceleration of his ... illness. It has begun to affect his brain. Syphilis.' Thouron broke off, clearly embarrassed to speak the word in Léonie's presence.

Baillard came round from behind the settee and sat down beside Léonie.

'Tell Inspector Thouron what you know,' he said. 'Leave nothing out.'

Léonie took another drink. The alcohol burned her throat, but it killed the sour taste in her mouth.

What need for concealment now?

She began to talk, detailing everything that had happened – from the false burial in Montmartre, their flight from Paris after the attack, their arrival in Rennes-les-Bains, the wedding in Carcassonne and the storm, to the bloody and dishonourable events of this evening in the woods of the Domaine de la Cade.

March, September, October.

*

Upstairs, Isolde was still held captive by the torment that had overtaken her the instant she saw Anatole fall.

Images, thoughts, glided in and out of her mind. Her eyes flickered half open. For a fleeting, joyful moment, she thought herself lying in Anatole's arms with the light of the candle reflected in his brown eyes, but the vision faded. The skin began to slip from his face, revealing the skull beneath, leaving only bone and teeth and black holes where his eyes had been.

And always the whisperings, the voices, Constant's malicious silver tones insinuating themselves. She felt herself tossing and turning upon the pillow, trying to rid her head of the echo, but succeeding only in making the cacophony louder. Which the voice, which the echo?

She dreamed she saw their son, crying for the father he had never known, separated from Anatole as if behind a pane of glass. She cried out to them both, but no sound came from her lips and they were beyond hearing.

Memories, dreams, premonitions. A mind shaken loose from its moorings by grief.

PART X

The Lake
October 2007

CHAPTER 83

When Meredith woke again, Hal was gone.

She put out her hand to the space in the bed where he had slept beside her. The sheet was cold, but the soft smell of him on the pillow and the impression where his head had rested remained. She smiled. No sense in thinking about anything beyond here, and now, but she had no regrets.

The shutters were closed and it was dark in the room. Meredith looked at the time. Eight o'clock. She guessed Hal didn't want the maids to see him and had gone back to his own room.

For a while, she lay burrowed deep in the covers, thinking about Hal, about emotions she had allowed herself to feel last night. Then, her thoughts drifted to Léonie, the girl with the copper hair, her other night-time companion.

I cannot sleep.

The words Meredith remembered from her dream, heard and yet not spoken. The sense of pity, of restlessness; the fact that Léonie wanted something from her.

Slipping out of bed, Meredith pulled on a pair of thick socks to keep her feet warm. Hal had forgotten his sweater, lying in a heap by the chair where he had tossed it last night. She held it to her face, breathing in the scent of him, then she put it on. It was way too big and baggy, but it was nice to wear it.

For a while, she sat looking at the portrait. The photograph of the sepia soldier, Great-great-grandfather Vernier, was tucked into the corner of the frame where she'd put it last night. Meredith felt the tug of possibility. The discordant ideas that had been massing in her mind had settled during the course of the night. Her mind was clear.

The obvious first step was to find out if Anatole Vernier had been married, although it was easier said than done. She also needed to find out how he and Léonie Vernier were connected to Isolde Lascombe. Had they lived in the house in 1891, around the time the photograph had been taken, or were they just visitors? As her online detective work yesterday had reminded her, most ordinary people didn't appear on the internet. Then, as now. Even if you trawled through genealogy sites, you needed names and dates and towns of birth and death to even have a chance of discovering anything.

She booted up the computer. There wasn't a reply from Mary yet, but she sent another email to Chapel Hill all the same, filling her in on the last twenty-four hours and asking if she'd have time to check out a couple more things. She said nothing about Hal, or Léonie. No sense giving her cause to worry.

Meredith went through to the bathroom to fill the kettle. While she was waiting for the water to boil, she ran her eyes along the spines of the books on the shelf above the bureau. Her attention was caught by one entitled *Diables et esprits maléfiques et phantômes de la montagne*. She took it out and opened it. The flyleaf told her it was a new edition of an earlier book by a local author, Audric S. Baillard, who had lived in nearby Los Seres and died in 2005. There was no date of original publication, but according to the reviews on the back, it was considered the definitive text on Pyrenean mountain folklore.

The book was divided into stories by region. The illustration for the section on Rennes-les-Bains was a black-and-white photograph of the place des Deux Rennes taken around 1900, when it was known as the place du Pérou. Meredith smiled. It seemed so familiar. She could even pick out the exact spot, beneath the spreading branches of the *platanes*, where her ancestor had stood.

The kettle whistled and clicked off. She poured a sachet of hot chocolate into a cup, stirred in two sugars, then took the book to the window and began to read.

The stories in the collection were similar from place to place – myths of demons and devils that were generations, even millennia, old; a linking of folklore with natural phenomena: the Devil's Armchair, the Horned Mountain, the Devil's Lake – all the names she'd come across already on the map. She flicked back to the imprint page again, checking there really was no clue as to when the book had first been published. The latest story was from the early 1900s, so given that the author had only died a couple of years ago, she guessed he'd gathered the stories more recently.

Baillard's style was clear and sparse, giving the factual information with the minimum of embellishment. With excitement, Meredith discovered that there was a whole section on the Domaine de la Cade. The property had come into the hands of the Lascombe family during the Wars of Religion, a series of conflicts fought between the Catholics and Huguenots from 1562 to 1598. Jules Lascombe had inherited the property on the death of his father, Guy Lascombe, in 1865. He had married an Isolde Labourde in 1885, and died without issue in 1891. She smiled at another piece of the puzzle falling into place, looking over at the ageless Isolde, Jules's widow, behind the glass of the portrait. Then it occurred to her that she hadn't noticed Isolde's name on the Lascombe-Bousquet family tomb in Rennes-les-Bains. Why not?

Something else to check out.

She carried on reading. Baillard moved to the legends associated with the Domaine. There had been, for many years, rumours of a vicious wild beast that terrorised the countryside around Rennes-les-Bains, attacking children and land workers on isolated farms. The distinguishing feature of the attacks was claw marks, three wide gashes across the face. Unusual marks.

Meredith stopped again, thinking of the injuries sustained by Hal's father while his car lay in the river gorge, and the defaced statue of Mary set on the Visigoth pillar in the approach to the church in Rennes-le-Château. Hard on its heels, the memory of a fragment of her nightmare came back to her – the image of a tapestry hanging on a poorly lit stair. The sensation of being chased, claws and black fur touching her skin, sliding over her hands.

Un, deux, trois, loup.

Then back to the graveyard in Rennes-les-Bains and the recollection of one of the names on the war memorial to the dead of the First World War: Saint-Loup.

There were many deaths and disappearances recorded between 1870 and 1885. A period of relative calm followed, then there was an intensification of rumours from the autumn of 1891 onwards and a growing belief that the creature – a demon in local folklore – was harboured within a Visigoth sepulchre that lay within the grounds of the Domaine de la Cade. There were deaths – unattributed attacks – intermittently over the next six years, but then the attacks came to an abrupt end in 1897. The author didn't actually say so, but he implied that the end of the terror was connected to the fact that parts of the house were ruined by fire and the sepulchre destroyed.

Meredith curled up tightly in the chair and sipped her hot chocolate. It was strange that, in a work devoted to folklore and legend, there was no reference to the Tarot deck. Audric Baillard must have heard about the cards during his research. The deck was not only inspired by the local landscape and printed by the Bousquet family, but also fell within the exact period of time covered by the book.

A deliberate omission?

Then, she felt it again. A chill in the air that had not been there before. The fleeting sense of there being someone there, not far away; not in the room, but close by.

Léonie?

Meredith stood up, finding herself drawn to the window. She unfastened the long metal catch, pulled back the two tall panes of glass and pushed open the shutters, letting them fall back against the wall. The trees were swaying, sighing as the wind wound itself around the ancient trunks, and the air seemed restless, carrying the memory of the echo of the music within it. Notes drifting on the breeze. The melody of the place itself.

As Meredith cast her eyes over the grounds, she caught a movement out of the corner of her eye and saw – thought she saw – a graceful figure in a long cloak, with the hood pulled up over its head, emerge from the lee of the building.

The wind seemed to be gathering force, racing now through the arched opening cut into the high box hedge that led to the wild meadows and rough grass beyond. Distant as it was, she could just make out the white crests as it sent the water of the lake lapping against the edge and up over onto the grass.

The outline, the impression, the figure kept to the shadows, skimming beneath the rising gaze of the pale sun, which darted in and out of the thin strata of clouds that chased across the pink sky. She seemed to glide over the grass, covered with the slightest sheen of dew. Meredith caught the smell of earth, of autumn, of burned stubble, of bonfires. Of bones.

She watched in captivated silence as the figure made its way – *her* way, Meredith felt sure – to the far side of the ornamental lake. For a moment, it stopped and stood on a small promontory overlooking the water. Meredith's vision seemed to narrow right in, like a camera close up. She imagined the hood falling back from the girl's face. It was pale and perfectly symmetrical, with emerald eyes that once had glinted. Shade without colour. The curls fell, like twists of beaten gold, transparent in the morning light, over the shoulders of her red dress and down to her waist. Shape without form. She seemed to hold Meredith's gaze, reflecting her own hopes and fears and imaginings.

'Léonie?' Meredith whispered into the silence.

For a while longer, she kept vigil at the window, staring at the place on the far side of the lake where the figure had stood. But now the air was still. Nothing stirred in the shadows.

Finally, she pulled back inside and shut the window.

A few days ago – hours even – she would have feared the worst. Would have looked at her reflection in the mirror and seen Jeanette's face staring out at her.

Not now.

Meredith couldn't account for it, but everything had changed. Her mind felt clear. She was fine. She wasn't frightened, she wasn't going crazy. The sightings, the visitations were a sequence, like a piece of music. Beneath the bridge in Rennes-les-Bains – water. On the Sougraigne road – earth. Here in the hotel – particularly in this specific room, where Léonie's presence was strongest – air.

Swords, the suit of air, represented intelligence and intellect. Cups, the suit associated with water, the emotions. Pentacles, the suit of earth, of physical reality, of treasure. Of the four suits, only fire was missing. Wands, the suit of fire, energy and conflict.

The story is in the cards.

Or maybe the quartet was completed in the past and not the present. In the fire that had destroyed much of the Domaine de la Cade more than a hundred years ago?

Full of energy, Meredith went back to the replica Tarot deck, turning over each card and staring again at the images, willing them to give up their secrets. As she laid them out, one by one, she set her thoughts free. She thought of how the Visigoths buried their kings and noblemen, with their treasure, in hidden graves rather than graveyards. Secret chambers below the river, diverting its course for long enough to excavate the site and prepare the burial chamber.

If the original deck had survived the fire, hidden safe within the grounds of the Domaine de la Cade, then where more secure than an ancient Visigoth burial site? The sepulchre itself, according to Baillard's book, dated back to that same period. If there were a river in the grounds, it would be the perfect hiding place. In plain view, yet totally inaccessible.

Outside, finally, sunlight split through the clouds.

Meredith felt dizzy through lack of sleep, but she was buzzing with adrenaline. She glanced at the clock. Hal had said Dr O'Donnell was coming at ten, but that was still an hour away.

Plenty of time for what she had in mind.

Hal was standing in his bedroom in the staff quarters thinking of Meredith.

After soothing her nightmare, he'd found himself wide awake. Not wanting to disturb her by turning on the light, in the end he'd decided to slip away, back to his own room, to go over his notes before the meeting with Shelagh O'Donnell. He wanted to be prepared.

He glanced at his watch. Nine o'clock. Still an hour to wait before he saw Meredith again.

His windows, on the top floor, looked out to the south and to the east, giving him an uninterrupted view over the lawns and the lake at the back, the kitchen and service areas to the side. He watched one of the porters throw a black refuse bag into the bin. Another was standing, his arms crossed to keep warm, smoking a cigarette. His breath puffed white clouds into the clear morning air.

Hal was too nervous to settle. He knew he shouldn't get his hopes up that Dr O'Donnell was going to turn out to have all the answers, but he couldn't help himself. At the very least, she ought to be able to give him some information about the night his dad died. She might remember something that would force the police to treat it as a suspicious death rather than a traffic accident.

His thoughts strayed back to Meredith again. He smiled. Maybe, when it was all over, she wouldn't mind if he went to visit her in the States. He brought himself up short. It was ridiculous to be thinking along such lines after only a couple of days, but he knew. He hadn't felt so strongly about anyone for a long time. Ever.

And what was to stop him? No job, an empty flat in London. He might as well be in America as anywhere. He could do whatever the hell he liked. He'd have money. He knew his uncle would buy him out.

Hal stood at his high window, watching the life of the hotel go on silently below. The phone on his bedside table rang. It was Eloise in reception, telling him his guest had arrived.

'She's nearly an hour early.'

'Shall I ask her to wait?' Eloise asked.

Hal hesitated. 'No, it's fine. I'll be right down.'

He took his jacket from the back of the chair, then rushed down two flights of narrow service stairs. At the bottom, he paused to slip his arms into his jacket and to make a call from the staff phone.

CHAPTER 84

Meredith was dressed to go out when her cell rang.

'Hi, you,' she said, experiencing a kick of pleasure at the sound of Hal's voice.

'Meredith,' he said. 'She's here.'

For a second, she thought he meant Léonie.

'Who's here?' she said, her thoughts short-circuiting for a moment.

'Dr O'Donnell. I'm in reception now. Can you come down and join us?' She heard the smile in his voice. 'If that's OK?'

Meredith realised that her expedition to the lake would have to wait a little while longer.

'It's OK,' she said. 'I'll be there as soon as I can.'

She peeled off her extra layers, replaced Hal's sweater with a red crew-neck of her own, then let herself out of her room. As she walked along the landing, her heart gave a little leap at the sight of Hal below. He was talking with a tall, dark-haired woman, who she recognised. Meredith frowned, then she remembered. The place des Deux Rennes the night she arrived, the woman leaning against the wall, smoking.

Hal's face lit up as she approached.

'Hi,' she said, giving him a quick kiss on the cheek, then offering her hand to Dr O'Donnell. 'I'm Meredith. We exchanged a couple of words the night of the funeral,' Meredith said. 'Outside the pizzeria in the square?'

Dr O'Donnell's face lightened. 'That's right, I thought I knew you.'

'I'll get us coffee brought to the bar,' Hal said. 'It will be quiet there.'

Meredith and Dr O'Donnell followed him through, Meredith asking the older woman general questions to break the ice. How long she'd lived in Rennes-les-Bains, what her connection with the area was, what she did for a living. Usual sort of stuff.

Shelagh O'Donnell answered easily enough, but there was a nervous tension behind everything she said. She was very thin. Her eyes were constantly in motion and she repeatedly rubbed her fingertips against her thumb. Meredith placed her at not more than early thirties, but she had the lined skin of someone older. She could see why the police might not have taken her late-night observations seriously.

They sat at the same table in the corner that they had occupied the previous evening with Hal's uncle. The atmosphere was very different in the daytime. Wine and cocktails had given way to beeswax polish and fresh flowers. A stack of boxes was waiting on the bar to be unpacked.

There was a pause while Hal poured the coffee. Dr O'Donnell took hers black. As she stirred in her sugar, Meredith noticed the red scars on her wrists that she'd spotted the first time round and wondered what had happened.

'Before we start,' Hal said, 'I want to thank you for agreeing to see us, Dr O'Donnell.'

Meredith was pleased he sounded calm and rational.

She nodded. 'I knew your father. He was a lovely man. But I really don't have anything to tell you.'

Hal smiled. 'I understand, and I know you've been through all this, but if you could just bear with me.'

'I'll do my best,' she replied, looking doubtful.

'I appreciate the accident was more than a month ago, but there are things about the investigation I'm not happy with. I was hoping you might be able to tell me a little about the actual night. The police said you thought you had heard something?'

Shelagh darted her eyes to Meredith, then to Hal, then away again. 'They're still saying Seymour went off the road because he was drunk?'

'That's what I find hard to accept.'

Shelagh picked nervously at a thread on her pants.

'How did you meet Hal's father?' Meredith asked, hoping to give her a bit of confidence.

Hal was listening intently.

'That night in the square, you asked me what *bien-aimé* meant.'

'That's right.'

'Well, Seymour was just that. Someone everyone liked. Everyone admired him, too, even if they didn't really know him. He was always polite, courteous to waiters, shop-keepers, treated everybody with respect, unlike ...' She broke off. Meredith and Hal exchanged a look, guessing she was comparing Seymour to Julian Lawrence. 'He wasn't here much, of course,' she continued quickly, 'but I got to know him when ...'

Now she was twisting a button on her jacket.

'Yes?' encouraged Meredith. 'You got to know him when ...?'

Shelagh took a deep breath. 'I went through a difficult time in my life a couple of years back. I was working on an archaeological dig not far from here, in the Sabarthès mountains, and got drawn into something. Made some bad decisions.' She paused. 'Since then, things have been hard. My health's not good, so I can only manage a few hours a week, doing a little valuation work at the *ateliers* in Couiza.' She sighed. 'I came to Rennes-les-Bains to live about eighteen months ago now. I have a friend, Alice, who lives in a village not far from here, Los Seres, with her husband and daughter, so it was a logical place to come.'

Meredith recognised the name. 'Los Seres is where the author Audric S. Baillard came from, right?'

Hal raised his eyebrows.

'I was reading a book of his earlier. One of your dad's *vide-grenier* bargains.'

Hal smiled, pleased she'd remembered.

Shelagh's expression darkened. 'That's him. Alice knew him well. I met him too.'

Meredith could see from the look on Hal's face that the conversation had triggered another thought, but he didn't say anything.

'The point is, I had been having problems. Drinking too much.' Shelagh turned to Hal. 'I met your dad in a bar in Couiza. I was tired, I'd probably had one too many. We got talking. He was kind, insisted he drive me back to Rennes-les-Bains. Nothing dodgy about it. Next morning, he turned up and took me back to Couiza to pick up my car.' She paused. 'Never mentioned it again, but after that, he always dropped in when he was over here from England.'

Hal nodded. 'So you don't believe he would have got behind the wheel if he was in no state to drive?'

Shelagh shrugged. 'I can't say for certain, but no, I just can't see it.'

Meredith still thought they were both a little naive. Plenty of people said one thing and did another, but Shelagh's evident admiration and respect for Hal's father impressed her all the same.

'The police told Hal that you'd thought you heard the accident but didn't realise what it was until the next morning.'

Shelagh raised her coffee cup to her mouth with an unsteady hand, took a couple of sips, then put it back in the saucer with a rattle.

'To be honest, I don't know what I heard. If it was connected at all.'

'Go on.'

'But definitely something – not the usual screech of brakes or tyres when people take the bend too fast, but just a kind of rumbling, I guess.'

'What time was this?'

'About one o'clock or thereabouts. I was still up, listening to music. I got up and looked out of the window, but I couldn't see anything. It was completely dark, completely quiet. I just assumed a car had gone past. It was only in the morning when I saw the police and ambulance down at the river that I wondered.'

Hal looked disappointed, but Meredith leaned forward.

'Wait up,' she said, 'let me get this straight. You're saying you looked out and there were no headlights. Right?'

Shelagh nodded.

'And you told the police this?'

'I'm not sure if I did. Does it matter?'

'Think about it,' Meredith said quickly. 'Even if your father was way over the limit, Hal – I'm not saying he was – would he really be driving with no lights?'

Hal shook his head. 'No, but if the car went over the bridge into the water, they could have been smashed.'

'Also, the police told you Shelagh heard a screech of brakes, et cetera, right?'

He nodded.

'Except Shelagh's just told us that's precisely what she didn't hear.'

'I still don't—'

Meredith marked the points out on her fingers. 'First, why is the police report inaccurate? Second – and, I admit, this is speculation – if your father did lose control on the bend and went over, surely there would have been a) more noise and b) something to see. I can't believe all the lights would have blown.'

Hal's expression started to change. 'Are you suggesting the car might have been rolled over the edge? Rather than driven?'

'It's an explanation,' Meredith said.

They caught one another's eye, their roles reversed. Hal doubtful, Meredith building a case.

'There is something else,' Shelagh said. They both turned to her, for a moment almost having forgotten she was there. 'When I turned in, maybe a quarter of an hour later, I heard another car on the road. Because of earlier, it made me look out.'

'And?' said Hal.

'It was a blue Peugeot, heading south in the direction of Sougraigne. About one-thirty. It only occurred to me the following morning that if they'd come through the town so soon after the accident, the driver couldn't have failed to see Seymour's car in the river. Why didn't they notify the police then?'

Meredith and Hal looked at one another, thinking of the car parked round the back in the staff lot.

'How could you be sure it was a blue Peugeot?' Hal asked, keeping his voice level. 'You said it was dark.'

Shelagh flushed. 'It's the exact same type and model as my car. Everyone's got one round here,' she said defensively. 'Besides, there's a street lamp outside my bedroom window.'

'What did the police say when you told them?'

'They didn't seem to think it was important.' She glanced at the door, then stood up. 'I'm sorry, I've got to make a move.'

Meredith and Hal did the same.

'Look,' he said, 'I know this is an imposition, but is there any way I could persuade you to come to the police station in Couiza with me? Tell them what you've just told us.'

'I don't know,' she said. 'I've already made a statement.'

'I know, but if we went together . . .' he persisted. 'I've seen the accident report and most of what you've told me isn't in the file.' He pushed his fingers through his mop of hair. 'I just want to get to the bottom of it. For my dad's sake.'

From the haunted expression on her face, Meredith could see Shelagh was finding it difficult. She clearly wanted nothing to do with the police. But her affection for Hal's father won out. She nodded.

Hal sighed with relief. 'Thank you,' he said. 'Thank you so much. I'll pick you up at, say, twelve. Is that convenient?'

Shelagh nodded again. 'I have a couple of errands to run this morning – it's why I was early coming up here – but I'll be home by eleven.'

'Right you are. And home is?'

Shelagh gave Hal her address. They all shook hands – a little awkward in the circumstances – then made their way back to the lobby. Meredith headed back to her room, leaving Hal to walk Dr O'Donnell to her car.

Neither of them heard the sound of another door – the door separating the bar from the offices at the back – click shut.

CHAPTER 85

Julian Lawrence was breathing fast, his blood pounding in his temples. He rummaged in his jacket pocket for his cigarettes and lighter. His hand was shaking so badly it took several attempts to light it.

The police commissaire had said someone had come forward – an English woman called Shelagh O'Donnell – but that she hadn't seen anything. The name had rung a bell, but Julian had let it go. They'd said she was a drinker and since the police didn't seem to take her seriously, he hadn't either.

When she'd turned up at the hotel this morning, even then he hadn't put two and two together. The irony was that he'd only slipped into the office at the back of the bar to listen to the conversation between her, Hal and Meredith Martin because he'd recognised O'Donnell from one of the antique dealerships in Couiza and assumed Ms Martin had invited her here to discuss the Bousquet Tarot.

Having listened in, he realised why O'Donnell's name was familiar. In July 2005, there'd been an incident at an archaeological dig site in the Sabarthès mountains. Julian couldn't remember the exact details, but several people had been killed, including a well-known local author whose name escaped him. None of that mattered.

What did matter was that she had seen his car. Julian was sure it would be impossible to prove it was his – as O'Donnell had said, everyone around here had one – but it might be just enough to tip the balance into Hal persuading the police to look again.

He thought it unlikely that O'Donnell had associated the Peugeot with the Domaine de la Cade, otherwise she would hardly have come up here this morning. But he couldn't risk her making the connection.

Julian looked at the time. He'd had another call this morning about the money he owed. Nothing threatened, but the undercurrent was clear. He didn't have time to deal with O'Donnell, but, yet again, his hand was being forced, just as it had been with his brother.

He glanced up at the painting on the wall above his desk: the old Tarot symbol, offering infinite possibilities, while he felt increasingly trapped.

On the shelf below it were objects he had found during his excavations of the estate. He had been slow to accept that the ruined sepulchre was just that: a few old stones, nothing else. But he had turned up one or two items. An expensive, although damaged, timepiece bearing the initials A.V., and a silver locket with two miniatures inside, both taken from graves he'd discovered by the lake.

This was what he cared about: the past. Finding the cards. Not sorting out the problems of the present.

Julian went to the tantalus on the sideboard and poured himself a whisky to steady his nerves. He drained it down in one, then glanced again at the clock.

Ten-fifteen.

He took his jacket from the back of the door, put a mint in his mouth, grabbed his car keys and headed out.

Julian left the car unlocked in the parking area on the outskirts of Rennes-les-Bains, then walked quickly down towards the small side street where his contact in the police had confirmed O'Donnell lived.

He loosened the tie at his neck. There were patches of sweat under his arms. He couldn't believe how complicated everything had become. All he had wanted was to find the cards, then sell the cards. After that, everything else would fall into place. No more debt, no more bargains he couldn't keep.

Julian hadn't thought about what he was going to say to O'Donnell, only that he could not allow her to go with Hal to the commissariat.

When he turned the corner, he saw her sitting cross-legged on the low wall that separated the terrace of her property from the deserted public footpath that led along the river. She was smoking and talking on a mobile phone.

What was she saying?

Julian stopped. Though he could hear her voice, the one-sided conversation was muffled by the pounding of the blood in his head.

He stepped closer. Dr O'Donnell leaned forward and with sharp stabbing movements extinguished a cigarette in a silver ashtray. Certain words leapt out at him.

'I've got to see about the car.'

Julian put his hand out to steady himself. If she'd worked it out already, there was no way she'd listen to reason. Just like his brother. He looked round, no longer thinking straight. There was a stick lying on the ground, half sticking out of the hedge. He picked it up. She was still talking, on and on, telling lies. Why wouldn't she stop talking?

Julian lifted the stick and brought it down upon her head.

Shelagh O'Donnell cried out in shock, so he hit her again to stop her making any noise. She fell forward onto the terrace.

Julian flung the weapon away from him in disbelief at what he'd done. For a moment, he stood dead still. Then, horrified, he kicked the stick back into the hedge and headed back to his car before anyone saw him.

CHAPTER 86

Having told Hal she intended to look for the Tarot deck, Meredith had left him trying to fix the meeting at the police commissariat in Couiza.

Dressed warmly in her scruffiest clothes for her expedition, she'd stopped at the front desk to ask the nice receptionist if she knew where she might borrow a shovel. Eloise had made no reaction to this odd request, simply suggesting that the gardener should be working in the grounds and might be able to help.

'Thank you. I'll ask him,' Meredith had said, before going out through the glass doors onto the terrace. The early-morning mist had almost burned away, although the grass was glistening with a silver dew.

There was already a heady smell of Hallowe'en bonfires in the air. Meredith breathed it in, the smell of fall taking her back to her childhood. She and Mary carving faces in pumpkins for lanterns, Bill helping to get her trick-or-treat costume ready. She usually went out as a ghost, in a white bed sheet with two holes cut for the eyes and a scary mouth painted on in black marker.

As she ran lightly down the steps to the gravel path, she wondered what Mary and Bill were doing right now. Then she laughed. It would be a quarter after five in the morning back home. Everyone would still be asleep. But she made a mental note to call later to wish them happy Hallowe'en.

The gardener was nowhere to be seen, but his barrow was there. She hesitated, then took the small trowel lying on top of the leaves, tucked it in her pocket and struck out across the lawns towards the lake. She'd bring it back as soon as she could.

Somehow, Meredith felt she was following in the footsteps of the figure she'd seen on the lawns earlier.

Seen? Imagined?

She found herself glancing back at the façade of the hotel, at one point stopping to figure out which was her window, and whether she could possibly have seen what she thought she had from such a long way off.

As she completed the path around the left-hand side of the lake, the ground began to rise. She climbed up a grassy slope to a small promontory that overlooked the water, straight across to the hotel. She was convinced this was precisely where she had seen the figure standing earlier.

Imagined.

There was a curved stone bench in the shape of a crescent moon. Meredith wiped it with her gloves, then sat down. As always, by deep water, thoughts of Jeanette rushed into her mind, and the way she had chosen to end her life. Walking into Lake Michigan with her pockets weighted down with stones. Like Virginia Woolf, Meredith had learned years later at high school, although she doubted her mother had had the English writer in her mind.

But as Meredith sat looking out over the lake, she felt peaceful. Though she couldn't help but think of Jeanette, her thoughts weren't accompanied by the usual feelings of guilt. No thumping heart, no rush of shame, no regret. This was a place of reflection, to be calm and private. The rattling of the crows in the trees, the higher-pitched twitterings of sparrows in the thick, high box hedge at her back; isolated from the house by the expanse of water yet still in plain view.

She lingered a while longer. Two hours earlier, she'd been desperate to get out and start looking for the ruins of the sepulchre. Now, she felt she had plenty of time. Given how nervous Shelagh O'Donnell had been, she figured Hal would have his hands full. She didn't expect him back before one.

She pulled out her cell and checked she had a signal. He could call if he needed to get in touch with her.

Careful on the wet grass, Meredith made her way back down to the level ground. In one direction, the path led around the lake and back towards the house. In the other, to the left, a more overgrown track went into the beech woods.

Meredith took the left-hand path and, within minutes, she was deep into the trees, winding through the dappled sunlight. The track led to a criss-cross of interconnecting paths, all pretty similar. Some led uphill, others seemed to slope down towards the valley. Her goal was to find the ruins of the Visigoth sepulchre, then, from there, work out if there was a place nearby where the cards might have been hidden. Anything too obvious and they would have been found years ago.

Meredith set off down a path that led to a small clearing. After a few minutes, the hillside dipped away sharply. The ground beneath her feet changed. She braced her legs, taking it slowly on the slippery stones and gravel, dislodging pine cones and fallen branches, until finally she found herself standing on some kind of natural platform, almost like a bridge. Underneath it, intersecting it at right angles, was a strip of brown earth leading down through the green woodland all around it.

In the distance, through a break in the trees, Meredith could pick out on the far hill a cluster of stone megaliths, grey among the wooded green, possibly the same ones Hal had pointed out to her on their way to Rennes-le-Château.

The hairs on the back of her neck stood on end.

She realised that, from here, pretty much all the natural landmarks Hal had mentioned – the fauteuil du Diable, the *bénitier*, the étang du Diable – were visible. More than that, from this one spot, all the locations used as backdrops to the cards were also evident.

The sepulchre dated back to Visigoth times. So it stood to reason there might be other Visigoth burial sites within the grounds. Meredith looked around. And this, to her inexpert eye at least, looked much like a dry riverbed.

Trying to keep her excitement in check, she looked around for a way down. There wasn't an obvious one. She hesitated, crouched and manoeuvred herself round, then lowered herself over the edge. She hung suspended in the air on her elbows, then let herself go, dropping for a fraction of a heart-stopping second, until her feet found the ground.

It looked like the bed of a winterbourne at the end of a dry summer, but slick with light fall drizzle. Taking care not to slip on wet topsoil, Meredith cast her eyes about her.

At first, there seemed no break in the undergrowth. Then, a little further, just before the track took another dip like a helter-skelter at a fairground, Meredith noticed a shallow depression. She moved closer until she could make out a flat grey stone, peeking out from beneath the roots of a spreading juniper bush, with its scratchy needle-like leaves and green and purple fruit. The depression wasn't big enough to be a grave itself, but the stone didn't look like it had been put there by chance. Meredith got out her phone and took a couple of photos, then reached in and pulled at the knotted undergrowth. The thin branches were strong and wiry, but she managed to pull them far enough apart to see into the dank green space around the roots.

She felt a spark of adrenaline. There was a ring of stones, eight in all, and she realised the pattern echoed the shape of the crown of stars on the image of La Force. And she could see the landscape right here was especially reminiscent in colour and tone of that depicted on the card.

With growing anticipation, Meredith thrust her hands into the foliage, feeling the green slime and mud seeping through the tips of her cheap woollen gloves, and dragged clear the biggest of the stones. She wiped the surface clean, then gave a sigh of satisfaction. Painted in black tar or paint was a five-pointed star set within a circle.

The symbol for the suit of pentacles. The treasure suit.

She took a couple more photos, put that stone to one side, then pulled the stolen trowel from her pocket and started to dig, scraping against stones and shards of unfired clay tiles until she had worked one of the larger pieces free. It looked like a roof tile, although she wondered how such a thing was buried out here, so far from the house.

Then the metal head of the trowel hit something substantial. Not wanting to damage anything, Meredith put it to one side and finished the job by hand, burrowing at the mud and worms and black beetles, pulling off her gloves and letting her fingers be her eyes.

Finally, she felt a piece of heavy material, a waxed cloth. She pushed her head under the leaves to look and peeled the corners back to reveal the beautiful lacquered lid of a small chest, with a mother-of-pearl inlay. It looked like a jewellery case or a lady's workbox, pretty and clearly expensive. On the top were two initials in dull, corroded brass: L.V.

Meredith caught her breath. Léonie Vernier? Could it be?

She went to open the lid, then hesitated. This is what she'd come to find, but she wasn't sure now that she'd expected to be successful. What if the cards were inside? What would it mean? Did she even want to see them?

The story is in the cards.

She wiped her palms on her jeans, then slowly she opened the lid. The box was full of spools of thread, ribbons and thimbles. A sewing box – was that all she'd found? The inside of the padded lid was studded with needles and pins. But with fingers raw from the cold and the digging, Meredith removed some of the cotton reels, burrowing through felt and cloth, and there they were.

The top card – with the same green back, the delicate patterns of tree branches threaded through in gold and silver, although the colour was chalkier, clearly painted by hand with a brush rather than made by a machine. She ran her fingers over the surface. A different texture: rough, not smooth. More like parchment than the modern plastic-coated reproduction deck.

Meredith took a deep breath, summoning the courage to turn the top card over.

Her own face stared up at her. Card XI. La Justice.

As she gazed at the hand-painted image, once more she was aware of whispering inside her head. Not like the voices that had hounded her mother, but gentle and soft; the voice she had heard in her dream, carried on the air, slipping between the branches and trunks of the fall trees.

Here, in this place, time moves away towards eternity.

In a rush, she felt the solitude press down upon her. The sounds of the wood that had been so gentle, so reassuring, now seemed oppressive, threatening. She pulled her phone from her pocket, checked the time. Maybe she should give Hal a call. The desire to hear another human voice – his voice – stabbed at her. She thought better of it. He wouldn't want to be disturbed in the middle of his meeting with the police, it wasn't fair. She hesitated, then texted him telling him where she was.

Feeling light-headed, Meredith stood up. The most logical move now would be to take the cards and go back to the house. Study them properly in the comfort of her own room, with all her notes, access to the internet, the reproduction deck to hand to compare them with.

But now she could hear Léonie's voice again. In the turning of a moment, the whole world seemed to have shrunk to this one place. The smell of the soil in her nostrils, the grit and soil under her nails, the dampness that seeped from the earth and into her bones.

Except this is not the place.

Something was calling her on deeper into the woods. The wind was getting louder, more forceful, carrying something more than just the noises of the forest. Music heard but not heard. She could pick out a faint melody in the rustling of the fallen leaves, the tapping of the bare branches of the beech trees a little further off.

Single notes, a mournful melody in a minor key, and always the words in her head leading her on to the ruined sepulchre.

Aïci lo tems s'en, va res l'eternitat.

PART XI

The Sepulchre
November 1891–October 1897

CHAPTER 87

Anatole was buried in the grounds of the Domaine de la Cade. The spot chosen was the little promontory overlooking the valley at the far side of the lake, in the green shade, close by the crescent stone bench where Isolde often sat.

Abbé Saunière officiated at the meagre ceremony. Léonie, Audric Baillard, Maître Fromilhague and Madame Bousquet were the only mourners.

Isolde remained under constant watch in her chamber, unaware even that the funeral was taking place. Locked within her silent and suspended world, she did not know how fast or how slowly time was passing, if indeed time had ceased or if all experience was contained in the chime of a single minute. Her existence had shrunk to the four walls of her head. She knew light and dark, that sometimes the fever burned in her and sometimes the cold, but also that she was trapped somewhere between two worlds.

The same group paid their respects a day later to Dr Gabignaud in the graveyard of the parish church in Rennes-les-Bains, this time the congregation swelled by the people of the town who had known and admired the young man. Dr Courrent gave the address, praising Gabignaud's hard work, his passion, his sense of duty. But Léonie felt the hostility of the congregation, the silent message that it was again the Domaine de la Cade that had brought horror to their town. She did not blame them. She felt her guilt keenly and believed she deserved their approbation.

In the bare beech woods, snow fell early, blanketing the lawns and the park in white. The lake froze and lay a mirror of ice beneath the lowering clouds. Numb with grief and the responsibilities thrust suddenly on her young shoulders, Léonie remained in the Domaine de la Cade and rarely ventured out.

The household fell into a joyless routine, day after endless day the same. A new medical recruit, Gabignaud's replacement as Dr Courrent's assistant, came daily from the town to monitor Isolde's progress.

'Madame Vernier's pulse is fast tonight,' he said one evening in mid-November, unhooking his stethoscope from his neck. 'The severity of grief, the strain upon her due to her condition, well, I fear for the full restoration of her faculties the longer this state persists.'

'And the child?' Léonie asked. It seemed impossible that the baby could thrive while his mother declined.

'The baby is strong,' the doctor said. 'I don't know how, but it has the will to live. We'll see.'

The weather deepened in December. Blustery winds drove in from the north, bringing with them hail and ice that assaulted the roof and windows of the house in waves.

The Aude valley was frozen in misery. Those without shelter, if fortunate, were taken in by their neighbours. Oxen starved in the fields, their hooves trapped and rotting in the mud and ice. The rivers froze. The tracks were impassable. There was no food, for man nor beast. The tinkling bell of the sacristan rang out over the fields as Christ was carried through the countryside to grace the lips of another dying sinner, over paths concealed and made treacherous beneath snow. It seemed that all living things would, one by one, simply cease to exist. No light, no warmth – like candles blown out.

In the parish church of Rennes-les-Bains, Curé Boudet preached masses for the dead and the bell tolled out its mournful passing note. In Coustaussa, Curé Gélis opened his doors and offered the cold flagstones of the presbytery floor to the homeless. In Rennes-le-Château, Abbé Saunière preached of the evil stalking the countryside and urged his congregation to seek salvation in the arms of the one true church.

At the Domaine de la Cade, the staff, although shaken by what had taken place and their part in the matter, remained steadfast. In Isolde's continuing indisposition, they accepted Léonie as mistress of the house. But Marieta was alarmed as sorrow stole from Léonie her appetite and rest, and she grew thin and pale. Her eyes lost their shine. But her courage held. She had made a promise to Anatole to protect Isolde and their child and was determined not to let him down.

Victor Constant was wanted for the murder of Marguerite Vernier in Paris, the murder of Anatole Vernier in Rennes-les-Bains and the attempted murder of Isolde Vernier, formerly Lascombe. There was also a prosecution pending arising out of the attack on the prostitute in Carcassonne. It was suggested – and accepted without further investigation – that Dr Gabignaud, Charles Denarnaud and a third man – had been killed on Constant's orders, even if it had not been his finger on the trigger.

The town disapproved of the news that Anatole and Isolde had married in secret, more at the haste of it than because he was the nephew of her first husband. But given the fact that they had been legally husband and wife, and there was to be a child, it seemed possible the situation at the Domaine de la Cade would come to be, if not accepted, at least tolerated in time.

The log pile against the scullery wall diminished. Isolde showed little sign of recovering her mental faculties, although the baby grew and flourished inside her. Léonie sat beside her, talking about Anatole, about their childhood, about the changes on the estate. Day and night, in her chamber on the first floor of the Domaine de la Cade, a good fire crackled and spat in the hearth. The hours of sunlight were short, barely warming the sky before dark fell over the land once again.

Enslaved by grief, Isolde stood yet at a crossroads between the world from which she had taken temporary leave and the undiscovered country beyond. The voices that were always with her whispered how, if she fared forward, she would find Anatole waiting for her. There was nothing to fear. In moments of what she believed were grace, she longed to die and be with him. But then she would sense the child move and know the spirit of his son wishing to be born was too strong.

On a dull and soundless December afternoon, with nothing to mark it from those days that had come before or those that were to follow, Isolde felt sensation return to her limbs. At first, it was her fingers. So subtle as to be almost mistaken for something else. An automatic response, not one of purpose. A tingling at the tips and beneath her almond-shaped nails. Then, a twitching of her feet beneath the covers. Then, a pricking on the skin at the base of her neck.

She moved her hand and the hand obeyed.

Isolde heard a noise. Not, this time, the ceaseless whispering that was always with her, but the normal, domestic sound of a chair leg against the floor. For the first time in months, it was not distorted or amplified or subdued by time or light, but knocking on her consciousness without refraction.

She sensed someone leaning over her, the warmth of breath on her face.

'Madama?'

Isolde allowed her eyes to flutter open. She heard the intake of breath, then feet running and a door flung open, shouting in the passageway, coils of sound winding up from the hall below, growing in intensity, growing in certainty.

'*Madomaisèla Léonie! Madama s'éveille!*'

Isolde blinked at the brightness. More noise, then the touch of cold fingers taking her hand. Slowly, she turned her head to one side and saw her niece's thoughtful young face looking down at her.

'Léonie?'

She felt her fingers being squeezed. 'I am here.'

'Léonie . . .' she whispered. 'Yes.'

Léonie's voice faltered. 'Anatole, he . . .'

Isolde took her hand. 'I know,' she said quietly.

Isolde's convalescence was slow. For the sake of her child, she walked, and ate, and slept, but though she grew stronger, the light had gone from her eyes. The loss of Anatole haddetached her from herself. Everything she thought and saw, felt and smelt, touched chords of painful remembrance.

Most evenings, she sat with Léonie in the drawing room talking of Anatole, her white fingers resting on her growing stomach. Léonie would listen while Isolde recited the whole story of their love affair, from the instant of their first meeting to the hoax at the Cimetière de Montmartre, and the short-lived joy of their wedding in Carcassonne on the eve of the great storm. The same memories, over and over again.

But however many times Isolde told the story, the ending remained the same. A once-upon-a-time cheated of its happy ever after.

*

The winter passed. The snow stopped falling, although a crisp frost still covered the morning in sharp whiteness in February.

At the Domaine de la Cade, Léonie and Isolde remained locked together in their sorrow, bereaved, watching the shadows on the lawns. They had few visitors, save for Audric Baillard and Madame Bousquet, who proved to be both a generous friend and a kind neighbour.

From time to time, Monsieur Baillard brought news of the police hunt for Victor Constant. He had disappeared from the Hôtel de la Reine in Rennes-les-Bains on the night of the 31st October and had not been seen since.

The police had enquired for him in the various health spas and asylums specialising in treating men with his condition, but met with no luck. Attempts were made by the state to seize his considerable assets. There was a price on his head. Even so, there were no sightings, no rumours.

On the 25th March, by unhappy coincidence the anniversary of Isolde's false burial in the Cimetière de Montmartre, Léonie received an official letter from Inspector Thouron. He informed her that since they now believed Constant had fled the country, perhaps over the border into Andorra or Spain, they were scaling down the manhunt. He reassured her that the fugitive would be arrested and guillotined should he ever return to France and hoped, therefore, that Madame and Mademoiselle Vernier would feel no alarm that Constant would concern them further.

At the tail end of March, when inclement conditions had kept them inside for some days, Léonie found herself taking up her pen to write to Anatole's friend and former neighbour, Achille Debussy, now calling himself Claude, though she could not bring herself to use it. Léonie could only assume, as his reputation had risen, that he thought it would sound more distinguished in the concert halls.

Once the police had finished with it, their apartment had been cleaned and cleared. Without Du Pont's largesse, they could no longer afford the rent. Besides, Léonie couldn't contemplate the thought of ever returning to the rue de Berlin, with all its memories of their mother and her brother, of a childhood she now realised Marguerite had worked so hard to provide. It was a source of great regret that Léonie had, so often, been impatient with her mother. She understood more now, but it was too late.

But, at the same time, she found herself missing Paris itself, for the life she had thought she would have. The correspondence both filled an absence in her confined life and, more important, helped keep a link with Anatole. Achille told her what was happening in the streets and boulevards they had once called home, gossip about who was in conflict with whom, all the petty rivalries at the Académie, the authors in favour or disgraced, the artists fighting, the composers snubbed, the scandals and the affairs.

Léonie did not want to care for a world that was now so distant, so closed to her, but it reminded her of conversations with Anatole. Sometimes, in the old days, when he returned home after a night out with Achille at Le Chat Noir, he would come into her room, throw himself into the old armchair at the foot of her bed, and she, with her covers drawn up to her chin, would listen to his stories. Debussy wrote mostly of himself, covering page after page with his spidery writing. Léonie did not mind. It took her thoughts away from her misery. She smiled when he wrote of his Sunday-morning visits to the church of Saint-Gervais to listen to the Gregorian chant with his atheistic friends, sitting with their defiant backs to the altar, thereby offending both the congregation and the officiating priest.

Léonie could not contemplate leaving Isolde. In any case, Inspector Thouron had suggested she did not return to Paris, even for her mother's funeral, in case Constant tried to find her. It was a quiet affair at the Cimetière de Passy in the 16th *arrondissement*. The tomb had been paid for by Du Pont as a last act of generosity. In truth, although Léonie had felt guilty for failing her mother, she was grateful not to have to go. But, at her request, Achille and Gaby Dupont made regular visits to the graveyard to lay flowers on Marguerite's grave. It was close to that of the painter Édouard Manet, Achille wrote, a peaceful and shaded spot. Léonie thought her mother would be content to lie among such company.

The weather changed as April came in, arriving like a general upon the battlefield. Aggressive, loud, bellicose. Squalls of scudding clouds skated across the peaks of the mountains. The days grew a little longer, the mornings a little lighter. Marieta got out her needles and threads. She put generous pleats into Isolde's *chemises* and let out the panels on her skirts to accommodate her changing shape.

Purple, white and pink valley flowers pushed tentative shoots through the crusted rim of the earth, raising their faces to the light. The smatterings of colour, like dabs of paint dripped from a brush, grew stronger, more frequent, vibrating in the green of the borders and the paths.

May tiptoed shyly in, hinting at the promise of longer days to come, of dappled sunlight on still water. Léonie ventured down into Rennes-les-Bains a little more often, to visit Monsieur Baillard or take afternoon tea with Madame Bousquet in the salon of the Hôtel de la Reine. Outside the modest town houses, canaries sang in cages now hung out of doors. The lemon and orange trees were in blossom, their sharp scents filling the streets. On every corner, early fresh fruits brought over the mountains from Spain were sold from wooden carts.

Soon, the Domaine de la Cade was glorious beneath an endless blue sky. The bright June sun struck the gleaming white peaks of the Pyrenees. Summer, at last, had come.

From Paris, Achille wrote that Maître Maeterlinck had granted permission to set his new drama, *Pelléas et Mélisande*, to music. He also sent a copy of Zola's *La Débâcle*, which was set during the summer of 1870, enclosing a personal note saying he knew it would have been of interest to Anatole, as it was to him, as sons of convicted Communards. Léonie struggled with the novel but appreciated the sentiment that had caused Achille to make her so thoughtful a gift.

She did not allow her thoughts to return to the Tarot cards. They were tied up with the terrible events of Hallowe'en. She packed away her incomplete set of drawings, too, leaving La Diable and La Tour unfinished. They were too painful a reminder of her brother and her mother. Nor did Léonie return to the glade ringed with the wild juniper. Its proximity to the clearing where the duel had taken place, where Anatole had died, was too much for her heart to bear.

Isolde's pains started early on the morning of Friday, 24th June, the feast day of Saint John the Baptist.

Monsieur Baillard, with his network of friends and comrades, secured the services of a *sage-femme* from his native village of Los Seres. Both she and the lying-in nurse arrived in good time for the birth.

By lunchtime, Isolde was considerably advanced. Léonie bathed her forehead with cold cloths and opened the windows to let into the chamber the fresh air and the scent of the juniper and honeysuckle from the gardens below. Marieta dabbed her lips with a sponge soaked in sweet white wine and honey.

By teatime, Isolde had been delivered of a boy, in good health and with an impressive pair of lungs.

Léonie had hoped that the birth would mark the beginning of Isolde's return to full health. That she would become less listless, less fragile, less separate from the world around her. Léonie – indeed, the whole household – expected that a child, Anatole's child, would bring with him the love and purpose Isolde so needed.

But a black shadow descended over Isolde some three days after the birth. She made enquiries as to her son's condition and welfare, but it was clear she was struggling to save herself from falling into the same stricken state that had afflicted her in the immediate aftermath of Anatole's murder. Her tiny son, so much the mirror of his father, served more to remind her of what she had lost than give her reason to continue.

The services of a wet nurse were employed.

As the summer progressed, Isolde showed no signs of improvement. She did her duty by her son when called upon to do so, but otherwise lived in a world of her own, persecuted endlessly by the voices in her head.

Léonie fell in love with her nephew without reservation or condition. Louis-Anatole was a sunny-natured baby, with Anatole's black hair and long lashes, framing startling grey eyes, inherited from his mother. In the delight of the child's company, Léonie sometimes forgot for hours at a time the tragedy that had overtaken them.

As the fearsomely hot July and August days marched on, from time to time Léonie would awake in the morning with a sense of hope, a lightness in her step. Her love and her determination to keep any harm from coming to Anatole's son helped her to recover her spirits.

CHAPTER 88

Autumn became winter, became another spring. There was still no word of Victor Constant and, without ever voicing the hope out loud, Léonie allowed herself to believe he was dead. Besides, her nephew and her duties on the estate occupied most of her time.

The August of 1893 was as hot and dry as the African deserts. The drought was followed by torrential inundations throughout the Languedoc, washing away sections of land on the plains, revealing long-hidden caves and *cachettes* beneath the mud.

Life at the Domaine de la Cade went on.

Debussy remained a regular correspondent. That December, he wrote with Christmas greetings and to tell Léonie that the Société Nationale was to present in concert a performance of *Prélude à l'après-midi d'un faune*, a new composition intended as the first of a suite of three pieces. As she read his naturalistic descriptions of the faun in his glade, Léonie was put in mind of the clearing within which she had, two years before, discovered the deck of cards. For the first time, she was tempted to retrace her steps to the spot and see if the Tarot deck was still there. But remembering what her uncle had unleashed, what he had written, and Monsieur Baillard's warnings of two years ago, she did not.

So rather than the boulevards of Paris, her world continued to be bounded by the beech woods to the east, the long driveway to the north, the lawns to the south. She was sustained by her few friendships, the loyalty of Pascal and Marieta, her duty to and affection for Isolde, but most of all by her love of her nephew.

Louis-Anatole was a great favourite in the town and the household. Nicknamed *pichon*, little one, he was mischievous, though always charming and full of curiosity, much like his aunt. As he grew older, he and Léonie walked the pathways and woods of the Domaine de la Cade. He was taken fishing by Pascal, who also taught him to swim in the lake. In the kitchen, Marieta would sometimes permit him to scrape the mixing bowl and lick the wooden spoon when she had been cooking – raspberry soufflé, chocolate puddings. As he balanced on the old three-legged stool set hard against the rim of the kitchen table, one of the maid's aprons reaching down to his ankles, Marieta would teach him to knead dough for bread.

When Léonie took him to visit Rennes-les-Bains, his favourite treat was to sit at the pavement café that Anatole had so loved. With his dark curls, white ruffed shirt and nut-brown velvet trousers drawn tight at the knee, he sat with his legs hanging down from the high wooden stool, drinking cherry syrup or freshly pressed apples, and eating chocolate creams.

On his third birthday, Madame Bousquet presented Louis-Anatole with a bamboo fishing rod. The following Christmas, Maître Fromilhague sent a box of tin soldiers to the house and presented the compliments of the season to Léonie.

He was a regular visitor, too, to the house of Audric Baillard, who told him stories of medieval times and the honour of the *chevaliers* who had defended the independence of the Midi against the northern invaders. Better than the pages of sooty history books, Monsieur Baillard's stories brought the past to life. Louis-Anatole's favourite was the siege of Carcassonne in 1209 and the brave men, women, even children little older than he who had fled to the hidden villages of the Haute Vallée.

When he was four years old, Audric Baillard gave him a replica of a medieval battle sword, its hilt engraved and carved with his initials. Léonie bought him a small pony, with white mane and tail and flash on its nose, acquired in Quillan, with the assistance of one of Pascal's many cousins. For the duration of that hot summer, Louis-Anatole was a knight-at-arms, fighting the French or victorious at the joust, knocking tin cans from a wooden fence set up by Pascal on the rear lawns.

From the drawing-room window, Léonie would watch and remember how, as a little girl, she had watched Anatole run and hide and climb trees in the Parc Monceau with much the same sense of envy at his freedom.

Louis-Anatole also showed a marked talent for music, the money wasted on keyboard lessons for Anatole in his youth paying dividends in his son. Léonie engaged a piano teacher from Limoux. Once a week, the professor would rumble up the long drive in the dog cart, with his white neckerchief and pinned stocks and untrimmed beard, and for two hours drill Louis-Anatole in five-finger exercises and scales. Each week, as he took his departure, he would press Léonie to make the boy practise with glasses of water balanced upon the backs of his hands. Léonie and Louis-Anatole would nod and, for a day or two following, he would attempt to do so. But then the water would spill, soaking Louis-Anatole's velvet breeches or staining the wide hems of Léonie's skirts, and they would laugh and play noisy duets instead.

When he was alone, often the boy would tiptoe to the piano and experiment. Léonie would stand on the landing at the top of the stairs, unobserved. His favourite key appeared to be A minor, and Léonie would think of the music she had stolen so long ago from the sepulchre, concealed still in the piano stool, and wonder if she should take it out for him. But, again, fearing the power of it and all it was connected to, she let things lie.

Isolde remained in a twilight world, drifting through the rooms and the passageways of the Domaine de la Cade like a wraith. She spoke little. She was kind, but distant, to her son and much loved by the servants. Only when she was alone with Léonie did something deeper seem to spark inside her. Then, for a fleeting second, grief and memory would blaze in her eyes, before the veil came down once more.

Some days were better than others, like the sun coming out from behind the cloud. But then the voices would start once more. Isolde would clasp her hands over her ears and weep and Marieta would gently lead her back to the privacy and half-light of her chamber until better times returned. The periods of peace grew shorter. The periods of torment grew more intense. Anatole was never far from her mind. For his part, Louis-Anatole accepted his mother as she was – he had never known her any different.

All in all, it was not the life Léonie had imagined for herself. She would have wished for love, for a chance to see more of the world, to be herself. But she loved her nephew and pitied Isolde and, determined to keep her word to Anatole, she did not waver in her duty.

The seasons passed. Each year followed much like the one before. Snow lay thick upon the tomb of Marguerite Vernier in Paris; the briars grew tangled around the more modest grave of Anatole overlooking the lake at the Domaine de la Cade.

Earth, wind, water and fire – the unchanging pattern of the natural world.

*

Their peaceful existence was not to last.

Between Christmas and the New Year of 1897, there was a succession of signs – omens, warnings even – that things were not right in the valley.

In Quillan, a chimney sweep's boy fell and broke his neck. In Espéraza, fire broke out in the hat factory, killing four of the Spanish female workers. In the *atelier* of the Bousquet family, an apprentice became trapped in the hot metal printing press and lost all four fingers on his right hand.

For Léonie, the general disquiet became specific when Monsieur Baillard came to give her the unwelcome news that he was obliged to quit Rennes-les-Bains. It was the time of local winter fairs – in Brenac on 19th January, Campagne-sur-Aude on the 20th and Belvianes on the 22nd – and his presence was expected. After that, he was obliged to make his way higher into the mountains. His eyes veiled with concern, he explained that there were obligations, older and more binding than his unofficial guardianship of Louis-Anatole, which he could delay no longer. He gave his word that he would return before the feast day of Saint Martin in November, when the rents were collected.

Léonie greatly regretted his decision, especially since he would be away for so long, but knew she had no right to ask him to stay. His sudden departure, and the rather vague reasons for it, reminded her of how little she really knew about her friend and protector. She did not even know for certain how old he was, although Louis-Anatole had declared that he must be at least seven hundred years old to have so many stories to tell.

Mere days after Audric Baillard's departure, scandal erupted in neighbouring Rennes-le-Château. The Abbé Saunière's restoration of his church was all but completed. But when the statuary ordered from a specialist supplier in Toulouse was delivered, and among them was a *bénitier* – a stoup for holy water – resting on the shoulders of a twisted demon, voices were raised in objection. Such a monstrous object, as other of the statues, was unsuitable for a house of worship. Letters of protest were sent to the *mairie* and to the Bishop, demanding that Saunière be brought to account. Demanding, too, that the priest no longer be permitted to dig in the graveyard.

Léonie had not known about the night-time excavations around the church, nor that Saunière was said to spend the hours between dusk and dawn walking the nearby mountainside, looking for treasure. She had always thought him devoted to his parish. Her unease came from the fact that certain of the statues were so precisely a match for those within the sepulchre. It was as if someone was guiding Abbé Saunière's hand and, at the same time, working to cause trouble against him. But with Audric Baillard absent, there was no one with whom she could discuss her fears.

The discontent spread down the mountain to the valley and Rennes-les-Bains. There again were whisperings that the troubles that had beset the town some years back had returned. There were rumours of secret tunnels running between Rennes-le-Château and Rennes-les-Bains, of Visigoth burial chambers. And, to Léonie's distress, allegations that the Domaine de la Cade was again the refuge of a wild beast started to gather force. Dogs, goats, even oxen were attacked, by wolves or mountain cats that appeared to be afraid neither of the traps nor the hunters' guns. It was an unnatural creature, or so the rumours spread.

Although Pascal and Marieta tried hard to keep the gossip from reaching Léonie's ears, some of the more malicious stories pierced her consciousness all the same.

As a cold and wet spring arrived, the rumours of supernatural occurrences at the Domaine de la Cade grew more frequent. Sightings of ghosts and demons, it was said, even of satanic rituals conducted under cover of night in the sepulchre. It was a return to the dark days of Jules

Lascombe's time as master of the house. The bitter and the jealous pointed to the events of Hallowe'en 1891 and claimed the ground was restless. Seeking retribution for past sins.

Old spells, ancient words in the traditional language, were scratched on rocks at the roadside to ward off the demon that now, as before, stalked the valley. Pentagrams were daubed in black tar on stones at the roadside. Votive offerings of flowers and ribbons were left at unmarked shrines.

Had Léonie not known that such a thing was impossible, she would have suspected the hand of Victor Constant in the rumours and gossip. She chastised herself for such thoughts.

Constant was dead. The police thought so. He had to be dead. Why would he have let them be for nearly six years, only to return now?

CHAPTER 89

CARCASSONNE

Throughout the summer, the stories about the Domaine de la Cade continued to circulate. Indeed, the atmosphere on the last occasion she had taken Louis-Anatole into Rennes-les-Bains had been so unpleasant that Léonie resolved not to visit for the foreseeable future. Silence or suspicious glances, where once there had been greetings and smiles.

As the heat intensified, Léonie felt in need of a break from her responsibilities, the confinement of the estate and the hostility of the town. And it would be good for Louis-Anatole. He needed to have wider horizons too.

As part of the celebrations for the anniversary of the storming of the Bastille, she discovered there was to be a display of fireworks in Carcassonne on the 14th July. Léonie had not set foot in the city since her ill-fated visit with Anatole and Isolde, but time had softened her memories and the thought of her nephew's delight gave her courage.

She was determined, too, to persuade Isolde to accompany them. Her nerves had been worse of late – insisting people were watching her from the far side of the lake, that there were faces under the water – and she saw smoke in the woods even when no fires were set. Perhaps, if she was away from the Domaine de la Cade, the bustle of ordinary life would help her to improve.

'It would do us all so much good to be away from here for a while,' Léonie pleaded, taking Isolde's hand. 'It would mean so much to me. And Louis-Anatole. Come with us, please.'

Isolde looked up at her with her beautiful but empty eyes, and nodded.

'If you wish it,' she said.

Léonie was so astonished that she flung her arms around Isolde. She was alarmed at how thin Isolde felt beneath her clothes and corset but saw her quick acquiescence as a sign that her sister-in-law was, at last, ready to look to the future. Finally, she would start to get to know her beautiful son.

It was a small party that set out by train to Carcassonne.

Marieta did not take her eyes off her mistress, so it fell to Pascal to occupy Louis-Anatole with military tales. He told stories about the current exploits of the French army in western Africa, talking with such relish of the deserts and roaring waterfalls that Léonie suspected he had borrowed his descriptions from the writings of Monsieur Jules Verne rather than from the newspapers. Louis-Anatole, for his part, entertained the carriage with Monsieur Baillard's tales of medieval knights. A thoroughly satisfying and bloodthirsty journey was passed by both.

They arrived at lunchtime on the fourteenth and found lodgings in the lower Bastide, by the cathédrale Saint-Michel. Léonie and Louis-Anatole passed the remainder of the afternoon sightseeing and eating ices in Square Gambetta.

When they returned to their rooms at six o'clock, Léonie found Isolde lying on a couch at the window overlooking the gardens of the boulevard Barbès and realised, with a sinking feeling, that she did not intend to come with them to view the fireworks. When the time came to venture out for the evening *spectacle*, Isolde confided that she did not feel equal to the crowds. Louis-Anatole was not disappointed, for, in truth, he never expected his mother's company. But Léonie allowed herself an uncharacteristic moment of irritation that, even on this one special occasion, Isolde did not rouse herself for her son.

Leaving Marieta with her mistress, Léonie and Louis-Anatole set out with Pascal. The *spectacle* had been planned and paid for by a local industrialist, Monsieur Sabatier, the inventor of the L'Or-Kina aperitif and 'La Reine des Liqueurs', and his presence was everywhere, in the promotional leaflets that Louis-Anatole collected in his small fists and on posters affixed to the walls of buildings.

As daylight started to retreat, crowds began to mass on the right bank of the Aude in the *quartier* Trivalle, gazing up at the restored ramparts of the Cité, not far from the church of Saint-Gimer where Léonie had sheltered with Victor Constant. She pushed the memory from her mind.

On the left bank, they gathered outside the Hôpital des Malades, every handhold and foothold occupied. Children balanced on the wall beside the chapelle de Saint-Vincent-de-Paul. Shop girls and boot boys, families from the grand houses. In the Bastide, they gathered at the Porte des Jacobins and along the riverbank. No one knew quite what to expect.

'Up you come, *pichon*,' said Pascal, swinging the boy onto his shoulders.

Léonie, Pascal and Louis-Anatole took a position on the Pont Vieux, squeezing into one of the pointed *becs* – the alcoves – that overlooked the water. As darkness fell, diners from the nearby restaurants swelled the numbers on the old bridge. The crowd became a crush. Léonie glanced up at her nephew, worrying perhaps that the noise and the smell of gunpowder would be alarming, but she was delighted to see the same look of intense concentration on Louis-Anatole's face that she remembered seeing on Anatole's when he had come across a particular rare book.

Louis-Anatole clapped his hands as the *embrasement de la Cité* began, enveloping the medieval walls in a fury of orange and red flames, sparks and smoke of all colours. Rockets shot up into the night sky and exploded.

Clouds of acrid vapours rolled down from the hill and over the river, stinging the watchers' eyes, but the magnificence of the spectacle more than compensated for the discomfort. The blue sky was purple now, glowing with green and white and red fireworks as the citadel was enveloped in flame and fury and brilliant light.

Léonie felt Louis-Anatole's small, hot hand creep onto her shoulder. She covered it with her own, feeling full of hope. Perhaps the grief, the remorse, that had dominated her life for so long would loosen its grip and allow thoughts of a brighter future.

'*À l'avenir,*' she said under her breath.

Louis-Anatole heard her. '*A l'avenir,* Tante Léonie,' he cheered, then added: 'If I am good, may we come again next year?'

When the display was over and the crowds dispersed, Pascal carried the sleepy boy back to their boarding house.

Léonie put him to bed. Promising they would have such an adventure again, she kissed him goodnight and retired, leaving a candle burning, as always, to keep away the monsters of the night. She was bone-tired, exhausted by the excitements of the day and her emotions. But finally, the guilt she felt at having led Victor Constant to Anatole and Isolde, kept at bay all day, wormed its way into her mind. It was impossible to be in Carcassonne without wishing she could put the clock back. That she had not disobeyed Anatole, that she had not been so easily charmed in the church, wishing that tragedy had passed them by.

Not wanting her relentless thoughts to keep her awake, Léonie mixed herself a sleeping draught. She watched while the white powder dissolved in a glass of hot brandy, then drank it slowly.

Dawn crept over the Aude as the pale morning light gave shape back to the world.

The water was as flat as a looking glass, barely moving in the quiet of the dawn, as the old boatman, Tistou, steered his heavy, flat barge upstream towards the Païchérou weir. This far upriver there was little evidence of the celebrations for the *fête nationale*. No spent cases, no streamers or advertisements, no lingering smell of gunpowder or singed paper.

His pole caught on something in the water. He adjusted his balance with practised ease, and slowly turned his barge around. The water lapped close to the wooden rim of the boat but did not spill over.

Anchoring the craft by plunging his wooden pole deep into the mud, Tistou knelt down and peered into the water. Beneath the green surface, he could just make out the shape of a woman. He threw up a word of thanks that she was face down – the glazed dead eyes of the drowned were hard to forget, the blue-rimmed lips and the look of defeat etched on the skin. And he didn't think she had been long in the water. Her body had not yet had time to change.

The woman looked strangely peaceful, her long blonde hair swaying back and forth, back and forth, like river weed. Tistou was mesmerised by the motion. Her back was arched, her arms and legs trailing down beneath her skirts, as if she was somehow attached to the riverbed.

Another suicide, he thought.

Tistou braced his legs and, locking his bent knees against the thwarts, he stretched over and grabbed a fistful of the woman's grey morning dress. Even sodden and made slimy by the river, he could feel the quality of the cloth. The barge

598

rocked dangerously, but Tistou had done this countless times and knew where the tipping point lay. He took a deep breath, then pulled again, clutching at the collar of her dress to get a better purchase.

'*Un, deux, trois, allez,*' he muttered, as the body slithered over the side into the hull of the boat.

Tistou wiped his forehead with his neckerchief, then he crossed himself. It was an act of instinct, not belief.

He turned the body over. A woman, no longer in the first flush of youth, but beautiful still. Her grey eyes were open and her hair had come loose in the water, but she was clearly a gentlewoman. Her white hands were soft, not those of one who worked for her living.

The son of a draper and a seamstress, Tistou knew good Egyptian cotton when he saw it. He found the tailor's mark – Parisian – still legible on the collar. She was wearing a silver locket around her neck – solid, not plate – with two miniatures inside, of the lady herself and a young, dark-haired man. Tistou left it be. He was an honest man – not like the scavengers who worked the weirs closer to the centre of town, and who would strip a corpse before turning it in to the authorities.

The moment the proprietor told her that there were two gentlemen wishing to speak to her, Léonie knew.

Indeed, from the moment Marieta had shaken her awake to say her mistress was not in her bed, Léonie had known. She had reported Isolde missing at first light, given a description and the clothes she might be wearing, then had sat by the window, feeling the chill of another death, another loss, seep into her bones. She did not cry, she did not think, she just sat looking out onto the quiet streets of Carcassonne knowing that, despite her best efforts, she had failed again. All these years she had cared for, and loved, her sister-in-law, but, in the end, she had not kept her safe.

The truth was that Isolde had died at the moment Anatole's heart had stopped beating.

'I'll come now,' she said.

Behind her, Marieta began to cry. Léonie took her hands – she knew how she had loved her mistress. She asked her to look after Louis-Anatole, then descended to the lobby to hear the worst.

They were obliged to remain for a couple of days while the formalities were observed and the paperwork signed, but there was little doubt as to the verdict: suicide by drowning while the balance of the mind was disturbed.

It was a dull, overcast and soundless July day when Léonie brought Isolde back to the Domaine de la Cade for the last time. Guilty of the cardinal sin of taking her own life, Isolde would not be allowed by the Church to rest within hallowed ground. Besides, Léonie could not bear the thought of her being buried in the Lascombe family vault.

Instead, she secured the services of Curé Gélis from Coustaussa, the priest of the village midway between Couiza and Rennes-les-Bains, to conduct a private memorial within the grounds of the Domaine de la Cade. She would have approached the Abbé Saunière, but since he was still suffering at the hands of his critics, she did not think it fair to add to his troubles.

At dusk on 20th July 1897, they buried Isolde beside her Anatole in the peaceful patch of ground on the promontory overlooking the lake. A new, modest headstone set flat into the grass recorded their names and dates.

Léonie listened to the murmured prayers, holding tight to Louis-Anatole's hand, and remembered how she had already paid her respects to Isolde in a graveyard in Paris six years ago. The memory swooped down upon her, so intense that she caught her breath. Standing in their old drawing room in the rue de Berlin, hands clasped before a closed casket, a single palm leaf floating in the glass bowl on the sideboard. The sickly aroma of ritual and death that had insinuated itself into every corner of the apartment, the burning of incense and candles to mask the cloying sweetness of the corpse. Except, of course, there had been no corpse. And on the floor below, Achille hammering endlessly on the piano, black notes and white seeping up through the floorboards until Léonie thought she would be driven mad with his playing. She had not known Isolde then, so that first funeral had hardly touched her. Now, her face was wet with tears. For the loss of her beloved sister-in-law, for the pity of it all. When she heard the thud of earth on the wooden lid of the coffin, her only consolation was that Anatole had been spared this day.

As if sensing her mood, Louis-Anatole reached up and curled his little arm around her waist.

'Don't worry, Tante Léonie. I will look after you.'

CHAPTER 90

The private drawing room on the first floor of a hotel on the Spanish side of the Pyrenees was full of acrid smoke from the Turkish cigarettes the resident guest had smoked since his arrival some weeks before.

It was a warm day in August, yet he was dressed as for midwinter in a thick grey greatcoat and soft calfskin gloves. His frame was emaciated and his head bobbed slightly in perpetual motion, as if disagreeing with a question no one else could hear asked. With a hand that shook, he raised a glass of liquorice beer to his lips. He drank carefully through a mouth scabbed in the corners. But his eyes still held the power to command, drilling into the souls of those observed like the jab of a stiletto.

A knock, and his man entered the drawing room.

'What news?' Constant said.

'They say she is drowned. By her own hand.'

For a moment, he felt his burden lift from him.

'And the other?'

'She cares for the child,' the servant replied.

Constant made no answer. The years of exile, the remorseless progress of the disease was destroying him. His body was failing; he could no longer walk easily. But, if anything, his physical deterioration seemed to have sharpened his mind. Six years ago, at the Domaine de la Cade, he had been forced to act more absolutely than he had intended. He had been deprived of the pleasure of enjoying his revenge. His interest in ruining Vernier's sister had been only for the purpose of torturing Vernier himself with the knowledge, so the failure of that part of his plan mattered less to him. But the quick and clean death meted out to Vernier disappointed him still, and now it seemed he had been cheated of seeing Isolde die as well.

His precipitate flight over the border to Spain meant that Constant had not learned for some twelve months after the events of Hallowe'en 1891 that the whore had not only survived his bullet, but had lived to give birth to a son. The fact that she had escaped him again had played obsessively on his mind since then.

It was the desire to complete his revenge that had kept him patient. The attempts to seize his assets had almost ruined him. It had taken all the skill and immorality of his lawyers to protect his wealth and his whereabouts.

Constant had been forced to be cautious and circumspect, staying in exile on the far side of the border until all interest in him had died down. Then last winter, Inspector Thouron had been promoted and assigned to the investigation into the conduct of the army officer Dreyfus, which was so occupying the Parisian police force. He no longer had time for an old case. More significantly, word had reached him that Inspector Bouchou of the Carcassonne *gendarmerie* had retired four weeks past. At last, the way was clear for Constant to return quietly to France.

In the spring, he had sent his man ahead to prepare the ground. With anonymous letters to the town hall and the Church authorities in Rennes-le-Chateau, it had been easy to fan the flames of a whispering campaign against the Abbé Saunière, a priest associated particularly with the Domaine de la Cade and the events Constant had discovered had taken place in Jules Lascombe's day.

It was his paid associates who had set the story running of a beast stalking the mountain valleys and attacking livestock. His servant travelled from village to village, stirring up the crowds and spreading rumours that the sepulchre in the grounds of the Domaine de la Cade was once again the centre of occult activity. It had been easy. He began with beggars who slept out of doors or found shelter beneath the drayman's cart, the winter shepherds in their isolation on the mountains, those who followed the assizes from town to town. He dripped Constant's poison into the ears of drapers and glaziers, boot boys from the big houses, cleaners and pantry maids.

The villagers were superstitious and gullible. Tradition, myth and history confirmed his calumnies. A whisper here and there that the marks were not those of an animal's claws. That strange wailings were heard in the night. That there was a putrid stench. All evidence that a demon was come to demand retribution for the unnatural state of affairs at the Domaine de la Cade – an aunt taken in marriage by her husband's nephew. And now all three were dead. What else could it be, but a judgement?

With invisible threads, Constant drew his net around the Domaine de la Cade.

Now, with Bouchou's retirement – and his instinct that the young man taking over in Carcassonne would have little time for crimes committed in a remote village several years before – Constant believed the time was right to act. Also, his time was running out. Despite the expensive remedies and treatments, the mercury, the waters, the laudanum, he knew he was dying. He knew he did not have long before his mind, too, would fail. He recognised the signs, could diagnose himself as accurately as any quack. The only thing he now feared was the brief, final flare of lucidity, before the shadows descended for good.

Constant planned to cross the border at the beginning of September and return to Rennes-les-Bains. Vernier was dead. Isolde was dead. But there was still the boy.

From the pocket of his waistcoat, he pulled the time-piece stolen from Vernier in the passage des Panoramas. As the Spanish shadows lengthened, he turned it over in his decaying, syphilitic hands, thinking of his Isolde and of how she had betrayed him.

CHAPTER 91

On 20th September, the anniversary of Marguerite Vernier's murder, another child went missing. It was the first for more than a month, taken from the bank of the river downstream of Sougraigne. The girl's body was found close to the fontaine des Amours, her face disfigured by claw marks. Unlike the forgotten children, the dispossessed, she was the beloved youngest child of a large family with relations in many of the villages of the Aude and the Salz. Léonie tried not to pay attention to the coincidence of the date.

Two days after that, a boy vanished from the woods not far from the lac de Barrenc, the mountain lake supposedly inhabited by a devil. He, too, was from a good family. He, too, had been savaged by an animal.

While there was still hope that the boy might be found unharmed, she offered the assistance of both inside and outside staff to participate in the search parties. It was refused. For Louis-Anatole's sake, she maintained a veneer of calm, but for the first time, she began to accept that they might have to leave the Domaine de la Cade, until the storm had blown over.

Maître Fromilhague and Madame Bousquet maintained it was obviously the work of wild dogs or wolves come down from the mountains. During the hours of daylight,

Léonie also dismissed the rumours of a demon or supernatural creature. But as dusk fell, her knowledge of the history of the sepulchre and the presence of the cards within the grounds made her nervous, less certain. Alone, now, she wished more than anything that Audric Baillard would return and advise her on what she should do for the best.

As the mood of the town grew increasingly ugly, the Domaine became the target for petty acts of vandalism. Léonie returned from walking in the woods one afternoon to see a cluster of servants standing around the door to one of the outbuildings.

'What is it?' she asked.

Pascal spun round, a look of horror in his eyes, blocking her view with his wide, solid frame.

'Nothing, Madama.'

Léonie looked at his face, then to the gardener and his son, Emile. She took a step closer.

'Pascal?'

'Please, Madama, it's not for your eyes.'

'Come now,' she said lightly. 'I am mistress of this estate. Whatever you are concealing cannot be so bad.'

Still Pascal did not move. Léonie reached out her gloved hand and touched him on the arm.

'If you please.'

All eyes were on Pascal, who, for a moment, remained steadfast, then slowly stepped aside to allow Léonie sight of what he so keenly wished to hide.

The skinned corpse of a rabbit, some days old, had been impaled to the door with a heavy furrier's nail. A swarm of flies buzzed furiously around a crude cross daubed on the wood in blood and, beneath it, words printed in black tar: PAR CE SIGNE TU LE VAINCRAS.

Léonie's hand flew to her mouth, but she was determined to keep her composure.

'How unpleasant. See it is disposed of, Pascal,' she said. She looked round at the assembled company, seeing her own fear reflected in their superstitious eyes. 'And I would be grateful for your discretion. All of you.'

Still, Léonie's resolve did not waver. She was determined not to be driven from the Domaine de la Cade, certainly not before Monsieur Baillard returned. He had said he would be back by the feast day of Saint Martin. She had sent letters via his old lodgings in the rue de l'Hermite with increasing frequency of late but had no way of knowing if any had found him.

The situation worsened. Another child, the daughter of a local lawyer and his wife, disappeared on 22nd October. Léonie recognised the date as the anniversary of Anatole and Isolde's clandestine marriage and, when the child's body was recovered beside the fauteuil du Diable, with a sprig of wild juniper pushed between her hands, Léonie could no longer pretend that the message was not left for her.

Two days later, a burning rag soaked in oil and goose fat was pushed through one of the windows of the library that had been left partially open. It was discovered before any serious damage was done, but the household became even more timid, more watchful, unhappy.

Léonie's friends and allies in the town – and Pascal and Marieta too – tried their best to persuade her accusers that they were mistaken in believing that there was any such beast quartered within the estate, but the town had made up its narrow mind. They believed it was incontrovertible that the old devil of the mountain had returned to claim his own, as he had in Jules Lascombe's time.

No smoke without fire.

However hard she tried, Léonie now could not deny the hand of Victor Constant in the persecution. Who else could it be? Her brother was dead, Isolde was dead, she had foolishly thought it was over. Now, she realised that nothing would be enough to assuage Constant's desire for retribution. He would keep going until he had destroyed everything that had ever mattered to Anatole.

For the first time, and the only time, Léonie gave in. She sank to the floor, overwhelmed with fear and grief and anger, and wept and wept until she was hollow.

The following day, Léonie attempted to persuade the *gendarmerie* that there was a campaign of persecution being waged against the Domaine de la Cade and that she, and everyone on the estate, was in danger. She begged the *mairie* to intervene, pleaded with Maître Fromilhague to intercede on her behalf, but to no avail. The Domaine stood alone. Léonie realised, now, this had been Constant's intention all along, to stir up the town into a frenzy of hate against them.

Isolated with her fears and suspicions, Léonie tried to plan. If Constant had returned to Rennes-les-Bains, which she suspected he had, then he could not fail to know that Isolde herself was dead. The fact that the persecution continued made it clear that she had to protect Louis-Anatole. She had to get him out of Constant's reach.

It was a plan easier to execute in thought than in deed. What income she had, once the lawyers had taken their share of the complications of inheritance, was tied up in the estate.

The truth was that Léonie had nowhere to go. She had no family in Paris, and she could hardly impose herself upon Debussy and his wife. Other than Audric Baillard, Madame Bousquet and Maître Fromilhague, she had few friends.

All the same, Léonie planned to smuggle Louis-Anatole away. She hoped he would be able to return to the Domaine de la Cade before too long – it was his home and she would not allow Constant to deprive him of his birthright – but his safety had to come first.

Confiding in no one but Pascal and Marieta, she prepared for departure. From what had gone before, she felt certain that Constant would make his final move against them on Hallowe'en. It was not only the anniversary of Anatole's death, but Isolde had once told her that it had been on Hallowe'en in 1890 that she had informed Constant that their short-lived affair must end. From that, all things had followed.

Léonie resolved that if he came on the veille de la Toussaint, he would find them gone.

Her heart thudding with anticipation, Léonie steeled herself and, on the afternoon of 31st October, she finally returned to the clearing where the juniper grew wild. However unlikely it was that he should stumble upon them in such an expanse of woodland, she could not risk leaving the Tarot cards there for Constant to find. Until she and Louis-Anatole could safely return – and in Monsieur Baillard's continuing absence – she had in mind that she would give them for safekeeping to Madame Bousquet.

She was on the point of exiting through the doors onto the terrace when she heard Marieta calling her name. With a guilty start, she turned back.

'What is it?'

'A letter, Madama,' Marieta said, holding out an envelope.

Léonie frowned. After the events of the past months, she treated everything with caution. She glanced down and did not recognise the hand.

'From whom?'

'The boy said from Coustaussa.'

Léonie opened it. To her surprise, the letter was from the elderly priest, Antoine Gélis, requesting her to call upon him that afternoon on a matter of some urgency. Since he was known to be something of a recluse – Léonie had met him only twice in six years, once in the company of Henri Boudet in Rennes-les-Bains on the occasion of Louis-Anatole's baptism, and at Isolde's burial – she was puzzled.

'Is there any reply, Madama?' Marieta enquired.

Léonie looked up. 'Is the boy still here?'

'He is.'

'Bring him in, will you?'

A small, thin child in an open-necked shirt and holding his cap in clenched hands was ushered into the hall. He looked dumbstruck with terror.

'There is no need to be frightened,' Léonie said. 'You have done nothing wrong. I only wish to ask if Curé Gélis himself gave you this letter?'

He shook his head.

Léonie smiled. 'Can you tell me who did?'

Marieta pushed the boy. 'The mistress asked you a question.'

Little by little, hindered rather than helped by Marieta's interventions, Léonie managed to tease out the bare bones of the matter. Alfred was staying with his *grandmère* in the village of Coustaussa. He had been playing in the ruins of the *château-fort* when a man came out of the front door of the presbytery and offered him a *sou* to deliver an urgent letter to the Domaine de la Cade.

'Curé Gélis has a niece who does errands for him, Madama Léonie,' Marieta said. 'Prepares his meals. Sees to his laundry.'

'Was the man a servant or a gentleman?'

Alfred shrugged. Realising she would learn nothing more from the boy, Léonie dismissed him.

'Will you go, Madama?' asked Marieta.

Léonie considered. There was a great deal to do before their departure. Conversely, she could not believe that

Curé Gélis would have sent such a communication without good reason.

'I shall,' she said, after a moment's hesitation. 'Ask Pascal to meet me at the front of the house with the gig.'

They left the Domaine de la Cade at a half past three.

The air was heavy with the scent of autumn fires. Sprigs of boxwood and rosemary were tied on the door frames of the houses and farms they passed on the way. At the crossroads, impromptu roadside shrines had sprung up for Hallowe'en. Ancient prayers and invocations scribbled on scraps of paper and cloth were laid as offerings.

Léonie knew that already in the graveyards of Rennes-les-Bains and Rennes-le-Château – indeed, in every mountain parish – widows draped in black crêpe and veils would be kneeling before ancient tombs, praying for deliverance for those they had loved. More so this year, with the blight that had fallen over the region.

Pascal drove the horses hard, until sweat steamed up from their backs and their nostrils flared wide. Even so, the four o'clock bells were ringing by the time they had covered the distance from Rennes-les-Bains to Coustaussa.

Leaving Pascal with the carriage and horses, Léonie walked through the deserted village. Coustaussa was tiny, no more than a handful of houses – no *boulangerie*, no café – so she found the presbytery, which adjoined the church, with little difficulty. There appeared to be no signs of life inside.

With a growing sense of unease, she knocked on the heavy door. No one came. She rapped again, a little louder.

'Curé Gélis?'

After a few moments, Léonie decided to try the church instead. She followed the darkening line of the stone building around to the back. All the doors, to front and side, were locked. A guttering oil lamp hung miserably from a bent iron hook.

Léonie made for the dwelling on the opposite side of the street and knocked. After a shuffling of feet from within, an elderly woman slid back the metal grille set within a hatch in the door.

'Who is it?'

'I have a rendezvous with Curé Gélis, but there is no answer.'

The woman looked at Léonie with sullen and distrustful eyes, saying nothing. Léonie dug into her pocket and produced a *sou*.

'*Ritou* is not there,' she said, taking the coin.

'*Ritou?*'

'The priest. Gone to Couiza.'

Léonie stared. 'That cannot be. I received a letter from him not two hours past inviting me to call upon him.'

'Saw him leave,' the woman said, with evident pleasure. 'You're the second to come calling.'

Léonie threw out her hand and stopped the woman from closing the grille, leaving a fraction of light dripping from inside out onto the street.

'What manner of person? A man, a woman?'

Silence. Léonie produced a second coin.

'French,' the old woman said, spitting out the word like the insult it was intended to be.

'When was this?'

'An hour or so ago, maybe more.'

Léonie turned away, hearing the grille slam shut behind her. She could only assume that in the time it had taken the boy to make the journey on foot from Coustaussa to the Domaine de la Cade, Curé Gélis had given up waiting and been unable to delay his departure longer. Or perhaps he had been called to attend to some more urgent matter? Or could she see Constant's hand in this? She was now desperate to be back at the Domaine de la Cade.

*

Pascal drove the horses even faster on the return journey, but every minute seemed to stretch. Léonie almost cried out with relief when the lights of the Domaine de la Cade came into view. When Pascal slowed on the icy drive, Léonie felt like jumping down and running ahead.

She threw herself out of the gig as soon as they stopped. She ran to the front steps, possessed by a nameless dread that something might have happened in her absence, and hurtled into the hall.

Louis-Anatole came running towards her. 'He's here!' he cried.

Léonie's blood turned to ice in her veins.

CHAPTER 92

'*B*onjorn, Madomaisèla,' came a voice from the shadows. At first, Léonie thought her ears were deceiving her, then he stepped out of the gloom to greet her.

Léonie leapt forward, her hands outstretched. 'Monsieur Baillard!' she cried. 'You are most welcome, most welcome.'

He smiled down at Louis-Anatole, hopping from foot to foot beside him.

'This young man has looked after me very well,' he said. 'He has been amusing me by playing the piano.'

Without waiting for further invitation, Louis-Anatole ran back to the piano stool.

'I found this in the piano stool. I have been learning it on my own.'

A haunting melody in the key of A minor, lilting and gentle, his small hands struggling not to split the chords. Music, at last, heard.

Sepulchre 1891.

Léonie felt tears brim in her eyes. With Monsieur Baillard beside her, she stood listening until the last chord faded away.

Louis-Anatole dropped his hands into his lap, took a deep breath, as if listening to the reverberations in the almost silence, then turned to face them with a look of pride on his face.

'There,' he said, 'I have been practising for you, Tante Léonie.'

'You have a great talent,' said Monsieur Baillard, applauding. 'I commend you.'

Louis-Anatole beamed with pleasure. 'If I cannot be a soldier when I am a man, then I shall be a famous pianist.'

'Noble occupations, both,' laughed Baillard. 'But now, my accomplished young friend, there are matters your *tante* and I must discuss. If you will excuse us?'

'But I—'

'It will not be for long,' he said firmly.

Léonie smiled. 'We will call for you when we are finished, *mon brave*.'

Louis-Anatole sighed, then ran off towards the kitchens, calling for Marieta.

Monsieur Baillard's face grew serious. 'Come, tell me all that has happened since January last.'

They went into the drawing room. Under his precise and careful questioning, Léonie told him everything, including her suspicions that Victor Constant had returned to Rennes-les-Bains.

'I did write,' she said, unable to keep the reproach from her voice, 'but I had no way of knowing if you had received any of my communications.'

'Some I did, others I suspect went astray,' he said in a sombre tone. 'The tragic news of Madama Isolde's death I learned only when I returned this afternoon. I was sorry to hear it.'

Léonie looked at him, seeing how tired and frail he looked. She sighed.

'In truth, it was a release,' she said, something she had been unable to say to anyone else. 'She had never been happy since Anatole's death.' She clasped her hands together. 'I have missed your company and your advice.'

He pressed the tips of his fingers together, as if in prayer. 'If it had not been a matter of great personal importance,' he said softly, 'I would not have left you. But I had received word that a person . . . a person for whom I have been waiting for many, many years had returned. But . . .' He paused, and in the silence, Léonie heard the raw pain behind the simple words. 'But it was not she.'

Léonie was momentarily diverted. She had heard him talk only once before with such affection but had received the impression that the girl of whom he spoke with such tenderness was some years dead.

'I am not certain I understand you, Monsieur Baillard,' she said carefully.

'No,' he said softly. Then a look of determination came over his features. 'Had I known, I would not have left Rennes-les-Bains.' He sighed. 'But I took advantage of my journey to prepare some refuge for you and Louis-Anatole.'

Léonie's eyes widened. 'But I only came to that decision a week ago. Less. You have been gone for ten months. How could you have . . .'

He gave a slow smile. 'I feared, long ago, that it would be necessary.'

'But how—'

He raised his hand. 'Your suspicions are correct. Constant has returned.'

Even though she knew it, Léonie fell still. 'If you have evidence, we must inform the authorities. They have refused to take my concerns seriously.'

'I have no evidence, only assured suspicions. But, as you have realised, Constant is here for a purpose. You must leave tonight. My house in the mountains is prepared and waiting for you. I will give directions to Pascal.' He paused. 'He and Marieta will travel with you?'

Léonie nodded. 'I have confided my intentions to them.'

'You may remain in Los Seres for as long as you wish. Certainly until it is safe to return.'

For a moment, the relief that it was not all on her shoulders overwhelmed her.

'Thank you,' she said eventually. With tears in her eyes, Léonie looked around the room. 'I shall be sorry to leave this house,' she said softly. 'For my mother and for Isolde, it was an unhappy place. But for me, despite the sorrows that have been contained here, it has been a home.'

She stopped. 'There is one thing I must confess to you, Monsieur Baillard.'

'Yes?'

'When we first met, I gave you my word that I would not return to the sepulchre,' she said. 'That promise I kept. But as for the Tarot deck, I must tell you that, after I took my leave of you that day in Rennes-les-Bains – before the duel and Anatole—' Her voice broke.

'I remember,' he said gently.

Léonie took a breath. 'That day, I took it upon myself to go into the woods to see if I might find the *cachette* for myself. I wanted only to see if the cards might still be there.'

She looked at Monsieur Baillard, expecting to see disappointment, even reproof, on his face. To her surprise, he was smiling.

'And you came upon the place.'

'I did. But I give you my word,' Léonie said, rushing on, 'I returned them to their hiding place.' She paused. 'Now, knowing everything I know, I would not leave them here, within the grounds where Constant might discover them. There is no knowing what a man such as that . . .'

As she was speaking, Audric Baillard reached into the large white pocket of his suit. He took out a square of black silk, a familiar parcel of material, and opened it up. The image of La Force was visible on the top.

'You have them!' Léonie exclaimed. Then she stopped. 'How did you know I had been there?'

'Obligingly, you left your gloves as a memento. Do you not remember?'

618

Léonie flushed, remembering the panic of that afternoon when she heard Marieta and Pascal calling her.

'I went because, like you, I do not believe these cards should be in the possession of Victor Constant. And ...' He fixed her with his gaze. 'And because I fear we might have need of them.'

Léonie shook her head. 'You warned me against using the power of the cards.'

He raised his hand. 'Unless or until there was no other choice. I regret that hour is at hand.'

Léonie felt her heart skip a beat. 'We should leave now, all of us.' She stood up. 'Now, before anything happens.'

'Ah, Léonie,' Baillard said, with such tenderness that all of her last defences fell away.

Tears filled her eyes. Now she understood. If she ran now, she would be running forever. Always looking over her shoulder, wondering if Constant was there, waiting in the shadows.

Il était une fois. Once upon a time.

She found herself remembering their happy first weeks at the Domaine de la Cade – she and Anatole and Isolde. How, in that long-ago autumn of 1891, it was the darkness she had feared most after the bright lights of Paris. She had been another girl then, innocent, untouched by darkness or grief. A child.

'If I stay and use the cards ...'

Audric Baillard met her gaze, his eyes full of grief.

'I give you my word that I will protect Louis-Anatole. He will be safe.'

They both turned to the sound of running feet in the hall. Moments later, the drawing-room door burst open and Pascal strode into the room.

'Madama Léonie, Sénher Baillard, they have forced their way through the gates!'

Léonie ran to the window. On the distant horizon, she could see a line of flaming torches, gold against the black night sky.

Then, from within the house, she heard the sound of glass breaking.

CHAPTER 93

Suddenly, the room seemed to be full. Louis-Anatole broke free of Marieta and threw himself at Léonie. His bottom lip was quivering, but he was trying to be brave.

'Who are they?' he said in a small voice.

Léonie squeezed him tightly. 'They are bad men, *mon brave*. But we will not let them frighten us.'

She cupped her hands to the glass. The mob was still some way off, but they were advancing on the house. Every invader held a burning torch in one hand, a weapon in the other.

'So many,' she murmured. 'How has he turned the whole town against us?'

'He played upon their natural superstitions,' Baillard replied. 'Republican or Royalist, they have grown up hearing stories of the demon that stalks the land.'

'Asmodeus.'

'Different names for different times, but always the same face. And if the good people of the town profess not to believe such stories during the hours of daylight, at night their older souls whisper to them in the dark. Of supernatural beings that rip and tear and cannot be killed, of sombre and forbidden places where spiders spin their webs.'

Léonie knew he was right. She remembered the night of the riot at the Palais Garnier in Paris when the veneer of civility fell so quickly away. How easily a crowd became a mob.

She could see the flames darting and licking the black air, reflecting off the leaves of the tall sweet chestnut trees that lined the driveway. She dragged the curtain across and stepped back from the window.

'To hound my brother and Isolde into their graves, even that seems not enough,' she said, keeping her voice level. 'Can we not reason with them?' She looked at Pascal, who shook his head in despair.

'The time for talking has passed,' Baillard replied. 'There comes always a moment when the desire to act, however ill the cause, is stronger than the wish to listen.'

'We can fight them off,' Pascal said, although Léonie could see the fear in his eyes.

'A good soldier knows when to stand and face his enemies, and when to withdraw,' said Baillard. 'Tonight we will not fight.' Then his expression hardened. 'Is the gig ready?'

Pascal nodded. 'Ready and waiting in the clearing by the sepulchre. It should be far enough away to evade their attention. I have hopes I can get us out from there without being observed.'

'*Ben, ben.* Good. We will go from the back, cutting across the path and into the woods, praying their target is the house itself in the first instance.'

'What of the servants?' Léonie asked. 'We cannot leave them.'

A deep flush spread over Pascal's broad, honest face. 'They will not go,' he said. 'They wish to defend the house.'

'I do not want anyone to come to harm on our account, Pascal,' Léonie said.

'I will tell them, Madama, but I do not think it will alter their resolve.'

Léonie could see his eyes were resolute.

'Thank you,' she said quietly.

Pascal nodded, then left the room. No one spoke for a moment. Then the urgency of the situation pressed down upon them once more.

'Léonie,' said Baillard, 'bring only what is absolutely essential. Marieta, fetch Madama Léonie's valise and furs. It will be a long and cold journey.'

Marieta swallowed a sob.

'In my travelling valise, Marieta, already packed, there is a small wallet of paper, inside my workbox. Paintings, about so big.' Léonie made the shape of a missal with her hands. 'Take the workbox with you. Keep it safe. But bring me the wallet, will you?'

Marieta nodded and rushed into the hall.

Léonie waited until she had gone, then turned back to Monsieur Baillard.

'Is there any hope?' Léonie whispered, so Louis-Anatole would not hear.

'There is always hope.'

'This is not your battle either, Audric,' she said. 'There is still time.'

'Sajhë,' he said softly. 'My friends call me Sajhë.'

She smiled, honoured by the unexpected confidence. 'Very well, Sajhë. You told me once, many years ago now, that it was the living, not the dead, who would be most in need of my services. Do you remember?' She glanced down at the little boy. 'He is all that matters now. If you take him, then I will know at least that I have not failed in my duty.'

He smiled. 'Love – true love – endures, Léonie. Your brother, Isolde, your mother, they knew this. They are not lost to you.'

Léonie remembered Isolde's words to her as they sat upon the stone bench on the promontory the day after the very first supper party at the Domaine de la Cade. She had been speaking of her love for Anatole, although Léonie had not known it at that time. A love so strong that, without it, Isolde's life had been intolerable. She would have wished for such a love for herself.

'Will you give me your word that you will take Louis-Anatole to Los Seres? I would not forgive myself if harm came to you.'

He shook his head. 'It is not yet my time, Léonie. There is much I must still do before I am allowed to make that journey.'

She darted a glance at the familiar yellow handkerchief, a silken square of colour just visible in the pocket of his jacket, and was about to speak when Marieta reappeared in the doorway with the wallet of paintings. She passed them to Léonie, then held out Louis-Anatole's outdoor clothes.

'Here,' she said. 'Quick, now.'

He obediently went to Marieta and allowed himself to be dressed, but then darted away from her and into the hall.

'Louis-Anatole!' Léonie called after him. 'There is no time to waste.'

He appeared back with the piece of piano music in his hand. 'We will not wish to be without music where we are going,' he said, looking round at the taut faces of the adults. 'Well, we would not!'

Her heart breaking, Léonie crouched down. 'You are quite right.'

'Although,' he faltered, 'I do not know where it is we are going.'

Outside the house, a shout erupted. Fuelled by fear and the darkness and the terror of all things that were abroad on the Eve of All Saints, the men armed with clubs and hunting rifles began their advance on the house.

'And so it begins,' Baillard said.

Léonie stood up, feeling her nephew's little hand slide into hers.

'*Corage*, Léonie,' Baillard said. Their eyes locked. Slowly, as if even now reluctant, he passed her the deck of Tarot cards. 'You remember your uncle's writings?'

'Perfectly.'

He gave a slight smile. 'Even though you returned the book to the library and led me to believe you never revisited it?' he chided gently.

Léonie smiled. 'I may, once or twice, have reacquainted myself with its contents despite your counsel.'

Baillard nodded. 'It is fortunate, perhaps. The old are not always wise.' He paused. 'But you understand that your fate is tied up with this? If you choose to breathe life into the paintings you have done, if you call forth the demon, you know he will take you too?'

Her heart lurched, but her courage and determination were stronger than her fear.

'I do.'

'I wish it were not so,' he said. 'If there was any other way . . .'

Léonie put her hand on his arm. 'But there is not, my friend.' She took a deep breath. 'What I do not understand is why the demon, Asmodeus, did not take my uncle.'

Baillard frowned. 'Your uncle did not wish to forfeit his life and so fought the demon he had raised.'

'But what if I do not know what to do? In that moment. If I fail.'

'It will become clear. I do not think you will fail.'

Their eyes met, then Léonie took the black silk package, put it in the pocket of her cloak, then rushed to the mantelshelf above the fire and took a box of matches balanced on the corner of the marble surround.

On her tiptoes, she placed a kiss upon Baillard's forehead. 'Thank you, Sajhë,' she whispered. 'For the cards. For everything.'

*

The hall was dark as Léonie, Audric Baillard, Louis-Anatole and Marieta emerged from the drawing room.

In every corner, every nook, Léonie could hear or see signs of activity. The gardener's son, Emile, now a strong and tall man, was organising the indoor staff with any weapon he could lay his hands on. An old musket, a cutlass taken from the display cases, sticks. The outdoor servants were armed with hunting rifles, rakes, spades and hoes.

Léonie felt Louis-Anatole's shock at the familiar faces of his day-to-day life transformed. His hand tightened in hers.

She stopped and set her voice high and clear.

'I do not wish you to risk your lives,' she said. 'You are loyal and brave – I know my late brother and Madama Isolde would feel the same, were they here to witness this – but this is not a fight we can win.' She looked around the hall, taking in their faces. 'Please, I beg you, leave now while you have the chance. Go back to your families and your children.'

No one moved. The glass of the black-and-white framed portrait hanging above the piano glinted, catching her eye. Léonie hesitated. The souvenir of a sunny afternoon in the place du Pérou, so long ago: Anatole seated, Isolde and herself standing behind, all three of them content in one another's company. For a moment, she was tempted to take the photograph with her. But mindful of the instruction to take only what was essential, she stayed her hand. The portrait remained where it had always been, as if keeping watch over the house and those in it.

'Thank you, my friends,' she said. 'I consider myself fortunate to have those of such courage and loyalty around me.'

Léonie and Louis-Anatole slipped through the glazed metal doors onto the terrace, with Baillard and Marieta following. From the assembled crowd behind her, a voice rang out and brought tears to her eyes.

'Good luck, Madama Léonie. And to you, *pichon*. We will be here when you return.'

'*Et à vous aussi*,' the little boy replied in his sweet voice.

Outside, the frost nipped at their cheeks and made their ears hurt. Léonie pulled her hood up over her head. They could hear the mob on the far side of the house, still some way off, but the sound was terrifying.

'Where are we going?' Louis-Anatole whispered.

Léonie heard the fear in his voice. 'Through the woods to where Pascal is waiting with the gig,' she said.

'Why is he waiting there?'

'Because we do not want anyone to see us or hear us,' she said quickly. 'We need to be very, very quiet. Then we will ride to Monsieur Baillard's house in the mountains.'

'Is it a long way?'

'It is.'

Louis-Anatole said nothing for a moment. 'Will we be coming back?' he asked.

Léonie bit her lip. 'Think of it as a game of *cache-cache*. Just a game.' She put her finger to her lips. 'But we must hurry now, Louis-Anatole. And remember, be very quiet.'

'And very brave.'

Léonie's fingers closed around the deck of cards in her pocket. 'Yes,' she murmured. 'Very brave.'

CHAPTER 94

'*Mettez le feu!*'
On Constant's order, the mob plunged their torches into the woody base of the box hedge. The hedge began to burn, first the network of branches, then the trunks, crackling and spitting like the fireworks on the walls of La Cité of Carcassonne. The fire rose and swayed and took hold.

Then the cold voice came again. '*À l'attaque!*'

Now the men were swarming across the lawns, around the lake, trampling across the flower borders. They leapt up the steps to the terrace, pushing over the ornamental planters.

Constant followed, limping, at a distance, a cigarette in his hand and leaning heavily on his stick, as if following a parade on the Champs-Élysées.

At four o'clock that afternoon – when he was certain that Léonie Vernier was already on her way to Coustaussa – Constant had delivered the body of another dead child to its parents, carried on an ox cart to the place du Pérou. It had taken little skill, even with his depleted energies, to catch the attention of the crowd. Such terrible injuries could not be inflicted by an animal, but only by something unnatural. A creature being concealed at the Domaine de la Cade. A devil, a demon.

A groom from the Domaine had been in Rennes-les-Bains at the time. The small crowd had turned on him, demanding to know where the creature was kept. The more he denied it, the more inflamed the crowd became.

It was Constant himself who suggested they storm the house to see for themselves. Within moments, the idea had taken hold and become their own. A little later, he allowed them to persuade him to organise the assault on the Domaine de la Cade.

Constant paused at the foot of the steps, exhausted by the effort of walking. He watched the mob divide into two columns, spreading out to front and side, swarming up the stone stairs onto the terrace at the back of the house.

The striped awning that ran the length of the terrace went up first, sparked by a boy climbing up the ivy and wedging his flaming torch into the folds of material at the end. Although damp from the October air, the material caught and ignited in seconds. The smell of oil and canvas and fire filled the night in a cloud of choking black smoke.

The sight of the fire seemed to inflame the passions of the villagers. The first window was broken, the glass shattering at the end of a steel-capped boot. One by one, the elegant rooms were breached by the violence of the crowd, jabbing their torches in to ignite the curtains.

Three others picked up a stone urn and used it as a battering ram on the door. Glass and metal buckled as the frame gave way. The trio dropped the urn and the mob flooded into the hall and the library. With rags soaked in oil and tar, they set fire to the shelves. One by one, the books ignited, the dry paper and antique leather bindings catching as easily as straw. Crackling and spitting, the flames leapt from one shelf to the next.

With faces distorted by rage and envy, they upturned the table where Léonie had sat and first read *Les Tarots* and ripped the stepladder from the wall, struggling with the brass fittings. Flames licked around the edge of the rugs, then blazed into full-scale fire.

The mob exploded into the chequerboard hallway. Walking slowly, throwing his legs awkwardly out before him, Constant followed them to witness his ramshackle army meet the defenders of the house.

The servants were heavily outnumbered, but they fought bravely. They, too, had suffered from the rumours. They were defending their characters, as well as the reputation of the Domaine de la Cade.

A young footman delivered a glancing blow to a man coming towards him. The villager stumbled back, blood streaming from his head.

They all knew one another, had grown up together, were cousins, friends, neighbours, yet they fought as enemies. Emile was brought down by a vicious kick from a man who had once carried him on his shoulders to school.

The shouting grew louder.

The groundsmen, armed with hunting rifles, shot into the mob, hitting one man in the arm, another in the leg. Blood burst through split skin, arms raised to ward off the blows. But by the sheer force of numbers, the house was overwhelmed. The old gardener fell first, hearing the bone in his leg snap as a foot came down upon it. Emile lasted a little longer, until he was seized by two men and beaten until he collapsed. Men, with whose sons Emile had once played, picked him up and hurled him over the banisters. He seemed to hang in the air for a fraction of a second, then fell, head over heels, to the bottom of the stairs. He landed with his arms and legs splayed at an unnatural angle. Only a single trickle of blood dribbled from the corner of his mouth, but his eyes were dead.

Constant stood at the foot of the stairs, holding his hand up to shield his face against the heat and soot, waiting as his man ran across the hall to report.

'I have searched everywhere. They are not here,' he gasped. 'It seems they left with an old man and the house-keeper some quarter of an hour ago.'

'On foot?'

He nodded. 'I found this, Monsieur. In the drawing room.'

Victor Constant took it in his trembling hand. It was a Tarot card, an image of a grotesque devil with two lovers chained at its feet. He tried to focus, the smoke taking his vision from him. As he looked, it seemed that the demon was moving, twisting as if under a burden. The lovers came to resemble Vernier and Isolde.

He rubbed his painful eyes with his gloved fingers. Then an idea came to him.

'When you have dealt with Gélis, leave this Tarot card with the body, then return here. It will confuse matters, if nothing else. The whole of Coustaussa knows the girl was there.'

The manservant nodded. 'And you, Monsieur?'

'Help me to the carriage. A child, two women and an old man? I do not believe they can have gone far. More likely, they will be hiding somewhere within the grounds. The estate is steeply wooded. There is only one place they are likely to be.'

'And them?' The servant jerked his head in the direction of the mob.

The sounds of screaming were rising in crescendo as the battle reached its zenith. Soon the looting would begin. Even if Vernier's son did survive tonight, there would be nothing for him to come back to. He would be destitute.

'Leave them to it,' he said.

CHAPTER 95

It was hard going in the dark through the woods. Louis-Anatole was a strong boy and Monsieur Baillard, despite his age, was surprisingly fast on his feet, but they made slow progress. They could not risk lighting the lamp they had brought for fear of drawing the mob's attention.

Léonie found that her feet knew the path she had so long avoided towards the sepulchre. As she walked, climbing uphill, her cape stirring up the fallen autumn leaves, she thought of all the journeys she had made around the estate – the glade with the wild juniper; the clearing where Anatole had fallen; the tombs of her brother and Isolde, side by side on the promontory on the far side of the lake – and her heart wept at the thought that she might never see any of it again. Having so long felt confined by her narrow existence, now the time had come to leave, she realised she did not wish to go. The rocks, the hills, the copses, the wooded pathways – she felt as if each was seamed into the structure of the person she had become.

'Are we nearly there, Tante Léonie?' said Louis-Anatole in a small voice. 'My boots are pinching me.'

'Almost,' she said, squeezing his hand. 'Be careful not to slip.'

'Do you know,' he said, in a voice that gave the lie to his words, 'I am not in the least afraid of spiders.'

They arrived at the clearing and slowed their pace. The avenue of yews Léonie remembered from her first visit seemed more knotted by time and the canopy less penetrable than before.

Pascal was waiting. Two weak lamps on the sides of the gig spluttered in the cold air.

'What place is this, Tante Léonie?' said Louis-Anatole, curiosity for the moment driving away his fear. 'Are we still within our grounds?'

'We are. This is the old mausoleum. Like a grave.'

'Where they bury people?'

'Sometimes.'

'Why are Papa and Maman not buried here?'

She hesitated. 'Because they preferred to be outside, among the trees and the flowers. They lie together by the lake.'

Louis-Anatole frowned. 'So they can hear the birds?'

Léonie smiled. 'That's right.'

'Are there ghosts?' he said, stepping forward. 'Is that why you have never brought me here?'

Léonie grabbed him. 'There is no time to explore now.'

His face fell. 'Can I not go inside?'

'Not now.'

'Are there spiders?'

'There might be, but since you are not afraid of spiders, you would not mind.'

He nodded, but he had turned quite pale. 'Why don't we come back another day? When it is light.'

She felt Monsieur Baillard's hand on her arm.

'We cannot delay any longer,' said Pascal. 'We must cover as much distance as we can before Constant realises we are not within the house.' He bent down and swung Louis-Anatole into the gig. 'So, *pichon*, you are ready for a midnight adventure?'

Louis-Anatole nodded.

'It's a long way.'

'Further than the lac de Barrenc?'

'Even further than that,' replied Pascal.

'I shall not mind,' Louis said. 'Marieta will play with me?'

'She will.'

'And Tante Léonie will tell me stories.'

The adults cast desperate glances at one another. In silence, Monsieur Baillard and Marieta climbed into the carriage, with Pascal settled on the driver's seat.

'Come on, Tante Léonie,' Louis-Anatole said.

Léonie closed the carriage door with a snap. 'Keep him safe.'

'You do not have to do this,' Baillard suddenly said. 'Constant is a sick man. It is possible that time and the natural run of things will bring this vendetta to an end, and soon. If you wait, all this may pass of its own volition.'

Léonie put her hand on his arm. 'It is possible, but I cannot take that risk. It might be three years, five, even ten. I cannot allow Louis-Anatole to grow up under such a shadow, always wondering, always looking out into the darkness. Thinking there is someone out there waiting to cause him harm.'

A memory of Anatole looking down at the street from their old apartment in the rue de Berlin. Another, of Isolde's haunted face gazing ever out at the horizon, seeing danger in the smallest thing.

She took a deep breath. 'I will not have Louis-Anatole live such a life. It has to end. Now, tonight, here.' She smiled. 'You believe this too, Sajhë.'

For a moment, in the flickering light of the lamps, their eyes met. Then, he nodded.

'I will return the cards to their ancient place,' he said quietly, 'when the boy is safe and there are no eyes to see me. You may trust me with that.'

'Tante Léonie?' said Louis-Anatole again, a little more anxiously.

'*Petit*, there is something I must do,' she said, keeping her voice level, 'which means I cannot come with you at this moment. You will be quite safe with Pascal and Marieta and Monsieur Baillard.'

His face crumpled as he reached out his arms to her, instinctively understanding that this was more than a temporary separation.

'No!' he cried. 'I don't want to leave you. I won't leave you.'

He threw himself across the seat and hurled his arms around Léonie's neck. She kissed him, then firmly detached herself from him.

'No!' the little boy shouted, struggling.

'Be good for Marieta,' she said, the words catching in her throat. 'And look after Monsieur Baillard and Pascal.'

Stepping back, she slapped her hand on the side of the carriage. 'Go!' she cried. 'Go!'

Pascal cracked the whip and the gig jerked forward. Léonie tried to close her ears to the sound of Louis-Anatole's voice calling out for her, getting fainter as he was carried away.

Blinded by tears, Léonie turned to face the old stone chapel. In the distance, the sky was glowing orange, filled with sparks and clouds of smoke, grey against the black night sky.

The house was burning.

She hardened her resolve. Then she turned the handle, pushed open the door and stepped over the threshold into the sepulchre.

CHAPTER 96

Cold air rushed to meet her.

Léonie pulled the box of matches from her pocket, opened the glass door of the lamp she had brought from the house and held a flame to the wick until it caught.

The blue eyes of Asmodeus fixed themselves upon her. Her heart rattling in her chest, Léonie stepped further into the nave. The paintings on the wall seemed to sway as she walked slowly up towards the altar. Grit on the flagstones scratched beneath the soles of her boots, loud in the silence of the tomb.

She was unsure what she should do first. In one pocket, she had the cards. In the other, the leather wallet containing the pieces of folded paper, the paintings she had attempted – of herself, of Anatole, of Isolde – from which she had not wished to be parted.

She had returned to her uncle's volume on several occasions, poring over the handwritten text, until she was word-perfect. Léonie understood that it was not the cards alone, nor the music, nor the place, but the combination of all three within the boundaries of the sepulchre that had the power to summon the ghosts who inhabited these ancient places. But still, despite this, a doubt remained over Monsieur Baillard's explanation of how the vivid life contained within the cards, and the music carried on the wind, might work one upon the other.

Could it be so?

And if the myths were the literal truth, then she knew that there would be no way back. The spirits would claim her. They had tried once before – and failed – but tonight she would willingly let them take her if they would take Constant too.

And Louis-Anatole will be safe.

A scratching sound, a tapping, made her jump. She cast her eyes around, looking for the source of the noise, before realising it was only the bare branches of a tree outside, knocking against the window.

Putting the lamp on the ground, Léonie lit each of the old tallow candles set in metal sconces on the wall. Drops of grease began to slide down the dead wicks, solidifying on the cold metal, but gradually each took and the sepulchre was filled with yellow, flickering light.

Léonie moved forward, feeling as if the eight tableaux within the apse were watching her every move, until she found the space before the altar where, a generation and more before, Jules Lascombe had spelled out the name of the Domaine in letters upon the stone floor. C-A-D-E.

She took the Tarot cards from her pocket, unwrapped them and placed the whole deck in the centre of the square, her late uncle's words reverberating in her head. Her leather wallet she placed beside the deck, undoing the ties but not taking the paintings out.

Through the power of which I would walk in another dimension.

Léonie raised her head. There was a moment of stillness then. Outside the chamber, she could hear the wind moving through the trees. She listened harder. The smoke still rose undisturbed from the candles, but now she thought she could almost discern the sound of music, thin notes, a high-pitched whistling as the wind threaded itself through the branches of the beech woods and the avenue of yew trees.

Then it came, slippery, in under the door, through the gaps between the lead and the stained glass of the windows.

There was a rushing of air and the sensation that I was not alone.

Léonie smiled, remembering the words on the page. She was not frightened now; she was curious. And then, as she looked up to the octagonal apse, she thought perhaps that she saw the face of La Force move. The faintest smile played across the painted face. And for an instant, the girl looked precisely like her – like her own face she had painted into her copies of the Tarot images. The same copper hair, the same green eyes, the same direct gaze.

My self and my other selves, both past and yet to come, were equally present.

Around her now, Léonie was aware of movement. Spirits, or the cards come to life, she could not say. The Lovers, to her hopeful and willing eyes, so clearly taking on the beloved features of Anatole and Isolde. For a fleeting moment, Léonie thought she could recognise the features of Louis-Anatole shimmering behind the image of La Justice, sitting with her scales and a run of notes around the rim of her long skirts, the boy she knew contained within the outline of the woman on the card. Then, out of the corner of her eye, only for a second, the features of Audric Baillard – Sajhë – seemed to imprint themselves upon the young face of Le Pagad.

Léonie stood completely still, letting the music wash over her. The faces and the costumes and the landscapes seemed to move, to shift and shimmer like stars, revolving in the silver air as if held by the invisible current of music. She lost any sense of herself. Dimension, space, time, mass, all vanished now to insignificance.

The vibrations, the rustling of the air – the ghosts, she supposed – brushed against her shoulders and neck, skimmed her forehead, surrounded her, gentle, kind, but without ever really touching. A silent chaos was growing, a cacophony of noiseless whispering and sighing.

Léonie reached her arms out in front of her. She felt herself weightless, transparent, as if floating in water, although her dress still hung red around her, the cloak black on her shoulders. They were waiting for her to join them. She turned over her outstretched hands and saw, quite clearly, the infinity symbol appear on the pale skin of her palms. Like a figure of eight.

'Aïci lo tems s'en, va res l'eternitat.'

The words fell silver from her lips. Now, after waiting so long, there was no mistaking their meaning.

Here, in this place, time moves away towards eternity.

Léonie smiled and – with the thought of Louis-Anatole behind her, her mother and brother and aunt before her – she stepped forward into the light.

The jolting over the rough ground had caused him great discomfort, opening several of the sores on his hands and on his back.

Constant descended from the carriage.

He poked the ground with his walking stick. Two horses had stood here – and recently. The wheel ruts suggested only one carriage and appeared to lead away from, rather than towards, the sepulchre.

'Wait here,' he instructed.

Constant felt the curious force of the wind insinuating itself between the tightly knit trunks of the avenue of yews that led to the door of the tomb. With his free hand, he held his greatcoat tight around his throat against the strengthening currents. He sniffed. His sense of smell was almost gone, but he could just pick out an unpleasant odour, a peculiar mixture of incense and the malodorous scent of rotting seaweed on the shore.

Though his eyes were watering with the cold, he could see there were lights burning inside. The thought that the boy might be hiding there powered him forward. He strode ahead, paying no attention to the rushing sound, almost like water, nor to the whistling, like wind chasing down the telegraph wires.

It was almost like music.

He refused to be diverted by whatever tricks Léonie Vernier might or might not be attempting with the light or smoke or sound.

Constant approached the heavy door and turned the handle. At first, it did not shift. He tried again and this time, all at once, it fell open. Constant almost lost his balance and half stepped, half fell into the sepulchre.

Straight away, he saw her, standing with her back to him in front of a small altar set within an eight-sided apse. Indeed, she was making no attempt to conceal herself. Of the boy, there was no sign.

His chin jutting forward, his eyes darting to left and right, Constant processed up the nave, his stick tapping on the flagstones as his feet fell awkwardly from step to step. There was an empty plinth just inside the door, jagged on the top as if the statue had been torn from it. Familiar plaster saints, set around the walls behind the modest rows of empty pews, marked his passing as he drew nearer to the altar.

'Mademoiselle Vernier,' he said, confused by her inattention.

Still she did not move. Indeed, she seemed unaware of his presence.

Constant stopped and looked down at the pile of cards strewn on the stone floor before the altar. 'What absurdity is this?' he said, and stepped into the square.

Now Léonie turned to face him. The hood fell from her face. Constant threw up his diseased hands to shield his eyes from the light. The smile slipped from his lips. He did not understand. He could see the girl's features, the same direct gaze, the hair now tumbling loose as it had been in the portrait he had stolen from the rue de Berlin, but she was transformed into something other.

As he stood there, captivated and blinded, she began to change. The bones, the sinews, the skull beneath the skin started to push through.

Constant screamed.

Something swooped down upon him and the silence he had not recognised as silence was broken in a disharmony of shrieking. He clamped his hands over his ears to stop the creatures from entering his head, but his fingers were pulled away by talons and claws, even though not a mark was laid upon him.

It seemed as if the painted figures had stepped down from the wall, each now transformed into a dark version of their fairer selves. Nails turned to talons, fingers to claws, eyes to fire and ice. Constant buried his head in his chest, dropping his stick as he curled his arms over his face to protect himself. He fell to his knees, gasped for breath as his heart began to lose its rhythm. He tried to move forward, out of the square on the ground, but an invisible force, like an overwhelming wind, kept pushing him back. The howling, the vibrating of the music was getting louder. It seemed to come from outside as well as in, echoing inside his head. Splitting open his mind.

'No!' he shouted.

But the voices were increasing in volume and intensity. Uncomprehending, he looked for Léonie Vernier. He could no longer see her at all. The light was too bright, the air shimmering with incandescent smoke.

Then, behind him, or rather from beneath the very surface of his skin, came a different noise. A scraping, like the claws of a wild animal, grating along the surface of his bones. He flinched and jerked, crying out in agony, then fell to the floor in a rushing of air.

And suddenly, crouched on his chest, with a reek of fish and pitch, was a demon, gaunt and twisted, with red leathery skin, a horned brow and strange, penetrating blue eyes. The demon that he knew could not exist. Did not exist. Yet the face of Asmodeus was looking down upon him.

'No!' His mouth opened in one final howl, before the devil took him.

Instantly, the air in the sepulchre was still. The whisperings and sighings of the spirits grew fainter until, at last, there was silence. The cards lay scattered on the ground. The faces upon the wall became flat and two-dimensional once more, but their expressions and attitudes had shifted subtly. Each bore an unmistakable resemblance to those who had lived – and died – in the Domaine de la Cade. Like Léonie's paintings.

Outside in the clearing, Constant's manservant cowered from the wind, the smoke and the light. He heard his master scream, once, then again. The inhuman sound kept him too petrified to move.

Only now, when all had fallen quiet and the lights within the sepulchre had steadied, did he summon the courage to come out of his hiding place. Slowly, he approached the heavy door and found it slightly ajar. His tentative hand encountered no resistance.

'Monsieur?'

He stepped inside and called again. 'Monsieur?'

A draught, like an exhalation, emptied the sepulchre of smoke in a single, cool breath, leaving the place lit by the lamp on the wall.

He saw the body of his master immediately. He was lying face down on the ground, in front of the altar, a deck of playing cards scattered all about him. The servant rushed forward and rolled his master's emaciated form onto its back, then recoiled. Across Constant's face were three deep, red gashes, like the savage marks of a wild animal.

The man crossed himself mechanically and leaned forward to close his master's wide, horrified eyes. Then his hand stopped as he noticed the rectangular card lying across Constant's chest, over his heart. Le Diable.

Had it been there all along?

Uncomprehending, the servant's hand went to his pocket, where he could swear he had placed the card his master had instructed him to leave with the body of Curé Gélis in Coustaussa. The pocket was empty.

Had he dropped it? What other explanation could there be?

There was a moment of recognition, then the manservant staggered back from his master's body and started to run down the nave, past the unseeing eyes of the statues, out of the sepulchre, away from the grimacing face on the card.

In the valley below, the midnight bell began to toll.

PART XII

The Ruins
October 2007

CHAPTER 97

'**D**r O'Donnell!' Hal shouted again.

It was ten past twelve. For more than fifteen minutes, he'd been waiting outside Shelagh O'Donnell's house. Neither of her neighbours was in, so he'd gone for a walk, come back and started knocking again. Still nothing.

Hal knew he was in the right place – he'd checked the address several times – and he didn't think she could have forgotten. He was trying to stay optimistic, but it was becoming more of a challenge with every second that passed. Where was she? The traffic was bad this morning, so maybe she'd got held up? Maybe she was in the shower and hadn't heard him?

The most likely scenario, of course, was that Shelagh had thought better of going with him to the police. Her dislike of authority was clear and Hal could easily see her losing what little nerve she had without him and Meredith there to back her up.

He pushed his fingers through his hair, took a step back and looked up at the shuttered windows. The house stood in the middle of a pretty row next to the River Aude, overlooking the water, shielded on one side from the walkway by a fence of green angle iron and split bamboo canes. It occurred to him that he might be able to see into the garden from the back. He followed the line of the buildings, then doubled back on himself. It was hard to tell which house was which from the back, but he matched the colour wash of the walls – one house was painted pale blue, another a thin yellow – until he was confident he knew which was Shelagh O'Donnell's property.

There was a low wall at right angles to the hedge. Hal walked closer to get a glimpse of the terrace. Hope sparked in his chest. It looked as if there was someone there.

'Dr O'Donnell? It's me, Hal Lawrence.'

There was no answer.

'Dr O'Donnell? It's a quarter past twelve.'

She appeared to be lying face down on the small terrace next to the house. It was a sheltered spot and the sun was surprisingly warm for the tail end of October, but it was hardly sunbathing weather. Perhaps she was reading a book; he couldn't see. But whatever she was doing, he thought with irritation, she had clearly decided to ignore him – to pretend he wasn't there. His view was obscured by a pair of unkempt planters.

His phone vibrated in his pocket. His mind only half on it, he pulled it out and read the message.

'Found them. Going to sepulchre now. xx.'

Hal stared blankly at the words on the screen, then he smiled, understanding Meredith's message.

'At least someone's having a productive morning,' he muttered. It spurred him on. After all the effort he'd put in to persuading the commissaire to see them, he wasn't going to let Shelagh duck out.

'Dr O'Donnell!' he called out again. 'I know you're there.'

Now he was starting to wonder. Even if she had changed her mind, it was odd that she was taking no notice at all. He was making enough noise. He hesitated, then pulled himself up and climbed over the wall. There was a heavy

648

stick lying on the terrace, half pushed under the hedge. He picked it up, then noticed there was blood on it.

With a very bad feeling, Hal ran across the terrace to where Shelagh O'Donnell was lying. One look was enough to see she'd been struck, and more than once. He checked her pulse. She was still breathing, although it was touch-and-go.

Hal pulled the phone from his pocket and dialled for an ambulance. '*Vite!*' he shouted, after he'd given the address three times. '*Oui, elle souffle! Mais vite, alors!*'

Rushing into the house, Hal found a blanket draped over the back of the sofa. He laid it carefully over Shelagh to keep her warm, knowing he shouldn't attempt to move her, then went through the house to the street. He felt guilty about what he was about to do, but he couldn't wait for the paramedics.

Hal hammered on the neighbour's door. When she answered, he told the startled woman there'd been an accident, asked her to stay with Dr O'Donnell until the ambulance arrived, then bolted to his car before she had a chance to object.

He put his foot on the accelerator. There was only one person who could be responsible. He had to get back to the Domaine de la Cade. And find Meredith.

Julian Lawrence charged up the front steps of the hotel. What had he done?

There were beads of sweat running down his face and soaking into the collar of his shirt. He stumbled into the reception. He needed to calm down. Then work out what to do.

'Monsieur? Monsieur Lawrence?'

He swung round to see the receptionist waving at him.

'Monsieur Lawrence,' Eloise started, then broke off. 'Are you all right?'

'What is it?' he snapped.

She flinched. 'Your nephew asked me to give you this.'

Julian snatched the paper from Eloise's outstretched hands. The note was from Hal, curt and to the point, saying he wanted to meet at two o'clock.

Julian screwed up the paper in his fist. 'What time did he leave this?' he demanded.

'About ten-thirty, Monsieur, just after you went out.'

'Is my nephew in the hotel now?'

'I believe he went to Rennes-les-Bains just before noon. To my knowledge, he hasn't yet come back.'

'Was the American girl with him?'

'No. She went out into the gardens,' she replied coldly.

'How long ago was this?'

'At least one hour, Monsieur.'

'Did she say what she was doing? Where she was going? Did you hear anything between her and my nephew, Eloise? Anything?'

Her growing alarm at his manner showed in her eyes, but she answered.

'No, but when she went out to the gardens, she asked if she might borrow a – I don't know the English word – *une pelle.*'

Julian starred at her. 'A spade?'

Eloise leapt back in alarm as Julian smacked his hands down on the desk, leaving two palm prints on the counter. Ms Martin would hardly ask for a spade if she didn't intend to dig. And she had waited until she knew he had left the hotel.

'The cards,' he muttered. 'She knows where they are.'

'*Qu'est-ce qu'il y a, monsieur?*' said Eloise, nervous now. '*Vous semblez—*'

Julian turned on his heel and strode out onto the terrace.

'What shall I say when your nephew comes back?' Eloise called after him.

He didn't answer.

CHAPTER 98

There was an avenue of yew trees straight ahead and the echo of an old path. It seemed to lead nowhere, but as Meredith looked closer, she could see the outline of foundations and a few broken stones on the ground. There was once a building here.

This is the place.

Holding the box containing the deck of cards, she walked slowly towards where the sepulchre had stood. She could feel the abandonment and isolation of the place through the soles of her muddy boots.

Meredith bit back her disappointment. A few blocks, the remains of an outer wall – otherwise just empty space. Grass as far as the eye could see.

Look closer.

Meredith looked into the space. Now she saw that the surface was not entirely flat. With a little imagination, she realised she could just about work out the footprint of the original building. A patch of ground, maybe twenty feet long by ten feet wide, like a sunken garden. Clutching the handles of the box a little more tightly, she stepped forward. Only as she was doing so did Meredith realise she'd lifted her foot.

As if stepping over a threshold.

Straight away, the light seemed to change. To grow denser, more opaque. The roaring of the wind in her ears was louder, like a high, repeated note or the buzz along telephone wires in the breeze. And she could detect the slightest scent of incense, the heady smell of stone and ancient worship hanging in the air.

She put the box down, then looked around. Some trick of the air made a soft mist rise from the damp soil. Then pinpricks of light began to appear, one by one, hanging suspended around the periphery of the ruin, as if some invisible hand was lighting a set of tiny candles. As each halo of light connected to the rest, they gave shape to the vanished walls of the sepulchre. Through the veil of thin cloud, Meredith thought she saw the outline of letters on the ground – C-A-D-E. As she stepped forward, the surface beneath her boots felt different too. No longer earth and grass, but hard, cold flagstones.

Meredith knelt down. Oblivious to the wet seeping through the knees of her jeans, she took out the deck and shut the lid, then laid her jacket, inside out, across the workbox. She shuffled the cards, as Laura had showed her in Paris, then cut the deck into three separate piles with her left hand. She put them back together – middle, top, bottom – and placed the entire deck face down on her makeshift table.

I cannot sleep.

Meredith knew she could not attempt a reading for herself. Every time she read through the notes she'd made, she was more confused by the meanings than before. She just intended to turn the cards – perhaps eight, respecting the relationship of the music with the place – until some pattern emerged.

Until, as Laura promised, the cards told the story.

She drew the first card and smiled to see the familiar features of La Justice. Despite the shuffling and cutting of the cards, it was the same card that had been on the top when she found the deck hidden in the dry riverbed.

The second card was La Tour, a card of conflict and threat. She placed it beside the first, then drew again. The clear blue eyes of Le Pagad looked up at her, one hand pointing to heaven and one to earth, the infinity symbol above his head. It was a slightly menacing figure, neither clearly good, nor clearly bad. As she stared, Meredith started to think she knew his face, although she could not yet recognise him.

Card four made her smile again: Le Mat. Anatole Vernier, in his white suit and boater, walking stick in hand, as painted by his sister. La Prêtresse followed him, Isolde Vernier, elegant and sophisticated. Then Les Amoureux, Isolde and Anatole together.

Card seven was Le Diable. Her hand hovered over the card a moment, watching while the malevolent features of Asmodeus took shape before her eyes. The demon, the personification of the terrors and mountain hauntings related by Audric Baillard in his book. Stories of evil, past and present.

Meredith knew now, from the sequence she had drawn, what the last card would be. Each of the *dramatis personae* were here, portrayed in the cards Léonie had painted, yet modified or somehow transformed to tell a specific story.

With the smell of the incense in her nose and the colours of the past fixed in her imagination, Meredith felt time sliding away. A continuous present, everything that had come before and everything that was yet to come, joined in this act of the laying out of the cards.

Things slipping between past and present.

She touched the final card with the tips of her fingers and, without even turning it over, Meredith felt Léonie step out of the shadows.

Card VIII: La Force.

Leaving it still unturned, she sat back on the ground and looked at the octave of cards laid out on the box. Then she realised that the images were starting to shift. She found her eye drawn to Le Mat. At first, it was just a spot of colour that had not been there before. A speck of blood, almost too small to see, growing larger, blossoming, red against the white of Anatole's suit. Covering his heart. For a moment, the painted eyes seemed to hold her in his gaze.

Meredith caught her breath, appalled yet unable to tear herself away, as she realised she was watching Anatole Vernier die. The figure fell slowly to the bottom of the painted ground, revealing the mountains of Soularac and Bézu in the background.

Desperate not to see more, yet feeling she had no choice, a movement on the adjacent card drew her. Meredith turned to La Prêtresse. To start with, the beautiful face of Isolde Vernier looked calmly up at her from card II, serene in a long blue dress and white gloves. Then her features started to change, the colour shifting from pink to blue. Her eyes widened, her arms seemed to glide above her head, as if she was swimming, floating.

Drowning.

And Meredith, thinking of her own mother sinking beneath the water, felt grief catch in her throat.

The card seemed to become darker, as Isolde's skirts billowed in the water around stockinged legs, shimmering silk in the opaque green underwater world, slimy fingers slipping the ivory shoes from her feet.

Isolde's eyes fell shut, but as they did, Meredith saw that the expression shining out of them was release, not fear, not the horror of drowning. How could that be? Had her life become such a burden to her that she wanted to die?

She glanced to the end of the row, at Le Diable, and smiled. The two figures imprisoned at the feet of the demon were no longer there. The chains hung empty around the base of the plinth. Asmodeus was alone.

Meredith took a deep breath. If the cards could speak the story of what had happened, what of Léonie? She reached out but still could not bring herself to turn the last card. She was desperate to know the truth, yet feared the story she might see in the shifting images.

She tucked her nail under the corner of the card, closed her eyes and silently counted to three. Then she looked.

The face of the card was blank.

She picked it up and turned it over, then back again. The card was still blank, completely white; not even the greens and blues of the Midi landscape remained.

A sound interrupted her thoughts: the crunch of stones knocked out of place on the path, the wild beating of a bird on the wing as it flew up out of the tree.

Meredith stood up. 'Hal?'

Possibilities flashed into her mind, none of them reassuring. She pushed them out. It had to be Hal. She'd told him where she was going. No one else knew she was here.

'Hal? Is that you?'

The footsteps were getting nearer. Someone walking fast through the woods, the swish of displaced leaves, the crack of twigs underfoot.

'Hal?' she said again, uneasy now.

Meredith wasn't sure what to do. The smart thing would be to run, not stick around waiting to see what the person wanted. If, indeed, there was someone there.

No, the smart thing is not to overreact.

She tried to tell herself it was just another guest out for a walk in the woods, like her. All the same, she moved quickly to pack away the cards. Now she noticed that several others were blank. La Tour and Le Pagad were empty too.

With fingers made clumsy by nerves and the cold, she snatched at the cards. She had the sensation of a spider running over her bare skin and flicked at her wrist to get it off. There was nothing there, although she could still feel it.

There was a different smell now too. No longer the scent of fallen leaves and ancient stone or the incense she'd imagined a few minutes earlier, but the stink of the sea on some stagnant estuary. And the smell of fire; not the familiar autumn bonfires down in the valley, but hot ash and acrid smoke.

The moment passed. Meredith blinked and pulled herself back. Then, out of the corner of her eye, she noticed a movement. There was some kind of animal, its fur black and matted, moving low through the undergrowth, circling the glade. She froze. It looked the size of a wolf or a wild boar. It seemed to spring from leg to leg. Meredith clutched the cards more tightly. Now she could make out obscenely misshapen front legs, and leathery, blistered skin. For a second, the creature turned its piercing blue gaze on her. She felt a sharp pain in her chest, like the point of a knife. Then the creature turned away and the pressure on her heart was released.

Startled by a sharp noise, she looked down and saw the scales of justice slip from the hand of the figure on card XI. Heard the clatter as the brass dishes and iron weights fell to the stone floor of the painting and scattered.

Coming to get you.

The two stories had merged, as Laura had predicted they would. The past and the present, brought together by the cards.

Meredith felt the hairs on her neck prickle, and realised that while she had been staring into the woods, trying to see what was out there in the gloom of the forest, she had forgotten the threat from the opposite direction.

It was too late to run.

Someone – something – was already behind her.

CHAPTER 99

'Give me the cards,' he said.

Meredith's heart leapt into her mouth at the sound of his voice.

She spun round, clutching the cards tightly, then recoiled. Julian Lawrence looked quite wild, as if he didn't really know where he was. His shirt was open at the neck and he was sweating heavily. There was the sour smell of whisky on his breath.

'There's something in the woods,' she said, the words bursting out of her mouth before she had a chance to think. 'A wolf or something, I'm telling you. I saw it. Outside the walls.'

He stopped, confusion clouding his desperate eyes. 'Walls? What walls? What are you talking about?'

Meredith glanced around. The candles were still flickering, sending shadows outlining the shape of the Visigoth tomb.

'Can't you see them?' she asked. 'It's so clear. The lights shining where the sepulchre used to be?'

A sly smile moved across his lips. 'Ah, I see what you're doing,' he said. 'But it won't work. Wolves, animals, ghosts – all highly diverting, but you're not going to stop me from getting what I want.' He took another step closer. 'Give me the cards.'

Meredith stumbled back. She was on his property, she was digging up his grounds without permission. She was the one in the wrong, not him. But the look on his face turned her blood cold. Piercing blue eyes, his pupils dilated. Fear trickled down her spine when she thought of how isolated they were, miles from anywhere, in the woods.

She needed to keep some kind of leverage. She watched cautiously as he glanced around the clearing.

'Did you find the deck here?' he said. 'No, I dug here. It wasn't here.'

Until now, Meredith hadn't really believed Hal's suspicions about his uncle. Even if Dr O'Donnell was right and it had been Julian Lawrence's blue car on the road just after the accident, failing to stop was not the same as having had something to do with the accident in the first place. But now, she wasn't so sure.

'Hal will be here any moment,' she said.

'And what difference does that make?'

She glanced around, trying to figure out if she could run. She was younger and fitter than him. But she didn't want to abandon Léonie's workbox on the ground. And even if Julian thought she was just trying to scare him with talk of wolves, she knew she had seen something, some predator, skulking around the edges of the clearing.

'Give me the cards and I won't hurt you,' he said.

Meredith met his gaze. 'I don't believe you.'

'I don't think it matters whether you believe me or not,' he said, then he lost his temper: 'Give them to me!'

Meredith clutched the cards to her, then she smelt it again – stronger than before – a stomach-churning stench of rotting fish and an even more pervasive smell of fire.

Julian was oblivious to everything but the cards. He kept walking towards her, getting closer and closer, holding out his hand.

'Get away from her!'

They both spun round, as Hal came running out of the woods, heading for his uncle.

Julian drew back his arm and caught him under the jaw with his fist. Taken by surprise, Hal went down.

'Hal!' Meredith shouted.

Hal lashed out at his uncle, striking him on the side of the knee. Julian stumbled but stayed on his feet. Hal struggled to get up, but although Julian was older and much heavier, he knew how to fight. He clenched his hands together and brought them down with force on the back of Hal's neck.

Caught between protecting Hal and protecting the cards, Meredith quickly put the cards in her pocket, then ran to where Hal lay unconscious on the ground.

Julian has nothing to lose.

'Pass me the cards.'

There was another gust of wind, carrying the smell of burning. This time, Julian smelt it too. Confusion flickered briefly in his eyes.

'I'll kill you if I have to,' he said, so casually that it made the threat all the more believable. Meredith didn't reply. Now the flickering candlelight she had imagined on the walls of the sepulchre was turning to leaping orange and gold flames. The sepulchre was burning. Black smoke was enveloping the clearing, licking at the stones. Meredith imagined she could hear the crackle of paint on the plaster saints as they started to scorch. The glass in the windows exploded outwards as the metal frames buckled.

'Can't you see it?' she shouted above the noise. 'Can't you see what's happening?'

She saw alarm flood across his face, then a look of pure horror fill his eyes. Meredith turned, but she was too slow to see it clearly. Something rushed past her, some kind of animal, with black, matted fur. With a strange jerking movement, it leapt.

Julian screamed.

Meredith watched in horror as he fell, trying to propel himself backwards on the ground. He threw up his arms, as if wrestling with some invisible creature, striking out at the empty air. His hands were clawing at his throat, tearing at the skin, as if trying to free himself from the grasp of a hand.

And Meredith heard the whispering, a different voice, deeper and louder than Léonie's, reverberating inside her head. She didn't recognise the words, but she understood the meaning.

Fujhi, poudes; escapa, non.

Flee you may, escape you cannot.

She saw the fight go out of Julian and he fell back onto the ground.

An immediate silence descended on the glade. Meredith looked blindly around. She was standing on a bare patch of grass. No flames, no walls, no smell of the grave or the sea.

Hal was stirring, raising himself up on one elbow. He put his hand to his face, then held out his palm, sticky with blood.

'What the hell happened?'

Meredith ran over and put her arms around him. 'He hit you.'

Hal blinked, then turned his head to where his uncle lay on the ground. His eyes widened. 'Did you . . .?'

'No,' she said quickly. 'I didn't touch him. I don't know what happened. One minute he was . . .' She stopped, not knowing how she could possibly describe to Hal what she'd seen.

'Heart attack?'

Meredith bent down beside Julian. His face was chalk white, tinged with blue around his lips and nose.

'He's still alive,' she said, pulling her cell phone from her pocket and tossing it to Hal. 'Call. If the paramedics are fast.'

He caught it but made no move to dial. She saw the look in his eye and knew what he was thinking.

'No,' she said softly. 'Not like this.'

He held her gaze for a moment, his blue eyes flickering with hurt. A magician, with power over life and death.

'Make the call, Hal.'

Meredith saw his eyes cloud over, then he came back to himself. Justice, not revenge. He began to punch in the number.

Meredith crouched down again beside Julian. His palms lay exposed to the air. There was a strange red mark on each, like a figure of eight. She put her hand on his chest and then realised. He was no longer breathing.

'Hal,' she said, shaking her head. 'It's too late.'

CHAPTER 100

Eleven days later, Meredith stood on the promontory overlooking the lake at the Domaine de la Cade, watching as a wooden casket was lowered into the ground.

It was a small party. Herself and Hal, now the legal owner of the hotel, together with Shelagh O'Donnell, still bearing the evidence of Julian's attack. The local priest was there and a representative from the *mairie*. After some persuasion, the town hall had given permission for the service to go ahead on the grounds that the site could be identified as the place where Anatole and Isolde Vernier were buried. Julian Lawrence had plundered the graves, but not disturbed the bones.

Now, after more than a hundred years, Léonie could finally be laid to rest beside the bodies of her beloved brother and his wife.

Relief caught in Meredith's throat. It was the end of the story.

In the hours after Julian's death, Léonie's remains had been unearthed in a shallow grave beneath the ruins of the sepulchre. It looked as if she had simply lain down on the ground to rest. No one could account for the fact that she had not been found before, given the extensive excavations that had been carried out on the site. Nor why her bones had not been scattered by wild animals.

But Meredith had stood at the foot of the grave and seen how the colours of the earth beneath Léonie's sleeping body, the burnished hues of the leaves above her and the faded fragments of material that still clothed her body and kept her warm, matched the illustration on one of the Tarot cards. Not the replica deck, but the original. Card VIII: La Force.

Earth, air, fire, water.

Caught up in the formalities, it had been impossible to find out precisely what had happened to Léonie on the night of 31st October 1897. There had been a fire at the Domaine de la Cade, that much was on record. It had broken out around dusk and, in the course of a few hours, destroyed part of the main house. The library and the study were the worst damaged. There was evidence that the fire had been started deliberately.

The following morning, All Saints' Day, several bodies had been recovered from the smouldering ruins – servants, it was presumed, who had found themselves trapped by the flames. And there were other victims, men who didn't work on the estate, from Rennes-les-Bains itself.

It was not clear why Léonie Vernier had chosen – or been forced – to remain behind when other inhabitants of the Domaine de la Cade, her nephew Louis-Anatole among them, fled. There was also no explanation of how the fire had spread so fast and destroyed the sepulchre too. The *Courrier d'Aude* and other local newspapers of the time made mention of the high winds that night, but even so, could they have bridged the gap between the house and the Visigoth tomb in the woods?

Meredith knew she would figure it out. In time, she'd fit all the pieces together.

Sunlight glanced off the surface of the water, the trees and the landscape that had held its secrets for so long. A breath of wind whispered across the grounds, through the valley. The priest's voice, clear and timeless, called Meredith back to the present.

'*In nomine Patri, et Filii et Spiritus Sancti.* In the name of the Father, the Son and the Holy Ghost.'

She felt Hal take her hand.

Amen. So be it.

The curé, tall in his heavy black felt cloak, smiled at her. The tip of his nose was red, she noticed.

'Mademoiselle Martin, *c'est à vous, alors.*'

She took a deep breath. Now the moment had come, she was suddenly reluctant. She felt Hal squeeze her fingers, then gently let her go.

Struggling to keep her emotions in check, Meredith stepped forward to the edge of the grave. From her pocket, she took two items recovered from Julian Lawrence's study: a silver locket and a gentleman's fob watch. Both were simply inscribed with initials and a date: 22 October 1891, commemorating the marriage of Anatole Vernier to Isolde Lascombe. Meredith hesitated, then dropped them gently into the ground where they belonged, beside their graves.

She glanced up at Hal, who smiled and gave the slightest nod. She took another deep breath, then pulled out an envelope: the piece of music, Meredith's treasured heirloom, carried by Louis-Anatole across the water from France to America, and down the generations to her. It was hard not to keep it, but Meredith knew it belonged with Léonie.

She looked down at the small slate plaque set into the ground, grey against the grass:

LÉONIE VERNIER.

22 AOUT 1874 – 31 OCTOBRE 1897.

REQUIESCAT IN PACE.

Meredith let the envelope go. It twisted, then spiralled down through the still air, a flash of white slowly falling from her black-gloved fingers.

Let the dead rest.

She stepped back, hands clasped in front of her, head bowed. For a moment, the small group stood in silence, paying their final respects. Then Meredith nodded to the priest.

'*Merci, Monsieur le Curé.*'

'*Je vous en prie.*'

Pressing his hands together, he seemed to draw in all those gathered on the promontory, then led the small party back down the hill and round the lake. As they struck out across the lawns, bright with morning dew, the rising sun was reflected like flames in the windows of the house.

Meredith stopped. 'Can you give me a minute?'

Hal nodded. 'I'll see them settled inside, then come back for you.'

She watched as he walked away, up onto the terrace, then she turned back to look across the lake. She wanted to linger a while longer.

Meredith pulled her coat tightly around her. Her toes and fingers were numb and her eyes were stinging. She didn't want to leave the Domaine de la Cade, but she knew it was time. This time tomorrow, she'd be on her way back to Paris. The day after, she'd be on a plane above the Atlantic on her way home. Then she'd have to figure out where the hell to go from there.

Work out if she and Hal had a future.

Meredith looked across the sleeping waters, flat as a mirror, to the promontory. Then, beside the old stone seat, Meredith thought she saw a figure, a shimmering outline in a white-and-green dress, tapered at the waist, full at the hem and arms. Her hair hung loose around her. The trees behind her, silver with hoar frost, shone like metal.

Meredith thought she heard the music once more, although she wasn't sure if it was inside her mind or from deep within the earth.

She stood in silence, waiting. Watching. There was a flash on the water, a refraction of the light perhaps, and Meredith saw Léonie raise her hand. A slim arm silhouetted against the white sky. Long fingers encased in black gloves.

She thought of the Tarot cards. Léonie's cards, painted by her more than a hundred years ago to tell her story and that of the people she had loved. In the confusion and chaos of the hours immediately after Julian's death on Hallowe'en – while Hal had been at the commissariat and calls were going backwards and forwards between the hospital, where Shelagh was being treated, and the morgue where Julian's body had been taken – Meredith had quietly, and without any fuss, replaced the cards in Léonie's workbox and returned it to the ancient hiding place in the woods.

They, too, belonged in the ground.

Her eyes stayed fixed on the middle distance, but the image was fading. It was the desire for justice that had kept Léonie here until the full story was told. Now she could rest in peace in the quiet ground she had loved so well.

Meredith felt Hal come up and stand beside her. 'How's it going?' he said quietly.

Let the dead sleep.

Meredith knew Hal was struggling. Over the past eleven days, they had talked and talked. She had told him everything that had happened, leading up to the moment when he burst into the clearing, minutes behind his uncle – about Léonie, about her Tarot reading in Paris, about the obsession stretching back more than a hundred years that had taken so many lives, about the stories of the demon and the music of the place, about how she felt she had somehow been drawn to the Domaine de la Cade. Myths, legends, facts, history, all jumbled up together.

666

'I'm good,' she said. 'A little cold.'

Meredith kept her eyes fixed on the middle distance. The light was changing. Even the birds had stopped singing.

'What I still don't understand,' Hal said, pushing his hands deep into his pockets, 'is why you? I mean, obviously there's the family connection with the Verniers, but even so . . .'

He trailed off, not sure where he was going.

'Maybe,' she said, 'because I don't believe in ghosts.'

Now she was no longer aware of Hal, of the pale-purple light spreading through the valley of the Aude. Only of the face of the girl on the other side of the water. Slipping away like the echo of a note.

Grey, to white, to nothing.

Meredith raised her hand, as if to wave, as the shimmering outline faded finally to absence. Slowly, she lowered her arm.

Requiescat in pace.

'Are you sure you're OK?' Hal said again. He sounded worried.

She nodded slowly.

For a few minutes more, Meredith stood staring into the empty space, unwilling to break her connection with the place. She took a deep breath and reached for Hal. He felt warm – solid flesh and blood.

'Let's head back,' she said.

Hand in hand, they turned and walked across the lawns towards the terrace. Their thoughts were running down very different paths. Hal was thinking of coffee. Meredith was thinking of Léonie. And how much she was going to miss her.

CODA

Three Years Later

SUNDAY, 31ST OCTOBER 2010

'Ladies and gentlemen, good evening. My name is Mark and it's my great honour to welcome Ms Meredith Martin here tonight.'

There was a burst of enthusiastic, if sparse, applause, then a hush descended over the tiny independent bookstore. Hal, sitting in the front row, smiled encouragement at her. Standing at the back, her arms folded, was her publisher, who gave the thumbs-up sign.

'As many of you know,' the manager continued, 'Ms Martin is the author of the acclaimed biography of the French composer Claude Debussy, which came out last year to rave reviews. However, what you may not know . . .'

Mark was an old friend, and Meredith had a horrible feeling he was going to start way back, taking the audience all the way through elementary school, high school and university, before he even got on to the subject of the book.

She let her mind wander, running down familiar paths. She thought about everything that had happened to bring her to this point. Three years of research, evidence, checking and double-checking, trying to fit together the pieces of Léonie's history while struggling to finish and deliver her biography of Debussy on time.

Meredith never did discover if Lilly Debussy had visited Rennes-les-Bains, but once back in America, she'd learned that the Verniers and the Debussys had been neighbours in the rue de Berlin in Paris. And when Meredith visited Debussy's grave in the Cimetière de Passy in the 16th *arrondissement*, where Manet and Morisot, Fauré and André Messager were also buried, she had found, hidden in a corner of the cemetery beneath the trees, the tomb of Marguerite Vernier.

The following year, back in Paris with Hal, Meredith had paid a visit to lay flowers on the grave.

As soon as she'd delivered the manuscript in the spring of 2008, Meredith had concentrated full time on researching the Domaine de la Cade and how her family had emigrated from France to America.

She started with Léonie. The more Meredith read about Rennes-les-Bains and the theories surrounding Abbé Saunière and Rennes-le-Château, the more she agreed with Hal that it was all part of a smokescreen to draw attention away from what had happened at the Domaine de la Cade. She was inclined to think that the three corpses discovered in the 1950s in the garden of Abbé Saunière's home in Rennes-le-Château were connected to the events of 31st October 1897 in the Domaine de la Cade.

Meredith suspected that one of the bodies was that of Victor Constant, the man who murdered Anatole and Marguerite Vernier. Records showed that Constant had fled to Spain and been treated in several clinics for third-stage syphilis, but that he had returned to France in the fall of 1897. The second might have been Constant's manservant, who was known to have been among the mob that attacked the house and caused the fire. His body had never been found. The third was harder to account for. A twisted spine, abnormally long arms, a person of no more than four feet in height.

The other event that caught Meredith's attention was the murder of Curé Antoine Gélis of Coustaussa, some time during the same night in October 1897. Gélis was a recluse. On the surface, his death seemed unconnected with the events at the Domaine de la Cade, apart from the coincidence of the date. He had been attacked first with his own fire tongs, then with an axe lying in the grate of the old presbytery. The *Courrier d'Aude* reported that there were fourteen wounds to his head and multiple skull fractures.

It was a particularly savage and apparently motiveless murder. The killer was never found. All the local newspapers of the time carried the story, and the details were much the same. Having killed the old man, the murderer laid out the body, crossing the old man's hands across his chest. The house had been searched and a strongbox forced open, but it was said by a niece who looked after him to be empty anyway. Nothing appeared to have been taken.

When Meredith researched a little deeper, she discovered two details buried deep in one of the newspaper reports. First, that on the afternoon of Hallowe'en, a girl matching the description of Léonie Vernier visited the presbytery in Coustaussa. Second, that a Tarot card had been left pushed between the fingers of the dead man's left hand.

Card XV: Le Diable.

When Meredith had read that, recalling what had happened in the ruins of the sepulchre, she thought she understood. The devil, through his servant Asmodeus, had taken another of his own.

As for who had placed Léonie's workbox and the original cards in their hiding place beneath the winterbourne, that remained unresolved. Meredith imagined Louis-Anatole creeping back into the Domaine de la Cade under cover of night and replacing the cards where they belonged in memory of his aunt. Her head told her it was more likely to have been a man called Audric Baillard, whose role in the story she'd not yet completely worked out.

The genealogical information was more straightforward to pin down. With the assistance of the same lady in the town hall in Rennes-les-Bains, who turned out to be both resourceful and extremely efficient, during the summer and early fall, Meredith had put together Louis-Anatole's history. The son of Anatole and Isolde, he had grown up in the care of Audric Baillard in Los Seres, a small village in the Sabarthès. After Léonie's death, Louis-Anatole had never returned to the Domaine de la Cade and the estate had been allowed to go to ruin. Meredith assumed Louis-Anatole's guardian was the father, maybe even grandfather, of the Audric S. Baillard who had written *Diables et esprits maléfiques et phantômes de la montagne*.

Louis-Anatole Vernier, together with a family servant, Pascal Barthes, had enlisted in the French army in 1914 and seen active service. Pascal was much decorated but did not survive the war. Louis-Anatole did and, when peace was declared in 1918, he made his way to America, officially signing over the abandoned Domaine de la Cade to his Bousquet relations. To start with, he paid his way playing piano on the steamboats and in vaudeville. Although Meredith couldn't prove it, she liked to think he might have at least crossed paths with another vaudeville performer, Paul Foster Case.

Louis-Anatole settled outside Milwaukee, in what was now Mitchell Park. It had been pretty easy to uncover the next chapter of the story. He fell in love with a married woman, Lillian Matthews, who became pregnant and had a daughter, Louisa. Soon after, the affair ended and Lillian and Louis-Anatole appeared to have lost touch. There was no evidence of contact between father and daughter that Meredith could find, although she hoped Louis-Anatole might have followed his daughter's progress from a distance.

Louisa inherited her father's musical talent. She became a professional pianist, in the concert halls of 1930s' America rather than on the steamboats of the Mississippi. After her debut at a small venue in Milwaukee, she found a package waiting for her at the stage door. It contained a single photograph of a young man in uniform and a piece of piano music: *Sepulchre 1891*.

On the eve of the Second World War, Louisa became engaged to a fellow musician, a violinist whom she'd met on the circuit. Jack Martin was nervous and volatile, even before his experiences in a Burmese prisoner-of-war camp ruined him. He returned to America, addicted to drugs, suffering hallucinations and nightmares. He and Louisa had a daughter, Jeanette, but they were clearly not happy. When Jack disappeared from the scene in the 1950s, Meredith imagined Louisa had not been sorry.

Three years of painstaking research, and she'd made it right up to date. Jeanette had inherited the beauty, the talent, the character of her grandfather, Louis-Anatole, and her mother, Louisa, but also the fragility, the vulnerability of her French great-grandmother Isolde and her father, Jack.

Meredith looked down at the back cover of the book, resting in her lap. A reproduction of the photograph of Léonie, Anatole and Isolde, taken in the square in Rennes-les-Bains in 1891. Her family.

Mark was still talking. Hal caught her eye, and mimed zippering his mouth shut.

Meredith grinned. Hal had moved to America in October two years ago: the best birthday present Meredith could have wished for. The legal side of things down in Rennes-les-Bains had been complicated. Probate had taken a while and there had been problems with ascertaining exactly how Julian Lawrence had died. Not a stroke, not a heart attack. There were no visible signs of any trauma whatsoever, apart from some unexplained scarring on the palms of his hands. His heart had just stopped beating.

Had he survived, it was unlikely he would have faced charges for either the murder of his brother or the attempted murder of Shelagh O'Donnell. The circumstantial evidence in both cases was persuasive, but the police were reluctant to reopen the inquest into Seymour's death in the circumstances. Shelagh had not seen her attacker and there were no witnesses.

There was, however, clear evidence of fraud and that Julian Lawrence had been skimming the profits from the hotel and borrowing against it for years to fund his obsession. Several valuable Visigoth artefacts, all illegally obtained, were recovered. In his safe were charts showing his detailed excavations of the grounds and notebook after notebook of scribblings about a particular deck of Tarot cards. When Meredith was questioned, in November 2007, she admitted she had a replica copy of the same deck, but that the originals were believed to have been destroyed in the fire of 1897.

Hal had sold the Domaine de la Cade in March 2008. There was no money in the business, only debts, and he was ready to move on. But he'd stayed in touch with Shelagh O'Donnell, who now lived in Quillan, and she told them that an English couple, with two teenage children, had taken over and successfully transformed the business into one of the leading family hotels in the Midi.

'So, ladies and gentlemen, please put your hands together for Meredith Martin.'

There was an explosion of riotous clapping, not least, Meredith suspected, because Mark had finally stopped.

She took a deep breath, composed herself and stood up.

'Thank you for that generous introduction, Mark,' she said. 'It's great to be here. The genesis of this book, as some of you know, comes from a trip I made while I was working on my biography of Debussy. My research took me to a delightful town in the Pyrenees called Rennes-les-Bains, and, from there, into an investigation of my own family background. This memoir is my attempt to lay the ghosts of the past to rest.' She paused. 'The heroine of the book, if you like, is a woman named Léonie Vernier. Without her, I wouldn't be here today.' She smiled. 'But the book is dedicated to Mary, my mother. I wouldn't be here without her either.'

Meredith saw Hal hand a tissue to Mary, who was sitting between him and Bill in the front row.

'It was Mary who brought music into my life. It was she who encouraged me to keep asking questions and to never close my mind to any possibility. It was she who taught me to always stick with it, however hard things got. Most importantly,' she grinned, lightening the tone a little, 'and especially appropriate tonight, I guess, it was Mary who showed me how to carve the best Hallowe'en pumpkins ever!'

The gathering of friends and family laughed.

Meredith waited, now excited as well as nervous, until silence fell over the room once more. She lifted the book and began to read.

This story begins in a city of bones. In the alleyways of the dead. In the silent boulevards and promenades and impasses of the Cimetière de Montmartre in Paris, a place inhabited by tombs and stone angels and the loitering ghosts of those forgotten before they are even cold in their graves.

As her words floated out over the audience, becoming part of the mass of stories to be told that Hallowe'en night, the comfortable sounds of the old building were Meredith's accompaniment. Chairs creaking on the wooden floorboards, the spluttering of water pipes, the blare of horns from cars in the street outside, the coffee percolator wheezing in the corner. From the bar next door, the strains of a piano coming through the walls.

Meredith slowed down as she came to the end of her reading.

For, in truth, this story begins not with the absence of bones in a Parisian graveyard, but with a deck of cards.
With the Vernier Tarot.

There was a moment of silence, and then the applause began.

Meredith exhaled with relief. As she looked out at her friends, her family, her colleagues, for a fraction of a second, there in the shifting of the light, she imagined she saw a girl with long copper hair and bright-green eyes, standing at the back of the room, smiling.

Meredith smiled back. But when she looked again, there was no one there.

She thought of all the ghosts that touched her life. Marguerite Vernier in the Cimetière de Passy. Of the cemetery in Milwaukee, close to the point where the three rivers met, where her great-grandfather Louis-Anatole Vernier – soldier of France, citizen of America – had been laid to rest. Of Louisa Martin, pianist, her ashes scattered to the winds. Jeanette, buried on the shores of Lake Michigan. But most of all, she thought of Léonie, sleeping peacefully in the ground at the Domaine de la Cade.

Air, water, fire, earth.

'Thank you,' Meredith said, as the applause died down. 'And thank you all very much for coming.'

AUTHOR'S NOTE ON THE VERNIER TAROT

The Vernier Tarot is an imaginary deck, designed for *Sepulchre*, painted by artist Finn Campbell-Notman and based on the classic Rider Waite deck (1910).

Experts cannot agree on the antique origins of the Tarot: Persia, China, Ancient Egypt, Turkey, India – all have claims. But the format of the cards we associate now with Tarot is usually accepted to date from mid-fifteenth-century Italy. There are hundreds of decks – and more come onto the market every year. The most popular continue to be the Marseille Tarot, with its distinctive, bright yellow, blue and red illustrations, and the narrative Universal Waite deck, devised in 1916 by the English occultist Arthur Edward Waite and with illustrations by the American artist Pamela Colman Smith. The deck used by Solitaire in the James Bond film *Live and Let Die*, painted by the artist Fergus Hall, drew strongly from the Universal Waite Tarot.

For those wishing to find out more about Tarot, there are plenty of books and websites. The best all-round guide is Rachel Pollack's *The Complete Illustrated Guide to Tarot*, published by Element (1999).

ACKNOWLEDGEMENTS

I have been extremely fortunate to have the support, advice and practical help of so many people during the course of writing *Sepulchre*. It goes without saying that any mistakes, in fact or interpretation, are mine.

My agent Mark Lucas continues to be not only a superb editor and a good friend, but also the purveyor of multicoloured Post-it notes – this time, red! Thanks, too, to everyone at LAW for their hard work and support, especially Alice Saunders, Lucinda Bettridge and Petra Lewis. Also, Nicki Kennedy for her enthusiasm, Sam Edenborough and the team at ILA.

In the UK, I'm lucky to be published by Orion. Thanks to Malcolm Edwards and Susan Lamb, publisher Jon Wood, editor Genevieve Pegg, copy-editor Jane Selley, Gaby Young in publicity, Mark Rusher in Marketing and Jo Carpenter and Dallas Manderson in sales. A huge thanks to Francesca Main, Kate Moreton and copyeditor Holly Kyte for all their hard work for this 2022 new edition.

In the US, I'd like to thank George Lucas and my wonderful editor at Putnam, Rachel Kahan. Also, at Droemer in Germany, Annette Weber; at Lattès in France, Phillipe Dorey and Isabelle Laffont.

A special thank you to author and composer Greg Nunes, who helped with the Fibonacci passages and who composed the beautiful piece of music, *Sepulchre 1891*, which appears in the book and on the audio version. I'm also very grateful to Finn Campbell-Notman and the art department at Orion for the eight Vernier Tarot cards.

My gratitude to Tarot readers and enthusiasts on both sides of the Atlantic, who were generous with their advice, suggestions and experiences – I would especially like to thank Sue, Louise, Estelle and Paul; Mysteries in Covent Garden; Ruby (aka the novelist Jill Dawson) for doing a reading for Meredith; as well as those who prefer to remain anonymous.

In France, thanks to Martine Rouche and Claudine l'Hôte-Azema in Mirepoix; to Régine Foucher in Rennes-les-Bains; to Michelle and Roland Hill for giving me sight of the diary; to Madame Breithaupt and her team in Carcassonne; and to Pierre Sanchez and Chantal Billautou for all the practical help over the past eighteen years.

A huge thank you to friends, especially Robert Dye, Lucinda Montefiore, Kate and Bob Hingston, Peter Clayton, Sarah Mansell, Tim Bouquet, Cath and Pat O'Hanlon, Bob and Maria Pulley, Paul Arnott, Lydia Conway, Amanda Ross, Tessa Ross, Kamila Shamsie and Rachel Holmes. Special mention must go to the Rennes-les-Bains research gang of Maria Rejt, Jon Evans and Richard Bridges, all of whom have spent more time than they might have wanted at that pizzeria!

Most of all, my love and gratitude to my family, most particularly my fabulous parents, Richard and Barbara Mosse, and my mother-in-law, Rosie Turner, who keeps everything on track.

Our daughter, Martha, is always happy and enthusiastic, upbeat and supportive, never doubting the book will get finished. Felix spent months and months walking the Sussex Downs, brainstorming ideas, making plot suggestions, offering editorial insights and ideas – without his input, *Sepulchre* would be a very different book.

Finally, as always, Greg. His love and faith, providing everything from editorial and practical advice to all that backing up of files and food night after night, makes all the difference to everything. As it always has.

Pas à pas . . . every step of the way.

QUESTIONS FOR
READING GROUPS

PERSPECTIVE

1. *Sepulchre* begins with an intimidating yet picturesque scene in a Parisian graveyard. The reader sees the action from Léonie's point of view – but Léonie has been deceived and doesn't really know what is going on. When did you first begin to pick up clues to the nature of the tragic intrigue?

2. 'The soul of another person is a dark forest in which one must tread carefully.' Claude Debussy was famously single-minded, yet he understood the profound nature of imagining oneself in another's emotions and thoughts. Did you feel like an eavesdropper in Léonie's world?

SETTING

3. At the end of the first section, Léonie and her beloved brother flee Paris. Were you sorry to leave the French capital behind? Did you enjoy it when there were later glimpses of Parisian action, such as Constant's murder of Marguerite and Laboughe's police investigation?

4. If you have read *Labyrinth*, you will know that most of the action takes place in the great, fortified medieval city of Carcassonne. By contrast, Rennes-les-Bains is a small, isolated spa town in the Pyrenees and the estate of the Domaine de la Cade is an imagined place. What difference did this make to your enjoyment of the descriptions of the landscape in *Sepulchre*?

CHARACTER

5. Léonie is – at least at first – a charmingly innocent though headstrong young woman. In fact, she is almost still a girl. In the modern section of *Sepulchre*, the hero – Meredith Martin – is much more worldly-wise, perhaps even a little sceptical. Did you enjoy the contrast between the two heroines?

6. Two of the characters you may have met in *Labyrinth* reappear in *Sepulchre* – one in 1891 and one in 2007. Was that a surprise? If you have read *Labyrinth*, did it make a difference when you realised that, in the modern section of *Sepulchre*, the *Labyrinth* story has already finished and one of those two characters has, more than 100 years later, died?

HISTORY

7. Léonie's father was exiled after the bloodbath of the Paris Commune. Her neighbour, Claude Debussy, was at the forefront of a transformation in classical music and a devotee of the new fashion for occult experiments. Did you feel the need to 'read up' on late nineteenth-century France, or did you feel that the

author gave you enough background to understand her characters in their historical context?

8. Rennes-les-Bains is a neighbouring village of Rennes-le-Château and the 'mysteries' of Abbé Saunière. Later, it is an intrigue concerning the Tarot that first draws Meredith into Léonie's drama. Perhaps you knew about Saunière or the Tarot before reading *Sepulchre*. Do you think the knowledge made any difference to your enjoyment of the story?

SUPERNATURAL

9. The landscape that Léonie discovers at the Domaine de la Cade is many people's idea of a perfect retreat from the world – a lovely house, a beautiful setting close to nature. Yet it is surrounded by place names that seem to summon evil – the Horned Mountain, the Devil's Lake, the Dead Man. Do you believe that a place can be inhabited by evil? Did you believe that the imaginary Domaine was inhabited by evil?

10. The author is a great admirer of the ghost stories of M.R. James and Algernon Blackwood. Do you think you need to believe in the supernatural to be able to enjoy a story – like *Sepulchre* – that has paranormal elements such as the demon?

Suggested Further Reading

Ancient Sorceries and Other Weird Stories by Algernon Blackwood

Casting the Runes and Other Ghost Stories by M.R. James

Collected Stories by Edgar Allan Poe

Debussy and his World edited by Jane F. Fulcher

L'Aude en Cartes Postales – Tome 1 by Marthe Moreau

La Rivière aux Bois Dormant by Jean-Pierre Monteil

Mémoire des Rues – Paris 9e by Philippe Roy

Mémoire en images – Carcassonne éditions by Alan Sutton

Mysteries of Templar Treasure and the Holy Grail by Lionel and Patricia Fanthorp

Selected Short Stories by Guy de Maupassant

The Cambridge Companion to Debussy edited by Simon Tresize

The Complete Illustrated Guide to the Tarot by Rachel Pollack

The Life of Debussy by Roger Nichols

The Occult Tradition by David S. Katz

The Turn of the Screw by Henry James

The
SEPULCHRE TOUR

Introduction

The medieval Cité of Carcassonne sits on a small hill alongside the river Aude, but on the far bank stands the nineteenth-century *bastide*. Find the lock on the Canal du Midi, round the railway station and up the steep hill to the Cimetière Saint-Vincent. Find a spot between the ornate tombs with an uninterrupted view south.

From here, the history of Carcassonne is easily discerned. In the foreground, from the turn of the century, the Hotel du Terminus, in the middle distance the battlements of the biscuit-coloured fortress and, on the far horizon, the green hills and snowy peaks of the Pyrenees.

It was here that I first met, in my imagination, those fashionable Parisians Léonie and Anatole Vernier . . . and had an inkling of the tragedy that awaited them in the distant wooded hillside above the run-down spa of Rennes-les-Bains and the mysterious Rennes-le-Château.

Kate Moss.

Carcassonne, 15 May 2008

1. Parc Monceau

After lunch, taking advantage of the mild and pleasant afternoon, Marguerite and Léonie went walking in the Parc Monceau, a favourite haunt of the ambassadors' children from the embassies nearby. A group of boys were playing un, deux, trois, loup *with great exuberance, shouting and yelling encouragement to one another . . . From the look on her mother's face, Léonie knew she too was remembering the past. She took advantage to ask a question.*

'Why is it that you were not happy at the Domaine de la Cade?' p122

Take the métro to Monceau and have a look round the lovely park where Léonie and Marguerite strolled. You too may see children from the fine houses nearby in the *impasse* Velasquez. There are also some intriguing pyramids. Then leave the park the way you came in, by the *métro* station on the north side. Take care crossing the boulevard de Courcelles, then aim north-west up rue Georges Berger. Cross

Villiers and Tocqueville into rue Legendre and you will find, on the left, just after place Lévis . . .

2.Square Claude Debussy

Meredith found the rue Cardinet easily and identified the block where Lilly and Debussy had lived. She felt a prick of disappointment. From the outside it was plain, nondescript, dull. There was no character to it. In letters, Debussy talked of the modest apartment with affection, describing the watercolours on the walls, the oil paintings.　　　　　　　　p76

If you are lucky it will be market day on rue de Lévis. Follow it down to place Prosper-Goubaux, then cross to take the south-east rue de Constantinople. It will lead you past some extraordinary views of multiple rail lines coming into Saint-Lazare. The roads flyover the tracks. Imagine how 1890s steam trains would have looked and sounded.

At place d'Europe, suspended over the railway intersection, go east into the . . .

3. Rue de Liège / rue de Berlin

There was a green woollen shawl hanging over the back of the chaise longue. Léonie wrapped it around her shoulders, turned down the gas lamp and curled up in her favourite armchair, her legs tucked beneath her. Suddenly, from the floor beneath, the sound of music began to filter up through the floorboards. Léonie smiled. Achille at his piano again. She looked to the clock on the mantelshelf. Past midnight. p46

Many French provincial cities still have roads with German names. In Germany, many towns have French names. In Berlin itself, an important square is named after Paris – the Pariser Platz. But, as far as I am aware, there isn't a single German road name that remains in the French capital because of what one French politician called the 'anti-German madness' of the Great War when the rue de Berlin, – where Léonie, Anatole and Marguerite and Claude Achille Debussy lived – changed its name to the rue de Liège.

Follow halfway along Liège, then turn right onto the rue d'Amsterdam. This will lead you south to . . .

4. La Gare Saint-Lazare

On their arrival at the Gare Saint-Lazare, Anatole had their baggage moved to a second cab. He made a great play of chatting with the driver, but Léonie noticed that he was sweating, even though it was cold. His cheeks were flushed and his temples slicked with beads of perspiration.

'Are you unwell?' p124

Léonie had no idea at the time that Anatole was attempting to throw Constant off their scent – to make it difficult for them to be traced south as trains from Saint-Lazare were mostly bound for Normandy and the Channel. Today, the clock sculpture is a well-known meeting point, a surreal expression of the daily maze of criss-crossed intentions as commuters arrive at and depart this central Paris station.

Head south down the rue du Havre, then east along the boulevard Haussmann to the intersection with the . . .

5. Rue de la Chaussée d'Antin

After five minutes Meredith stopped to get her bearings and saw she'd ended up in the rue de la Chaussée d'Antin. In Debussy's day, the notorious Cabaret Grande-Pinte had stood at the top of the street, near the plate de la Trinité . . . And at the bottom, pretty much where she was standing, was Edmond Bailly's notorious esoteric bookstore. There, in the glory days of the turn of the century, poets and occultists and composers had met to talk through new ideas, of mysticism and alternative worlds. In Bailly's bookshop, the prickly young Debussy would not have had to explain himself. p94

As Meredith found, Edmond Bailly's esoteric bookshop – sadly – no longer exists. Neither does Laura's Tarot reading parlour, though there are many like it that do.

Going this way, it is hard to avoid the *Grands Magasins* – the Galeries Lafayette and so on. But follow the boulevard Haussmann for about 500m. On the right-hand side, you will come across the modest entrance to the . . .

6. Passage des Panoramas

Certain now he was being marked, Anatole darted right into the Passage des Panoramas . . . The few remaining gas lamps burned with a cold blue light as he passed along the narrow row of glass fronted shops selling stamps and ex-voto trinkets, the furniture-maker displaying an ancient cabinet with dilapidated gilding, the various antiques dealers and sellers of objets d'art. p51

The passage des Panoramas is an atmospheric shopping arcade, named for an early nineteenth-century attraction showing panoramic views of great cities installed at one end. Today it is intriguingly crowded with stamp and post-

card shops, restaurants and the legendary Parisian printer and engraver Stern, present in the Passage since 1834. I am certain that this is where Anatole had his calling cards printed.

Walk all the way to the end, turn right, then swiftly left onto rue Vivienne. Walk south towards the Bourse – the stock exchange – then turn right and follow the rue du 4 Septembre to the . . .

7. Place de l'Opéra

Another omnibus passed between Léonie and the magnificent façade of the Palais Garnier on its way to the boulevard Haus-mann, the conductor whistling on the upper deck as he punched tickets. An intoxicated soldier with a Tonquin medal pinned to his breast stumbled back and forth, singing an old army song. Léonie even saw a clown with a whitened face under his black domino felt cap, his costume covered in gold spangles.

'How could he leave me waiting?' p10

As well as the anti-Wagner riot that Léonie gets caught up in, in 1891 other dangers stalked the French capital, with 30,000 unemployed men in central Paris alone. Outside the city, the iron foundries of the Creusot company were already at work on the artillery for the next – apparently inevitable – war. In the *Revue Illustrée*, a journalist considered French prosperity and remarked: 'When walking with pockets jingling with gold through the forests of contemporary Europe, it's probably a good idea to have the butt of a revolver visible in your waistband.'

Leave the place de l'Opéra by the boulevard des Capucines, west towards Madeleine. After 150m or so, take a left onto rue Cambon, then follow it south until the junction with rue Saint-Honoré and the restaurant . . .

8. Voisin's

Marguerite Vernier disembarked the fiacre at the corner of the rue Cambon and the rue Saint-Honoré, accompanied by General Georges Du Pont. While her escort settled the fare, she pulled her stole around her against the chill of the evening and smiled with satisfaction. Voisin's was the best restaurant in town, the famous windows curtained, as ever, with the finest Brittany lace. It was a measure of Du Pont's growing regard for her that he had brought her here. p29

During the famine of 1870, when the Parisian Communards were blockaded by an alliance of French loyalist and Prussian troops, the menu at Voisin's, the 'best restaurant in town', included elephant soup, bear ribs and kangaroo stew, all animals 'liberated' from the zoo. Now the only place to eat on this intersection is the charity kitchen at the Polish church.

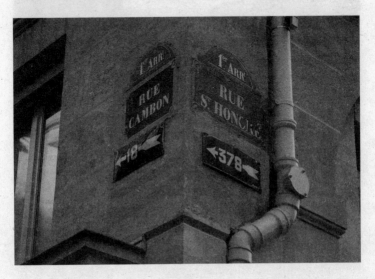

From the corner of Cambon and Saint-Honoré, it is only a short step south onto the rue de Rivoli and along the railings of the Tuileries Gardens towards Concorde. From here you can take the *métro* to the Gare Montparnasse and flee south, like Léonie and Anatole, to **Rennes-les-Bains**.

RENNES-LE-BAINS

∞

9. The River Salz

But once she hit the autoroute, things calmed down. She start-
ed to feel confident enough to turn on the radio. She found a
station, Classique, on preset and turned the volume up high.
The usual. Bach, Mozart, Puccini, even a little Debussy. By six
o'clock, feeling a mixture of anticipation and excitement, she was
driving into the town she'd thought about for so long.   p197

The D14 road, as it emerges from the woods and the gorges, runs alongside a sheer wall of rock. There are parking spaces opposite the great blockhouse of the Thermal
Spa. From here, you can follow in Meredith's footsteps,
steeply down the allée des Bains de la Reine to the banks
of the River Salz, past the open-air swimming pool filled
with hot, mineral-rich spa water. Except that when Meredith visited it was closed. Over 100 years previously, Léonie
came this way too, and saw the rich, ailing visitors, pam-
pered with servants and towels.

10. The Far Bank

There was a different atmosphere on the far side of the river . . . a more enduring landscape, less influenced by people and fashions. The rough-hewn jutting hillside seemed to rise straight out of the ground in front of her, The variegated greens and browns and coppers of the bushes and trees taking on the rich hues of dusk. It should have been a landscape that appealed, but something felt wrong about it. Two-dimensional, somehow, as if the true character of the place was concealed beneath a painted exterior. p189

Down on the riverbank, you can turn left and make your way towards a low concrete bridge and a storm drain where Meredith saw a face in the water – 'a modern-day Ophelia'. Turn the other way, past the swimming pool, into an artificial gorge created by tall narrow houses, deceptively short up on the road but, in the river cutting, stretching two or even three stories down towards the water.

Further upriver, on the far bank, close to the iron footbridge – the Pont de Fer – is a small pool of hot spring water, enclosed by the foundations of a large pink building. People bathe here even in winter with the thermometer at zero, steam rising enigmatically from the surface.

11. The Flood

Léonie intended to walk to the poste restante via the road in which Monsieur Baillard's lodgings were to be found to make the story she had told true. To her delight, the blue shutters of his tiny house were pinned back. p474

There is a steep stone stair that climbs up out of the river gorge to the cluster of intertwined streets that make up the heart of Rennes-les-Bains. These are the roads and alleyways which Léonie explored, virtually unchanged in layout. From the confinement of the river cutting, you emerge into tight lanes. Many homes sport the traditional bright- or grey-blue shutters. A plaque near the corner of the rue de la Poste, close by where I imagine Audric Baillard's house to be, shows the frightening depth reached by the flood waters in the terrible rains of 25th October 1891, at eye-level on the wall.

12. The Bridge

Marieta led them down a shadowed passageway between the houses. They emerged into bright sunlight on an old arched stone bridge. Far, far below, the water flowed over flat rocks. Léonie caught her breath, made dizzy by the sensation of light and space and height. pp150-1

Of course, Isolde's maid Marieta met Léonie and her brother in the place du Pérou. From there, they made their way towards the river. Today, as well as the pedestrian Pont de Fer, you can see the narrow – but solid-looking – stone road bridge. Once they had crossed, Marieta took Léonie and Anatole by a woodland path – the short cut to Isolde Lascombe's beautiful but unlucky *domaine*.

13. La Place des Deux Rennes

Suddenly she saw it. The photograph of the young soldier, her ancestor, had been taken here, the precise spot framed by the buildings leading to the Pont Vieux, between a line of platanes and the wooded hillside glimpsed through the gap in the houses. pp198–9

The heart of the town is the place des Deux Rennes – the place known by Léonie as the place du Pérou. Here Meredith witnessed the funeral *cortège* of Hal's father and discovered the coincidence of dates – 31st October 1891 – on the gravestones in the churchyard just around the corner. And, of course, the first substantial clue that she is linked by personal family history to this village in the Pyrenees.

14. Route des Deux Rennes

To pass the time, Meredith walked past the Jardin Paul Courrent, then right up a very steep road that seemed to run straight into the hillside itself. . . . She read the tourist information board, a rustic wooden sign advertising walks to local landmarks: L'Homme Mort, La Cabanasse, La Source de la Madeleine, and a cross-country route to a neighbouring village, Rennes-le-Château.

p193

Head further south down the main street – the Gran'Rue – to the rural route des Deux Rennes, so called because it

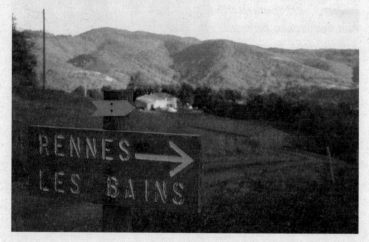

links Rennes-les-Bains, the spa town in the valley of the River Salz, with the hilltop Rennes-le-Château. Apparently, in the 1890s, Bérenger Saunière and Henri Boudet, the two town priests, would regularly tramp this very path, on friendly mutual visits or solitary explorations of a countryside studded with ill-omened landmarks – the Dead Man, the Devil's Lake, the Horned Mountain.

15. Domaine de la Cade

Meredith found the road to Sougraigne marked on the brochure and turned left. She rubbed her eyes, aware that she was too beat to be driving. The bushes and telegraph poles at the verge seemed to be swaying, vibrating. . . . Meredith slammed on the brakes. There was someone standing right in the middle of the road. A woman in a long red cloak, the hood pulled up over her head.   pp200–1

Meredith left Rennes-les-Bains driving south, but at the very exit to the village she found a left turn across the salt River Salz towards Sougraigne. Had she driven on through Sougraigne towards Fourtou, she could have visited the briny source – the *Fontaine Salée* –
and the ruined excise building controlling the tax on salt instituted in the early seventeenth century. But Meredith turned off after only a couple of thousand metres, onto a rising track leading up into the heavily wooded hills that overlook Rennes-les-Bains – the refurbished driveway that, if it did exist, would lead you to the Domaine de la Cade, hidden in the trees but within range of the mournful bell of the village church.

16. From Rennes-les-Bains to Rennes-le-Château

'I'm taking you the back way, cross-country to Rennes-le-Château. Much quicker than heading into Couiza and out again,' said Hal.

The road doubled back and twisted up on itself as it climbed through the wooded hills. A final hairpin bend, and then they were out of the woods and into wide expanses of meadows and pasture. p311

Because he knew the back roads, it was Hal who drove Meredith to see the parish of Bérenger Saunière. It is a difficult country road, narrow and easy to get lost. Often used by large farm vehicles, it is sometimes necessary to reverse long distances in order to allow oncoming traffic to pass. Great care should be taken by anyone who chooses to follow the route Hal took.

Hal and Meredith left Rennes-les-Bains heading south and took a right turn, signposted Labadous, 2.1km after the turning for Sougraigne. They drove along a beautiful valley road, emerging from the trees 1.5km further on to see an impressive limestone ridge in the distance. After one more kilometre, they reached the village of Coume Sourde. Once out of the village, scars in the ground began to reveal soil that was red in colour rather than brown. A little further and – because they were lucky and enjoyed clear October weather – the sharp-toothed white peaks of the snowy Pyrenees appeared.

About 6.2 km in total from the Sougraigne turning just outside Rennes-les-Bains, they had their first glimpse of the hilltop village of Rennes-le-Château profiled against the western sky. They drove on 2.5km across a sloping plain, looking out for wild thyme and broom and an abandoned windmill on a promontory to the left. Then there was a sharp left turn up towards the village, which appeared silhouetted on the skyline.

Meredith peered through the windshield as Hal edged the car up the last bend in the road, and suddenly they had arrived.

Set high on the vertiginous hillside above them was a collection of houses and other buildings. There was a painted board welcoming them to Rennes-le-Château: Son site. Ses mystères. p317

Hal followed signs to the P1 Belvedère car park and parked near the water tower, not far from a long bronze map identifying the many visible mountains, including the Pic de Soularac, the imagined location of the *Labyrinth* cave.

17. The Sundial

Immediately behind them there was a circular stone water tower. A square sundial painted on the south-facing curve marked the summer and winter solstices. At the top, there was an inscription. She shielded her eyes to read it: Aici le tems s'en / Va res l'Eternitat. p317

Visit the 'dusty parking lot' today and you will see no sign of the obscure motto on the wall of the water tower. It has been painted out.

18. La Tour Magdala

'What's that?' asked Meredith, pointing at a squat, crenellated tower built overlooking the valley.

'The Tour Magdala,' he replied. 'Saunière built the belvedere – the stone walkway that runs along the south side of his gardens – with this incredible view, at the very end of the

renovation programme, 1898, 1899. The tower was to house his library.'

'The original collection's not in there surely?'

'I doubt it,' he said. 'I suspect they've done what my dad did at the Domaine de la Cade – put a few replacement volumes in the cases, for atmosphere.'

The Tour Magdala is just to the right of the car park. It overhangs the vast valley. Actually, if you know what you are looking for, it can be picked out from the road well before Couiza as you drive south from Limoux, a striking profile against the skyline. It is said that twenty-two towns and villages can be seen from its walls.

19. La Villa Béthania

'The Villa Béthania here,' he pointed up at the impressive house, 'Saunière built for guests rather than for himself. When I came with Dad, it was open to the public, but in a totally haphazard way. You'd wander into one of the rooms and see a waxwork figure of Saunière sitting up in bed.'

Turn away from the extraordinary view and walk down the narrow village street that runs along the railings of Saunière's garden. You will find his elegant guest house on the left – impressive for a Carcassonne town house, still more so in its astonishing hilltop location.

20. The Church

'That inscription – TERRIBILIS EST LOCUS ISTE – is another reason all the conspiracy theories surrounding Rennes-le-Château took hold,' he said, clearing his throat. 'The phrase actually translates as "this place is awe-inspiring", terribilis in the Old Testament sense rather than terrible in the modern sense, but you can imagine how it's been interpreted.' pp330–1

The inscription can be read over the door of the sanitised church, with its dreadful piped music and exhortation that 'you are the treasure' – a reference to the so-called 'mystery of Rennes-le-Château'. Nearby is a statue of the Virgin supported by – apparently – a Visigoth pillar, perhaps the hollow prism of stone inside which Saunière discovered his treasure or parchments. The pillar has been carved with two post-Visigoth messages: '*Pénitence, Pénitence*' and '*Mission 1891*'. As Meredith thought: 'That date again . . .'

21. Asmodeus

Meredith was staring at the stoup for holy water on the immediate left of the door. The bénitier was balanced on the shoulders of a three-foot-high statue of a devil. The malevolent red face, the twisted body, the unnerving, piercing blue eyes. She'd seen the demon before. At least, an image of him. Lying on the table in Paris as Laura spread out the major arcana at the beginning of the reading. Le Diable. Card XV of the Bousquet Tarot. pp331-2

Above the holy water stoup, the four plaster apostles are making the sign of the cross. An inscription below them reads: 'Through this sign, you shall conquer him.' The motto strikes most people as unusual, because it refers so explicitly to the demon – 'him' – as if the sign of the cross were a piece of practical knowledge, like knot-tying, and as if the demon were a commonplace adversary with whom confrontation is inevitable. Or have I, like others perhaps, read too much into it?

22. The Cemetery

They walked on in silence until they reached the high, solid metal gates protecting the graveyard. Meredith tilted her head back to read the inscription set in a porcelain pendant above the locked gates: 'Memento homo quia pulvis es et in pulverem reverteris.'

"Which means?" Hal asked.

'Dust to dust,' she said.

pp320–1

Perhaps it isn't surprising to find the cemetery locked. Over the years, especially since the publication of Dan Brown's *The Da Vinci Code*, many visitors have failed to respect the graveyard, even going so far as to vandalise the tombs. The sad message on the locked gates, printed from a home computer and protected from the weather with a cheap plastic pocket, confirms that access to the cemetery is restricted to the relatives of its dead. Above the gates, the stone lintel is carved with a skull-and-crossbones.

23. Coustaussa

The storm hit the Haute Vallée at a little after eight o'clock in the evening, just as the train carrying Léonie, Anatole and Isolde south approached the station at Limoux. Thunder, then a jagged fork of lightning slashed the purple sky. Isolde cried out and Anatole took her hand.

'It will be all right, I promise you.' p427

Driving away from Rennes-le-Château, it is possible to follow a steep sequence of hairpin bends that leads down to Couiza, where Léonie and Anatole left the train on arrival in the Pyrenees. About a third of the way down from the hilltop village, there is a parking place – just a space to pull in – on the right-hand side of the road. It overlooks the valley in which thunderstorms so often become trapped. Away to the left, on a high hill above the river and the railway line, is the village of Montazels, birthplace of Bérenger Saunière. Away to the right, you can also clearly see the ruined *château* of the village of Coustaussa, whose real-life priest was murdered in 1897, the year in which the imaginary Domaine de la Cade was burnt down.

24. The Landscape

Higher and steeper they went, along a dappled track of stones and fallen leaves, venturing ever deeper into the thick forest. Before long, the path opened out into a wider country track.

Léonie turned and looked back in the direction they had come. Now she could see, steeply below them but close still, the red and grey sloping roofs of Rennes-les-Bains. She could even identify the hotels and the central square where they had disembarked the carriage. The water shimmered and teased, a ribbon of green and silver, even red with the reflection of autumn leaves, running as smooth as silk.

p151

Although the pomp and opulence of the 1890s spa has long since given way – there is an air of ghost town that hangs over Rennes-les-Bains in winter – it is, for all that, a beautiful and peaceful place. The trees are deep green, copper and gold, the paths between them sinuous and intriguing. When I raise my eyes to the horizon, if I am lucky and the sky is clear, I can see the Pyrenees – even pick out Saint-Barthélémy towering above Montségur. Here, I feel sure, no storyteller could ever be lost for inspiration or any visitor fail to be charmed by the beauty and splendour of a natural landscape sculpted by time in forest, rivers, limestone and brown and red earth.

Photographs © Mark Rusher

Discover Kate Mosse

storytelling at its most captivating

8 MILLION BOOKS SOLD

'A powerful storyteller with an
abundant imagination'

Daily Telegraph